DAVID WEBER

IN ENEMY HANDS

This is a work of fiction. All the characters and events por-
trayed in this book are fictional, and any resemblance to real
people or incidents is purely coincidental.

A Baen Books Original

Baen Publishing Enterprises
P.O. Box 1403
Riverdale, NY 10471

ISBN: 0-671-87793-3

Cover art by David Mattingly

First printing, August 1997

Distributed by Simon & Schuster
1230 Avenue of the Americas
New York, NY 10020

Library of Congress Cataloging-in-Publication Data

Weber, David, M. 1952–
      In enemy hands / David M. Weber
            p.   cm.
      ISBN 0-671-87793-3 (hardcover)
      I. Title
   PS3573.E217I5   1997
   813'.54—dc21   97-3192
                                                      CIP

Typeset by Windhaven Press, Auburn, NH
Printed in the United States of America

For Sharon, who loves me anyway.

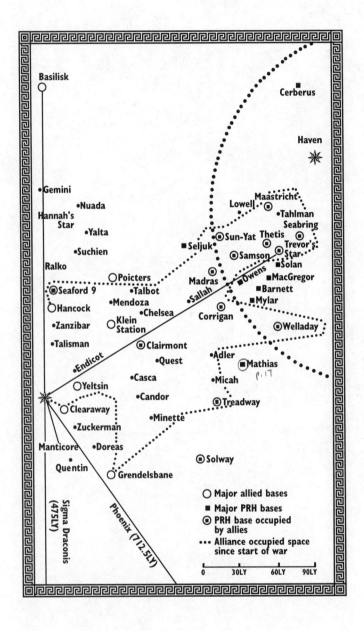

Basilisk

Cerberus

Haven

Gemini

Nuada

Maastricht
Lowell
Tahlman
Hannah's
Star
Yalta
Seabring
Sun-Yat
Thetis
Suchien
Seljuk
Trevor's
Samson
Star
Ralko
Solan
Poicters
Madras
Owens
MacGregor
Seaford 9
Talbot
Barnett
Hancock
Mendoza
Sallah
Mylar
Chelsea
Zanzibar
Klein
Corrigan
Station
Talisman
Welladay
Clairmont
Quest
Adler
Casca
Mathias
Yeltsin
Micah
p. 17
Candor
Clearaway
Treadway
Minette
Zuckerman
Manticore
Doreas
Quentin
Solway
Grendelsbane

○ Major allied bases
■ Major PRH bases
◉ PRH base occupied
   by allies
••• Alliance occupied space
    since start of war

Endicot

Sigma Draconis
(475LY)

Phoenix (712.5LY)

| 0 | 30LY | 60LY | 90LY |

• Prologue

"I think it's a mistake—a big one." Cordelia Ransom's blue eyes glittered, but the passionate voice which had raised and swayed so many chanting crowds was cold, almost flat. Which, Rob Pierre reflected, proved her emotions were truly engaged on this issue.

"I obviously don't, or I wouldn't have suggested it," he told her, meeting her eyes levelly while he sought to put enough iron into his deliberately calm reply to override her chill intensity. He succeeded in that, for the most part, but it wasn't as easy as it should have been, and he knew it. He just hoped *she* didn't.

Officially, Pierre was the most powerful man in the People's Republic of Haven. As the creator and head of the Committee of Public Safety, his word was law and his power over the PRH's citizens absolute. Yet even he faced limits—including the one which had finally decided him his proposal was necessary—and the fact that most of them were invisible to those beyond the ranks of the Committee's membership made them no less real.

His was a revolutionary government which had imposed itself upon the Republic by force. Everyone knew it had extended its grasp far beyond the caretaker role the People's Quorum had envisioned when it voted to ratify his creation of the Committee and named him its chairman. The Quorum had thought it was setting up little more than a caretaker panel to restore domestic stability as quickly as possible . . . what it had gotten was a revolution run by a multiheaded dictatorship which was quite prepared to use coercion, suppression, and outright terror tactics to maintain

1

its grasp and promote its own agenda. That was the heart of his problem. By using force and ruthlessness to reach so far beyond what the Quorum had expected and authorized, he'd made his power real and undeniable, but he'd also deprived his *authority* (which, he conceded, was not—quite—the same thing) of that subtle and elusive quality called "legitimacy."

A rule imposed by violence or the threat of violence could be overturned the same way, and as a creature of force, his Committee had no recourse to the rule of law or custom to support it. It was odd how little thought people gave to governments which *could* claim those supports, he thought moodily. Or of how the destruction of a society's underlying social contract, even if the contract in question had been a bad one, smashed the stability of that society until a new contract, acknowledged by its members as legitimate, replaced it. Pierre himself had certainly underestimated the consequences when he set out upon the revolutionary's path. He'd known there had to be a period of unrest and uncertainty, but somehow he'd assumed that once he and his colleagues got past those initial rough spots, the simple passage of time would be sufficient to legitimize their authority in the eyes of those they ruled. That was how it *ought* to have worked, he told himself yet again. However they'd gotten to where they were, they had at least as strong a claim to their places as the Legislaturalists they'd destroyed to get here had ever had. And unlike the Legislaturalists, Pierre had become a revolutionary in the first place because he genuinely believed in reform. Yet by the very act of seizing power, he had created a situation in which the ability to *take* that power was all that truly mattered to those who might compete for authority, for his own actions had eliminated not only all previously existing avenues to it but also any "legitimate" constraints upon the use of force.

All of which meant that the seemingly all-powerful Committee of Public Safety was, in fact, a far more fragile edifice than it appeared. Its members were careful to display their confidence to the Dolists and Proles they'd mobilized, but Pierre and his colleagues knew that any number of unsuspected plotters could be working to overthrow them at any moment. Why not? Hadn't *they* overthrown the Republic's previous lords and masters? Hadn't the Legislaturalists' long monopolization of the power of the state produced crackpots and fanatics in profusion? And hadn't the Committee itself crushed enough "enemies of the People" to guarantee its members potential—and passionate—enemies galore?

Of course they had, and some of them had demonstrated a dangerous willingness to act on that enmity. Fortunately, most of the outright lunatics, like the Zeroists, who had supported Charles Froidan's demands that all money be abolished, had been too incompetent to plan a bottle party, much less stage a coup. Others, like the Parnassians, whose platform had included the execution of all bureaucrats on the grounds that their choice of employment was *prima facie* evidence of treason against the People, had been reasonably competent conspirators but guilty of bad timing. By moving too soon, they'd made too many enemies among their competing extremists, and Pierre and State Security had managed to play one faction off against the other to destroy them. (Actually, that had been one of Pierre's harder decisions, for he'd discovered that, having dealt with the enormous, glacially paced bureaucracy bequeathed to him by the Legislaturalists, he felt a certain personal sympathy for the Parnassians' views. In the end, however, he had decided—not without regret—that the Committee required the bureaucrats to keep the Republic running.)

Some of their enemies, however, like LaBoeuf's Levelers, might have been lunatics but had certainly been capable of excellent timing and good security. Their idea of a proper society made anarchy look positively regimented by comparison, but they'd been organized enough to get several million people killed in less than a day of heavy fighting. It was amazing what a few kinetic bombardment strikes and pee-wee nukes could do to a city of thirty-six million souls, he thought. Actually, they'd been lucky to get off as lightly as they had . . . and at least none of the Levelers' known leadership had survived the bloodbath. Of course, it was almost certain that at least some of their inner cadre actually held seats on the Committee itself. They had to for the Levelers to have come so close to success, and *they* remained unidentified so far . . . whoever they were.

Under the circumstances, Pierre supposed he shouldn't be surprised to find that his initial ardor for reform was being ground away by his constantly growing, persistently unshakable sense of insecurity. Bad enough when that feeling of vulnerability had been genuine paranoia, with no basis in fact. Now that he had proof he not only had enemies but that they could be deadly dangerous, he was desperate to reach out for anything which might lend the Committee even a tiny bit more stability, strengthen his hand in any way he could. That, coupled with the equally desperate need to win the war to which the previous regime had committed the Republic, was the reason for his present proposal, and he glanced at Oscar Saint-Just for support.

To an outside observer, Saint-Just must clearly have been the second most powerful member of the triumvirate which ruled the Committee and hence the PRH. In fact, some might consider him even more powerful—tactically, at least—than Pierre himself, for Saint-Just's was the iron fist which commanded the Office of State Security. But once again, appearances could be deceiving. As head of the SS, Saint-Just was the Committee's executioner, with a power base which was far more readily apparent than Ransom's. Yet the very reasons Pierre was willing to trust him with that authority underscored the fact that Saint-Just could never be the threat Ransom might someday become. Unlike Cordelia, Oscar knew his reputation as the Republic's chief warden would preclude his maintaining himself indefinitely in power even if he somehow managed to seize it. He was the focal point of all the fear, hatred, and resentment the

Committee of Public Safety had engendered . . . on top of which, he genuinely had no desire to supplant his leader. Pierre had given him sufficient opportunities to prove otherwise, but Saint-Just had taken none of them, for he knew his own limitations.

Ransom didn't, and that was why Pierre would never have given her the position Saint-Just occupied. She was too unpredictable—which translated into "unreliable" in his mind. And where he was determined to at least attempt to build something constructive atop the bones of the old, murdered power structure, she often seemed more interested in the exercise of power than in the ends to which it was exercised. She was always at her best whipping up the Proles' mob mentality, and it was her ability to direct that mentality against targets other than Pierre and his regime which made her so valuable. Yet it also gave her Office of Public Information the first opportunity to put its spin on each issue as it came along, which gave her a degree of power—intangible, but frighteningly real—that made her very nearly Saint-Just's equal. And, Pierre reminded himself, Cordelia had more than her fair share of cronies within Oscar's own SS, as well. She'd been one of the Committee of Public Safety's roving headsmen immediately after the coup, before he moved her to Public Information, and she retained personal contacts with the men and women with whom she'd served. The fact that she and Oscar were both fierce empire-builders (although, Pierre suspected, for quite different reasons) only made the situation worse in many ways, but at least it let him play them off against one another, maintaining their "constituencies" in a delicate, sometimes precarious balance he could force to support his own position rather than undermining it.

"I understand Cordelia's concerns, Rob," Saint-Just said, answering Pierre's unspoken appeal after a long, pregnant moment. He tipped back his chair, leaning away from the crystal-topped conference table, and steepled his fingers across his chest in a posture that made him look even more like someone's harmless, nondescript uncle. "We've spent over five T-years convincing everyone the Navy was responsible for the Harris Assassination, and while we've, ah, *removed* virtually all the precoup senior officers, putting my commissioners aboard the Navy's ships hasn't won us many fans among their replacements. Whether we want to admit it or not, granting political agents—we might as well be honest and call them spies—veto authority over line officers helps explain the fiascoes the fleet keeps sailing into . . . and the officer corps knows that, too. When you add all that to the number of officers we've shot or locked up 'to encourage the others,' it could certainly be argued that taking our boot off their necks is a questionable decision, at best . . . even if it *was* the Navy that saved our asses from LaBoeuf's maniacs. I mean, let's not fool ourselves here; *anyone* would have looked good compared to the Levelers. Don't forget that part of their platform called for shooting anyone above the rank of lieutenant commander or major for the 'military-industrial complex's treasonous misconduct of the war.' There's no guarantee the Navy would back us against someone less, um, *energetic* than they were."

His tenor was as mild and colorless as the rest of him, yet Ransom's eyes hardened behind their glitter as she heard the "But" he hadn't quite voiced. Pierre heard the qualification as well, and his own eyes narrowed.

"But compared to our other options?" he said softly, inviting Saint-Just to continue, and the SS chief shrugged.

"Compared to our other options, I don't see a lot of choice. The Manties keep handing our fleet commanders their heads, and we keep blaming *them* for it. After a point, that becomes bad propaganda as well as bad strategy. Let's face it, Cordelia," Saint-Just swiveled those nondescript eyes to his golden-haired colleague, "it gets awfully hard for Public Information to keep rallying public support behind our 'gallant defenders' when *we* seem to be killing as many of them as the Manties are!"

"Maybe it does," Ransom countered, "but that's less risky than letting the military get a foot into the door." She switched the full force of her personality to Pierre. "If we put someone from the military on the Committee, how do we keep him or her from finding out things we don't want the military to know? Like who *really* killed off the Harris government?"

"There's not much chance of that," Saint-Just pointed out reasonably. "There was never any hard evidence of our activities . . . and aside from a few people who had a hand of their own in the operation, there's no one left who could challenge our version of what happened." He gave a chill smile. "Anyone who knows anything—and is still alive—could only incriminate himself if he tried to talk about it. Besides, I've made damned sure all of StateSec's internal records reflect the official line. Anyone who wants to challenge all that 'impartial evidence' is obviously a counter-revolutionary enemy of the People."

" 'Not much chance' isn't the same thing as no chance at all," Ransom retorted.

Her tone was sharper than usual, for manipulator or not, she truly believed in the concept of enemies of the People, and her suspicion of the military was almost obsessive. Despite her need to produce pro-war propaganda which extolled the Navy's virtues as the Republic's protectors, her personal hatred for it was the next best thing to pathological. She loathed and despised it as a decadent, degenerate institution whose traditions still tied it to the old regime and probably inspired it to plot the Committee's overthrow in order to restore the Legislaturalists. Even worse, its persistent failures to throw the enemy back and save the Republic—which was probably at least partly due to its disloyalty—only reinforced her contempt with fear that it would fail to save *her*, and it was starting to get out of hand. In fact, her increasingly irrational antimilitary biases were a main reason for Pierre's decision that he needed someone *from* the military as a counterbalance.

He often thought it was odd that so much of her hatred should be fixed on the military, for unlike him, Ransom had come up through the action arm of the Citizens' Rights

Union. She'd spent the better part of forty T-years fighting not the military, which had virtually never intervened in domestic security matters, but the minions of Internal Security, and Pierre would have expected her passionate hate to be focused there. But it wasn't. She worked well with Oscar Saint-Just, one-time second-in-command of InSec, and she never seemed to hold past connections to InSec against any of State Security's current personnel. Perhaps, he thought, that was because she and InSec had played the same game by the same rules. They'd been enemies, but enemies who understood one another, and Ransom the not-so-ex-terrorist had absolutely no understanding of or sympathy for the traditions and values of the military community.

But whatever the source of her attitudes, neither Pierre nor Saint-Just shared their virulent intensity. Enemies of the *Committee*, yes; they had positive proof those were out there. But unlike Ransom, they could draw a clear distinction between the Committee and the PRH itself, just as they could accept that military failures were not incontrovertible proof of treasonous intentions. She couldn't. Perhaps that was because they were more pragmatic than she, or perhaps it was because each of them, in his own way, was actually trying to *build* something while Cordelia was still committed to tearing things down. Personally, Pierre suspected it was because her egoism and paranoia were reinforcing one another. In her own mind the People, the Committee of Public Safety, and Cordelia Ransom had become one and the same thing. He who opposed—or failed—any part of her personal Trinity was the enemy of them all, so simple self-defense required her to be eternally vigilant to ferret out and crush the People's enemies before *they* got *her*.

"And even if your cover holds up perfectly," she went on forcefully, "how can you even *consider* trusting anyone from the officer corps? You said it yourself: we've killed too many of them and made too many others—and their families—disappear. They'll never forgive us for that!"

"I think you underestimate the power of self-interest," Pierre replied for StateSec's commander. "Whoever we offer a slice of the pie to will have his own reasons to keep us in the saddle. For one thing, everyone will know he had to make some major accommodations with us to get the slot, and any power he has will depend on our patronage. And if we ease up on the officers—"

"They'll think *he's* the one to thank for it and have even more reason to be loyal to him rather than to us!" Ransom half snapped.

"Maybe," Pierre conceded. "But maybe not, too. Especially if we see to it that *we* put his advice into practice and do it very openly." Ransom started to open her mouth again, but his raised hand stopped her—for the moment. "I'm not suggesting that whoever we pick won't get at least some of the credit. For that matter, he'll probably get almost all of it, initially. But if we're going to win this war, we have to enlist our military as something more than slave labor. We've tried 'collective responsibility' with some success— after all," he smiled thinly, "knowing your family will suffer for your failures gives you a powerful incentive. But it's also counterproductive, and it produces *obedience*, not allegiance. By threatening their families, we become as much the enemy as the Manties. Probably even more than the Manties, for a lot of them. The Manties may be trying to kill *them*, but the Alliance isn't threatening to kill their wives or husbands or children.

"Frankly, it would be irrational for the officer corps to trust us under the present circumstances, and I think our past failures demonstrate that we have to 'rehabilitate' ourselves in their eyes if we expect them to become an effective—*motivated*—fighting force. We were incredibly lucky that the Navy didn't just stand by and watch the Levelers roll over us. In fact, I remind you that only one ship of the wall—just *one*, and not even a unit of the Capital Fleet, at that—had the initiative and nerve to intervene. If *Rousseau* had stayed out of it, you and Oscar and I would all be dead now, and we can't count on that sort of support again without demonstrating that we at least know we owe the people who saved our hides a debt. And the only way *I* can see to do that is to give them a voice at the highest level, make sure the rank and file know we've done it, and actually pay that voice some attention . . . publicly, at least."

"Publicly?" Ransom repeated with a cocked eyebrow and an arrested expression, and Pierre nodded.

"Publicly. Oscar and I have already discussed the sort of insurance policy we'll need if our tame war dog gets out of hand. Oscar?"

"I've considered each of the officers Rob's nominated," the SS man told Ransom. "It wasn't too hard to edit their records and their people's commissioners' reports. Any one of them will look like a knight in shining armor when we introduce him to the public, and all of them are quite competent in their own field, but we've got enough time bombs hidden in their dossiers to blow them away any time we have to. Of course," he smiled thinly, "it *would* be convenient if the officer in question were already dead before we make those bombs public. It's ever so much harder for a dead man to defend himself."

"I see." It was Ransom's turn to lean back and rub her chin in thought, and she nodded slowly. "All right, that's a good first step," she admitted finally. Her tone was still grudging, but it was no longer adamant. "I'll want a good look at those 'time bombs,' though. If we want this talking head to be vulnerable to charges down the road, Public Information's going to have to be careful about just how we initially build him up for public consumption. We wouldn't want any avoidable inconsistencies in there."

"No problem," Saint-Just assured her, and she nodded some more. But her expression was still dissatisfied, and she let her chair snap back upright as she stopped rubbing her jaw and leaned over the table towards Pierre.

"This is all well and good as far as it goes, Rob," she said, "but it's still a hell of a risk. And we're going to be sending some very mixed signals, however we do it. I mean, we just shot Admiral Girardi for losing Trevor's Star, and whatever we may have told the Proles, we all know it wasn't entirely his fault." Pierre was a bit surprised she was willing to make even that much of a concession to a Navy officer, but perhaps it was because even she had to admit dead men could no longer plot treason. "The Navy's senior officers certainly don't think it was, anyway. They're convinced we only shot him to 'prove' to the Mob that it wasn't *our* fault, and even some *enlisted* personnel resented our turning him into a 'scapegoat'! I don't see your proposal making much of a dent in that any time soon."

"Ah, but that's because you don't know who I'm planning to appoint!" Pierre said, then sat without another word, grinning at her. She glared at him, trying to pretend his effort to play on her impatience wasn't working. Unfortunately, they both knew it was. The better part of a full minute dragged past, then she shrugged impatiently.

"So tell me already!"

"Esther McQueen," Pierre said simply, and Ransom jerked upright in her chair.

"You're joking!" she snapped, and her face darkened when Pierre only shook his head. "Well, you damned well *ought* to be! Damn it, Oscar!" The glare she turned on Saint-Just should have been sufficient to incinerate the SS chief on the spot. "The woman's personal popularity is already at dangerous levels, and your own spy's reported that she's got ambitions—and plans—of her own. Are you seriously suggesting putting a loaded pulser into the hands of someone we *know* is looking for one already?"

"First of all, her ambition may be our best ally," Pierre said before Saint-Just could reply. "Yes, Brigadier Fontein's warned us that she has her own agenda. In fact, she's made one or two efforts to set up some sort of clandestine network among her fellow flag officers. But she hasn't met with much success, because they know what she has in mind as well as we do. Most of them are too cowed to stick their necks out, and the ones who aren't consider her as much a political animal as a military one. Given the, um,

finality with which politics are played these days, they're
not about to trust even one of their own if she's shown she
wants to join the game. If, on the other hand, we give her
a place at the table, that very ambition will give her every
reason to make sure the Committee—and, with it, *her*
power base—survives."

"Hmph!" Ransom relaxed just a bit and folded her arms
across her chest as she considered. Then she shook her
head again, but this time the gesture was slower and more
thoughtful. "All right," she said at last, "let's assume you
have a point there. But she's still dangerous. The Mob sees
her as the Committee's savior against the Levelers—hell,
half the damned *Committee* thinks she can walk on water
right now! But we don't even know that she actually
intended to save us at all, do we? If her pinnace hadn't
crashed, she might just have kept right on rolling with the
momentum and finished us off herself!"

"She might have, but I don't believe for a minute she
planned to," Pierre said, just a bit more emphatically than
his level of confidence deserved. "The Committee at least
has the legitimacy of the original resolution which created
it, not to mention almost six T-years as the Republic's
functioning government. Even if she'd managed to wipe
us out herself, what would she have had for a power
base? Remember that only her own flagship supported
her when she came to *rescue* us, and she was clearly
doing her duty then. There's no way she could have
counted on the rest of the Fleet to support any sort of
putsch on her part, especially not given her reputation
for political ambition."

"It sounds to me like you're trying to convince *yourself*
of that," Ransom muttered darkly. "And even assuming
you're right, doesn't your logic undercut your own argument
for giving her a seat at the table? If the rest of the officer
corps see her as a political animal, why should appointing
her to the Committee convince them to support us?"

"Because political animal or not, she's also the best field
commander we've got, and they know *that*, too," Saint-Just

answered. "They don't distrust her competence, Cordelia—just her motives. In a sense, that gives us the best of both worlds: an officer whose ability is recognized by her peers, but whose reputation for political ambition sets her apart from the 'real' Navy."

"If she's that damned good, how did we lose Trevor's Star?" Ransom demanded, and Pierre hid a smile behind his hand. Cordelia's ministry had turned Trevor's Star into a sort of metaphorical redoubt for the entire People's Republic—the "line in the stars," the point from which no retreat could even be contemplated—despite his own suggestions that she might want to tone the rhetoric down just a bit. To be sure, the system *had* been of enormous strategic importance, and the military consequences of its loss were what had originally inspired him to look for a naval representative for the Committee. Yet viewed against the sheer size of the Republic, even Trevor's Star was ultimately expendable. What was *not* expendable was public morale or the People's Navy's will to fight, both of which had taken yet another nose dive when "the line in the stars" fell to the Royal Manticoran Navy's Sixth Fleet.

"We lost Trevor's Star," he told Ransom, "because the Manties have better ships and their technology is still better than ours. And because—thanks in no small part to our own policy of shooting losing admirals—their senior officers go right on accruing experience while ours keep suffering from a severe case of being dead."

His caustic tone widened her eyes, and he gave her a thin smile.

"McQueen may not have been able to hold the system, but at least she inflicted heavy losses on the Manties. In fact, given the relative sizes of our navies, the Alliance's proportional losses were probably worse than ours, at least before the final engagement. Her captains and junior squadron commanders gained a lot of experience during the fighting, too, and we managed to rotate about a third of them home to pass that along. But it was obvious at least a year ago that White Haven was going to take the system eventually. That's why I pulled McQueen out and sent Girardi in to take the heat." Ransom quirked an eyebrow, and Pierre shrugged. "I didn't want to lose her, and given our existing policies, we'd have had no choice but to shoot her if she'd still been in command when Trevor's Star went down." He smiled wryly. "After last month's excitement, I'm inclined to see that as one of my more brilliant moves of the war."

"Hmph!" Ransom repeated, sliding lower in her chair once more and frowning down at the conference table. "You're sure McQueen is the one you want for this? I have to tell you that the more you tell me about how competent she is, the more nervous you make me."

"Competent in her own area is one thing; competent in *our* area is another," Pierre said confidently. "Her reach considerably exceeds her grasp on the political side, and it'll take her a while to figure out how the rules work on our side of the street. Oscar and I will keep a close eye on her, and if it starts to look like she's figured it out, well, accidents happen."

"And whatever negative considerations might attach to choosing *her*," Saint-Just said, "she's a better choice than the next candidate in line."

"Which candidate would that be?" Ransom asked.

"Before our raid on the Manties' commerce in Silesia blew up in our faces, Javier Giscard would have been an even better choice than McQueen. As it is, he's completely ineligible, at least for now. His political views are more acceptable than McQueen's—in fact, Commissioner Pritchard continues to speak very highly of him—and in fairness to him, what happened to his plan wasn't his fault. In fact, our decision to recall him was probably a mistake. But we *did* recall him, and he's still on probation for his 'failure.'" Ransom cocked her head, and Saint-Just shrugged. "It's only a formality—he's too good for us to shoot unless we absolutely have to—but we can't rehabilitate him overnight."

"All right, I can see that," Ransom nodded, "but that just tells me who the next candidate *isn't*."

"Sorry," Saint-Just apologized. "I got distracted. In answer to your question, McQueen's only real competition is Thomas Theisman. He's considerably junior to her, but he was the only flag officer to emerge from Operation Dagger with a reputation as a fighter, and he distinguished himself in the Trevor's Star fighting before we pulled him out. His stand at Seabring is one of the very few victories we've had to crow over, but while the Navy respects him as a tactician and a strategist, he's been very careful to remain totally apolitical."

"And that's a disadvantage?" Ransom sounded surprised, and Pierre shook his head at her.

"You're slipping, Cordelia," he said mildly. "There's only one reason for him to be *apolitical*, and it's not because he admires us. He might choose to avoid the political game because of its inherent risks, but no one with his combat record could be an idiot, and only an idiot wouldn't see that there are all sorts of small ways he could send us signals that he's an obedient little boy. They wouldn't have to be *sincere*, but they wouldn't cost him anything to send."

"His people's commissioner agrees with that assessment," Saint-Just put in. "Citizen Commissioner LePic's reports make it clear that he rather admires Theisman as an officer and a man, and he's convinced Theisman is loyal to the *Republic*. But he's also cautioned us that Theisman is less than pleased with several of *our* policies. The admiral's been careful not to say so, but his attitude gives him away."

"I see," Ransom said, and her voice was far grimmer than it had been.

"At any rate," Pierre said, trying to reclaim the conversation before Ransom's suspicions had time to come fully to life, "Theisman was acceptable from the professional viewpoint, but he's a Brutus, and we need a Cassius. McQueen's aspirations may make her dangerous, but ambition is more predictable than principle."

"I can't argue with that," Ransom muttered. She frowned down at the table again, then nodded. "All right, Rob. I know you and Oscar are going to put her in whatever I say, and I have to admit that your arguments make sense in at least some ways. Just be *very* sure you keep an eye on her. The last thing we need is for a politically ambitious admiral to put together a real military coup against *us*."

"That *would* be rather a case of hoisting us with our own petard," Pierre agreed.

"But whatever we do with McQueen, I'm concerned by what you've said about Theisman," Ransom went on. "I gather that with McQueen diverted to political duties, Theisman will take her place as our best commander in the officer corps' estimation?" Saint-Just nodded, and her frown deepened. "In that case, I think it might be a good idea to take a close personal look at Citizen Admiral Theisman."

"'Personal' as in you're thinking of taking it yourself?" Pierre asked in a carefully casual tone.

"Maybe." Ransom plucked at her lower lip for a moment. "He's stationed at Barnett now?"

"System commander," Saint-Just confirmed. "We needed to put someone good in charge of DuQuesne."

Ransom nodded. The Manticoran Alliance's capture of Trevor's Star gave it a near-impregnable position between the heart of the People's Republic and the Barnett System, but the massive infrastructure of DuQuesne Base and all the other military installations of the system remained. Barnett had been intended as the jump-off point for the inevitable war against Manticore, and the Legislaturalist regime had spent twenty T-years building it up for its task. However much the Manties might want to let it wither on the vine, they couldn't afford to leave it intact in their rear, for unlike wet-navy ships, starships could easily avoid interception if they planned their routes through hyper-space with even moderate care. Reinforcements—or fresh attack forces—might take time to reach Barnett on such roundabout courses, but they could get there.

The Manties, however, could get there more quickly. While their Sixth Fleet had been busy taking Trevor's Star, other Allied task forces had taken advantage of the People's Navy's distraction and snapped up the forward bases of

Treadway, Solway, and Mathias. They'd captured the naval facilities in Treadway virtually intact, which was bad enough, but they'd also broken through the arc of bases which had guarded Barnett's southeastern flank . . . and that didn't even consider what the loss of Trevor's Star implied. With the capture of *that* system, the Royal Manticoran Navy had attained control of every terminus of the Manticore Wormhole Junction, and that meant convoys—and task forces—could move directly from the Manticore Binary System to Trevor's Star and come down on Barnett from the north.

For all practical purposes, then, Barnett was doomed, yet the Manties had taken their own pounding to capture Trevor's Star. They'd need at least a little time to reorganize and catch their breath, and once they were ready to move again, Barnett was almost certain to attract their immediate attention away from the Republic's core and back out towards the frontier. That made holding the system as long as possible, even if only as a diversionary measure, critically important, which, in turn, required the services of a competent system CO.

"From the way you've been talking, I assume you don't intend for him to ride the base down in flames, though," Ransom observed after a moment, and Pierre nodded. "In that case, I think I should take a little trip down to Barnett to form a personal impression of him," she said. "After all, Public Information's going to have to deal with whatever finally happens there, and if he looks too politically unreliable, we might want to *leave* him there . . . and write a truly epic piece about his gallant but doomed battle to fend off the attacking Manticoran hordes. Sort of a Theisman's Last Stand."

"Unless you see something LePic's entirely missed, he's still going to be too valuable to throw away," Saint-Just cautioned.

"Oscar, for a cold-blooded spook, you can be entirely too squeamish," Ransom said severely. "The only good threat is a dead one, however unlikely a danger it may seem. And when your navy's getting its ass kicked as thoroughly as ours is, the occasional dead hero can be worth a hell of a lot more than the same officer was ever worth alive. Besides, it amuses me to turn potential threats into propaganda assets."

She smiled that thin, cold, *hungry* smile which frightened even Oscar Saint-Just, and Pierre shrugged. Oscar was right about Theisman's value, and Pierre had no intention of simply throwing the man away, whatever Cordelia wanted. On the other hand, Cordelia was the Mob's darling, the spokeswoman and focus of its urge to violence. If she decided that she simply had to add Theisman's head to the ones already mounted on her wall, Pierre was prepared to give it to her—especially if handing him over bought Cordelia's (and Public Information's) support for adding McQueen to the Committee. Not that he intended to tell her so.

"That's a three-week trip one way," he pointed out instead. "Can you afford to be off Haven that long?"

"I don't see why not," she replied. "You're not going to convene any more meetings of the full Committee for the next two or three months, are you?" He shook his head, and she shrugged. "In that case, you and Oscar won't need my vote to keep the machinery running, and I've got *Tepes* set up to function as a mobile command post for Public Information. Nothing says all of our propaganda has to originate here on Haven and move outwards, you know. My deputy can handle routine decisions here in my absence, and we'll produce any new material aboard *Tepes*. As long as I'm in a position to vet it before release, we can dump it into the provincial nets and let it work inward from the frontier just as well as outward from the center."

"All right," he said after a moment, his tone mild. "If you want to look the situation over and you feel comfortable about managing Public Information from there, I think we can spare you long enough for the trip. Be sure you take along enough security, though."

"I will," Ransom promised. "And I'll take a complete tech section from the ministry, too. We'll get lots of stock footage, do some interviews with personnel there for release after the system falls—that sort of thing. After all, if we can't hold it in the first place, we might as well get as much advantage out of *losing* it as we can!"

• Chapter One

The atmospheric dust count was up today. Concentrations weren't enough to bother native Graysons after almost a thousand years of adaptive evolution, but they were more than sufficient to worry someone from a planet with lower levels of heavy metals.

Admiral of the Green Hamish Alexander, Thirteenth Earl of White Haven and designated commander of Eighth Fleet (assuming it ever got itself put together), was a native of the planet Manticore, and the capital world of the Star Kingdom of Manticore did *not* boast such levels. He felt mildly conspicuous as the only breath-masked member of the entourage on the landing pad, but the better part of a century of naval service had given him a healthy respect for environmental hazards. He was perfectly willing to feel a little conspicuous if that was the price of avoiding airborne lead and cadmium.

He was also the only person on the pad who wore the space-black-and-gold of the Royal Manticoran Navy. Over half of his companions were in civilian dress, including the two women who wore the ankle-length skirts and long, tabardlike vests of traditional Grayson fashion. Those in uniform, however, were about equally divided between the green-on-green of the Harrington Steadholder's Guard and the blue-on-blue of the Grayson Space Navy. Even Lieutenant Robards, White Haven's aide, was a Grayson. The admiral had found that a little disconcerting at first. He was much more accustomed to having members of allied navies come to the Star Kingdom than to meeting them on their home turf, but he'd quickly become comfortable with the new arrangement, and he had to admit it made sense. Eighth Fleet would be the first Allied fleet which was actually composed of more non-Manticoran than RMN units. Given the "seniority" of the Manticoran Navy, there'd never been much question that the RMN would provide the fleet commander, but a good two-thirds of its starships would be drawn from the explosively expanding GSN and the far smaller Erewhon Navy. As such, White Haven, as CO 8 FLT (Designate), really had no choice but to build his staff around a Grayson core, and he'd spent the last month and a half doing just that.

All in all, he'd been impressed by what he'd discovered in the process. The GSN's expansion had spread its officer corps thin—indeed, something like twelve percent of all "Grayson" officers were actually Manticorans on loan from the Star Kingdom—and its institutional inexperience showed, but it was almost aggressively competent. Grayson squadron and task force commanders seemed to take nothing at all for granted, for they knew how quickly most of their officers had been pushed up to their present ranks. They drilled their subordinates mercilessly, and their tactical and maneuvering orders spelled out their intentions with a degree of precision which sometimes produced results that were a little too mechanical for White Haven's taste. He was more accustomed to the Manticoran tradition in which officers of a certain rank were supposed to handle the details themselves, without specific direction from higher authority. Yet he was willing to admit that a navy as "young" as the GSN probably required more detailed orders . . . and if Grayson fleet maneuvers were sometimes mechanical, he'd never seen the kind of raggedness which could creep in when a flag officer assumed—incorrectly— that his subordinates understood what he had in mind.

But if the earl sometimes wished Grayson admirals would grant their subordinates a little more initiative, he'd been both astounded and delighted by the GSN's relentless emphasis on actual shipboard drills, not just computer simulations, and their willingness to expend munitions in live-fire exercises. RMN tradition favored the same approach, but the Manticoran Admiralty had always been forced to fight Parliament tooth and nail for the funding it required. High Admiral Matthews, the GSN's military commander-in-chief, on the other hand, had the enthusiastic support of Protector Benjamin and a solid majority of the Planetary Chamber, Steadholder and Steader alike. Perhaps that support owed something to the fact that the current war with Haven had brought deep-space combat to Yeltsin's Star four times in less than eight T-years, whereas no one had dared attack the Manticore Binary System directly in almost three centuries, but White Haven suspected that it owed an equal debt to the woman he and his companions had gathered to welcome home.

His lips quirked and the blue eyes which could assume the chill of arctic ice twinkled at that thought. Lady Dame Honor Harrington, Countess Harrington, was only a captain of the list, as far as the RMN was concerned, and she'd earned a reputation (among her many domestic political enemies, at any rate) as a dangerous, hot-tempered, undisciplined loose warhead. But here in Yeltsin she carried the rank of a full admiral in the GSN, not to mention the title of Steadholder Harrington. She was the second-ranking officer of Grayson's Navy, one of the eighty great nobles who governed the planet, the wealthiest woman—or, for that matter, man—in Grayson history, the only living holder of the Star of Grayson (which also happened to make her Protector Benjamin's official Champion), *and* the woman who had saved the system from foreign conquest, not just once, but twice. White Haven himself was deeply respected by the Grayson Navy and people, for he was the officer who'd overseen the conquest of their fratricidal sister world of Masada and won the Third Battle of Grayson to open the war with Haven, but he remained a "foreigner." Honor Harrington didn't. She had become one of their own, and in the process, whether she knew it or not, she'd also become the patron saint of their fleet.

She probably *didn't* know it, White Haven reflected. It

wasn't the sort of thing which would occur to her . . . which no doubt helped explain why it was true. But White Haven and every other Manticoran working with the GSN certainly knew. How could they not? The ultimate touchstone for every Grayson training concept or tactical innovation could be contained in the three words "Lady Harrington says" or their companion "Lady Harrington would." The near idolatry with which the GSN had adopted the precepts and example of a single individual, however competent, would have been terrifying if that individual's fundamental philosophy had not included the need to continuously question her *own* concepts. Somehow, and White Haven wasn't certain precisely how, Honor Harrington had also managed to transmit *that* portion of her personality to the navy so enthusiastically forming itself in her image, and he was profoundly grateful that she had.

Of course, the GSN had given her a much freer hand than the Manticoran Admiralty had ever given any RMN admiral, but that made her accomplishments no less impressive. High Admiral Matthews had admitted to White Haven that he'd all but dragooned her into GSN service expressly to pick her brain, and that was something the earl readily understood. Very few fleets could match the experience of the Royal Manticoran Navy, and for all her political problems back home, Harrington's professional reputation had been second to none in the navy of her birth kingdom. Even if it hadn't seen her in action itself, any navy in the GSN's position would have been prepared to do just about anything to get her into its uniform. And, White Haven thought, given how intensely the Graysons had listened to her, and how eager they'd been to utilize her as a training resource, it would actually have been surprising if she *had* realized how deeply she'd impressed her own personality and philosophy upon them. They'd adopted her concepts so readily that it must have seemed to her as if *she* were adapting to *their* philosophy. Oh, yes. He understood how it had all happened. Yet that made it no less ironic that, in so many ways, the Grayson Space

Navy was actually closer to the ideal of the Manticoran Navy than the RMN itself.

It also, he admitted, had offered him a new and valuable perspective on Harrington herself. He was familiar with the sycophantic personalities which all too often attached themselves to a successful officer, just as he recognized the more extreme forms of unquestioning hero worship when he saw them, and he'd found some of both of those here on Grayson where Harrington was concerned. But when a single, foreign-born woman could walk into a theocratic, male-dominated society and win the personal devotion of a group so disparate that it contained not simply that society's navy but old-line Grayson male supremacists like Howard Clinkscales, Harrington Steading's regent; reformers like Benjamin IX, the planet's reigning monarch; religious leaders like the Reverend Jeremiah Sullivan, spiritual head of the Church of Humanity Unchained; urbane and polished statesmen like Lord Henry Prestwick, Grayson's Chancellor; and even ex-Havenite officers like Alfredo Yu, now a GSN admiral, she had to be something quite out of the ordinary. White Haven had seen that in her the very first time he'd met her, despite the physical wounds and the grief and sense of guilt she'd carried away from the Second Battle of Yeltsin, but then he'd been in the position of her senior officer, looking down a steep gradient of rank, military and social alike. These days, she matched his naval rank (in Grayson service, at least) and, as a Steadholder, however new her title, took social precedence over even one of the oldest of Manticore's earldoms.

Hamish Alexander wasn't the sort to feel diminished by anyone. One of the small number of people who could address his Queen in private by her given name, he was also the single most respected strategist of the Manticoran Alliance. His reputation was firmly based on achievement, and he knew it, just as he knew he truly was the equal or superior of any serving officer in any other navy in space. He wasn't arrogant—or he tried not to be—yet he knew who and what he was, and it would have been foolish to pretend he didn't. But he also knew Harrington had begun her career without the advantage of an aristocratic name or the family alliances and patronage which went with it. However much White Haven might have earned by merit, and however much he'd given back in part payment for the opportunities he'd enjoyed by an accident of birth, he could never forget or deny that his family's position had given him a starting advantage Harrington had never had. Yet here on Grayson she'd been given a chance to show all that she could do and be, and what she had accomplished was almost humbling to the man who was Earl of White Haven.

She was barely half his age, and this entire section of the galaxy had entered the dark valley of a war whose like had not been seen in centuries. Not a war of negotiated peaces or even conquest, but one in which the losing side would be destroyed, not merely defeated. It had already raged for going on six T-years, and despite the Allies' recent successes, there was no end in sight. In a society in which the prolong treatment stretched life spans to as much as three hundred-plus years, advancement to the senior ranks of any navy could be glacially slow, although the RMN's prewar expansion had kept things from being quite that bad, professionally speaking, for its officers. Compared to navies like those of the Solarian League, promotion had actually been quite rapid, and now the war had kicked the door to senior rank wide. Even victorious admirals sometimes died, and the Navy's expansion rate had trebled since the start of open hostilities. Where would someone like an Honor Harrington end this war . . . assuming that she survived? What sort of mark would she make upon it? It was obvious—to everyone but her, perhaps—that she would figure in whatever histories were finally written, but would she attain the exalted rank in her birth navy which her abilities deserved? And if she did, what would she *do* with it?

Those questions had come to fascinate White Haven. Perhaps it was because, in a sense, she'd been his hostess since his arrival in Yeltsin. She'd been generous enough to offer him the opportunity to stay at Harrington House, the official residence from which she governed Harrington Steading when she was on Grayson, while he was here. It made sense, given that Alvarez Field, the GSN's major new planetary base and site of its new Bernard Yanakov Tactical Simulation Center, was only thirty minutes away by air car. At least until Eighth Fleet's units were physically assembled, most training exercises had to be done in sims, whatever the Graysons—or White Haven—might have preferred. That meant he had to be located someplace handy to Alvarez's simulators, and by inviting him to stay at Harrington House while she herself was temporarily stuck back in the Star Kingdom, Harrington had given the imprimatur of her approval to his relationship with the GSN. He probably hadn't needed it, and he was quite certain she hadn't reasoned it out in those terms, but he was also experienced enough not to turn down any advantage that came his way.

Yet living in her house, his needs seen to by her servants, speaking with her fellow Grayson officers, her regent, her security staff . . . In a very real way, it had felt sometimes as if he were uncovering facets of her personality which could be discovered only in her absence. It was silly, perhaps. He was ninety-three T-years old, yet he was fascinated—almost mesmerized—by the accomplishments of a woman to whom he'd spoken perhaps a dozen times. In one sense, he scarcely knew her at all, but in another, he'd come to know her as he'd known very few people in his life, and a part of him looked forward to somehow reconciling the difference between those two views of her.

Honor Harrington leaned back in the pinnace seat and tried not to smile as Major Andrew LaFollet, second-in-command of the Harrington Steadholder's Guard and her personal armsman, crawled as far under the seat in front of her as he could get.

"Come on, now, Jason," he wheedled. His soft Grayson accent was well suited to coaxing, and he was using that advantage to the full. "We're due to hit atmosphere any minute now. You have to come on out . . . please?"

Only a cheery chirp answered, and Honor heard him sigh. He tried to crawl still further under the seat, then backed out and sat up grumpily on the decksole. His auburn hair was tousled and his gray eyes dared any of his subordinates to say one word—just *one*—about his current, less than dignified preoccupation, but no one accepted the challenge. Indeed, Honor's other armsmen were busy looking at anything *except* him, and their expressions were admirably, one might almost say determinedly, grave.

LaFollet watched them not watching him for a long moment, then sighed again. His own mouth twitched in a small grin, and he turned his eyes to the slender brown-and-white dappled treecat curled up in the seat beside Honor's.

"I don't want to sound like I'm criticizing," he told the 'cat, "but maybe *you* should fish him out."

"He has a point, Sam," Honor observed, feeling her right cheek dimple as her smile grew broader. "He *is* your son. And unlike Andrew, you'd fit under the seat."

Samantha only looked at her, green eyes dancing, and her lazy yawn bared needle-sharp white fangs. Two more prick-eared heads, each far smaller than her own, rose drowsily from the warm nest she'd formed by curling about their owners, and she reached out with one gentle true-hand to push them back down. Then she turned her gaze to the larger, cream-and-gray 'cat lying across Honor's lap, and Honor felt the faint echoes of a deep, intricate mental flow as Nimitz raised his head to gaze back. None of the humans present could tell exactly what Samantha was saying to her mate—indeed, no one but Honor even "heard" it at all—but everyone grasped her meaning when Nimitz heaved a sigh of his own, flicked his ears in agreement, and slithered to the deck.

He flowed along the aisle using all three sets of limbs, then settled down beside the seat LaFollet had tried to climb under. He crossed his true-hands on the decksole and rested his chin on them, gazing under the seat, and once again Honor felt the echoes of someone else's thoughts. She also felt Nimitz's mingled amusement, pride, and exasperation as he addressed himself firmly to the most adventuresome of his offspring.

As far as she knew, no other human had ever been able to sense the emotions of a treecat, and certainly no one had ever been able to sense the emotions of other humans *through* their adopted partner, but for all its unheard of strength, her link to Nimitz remained too unclear for her to follow his actual thoughts. That didn't keep her from realizing that he was taking the time to form those thoughts very clearly and distinctly, and she suspected he was also keeping them as simple as he could . . . which only made sense when he was directing them to a kitten who was barely four months old.

Nothing happened for several seconds, and then she sensed the equivalent of a mental sigh of resignation and a tiny duplicate of Nimitz poked its head out from under the seat. James MacGuiness, Honor's personal steward, had given Jason his name in honor of the kitten's intrepid voyages of exploration, and Honor knew she should have expected the marvelous new puzzle of the pinnace to suck him into wandering. She wished he weren't quite so curious, but that was a trait all 'cats—and especially young ones— shared. Indeed, there was something almost appalling about the compulsion to explore which afflicted *all* of Samantha and Nimitz's kittens. Jason was simply the worst of them, with a taste for solo boldness worthy of his name, and Honor sometimes wondered how any treecat survived to maturity if they were all this curious in the wild. But this crop wasn't *in* the wild, and at least every human in the pinnace knew to keep an eye out for the kids.

And so did the treecats. Even as she watched Nimitz gather Jason in with one agile, long-fingered true-hand, another brown-and-white female came hopping from seat back to seat back with yet a fourth kitten. Honor recognized the new kitten as Achilles, Jason's barely less audacious brother, and smiled again as she watched his nursemaid haul him—wiggling and squirming in protest the entire way—back to his mother.

She wondered if even MacGuiness truly realized just how rare a sight for human eyes that was. Treecats who adopted humans almost never mated and produced offspring, and in those very rare cases in which they did, mothers invariably returned to their own or their mates' native clans to give birth and then fostered their children with other females of the clan. Outside the Sphinx Forestry Commission, only a tiny handful of humans had ever seen infant 'cats in the wild, and as far as Honor knew, *no one* had ever seen infants whose parents had introduced them into human society from birth.

But that was precisely what Nimitz and Samantha had done, and their refusal to conform to the expected pattern had caught both Honor and the Navy off guard. The RMN had been forced long ago to evolve special rules for the rare instances in which it had to deal with a pregnant treecat who'd bonded to one of its personnel. That was why Honor had been reassigned to the Manticore Binary System eight months ago on her return from the Silesian Confederacy. It both got Samantha away from radiation hazards and other risks associated with service in space and put her within easy reach of Sphinx and her own or Nimitz's clan. Of course, the fact that Samantha had never adopted Honor in the usual sense had put her case outside normal parameters to begin with, but the death of the person she *had* adopted had left Nimitz and Honor as her sole family. In the wake of that devastating loss, the Admiralty had decided, Honor qualified for the maternity leave normally granted to both halves of an adoption bond. Besides, it had given them a chance to assign her to the Weapons Development Board for the duration of said leave. She'd been an obvious choice to give the Board feedback on how well its latest brainchildren had worked in the field, since she was the only person who'd ever commanded a squadron—albeit only one of armed merchant cruisers—equipped with them, and to her own surprise, she'd actually enjoyed the duty.

But despite all the Navy efforts to accommodate her needs, Samantha had proven persistently unconventional. Perhaps that was to have been expected. Virtually all of the very few female 'cats who'd ever adopted had bonded to Forestry Commission rangers and never left Sphinx. Honor had run a check. No law or regulation required the registry of treecat adoptions, so the records she'd been able to consult had to have been incomplete, but as nearly as she could determine, in well over five T-centuries, only eight female 'cats had *ever* adopted anyone except a ranger . . . and that number included Samantha. That probably should have warned her that Samantha was unlikely to feel bound by whatever parenting conventions were "normal" for 'cats, but she'd still been surprised when Nimitz made it clear that Samantha wanted and intended to return to Grayson—with her kittens—when he and Honor did.

That had seemed like a very bad idea to Honor. She and Nimitz were scheduled to resume shipboard duty soon after her return, which would leave Samantha all alone with four rambunctious young on an alien planet whose environment included invisible and insidious risk factors which could kill even an adult 'cat, much less a kitten. Worse, she and her children would be the *only* treecats on the planet, leaving her as a first-time mother with no older and more experienced mothers of her own kind to whom to turn for advice or assistance.

Honor had tried to make those points to Nimitz and Samantha, and she'd been confident *Nimitz* grasped them. But she hadn't been certain Samantha understood even with Nimitz to explain them to her. Telepathy was all very well, but Samantha had seemed so blithely unconcerned by Honor's arguments that she'd doubted the message was getting through.

Until the week before their departure for Grayson, that was. It had never occurred to Honor to wonder about just how much seniority Samantha had among her own kind.

She was quite a bit younger than Nimitz, and Honor had simply assumed that the wishes of a 'cat of her relative youth couldn't carry a great deal of weight with a clan to which she belonged only "by marriage." But she'd been forced to reconsider that assumption rather radically when no less than eight members of Nimitz's clan—three of them female, all older than Samantha—arrived on her doorstep. She'd been staying in her parent's rambling, five-hundred-year-old house on the flanks of the Copperwall Mountains when they turned up, and she'd hardly been able to believe her own eyes.

She'd been certain at first that there was some mistake when MacGuiness answered the front doorbell and the newcomers had walked calmly inside, but Nimitz and Samantha had greeted them with purrs of pleasure and the unmistakable air of hosts welcoming expected guests. The thought of trying to chase them back outside had never even occurred to Honor—one simply didn't do things like that with treecats—and the eight of them had hopped up onto her parents' dining room table and regarded her expectantly. Her sense of shock had made her a bit slow, but a sharp nudge over her link to Nimitz had reminded her of her manners, and she'd introduced herself to her surprise guests while MacGuiness disappeared into the kitchen in search of the celery all 'cats loved.

Each 'cat had acknowledged her self-introduction gravely, and though it was considered bad form to assign names to 'cats unless the 'cat in question had adopted the namer, there were so many of them that Honor *had* to call them something just to keep them all straight. Given her taste for naval history, the five males had ended up dubbed Nelson, Togo, Hood, Farragut, and Hipper, but naming the females had been harder. Since so few of them adopted, it had seemed particularly important to come up with names which reflected their personalities, and Honor had needed several days to get to know them well enough to feel comfortable naming them.

In the end, the apparent social dynamics of the group

had done it for her. The eldest of the three had become
Hera, for it was obvious that every one of the males—
except, perhaps, Nimitz—deferred utterly to her authority.
If she was the head of this small slice of a clan, however,
the 'cat Honor had dubbed Athena was obviously her exec
and general advisor. The third female, Artemis, was barely
older than Samantha, but she was also the feistiest of the
ladies and the one who'd taken on the task of teaching the
kittens the rudiments of hunting and stalking.

Honor still felt uncomfortable over having assigned
names at all, but the newcomers had accepted their new
appellations with cheerful approval. They'd also proceeded
to settle down as if they'd always been members of her
household . . . and given every sign that they intended to
remain as such.

Yet if *they*'d been calm about it, the humans of Sphinx
had not.

Despite the fact that Honor knew more about treecats
than ninety-nine percent of her fellow Sphinxians, she'd
had no more idea of how to proceed than anyone else did.
It was clear Samantha and Nimitz had invited the others
to join them, but she'd taken a while to grasp that it wasn't
just for an extended visit or to take the kittens back to
Nimitz's clan. And when she finally *did* realize Samantha
actually intended for the newcomers to accompany her and
Nimitz back to Grayson, it really hit the fan.

Treecats were a protected species. More than that, the
Ninth Amendment to the Star Kingdom's Constitution
expressly granted them special status as the indigenous
intelligent species of Sphinx. The laws which protected their
corporate claim to just over a third of Sphinx's surface in
perpetuity and guarded them from exploitation were, to
say the least, firm, but the people who'd drafted those laws
had never anticipated a situation such as this. Adoption
bonds had much the same legal status as marriages, which
helped explain the Admiralty regulations sending pregnant
'cats and their humans home, but the fact that Samantha
hadn't adopted Honor had already put their relationship

on the fringes of established precedence. It was unheard of for a single human to have two 'cats, although no one had been prepared to comment when it was obvious Samantha and Nimitz were mated. But *eight more* of them? No one had ever even contemplated a situation in which one human found herself the focus of no less than *ten* treecats (not to mention the kittens) . . . all of whom seemed intent on following said human off-planet!

The Forestry Commission had pitched a fit, and a dozen rangers had descended on the Harrington Homestead, grimly determined to rescue the eight "wild" 'cats from any chance of exploitation. But once there, they'd been faced by their rescuees' determination not to be rescued. Two of the rangers had been accompanied by their own 'cats, whose reactions had made it plain that *they* felt Samantha and Nimitz's friends had the right to go wherever they wanted to go with whomever they chose to go there with . . . however hot and bothered it might make humans.

But once the Forestry Commission had retreated in confusion, the Admiralty's minions had moved in. They'd wanted Honor to leave Samantha on Sphinx with Nimitz's clan—which, in fact, had been her original intention. Honor couldn't blame BuPers for being just a bit put out with her for changing her mind (although, to be fair, *she* wasn't precisely the one whose mind had changed), but she did think they'd overreacted when they all but commanded her to leave Samantha, the kittens, and—especially!—the eight "wild" adults on Sphinx. They hadn't quite made it a nondiscretionary order, but they *had* specifically denied her the right to take any 'cat other than Nimitz with her aboard the military transport whose use her orders to Grayson authorized.

Unfortunately for Their Lordships, the Articles of War didn't *require* naval personnel to use naval shipping to reach their assigned duty stations, and once she'd accepted that her six-limbed friends were serious, Honor had given in and provided alternate transportation. At first, she'd intended to buy passage aboard a passenger liner. Then she'd considered chartering a small private vessel. What she *hadn't* considered—until Willard Neufsteiler, her chief financial manager, suggested it—was buying a ship of her own.

Since even a small, unarmed, bare-bones civilian starship cost about seventy million dollars, the idea of purchasing one had seemed extravagant, to say the least. But as Willard had pointed out, she was worth over three and a half *billion* by now, and if she bought the ship as a corporate asset of her Grayson-headquartered Sky Domes, Ltd., she would owe no licensing fees (in light of her steadholder's status), while the purchase would provide a substantial tax write-off in the Star Kingdom. Not only that, he'd been able to negotiate a very attractive price with the Hauptman Cartel for an only slightly used vessel much larger and more capable than she'd thought possible. And, he'd argued persuasively, her growing financial empire required more and more trips back and forth between Yeltsin's Star and Manticore by her various managers and factors. The flexibility and independence from passenger liner schedules which a privately owned vessel would provide would grow only more useful as time passed.

And so, to her considerable bemusement, she'd returned to Grayson not aboard an RMN or GSN cruiser or destroyer and not accompanied by a single treecat. Instead, she'd returned in state aboard the fifty-k-ton, private registry *Star Falcon*-class yacht RMS *Paul Tankersley* accompanied by *fourteen* treecats, and somewhere in the course of the voyage, she'd realized what she was really doing.

She was helping Samantha and Nimitz establish the first extra-Sphinxian colony of treecats. For whatever reason, her two friends and—obviously—the rest of Nimitz's clan had decided it was time to plant their kind on another planet, and that represented a quantum leap in their relationship with humanity. It might also prove that they were more intelligent than even Honor had suspected.

She knew Nimitz, at least, understood that the Star

Kingdom was at war, and he'd had entirely too close a view, on occasion, of what humanity's weapons were capable of in ship-to-ship combat. It was entirely possible that other 'cats had seen what could happen when those weapons were used against planetary targets and shared the information with him, or perhaps he'd simply extrapolated the possible consequences from what he'd seen himself. Whatever anyone else might think, Honor had always known he was brighter than most two-footed people, and she'd asked him pointblank if an awareness of the military threat was behind this extraordinary departure in the behavior of his species. As always, there'd been a frustrating fuzziness to some of the nuances of his reply, but the gist of it had come through clearly enough.

Yes, he and Samantha *did* understand what nuclear or kinetic weaponry could mean for planetary targets, and they—or they and his clan, Honor wasn't entirely clear on that point—had decided it was time the 'cats stopped keeping all their eggs in one basket. She couldn't be certain, but she suspected that it wouldn't be long before other adopted humans were tapped to help move core colony groups from Sphinx to Manticore and Gryphon, the other two habitable worlds of the Manticore System, and that headed her towards other speculations. She'd become convinced over the years that 'cats in general were considerably smarter than they chose to admit, and she could see several advantages which might accrue from concealing their full capabilities. No humans who'd ever been adopted could doubt the depth, strength, and reality of the bonds between them and "their" 'cats. Honor knew—didn't think; *knew*—that Nimitz loved her just as fiercely as she loved him. But at any given time, only a minute percentage of the 'cats' total population ever adopted, and she'd sometimes wondered if perhaps those who did filled the role of scouts or observers for the rest of their species.

Did Nimitz report back to his clan on all that he'd seen and done with her between their visits home? Had the 'cats decided long ago that they needed to keep an eye on the humans, who had invaded their world? Given the ability of humanity's technology to destroy, as well as help, observing and studying the newcomers certainly would have made sense. Honor had never asked Nimitz outright if he reported to his clan, but she'd gradually become certain he did. Not that it bothered her. *She* certainly discussed the events they'd shared—including his part in them—with other humans, so how could she possibly object to his sharing them with his own family?

But his clan's decision to establish extraplanetary colonies suggested a more highly developed policy-making ability than even the most free thinking 'cat experts had been prepared to posit. Not only did it require them to carry out some pretty sophisticated threat analysis, but it presupposed an ability to formulate a *generational* strategy for their clan and, quite possibly, their entire species. That was a sobering thought, and once it sank in, it was going to require those "experts" to undertake some substantial reevaluation of their hypotheses. And especially, Honor had thought with a smile, the theories woven in efforts to explain why seven of Manticore's last nine monarchs had all been adopted on state visits to Sphinx. If she was right in her latest hunch, that indicated the 'cats had an awareness of human political structures whose sophistication no one had ever suspected in his or her wildest dreams.

In the meantime, however, she had to deal with the more immediate consequences of the decision to immigrate. At least it had provided Samantha and Nimitz with a generous number of baby-sitters, and given the appalling energy and inquisitiveness of their offspring, that was a not inconsequential benefit. More than that, the others had shown a far greater willingness to interact with humans than most "wild" 'cats did. Honor hadn't tried them in a large crowd yet, but neither MacGuiness nor her twelve armsmen bothered them in any way. In fact, each of the eight newcomers had been taken around the entire crowd of humans and formally and individually introduced by Nimitz or Samantha. Most of them had followed Nimitz's example and adopted the custom of shaking hands, and the nods and ear flicks and flirted tails of the ones who hadn't had clearly been intended as formal gestures of greeting.

They'd taken the move aboard ship with equal aplomb, and they'd abided by Honor's strict injunctions not to go running about unaccompanied by a human. Like Nimitz and Samantha, they clearly understood human technology could kill by accident, as well as design, and they'd not only exhibited their own willingness to avoid such dangers but guarded the kittens against any similar risk with undeviating attentiveness.

But within thirty minutes, the GSN pinnace which had come up to collect Honor and her party from the *Tankersley* would deliver them all to the pad at Harrington Space Facility. And as Hera, the seat-hopping nursemaid, deposited Achilles in the seat with Samantha, Honor found herself wondering how well the Graysons would handle their planet's invasion by treecats.

Grayson's human settlers had always faced serious environmental limitations. In many respects, the entire planet could have been considered a vast toxic waste dump, where human-habitable enclaves could be carved out only through unremitting effort and where draconian birth control had been required for a millennium. The situation had grown steadily better over the past three T-centuries and—especially—the last decade. When Grayson first joined the Manticoran Alliance, it had been laboriously pulling itself up by its own bootstraps via space-based industry and orbital farms. That process had been hugely accelerated when a youthful engineer named Adam Gerrick came to his newly installed Steadholder's office with a proposal to build entire planetary farms under domes constructed of the advanced materials the Alliance had made available. His audacious plan had been well beyond the resources of Harrington Steading . . . but not beyond the off-world resources of *Countess* Harrington, and by now Honor's Grayson Sky Domes, Ltd., was busy doming entire towns and cities, as well as farms.

That was one of several reasons her personal wealth was

expanding at an almost geometric rate. There were others, of course. As Willard had promised her, once her working capital passed a certain point, it became almost a self-sustaining reaction. She was even beginning to understand the inner workings of high finance, though she remained far out of the class of a wily old financier like Neufsteiler. But the impact on Grayson had been to provide an enormous expansion in safe habitats and relax many of the traditional restrictions on birth rates.

Now she—or, more precisely, Nimitz's clan—proposed to introduce a second intelligent species into that mix. To be sure, it might be some time before most Graysons fully grasped that the 'cats were another *intelligent* species, but Honor expected them to make the leap at *least* as quickly as Manticorans would have. She and Nimitz had been entirely too visible here for the people of Grayson to be able to ignore the fact of his intelligence, whereas few non-Sphinxians came face-to-face with 'cats back in the Star Kingdom. In a sense, the fact that treecats were an accepted part of the "scenery" there actually made it easier for native Manticorans to overlook their intelligence. Where the Graysons saw Nimitz as a new, fascinating species to be carefully studied and enjoyed, Manticorans were almost blasé, comfortable with what they already "knew."

It had been rather refreshing for both Honor and Nimitz to meet an entire planet of people who were willing to accept the 'cat on his own terms, but it did mean the Graysons were also more likely to grasp that Nimitz and Samantha's new friends were, in effect, the opening wedge of an invasion. A friendly one, perhaps, but still an invasion. One of Honor's traditional authorities as Steadholder Harrington was to decide how many and which emigrants would be allowed into her steading. In Grayson's grim, early days, it had also been the steadholder's harsh duty to determine which of his steaders had to die if that was what was required to balance population against the maximum strain his steading could bear, and Honor was unspeakably grateful that decisions like that were no longer necessary.

Yet Grayson remained a planet with a commitment to the tradition of balancing people against resources which would have delighted the most rabid of Old Earth's pre-space Greens, and that was the environment into which Honor proposed to introduce treecats.

The good news was that 'cat populations grew far more slowly than their multiple-birth reproductive patterns might suggest. Samantha's four-kitten litter was of about average size, but most females littered no more than once every eight to ten T-years. Given that they lived about two hundred years and remained fertile for a hundred and fifty, that still meant a single mated pair could produce a staggering number of offspring, but the process took much longer than initial impressions might suggest. And it was inevitable that human and 'cat societies were going to be much more intimately intertwined here on Grayson, which lacked the endless forests that provided Sphinx with virtually unlimited habitat for its native sentients. Here, 'cats would have to share the life-sustaining enclaves of humanity, and Honor wondered just how that would affect their adoption rate.

But whether they adopted in larger numbers or not, they were going to have to find their own niche in this new, radically different environment. From what she knew of 'cats, she was confident they could—and would. And, she thought, do it in a way which made them valued citizens. In the meantime, she had the legal authority to start their colony out in Harrington, and given her steaders' fascination with and pride in "their" treecat Nimitz, she expected the initial stages to go quite well.

In fact, she thought with a lurking smile, the biggest problem was likely to be that there were too few 'cats to go around!

The pinnace touched down with delicate precision.

The waiting greeters stood patiently outside the yellow warning line as the pilot brought up his belly tractors, killed his counter-grav, and powered down his other systems, and then the hatch slid open. This was the point, under other circumstances, at which the band would have broken into the Steadholder's March, but Lady Harrington had issued stern orders to leave the band home . . . and accompanied them with remarkably grisly threats about what would happen if it wasn't. Instead, Howard Clinkscales and Katherine Mayhew, as the two senior members of the greeting party, headed for the foot of the ramp as soon as the green safety light flashed. White Haven, as the senior Manticoran representative, and Honor's personal maid Miranda LaFollet, as the next most senior member of Honor's Grayson household, followed on their heels.

Lady Harrington's treecat rode her shoulder, but that was to be expected. What White Haven *hadn't* expected was that she would wear RMN uniform, not that of the Grayson Navy, and his eyes narrowed in approval. The last time he'd seen her in Manticoran uniform, her collar had carried a single gold planet and her cuffs had borne the four narrow stripes of a senior-grade captain. Today, there were *paired* planets on her collar, and her fourth cuff stripe was the broad one of a commodore. No one had told him her promotion had come through, but he was delighted to see it. It still fell far short of the rank she deserved, yet it was certainly a step in the right direction . . . and an indication that the Opposition's political vendetta against her had weakened even further.

She also, he noted, had acquired the Saganami Cross to go with her Star of Grayson, Manticore Cross, Order of Gallantry, Sidemore Presidential Medal, and CGM with cluster. She was assembling quite a crop of medals, he reflected, and his eyes darkened at the thought. He knew better than most how hard earned each of those bits of metal and ribbon had been, and he had nightmares enough of his own, on the bad nights, to guess how much she still paid for them from time to time.

Then his mood lightened, and he hid a potentially impolitic smile as Katherine Mayhew hurried forward. Virtually all Graysons were short by Manticoran standards, but Katherine was small even for a Grayson woman. Protector Benjamin's senior wife, effectively the Queen Consort of Grayson, was almost fifty centimeters shorter than Lady Harrington, and her gorgeous gown and vest were jewel-bright beside Lady Harrington's black and gold. But silly as they could have looked next to one another, there was no sense of awkwardness between them, and their obvious friendship went well beyond the official cordiality to be expected between a head of state's wife and one of his most powerful vassals.

Then Harrington turned from Madam Mayhew to Howard Clinkscales, and White Haven's eyebrows rose as she hugged the old dinosaur. Such public physical familiarity between the sexes was virtually unheard of on Grayson, and Harrington had never struck the earl as the sort given to casual gestures of affection. But then he saw Clinkscales' expression and realized there was nothing casual about it.

He was still filing that bit of information away when another treecat flowed through the pinnace hatch. For a moment, White Haven assumed the newcomer must be the mate of Harrington's . . . Nimitz. That was the name. But that assumption vanished as a second, and then a third, a fourth, and a *fifth* 'cat followed. A veritable procession of treecats, four of them carrying the tiny, wigglesome shapes of treekittens, trooped down the ramp, and no one had mentioned anything about *this* to him. From the reactions of the people around him, no one had mentioned it to anyone else, either, and White Haven felt a sudden, almost uncontrollable urge to laugh at Honor Harrington's unending ability to stand the status quo on its head.

Honor smiled wryly as Katherine Mayhew broke off in midsentence. She'd considered sending word ahead, but *Tankersley* was a fast ship. The *Star Falcons* were a civilian version of what had been a military/diplomatic courier vessel used to transport dispatches or relatively small groups of passengers when speed was of the essence. *Tankersley* would never make an efficient freight carrier, but her speed meant that even the fastest mail ship would only have provided the Graysons with a day or two of warning of the 'cat invasion. Given Honor's own uncertainty over how they might react to the news and how quickly her arrival would have followed upon it, she'd decided it was better to wait until she could deliver it personally. She still thought that had been the right move, but she also felt undeniably nervous when the ripples of silence spread out as the 'cats followed her down the ramp and assembled in a neat line behind her. They sat up on their four rearmost limbs, most of those who weren't occupied restraining a kitten who urgently wanted *down* grooming their whiskers, and the Graysons stared back at them.

"Howard, Katherine," she said to Clinkscales and Madam Mayhew, "allow me to introduce the newest citizens of Harrington Steading. These are—" she turned to face them, pointing to each in turn "—Samantha, Nimitz's mate, and her friends Hera, Nelson, Farragut, Artemis, Hipper, Togo, Hood, and Athena. The kittens are Jason, Cassandra, Achilles, and Andromeda. Going the other way," she informed the 'cats, "these are Howard Clinkscales, Katherine Mayhew, Miranda LaFollet, Earl Whi—"

She broke off in astonishment as Farragut's eyes met Miranda's. Only the 'cat's head moved, yet Honor felt the shock like a hammer blow, reverberating down her link to Nimitz. It sang and echoed through her, and then Farragut bounded forward in a cream-and-gray streak. He left the ground two meters from Miranda, in a prodigious spring, and Honor heard Andrew inhale sharply behind her. Her armsman was only too aware of what a treecat's claws could do, and he started to shout a warning to his sister. Only Miranda needed no warning. Her eyes—the same clear gray as her brother's—were wide and soft, as filled with surprise as wonder, but her arms reached out instinctively, and Farragut's leap deposited him within them so naturally that it seemed inevitable. They tightened instantly, cradling the 'cat against her, and his high, buzzing purr filled the afternoon air as he hugged her neck and rubbed his cheek ecstatically against hers.

"Well!" Honor said after a moment, letting the word out in an explosive gust. "I see at least *one* introduction just became superfluous." Miranda didn't even look up from Farragut, but Katherine Mayhew cleared her throat.

"Ah, is that what I think it is?" she asked, and Honor nodded.

"Indeed it is. You've just witnessed the first adoption of a Grayson by a Sphinx treecat . . . and Lord only knows where the lightning may strike next."

"Is it truly that random, My Lady?" Clinkscales asked, the edge of yearning in his voice controlled by the habits of a lifetime of discipline, and Honor shrugged.

"No, it's not random, Howard. Unfortunately, no one's ever been able to figure out what criteria the 'cats go by. From my own observation, I'd say each of them uses a completely unique set of value judgments, and I doubt most of *them* realize that they're likely to adopt before they meet the 'right' person."

"I see." Her regent gazed at Miranda and Farragut for another moment, then gave the remaining 'cats a glance and shook himself. "Well, in the meantime, My Lady, welcome home. I'm delighted to see you for several reasons, not least—" he smiled almost impishly "—the heap of paperwork which has accumulated in your absence."

"You're a sadist, Howard," Honor observed with a smile. "In this case, however, you're going to have to wait a bit before you can drag me off to the office." His eyes twinkled back at her, and she reached past him to extend a hand to Earl White Haven. "Hello, My Lord. It's good to see you again."

"And to see you, Milady," White Haven responded. Technically, Commodore Harrington should have greeted Admiral White Haven with strict military formality. Steadholder Harrington, on the other hand, freshly returned to her own steading, was senior to anyone short of Protector Benjamin himself, and the instinctive grace with which she'd split the difference between her two personae impressed the earl. The last time he'd spoken to her, here on Grayson before her return to Manticoran service, he'd recognized how she'd grown and matured in her new role of great feudal lady. Clearly she'd gone right on maturing, and he wondered once again if she even began to grasp all the ways in which she'd changed.

"I'm sorry about all the hoopla," she went on easily, "and Their Lordships sent both my own orders and dispatches for you along with me." Her eyes went past him, to the other local dignitaries, military personnel, and armsmen waiting to greet her, and she smiled another of the crooked smiles the artificial nerves in the left side of her face imposed. "I suspect I'll be rather occupied saying hello for the next half-hour or so, My Lord," she continued, "and then I have to get Sam, the kids, and the rest of the 'cats settled in Harrington House. May I impose upon you and ask you to wait for your dispatches while I finish putting out all my various fires?"

"Of course you may, Milady," the earl replied with a chuckle, and released her hand with a final squeeze.

"Thank you, My Lord. Thank you very much," Honor said with true feeling, and turned to greet the wave of people crowding forward to welcome her home.

• Chapter Two

Hamish Alexander stepped into Harrington House's library with what an unbiased observer almost certainly would have called a furtive air, looked around carefully, then relaxed. The enormous room was empty, and he loosened the collar of his mess dress tunic with heartfelt relief as he crossed the huge Harrington coat of arms inlaid into the parquet floor. The sound of music followed him through the open door, but distance had swallowed the background murmur of voices, and the click of his heels on polished wood carried clearly.

He unclipped the archaic sword which was mandatory with mess dress and laid it atop one of the book-lined room's terminals, then lowered himself into the comfortable chair at the data station and stretched hugely. The library had become one of his favorite places in Harrington House. If its contents had been chosen to reflect Honor Harrington's tastes, then the two of them had more common interests than he'd realized, but the big room's tasteful, comfortable furnishings and quiet— *especially* quiet, he thought with a grin—were also factors in his feelings.

His grin grew as he finished stretching and tipped the chair back. His birth had exposed him to the most formal parties of the Star Kingdom's social elite at a very early age, but that didn't mean he'd ever learned to enjoy such evenings. His parents had seen to it that he learned to *pretend* he did, and there were occasions when pretense merged—temporarily, at least—with reality. But by and large, he would have preferred an old-fashioned, pre-space root canal to at least half the parties he'd attended, and tonight's formal ball had pushed him into active flight.

It wasn't that he didn't like his hosts, for he found Graysons admirable in many ways, from their refusal to admit any task might be beyond their capabilities to their courage, basic decency, and inventiveness. He was perfectly comfortable in professional conferences with their officers and enlisted personnel, and he seldom had any problem connecting with even their civilians on a pragmatic level. But their notion of classical music was enough to set his teeth on edge, and they *insisted* on playing it at affairs like tonight's. Worse, Grayson's entire society was in a state of flux which only made his fundamental dislike for formal social gatherings even stronger here than it was back home, yet there was no graceful way for him to avoid them.

At least a third of his mission to Yeltsin's Star was as much diplomatic as military. He was the older brother of the Cromarty Government's second ranking minister, *and* he'd served as Third Space Lord, an appointment with almost as many political as military implications, for three T-years during the Duke of Cromarty's immediately previous stint as Prime Minister. As such, he found himself required to interact with Grayson political circles at the highest level, and since so much of politics was conducted under the guise of social activities, that meant he had to spend most of his theoretically "free" evenings at some party or another. Musical tastes aside, the rapidly changing mores of Grayson society could make that particularly wearing for someone from the Star Kingdom, where the notion that anyone could possibly consider men and women as anything but equals was as bizarre as the idea of treating a fever by bleeding, and tonight that persistent background sense of tension was only exacerbated by the professional concerns the latest dispatches from home had awakened in his mind.

Things would have been simpler, he mused, tipping even further back and resting his heels on the counter beside his dress sword, if Grayson society had simply stayed frozen where it had been before the planet joined the Alliance. In that case, he could have written its people off as a batch of backward barbarians—admirable in many ways, but still barbarians—and fitted himself into the proper role for interacting with them like an actor in a historical holo-drama. It wouldn't have been necessary to actually understand them; all he would have required was the right set of social cues to pretend he did.

Unfortunately, these days Grayson's social elite were as confused about what constituted proper behavior as any outsider. They *were* trying. White Haven had to give them that, and he rather admired how much they'd achieved in such a short period, but there was an underlying air of uncertainty. Some of society's grande dames resented the changes in the rules they'd learned as girls even more than the unreconstructed male conservatives resented their loss of privilege. Those groups formed a sort of natural alliance that clustered somewhere just beyond the reception line and radiated a prickly intensity as they clung grimly to the old rules and forms . . . which, of course, brought them into direct collision with their (mainly) younger counterparts who had embraced the notion of female equality with militant fervor.

Personally, White Haven found the more enthusiastic reformers more wearing than the reactionaries. He couldn't fault their motives, but the fact was that Benjamin IX had imposed a top-down revolution on his home world. He was remaking what had been, whatever its faults, a stable social order which had changed only slowly and incrementally over the last six or seven hundred years. With a very few exceptions, that social order's current members had only the vaguest notion of where they were headed, and many of the reformers seemed to believe stridency could substitute for direction. The earl was confident that most of them would get over it—they'd only been at it for a few years, and they were bound to figure *some* of it out with time—but at the moment, their main function at social gatherings seemed to be to make everyone else uncomfortable by aggressively demonstrating their rejection of the old order.

And, of course, the conflict between the old guard and the new put White Haven and other Manticorans squarely in a crossfire. The reactionaries regarded the foreigners as the sources of the infection which had attacked all they knew and held dear, while the reformers took it for granted that the Manticorans must agree with *them* . . . even though it was painfully obvious that all the reformers didn't agree with one another! Walking that sort of tightrope without giving offense—or, at least, *further* offense—to *someone* was almost as exhausting as it was irritating, and White Haven was heartily tired of it.

To be fair, the situation was better here. Harrington Steading had attracted the most open-minded citizens from Grayson's other steadings from the outset, for only people like that had been willing to relocate themselves and their families in order to live under the personal rule of the first female steadholder in their planet's history. More than that, the people at the party he'd just escaped had been given ample opportunity to see their Steadholder in action in political and social terms, as well as military ones. Whether she realized it or not, her status as their liege lady made her the ultimate arbiter of custom in her steading, and her steaders had watched her carefully and adapted their etiquette to fit her reactions to it. All of that left White Haven feeling far more at ease in Harrington than in most of Grayson's other steadings, and he'd actually enjoyed at least the early phases of tonight's ball to welcome Lady Harrington home. His need to escape it was more a matter of cumulative fatigue than anything else.

Besides, he had a lot on his mind after scanning the orders and briefing documents Lady Harrington had brought with her. He'd been pleased to learn that she would be assigned to Eighth Fleet, but some of the Office of Naval Intelligence's reports made for disquieting reading, and he was supposed to brief High Admiral Matthews and Command Central on them as soon as possible. That was one of the main reasons for sneaking away from the party early. He needed to think about the data and fit the pieces together. And, he confessed, he had to decide how he felt about other aspects of the total package, for grim as some of ONI's analyses of the Peeps' activities might be, the notes on the RMN's own Weapons Development Board's recommendations actually worried him even more.

The notion of making far-reaching and fundamental changes in the Fleet's weapons mix at a time when the Star Kingdom was fighting for its very life struck him as highly questionable. He'd waged a bitter, decades-long prewar battle against the efforts of the material strategists of the *jeune école* to introduce half-baked weapon systems before they were fully tested. At times the battle of ideas had spilled over into venomous personal exchanges, and he deeply regretted the vicious feuds which those had spawned between some within the RMN's senior ranks, but he'd never dared let that affect his resistance. The *jeune école* was so in love with the idea of developing decisive advantages out of new technological departures that they seemed to believe any new idea was good simply because it *was* new, regardless of its actual tactical virtues or vices. Nothing he'd seen lately convinced him that they'd learned a thing from the present war, which meant—

His half-drifting thoughts broke off as someone else's heels clicked on the library floor. He snatched his feet off the console and let the chair snap upright, spinning it to face the door, then paused. He'd acquired far too much polish over the years to let consternation show, but it was harder to conceal than usual as he realized his hostess had caught him hiding from her party.

She stood just inside the doorway, tall and slender in the deceptively simple white gown and jade-green vest which had, for all intents and purposes, become her civilian "uniform," with Andrew LaFollet standing at her shoulder. Her brown hair spilled far down her back, in sharp contrast to the short-clipped fuzz she'd favored the first time White Haven saw her, and the golden Harrington Key and equally golden Star of Grayson glittered on her breast. She made a striking picture, he thought, and rose respectfully to greet her.

Honor watched the earl stand and smiled at his surprised expression. Of course, she told herself, stepping towards him to extend her hand, he didn't know that Harrington House's security systems had kept her advised of his location all evening long.

He bent over her hand, kissing it in proper Grayson fashion, then straightened, still holding it in a light clasp. White Haven was a tall, broad shouldered man, yet he and Honor stood virtually eye to eye, and she felt Nimitz's interested examination of the earl as the 'cat rose a bit higher on her shoulder.

"I see you've found my own preferred hiding place, My Lord," she observed.

"Hiding place?" White Haven replied politely.

"Of course." She glanced at LaFollet, and her armsman read the silent order in her eyes. He still didn't much like the idea of leaving her back unguarded, but even he had to admit she should be safe enough here, so he gave a small half-bow of surrender and withdrew. The library door closed behind him, and Honor walked past White Haven to the main data console in a rustle of skirts. She lifted Nimitz to the perch installed above the console especially for him, and he gave a soft, half-scolding, half-laughing sound and snatched playfully at her hand. But that was an old game, and she evaded him easily and gave him a gentle swat on the muzzle before she turned back to the earl.

"I've never really enjoyed parties, My Lord," she admitted. "I suppose it's because I still feel out of place at them, but Mike Henke and Admiral Courvosier taught me to at least *pretend* I'm having a good time." She gave him another of her off-center smiles, and he nodded as though he hadn't already known that. Raoul Courvosier had been one of his closest friends, as well as Harrington's professional mentor, and over the years, Raoul had let fall even more about his favorite student than he himself, perhaps, had realized.

"At any rate," she went on, stepping back to prop a hip on the corner of the console behind her, "I decided that since I'm a steadholder now, I have the authority to at least provide myself with a hidey hole. That's why the staff has orders to keep the library clear on party nights to provide a place where I can clear my head between skirmishes."

"I didn't know, Milady," White Haven said, reaching for his dress sword as he prepared to withdraw, but she shook her head quickly.

"I'm not trying to evict you, My Lord," she assured him. "As a matter of fact, Security saw you headed this way and passed the word to Andrew. That's why I'm here myself . . . and if you hadn't found your way here on your own, Mac would be gently nudging you in this direction about now."

"Ah?" White Haven cocked his head, and her smile turned wry as she shrugged.

"I've just come from a stint on the Weapons Development Board, and Admiral Caparelli felt you might have some, um, concerns over certain of its recommendations. Because of that, he specifically instructed me to brief you on what the Board's been up to. Since neither of us seems particularly addicted to the social life, and since I know you'll be talking to High Admiral Matthews and his staff about them in the next few days, I'd rather hoped I could create an opportunity to answer any of your questions that I can tonight."

"I see." White Haven rubbed his chin as he considered her confident, self-assured manner and found himself impressed yet again by all the ways in which she'd grown into her many roles. He knew he shouldn't be, yet he couldn't help comparing her to the focused military officer, painfully ignorant of and filled with contempt for politics (or at least *politicians*), whom he'd first met here in Yeltsin.

There was no sign of that officer's political ignorance in this poised stateswoman, and the transformation still astounded him. Partly, he supposed, that stemmed from the fact that he belonged to the first Manticoran prolong generation. Whatever his own life expectancy, he'd grown up in a society where people still died after little more than a T-century, and at the deepest levels, the assumptions of that earlier society remained a part of his mental baggage. At ninety-two, anyone as young as Honor Harrington still seemed a child to him, and the fact that her own *third*-generation treatments froze the aging process at a far earlier point only made it worse. *He* at least had streaks of white in his hair and what he preferred to think of as "character lines" around his eyes, whereas *she* looked like a pre-prolong nineteen or twenty!

But she wasn't a child, he reminded himself. In fact, she was fifty-two, and as smart—and tough, mentally as well as physically—as anyone he was ever likely to meet. She was also a person who had always accepted the responsibilities which came her way, whether she'd sought them or not, and that made it almost inevitable that she should "grow" into her role as Steadholder Harrington. She couldn't have done anything else without being *someone* else.

None of which made her accomplishments any less admirable. It only meant it was damned well time he stopped thinking of her as a brilliant, talented, gifted junior officer and began thinking of Admiral Lady Harrington, GSN, as his equal.

Those thoughts flickered through his brain almost too quickly to keep track of, and then he smiled at her.

"I see," he repeated, and sat back down in the chair he'd vacated. Honor returned his smile and turned the chair at her own data station to face him, then sat and made a small gesture which invited him to begin.

"Actually," he said after a moment, "I'm at least as concerned over some of ONI's reports as I am about the WDB. The Admiralty's kept me generally abreast of developments, but the analyses you brought out with you are both more detailed and rather more pessimistic than anything else I've seen. They also seem to contain a lot of new data, and I can't help wondering about that data's reliability. Did you have the chance to discuss any of this with someone at ONI before you left the Star Kingdom?"

"As a matter of fact, Admiral Givens and I spoke about it at some length month before last," Honor replied. "We didn't go into any detail on the operational side—ONI's actual information-gathering activities are classified on a need-to-know basis, and I didn't need to—but the WDB needed the most complete background available before it wrote its recommendations. From what she told me then, I'd say *she's* convinced of her sources' reliability, and given how well she and ONI have read the Peeps since the shooting actually started—"

She shrugged, knowing White Haven understood what she'd left unspoken. The actual outbreak of hostilities had taken the Office of Naval Intelligence by surprise, and Admiral Givens and her analysts had been given no more reason than anyone else to expect (or predict) the Harris Assassination or the creation of the Committee of Public Safety. But those failures aside, ONI's spooks had done a sterling job of dissecting Peep capabilities and probable intentions.

"I gathered the impression," she went on after a moment, choosing her words with care, "that a good deal of the raw data is coming from new human intelligence sources."

She held White Haven's eyes until he nodded once more. "Human intelligence" was a more polite term than "spies," but even today, the many and varied technological means for gathering information fell short of what an alert, intelligently used pair of eyes and ears in the right place could deliver. The problem, of course, was assessing your spies' reliability, then getting their reports across interstellar distances. On the other hand, intelligence agencies had been working on the data transmission end of it ever since the Warshawski sail made hyper-travel a truly practical proposition.

"In particular," she continued, "I rather suspect, though

Admiral Givens didn't say so directly, that we have at least one source within the Peeps' embassy on Old Earth."

White Haven's eyebrows rose at that, but then his lips pursed as thoughtfulness replaced surprise. That actually made sense, he reflected. Ron Bergren, the Havenite foreign secretary under the old Legislaturalist government, had been the only member of Sidney Harris' cabinet to escape the massacre of the PRH's so-called military coup attempt. He'd survived for the simple reason that, at the time, he'd been in transit to Old Earth to explain to the Solarian League that the war with Manticore hadn't *really* been started by the Peeps, however things might look. Upon learning of the coup, he'd declared his enthusiastic loyalty to the Committee of Public Safety . . . and found as many reasons as possible why neither he, his wife, nor their three children should return to the People's Republic. That was probably wise of him, given the fact that over ninety percent of the members of the great Legislaturalist families had been executed or exiled to prison planets by the People's Courts, and he'd been helped by the fact that Old Earth was over eighteen hundred light-years from the Haven System.

The Manticore Wormhole Junction was closed to Peep traffic for obvious reasons, and the Cromarty Government had scored an enormous diplomatic triumph when it added the Erewhon Republic to the Manticoran Alliance seven years ago. Erewhon was only a single-system polity, but like the Star Kingdom itself, though on a lesser scale, it was far wealthier than any single system could normally expect to be, for it just happened to control the only *other* wormhole terminus connecting to League space from within twelve hundred light-years of the Peeps' capital. There'd been a degree of economic rivalry between Erewhon and Manticore in the past, but both of them had recognized the threat Haven posed to them, and Erewhon's admission to the Alliance had closed the Erewhon Wormhole to the Peeps. That meant even Peep courier boats, which routinely rode the upper edge of hyper-space's theta bands, required well over six months for the trip to Old Earth, whereas a courier from *Manticore* could reach the mother world in barely a week.

The diplomatic advantages for the Star Kingdom were obvious, but those for Ron Bergren personally were almost as great. He was well beyond the Committee's reach but already in place in Old Earth's diplomatic structure, where he'd represented the interests of his new masters with diligence and industry (after all, he still had relatives back home), and any attempt to recall him against his will could only result in his requesting political asylum from the League . . . or defecting to Manticore.

As a consequence, he was still technically the PRH's foreign secretary, although for all practical purposes he'd been reduced to the status of the Peeps' ambassador to Old Earth and the League. But even if Bergren himself truly was—or acted as if he were—loyal to the new regime, he'd taken a staff with him. Most of them were also Legislaturalists, and the possibility that one of *them* might have become a Manticoran agent—whether for money, vengeance, patriotic loyalty to the old regime, or any combination of the above—was excellent. And given the difference in transit times, the Star Kingdom would get such an agent's reports on any changes in the Peeps' relations with the League at least six months before the Committee of Public Safety could.

"At any rate," Honor observed after giving the earl a few minutes to consider what she'd already said, "the *nature* of the data clearly indicates that at least one major source is reporting from Old Earth. Look at the information on the Peeps' efforts to get around the tech embargo."

"I did," White Haven said sourly, and it was Honor's turn to nod soberly. The Solarian League's prewar embargo on technology transfers to the belligerents clearly favored the Star Kingdom, with its more active research and development establishments and superior educational system, and the RMN's technological advantages had been a major factor in its ability to carry the war to the Republic thus far.

But, White Haven reminded himself, some of the League's member systems had always resented the embargo, which the Star Kingdom had achieved only because of the economic clout bestowed by its vast merchant marine and control of the Manticore Wormhole Junction. And for all its undeniable size and power, the League was a rather ramshackle proposition in many ways. It might be called the *Solarian* League, but in actual fact Old Earth was simply first among equals, for every member world held a seat on the Executive Council . . . and each Council delegate held the right of veto. By long tradition, that veto right was used only rarely on domestic issues for two reasons. First, the League ministers' awareness that their policies *could* be vetoed by a single objector had for generations inspired them to recommend only center of the road domestic policies they could be fairly certain would command a broad consensus. And, second, any member world which used its veto right frivolously soon discovered that its fellows had any number of means of unilateral retaliation.

But if the League's domestic policies were coherent, its military and foreign policies were another matter, for it was far harder to forge a consensus on the diplomatic front. Much of that stemmed from the League's sheer size and power. Even the vast military machine the People's Republic had forged was less than a fourth the size of the League Navy, and the League's industrial base probably equaled that of all the rest of humanity combined. As a consequence, it was very difficult for anyone to convince the League's member worlds that anyone or anything represented a credible threat to them, and that sublime confidence was disastrous when it came to creating a harmonious foreign policy. The consequences of domestic policy decisions had a direct, perceptible impact upon the standard of living League citizens enjoyed; the absence of a rational *foreign* policy did not, and so each member world felt free to press for its own idiosyncratic ideal of "proper" policy . . . or simply to ignore the entire matter. And delegates to the Executive Council were far more likely to use their veto power to prevent "dangerous foreign adventures" than to cross their fellows on domestic matters.

That was why the Cromarty Government had been forced eventually to put the technology embargo in purely economic terms. The Star Kingdom had been less than subtle in the pressure applied, but nothing less than a threat to close the Manticore Junction to all League-registered shipping and to impose punishing duties on all League cargoes traveling in Manticoran bottoms had been sufficient to get the Council's attention. Cromarty had been perfectly well aware that such strong-arm tactics would generate resentment, but he'd also been convinced he had no other choice.

They'd worked . . . and they'd also produced even more resentment than he'd expected. Not only did many League leaders regard such a tough stance as a personal and diplomatic affront, but Cromarty's analysts had failed to appreciate quite how much money the Peeps would offer for League technology. Once combat made the Star Kingdom's edge obvious, even a financially strapped empire like the People's Republic had managed to come up with immense payments for anyone willing to sell them what they needed. For the League's arms merchants, being required to forgo that lucrative income was even more of an affront than Manticore's negotiating tactics, and from the evidence ONI had assembled, it seemed painfully apparent that *someone* in the League had decided to violate the embargo's restrictions after all.

Equally apparently, the leak in the embargo spurted both ways, for a source within the League Navy reported that the League's R&D types were now experimenting with their own version of the short-range FTL com system which was one of the RMN's most valuable tactical advantages. Their success was extremely limited to date, but they were headed in the right direction, and the progress they'd made, not to mention the basic concepts upon which their efforts appeared to be based, suggested that someone had been sharing data with them. It was always possible that an agent within the Allies' own military had passed the information on, but the Peeps, who'd seen the system in action and undoubtedly had sensor readings on it (not to mention the possibility that they might have captured a transmitter sufficiently intact to permit them to reverse-engineer it), were more likely suspects. And if they could, in fact, provide information to help the League develop that sort of capability, then a quid pro quo that sent more capable military hardware back to Haven in return would seem only fair.

"We've got some confirmation of technology transfers from other sources, as well," Honor told her guest quietly. "The seeking systems in Peep missiles have gotten much better in a very short period of time. We had a thirty to forty percent edge when the war began; BuWeaps estimates that our superiority's dropped to no more than ten percent at present. Fortunately, our countermeasures and general electronic warfare capability have continued to improve at a faster rate than theirs, so the effective *relative* increase in their missile accuracy is 'only' on the order of twenty percent, but that's still not good. Also," her eyes darkened, "we've had unconfirmed reports that the Peeps have begun deploying missile pods of their own."

"We have?" White Haven's voice was sharp. "I didn't see that mentioned in ONI's briefing documents!"

"As I say, it's unconfirmed . . . mainly because the ships we think may have encountered them haven't come home to tell us about them." Honor shrugged. "The Weapons Development Board was convinced of the accuracy of the reports in large part because they dovetailed so neatly with other, incremental improvements we're seeing across the board in the PN's technology. But ONI's taken the position that until we have something more definite, the existence of Peep pods has to be considered conjectural."

"'Conjectural'!" White Haven snorted harshly. "That's going to be a *lot* of help when they stick their damned 'conjectural' pods up some poor damned commander's—" He broke off suddenly and cleared his throat. "I mean, the first time one of our fleet commanders encounters them. I can't believe Pat Givens is being this coy about a threat like that!"

"I know exactly what you mean, My Lord," Honor said with a lurking smile for the word he hadn't let himself use in her presence. Was it possible Grayson mores were contaminating the Manticorans assigned here? And if they were, was that such a bad thing? Then she turned more serious and leaned slightly towards him.

"As for Admiral Givens, I don't know why she's failed to make the warning official. One possibility—and I offer it only as pure conjecture on my part, from some of the things I observed while at the WDB—is that she's less of a technician than a strategist. It seems to me that she's a bit more hesitant to commit herself on hardware issues than on operational or diplomatic ones." She shrugged apologetically. "I may be out of line on that, but it seemed that way to me." She saw no reason to add that what she and Nimitz had read of Givens' emotions was a major factor in her "conjecture."

"You may well be right," White Haven said. In fact, he was certain she was, and it was another sign of her own intelligence that she'd reached that conclusion from such a relatively junior position in the RMN.

"At any rate," Honor went on, "whether they're developing pods or not, general increases in their systems efficiency are turning up in almost every area. Fortunately, our latest estimates indicate that we have a certain margin of superiority even over the more recently introduced League hardware, but it's far thinner than the one we enjoy over the Peeps. It may be enough if we continue to exploit it aggressively, especially in view of the long turnaround time on any data or equipment flow between the League and the Peeps, and BuWeaps and the WDB hope to do just that. There's also been quite a bit of discussion with BuShips about ways we might be able to shoehorn more EW capability into our hulls without cutting into weapons volume, but it looks like we're beginning to reach a point of diminishing returns in that regard. That's one reason BuWeaps has been pushing the Ghost Rider Project so hard for the last T-year."

She glanced at the earl, who nodded in understanding. "Ghost Rider" was the code name assigned to what would hopefully turn out to be a whole new generation of electronic warfare. If things worked out as planned, the needed capabilities would be built into drone bodies, providing an EW capability which could be deployed in multiple, independent platforms. Ideally, a ship would be able to put out shells of drones, relatively simple-minded and limited compared to shipboard systems, but with each operating in a different mode to give much greater overall capability than onboard systems which might be more powerful but could operate in only a single mode at any one time.

"While I was with the Board, I saw some encouraging long-range reports on Ghost Rider," Honor went on after a moment. "The only hardware actually in the production pipeline are the new decoy missiles and the stealthed missile pods, and it'll be some time before any of the other goodies reach deployment status. I think Vice Admiral Adcock is right about how much the project will enhance our capabilities—eventually—but for now, the PN has definitely cut into our advantage."

"*And* their building rates are going up," White Haven muttered, and she nodded once more, her eyes very serious.

"That they are, My Lord. The total number of new hulls per month has continued to decline, but that's only because we've taken so many yards away from them. The yards they have left are showing a marked increase in output. They're turning out individual new ships much more quickly, even though their overall loss of yard space means they can build fewer of them *simultaneously*. Again, part of that increase could result from technology transfers, but it's more likely that it stems from more effective personnel management. Their building rates went into the toilet when they started drafting Dolists into the yards, but that trend has reversed in the past year or so. I think ONI is right that the reversal indicates both that their original, effectively unskilled labor force is learning to do its job more efficiently and that popular support for the war remains high, which produces a motivated work force. Without really substantial technology imports from the League, the limitations of their physical plant should keep them from matching our construction rates, but they're going to come a lot closer than they used to be able to."

"So Admiral Givens stands by the notion that Pierre and his crowd enjoy 'popular support,' does she?" White Haven cocked his head. "That business in Nouveau Paris didn't change her mind?"

"No, My Lord. Reports about exactly what happened are mixed, but since both ONI and the Special Intelligence Service agree that it's actually strengthened the Committee of Public Safety's position, I don't think we dare disagree."

She grinned, despite the gravity of the conversation, and White Haven smiled back. The Office of Naval Intelligence and the Special Intelligence Service, the umbrella agency coordinating its civilian counterparts, enjoyed a tradition of lively competition . . . and resentment. As was probably to be expected, ONI tended to be right more often on military matters, while SIS had a vastly better record on diplomatic and economic matters. Where their areas of expertise collided, however, disputes were both common and passionate. Having both of them actually agree on something was almost unheard of.

But then he remembered what they were talking about, and his smile faded.

"I don't think I *do* disagree," he said after a moment, "but I'm curious as to whether their reasoning coincides with my own. Did they share it with you?"

"In general terms," Honor replied. "I think their first point would be that the fighting took place in Nouveau Paris, nowhere else in the Haven System or, for that matter, anywhere else in the Republic. Since that business at

Malagasy and the mutiny in the Lannes System, we've had no reports of open resistance to the central government in any other system. That's not to say that there may not have been some, but if there were, they must have been on a small enough scale for their Office of Public Information to hush them up. That means that whoever controls the capital controls the provinces."

She paused, curving an eyebrow at him, and he nodded for her to go on.

"Their second point is that whoever was behind the coup attempt failed pretty spectacularly," she said. "Whether we take the official Public Information version of what happened or the less coherent—but probably more accurate—versions from other sources, it seems pretty clear that the bulk of their supporters were caught in the open. We've got reports that they used snowflake clusters on street mobs, My Lord." Her eyes were briefly haunted, as she remembered a time when pinnaces under *her* command had used similar weapons on unprotected targets. "They may have managed to get several million other people killed with them, but after that sort of . . . treatment, the 'Levelers' can't have a lot of manpower left. Not only have they been crushed themselves, but the example of what happened to them should make anyone else think twice about launching a similar attempt.

"Finally, all the available evidence suggests that it was the Navy which actually stopped them. Public Information insists it was State Security, Committee Security, the Public Order Police, and the Chairman's Guard, *supported* by the Navy, but all of our other sources suggest it was the other way around. The security forces certainly didn't just lie down and play dead, but their responses weren't coherent. ONI suggests that someone must have managed to compromise their command and control net, though we haven't been able to confirm that. But whatever happened, it was Navy kinetic strikes and air strikes and battle-armored Marines acting under Admiral McQueen's orders that broke the uprising's back, and McQueen didn't go on to take out the Committee herself.

That indicates a higher degree of military backing for the Pierre regime than we'd earlier estimated, and the reports that McQueen's been offered a seat on the Committee should only make that backing even stronger."

"So what you're saying," White Haven summarized when she paused once more, "is that the provinces have been brought into line, civilian resistance in the capital has been crushed, and the military has signed on?"

"Pretty much," Honor agreed, "though I don't think I'd put it precisely that way. I'd say that a particular *segment* of the civilian population of the capital was crushed. Given the amount of carnage and collateral casualties inflicted in the process, I suspect the bulk of the Dolists have decided to support the Committee as a source of stability which may be able to keep similar things from happening again. That goes quite a bit beyond the notion of civilians simply cowed into obedience by an iron fist, My Lord."

"Um." White Haven tilted his chair back once more, propping his elbows on its arms and lacing his fingers together in front of him, and frowned. Once again, he couldn't fault her analysis . . . or, perhaps more to the point, ONI's and BuShips' estimates of what stability within the People's Republic meant for the building race. The Peeps had definitely turned up the heat under their construction programs. Where it had once taken them very nearly twice as long to build a superdreadnought, they'd cut their disadvantage in half, and if there were no fresh domestic upheavals to disrupt their efforts. . . .

"However you look at it," he said slowly, "we're losing our margin of superiority. Not just in numbers—I saw the building rate increase coming months ago—but in *quality*, as well." He shook his head. "We can't afford that, Milady."

"I know," she replied quietly, and watched his eyes narrow as he turned his full attention upon her.

"On the other hand," he said, "I think this adds extra point to my concerns about the Weapons Development Board's recommendations."

"Concerns, My Lord?" she asked calmly.

"Fairly serious ones, as a matter of fact," he said. "Given that we're already looking at steepening numerical odds and improvements in the enemy's technology, this is no time to be tinkering with our own weapons mix by backing blue-sky projects." He snorted derisively, curling a mental lip at the preposterous proposals—and claims—put forth by the WDB white paper Harrington had delivered. He'd only skimmed the document, but that had been enough to show him it was more of the *jeune école*'s nonsense. "The last thing we can afford to do is split our efforts between too many projects—most of which are probably useless anyway. What we need to do is rationalize production plans to turn out the maximum number of weapons we *know* work rather than fritter away resources pursuing crackpot 'break-throughs.' Surely the need to concentrate on realizable technologies rather than harebrained, pie-in-the-sky, panacea boondoggles is one lesson people should have learned by now, if only from Old Earth's history!"

"The Board isn't precisely calling for 'boondoggles,' My Lord," Honor said in a slightly frosty tone, but he shook his head.

"I'm sure your aware of my, um, differences of opinion with Lady Hemphill and the *jeune école*," he said. "I've never denied that there's room for new technology—Ghost Rider is a prime example of a new system with real and immediate value—but there has to be a balance. We can't just throw a new weapon into service *because* it's new. It has to have a functional slot, and the Fleet requires a rigorous analysis of its advantages—and disadvantages—before it's deployed. The mere existence of a weapon, however potent, doesn't guarantee proper doctrine will be formulated for it, either. A system we haven't figured out how to employ properly could turn out to be more dangerous to us than to the enemy, especially if we commit so heavily to it that we skimp on other, battle-proven weapons."

Honor felt his disgust through her link to Nimitz, and

it surprised her. She knew White Haven was the acknowledged leader of the so-called "historical school" which
believed that the fundamental strategic truths didn't
change—that new weapon systems and technology simply
offered new and better ways to apply those truths, not that
they could create new ones—and his clashes with the *jeune
école* were legendary. But the depth and bitterness of the
weariness coloring his emotions startled her. It was almost
like combat fatigue, she realized, as if he'd fought so many
battles against the *jeune école* that he could no longer
summon the detachment to consider the WDB proposals
dispassionately.

She started to speak, but he held up a hand and went
on before she could.

"I realize that your stint on the Board was brief, Milady,
but just look at some of its proposals." He ticked the points
off on the fingers of his raised hand. "First, it wants us to
radically redesign our ships of the wall to produce a totally
untested class. Next, it wants us to *accelerate* the construction of light attack craft, when we've demonstrated
just about conclusively that even modern LACs are no
match, ton-for-ton, for properly designed starships, even
in a defensive role. Then it wants us to divert something
like ten percent of our building capacity from super-
dreadnoughts and dreadnoughts—and this, mind you, at
a time when the Peeps' building rates in those same classes
are going *up*—to build these so-called 'LAC-carriers' in
order to transport light attack craft across interstellar
distances as *offensive* units, not defensive ones. Not content
with that, it wants to strip the missile tubes out of our
existing ships of the wall and replace them with launchers
which will use up twelve percent more weapons volume
and fire missiles whose size effectively reduces magazine
capacity by *eighteen* percent?" He shook his head.

"No, Milady. This isn't just changing horses in midstream;
this is jumping off your horse without making sure you have
another one to land on, and you don't do that in the middle
of a war. Not if you want to *win* that war. This sounds too

much like a Sonja Hemphill wish list for me to endorse it."

"Then you're wrong, My Lord," Honor said, "and perhaps you should have *read* that white paper rather than just venting your spleen on it."

Her soprano's flat, biting incisiveness twitched White Haven upright in his chair, and she felt his astonishment through Nimitz. He was unused to hearing *anyone* speak to him like that, she realized, but she refused to retreat and held his eyes unflinchingly.

White Haven looked at his hostess, and it was as if he were truly seeing her for the first time. Very few officers below three-star rank dared cross swords with *him*, and even those who did seldom had the nerve to address him in such a cool, clipped tone. But Honor Harrington had the nerve, and her chocolate-brown eyes were very level— and hard. He blinked as he digested her demeanor, for it was painfully clear that all his undeniable experience, achievements, and seniority failed to overwhelm her. There was no hint of apology or hesitance in her manner, and her treecat raised his head to glance at White Haven from his perch above her.

"I beg your pardon?" The question came out more harshly than he'd intended, but she'd hit a raw nerve. He'd spent the better part of thirty T-years fighting "Horrible Hemphill's" mania for new toys. If not for him, the entire Navy might have found itself lumbered with the same weapons mix which had almost gotten Harrington's own ship killed on Basilisk Station ten years ago!

"I said you're wrong," Honor repeated, not yielding a millimeter before the cold anger in his voice. "I've had my own differences with Lady Hemphill, but the WDB recommendations are *not* her 'wish list.' Certainly she had a lot to do with pushing most of the new concepts into deployment. Be honest, My Lord—has there been a new tech development in the last thirty years that she *hasn't* been involved with? Whatever else she may be, she's imaginative and technically brilliant, and while it's true a lot of her ideas have proven operationally unsound, assuming *all* of them will *always* fail is as foolish as rejecting them out of hand simply because she proposed them. No one whose imagination is as fertile as hers can be wrong *all* the time, My Lord!"

"I'm *not* rejecting them simply because she proposed them," White Haven returned sharply. "I'm rejecting them because this package she rammed through the Board will disorder our production schedules and require us to develop whole new tactical doctrines—for weapons which probably won't work as well as she and her supporters think—in the middle of a damned war!"

"Before we continue this discussion, My Lord," Honor said very calmly, "I think you should know that the person who wrote the Board's final recommendations was me."

White Haven closed his mouth with a snap and stared at her. She didn't really need Nimitz to feel his astonished disbelief, and she suppressed a sudden desire to snort in exasperation. She'd always respected White Haven, both as an officer and a man, and she knew he'd taken a personal interest in her career since Admiral Courvosier's death. His guidance and advice had been invaluable to her on more than one occasion, but this time she felt a powerful sense of disappointment in him. She knew he was tired—one look at the deep lines etched around his ice-blue eyes and the thicker streaks of white in his black hair proved that—but he was better than this. He'd *better* be, anyway! The Navy—and the Alliance—needed him to throw his influence behind the right policies, not to retreat into dogmatic opposition of anything associated with Sonja Hemphill.

He started to say something more, but she beat him to it.

"Admiral, I'll be the first to acknowledge your successes, both before and since this war began. As a matter of fact, I've always been more comfortable with the historical school than the *jeune école* myself. But the Star Kingdom doesn't have the luxury of letting its senior officers battle one another to submission over this point. I assure you that I wasn't the only officer asked to comment on my personal experience with the hardware the Board's recommending. And if you'd checked the technical appendices rather than simply skimming the proposed changes in production priorities, you'd have seen that regardless of who first proposed them, every one of our recommendations has been modified to reflect actual combat experience.

"For example, the LACs to which you object are an entirely new model, with improvements even the ones I took to Silesia didn't have. The new compensators will make them *much* faster than anything else in space; BuShips has found a way to upgrade their beta nodes almost to alpha node strength, which will give them far stronger sidewalls than any previous LAC; and the new designs incorporate *extremely* powerful energy armaments—grasers, not lasers—in a spinal mount configuration. They won't be designed for broadside combat at all; their function will be to approach hostile starships obliquely, denying the enemy any down-the-throat shot until they close to decisive range, then turn simultaneously to attack single targets *en masse*. In many respects, it will be a reversion to the old wet-navy aircraft carrier . . . and with a lot of the same advantages for the LAC-carrier. It can deploy its assets from outside missile range, attack, and get out without ever coming under threat from a conventionally armed defender. And whether you and I like it or not, Lady Hemphill does have a point about LAC's expendability. They're so small and carry such small crews that we can trade a dozen of them for a heavy cruiser and come out ahead—not just in tonnage terms, but in loss of life, as well.

"Next, the new ships of the wall you object to are a logical extrapolation of the armament I had in Silesia. Where, I might remind you, Sir, my squadron, operating as single units outside any mutual support range, captured or destroyed an entire pirate squadron—plus a Peep light cruiser, two heavy cruisers, and a pair of *battlecruisers*—for the loss of a single armed merchant cruiser. Certainly building a superdreadnought around a hollow core would be a radical departure, and BuShips agrees that the new design will result in some reduction in structural strength. But it will also allow each SD to carry just over five hundred ten-missile pods and fire a salvo of six of them every twelve seconds. That's over five *thousand* missiles, at the rate of three hundred per minute, from a single ship which will sacrifice about thirty percent of its conventional armament to fit them in. I might also point out that the Ghost Rider remote platforms will make their pods even more useful, since it will allow the new design to deploy a complete, multilayered shell in a single salvo. Moreover, the new missile ships and the LAC-carriers between them will divert only twenty-five percent of the yard capacity currently devoted to conventional ships of the wall, assuming the recommended WDB ship mix is adopted.

"And as far as the new missiles are concerned, My Lord, did you even *look* at the performance parameters before you decided they were more of 'Horrible Hemphill's wish list'?" Honor demanded, unable to hide her exasperation.

"*Certainly* she came up with the concept, but R&D took it and ran with it. We're talking about a 'multistage' missile—one with three *separate* drives, which will give us a degree of tactical flexibility no previous navy could even dream of! We can preprogram the drives to come on-line with any timing and at any power setting we wish! Simply programming them to activate in immediate succession at maximum power would give us a hundred and eighty seconds of powered flight . . . and a powered attack range from rest of over fourteen and a half million kilometers with a terminal velocity of point-five-four cee. Or we can drop the drives' power settings to forty-six thousand gees and get five times the endurance—and a maximum powered missile envelope of over *sixty-five* million klicks with a terminal velocity of point-*eight-one* light-speed. That's a range of three-point-six *light-minutes*, and we can get even more than that if we use one or two 'stages' to accelerate the weapon, let it ride a ballistic course to a preprogrammed attack range, and then bring up the final 'stage' for terminal attack maneuvers at a full ninety-two thousand gravities. I don't know about you, My Lord, but I'll sacrifice eighteen percent of *my* total missile load for that performance envelope!"

White Haven tried to say something, but she rolled right on over him, and her flashing eyes were no longer cold.

"And finally, Sir, I submit to you that the fact that the Peeps are beginning to cut into our technology advantage is the strongest possible argument *for* these new systems. Of course we can't afford to dissipate our resources chasing after unworkable concepts just because they're exotic or fascinating! But the only thing that's let us maintain the upper hand, however narrowly, so far has been the fact that both our hardware *and* our tactics have been better than theirs. If you want to cite examples from Old Earth, let me paraphrase Admiral Saint-Vincent for you. 'Happen what will, the Star Kingdom must lead,' My Lord, because our survival depends even more heavily on our fleet's superiority now than Great Britain's did then!"

She stopped speaking abruptly, and White Haven shook himself. He felt dull spots of color burning on either cheek, but they weren't born of anger. They burned because he'd let himself be caught short this way, for however much he might wish differently, he couldn't deny her charge that he hadn't read the appendices. Nor could he deny that it was his own prejudice which had kept him from doing so. There was no question in his mind that he'd been right to fight Hemphill's efforts to introduce things like the grav lance or the pure energy torpedo armament into general service, and God only knew where things might have ended if she'd been allowed to implement her "spinal mount" main armament concept for ships of the wall! The idea of a capital ship which had no choice but to cross its own "T" for an enemy in order to engage it still made him cringe, and, he was certain, it would have the same effect on his hostess.

But that didn't alter the accuracy of her indictment. What would be madness in a ship of the wall might make perfectly good sense in something as small, agile—and (however little he might like it) expendable—as a LAC, and he hadn't even considered it. Nor had he made sufficient allowance for what the new central-core missile pod systems had allowed Harrington to accomplish in Silesia when he dismissed the concept's applicability to "real" warships. And, worst of all, he hadn't even bothered to look at the drive numbers on the new missiles or recognize their implications. And *all* of it, he admitted with still deeper chagrin, had stemmed from his instinctive, unreasoning, gut-level rejection of any project with which Sonja Hemphill was connected. Which meant he'd just exercised exactly the same knee-jerk reaction to technological change, albeit in the opposite direction, for which he'd always lambasted the *jeune école*.

And Honor Harrington had called him on it.

He blinked again and sat back in his chair, noting the slight flush in her cheeks, the light of battle in her eyes, the refusal to back down simply because the most successful fleet commander the RMN had produced in two centuries disagreed with her. And as he gazed at her, he realized something else, as well. He'd always been aware of her physical attractiveness. Her triangular, sharply-carved face, dominated by her strong nose and the huge, almond eyes she'd inherited from her mother, would never be conventionally beautiful. Indeed, in repose, it was too harsh, its features too strong, for that. But the personality behind it—the intelligence and character and strength of will— gave it the life and energy to make one forget that. Or perhaps she *was* beautiful, he thought. Beautiful as a hawk or falcon was, with a dangerous vitality that warned anyone who saw her that this woman was a force to be reckoned with. The slim, sinewy grace with which she moved only added to that image, and his mind had always recognized it.

But her attractiveness had simply been one more facet of an outstanding junior officer who'd somehow become his protégé, and his cerebral awareness that so much competence was wrapped in such a fascinating package had never moved beyond his forebrain. Perhaps that was because he'd never really seen her as anything *except* a naval officer, or perhaps it was because he'd always been attracted to women who were shorter than he . . . and who didn't have the hand-to-hand training to tie him into a pretzel. And, he admitted, whose ages were closer to his own. Perhaps there'd even been a sort of subconscious awareness on his part that it would be far better for both of them if he never *did* "see" just how attractive—to him—she had the potential to become.

But whatever it might have been, it had suddenly become irrelevant. In that moment, he no longer saw her simply as an officer, nor even as a head of government. In an odd sort of way, it seemed to be *because* of the way she'd taken him to task, as if that had somehow jarred him into a fundamental reevaluation—on an emotional, as well as an intellectual basis—of who and what she truly was. And among the many other things she might be, he realized now, she was an astonishingly fascinating woman . . . and one whom he suddenly feared (though fear, he admitted, was not precisely the proper word) he would never again be able to see solely as his protégé.

Honor's eyes went wide as the emotions flowing into her through Nimitz changed abruptly, and her own exasperation vanished, blown away by White Haven's sudden, intent focus on her. Not on what she'd been saying, but on *her*.

She pushed back in her chair and heard Nimitz thump down on the console behind her. Then the 'cat flowed over her shoulder and down into her lap, and she busied herself clasping him in her arms as if that could somehow make time stand still while she thought frantically.

This shouldn't—*couldn't*—be happening, and she wanted to shake Nimitz like a toy as the 'cat added his own approval of White Haven's reaction to the emotions pouring into her. Nimitz knew how much she'd loved Paul Tankersley, and, in his own way, the 'cat had loved Paul almost as fiercely. But he also saw no reason she shouldn't someday find another love, and his bone-deep purr was only too clear an indication of *his* reaction to the earl's sudden recognition of her attractiveness.

But if Nimitz couldn't see the potential disaster looming ahead, Honor certainly could. White Haven wasn't simply her superior officer; he was also Eighth Fleet's designated CO, while she was slated to command one of his squadrons. That put them in the same chain of command, which meant anything at all between them would be a violation of Article 119, and that was a court-martial offense for officers. Even worse, he was married—and not to just anyone. Lady Emily Alexander had been the Star Kingdom's most beloved HD actress before the terrible freak air car accident which had turned her into a permanent invalid. Even today, locked forever into a life-support chair and reduced essentially to the use of one hand and arm, she remained one of Manticore's foremost writer-producers . . . and one of its leading poets, as well.

Honor made her brain stop racing and drew a deep breath. She was being ridiculous. All she'd felt was a single surge of emotion, and it wasn't as if she hadn't felt spikes of admiration and even desire from other men since her link to Nimitz had changed! Things like that happened, she told herself firmly, and she'd never worried about it unless someone tried to act upon it. In fact, she'd often found it rather pleasant. Not because she felt any desire to offer the men in question encouragement—her relationship with Paul had made difficulties enough for her on conservative Grayson, and she didn't need to awaken old memories, personal or public—but because it was rather flattering. Especially, she admitted, for someone who'd spent thirty years feeling like an ugly duckling.

This was just another case of passing interest, she told herself even more firmly. The best thing she could do was pretend she was unaware of it and offer no encouragement. If she ever let White Haven suspect she'd recognized his feelings, it could only embarrass him. Besides, his enduring love for his invalid wife—and their devotion to one another—were legendary. Their marriage was one of the great, tragic love stories of the Star Kingdom, and Honor couldn't even imagine him turning away from Lady Emily, however attractive he found someone else.

Still, a small corner of her brain whispered, *there* were *those rumors about him and Admiral Kuzak. I suppose it's* possible *that—*

She chopped that thought off in a hurry and cleared her throat.

"Excuse me, My Lord," she said. "I didn't mean to lecture. I suppose part of my reaction stems from the fact that I've had my own doubts where Lady Hemphill is concerned. It may be that making the adjustment to supporting at least some of her concepts has given me a sort of evangelical fervor, but that's no excuse."

"Um." White Haven shook himself, blinked in bemusement, then waved away her apology with a smile. "No excuse is needed, Milady. I deserved every word of it . . . and if I *had* bothered to read the appendices, I could have avoided a well earned tongue-lashing." She felt his own confusion over his reaction still echoing below the surface of his thoughts, but no sign of it touched his expression, and she was grateful. Then he glanced at his chrono and twitched in surprise so artfully assumed it would have fooled even Honor if not for her link to Nimitz.

"I hadn't realized how late it's gotten," he announced, rising and reaching for his sword once more. "It's time I turned in, and I imagine your guests are about ready to depart." He clipped the sword to his belt and smiled again, and any disinterested observer would have thought that smile was completely natural. "Allow me to escort you back to the ballroom," he suggested, extending his arm, and she rose with a matching smile and set Nimitz back on her shoulder.

"Thank you, My Lord," she said, placing her hand on his elbow in approved Grayson fashion, and he swept her out of the library in style.

Andrew LaFollet fell in behind them, and his calmly attentive, utterly normal emotions were a soothing contrast to what Honor still sensed from White Haven—or, for that matter, felt herself—as she walked down the hall at the earl's side, chatting as if nothing at all had happened.

And, she told herself, nothing *had* happened. She told herself that firmly, almost fiercely, and by the time they reached the ballroom once more, she almost believed it.

• Chapter Three

"Good morning, Milady."

Honor turned her head and looked up as if to identify the new arrival, but it wasn't really necessary. She'd felt White Haven's approach through Nimitz long before he stepped into the sun-drenched dining room, and she summoned a smile of greeting.

"Good morning, My Lord. Will you join us?" She gestured at the well-spread breakfast table, and he returned her smile.

"I certainly will," he replied, "and the pancakes smell delicious." He spoke in an absolutely normal tone, with no echoes of the feelings she'd caught from him last night, and she felt a flood of relief . . . which she promptly scolded herself for feeling.

"What you're smelling aren't pancakes," she told him, and he cocked a questioning eyebrow. "They're waffles, and I'm afraid they're disgustingly rich the way I like them."

"Waffles?" White Haven repeated the unfamiliar word as if sampling it.

"Think of them as, oh, crunchy, quilted pancakes," she said. "They're something of a tradition here on Grayson—one I wish the Star Kingdom hadn't lost, even if it *is* a dietitian's despair. And Manticore had a lot better shot at retaining it, given the difference in our first wave's relative circumstances. On the other hand, you may have noticed that Graysons can be a little stubborn?" She turned her head to smile up over her shoulder at Andrew LaFollet, then quirked a roguish eyebrow at his sister, and the two of them chuckled as White Haven gave a wry nod. "Well, this is one of the things they simply made up their minds that they *would not* lose. I suspect the recipe's changed a little . . . but I wouldn't be willing to bet any money on it."

This time White Haven joined the LaFollets' laughter. The inhabitants of Grayson were nothing if not determined. Among other things, theirs was the only planet in the explored galaxy which had retained the ancient Gregorian calendar, despite the fact that it was totally unsuited to their planetary day or year. If anyone was likely to have preserved a traditional breakfast food in the midst of colonizing a disastrously hostile planet with a pathetically crippled tech base, they were certainly the people to do it.

He sniffed again as he slid into the chair facing Harrington's and ran his eyes over her oddly assorted breakfast party. Her treecat sat in a highchair to her right, wrinkling his whiskers at the earl in unmistakable greeting. White Haven gave him a courteous nod, then nodded in turn to Samantha, who sat in a matching chair to Nimitz's right. Miranda LaFollet sat to Harrington's left, and a third highchair sat to *her* left for Farragut. White Haven had rather more experience with 'cats than most Manticorans, given his family's long-standing alliance with the House of Winton. Enough monarchs and crown princes and princesses had been adopted over the past eight or nine generations for breakfast at Mount Royal Palace to seem somehow *wrong* if there weren't any treecats present, but it was unusual—to say the least—for the 'cats' numbers to equal those of the human diners.

Of course, he reminded himself, there were eleven more of them somewhere around Harrington House this morning. He wondered who was watching Samantha's kittens and wished whoever it was luck. From what he'd seen of her offspring yesterday, their nursemaids were going to need all the breaks they could get, and he was heartily glad that *he* wasn't one of them.

He smiled inside at the thought and returned his attention to the fascinating odors wafting in from the open door at the end of the dining room. They really *did* smell delicious . . . and the lush, buttery undertones warned him the "waffles" would be just as rich as Harrington had intimated. He cocked his head to look at her, noting the full cocoa mug beside her plate, and wondered how she could possibly stay so slender in the face of what was clearly a monumental sweet tooth. There had to be more to it than exercise alone, however many calories she burned up in her physical training program.

Honor felt his attention and sensed the speculation at its heart. She couldn't tell precisely what he was speculating upon, but it was very different from the sudden burst of almost visceral awareness she'd picked up from him last night. She wondered if she was glad for the difference, then gave herself a sharp mental shake. Of course she was glad! A goodly part of her had dreaded breakfast, for her night had not been restful. She'd gone back over those last few minutes in the library again and again, picking at them as she might have scratched at some maddening physical itch. And, as she'd told herself at the time, her spiraling afterthoughts had concluded that it was nothing to worry about. That it had been only a momentary thing, a flash of awareness which White Haven had no way of knowing she'd shared with him. Something he would put away in a back corner of his brain where it could not affect their professional relationship.

Unfortunately, a deep, inner part of her had refused to accept that comforting logic.

It had been ridiculous. She was over fifty T-years old, not a schoolgirl! She'd had no *business* lying awake speculating on what a man who'd never before shown the least awareness of her as a woman might be thinking about her. Especially not *this* man. Yet that was precisely what she'd done, and taking herself to task for it had done no good at all. She dropped her eyes to her own plate, looking at the butter and syrup-drenched wreckage of her second stack of waffles, and gave herself yet another mental kick.

What was *wrong* with her? She should be relieved that

he wasn't thinking about her that way, and she was. But a part of her didn't share that relief. Oh, no. Part of her felt almost petulant, angry with him because he *had* put his awareness of her attractiveness away somewhere . . . exactly as she'd half-prayed that he would. And as if to make her absurd dithering worse, there was an undertone of guilt, as if the petulance of that irrational part of her were somehow a betrayal of Paul Tankersley.

Her expression showed no trace of it, but Nimitz cocked his ears inquisitively as he felt her frustration with her own ridiculous fixation on someone else's momentary preoccupation, and she gritted mental teeth as she sensed his rousing interest. There was an undeniable edge of wicked delight in his emotions, and the laughter in his grass-green eyes would have been a dead giveaway even if their emotions hadn't been linked. It wasn't often she did something he found ridiculous to the point of hilarity, but it appeared that his empathic abilities gave him a rather different perspective. Well, that was fine for him, she thought moodily. Maybe *his* species was so accustomed to feeling others' emotions that they could take it in stride, however inappropriate the circumstances, but that was no reason he should be so indecently amused by *her* difficulties!

She concentrated on radiating an aggrieved sense of rebuke at him, but he only bared his fangs in a lazy, unmistakable laugh. And, just to make things worse, he sent her another strong pulse of that approval for White Haven.

She heard a quiet sound behind her and turned with a sense of relief for the distraction as MacGuiness stepped out of the pantry—*his* pantry, as every member of the Harrington House staff had been made thoroughly aware. The entire staff deferred to MacGuiness, and he was perfectly willing to delegate most tasks, but *he* was in charge of serving his captain's meals, and he gave White Haven a small half-bow.

"Good morning, My Lord. May I bring you coffee?"

"You may," White Haven said with a smile, "but I think

I'd prefer to start with a glass of juice and save the coffee to follow the waffles. I suspect I'll need something to chase the syrup through my system."

"Of course, My Lord," MacGuiness replied, and looked at Honor. "Are you ready for another serving, My Lady?" he asked.

"Um, yes. Yes, I am, Mac," she replied, and he smiled and turned back to his pantry.

His intervention, brief as it was, had been enough to redirect Honor's wandering thoughts, and she looked up at White Haven with a smile as something quite different from last night's admiration colored his emotions. His surprise was something she'd felt before, and while she generally didn't comment on it, it felt so *normal* compared to the other things she'd been worrying about that she found herself explaining.

"You're wondering why I don't look like a pre-space blimp, aren't you, My Lord?" she teased gently.

"I— That is—" White Haven blushed. Her direct, smiling question had caught him without a graceful response, and his blush deepened at her soft laugh.

"Don't worry, My Lord. Mike Henke teases me about it all the time, and the explanation's simple enough. I'm a genie."

The earl blinked briefly, his expression totally blank, then nodded in sudden understanding. It was considered extremely impolite to use the term "genie" to describe someone, but given Harrington's neurosurgeon father and— especially—geneticist mother, she was probably more comfortable with the label than many. For that matter, the prejudice against genetically engineered humans was slowly dying out as the last memories of Old Earth's Final War faded from the racial forebrain. But there had been no such prejudice in the early days of the Diaspora, and quite a few colonies had been established by genies specifically designed for their new environments.

"I wasn't aware of that, Milady," he said after a moment.

"We don't talk about it much, but I'd guess the majority

of Sphinxians are genies by now," she replied. He raised a polite eyebrow, and she shrugged. "Think about it," she suggested. "Heavy-grav planets are one of the most common 'hostile' environments. You know that even today most heavy-worlders have shorter than average life expectancies?" She looked at White Haven again, and he nodded. "That's because even with modern medicine you can't put a body designed for a single gravity onto a one-point-three or one-point-five-gravity planet and expect it to function properly. I, on the other hand—"

She made a graceful gesture with one hand, and he nodded slowly. "I knew about the modifications for Quelhollow, but those are much more readily apparent than what you seem to be talking about," he observed.

"Well, Quelhollow had some other environmental concerns, whereas *my* ancestors were more of a . . . generic design, I suppose. Basically, my muscle tissue is about twenty-five percent more efficient than a 'pure human's,' and there are a few changes to my respiratory and circulatory systems, plus some skeletal reinforcement. The idea was to fit us for heavy-grav planets generally, not one in particular, and the geneticists made the changes dominant, so that every parent would pass them on to every child."

"And your diet?"

"I don't get more efficient muscles and a stronger heart for free, My Lord," Honor said wryly. "My metabolism runs about twenty percent faster—a little more than that actually, but not much—to fuel the differences. Which is why I can afford to eat like this," she finished, grinning as MacGuiness put a third plate of waffles in front of her.

"Actually," she added, cutting into the stack, "I tend to stuff myself at breakfast, then have a relatively light—well, light for *me*, anyway—lunch. The overnight 'down time' leaves me needing more reactor mass in the morning."

"That's fascinating," White Haven murmured. "You say more than half of Sphinx has the same modification?"

"That's only an estimate, and it's not *one* modification. The Harringtons are descended from the Meyerdahl First

Wave, which was one of the first—in fact, I think it was *the* first—heavy-grav modification, and folks like us probably make up about twenty or twenty-five percent of the population. But there are several variations on the same theme, and worlds tend to attract colonists who can live there comfortably. When you add the free passages the government offered to recruit fresh colonists after the Plague of Twenty-Two AL, Sphinx wound up attracting an even bigger chunk of us than most, including a lot from the core worlds who wouldn't even have considered emigration otherwise. In many respects, the Meyerdahl genies are the most successful, in my modest opinion, though. Our musculature enhancement is certainly the most efficient, at any rate. But we do have one problem most of the others don't."

"Which is?"

"Most of us don't regenerate," she told him, touching the left side of her face. "Over eighty percent of us have a built-in genetic conflict with the regen therapies, and not even Beowulf has been able to figure out how to get around it yet. I'm pretty sure they will eventually, but for now—"

She shrugged, mildly surprised at herself for offering the explanation in the first place, and even more for giving so many details. It wasn't something she thought much about herself, and some people still had funny reactions to the entire notion of "genies." But the conversation had reminded her of something else, and she turned to Miranda.

"Is everything ready for the ground-breaking?" she asked, and Miranda nodded.

"Yes, My Lady. I went over the details with Colonel Hill one last time last night. Everything's in place, the Guard's satisfied with its crowd control measures, and Lord Prestwick will be here to express the Protector's personal thanks for your endowment."

Honor waved a hand to banish the importance of that last point, but Miranda, like her brother, had figured out that Honor's link to Nimitz let her sense the emotions of others. She appeared to have become even more aware of that in the three days since her own adoption, and Honor blinked as she realized her maid was *deliberately* using Nimitz to communicate her disagreement with Honor's attempt to minimize the significance of her gift to her adopted world.

Miranda held her gaze for a moment, and Honor blinked again. She'd become almost accustomed to having other treecats consciously use her link with Nimitz that way, but Miranda was the first human to do it, and Honor suddenly wondered if that stemmed from the fact that Miranda *wasn't* a Sphinxian. Was it possible that her lack of preconceptions about the 'cats' abilities actually left her better able to recognize—and utilize—those same abilities?

Perhaps. But at the moment, Miranda was concentrating on a gentle rebuke, and Honor sighed as she admitted the younger woman was probably right. Honor hadn't set up the endowment to curry favor with Protector Benjamin or anyone else. She'd done it because she felt it was important and necessary and because, unlike most Graysons, she had more money than she could possibly spend anyway, so she might as well do something useful with it. But that didn't change the fact that she *had* done it, and if the Chancellor of Grayson was going to come clear out here to thank her, the least she could do was respond graciously.

"All right, Miranda," she sighed. "I'll behave."

"I never doubted it, My Lady," Miranda replied with admirable gravity, then smiled. "But I'm afraid you *are* going to have to give your own speech in response to his."

Her gray eyes twinkled, and Honor swallowed a chuckle as Farragut bleeked a soft laugh from his person's far side. Honor's "maid" wasn't the sort of radical likely to storm the bastions of male supremacy, but she *was* a sturdy, self-confident individual, and that aspect of her personality had come strongly to the fore. Without even realizing it, she'd begun sinking a few mines under the bastions she was unprepared to assault frontally, and Honor was glad of it. For all intents and purposes, Miranda had become her social and public relations chief of staff, and her number-two political advisor, with at least as much insight as and a rather different perspective from Howard Clinkscales. That would have occasioned no comment back in the Star Kingdom, but it could have been a source of major consternation here on Grayson, where it had never been "proper" for women to dabble in politics, however indirectly. Worse, Miranda had moved smoothly into the role of coordinator, giving directions to a primarily male staff with an assurance which mirrored her Steadholder's.

It was possible that some of that assurance stemmed from an awareness that she shared in Honor's prestige and authority, but Honor thought that was only a very small part of it. Most of Miranda's competent assurance sprang from the fact that her native ability had finally been given a chance to reveal itself and that she was simply incapable of not rising to that sort of challenge.

And I wonder, Honor mused, *how much of a role that played in Farragut's decision to adopt her?*

"Did the Colonel say anything about the upper review stand?" Major LaFollet asked his sister, and Miranda shrugged.

"I think he thinks you're being paranoid, but he agreed to have the engineers check it out. And to put two or three armsmen up there to keep an eye on things. And we've adjusted the schedule to give you the time you wanted for you and Lord Clinkscales to meet privately with the Chancellor, My Lady."

LaFollet's on-duty expression relaxed enough to permit a small smile at the word "paranoid," but Honor sensed his satisfaction. The upper review stand actually overhung the area in which she would use the silver shovel for the official ground-breaking ceremony, and Andrew had disliked it from the outset. *Which,* she reflected, *I can live with. Andrew may be a little on the "paranoid" side, but given what Burdette and his maniacs tried—*

She brushed that thought aside and nodded.

"Good," she told her henchpeople, then frowned and rubbed the tip of her nose. "Speaking of Lord Clinkscales and meetings, Miranda, please run down Stuart Matthews for me. I want a thumbnail technical-side briefing on Sky Domes' to bring me up to speed before we meet with Lord Prestwick."

"Yes, My Lady. But don't forget the audience with Deacon Sanderson, either. I've scheduled that for fifteen-hundred tomorrow."

Miranda's tone was respectful, but Honor suppressed a sudden desire to smack herself on her forehead, for she *had* forgotten the meeting with Sanderson. And it promised to be an important one, considering that Sanderson was the personal aide and direct representative of Reverend Sullivan. Honor *hoped* the audience's purpose was to express Sullivan's support for her newest project. She had no reason to expect anything else, but she still didn't know Sullivan well, and the new Reverend was a far cry from the gentle man he had succeeded. No one could have doubted the strength of Julius Hanks' personal faith, and those who'd known him well had always recognized that, for all his soft-spokenness, he had a whim of steel and a central core of titanium, but he'd never been a confrontational personality. Instead, he'd achieved his ends by a sort of spiritual *akido*, turning his most vociferous opponents into allies with the magic of his humor and inescapable . . . well, *goodness*. Honor had no doubt that the Church would nominate him for canonization at the earliest possible moment, and anyone who'd ever met him would support his elevation to sainthood with enthusiasm.

But Jeremiah Sullivan was cut from very different cloth. Thanks to Nimitz, Honor knew that Sullivan's faith was as deep as Hanks' had been, but where Hanks had often seemed almost too gentle for the real world, Sullivan went through life like a whirlwind. He'd spent years as Hanks' right-hand assistant and (when needed) hatchet man, and he'd embraced virtually all of Hanks' policies when he replaced the previous Reverend at the head of the Sacristy. But his bracing, aggressive, sometimes oppressively energetic temperament made him a very different person, and the Church was still coming to grips with the change in its leadership.

In the long run, Honor expected Sullivan to be good for Grayson. He would accomplish whatever he did in ways which would never have occurred to Hanks, but his devotion to his God, his flock, his church, and his Protector—in that order—were beyond question.

Unfortunately, however, he was also rather more of a social conservative than Hanks had been. Or, rather, than Hanks had *become* following Grayson's alliance with Manticore. The new Reverend had been zealous in proclaiming the Church's continued backing for the Protector's reforms, and his attitude towards Steadholder Harrington could hardly have been more supportive, yet Honor knew the concept of a female steadholder didn't come naturally to him. In a very real sense, Sullivan was forcing himself to do what his intellect and his understanding of his faith required of him despite a lingering, deep-seated emotional distaste for the changes in his world—and his own world *view*—that required.

Honor respected him for that, but it also meant that she nursed a tiny, perpetual fear that sooner or later his emotions were going to get the better of reason and bring the two of them—or, worse, Protector Benjamin and him—into painful collision. And given who she'd picked to head the clinic—

"Excuse me, Milady." White Haven's voice broke into her reverie, and she gave her head an impatient shake and turned to face him. "I couldn't help overhearing," the earl went on. "May I ask just what you're breaking ground for?" He smiled wryly. "If you'll forgive my saying so, you *do* seem to have an unending flow of projects."

"This is a new steading, My Lord," Honor replied. "And, truth to tell, I sometimes think Harrington is Grayson's proving ground. My people are used to having their minds stretched, so we keep trying out new things here before we turn them loose on the conservatives. Don't we, Miranda?"

"I'm not sure I'd say 'we' do it, My Lady," her maid murmured, "but *someone* certainly does." She looked innocently at her Steadholder, and all three treecats bleeked in laughter.

"I'm keeping track," Honor told her, "and the day will come, Miranda LaFollet."

"What day would that be, My Lady?" Miranda asked demurely, eyes laughing.

"Don't worry," Honor said ominously. "You'll recognize it when it arrives." Miranda chuckled, and Honor glanced back at White Haven.

"As I was saying before the distraction, My Lord," she resumed, ignoring her maid and armsman as they joined the 'cats' laughter, "we tend to try things out here, and what we're trying out this time is Grayson's first modern genetic clinic."

"Ah?" White Haven raised his eyebrows attentively, and Honor felt his fresh flicker of interest. Most of it was simply that—interest in the project she was describing—but there was more to it, as well. A dancing fire around the edges of his emotions. It was . . . admiration, she realized, and felt her cheeks heat. Darn it! Whatever White Haven— or Miranda, or Lord Prestwick, or even Benjamin Mayhew— might think, there was *nothing* extraordinary about her decision to bankroll the clinic. The entire initial endowment came to barely forty million, and Graysons suffered from an appalling number of genetic defects—many, if not most, of them correctable by modern medicine—after a millennium's exposure to their planet's heavy metal concentrations. It would have been criminal for her *not* to get someone from the Star Kingdom out here to do something about that, so where did White Haven get off *admiring* her for it? What gave him the right to sit there and—

She snatched her own thoughts to a halt with a confused sense of shock. Dear God, something *was* wrong with her. This irrational anger—and anger, she knew, was precisely what it was—was alien to her. Worse, it *was* irrational. Neither Miranda nor White Haven had said or done a single thing which should have upset any rational human being. And Miranda's admiration *hadn't* upset her. But *White*

Haven's had, and a dagger of sheer disbelief went through her as she realized why.

She'd been wrong. His sudden awareness of her last night hadn't been one-sided after all, and she swallowed hard, reaching for her napkin and wiping her lips in an effort to buy herself a few more seconds' respite. Perhaps the earl's moment of recognition had begun one-sidedly, but it hadn't stayed that way, and that was the reason she'd found herself picking at it so long last night. For in the moment in which he'd truly seen her, some part of her had truly seen *him*. And now something infinitely worse had happened, for in the moment of her awareness, something stabbed at her through Nimitz. She heard the 'cat inhale sharply, felt his twitch of shock, but she couldn't sort out his reactions. She was too busy fighting to understand her own, for in that instant, her link to the 'cat had let her not simply see White Haven but *recognize* him.

There was a . . . resonance between them, one she'd never sensed before, even with Paul. She'd loved Paul Tankersley with all her heart. She *still* loved him, and the two of them had shared something she knew had been rare and perfect and wonderful. She no longer allowed herself to dwell upon it, but not a day passed in which she didn't miss his gentle strength, his tenderness and passion, and the knowledge that he'd loved her just as deeply as she had loved him. Yet for all that, she had never felt this . . . this sense of *symmetry*.

That wasn't the right word either, and she knew it. But there *was* no "right" word, and she wondered almost wildly how much of this moment was her, how much White Haven, and how much simply some bizarre malfunction of her link with Nimitz. No one else had ever been so closely tied to a 'cat. Surely that was the explanation! It was just a quirk in the flow, some sort of weird emotional spike which had fooled her into thinking it was something more.

Yet even as she thought that, she knew it was nonsense. It was as if a door she hadn't known was there had opened in her head and she'd looked through it to see deep inside White Haven. And what she saw there was herself.

There were differences, of course. There had to be. They didn't agree on everything. They didn't share all the same opinions. In fact, there was enormous scope for disagreement, argument, even quarrels. But where it mattered—where the wellsprings of their personalities rose and gave meaning to their lives—they were the *same*. The same qualities drove them, molded and pushed them, and Honor Harrington felt a sudden, aching need to reach out to him. It shocked and confused her, but she could no more have denied that desire than she could have stopped breathing, for she sensed the enormous potential singing unseen but inescapable between them. It wasn't sexual. Or, rather, it *was* sexual, but only as a part of the whole, for it went far, far beyond any sensual attraction. It was a hunger that went so deep and subsumed so much of her that sexuality *had* to be a part of it. No one had ever before evoked such an intense sense of shared capability within her, and she sensed the way they complemented one another, the unbeatable team they could become.

Yet that was impossible. It could never happen—could never be *allowed* to happen—for what she sensed and recognized in that moment went far beyond any *professional* team. It was a total package, almost a fusion, with implications she dared not truly consider.

Honor had never believed in "love at first sight" . . . which, a tiny part of herself told her quietly, was foolish in someone who'd actually experienced just that in the moment of her adoption by Nimitz. But that had been different, another part of her wailed. Nimitz wasn't human. He was her other half, her beloved companion, her champion and protector—as she was his—but at this moment . . .

She closed her eyes and inhaled deeply. Enough. This was more than simply ridiculous. Hamish Alexander was both her superior officer and a married man who loved his wife. Whatever momentary awareness he might have felt last night, he had never—*ever*—said a single word she could possibly construe as "romantic." Whatever was happening to her, *he* was in control of himself, and if he'd had even the faintest inkling of the sudden, ludicrous confusion whiplashing through her, he would have been disgusted. She knew it, and somehow she forced the fire out of her cheeks and looked up from her waffles with chocolate-dark eyes that showed no sign of her inner turmoil.

"Yes, My Lord," she heard herself say tranquilly. "The strides Grayson has made in industrial capacity and the ability to feed its people are remarkable, but I think, in the long run, that modern medicine is what's really going to have the greatest impact here. No doubt the fact that both of my own parents are physicians tends to prejudice my thinking in that regard—in fact, I've asked my mother to take a leave from her practice on Sphinx to set up our clinic here—but I don't really believe anyone who truly thinks things through could argue the point. After all, simply introducing prolong will bring about enormous changes, and when you add things like genetic repair and research, or—"

She listened to her own voice, letting it wash over her almost as if it were someone else's, and below its calm normality, she wondered despairingly what had come over her . . . and how to cope with it.

• Chapter Four

Citizen Admiral Thomas Theisman leaned back in the sinfully comfortable chair and rubbed his eyes with both hands, as if the act could somehow scrub away the burning ache of fatigue. It couldn't, of course, and he lowered his hands once more to smile bitterly at the opulent office which surrounded him. *At least the condemned man gets a comfortable cell*, he told himself. *Too bad they couldn't give me a few more ships of the wall to go with it.*

He grimaced as the familiar thought wended through its well-worn mental rut. It wasn't as if he were the only system CO who needed more tonnage; it was just that his need was a bit more desperate than most . . . and that he knew his command area had already been written off by the planners back home.

Not that anyone would tell him that in so many words. That wasn't the way things were done these days. Instead, commanders were sent out on hopeless missions to hold the unholdable with the knowledge that when—not if— they failed to achieve victory, their families would suffer for that "failure." Theisman couldn't deny that such measures could strengthen a CO's willingness to fight, but in his opinion, the cost was far too high for the return even from a purely military viewpoint, far less a moral one. Officers who knew both that they couldn't win and that their families were hostage for how hard they *tried* to win were prone to desperation. Theisman had seen it again and again. All too often, an admiral stood and fought to the death for an objective rather than break off and retreat or even adopt a more flexible strategy of maneuver (which might, after

91

all, be mistaken for a retreat by people's commissioners without the military experience to realize what was really happening), and in the process the toll in lost warships and trained personnel rose to even more disastrous levels. Not that anyone seemed able to convince the Office of State Security of that simple, painfully evident fact. Indeed, Theisman often suspected that his own lack of any immediate family was one reason the present command structure of the People's Navy regarded him with permanent low-grade suspicion. Since an officer with no family was less amenable to terrorization, it was inevitable that a regime which depended on terror to maintain its power would distrust him and watch perpetually for the first sign of "treason."

He snorted and let his chair snap upright, then stood to pace restlessly around his huge office while he pondered the paranoia of that last thought. Thomas Theisman had been born fifteen days after his unmarried Dolist mother's sixteenth birthday, and he often wondered what she had been like. All he had of her was a single holocube of a skinny teenager in the cheap, typically flashy garb and overdone cosmetics Dolists favored even now. She'd been almost pretty, in a washed out, rather vapid-looking sort of way, he often thought, and there'd been at least a glimmer of intelligence and a trace of character in that otherwise amorphous face. With a few more years of maturity, a little genuine education, and a reason to at least try to improve her life, she might even have grown into someone he would have liked to know. But he'd never had the opportunity to find out if she had, for she'd handed him over to one of the state-run crèches before he was six months old. He'd never seen her again, and he had even her holocube only because the senior matron of his crèche had violated regulations to let him keep it.

Which, he told himself now, rubbing the deep scar on his left cheek, *is probably a good thing. Since I've never met her—don't even know if she's still alive, for that matter*—*not even StateSec would threaten to shoot her to "motivate" me. Or I don't think they would, anyway.*

He grimaced again and stopped near the door of his office, turning to survey the site from which he governed his doomed domain.

It was, beyond a doubt, the biggest, most luxurious working space he'd ever had, for this was the nerve center of the Barnett System. Buried deep at the heart of DuQuesne Base, the largest military installation on the planet Enki, it was only a moment's walk from the War Room. Once second only to the Haven System itself among the People's Navy's command slots, it had been outfitted with all the luxury the old Legislaturalist officer corps had reserved to itself, and if the decor showed signs of wear and neglect, at least no one had gotten around to stripping the office of the "decadent trappings of elitism." Theisman supposed he was grateful for that. The only problem was that no amount of personal comfort could disguise the fact that he was in yet another of the hopeless positions the People's Republic and its Navy seemed to spend so much time stumbling into, and he couldn't quite suppress the suspicion that he was here *because* the situation was hopeless.

He put his hands behind him and gripped them together, rocking on his heels as he contemplated his unpalatable and probably brief future, and cursed himself yet again for his inability to play the political game properly. If only he'd been able to bring himself to kiss ass a little where the Committee of Public Safety or State Security were concerned he might not be in this office, looking down the barrel of a loaded pulser. He'd known all along that he was headed somewhere like this, he supposed. It wasn't because he'd been loyal to the old regime, for the old regime had given him very little reason to feel any devotion to it. Nor was it because he was *dis*loyal to the PRH, for whatever its faults might be, the People's Republic was his country, the star nation whose uniform he'd chosen to wear and which he'd sworn to defend.

No, the problem, as he was only too well aware, was that

he couldn't stomach the stupidity and waste and gratuitous violence wreaked in the name of discipline by half-wits who lacked the intelligence to see where their version of "discipline" must ultimately lead. Like many other officers, he'd found in the Legislaturalist purges a chance for the flag rank he could never have attained under the old regime, but his attitudes, as his military skills, had been shaped by his one-time mentor Alfredo Yu. And like Yu, Thomas Theisman believed in finding ways to maximize the strength of the raw material assigned to him, whether in terms of equipment or personnel, which required that an officer *lead*, not simply goad from behind.

But the crude tactics embraced by the SS rejected that tradition. Indeed, StateSec didn't *want* leaders in the military, for anyone who could motivate his people to follow him and give of their very best for him in the furnace of battle could only be regarded as a potential threat to the *new* regime. And that, Theisman told himself gloomily, was the real reason he was in this office. He'd made the mistake of convincing his personnel to follow him without devoting sufficient industry to personally espousing the Committee of Public Safety's platform, and that—despite a record as one of the Committee's most effective field commanders— had turned him into a dangerously ambitious disloyalist in StateSec's eyes.

He rubbed his scar once more, remembering the bloody chaos of the day he'd received it stopping a Manty thrust at the Seabring System. It hadn't mattered in the end, but his stand at Seabring had probably bought Trevor's Star another three or four months, possibly even more. It had also cost virtually his entire task force, for he'd been forced to engage dreadnoughts with battleships and battlecruisers. He knew he'd fought well, even brilliantly, but brilliance had been too little to overcome his units' individual inferiority. He'd had twice as many ships as his opponent but less than two-thirds the tonnage, and battleships and battlecruisers had no business fighting dreadnoughts even at two-to-one odds. Not even if they'd had technological parity. He'd managed to destroy only a single Manticoran dreadnought in return for the total destruction of seven battleships and eleven battlecruisers plus sufficient damage to send three more battleships—including PNS *Conquèrant*, his flagship—to the breakers, but he'd inflicted such a heavy pounding upon the enemy in reply that the opposing admiral had broken off to shepherd his cripples clear.

Eleven battlecruisers and ten obsolete, undersized, underarmed "capital ships" which had no business in the wall of battle anyway wasn't an exorbitant price for holding a star system . . . assuming that there'd been any point in holding it in the first place, and he tried to believe there had been. Oh, the First Battle of Seabring hadn't stopped the Manties cold, nor had it prevented Theisman's successor in command of the system from losing the *Second* Battle of Seabring or saved Trevor's Star in the long run. But it had at least slowed the enemy up, weakened him at least a little, cost him at least a few escorts and sent half a dozen dreadnoughts back to the yard for extensive repairs. And in a war in which the People's Navy could count its victories on the fingers of one man's hands, it had been a major boost to the Navy's morale . . . a point Theisman tried to remember when he reflected upon the nineteen thousand men and women who'd died winning it.

So here he was, servant of a government which had rewarded him with a chest full of medals for delivering even a passing victory at Seabring only to send him to Barnett to fill what had once been a premier command slot but now could end only in defeat whatever he did. And given that StateSec was still in the habit of shooting defeated admirals, it seemed highly probable that the Committee of Public Safety had finally concluded that it could dispense with the services of one Thomas Edward Theisman.

He snorted again, this time in bitter amusement, walked back to his oversized desk, and settled himself once more in his overly comfortable chair. It was possible he was being too pessimistic, he told himself. Of course, it was better to be overly pessimistic than optimistic in the current People's Republic, but perhaps Esther McQueen's elevation to the Committee of Public Safety was a hopeful sign. She would be the *only* military person on the Committee, and for all her brilliance in battle, she'd always been dangerously ambitious, even under the Legislaturalists. Isolated as she was among civilians with no understanding of the problems the Navy faced, and ambitious to boot, she was more likely to get caught up in playing the power game than in solving the Fleet's problems. And even if she was inclined to fight for the Navy, she looked like being too little and too late to save Theisman's bacon, but he couldn't quite quash a lingering hope that she *would* make a difference. Whatever her other faults, she'd been a Navy officer for over forty T-years, and she'd always been able to inspire loyalty in her immediate subordinates. Perhaps she would remember that loyalty cut both ways. . . or at least see the need to strengthen the Navy if only to keep her own constituency strong.

He snorted again—this time in exasperation with his masochistic need to believe the Republic might somehow survive despite the lunatics running it—and punched for a fresh file. He might have been handed a dead ship drifting steadily deeper into a gravity well, but that didn't change his responsibility to do the best he could with it until—

The quiet buzz of his com interrupted his thought. He punched the acceptance key, and the neat blocks of alphanumeric characters disappeared from his display as it dropped into split-screen com mode. Raven-haired, brown-eyed Citizen Captain Megan Hathaway, his chief of staff, and Citizen Commander Warner Caslet, his ops officer, looked out of the screen at him, and Theisman hid another grimace, for Caslet was one more bit of evidence that the Committee had decided it could manage without Thomas Theisman.

It wasn't Caslet's fault; in fact, he was an officer of superior quality whose services, under normal circumstances, Theisman would have been delighted to obtain.

But the citizen commander was a man under a cloud. Up until a little over a T-year ago, he'd been one of the rising young stars of the People's Navy, but that was before the results of Citizen Admiral Giscard's commerce raiding campaign in Silesia were reported back home . . . and before Caslet lost his own ship trying to save a Manticoran merchantman from homegrown Silesian pirates.

Theisman had seen the reports on the pirates in question, and even through the obvious censorship to which they'd been subjected before reaching him, he could understand why any officer worth the uniform he wore would have wanted to save *any* merchant crew from them. It had simply been Caslet's misfortune that the freighter he tried to rescue had turned out to be a disguised armed merchant cruiser of the Royal Manticoran Navy which had wound up taking *his* ship as well as finishing off the pirate vessels Caslet had engaged in order to save it.

Once in Manticoran custody, Caslet—with the approval of his people's commissioner—had shared his data on the pirates with his captors, and that, coupled with his effort to "save" them, had led the Manties to repatriate him and his senior officers rather than clapping them into a POW camp somewhere. Considered all in all, returning Caslet had been a mixed favor, for the only thing which had kept the SS from executing him for losing his ship under such circumstances was the fact that the Admiralty had issued every unit of Giscard's task force standing orders to come to the assistance of any *Andermani* merchant vessels threatened by pirates.

The idea, as far as Theisman had been able to discover, had been that by doing so Giscard's commerce raiders would win enough gratitude from the Andermani Empire for the Imperial Navy to overlook the next-door operations of the People's Navy and the spread of the war with Manticore to its doorstep. If that *had* been the idea, it certainly hadn't worked, as the Andermani's ferocious diplomatic protests had made abundantly clear, but those orders were what had saved Caslet's neck, for at the time he'd thought he was coming to the Manty Q-ship's rescue, the Q-ship in question had disguised itself as an Andermani freighter. Which meant, of course, that Caslet had simply been following his orders.

Whatever its other faults (and God knew they were legion), the current leadership at the Admiralty had at least managed to convince StateSec that shooting officers for *following* orders would have a . . . negative impact on naval operations. It was bad enough to know you would be shot for failing to execute orders, however impossible the task to which they assigned you, without knowing that you'd also be shot if you *did* execute them and things turned out badly anyway. Besides, officers who figured they had nothing to lose *whatever* they did were far more likely to turn upon their political masters, and thank God someone had been able to make the SS see at least that much!

The fact that they hadn't shot Caslet, however, didn't mean that the powers that were intended to forgive and forget, and he'd been denied a new command. Instead, and despite an otherwise brilliant command record, he'd been shuffled off to staff duty . . . and sent to Barnett, which promised to be even more of a dead end—with emphasis on the "dead"—than most backwater staff assignments.

On the other hand, it could *represent a chance for him to "redeem" himself by how he performs here*, Theisman thought. *If he does his job and we actually manage to hold out long enough to please our lords and masters, maybe they'll "rehabilitate" him. Hell, maybe they'll even pull* me *out in time. Yeah.* Sure *they will, Tommy.*

It was only then that he realized a face was missing. Dennis LePic, Barnett's senior people's commissioner and Theisman's personal watchdog, was a relatively decent sort, but he was also inquisitive and assertive and took his responsibilities seriously enough to be a general pain in the ass. He was smart enough to leave operational matters to the professionals upon whom he spied, but he insisted on being kept informed and routinely "shared" conferences between Theisman and his staffers. LePic's absence from the split screen was more than enough to raise Theisman's mental eyebrows, but he kept that, too, from showing. Any prudent officer assumed that *any* com channel, be it ever so secure, was bugged, and his voice displayed no surprise as he greeted his callers.

"Hello, Megan—Warner. What is it?"

"We've just received the latest ship movement report from the Admiralty, Citizen Admiral," Hathaway replied in exactly the same sort of calm tones. "We're looking at several more ships than we'd anticipated, and Warner and I thought we should bring you up to speed."

"That sounds reasonable," Theisman agreed, tipping his chair back once more, but Hathaway's response, however reasonable it might seem, obviously wasn't the real reason she'd commed him. They were due for a routine staff meeting in less than two hours, and even word that the Admiralty was sending him the entire Capital Fleet could have waited that long. "So just what sort of good news are we looking at?" he asked.

"For starters, they're sending us the Sixty-Second and Eighty-First Battle Squadrons," Caslet replied, and despite himself, Theisman's eyebrows did rise this time. "The Sixty-Second is twenty-five percent understrength, and the Eighty-First is short one ship, but that's still thirteen more of the wall, S— Citizen Admiral."

Theisman nodded. That was a much heavier reinforcement than he'd let himself anticipate. In fact, it would increase his wall of battle's strength by almost thirty percent, which might actually indicate that the Republic's rulers intended to make a serious fight for Barnett. They wouldn't be able to hold it even if they did, but if they gave him enough combat power he could at least make his defense buy the rest of the Navy a chunk of time big enough that it might actually *mean* something. But despite his surprise, he delivered a moderately quelling frown to his ops officer. Caslet had commanded his own ship long enough to know to avoid slips like the one he'd just almost made. Or perhaps it was *because* he'd commanded his own ship for so long that he had trouble remembering that the only people the Navy was allowed to address as "Sir" or "Ma'am" these days were its people's commissioners.

PNS *Vaubon* had been a light cruiser, and as light cruisers were wont to do, she'd spent most of her time cruising independently. However much he might have ridden herd on the revolutionary vocabularies of his subordinates, Caslet himself had gone for enormous stretches of time in which he'd *had* no superior—aside from his own commissioner— to whom to report directly. But whatever the reasons, an officer in his present position simply could not afford anything remotely suggestive of lack of enthusiasm for the new regime.

"That's certainly a good start," Theisman said after a moment. "Is there more?"

"Yes, Citizen Admiral," Hathaway said. "That's the heavy metal, but it looks like we're getting another destroyer flotilla, the better part of the Hundred Twenty-First Light Cruiser Squadron, and another half-dozen heavy cruisers. We may even be getting another battlecruiser, assuming we get to hang onto her." Except to someone who knew her very, very well, Hathaway's tone as she delivered her last sentence would have sounded completely normal, but Theisman *did* know her.

"We can always use more battlecruisers," he said easily. "Which one is she?"

"The *Tepes*, Citizen Admiral." Caslet's tone exactly matched Hathaway's, and Theisman felt his expression try to congeal as he realized the true reason Megan and Warner had commed without LePic—and probably only after making certain the commissioner had been diverted elsewhere by some very legitimate distraction.

The *Tepes*, he thought. One of the *Warlord*-class ships which had replaced the *Sultans* as the newest and most powerful battlecruisers in the Navy's inventory. But *Tepes* didn't belong to the Navy . . . and her crew consisted not of Navy personnel but of officers and enlisted personnel drawn from the Office of State Security.

Theisman hid a core-deep sense of disgust—and fear— as he considered the news. Like virtually all regular officers, even those who most ardently supported the new regime, he found the logic in diverting desperately needed warships from front-line task forces questionable, to say the least. But what he found frightening, and what he dared never voice aloud, was the other side of the logic. StateSec was amassing an entire fleet of warships which were either commanded by SS officers or even, as in *Tepes'* case, manned entirely by SS personnel.

Admittedly, much of StateSec's present manpower had come from discontented elements of the pre-coup People's Navy and Marines, but even with the aid of those volunteers, Oscar Saint-Just's thugs lacked the training and experience to make full, proper use in combat of the ships they controlled. Yet those vessels constituted what was, in effect, a second navy, and one had to wonder why it had been created. No doubt part of it was simple, if stupid, bureaucratic empire-building. Like any other parasite, StateSec had an insatiable appetite for ever more power, even at the expense of diverting strength from the fleets which actually had to face the enemy. Yet there was more to the creation of the SS's private fleet than mere egotism or muscle-flexing. It would be all but useless against the Manties, but that wasn't the real point. As the real Navy knew perfectly well, the *point* was to provide StateSec with a "navy" which could be relied upon to execute the coercive domestic missions Saint-Just might not fully trust the regular fleet to carry out against the Republic's own citizens. *Or,* Theisman thought grimly, *to execute missions against* Navy *personnel—or their dependents—like that idiocy in* Malagasy.

But what sent a chill down his spine—and explained LePic's absence—was that PNS *Tepes* had a very special reputation. Although her crew was drawn from the Office of State Security, she was permanently assigned to the Office of *Public Information*. She was, in fact, Committeewoman Cordelia Ransom's personal transport, and if the thought of diverting one of the Navy's most powerful battlecruisers to serve as a private yacht for the mistress of the Republic's propaganda machine and her personal crew of technicians seemed obscene, no one would ever dare say so. Just as no one would ever dare point out that Ransom's decision to visit the Barnett System could be far more dangerous to the officer charged with defending that system than any Manty task force.

"Well," Theisman heard himself say in brisk, efficient tones, "whether we get to keep *Tepes* or not, we can certainly use the other units! In fact, Warner, I want you to rethink our current forward pickets. If we're going to be seeing more ships of the wall, then I'd like to look at releasing Citizen Rear Admiral Tourville's battlecruisers from patrol duty here in Barnett."

"Yes, Citizen Admiral. We can do that," Caslet replied, eyes lowered as he keyed notes to himself into his console. "The destroyer reinforcements alone will more than compensate for the loss in sensor platforms. What did you want to do with them instead, Citizen Admiral?"

"I'd like to send his second and third divisions up to thicken the picket at Corrigan. That won't be enough to hold it when the Manties finally move in, but at least it could help force them to be a little more cautious about the way they scout the system. Let's put in enough firepower to make them think twice about recon sweeps with light cruisers."

"Yes, Citizen Admiral. And the rest of the squadron?"

"I think I'd like to detail them for a little aggressive sweeping of our own." Theisman tipped back his chair, and his voice was suddenly more thoughtful as he got past the warning that *Tepes* was en route to Barnett and began truly considering the rest of the news. "You say half a dozen heavy cruisers are in the pipeline, Warner?"

"Yes, Citizen Admiral."

"All right. In that case, let's give Tourville CruRon Fifty and half a destroyer flotilla or so in return for the battle-cruisers for Corrigan. That'll give him a nice little raiding force, with the speed to run away from anything it can't fight—unless, of course, it runs into a couple of divisions of Manty battlecruisers with their new compensators."

Theisman grimaced as he added the qualifier, and the more than half-defensive edge he couldn't quite keep out of his voice despite his best efforts irritated him immensely. At the same time, however, all four of the battlecruisers he intended to assign to the operation were *Warlords*, with the first fruits of the technology transfers from the Solarian League. The Manties' most recent *Reliant*-class still boasted a marginal advantage in weapons fit, and its electronic warfare capabilities offered it a substantial combat edge, but both those margins would be far smaller against a *Warlord* than anyone on the other side was likely to suspect. And, of course, if Tourville happened across something *older* than a *Reliant*, well . . .

"Yes, Citizen Admiral," Caslet said again. "Do you have a specific target in mind, or do you want Citizen Commander Ito and me to work up a list to choose from?"

"I think Adler or Madras," Theisman said. "They're still settling in at Adler, in particular, so a good hard jab there might at least draw them into diverting more force to their pickets there and away from Barnett. But let's not limit ourselves to what occurs off the top of my head. Go ahead and sit down with Ito, then give me what the two of you think are the best prospects." He paused a moment, rubbing an eyebrow, then nodded to himself. "And go ahead and think about possible multiple targets. I don't want to get carried away with my own aggressiveness here, but if we can scrape up the tonnage, hitting the bad guys in more than one place at a time could be a good idea. Even with these new reinforcements, we're unlikely to hold Barnett if they concentrate properly, so any chance to make them worry about *their* defenses is worth taking, I think."

"Yes, Citizen Admiral. We'll have something for you by this afternoon's brief."

"Good, Warner." Theisman smiled at his ops officer, then glanced back at Hathaway, and his voice was carefully normal again as he addressed her once more. "In the meantime, Megan, would you please see about locating Citizen Commissioner LePic and passing this information on to him, as well? This is a lot more firepower than I'd anticipated having available, and it could substantially change my contingency planning. Please tell him that I need to discuss the new possibilities it opens up and that I asked you to bring him up to speed on the new ship movement schedule before he and I put our heads together."

"Of course, Citizen Admiral," Hathaway replied as if she had no suspicion at all that Theisman was speaking for the recording devices all three of them were certain had been tapped into the entire conversation . . . or that everything before the chief of staff's first mention of the name *"Tepes"* had been so much window dressing.

"Thank you, Megan. And you, too, Warner," Theisman said very sincerely. "I appreciate it."

• Chapter Five

Five days after returning to Grayson, Honor left its surface once more. Her hasty scramble to cope with her responsibilities in such a short period had run her steading staff ragged, and she felt more than a little guilty about that. Especially since all of her Harringtons, from Howard Clinkscales down, had anticipated that she would be on-planet for at least four weeks. Even that would have been on the tight side for her to give proper personal attention to all the problems—and solutions—which had cropped up during her long absence, and she was unhappily certain that she'd left far too much undone.

But she also knew how capable Clinkscales was. In many ways, he was actually better at running Harrington Steading than she was, and besides, when the Conclave of Steadholders had invested her with her steadholdership, it had specifically recognized her commitment to the Royal Manticoran Navy and accepted that her duty as a naval officer would frequently pull her away from Harrington. *Or, to put it another way,* she told herself with bleak self-scorn, *I've got an outstanding exec and enough wiggle room to run away in the name of "duty" and dump the entire load on him.*

She gave herself a mental shake and gazed out the view port, stroking Nimitz with slow, gentle fingers as the sky turned indigo blue and then black beyond the armorplast. The 'cat curled in her lap, his soft purr buzzing through his bones and into her own, yet she knew he was much less relaxed than he might appear to other eyes. She felt him in the back of her brain, sharing her emotions and keeping watch upon them . . . and failing to understand.

She closed her eyes and leaned further back, tasting the faint but persistent trace of Nimitz's worry. There was no complaint or scolding in it, only a vague discomfort as, for the first time in his experience, he found himself unable to understand her emotions. There had been many times when he'd found human philosophical concepts odd or even downright perverse, just as there were certain forms of human enjoyment—like swimming—whose appeal were completely incomprehensible to him. But however hard he might have found it upon occasion to grasp *why* Honor felt something, never before had he been unable to understand *what* she felt.

This time he was. Which, she reflected, wasn't surprising, given how little idea *she* had of what was happening inside her. All she knew with certainty was that she had become increasingly and acutely uncomfortable in Hamish Alexander's presence.

It wasn't because of anything he'd done or said, and she could hardly blame the man for what he might feel in the privacy of his own mind. But even though his actions and behavior were precisely what they ought to have been, the flicker of admiration behind them refused to go out. It never turned into anything stronger than a flicker—*he*, at least, had himself under control, she thought bitterly—but it was always present, as if a part of him were automatically suppressing it without quite being able to eradicate it. Yet whether he knew it was there or not, *she* did, and that traitor part of herself which had sensed their inner resonance longed to reach out to what he kept so well concealed even from himself.

For the first time, her link to Nimitz was as much curse as blessing, for try as she might she simply could not pretend she was unaware of White Haven's banked inner glow, and her awareness jabbed at her, unsettling her efforts to maintain a matching self-control. Looking back now, she remembered the first few months after she'd realized how

Nimitz was tying her perceptions into the emotions of those about her. She'd tried, at first, to get him not to do that, because it had seemed wrong somehow. Dishonest. As if she were some sort of emotional voyeur, spying on the most intimate aspects of people who didn't even realize they *could* be spied upon. But Nimitz had never grasped why she felt that way, and she'd gradually come to realize that it was because treecats never perceived anyone any *other* way. The emotions of others were always there for a 'cat; he couldn't *not* perceive them, and trying not to was like trying to give up breathing.

And so she'd lost her struggle to remain blind, and, in time, she'd even come to forget that she'd ever tried to remain so. She'd become as accustomed as Nimitz himself was to sensing others' emotions, come to rely on it for guidance. It no longer seemed like spying because, as for the 'cats, every human she encountered was a blaze of emotions, feelings, attitudes which cried out to her. She could screen them, pay less attention to them, but she couldn't make them go away. One of Old Earth's over-crowded cultures—she couldn't remember which, but it might have been the Japanese—had had a saying about nakedness. Nakedness, they had said, is often seen but seldom looked at, and that was how she'd learned to handle the onslaught of other people's emotions. But not this time. This time whatever had struck that reverberation between her and White Haven had destroyed her ability to "see" his emotions without looking at them. Outwardly, she'd managed to be just as correct as he; inwardly, she felt as if she were walking an emotional tightrope, and her inability to find any rational reason to feel that way only made it even more maddening.

And so she was running away. She knew she was, and she knew it confused Nimitz. Perhaps the 'cat's inability to understand her feelings stemmed from the very clarity with which he and his kind perceived emotions. They always knew precisely what their humans felt, but not what those humans *thought*. From her own experience looking through

Nimitz's empathy, she knew emotions were bright, vivid things. They might be complex or confusing, but they were seldom ambiguous, for they were portraits painted in primary colors, and perhaps that was what made treecats such direct, uncomplicated sorts. After all, there was no point in one 'cat's trying to dissemble or hide his feelings from another of his own species. It was, she thought, as if in seeing so clearly and deeply into one another they beheld an enormous, textural richness humans could not . . . and as if that very richness washed out the subtler hues and indirect interpretations which were all most humans could rely upon. Perhaps, with no need to *analyze* what others felt, 'cats had never developed the capacity to do so, and so Nimitz lacked the ability to sort out feelings which she could not sort out herself.

It was an intriguing speculation, but it offered no answers. Nor could it turn her retreat into something besides flight or help her to explain her motives to Nimitz, and she felt . . . inadequate. As if her inability to do so meant she were somehow failing in her responsibilities. Yet what she felt even more strongly—beyond that raw edge of guilt at having saddled her subordinates with an unfair share of her own responsibilities—was relief. She needed to put distance between herself and White Haven while she figured out how to cope with her confusion and regained some sort of rational perspective. And perhaps that same separation would give him a chance to get over whatever it was he was feeling for her. Part of her brain prayed he would do just that, yet another part—the part which made this separation so necessary—hoped with equal strength that he wouldn't. But what mattered most was the need for *her* to get a grip on herself, which she manifestly wasn't going to manage with him as her house guest.

Yet neither could she evict him from Harrington House. Devising a pretext which wouldn't have reeked of discourtesy would have been difficult, though she suspected she could have found one that would have served for public consumption. But what might have satisfied outward appearance wouldn't have deceived White Haven, and she simply couldn't bring herself to offer him what could be construed as an insult. Besides, there was a simpler solution which also happened to be one which had always worked for her in the past. She was scheduled to take command of the Eighteenth Cruiser Squadron, and five of its eight units had already arrived at Yeltsin's Star. Until CruRon 18 passed formally under the command of Eighth Fleet, it remained part of the Grayson Navy's Home Fleet, and if explaining her real reasons for asking High Admiral Matthews to expedite her assumption of her duties had been out of the question, he'd seemed to sense the urgency she couldn't voice. He hadn't argued, at any rate, and his staff had cut the orders recalling her to active duty even more quickly than she'd hoped, which was why she and Nimitz were now bound for GNS *Jason Alvarez*, her new flagship.

Her nostrils flared as she inhaled deeply, and when she opened her eyes once more, they were calm. She reached out, mentally and emotionally, to her new command, and something deep inside her sighed in relief as she felt responsibility's familiar weight settle upon her shoulders . . . and push her maddening preoccupation with other matters out of the front of her brain. It didn't cause her distractions to magically disappear, but at least it gave her a respite which might—if she was lucky—last long enough for those competing elements to subside into their proper places.

A soft, musical chime warned her that the pinnace was beginning its final approach to *Alvarez*, and she watched out the port as her pilot turned onto a closing spiral designed to give her a direct view of the ship.

Alvarez lay quietly in her parking orbit, her double-ended, hammerhead hull's sleek flanks gleaming with the green and white lights of an "anchored" starship. At just over three hundred and forty thousand tons, she was less than five percent the size of Honor's last command, but HMS *Wayfarer* had been a converted merchant ship—a huge, slow, unarmored bulk-carrier's hull with weapons crammed in wherever space permitted. *Alvarez* was a warship, a heavy cruiser, designed to hit and run and equipped with the systems redundancy which *Wayfarer* had lacked. Despite her smaller size, she could survive and remain in action after suffering far heavier damage, and she was much, *much* faster and more maneuverable.

She also marked the beginning of a change in the way warships would be built, Honor reflected. Like RMN cruisers, *Alvarez* carried all her broadside weapons on a single deck, but she showed considerably fewer weapons hatches than her Manticoran contemporaries, and there was a reason for that.

Alvarez was the first Grayson-designed heavy cruiser, and while her electronic warfare suite and defensive systems were roughly equivalent to those of the RMN's *Star Knight* class—upon which her design was based—the Graysons had had their own ideas about her *offensive* systems. It had taken a large dose of . . . call it "self-confidence," Honor mused, for a navy with no history of deep-space warfare to depart from the combined conventional wisdom of the rest of the explored galaxy when writing the specifications for its first modern warship, but the GSN had done it. *Alvarez* carried less than half the energy weapons of a *Star Knight*, which substantially reduced the number of targets she could engage simultaneously. It also cost her a small but possibly significant percentage of her antimissile capability, since starships often used broadside energy batteries to back up their purpose-built point defense weapons during long-range missile duels. But by accepting that reduction in weapon numbers, the combined Grayson–Manticoran design team had been able to mount twenty percent more missile tubes *and* fit in graser projectors heavier than most battlecruisers mounted. Conventional wisdom held that an equal tonnage of heavy cruisers could not fight a battlecruiser and win . . . but Honor suspected conventional wisdom was wrong where the *Alvarezes* were concerned.

Not that Honor intended to match any of her ships

against Peep battlecruisers. She'd experienced more than her fair share of unequal fights against superior opponents, and she was more than willing to leave such affairs to others for a while.

Her lips quirked at the thought, and she surveyed the volume of space about *Alvarez* as the pinnace approached the cruiser's midships boat bay. Although their parking orbits were comparatively tight, the units of CruRon 18 were far enough apart to reduce most of the squadron's other ships to tiny gleams of reflected sunlight. But one ship—HMS *Prince Adrian*—lay less than thirty kilometers off *Alvarez's* port quarter. That was only proper, as she belonged to the officer who, as the senior-ranking captain of the squadron, would serve as its second in command, and Honor's smile grew warm with memories.

Adrian was smaller, much older, and less heavily armed than her flagship, but Captain Alistair McKeon had commanded her for almost six T-years now. If there was a more efficient ship in the Fleet, Honor had yet to see it . . . and she *knew* there was no more reliable CO—or friend—in *any* fleet.

Prince Adrian vanished beyond the corner of her view port as the pinnace cut its impeller wedge and went to reaction thrusters, and Honor reached up to tug her uniform beret out from under her left epaulet. She smoothed it out, and her smile faded as she twitched its soft fabric into the proper configuration, for it was black. For the first time in twenty-one T-years, she was about to assume a spacegoing command as an RMN officer without the white beret which designated a starship's commander. Indeed, she would never wear the white beret again, and the thought produced a fresh pang. Intellectually, she knew how lucky she'd been to command as many ships as she had, but she also knew she would always long for just one more . . . and that she would never receive it.

But that was the price of seniority, she told herself more briskly, settling the beret on her head. She adjusted it just so as the boat bay tractors reached out to the pinnace, then rose as a gentle vibration and another soft chime announced engagement of the mechanical docking arms. She lifted Nimitz to her shoulder, brushed her fingers over her braided hair and beret once more, and then, without even realizing it, ran those same fingers lightly over the six gold stars—each indicating a different hyper-capable command—on the breast of her tunic as she turned to face the hatch.

Captain Thomas Greentree, GSN, commanding officer of GNS *Jason Alvarez*, did his best to look unconcerned while Lady Harrington swam the tube. He was proud of his ship and his crew, confident they were up to any demand, but he was also acutely aware of just whose flagship *Alvarez* was about to become. Greentree had his reservations about the Manty newsfaxes, which he considered both intrusive and impertinent (not to mention sensationalist), and their decision to nickname Honor Harrington "the Salamander" because she always seemed to be where the fire was hottest offended him. No decently brought up Grayson would ever have pinned a name like that on a lady, he thought moodily, yet what bothered him most was that it was so apt. Graysons might have been unlikely to *think* of it, but they certainly used it once someone *else* thought of it. For that matter, even Greentree sometimes caught himself applying it to her—mentally, at least—though he always jerked himself up short the moment he realized he had.

But the real reason his personnel—and, he admitted, he himself—used that nickname was less because Lady Harrington was drawn to the fire than that the fire was drawn to *her*. She was like the bird in the ancient tales from Old Earth, he thought. Like the albatross, a harbinger of storms. That she had proved herself able to deal with those storms time and time again only made her even more impressive, and the Grayson Space Navy knew even better than most how well deserved (and hard earned) her reputation was. Greentree was proud that his ship had been chosen to carry her flag, yet with that honor came the opportunity to fall short of her standards, and he'd expected at least another three weeks to prepare for her arrival. *Alvarez* had just completed a scheduled major overhaul, and the yard had replaced her original electronic warfare section with all new hardware. The capabilities the new systems promised were exciting, but Greentree and his engineers were still working their way through the inevitable teething problems, and his tactical officers were just beginning the necessary simulator training.

There were similar, if less drastic, upgrades in most of the ship's departments, but Greentree was profoundly grateful that *Alvarez*'s flag bridge, at least, had been left untouched. And while he was being grateful for things, he reminded himself, he should remember to list the fact that Lady Harrington's full staff was on board to greet her. From her reputation, she would be tactful enough to stay off his neck until he got his problems sorted out, and the presence of her staff would allow her to keep herself too busy getting the entire squadron organized to notice any internal chaos aboard her flagship until he could get it squared away.

He certainly hoped she would, at any rate, he thought, and drew a deep breath as the side party snapped to attention and an old-fashioned bugle sounded the opening notes of the Steadholders' March. Lady Harrington caught the green grab bar and swung gracefully from the access tube's zero-gee into *Alvarez*'s onboard gravity, her treecat on her shoulder. She landed just outside the line painted on the deck, and her hand came up to her beret in salute as her trio of armsmen followed her from the tube.

"Permission to come aboard, Captain?"

Thomas Greentree was a Grayson. Despite his best efforts to adjust to new realities, he came from a male-dominated culture in which voices like that clear soprano had no business on the deck of a ship of war. Fortunately, that *particular* voice was one whose right to be just about anyplace it cared to be no Grayson officer would ever dream of questioning, and he snapped off a parade ground salute of his own.

"Permission granted, My Lady!" he replied, then held out his hand as she stepped across the painted line. "Welcome aboard, My Lady," he said in more normal tones, and hid a tiny flicker of surprise at the strength of her grip.

"Thank you, Captain." Honor surveyed the immaculate boat bay gallery, the side party, and the waiting honor guard and smiled. "I see *Alvarez* is still the best cruiser in the Fleet," she observed, and felt the pleasure of everyone in earshot at the compliment.

"I think she is, at any rate, My Lady," Greentree said, and if Honor sensed a few reservations behind that statement, she also sensed his determination to erase them as soon as possible. Well, that was fair enough. This ship had a reputation in the Grayson Navy, and Thomas Greentree was even better aware of that than she was. And unlike the last time Honor had assumed command of a GSN squadron, she'd actually managed to do her homework and scan the personnel packages on her new flagship's senior officers.

Even a casual glance at those records would have made it obvious that the Office of Personnel hadn't picked her flag captain at random. As a lieutenant, Greentree had served as assistant tactical officer aboard High Admiral Matthews' old ship, GNS *Covington*, the only Grayson cruiser to survive the original Peep attempt to conquer Yeltsin's Star by proxy. After Grayson formally joined the Alliance, he'd been detached to the Star Kingdom and an abbreviated, intensive stint at the RMN's Advanced Tactical Training Course, then sent back to Yeltsin to command one of the first new-build destroyers. His prewar record against the pirates who had once infested the area around Yeltsin was impressive, and he'd further distinguished himself commanding a light cruiser division in Fourth Yeltsin. From his file, he was one of those officers who made a habit of exceeding every responsibility that came his way, and she felt Nimitz's close, evaluating regard join hers as she looked back at him.

The captain was a chunky man. Like most Graysons, he

was shorter than she—in his case, by at least fifteen centimeters—and, although he was actually ten years her junior, he looked much older. His thick brown hair, worn long for a Grayson, was streaked with white under the high-peaked cap of the GSN, and crow's-feet framed his level brown eyes, evidence that his planet had gained access to the prolong treatments too late for him to receive them. Yet she detected no resentment for her own physical youth, and he moved with a muscular fitness which spoke of both self-confidence and as much gym time as he could pry loose from other concerns. In some ways, he reminded her of an older (physically, at least) Paul Tankersley, and he radiated that same inner sense of solid reliability.

All in all, she was inclined to approve of Captain Greentree, and that was good. As her flag captain, he would be her tactical deputy. It would be his job, even more than Alistair McKeon's, to transform her plans and intentions into successful action. His record had suggested that he was the right man for the job, but there was always the possibility that the record was wrong. Or, for that matter, that personality clashes no one could predict would doom what ought, on paper, to have been a superior command team. Her last flag captain had almost become a case in point. Not because of any shortcoming on *his* part, but because Honor herself had found it so difficult to forget the fact that he was an ex-Peep whose ship had killed Raoul Courvosier. Fortunately, the fact that Alfredo Yu was such a fundamentally good man, coupled with the empathic insight Nimitz gave her, had helped her overcome her prejudices, and Yu's performance had been critical to the victorious outcome of the Fourth Battle of Yeltsin.

But aside from an understandable amount of tension at meeting his new commodore, Greentree seemed to have himself and his command well in hand, and now he indicated the wiry, black-haired young man beside him.

"Commander Marchant, My Lady. My exec," the captain said. Marchant was extremely young for his rank, even in the Grayson Navy. Indeed, unlike his captain, he'd been young enough to receive the original, first-generation prolong treatment. His record, too, was exemplary, but the flicker of emotions Honor picked up as she reached out to shake his hand was very different from Greentree's. Behind the level facade of his startlingly green eyes, his feelings were tied into a tight, defensive knot, and she fought not to wince in sympathy.

"Commander," she said, keeping her voice completely normal.

"My Lady." His tone was tense and clipped—certainly not disrespectful, but with a tightness that reflected his inner turmoil.

She understood his discomfort, for she'd read his file, as well as Greentree's, and she knew Solomon Marchant was a distant cousin of the late, unlamented *Edmond* Marchant. Of course, that was true of a lot of people, given the huge, intricately linked clan structure Grayson's harsh conditions had created, and most members of the Marchant Clan were as decent and law-abiding as any. But Edmond Marchant had been the bigoted, reactionary cleric who'd attempted first to discredit and then to assassinate Honor to derail the reforms she and Protector Benjamin had brought to Grayson.

None of it had been Solomon's fault, and she doubted he'd even known Edmond, but it seemed obvious that the commander felt guilty. He was being grossly unfair to himself—and, in a sense, to her, if he expected her to blame him for someone else's bigotry—and his pain transmitted itself all too clearly to her. But he didn't know that, and she couldn't refer to it without simply making things worse.

"I'm pleased to meet you, Commander," she said instead. "I was impressed by the reasoning behind your essay on new convoy tactics in the *Proceedings*. I'd like to discuss it with you in somewhat greater detail."

"Ah, certainly, My Lady." Marchant's eyes flickered— less steady but much more human in that moment—and she gave his hand a squeeze. The tight knot at his center was still there, though it seemed to have eased just a bit. Getting it to unknot entirely would undoubtedly take time, but she seemed to have hit the right note for a beginning.

"And this officer, I'm certain, needs no introduction, My Lady," Captain Greentree went on, nodding to the dapper RMN commander beside him. Andreas Venizelos was as short as most Graysons, but he wore his exquisitely tailored uniform with panache. He was dark haired, slender, and wiry, with an aquiline nose and a sense of perfect poise and balance any treecat might have envied.

"No, indeed, Captain!" Honor extended her hand to Venizelos with an enormous smile. "It's wonderful to see you again, Andy. I seem to be making a habit out of seeing old friends on my staff whenever I have one!"

"Yes, Ma'am. So I've heard," Venizelos replied with a matching smile Honor was relieved to see. Not every officer would have been thrilled by the notion of giving up command of a light cruiser to accept a staff position. Of course, Venizelos had been scheduled to do just that long before Honor was tapped to command CruRon 18; all she'd done was grab him for *her* staff.

Only admirals and vice admirals were supposed to be allowed captains as their chiefs of staff, though an occasional rear admiral might get one, if he was a particular favorite of someone at the Admiralty. As a mere commodore, custom said Honor was limited to a commander or lieutenant commander, and she'd put in an immediate request for Venizelos when she'd found out he was available, but the decision to give him some senior staff experience before promoting him to captain junior grade had been made at a much higher level. Honor was certain he knew that . . . and wondered if he realized just what that meant. Experience as the chief of staff for an allied squadron with personnel and ships drawn from three different navies would be invaluable to him later in his career, and unless she missed her guess, BuPers had already earmarked him for an eventual flag of his own, probably sooner than he believed possible.

"Well!" She shook off her thoughts, clasped her hands

behind her, and rocked gently on her heels, contemplating her new subordinates for several seconds, then nodded. "I'll look forward to meeting the rest of your senior officers, Captain—and the rest of the staff, Andy—once I've had a chance to settle in."

"Of course, My Lady," Greentree replied. "May I escort you to your quarters?"

"Thank you, Captain. I'd appreciate that," Honor said, and gloved hands slapped pulser butts as the Marine honor guard snapped to attention. Greentree and Marchant accompanied her, each a precise, militarily correct half-pace behind, and she glanced back and smothered a chuckle as the rest of her entourage shook itself out into formation. Andrew LaFollet led the procession, following at her shoulder, with Venizelos at his side. MacGuiness came next, keeping an eagle eye on two third-class stewards weighed down with the last of her personal baggage, and James Candless and Robert Whitman, the other two members of her permanent security party, brought up the rear. Accustomed though she was becoming to playing the role of a three-ring circus, it still struck Honor as mildly ridiculous to have so many people trudging around behind her. Unfortunately, no one had offered her much choice in the matter.

She just hoped the lift would be big enough to cram everyone into it.

• Chapter Six

Esther McQueen's carefully trained face hid the mild surprise she still felt as Rob Pierre and Oscar Saint-Just both came to their feet at her arrival. They'd each done the same thing on every other occasion upon which she'd met with either or both of them, and oddly enough, she was certain the courteous gesture was genuine, not something assumed for the purposes of manipulation. Not because she would ever make the mistake of forgetting that both these men were consummate manipulators, but because, in their personal relations, both of them routinely demonstrated an old-fashioned courtesy which was almost grotesque against the backdrop of the Republic's current agony.

And agony it was, she thought grimly as she crossed the thick carpet of the small conference room to shake hands with her hosts. Her own encounter with the Levelers was proof enough of that . . . as were the huge mass graves which had been required to deal with the wreckage in its wake.

No one had managed to produce an accurate estimate of which side had killed how many, and McQueen was just as glad. According to Public Information, of course, virtually all the casualties had been inflicted by the insurrectionists, and McQueen didn't know whether to be grateful or furious. On the one hand, she had no desire to be remembered as a mass murderer, however necessary it had been. On the other, any thinking individual who heard those reports would know they were lies—you didn't use modern weapons in a city the size of Nouveau Paris without killing a lot of people, however pure your motives—and think she'd signed off on them.

The truth was, as she knew, that she was trapped in a no-win situation where the death toll was concerned . . . and not just with the public. She wasn't the one who'd popped off the pee-wee nukes the Levelers had smuggled into both of StateSec's major HQs here in the capital. Those bombs had done their job of taking out the only SS field forces which might have been deployed in sufficient strength to make a difference, and the Leveler leadership had obviously felt the slaughter of surrounding civilians was worth it. McQueen would have preferred to think she wasn't like that, but the same brutal self-honesty which made her such an effective field commander wouldn't let her.

The only real difference, she told herself, *is that at least I didn't start it. But I made up for that once I got rolling, didn't I? My kinetic strikes were "cleaner" than theirs were, but does it really matter to a six-year-old whether or not the flash that incinerates her comes from a fusion reaction?*

But that was the point, wasn't it? The Levelers *had* "started it," and the fact they'd opted for what were still quaintly called "weapons of mass destruction" from the outset only emphasized the nature of their thought processes. She'd known what they had in mind and seen how they were willing to go about accomplishing it, and she'd done what she had to do because the consequences of doing nothing would have been still worse. She'd had to make her decisions under pressure as dreadful as any she'd ever faced in the defense of Trevor's Star, but she'd had time to reconsider them in detail since, and she was convinced she'd made the right ones. The hellish part was that even knowing she'd done the right thing, even knowing she'd had no choice, she still had to live with the knowledge that she'd probably killed *at least* as many people as the Levelers.

Yeah? Well, maybe I did . . . but unlike them, at least I actually got some of the guilty ones along the way, by God!

So she had, she told herself, settling into the chair Saint-Just had pulled back from the table for her, and if her appointment to the Committee of Public Safety was her reward, well, the laborer was worthy of her hire. Besides, it required raw power to set anything as thoroughly screwed up as the People's Republic of Haven back to rights, and someday she'd have the power to get some *more* of the guilty ones . . . starting with the two in this conference room.

"I'm glad to see you're moving better, Citizen Admiral," Pierre said, opening the conversation, and McQueen smiled at him. The broken—"smashed" was probably a better choice of words—ribs she'd suffered when her pinnace went down near the end of the fighting had done major internal damage. Surgical repairs and quick heal had put most of that to rights swiftly enough, but quick heal was less effective on bones. They persisted in knitting at the old-fashioned rate evolution had designed into them and she'd done an unusually thorough job of reducing most of her right rib cage to splinters. Her ribs had needed over two T-months to glue themselves back together, and an edge of stiffness persisted even now.

"Thank you," she replied. "I'm *feeling* better, as well, Citizen Chairman, and—"

"Please, Citizen Admiral—Esther," Pierre broke in, raising one gently restraining hand. "We try not to be that formal in private, at least among ourselves."

"I see . . . Rob." The name tasted strange on her tongue, another one of those surreal touches like the courtesy with which he'd stood to greet her. She would never be naïve enough to believe this man saw her as anything except a temporarily necessary expedient, and she certainly had no intention of leaving *him* alive when the time came, yet here they sat, playing their parts with proper etiquette while the Republic burned.

"Thank you," she went on. "As I was saying, however, I *am* feeling much better. That's why I asked to see you and Ci—Oscar this morning. I'm ready to be put to work, but our earlier discussions were a little vague. I hoped you could explain just what it is you have in mind for me to do."

She gave him another smile, and he tipped back in his huge chair at the head of the table while he considered her request. All the chairs in the conference room were big and sinfully comfortable, but his was the most impressive of all, and as he propped his elbows on its arms to steeple his fingers under his chin like an enthroned monarch, McQueen was suddenly struck by the mental image of a spider at the center of its web. It was a hackneyed cliché, and she knew it, but it was also utterly appropriate.

Pierre sat for another long moment, contemplating the dark-haired, slightly-built woman at the far end of the table. Her green eyes were mildly, respectfully courteous, and despite the gold braid and the plethora of decorations on her meticulously correct uniform, she scarcely looked like a cold blooded and deadly military commander. On the other hand, Oscar Saint-Just hardly looked the part of StateSec's mastermind, either. It was a point worth bearing in mind, he mused, for he himself had used Saint-Just's harmless-looking exterior to lethal effect in the planning and execution of *his* coup.

But for now, at least, McQueen seemed to be toeing the line. Officially, she'd been a member of the Committee for almost three months, but she'd accepted the equally official position that her injuries precluded her from assuming her duties immediately. She had to have known better, for however painful it was, the damage had hardly been incapacitating, but she'd been willing to pretend otherwise rather than push. She probably didn't know that one of the main reasons for the delay had been to get Cordelia Ransom and her bitter antimilitary prejudices off Haven, of course. Cordelia might have agreed to back McQueen's elevation—openly, at least—but that hadn't lulled Pierre into thinking she truly accepted it, and he'd been unprepared to put up with the potential fireworks between her and the citizen admiral, at least until McQueen got her feet under her.

He'd had no intention of telling her so, however, and he'd taken the opportunity to watch how she responded as a gauge of her own willingness to accept limits. In the event, she'd waited patiently, accepting the official fiction that the delay was only to give her body time to heal, and Pierre knew from Saint-Just that she'd gone through the motions of getting clearance from her doctors before she asked for this meeting.

All of that was either a good sign or a very bad one. Her popularity with the Nouveau Paris Mob had skyrocketed once word of who'd stopped the Levelers spread. Public Information had done its best to play up the role of the other security forces—many of which, Pierre admitted, had in fact fought with infinitely greater tenacity and courage than he'd expected—but too many people had known the truth. And so McQueen's existing reputation as the admiral who'd held Trevor's Star for more than eighteen T-months had been enhanced by her decisiveness in preserving "the People's revolution." The fact that she'd probably killed at least as many of their friends and neighbors as the Levelers had meant little to the Mob's members. Ultimately, their approbation was nothing if not fickle, as few people had more reason to know than Rob S. Pierre, but for the moment, she was their darling, and she could have used that to demand an immediate and meaningful role on the Committee. As a matter of fact, he'd been afraid she might do just that, and he and Saint-Just had made quiet preparations for her to suffer sudden, unexpected medical complications if she had.

But she hadn't. Instead, she'd accepted the Committee's thanks and the offer of a seat on it, if not with modesty, without arrogance, either. That, too, had struck Pierre's mental antennae as reflecting exactly the right attitude, for any modesty on her part would had to have been false. She knew as well as he did who'd saved the Committee . . . and that she wouldn't have been offered a place on it even now if Pierre hadn't believed he needed her. Yet she also seemed prepared to take things as they came, without pushing or probing for openings, just as she had always—outwardly, at least—accepted her orders from the Admiralty. Assuming her actions accurately reflected what was going on inside her head, that was a very good thing, and Pierre allowed himself to hope that it was.

But he wasn't about to leap to any conclusions. The contingency plans she'd somehow put together right under Citizen Commissioner Fontein's nose had played a major—possibly even a decisive—part in saving the Committee, but she shouldn't have been able to make them. Of course, her ability to inspire the sort of personal loyalty that carried men and women into battle with her was one of the things which made her so valuable as a military officer. But it was also the kind of ability which might convince subordinates to go along with making unauthorized plans—or, to use an uglier turn of phrase, conspiring with her to circumvent civilian authority—and that was specifically what Oscar Saint-Just had chosen Erasmus Fontein as her commissioner to prevent.

Fontein was one of the best StateSec had, yet he *looked* like a complete incompetent. The theory, of which Pierre had approved, was that McQueen would feel relatively unthreatened (and hence less security conscious) if the individual assigned to watch her was an idiot, and Fontein had taken pains to convince her he was almost as inept as he looked. From all appearances, he'd succeeded, at least until the need to stop the Levelers had required him to take the mask off and act decisively in cooperation with her. Yet she'd *still* taken sufficient precautions to manage to conceal that contingency planning from him. Not just partially, but completely. His report had been scathingly self-honest, fully admitting that he'd been taken totally by surprise. Pierre was pleased by his candor; too many others would have been too busy trying to cover their own backsides to draw the proper conclusions and point them out, but Fontein was a professional. He'd made certain his superiors recognized the implications, and Pierre agreed with his warning. If she'd bothered to dissemble that well against someone she regarded as an idiot, she would be even more careful against people she knew *weren't* fools. And that was why her impeccable behavior worried Pierre almost more than immediate efforts to build a personal power base would have. His conversation with Cordelia notwithstanding, he knew Esther McQueen could easily prove a two-edged sword, and he had no intention of losing *his* fingers to her blade.

But he'd also discovered how easily someone in his position could double- and triple-think himself into doing nothing, even in the face of current disaster, because of potential dangers which might never materialize, and so he smiled and nodded to her.

"We really should have explained what we had in mind weeks ago, Esther, and I apologize for being so slow about bringing you up to speed. Obviously everything we've had on our hands in dealing with the fallout from the coup attempt has disorganized all our schedules, but to be perfectly honest, there were some political considerations, as well. As I'm sure you can appreciate, not all the Committee's members are exactly enthralled by the idea of giving the military direct representation on it."

"I can accept that their lack of enthusiasm exists without believing that it's justified," McQueen replied levelly.

"No reasonable person would expect *you* to believe it was." Pierre's voice was just as level, and their eyes met with the air of fencers testing one another's guards. It wasn't precisely a clash of wills, but it came far closer to one than anyone—besides Cordelia—had dared to offer Pierre in over a T-year, and he felt a small stir of pleasure as their foils met. "The prejudice exists, however," he continued, "and I wanted to let things settle down a bit before bringing you fully on board."

"May I take it that things have, in fact, settled down?"

"You may," Pierre agreed. He saw no reason to add that, given her popularity with the Mob, her appointment to the

Committee, window dressing though it had so far been, had played a major part in *helping* to settle things. Only a fool, which she manifestly was not, could have failed to realize that, but it wouldn't hurt if he could convince her that he thought she was foolish enough to believe that he thought she *didn't* know it. "In fact, if you hadn't asked for this meeting, I would have asked you to join Oscar and me tomorrow or the next day."

She tipped back in her own chair and quirked a wordless eyebrow, and he smiled. But then his smile faded, and his voice was much more serious as he leaned forward.

"The Levelers' coup attempt has exposed one new problem and reemphasized several we already knew about," he said. "The new one is the fact that the Levelers managed to infiltrate the Committee itself. On the purely military side, they couldn't have gotten their bombs in place or sabotaged our command net without inside help, and from a political viewpoint, they *had* to have been counting on putting at least some members of the present Committee on HD to legitimize their coup after the fighting. I'm sure they could have counted on getting a few obedient talking heads by putting pulsers to our temples, but crazy as the Leveler rank and file were, LaBoeuf and his inner cadre were smart and dangerous. My belief—and Oscar shares it—is that they would never have moved without the assurance of long-term, *willing* support from at least a portion of the Committee. Unfortunately, we haven't been able to identify those supporters, which means that we have a serious internal security problem that we didn't know about before.

"Oscar's people—" Pierre nodded to Saint-Just "—are working on that. We don't have much to go on yet, but they'll keep digging until they find the moles. In the meantime, we're considering a drastic downsizing of the Committee. At the moment, we're looking at a reduction of perhaps fifty percent in its present membership. We can't make a move that drastic immediately, of course, and we can't be positive that all the unreliable elements would be pruned away in the purge even when we do. What we *can* plan for, though, is to retain the people we trust the most."

He paused for a moment, watching McQueen's face. Telling her what he just had was tantamount to promising her that she would remain a member of the new leaner, meaner Committee, but she gave no sign of realizing that. Except for slightly pursed lips and a small nod of understanding, her calm, attentive expression never wavered.

"That, as I say, will have to wait, at least for a while," Pierre resumed, "but we can begin dealing with the problems we already knew about now. Between us, the Manties, and the Legislaturalists, our military has been monumentally screwed over, Esther. The Manties, at least, *ought* to be trying to beat us, but we—and I include the Committee of Public Safety and State Security in 'we'— have managed to do a pretty good job of gelding the Navy for them. Well, it's time we stopped blaming the Navy for failing and admit that it's got problems *we* created. Problems we want *you* to fix."

Despite her self-control, McQueen blinked in surprise. She hadn't expected this degree of frankness on the political front, much less such a candid admission of responsibility for the mess in which the Fleet found itself. The very brevity with which Pierre had made that admission only lent it greater weight, and she made herself think for several seconds before she replied.

"I can't disagree with what you've just said, Citizen Chairman," she said finally, speaking with deliberate formality. "I probably wouldn't have said it myself—not in so many words, at any rate—because it would be inappropriate for an officer on active duty to make such a . . . frank statement, but I'm extremely glad to hear *you* say it. If you and Committeeman Saint-Just really believe that, and if you're willing to support me, I think I can begin repairing the worst of the damage. I'll be honest, however. Without a reasonable degree of freedom of action, anything I can accomplish will be limited."

She paused, feeling a very faint prickle of sweat along her hairline as she committed herself openly. She'd just gone quite a bit further than Pierre had, and she knew it, but her expression showed no sign that she did.

"I see," Pierre murmured, and glanced at Saint-Just. Then he looked back at McQueen. "Before we get into spheres of authority and action, it might be a good idea to be certain we're agreed on just what needs fixing. Suppose *you* tell *us* what you think our worst military weaknesses are."

The ice was getting thin underfoot, but McQueen felt something very like the adrenaline rush of combat. It wasn't eagerness, exactly, but it was something very similar. And for all her ambition, she *was* an admiral. She'd spent decades learning her trade, and the Fleet was her life. Whatever else happened, she'd been given a chance to state the Navy's case to the one set of ears that really mattered, and she looked straight at the most powerful man in the People's Republic as she embraced the opportunity.

"Our biggest single problem," she said precisely, "is the fact that our officers have about as much initiative as a three-day corpse. I realize the military must be answerable to civilian authority. That was an article of faith even under the Legislaturalists, and it's even more true now than it was then. But there's a distinct difference between obedience to orders and being too terrified to take *any* action *without* orders, and quite frankly, StateSec has gone too far." Her green eyes swiveled to meet Saint-Just's levelly, without flinching.

"The pressures being brought to bear on all our personnel, but especially our officers, are too great. You can drive men and women into submission, but what a navy requires is leadership and intelligent initiative, not blind obedience. I'm not speaking about disobeying directives from higher authority; I'm talking about senior officers exercising their own discretion when situations arise which their orders don't *cover*. The recent coup attempt offers the clearest possible proof of the weakness lack of initiative creates. Let me remind you that even when the Levelers started detonating nuclear devices in the heart of Nouveau

Paris, not a single senior officer of the Capital Fleet moved to assist me. They were *afraid* to—afraid someone might think they were supporting the insurgents so that even if they survived the fighting, State Security would be waiting to shoot them when the smoke cleared."

She paused for breath, and Pierre felt a stir of anger. But then he made himself stop and think about *why* he felt it, and he grimaced wryly. It was her tone as much as what she'd said, he realized. She wasn't lashing out, for her voice was calm and level. She wasn't even lecturing. But neither was she being apologetic, and there was genuine passion in her eyes.

Well, you asked *her to tell you what was wrong, didn't you? If you don't like what you're hearing, whose fault is that? Hers? Or the people who* created *the mess?*

He didn't really care for the answers which suggested themselves to him, but he'd wanted her for this post because she might actually be able to do some good, and she could hardly do that without the insight to identify the problems in the first place. It was just that he wasn't used to having the military's case put to him quite that bluntly, and he hadn't made sufficient allowance for how hearing it would sting.

"Lack of initiative was certainly one of the problems I already recognized," he told her in a deliberately dispassionate voice. "From your tone, however, I assume you have others in mind, as well?"

"Citizen Chairman, I could go on for hours about all the problems we have," she said frankly. "Most of them, however, can be fixed by officers who believe they'll be backed up by their superiors and that honest mistakes— not treason, but honest *mistakes*—won't get them shot or their families imprisoned. Lack of initiative is only one symptom of the true problem, Sir. Our officers are too busy looking over their shoulders to concentrate on the enemy. They're not only afraid to act on their own, they're afraid *not* to follow orders which they know are no longer relevant by the time they receive them. And quite aside from any other concern, shooting officers who've done their best and failed also means they never get a chance to learn from their mistakes. The successful conduct of a war requires a professional military with confidence in itself and its support structure. At the moment, we're still trying to rebuild to the level of professional skill we had before the coup, and we *don't* have confidence in ourselves, the quality of our weapons, or—I'm sorry, but I have to say it—the support of our civilian leadership."

She sat back, suddenly aware that she'd gone further and spoken far more candidly than she'd intended when she walked into this room. And, she thought wonderingly, she'd done it without giving a single thought to how it might affect her own position. The events of the last six years must have eaten into her even more deeply than she'd thought, for her words had come from the heart, and ambition or no, she'd meant every one of them.

But the silence from the other two people at the table brought her back to earth quickly, and her right hand fisted in her lap under the concealing tabletop as she cursed herself for losing control of her tongue. Had she come this far only to blow her chance at the last minute?

Pierre looked speculatively at Saint-Just, and the commander of State Security frowned. Then he gave a shrug so tiny that only someone who knew him well would have recognized it. He nodded slightly, and Pierre turned back to McQueen.

"Believe it or not, I agree with you," he said quietly, and smiled a faint smile as, despite all she could do, her shoulders sagged in relief. "At the same time, however, I have to warn you that not everyone on the Committee— not even on the downsized version we're planning—will share that agreement. And to be completely honest, I have some serious reservations about how far we can afford to go, in the short term, at least, towards dealing with the problems you've identified. Obviously, what you would prefer is a return to a more classically organized military chain of command, but there are still unreliable elements in the military—if for no other reason, because our present policies have *created* them. I'm afraid we've painted ourselves into a corner that we can't get out of overnight."

He made the admission without even wincing, and McQueen felt her lips twitch in a brief, bitter smile at his choice of words. A "classically organized military chain of command" indeed. Well, that was one way of saying she wanted to throw the people's commissioners out the nearest airlock. Or perhaps she could cram them into her missile tubes and launch them at the enemy, where they might actually make *some* contribution to the war effort! She allowed herself to contemplate an entire broadside of Erasmus Fonteins for one shining moment, then gave herself a mental shake. She could daydream later; for now she had to concentrate on the matter in hand.

"I realize we can't change everything instantly," she said, "but neither can we afford to wait too long before we *start* making changes. The technology transfers we're getting from the Solarian League should help restore at least some confidence in our weapons, but technical superiority isn't the only reason the Manties are pushing us back. Their officers think for themselves. They adapt and modify their plans within the framework of the directives they've been given instead of following the letter of orders which may no longer make sense in the face of changing circumstances. And when one of their admirals gives an order, she gives it *herself.* She doesn't have to clear it with someone else, she knows it will be obeyed by the people she gives it to, and she knows that she won't be shot by her superiors just because she made a mistake."

She looked at the two men, wondering if she really wanted to finish her argument, and then gave a mental shrug. If candor was going to ruin everything, then it had already done so, in which case she might as well be hung for a sheep.

"*That's* what really gives the enemy their edge against us, gentlemen," she said flatly. "Manty officers face only one enemy."

Pierre rocked his chair back and forth for a few seconds, then cocked his head.

"I think we're in general agreement about the, um, nature of the problem," he said in a tone which suggested it might be just as well not to emphasize past errors much more strongly. "What I'd like to hear is how you would propose to change the current system to correct it."

"I'd like an opportunity to consider that at a little length, preferably with a small staff group with both a military and a political component, before I got into detailed proposals," McQueen said cautiously.

"Understood. But tell us how you'd begin."

"All right." She drew a deep breath, then plunged in. "The first thing I'd do would be to formally discontinue the policy of 'collective responsibility.' Shooting people for *their* mistakes is one thing; in my opinion, shooting people just because they're related to someone who screwed up not only strangles initiative but is actively counterproductive in terms of loyalty to the state.

"Second, I would take a very close look at every officer above the rank of commodore or brigadier. I would evaluate them on the basis of four qualities: competence, aggressiveness, loyalty to the Committee, and leadership ability. Precisely how those qualities should be balanced is one of the things I'd like to go into with that staff I mentioned earlier, and the interrelationships between them would mean the evaluations would have to be done on something of an individual basis, but it would give us a handle for eliminating dead wood. And there *is* dead wood out there, gentlemen. Strapped as we are for officers, operating shorthanded is better than handicapping ourselves with incompetents.

"Third, I would remove the people's commissioners from the chain of command." She saw Saint-Just stiffen but went on speaking before he could protest. "I'm not suggesting that we remove them from the ships—" *after all, you did say we have to start slowly, didn't you, Citizen Chairman?* "—nor am I suggesting that they should stop being the Committee's direct representatives. But however sound they may be ideologically, not all of them are competent to judge the military merits of battle plans and orders. And if we're going to be honest, some of them have personal axes to grind which have nothing to do with operational realities. All I'm suggesting is that they be restricted to passing on the Committee's directions and overseeing the general policy of the units to which they're attached without being required to sign off on actual ops plans and orders. If there's a difference of opinion between a commissioner and a flag officer, by all means let them report the matter to higher authority, but until a decision comes down from above, let the trained professional make the operational call. After all—" she smiled thinly "—if an admiral knows her commissioner is complaining to the Admiralty, State Security, and the Committee, she's going to think long and hard before she does anything too risky."

"I don't know. . . ." Pierre rubbed his chin and looked back at Saint-Just. "Oscar?"

"I can't say I care for the idea," Saint-Just said frankly, "but we invited the Citizen Admiral—Esther—to join the Committee because we felt we need a professional officer's advice. Under the circumstances, I'm not prepared to reject it out of hand without giving it some pretty careful thought."

"That sounds fair enough," Pierre agreed. "And her other recommendations?"

"Those make sense," Saint-Just said. "Mind you, I'm in two minds about how to proceed on the question of collective responsibility. I have to admit that we've reached a point of diminishing returns with it, but I'm also convinced it's still useful in some cases, and I'm worried about what Manty propaganda could do if we formally admit that we ever adopted the policy in the first place. Could we discontinue it without making a specific announcement to that effect? That would avoid the possible propaganda damage, and surely the fact that we've simply stopped doing it would percolate through the military fairly quickly."

"That's obviously a political decision," McQueen said, seeing an opportunity to give ground and sound reasonable. "From a purely military perspective, I think an announcement would be beneficial by providing a sense of closure, and a formal statement would end any lingering confusion as to our intentions much more quickly. On the other hand, there is indeed the potential for enemy propagandists to make capital out of it. Perhaps Committeewoman Ransom should be consulted."

"That won't be possible for at least a month or two," Pierre told her. "Cordelia is en route to Barnett."

"She is?" McQueen's mental antennae quivered at that. She'd met Thomas Theisman, and she respected his record, though she didn't know him well. He'd always struck her as a bit too politically puritanical, however. In her opinion, no officer could wield real power to affect the decisive decision points in a war unless she had the political clout to go with her rank. Under the Legislaturalists, that had meant family connections or debts that could be called in; under the new system, there were more . . . direct routes to it, but Theisman had never been interested in reaching for it under either set of rules. All the same, she hoped Ransom's visit to Barnett didn't mean Theisman was about to be "disappeared." The Navy needed any officer who could motivate his people the way he did, and they needed him where he was if they were going to hold Barnett long enough to make a difference.

"She is," Pierre confirmed, then smiled tightly. "And we might as well admit that having her away for a few weeks may not be an entirely bad thing. I'm sure you've observed that the Navy isn't exactly her favorite institution?"

"I'm afraid I have," McQueen admitted in a carefully neutral tone.

"Well, I expect her to pitch a fit when she hears what you have in mind," Pierre said almost philosophically, "and we're going to need Public Information's support, not just its acquiescence, if we're going to make this work. That means we'll have to bring her around somehow."

"May I assume from that that *you* intend to support the

changes I've suggested?" McQueen asked even more carefully, and Pierre smiled once more.

"I'm not certain I agree with all of them," he said frankly. "I think that staff group you suggested is an excellent idea, and I'd like you and Oscar to each nominate half its membership. But even if it signs off on all of your suggestions, *I'm* not the one who's going to be supporting them. *You* are . . . Citizen Secretary of War."

"Sec—?" McQueen managed to chop herself off before she repeated the title like an idiot, and Pierre nodded.

"Citizen Secretary Kline is one of the committee members whose loyalty Oscar and I have some doubts about," he admitted. "Under the circumstances, I think we can dispense with his services, and if you're going to take Cordelia on, you'll need the rank to do it." McQueen nodded, green eyes glowing despite her iron self-control, and he frowned slightly. "At the same time, Citizen Secretary, bear in mind that your appointment is provisional," he said in a much cooler tone, and she nodded once more.

Of course it was provisional. It had to be. They wouldn't dream of really trusting her until they decided that she was sufficiently tame, but that was all right. Even a provisional appointment would put her in a position from which she might actually be able to fix some of the things wrong with the Fleet, and if Rob Pierre wanted to play lion-tamer with her, that was fine with Esther McQueen.

Let him and Saint-Just decide I'm nice and tame, she thought, smiling brightly but soberly at the Chairman of the Committee of Public Safety. *After all, how many lion-tamers come close enough to a* wild *lion for it to eat them?*

• Chapter Seven

"Good morning, Milady."

Andreas Venizelos turned with a smile of greeting as Honor stepped out of the flag bridge lift with Andrew LaFollet at her elbow. Although her chief of staff had known her since the days when she was plain Commander Harrington, with no titles or feudal dignities, he'd adjusted to the presence of her armsmen without fuss or bother. In fact, he and LaFollet were well on their way to becoming friends, for which Honor was grateful.

Nimitz rode in his normal, half-standing perch on her shoulder. Like her Grayson vests, her uniform tunics were made of a fabric tough enough to resist light pulser fire— not because she expected assassins to lurk on her flag bridge, but because Nimitz's claws required it. His true-feet dug in at the level of her shoulder blade, and his hand-feet clung to the top of her shoulder as he looked around with bright, curious eyes, and the scimitar claws which would quickly have reduced any lesser fabric to shreds didn't even leave pick marks. Which was just as well, she thought, and smiled as she reflected on MacGuiness' probable reactions to that sort of carnage.

Nimitz caught her amusement and bleeked a laugh, flirting the tip of his prehensile tail cheerfully, as he plucked the same image from her thoughts. Like Honor, the 'cat had perked up in the last few days. In her case, it was being away from the perplexing puzzle Earl White Haven had come to represent, and, in a sense, that was also the reason for Nimitz's improved mood. There was still a low key echo—a sense of something not quite perfectly in synch—

in her emotions, but by and large the return to a familiar environment and new but well-understood challenges had restored her equilibrium and damped the emotional spikes he'd been unable to understand. Neither of them was so foolish as to think the problem was solved, but unlike Honor, Nimitz had the capability to let worries take care of themselves without rushing to meet them.

"Good morning, Andy." Honor nodded a reply to the chief of staff's greeting and crossed to her comfortable command chair and ran her fingers lightly over the keys to bring it on-line.

The flatscreen and holo displays flicked to life about her, presenting the full status of her squadron—or, at least, those units of it which were currently present—at a glance, and she gave a mental nod of satisfaction. There wasn't that much to see, with all her ships still in a Grayson parking orbit, but she sat back for a moment, watching the routine small craft traffic plying between them and the planet or moving on ship-to-ship courses. There was something almost sensually satisfying about watching her command live and breathe. In an odd sort of way, it was even more satisfying than it had been when she'd been given the GSN's First Battle Squadron and command of no less than six superdreadnoughts. Even one of those stupendous ships would have outmassed her entire present squadron by a factor of three, but perhaps that was the reason for the difference. Those ships had *been* stupendous, with a ponderous might and majesty that lacked the fleet-footed responsiveness of a cruiser squadron.

This, she realized suddenly, was probably the best squadron command she would ever have—unless, perhaps, she was ever fortunate enough to command her own battlecruiser squadron. Heavy cruisers were powerful units, too valuable to waste on secondary duties, yet small enough and numerous enough that they could be worked hard . . . or risked. There would always be *something* for squadrons like this to do, and those who commanded them would always enjoy a degree of freedom and independence from higher authority no ship of the wall would ever know. Capital ships must remain concentrated at crucial strategic points, but cruisers were not just the eyes and ears of the Fleet but its fingertips, as well. They were far more likely to be detached for independent operations, and she felt herself looking forward to forging *her* ships into the single, cohesive force she would wield as easily and naturally as she did the Harrington Sword.

She smiled at the simile and turned her chair around, putting her back to her displays to survey her staff. She was over a half-hour early for the regular morning conference, and most of her officers were busy with routine duties or collating one last bit of data for their upcoming briefings.

Like her squadron's ships, her staff reflected the composite nature of the fleet it would be joining. Unlike her BatRon One staff, however, she'd personally selected each member of her current team, either on the basis of personal experience with them or on the advice of Commodore Justin Ackroyd, current head of the GSN's Office of Personnel.

Venizelos, of course, she knew very well indeed, and her eyes rested on him with carefully hidden fondness as he bent over Lieutenant Commander McGinley's shoulder to discuss something on the ops officer's display. Honor could just hear the crisp, quiet murmur of his voice, and she smiled as she recalled the poker-faced, noncommittal, almost desperately detached officer she'd taken to Basilisk Station with her so many years ago. He'd changed a lot since then, yet he remained just as poised—and handsome—as ever, and his small stature was no handicap among Grayson's generally undersized population. In fact, he probably wished it *was* a problem. Given the fact that female births outnumbered male by three-to-one on Grayson, women were far more aggressive—in their own fashion—here than back in the Star Kingdom, and according to Honor's reports from MacGuiness, Venizelos was finding it necessary to beat off Grayson beauties with a stick.

She smothered a highly inappropriate giggle at the thought and turned her attention to the ops officer herself. Like Venizelos, Marcia McGinley was Manticoran, but unlike him—or, for that matter, Honor—McGinley wore Grayson uniform. The trim, brown-haired, gray-eyed lieutenant commander was barely thirty-seven, extremely young for her rank in the RMN, but like many of the Manticoran "loaners" in GSN service (including one Honor Harrington), she'd found rapid promotion in her adopted navy. She was also, according to Commodore Ackroyd—who'd hand-picked McGinley as one of his three final nominees for Honor's operations officer—extremely good at her job. From what Honor had seen so far, he'd been right about McGinley's competence, and it looked like the ops officer was going to be one of the off-duty spark plugs of the staff, as well.

Commander Howard Latham, her staff com officer, was the senior Grayson-born member of the staff, and he was as old for his rank (as a Grayson) as McGinley was young (for a Manticoran). Not that his service record had ever been less than exemplary, for his relative lack of seniority was entirely due to the serious injuries he'd suffered in a shuttle accident six years before Grayson joined the Alliance. Grayson's pre-Alliance medical science had done its best, yet its best hadn't been good enough to keep the damage from cutting short what had been a very promising career. But once Grayson had signed the treaty of alliance, modern medicine had been able to intervene retroactively and do a great deal to restore his "hopelessly crippled" legs.

Complete repair, unfortunately, had evaded even the Manticoran doctors—mainly because the healing process had been so far along. To really fix all that was wrong, the doctors would have been forced basically to destroy his legs all over again in order to start from scratch, and Latham had been entirely too good an officer to put back into the hospital for another two years. His mouth was bracketed by deep-etched pain lines, and he moved stiffly, but even when he had been invalided out of the Navy, he'd continued to work from a wheelchair as one of the GSN's civilian consultants. On his return to active duty, he'd spent two years working with the RMN to more fully integrate the Allies' FTL communications capability into squadron-level tactical and operational capabilities, and his present assignment was almost certainly the last stop on his career track before he received his own first starship command. Honor didn't know if he realized that, but she knew how glad *she* was to have him.

At fifty-five, Lieutenant (Senior-Grade) George LeMoyne, her Logistics and Supply Officer, was the oldest member of the staff, but anyone who thought his relatively low rank reflected lack of ability or performance would have been sadly mistaken. LeMoyne had joined the Royal Manticoran Navy straight out of high school (as the forfeit for a lost bet, according to him). Despite initial training as a small craft coxswain, he'd soon been moved over to the Bureau of Ships and assigned to BuShips Logistics Command, and despite his lack of formal education, he'd risen steadily in grade on the basis of sheer competence. Two T-years before the present war broke out, LeMoyne had attained the rank of master chief and the equivalent of at least three post-graduate degrees, and Admiral Cortez's BuPers had offered him a commission, then assigned him to Logistics Command's Grayson liaison group. His performance there had more than justified BuPers' faith in him, and Honor knew she'd be able to keep him for no more than a T-year or so before he was promoted to lieutenant commander and reassigned to one of the Manticore Binary System's three major Navy shipyards.

Lieutenant Commander Anson Lethridge, Honor's astrogator, was the only member of her staff who was neither Manticoran nor Grayson. Lethridge was from the Erewhon Republic and an officer of the Erewhon Navy. Dark-haired and eyed, he was heavyset and powerfully built. He was also one of the ugliest men Honor had ever seen, with rough features and a heavy brow that, coupled with his broad shoulders and long arms, lent him a hulking, almost brutish appearance at complete odds with his quick mind and endless energy, and she wondered why he'd never resorted to biosculpt. It was obvious that he was sensitive about the way he looked, for he went out of his way to deliberately cast himself as the butt of his own humor by making jokes about his appearance. Many of them were genuinely funny, but all carried their own bitter, biting edge, though Honor sometimes wondered if the rest of her staff realized that as clearly as she did. Of course, she'd spent twenty or thirty T-years convinced that *she* was ugly, too, and she empathized almost painfully with him. But whatever other problems Lethridge might have, he was a first-rate astrogator who manipulated courses and voyage times with an ease Honor could only envy.

She watched now as he gazed at his display, watching vectors shift and change while he played with the input values and variables. It was odd, she reflected, how often outward appearances were so completely misleading. Of every officer on her staff, her brutish astrogator was almost certainly the most gentle . . . despite the lengths to which he went to hide it.

The lift doors hissed open once more, drawing her eyes from Lethridge, and a small, fond smile curved her lips as her squadron's senior medical officer arrived on the bridge. Surgeon Commander Fritz Montoya was *Alvarez*'s surgeon and technically not a member of her staff at all, but she'd specifically requested him for *Alvarez*, and she made a point of including him in staff meetings.

By rights, a physician with his experience and demonstrated skill *should* have been home in the Star Kingdom on the staff of one of the major base hospitals, or else assigned to one of the lavishly equipped hospital ships which accompanied the Fleet Train. Some flag officers might have wondered why he wasn't in one of those other pigeon holes and been leery about accepting his services lest they discover there was a reason no one else had wanted him. But Honor had known Montoya for over twelve T-years . . . and knew he'd spent the time since they'd last served together systematically avoiding the promotion to captain which would have pulled him out of regular fleet deployments and seen him assigned to one of those base hospitals or hospital ships. She doubted he'd be able to avoid that fourth cuff ring much longer, but in the meantime she'd grabbed him and had no intention of letting him go, whatever BuPers might want. In addition to being (as she could attest from painful personal experience) one of the finest doctors around, he was a friend. And his Medical Branch commission meant he stood outside the normal chain of command, which gave him a certain detached perspective she'd found useful in the past.

The extremely young lieutenant commander who accompanied Montoya onto the bridge was the final Manticoran-born member of Honor's staff. His third cuff ring was so new it still squeaked, but Honor had known Scotty Tremaine since he was an ensign, and despite her ingrained distaste for anything that resembled favoritism, she'd done her best to shepherd his career. It was part of the payback she owed the Navy for the officers like her own first captain and Admiral Courvosier who'd shepherded *her* career, and she knew all about the skilled professional who hid behind his irrepressible surface persona. She'd been glad to get him as her staff electronics officer, although she knew he'd had a few reservations about the job—not about serving on her staff, but about the position itself. First and foremost, Tremaine was a small craft specialist who felt most at home as a boat bay officer or in charge of flight ops for a LAC squadron. That was where he was most comfortable and where he would really have preferred to remain . . . which was one reason Honor had picked him for his new job. It would do him good to stretch his mental muscles and push him into something beyond his beloved small craft. The experience would stand him in good stead down the road, just as his quick mental agility would stand him—and Honor—in good stead as they worked together to establish the exact parameters of his position's responsibilities.

They wouldn't be the only RMN officers working on that

particular problem, and Honor knew some of the others were going to approach the concept with negative preconceptions. She understood that, but she rejected their reservations . . . and not simply because she'd become as much a Grayson as a Manticoran. To be sure, the notion of devoting a staff-level slot to an officer specifically responsible for coordinating an entire squadron's or task force's electronic warfare systems, however logical, had never occurred to the RMN, which had always seen that sort of duty as one of the ops officer's responsibilities.

That was where most other navies assigned the responsibility, as well, but the Graysons, continuing their iconoclastic ways, had chosen to split the function off. They'd created the new staff position less than a T-year before, which meant it was as new in practice to Honor as to any other RMN officer, but both the Office of Personnel and Commodore Reston's Doctrine and Training Command had put a lot of thought into it before they'd acted. She'd known they were considering it before she'd left Yeltsin to return to Manticoran service, which put her at least a little ahead of her RMN contemporaries, many of whom were still busy grumbling about newfangled notions thought up by inexperienced amateurs without the common sense to leave things alone if they weren't broken. In Honor's experience, that was usually the first response of people who clung to tradition simply because it *was* tradition. That would have been enough by itself to incline her to give the concept a fair try, and like quite a few of the GSN's other heretical ideas, the arrangement appeared to be working out well in practice—a conclusion Scotty seemed to be coming to share as he settled into his new responsibilities.

As she watched, Tremaine crossed the bridge to the second youngest member of her staff. Lieutenant (Senior-Grade) Jasper Mayhew, her staff intelligence officer, was a distant relative of some sort of Protector Benjamin and only twenty-eight T-years old, with auburn hair as thick as Andrew LaFollet's and sky-blue eyes. Despite his extreme youth, Honor was confident of his abilities, and the fact that he'd been trained by Captain Gregory Paxton, who'd held the intelligence slot on her BatRon One staff, only made her more so. Besides, he and Scotty already worked together with the smoothness of long-time cronies, and little though she might choose to admit it (at least where Tremaine could hear her) she had great faith in the electronics officer's judgment.

Lieutenant Commander Michael Vorland, her staff chaplain, was the only one of her staffers who would be absent from this morning's meeting. A small, neat, balding man with gentle brown eyes and a fringe of sandy hair, Vorland actually wore antique wire-rimmed spectacles and steadfastly refused to avail himself of the corrective services available since Grayson joined the Manticoran Alliance. On the other hand, his lense prescription was modest, and Honor suspected that his refusal to discard them had less to do with old-fashioned prejudice than with preserving something which had become a part of his "uniform" over the years. No one could have presented a milder appearance, yet his slight frame hid a surprising physical strength and he could radiate an astounding degree of sheer moral presence at need.

It was obvious that he was also aware that the Manticoran members of her staff felt a bit uncomfortable where he was concerned. The RMN had no official chaplains, and it would have been surprising if there hadn't been a certain period of . . . adjustment. At the same time, the Grayson Navy had never been *without* its chaplains, and even the most skeptical of Manticorans had to admit that a mixed squadron required a clerical presence. Honor would really have preferred to call once more on the services of Abraham Jackson, who'd served as BatRon One's chaplain, but Jackson had been detached from active duty and assigned to Reverend Sullivan's personal staff, and although Vorland was a very different man, she sensed from him the same sort of open-minded, flexible strength she'd found in Jackson. At the moment, he was somewhere in Mackenzie Steading instead of aboard *Alvarez*, but Honor could hardly begrudge his absence. His only son was marrying his third wife today, and Vorland would be there to perform the wedding himself.

Honor rubbed the tip of her nose slowly, contemplating the strengths—and occasional weaknesses—already emerging from her new staffers. Even the ones with whom she had served before would be performing in new roles, assuming new responsibilities and relationships with her, but so far most of the surprises had been pleasant ones, and—

She heard a sudden sound behind her—a soft, almost slithery noise, followed by the flat, slapping sound of something flexible hitting the deck—and turned her head just in time to see a husky young man grab frantically for the armload of hardcopy binders he'd just spilled. He managed to snag one of them, but the others evaded his desperately reaching hands like missiles on preprogrammed evasion courses. The noise level as they hit the deck was remarkable, and Honor pressed her lips together to keep from smiling as the youngster's face went beet-red.

The color showed very clearly, for Ensign Carson Clinkscales, her flag lieutenant, was cursed with the fair, freckled complexion that went with his dark red hair and green eyes. He was enormously tall for a Grayson—at a hundred and ninety centimeters, he was taller than Honor herself, which was a claim very few Graysons could make— but he was also only twenty-one T-years old. He never seemed entirely certain what to do with his hands and feet, and he was agonizingly aware of Honor's reputation and rank . . . which only made his lingering, puppylike awkwardness worse. In many ways, he reminded her of young Aubrey Wanderman, a grav tech from her last ship who'd suffered from both inexperience and a massive case of hero worship. Except, of course, that Wanderman had always seemed to get things right where his job was concerned, and Clinkscales, well . . .

She'd never met a youngster who tried harder or applied himself more conscientiously to his duties, but if there was any way—any way at all—that something could go wrong for him it did so with an inevitability that was almost awesome. She devoutly hoped that he would outgrow his penchant for disasters, because she liked him a great deal—rather more, in fact, than she was prepared to let him guess. She'd bent one of her own rules by accepting him for her flag lieutenant, and she was determined to avoid even the suggestion that his status as Howard Clinkscales' nephew was going to buy him any favoritism. And in fairness to the youngster, he seemed to have all the right ingredients, if he could only get on top of his private jinx. Although he was the physical antithesis of Jared Sutton, her last flag lieutenant, his lingering shyness and determination to get things right—eventually—reminded her almost too strongly of Jared. She couldn't forget the way young Sutton had died, and his face wanted to superimpose itself on Clinkscales' whenever she let her guard down.

But there were no ghosts on the flag bridge just now, and she heard Venizelos chuckle—not softly, but not unkindly, either—as the ensign squatted to fumble after the binders. The chief of staff walked over to him and knelt to reach under a console for a folder which had slithered away from the main heap, then held it out with a smile.

"Don't sweat it, kid," Honor heard Venizelos say, though the commander had obviously pitched his voice only for Clinkscales' ears. "You should've seen *my* first disaster on a starship bridge. At least you're only dropping folders; *I* dropped an entire cup of coffee—cream, with two sugars—right in the XO's lap!"

Clinkscales stared at him for a moment, then grinned shyly and bobbed his head in gratitude, and Honor looked away once more. Clinkscales had obviously expected someone to tear a strip off him, and no doubt some senior officers would have done just that. Not on this staff, though, and she drew a deep breath of satisfaction, for the seemingly tiniest things were often the best indicators of a team's cohesion and quality.

"Yes, Sir. I'm sorry, Sir," Clinkscales told Venizelos quietly. "I just picked these up from CIC for Lieutenant Mayhew to distribute before the morning brief, and, well— " He broke off, looking down at the stack of binders. Some had popped open when he dropped them, spilling pages which had lost any sort of order in a confetti-like pile, and Venizelos squeezed the taller youngster's shoulder with his right hand. His left beckoned to Mayhew, and he smiled reassuringly.

"We've still got twenty minutes, Carson. You'll have time to get them sorted back out . . . but you should probably go ahead and get started on it."

"Yes, Sir. Right away, Sir!"

The intelligence officer arrived, and he and the ensign carted the scrambled binders off towards his console. Venizelos watched them go and nodded to a trio of yeomen, who quickly converged to lend additional hands to the problem, then glanced at Honor and gave her a wink before he turned to walk calmly back to his own console.

Yes, the chemistry's good, Honor thought, listening to Mayhew rag Clinkscales gently. The intelligence officer's own relatively junior rank made him a logical mentor for the ensign—senior enough to be an authority figure, yet junior enough not to be frightening—and Mayhew seemed to have slipped naturally into the role. *Still, I hope Carson does get over this fit of the clumsies. Andy's on the right track for now, and the others are following his lead, but sooner or later the kid's simply going to have to get it together. He* is *an officer—or the larval stage of one, anyway—and—*

Nimitz made a soft chiding sound from the back of her chair, and she chuckled as she reached up to caress his ears. He was right. Generations of young officers had survived maladroitness and embarrassment, and no doubt Carson would as well. And whether he did or not, it was her chief of staff's job to fret over it, not hers. Except, of course, that fretting was one of the privileges of command.

She chuckled again and lifted Nimitz down to her lap so she could rub his ears properly.

✦   ✦   ✦

"—so that's about it, Milady," Marcia McGinley finished up. "Command Central says it will be at least a month before the rest of the squadron assembles here, but we're on notice that we may be tasked for miscellaneous duties between now and then. Once Admiral White Haven takes over, our posture and deployment will be up to him."

"Understood, Marcia. Thank you." Honor tipped her chair back, moving her eyes to scan the faces gathered around the conference table in her flag briefing room. "Did you discuss this with Captain Greentree, Andy?"

"Yes, Milady," the chief of staff replied with a slight grin. "He hasn't heard anything more than we have, and nothing official's come in yet at all, but you know how the grapevine works."

"Ah?" Honor cocked an eyebrow, and Venizelos shrugged.

"His astrogator's just received an updated download on the Clairmont-Mathias Sector, Milady. That inspired me to do a little checking, and it turns out that System Control's expecting a JNMT convoy to arrive shortly. It's scheduled to move on to Quest, Clairmont, Adler, and Treadway, and a little birdie down in Command Central tells me that the dreadnought division escorting it is due to peel off here to join Eighth Fleet. Sounds to me like they're going to have to find some replacement escorts, Milady."

"I see." Honor rocked her chair gently from side to side, then nodded to Jasper Mayhew when the lieutenant raised a hand. "Yes, Jasper?"

"I think Commander Venizelos is on to something, My Lady," Mayhew said. "According to my latest update from High Admiral Matthews staff," he tapped the binder in front of him, one of the ones Clinkscales had delivered to the flag bridge, "most of the convoy's cargo is actually intended for Treadway, the endpoint of the voyage. I don't have detailed specs on it, but reading between the lines suggests that it's probably more hardware—and possibly some more personnel—to help upgrade the yard facilities we captured from the Peeps. One part of the convoy manifest that I *do* have, though, is the portion for Adler.

Apparently the Protector has agreed to provide Marines to garrison Samovar, the system's inhabited planet, until the Royal Army can take over. A large part of this convoy constitutes ammunition, ground equipment, and general support for those Marines, and there's also a fairly hefty load of humanitarian relief supplies. From the look of things, the system was in pretty poor shape before the Alliance threw the Peeps out, and the locals seem to prefer us to the old management."

"You say all this was included in your most recent download?"

"Yes, My Lady."

"Then I suspect you and Commander Venizelos are right about where we're likely to be headed shortly. And to be honest, I'm just as happy to hear it. We've got sixty percent of the squadron assembled, and I'd sooner put it to good use—and get some operational experience under our belts—than just sit up here in orbit. Andy," she turned back to Venizelos, "talk to your little bird at Command Central. 'Suggest' to him that we think we'd be ideal for this particular mission. After all—" she smiled one of her crooked smiles "—we might as well let the brass know we're bright-eyed and eager, right?"

"Yes, Milady." Venizelos' tone combined exactly the right degree of respect and resignation, and a quiet chuckle circled the table.

"And while the Commander is doing that, Carson," Honor went on, turning to her flag lieutenant, "I'd like you to contact Captain Greentree and Captain McKeon. Invite both of them to join me—and, I think, you, Andy, and you, too, Marcia—for supper tonight. If we're going to be volunteering for escort duty, I'd like to run a few squadron-level sims before we pull out, and we might as well get started planning them now."

"Yes, My Lady!" Clinkscales remained in his chair, but somehow he gave the impression of having risen, saluted, clicked his heels together, *and* bowed in acknowledgment, and Honor hid a grin.

"All right, then. I think that just about covers everything. Unless anyone has something else we need to look at?" No one did, and she nodded in satisfaction. "Good! In that case, I'll be in the gym for the next hour or so if anyone needs me. After that, Andy, I'd like to see some rough ideas from you and Marcia."

"Yes, Milady."

"Fine." Honor stood and lifted Nimitz from the back of her chair, setting him in his proper position on her shoulder as her subordinates rose to their feet as well. "A good brief, people. Thank you."

A gratified murmur answered her, and she smiled, nodded once more, and headed for the hatch and an overdue appointment with her sparring partner.

"Earl White Haven has arrived, Sir," the yeoman said. He stood aside to admit Hamish Alexander to the comfortably austere office, then withdrew and closed the old-fashioned door quietly behind him.

"Ah, Admiral White Haven!" High Admiral Wesley Matthews rose and walked quickly around his desk to extend his hand. "I apologize for interrupting your schedule, but thank you for coming so promptly."

"You didn't actually interrupt anything, High Admiral," White Haven reassured him. "My staff is running a battle simulation for Admiral Greenslade and Rear Admiral Ukovski, but we're only acting as umpires for this one. What can I do for you, Sir?"

"Please, sit down," Matthews invited. He waved his guest into one of the comfortable chairs before his desk, then settled himself into another one while he considered exactly how to approach his current concern. Things weren't made any easier by the fact that Hamish Alexander, despite the fact that he was both twice Matthews' own age and one of the most highly respected strategists and fleet commanders in the explored galaxy, was technically junior to him. In fact, Sixth Fleet, White Haven's last command, had out massed the entire Grayson Space Navy by a factor of around eight, which always made

Matthews feel a little awkward when dealing with the earl through the formal chain of command. But the high admiral was also unaccustomed to dodging responsibilities, and he crossed his legs, rested his folded hands on his raised right knee, and launched into the reason he'd invited White Haven here.

"As you know, My Lord," he began, "Lady Harrington has assumed command of her squadron several weeks sooner than we'd anticipated." White Haven leaned back with a brief nod of acknowledgment, but had there been a momentary flash of . . . something in those ice-blue eyes? "Needless to say, I was delighted to have her back, however temporarily," the high admiral continued, "and she's been settling into her new position with all her usual efficiency. In fact, that's the reason I wanted to see you."

"I beg your pardon?" White Haven blinked, and Matthews smiled wryly.

"As I'm sure you know even better than I, My Lord, every fleet is *always* short of cruisers, and Home Fleet is no exception. Given our need for pickets and scouts, as well as screening units, our light forces are stretched very tight." White Haven nodded once more. As Matthews said, cruisers were always in short supply, which was the reason cruiser skippers got so little rest . . . and why any ambitious junior officer lusted to become one.

"Unfortunately, that shortage seems to be even more widespread than usual," Matthews went on, "and everyone in the Alliance is looking around for any of them they can latch onto—including me. Specifically, Admiral, I'd like to 'borrow' Lady Harrington's squadron for a few weeks."

"Ah?" White Haven leaned further back and crossed his own legs. He was aware of a small, highly unusual spike of internal consternation, but no trace of it showed in his politely curved eyebrow.

"Yes. I realize CruRon Eighteen is still a GSN formation for the moment, but I also realize that its status could change very quickly as the rest of Eighth Fleet assembles here. Actually, you'd be justified right now in activating your fleet HQ and assuming control of the currently assembled forces, in my opinion. That's why I wanted to speak to you before I make any decisions."

"Exactly what mission did you have in mind, Sir?" White Haven asked after a moment.

"A fairly routine one, actually. We've got a major convoy—sixteen or seventeen freighters and transports— routed through Yeltsin to Clairmont-Mathias. They're scheduled to make deliveries to several systems, but these are all JNMTC ships, so transit times will be a lot shorter than you might think."

He paused until White Haven nodded understanding. The Joint Navy Military Transport Command was the brainchild of the RMN's Logistics Command and the GSN's Office of Supply. Logistics Command had pointed out that really big freighters and transports, while invaluable under many circumstances, weren't really ideal in terms of flexibility. Smaller ships in the four- to five-million-ton range couldn't carry as much cargo or as many personnel, but smaller size translated into a larger total number of hulls for the same cumulative tonnage, and that equated to more destinations which could be served simultaneously. In peacetime, operating costs would have doomed the proposal (after all, a four million-ton ship required the same crew and very nearly the same fuel and maintenance costs as an eight million-ton vessel), but faced with the war against the Peeps, military, rather than financial, efficiency had become the overriding priority.

The Joint Navy Military Transport Command, composed of midsized ships and normally assigned to the delivery of high-priority, time-critical cargoes (or delivery to potential combat hot spots), was the result. And as part of the same move to speed and streamline the transportation process, the ships designated for JNMTC use had been taken in hand by navy shipyards—Manticoran or Grayson, as available slips permitted—for overhaul. Time was too tight for their civilian grade inertial compensators and impellers to be altered, but they'd received light sidewalls and missile defense systems, upgraded sensors and rudimentary electronic warfare systems, and military hyper generators to permit them to reach as high as the eta bands. Since most merchantmen were designed to cruise no higher than the delta bands, their up-rated generators virtually doubled the sustained apparent velocity JNMTC ships could attain.

"Even so, however," Matthews pointed out, "the entire round trip is going to take something like two T-months, and it could run more if they have longer than expected layovers at any of their stops. That's why I wanted to talk to you before simply assigning Lady Harrington to the job. In many respects, her squadron would be a perfect fit. She's still short a quarter of her official strength, but those ships won't even arrive for at least another month, and six heavy cruisers should be enough to ride herd on the convoy. At the same time, since I didn't actually expect her to assume command so quickly, her ships haven't been assigned to any other pigeonholes, which means I can detach them without taking them away from any other pressing duty. And a routine mission like this would also give her an opportunity to shake down her crews and her staff. But with the activation date for your headquarters still up in the air, I wanted to clear it with you before detaching one of 'your' units for that long."

"I see. And I appreciate your thoughtfulness, Sir," White Haven replied, rubbing his chin as he thought. *Not that there's all that much to think about,* he told himself. *Until we activate Eighth Fleet, the ships belong to Matthews. And he's right that they'd be ideal for the job. So why does the idea bother me?*

He frowned mentally, probing for the answer to that question. The obvious explanation was that Matthews was also right about the perpetual scarcity of cruisers, which made White Haven as unhappy as any other fleet commander at the prospect of detaching a squadron of them. But much as he was tempted to accept that as the reason for his hesitation, he knew better. It wasn't as if Harrington's squadron would be gone all *that* long, and although High Admiral Matthews was right about how quickly Eighth Fleet was assembling, they both knew it would be at least three or four months before the new force was ready to move against Barnett. There'd be plenty of time for an officer of Harrington's caliber to complete the escort mission, return, absorb her remaining units, *and* settle comfortably into her slot in the fleet's table of organization.

So why *did* it bother him? He chewed the question a moment longer, but the answer had already suggested itself to him; he simply didn't want to look at it too closely, because he already felt guilty.

He snorted mentally as he admitted it. He didn't know precisely what he'd done, but he couldn't shake an inexplicable certainty that Honor Harrington's hurried departure from Harrington House was somehow his fault. She hadn't said or done anything to suggest such a possibility, yet he'd picked up a certain tension which hadn't been there before. An . . . uneasiness. Whatever it was, it had started that evening in the library, and he rubbed his chin harder to hide the tightening of his jaw muscles from Matthews as his mind ran back over their confrontation—if that was the word for it—and its aftermath.

Had he somehow given away his sudden, radically altered awareness of her? He'd tried not to, and after so many years of naval service and all too frequent exposures to the rough and tumble of the Star Kingdom's political strife, he would have sworn his face was well enough trained to hide anything he commanded it to. But that was the only reason he could think of why she might abruptly become so much more guarded—so . . . wary—where he was concerned. *Had* she picked up on it? Certainly she had an uncanny ability to read the people around her. He wasn't the only one to have noticed that, he reflected, recalling conversations with Mark Sarnow, Yancey Parks, and other flag officers under whom she'd served. Had her intuition or whatever it was she used detected his feelings? Had she misread his reaction, possibly even feared he might use his position as her soon to be commanding officer to attempt to *force* some sort of intimacy upon her?

Of course not! She knew him better than that—she *had* to! But even as he thought that, another small part of him wondered if perhaps she would have been as wrong to fear that as he preferred to think. He'd never done anything of the sort before, and he'd always believed there was no chance he ever would, for he'd despised anyone, man or woman, who attempted to exploit his or her position that way. Yet he also had to admit that he'd never felt anything quite like . . . like *whatever* it was he'd felt that night. *And, he admitted guiltily, you're not quite the saint you'd like your admiring public to believe, now are you, Hamish?*

He closed his eyes and inhaled deeply. He loved his wife. He'd loved her since the day he met her, and he would love her till the day he died, and she knew it. But she also knew, although they'd never discussed it, that he'd had more than one affair since the freak accident put her in her life-support chair. There was no way—could never be one, ever again—the two of them could enjoy a physical relationship. Both of them knew that, and so Emily looked the other way whenever one of his rare affairs blossomed. She knew they were only temporary, that his occasional lovers were all women he liked and trusted but did not *love*—not as he loved and would always love her. She was the one to whom he always returned, for they shared everything but the one form of intimacy they had lost forever. He knew that it hurt her, less because he was being "unfaithful" than because it reminded her of what she'd lost, and that his "infidelity" would cause her great pain if it ever became public, and so he was always circumspect . . . and always careful to avoid any relationship which could ever become more than friendship.

But now he was no longer certain of himself, and that hurt deep down inside, where his belief in himself, his ability to trust himself, lived. He'd never felt anything like that sudden, soaring moment when he looked at Honor Harrington and saw not merely an officer but a *woman* he'd never truly looked at before. It wasn't just that she was attractive, though she certainly was, in her own exotic, sharply carved way. He'd lost track of the stunning women—and men—he'd seen in a society in which biosculpt had become as common as teeth-straightening braces had been in pre-space days, and although mere physical beauty might still attract his eye, it was no longer capable of seizing his thoughts by the throat this way.

No, he was responding to something far deeper, some elemental part of her that called to something deep inside him. Aside from the occasional handshake or a touch on a shoulder or an elbow, he'd never even touched her, yet that something inside had roused for her as it never had for any of the women who'd been his lovers, and that scared him. It was one thing to turn to another for the physical intimacy he could no longer give Emily or receive from her; it was another thing entirely—a dark, frightening thing—to feel so strongly drawn to another woman. And especially to one who was not only half his own age but one of his subordinate officers. From every possible perspective, Honor Harrington could never be anything *but* a fellow officer to him, and he knew it.

But a part of you doesn't really believe *it, does it Hamish?* his conscience observed mercilessly. *And if you don't, and if she did pick up on it, then maybe she was right to put some distance between you. And while we're on the subject, My Lord, just what in* hell *do you intend to do about all this? Are you going to let yourself act like some testosterone-bullied adolescent, or are you going to remember that you're a Queen's officer . . . and that* she's *an officer, as well?*

He realized Matthews was looking at him rather intently and shook his head as if to discourage a nagging fly. No doubt Matthews wondered just what the problem was. The proposition was straightforward, as was the escort mission, and given who the Eighteenth Cruiser Squadron currently reported to, this entire meeting was little more than a professional courtesy.

"Excuse me, High Admiral," the earl apologized. "I'm afraid I started shoving ships and deployments around in my head and allowed myself to become distracted. As far as I'm concerned, Lady Harrington and her squadron would be an ideal choice for the mission you've described. Obviously, I'd like to have her present when we actually begin putting the fleet together. Despite her relatively junior Manticoran rank, I envision a major role for her in the coordination and deployment of my screening units, which will also let me take the best advantage of her GSN status. But there should be plenty of time to deal with all of that after her return. I appreciate your informing me of your intentions, of course, but I see no objection to them."

"Thank you, My Lord." Matthews stood, extending his hand once more, and walked the earl to the door as they shook hands again. "I suppose," the Grayson added with a wry smile as he personally opened the door for his guest, "that the real reason I wanted to discuss it with you was that I feel a bit guilty to be poaching Lady Harrington from you. There are never enough good officers in any navy, and when you get one like *her*, well—" He shrugged. "Any admiral I know would want to get his hands on her."

"Indeed he would, Sir," White Haven agreed. *But by the time she gets back*, he added mentally, *maybe* this *admiral will have gotten his head straightened out and realized he has to keep his hands in his pockets where she's concerned!*

• Chapter Eight

"All right, people—let's see some *enthusiasm!* We've got some Manty ass to kick!"

Citizen Rear Admiral Lester Tourville's thick mustache bristled aggressively over his fierce grin. Conformity had become the path to survival for most of the People's Navy's senior officers, but Tourville was and would always remain a character—indeed, almost a caricature. His climb from captain to rear admiral had been meteoric, yet he knew as well as anyone that the likelihood of his ever rising *above* rear admiral was essentially nonexistent. Not that it bothered him. Most of his more colorful mannerisms might be deliberate affectations, but underneath them he truly was the hard-charging warrior he parodied so well. Higher rank would only have diluted the impact his talents (and style) could exert at the squadron level. It would also require him to play the political game, and Tourville knew his limits. Even those idiots at StateSec were unlikely to execute a mere rear admiral who was constitutionally unable to fit the party mold—particularly if he was also a trouble-shooter who always came through—but a vice admiral or admiral with the same tendencies would quickly end up dead. All of which helped explain the "loose warhead" persona he'd gone to such lengths to perfect.

Of course, there were drawbacks to his relatively junior rank. Foremost among them was the fact that he would always be charged with executing someone else's orders, since any squadron he commanded would always belong to someone else's task force or fleet. On the other hand, any navy often had to detach squadrons for independent service. When that happened, any set of orders could offer only general guidance, with the squadron CO expected to use his own good sense to implement them, and that was as close to being his or her own master as any PN officer was likely to get these days. Besides, sometimes the person writing your orders actually knew what he was doing.

That was one of the reasons Tourville liked working for Citizen Admiral Theisman. The keen analyst hidden behind Tourville's bullheaded exterior rather doubted Theisman would be around much longer, for the citizen admiral had made the mistake of allowing himself to be promoted. A postgraduate degree in ass-kissing was required at Theisman's level, and the Barnett System CO lacked the ability to buff sufficient buttocks. That probably said something good about him as a human being, but it was a fatal flaw in the present day PRH. So far, Theisman— like Tourville—had always managed to deliver the goods, which kept him valuable to his masters. Unlike Tourville, he'd climbed too high to be allowed to remain apolitical. His purely military value would soon be outweighed by his political liabilities if he persisted in trying to remain his own man.

In the meantime, however, Theisman was one of the minority of senior officers who both saw what had to be done and was willing to risk saying so. He also had the guts to take calculated risks, despite the SS's habit of shooting those who tried and failed, and he was always careful to phrase his orders in ways which would protect the subordinates he sent out to run those risks from StateSec's wrath. Like Tourville's current orders.

"I commend your own enthusiasm, Citizen Rear Admiral," People's Commissioner Everard Honeker said dryly, "but let's not get carried away. Our orders are to carry out a reconnaissance in force, not to defeat the Alliance single-handedly!"

"Agreed. Agreed." Tourville waved one hand airily and drew a cigar from the breast pocket of his tunic. He shoved it into his mouth at precisely the right angle of jauntiness, lit it, and blew a stream of pungent smoke at the air return over his console. In point of fact, he didn't much care for cigars, but smoking had once more become fashionable over the past several years, and he'd decided cigars fitted his image. Now he couldn't get rid of the miserable things without admitting they'd been a mistake, and he was damned if he'd do that.

"A reconnaissance in force, Citizen Commissioner," he went on once he had the cigar drawing properly, "is just that, however: a reconnaissance *in force*. That means we get to kick the ass of anything that isn't capable of kicking *our* ass, and the Manties are kind of thin in the neighborhood just now. Seems to me the bastards've gotten a little overconfident. They've kicked us out of Trevor's Star and they're closing in on Barnett, and they figure we haven't got squat to stop 'em. They aren't too far wrong, either," he admitted, "but assuming the other side's gonna just lie down and die is never a good idea, and that's what they're doing in our sector. So, yes, Sir. Our orders are to pull a 'reconnaissance,' but when I find something to shoot, I'm damned well gonna shoot it!"

Honeker sighed, but he'd grown accustomed to Tourville's ebullience. There was no real point trying to resist it, for the citizen rear admiral seemed unaware that Honeker held his leash. Indeed, Honeker often thought of himself as being towed bodily along by the cheerful, clumsy eagerness of the Great Dane or Saint Bernard he was supposedly walking. It wasn't how things were supposed to be, but it had worked—so far, at least—and his political superiors gave him much of the credit for Tourville's successes. Besides, Honeker actually liked the citizen rear admiral . . . even if he *did* choose to play the role of someone who belonged on a holystoned wooden quarterdeck with a cutlass and a brace of flintlock pistols in his belt, bellowing orders over the roar of cannon.

"I don't have a problem with engaging the enemy, Citizen Rear Admiral." The commissioner heard a familiar, half-soothing note in his voice and hid a wry mental grimace. "I'm simply pointing out that your squadron represents a valuable asset. It shouldn't be risked unless the potential gain clearly justifies doing so."

"Of course not!" Tourville agreed genially through another cloud of aromatic smoke. Honeker would have felt a bit better if the citizen rear admiral's grin had been a little less fierce, but he decided to accept Tourville's agreement at face value. There would be time enough to argue when the moment came . . . and precious little point trying to make this cheerful, bloodthirsty adolescent see reason ahead of time, anyway.

Tourville watched the people's commissioner give up the argument with deep satisfaction. One thing he'd learned early on was that it was far better for one to appear overly aggressive, so that the Committee of Public Safety's spies were forced to rein one in, than to appear timid or hesitant. It was a lesson Citizen Admiral Theisman's own performance at the Fourth Battle of Yeltsin had underscored, and it had served Tourville well since the Harris Assassination. When he was certain Honeker had stopped objecting, he turned sharp, dark eyes on his chief of staff and jabbed the cigar at him like a pulser.

"All right, Yuri. Let's hear it," he commanded.

"Yes, Citizen Rear Admiral," Citizen Captain Yuri Bogdanovich replied. He'd been with Tourville long enough to learn to double-team their watchdog, and his crisp, cool tone was a deliberate contrast to his admiral's jovial ferocity. Now he straightened his shoulders, sitting upright with military precision, and activated the holo unit to project a floating star map above the table in PNS *Count Tilly's* flag briefing room.

"This is our general operations area, Citizen Rear Admiral, Citizen Commissioner. As you know, Citizen Admiral Theisman and Citizen Commissioner LePic have detached our second and third divisions to reinforce the Corrigan System pickets here." He touched a key, and the G6 primary of the Corrigan System pulsed brightly. "While that represents half our total unit strength, the ships in question are all *Sultans* or *Tigers*, whereas the units remaining under our immediate command are all *Warlords*. In addition, Barnett HQ has assigned us five *Scimitar* and three *Mars*-class heavy cruisers and six *Conqueror*-class light cruisers to replace them. Our cumulative loss in actual fighting strength is thus about equal to one *Sultan*-class, but we've gained three and a half times as many scouting platforms *and* a somewhat higher squadron acceleration curve in return. In other words, we've got more eyes, more speed, and almost as much punch as we had before. In addition, we've been assigned two fast minelayers—*Yarnowski* and *Simmons*—which have been reconfigured as freighters to provide logistical support."

Bogdanovich paused and glanced around the table to be sure his recap had sunk in, then cleared his throat and tapped more keys. Three more stars blinked in the display, and he highlighted the tiny characters of the system names beside them.

"Our current areas of interest are these three systems," he went on. "Sallah, Adler, and Micah. According to our latest intelligence dumps, the Manties have taken Adler and Micah, but we still hold Sallah. Unfortunately, the data on Sallah is over two weeks old, so with your permission, Citizen Commander Lowe and I recommend beginning our sweep there, then moving south to Adler and Micah before returning to Barnett."

"What sort of passage times are we looking at?" Tourville demanded.

"Just under nine and a half days to Sallah, Citizen Rear Admiral," Citizen Commander Karen Lowe, Tourville's staff astrogator, replied. "Sallah to Adler would be another three days, and Adler to Micah would be another thirty-one hours. Return passage from Micah to Barnett would be another nine-plus days."

"So the entire sweep, exclusive of any time we spend shooting Manties, would be—what?" Tourville squinted against his cigar smoke while he did the mental math. "About three T-weeks?"

"Yes, Citizen Rear Admiral. Call it five hundred twenty-four hours, or just under twenty-two days."

"How does that stack up against HQ's time limit, Yuri?"

"Citizen Admiral Theisman and Citizen Commissioner LePic have authorized up to four T-weeks," Bogdanovich replied in that same crisp tone. "There's also a provision allowing you and Citizen Commissioner Honeker to extend your operational time by up to another week if that seems justified."

"Um." Tourville drew heavily on his cigar, then took it from his mouth to examine its glowing end. Then he looked at Honeker. "Personally, Citizen Commissioner, I'd rather begin by sweeping straight through Adler and then on to Micah. We *know* we're going to find bad guys there, whereas Sallah's probably still in our hands." He barked a harsh laugh. "God knows there's nothing important enough there to justify a Manty attack on the place! Still," he put the cigar back in his mouth with an unhappy grunt, "I suppose we have to start at Sallah, anyway. HQ apparently wants to know what's going on there, and it's the longest leg of the mission. Do you concur?"

"I think so." There was an edge of caution in Honeker's reply. He'd been too quick to agree with Tourville a time or two, only to discover that the citizen rear admiral had sold him a bill of goods just so he could see a little action. The experience had taught him not to rush into anything, and he looked at Citizen Commander Shannon Foraker, Tourville's ops officer and the newest member of his staff. "What do we know about probable enemy forces in the area, Citizen Commander?"

"Not as much as I'd like, Sir," Foraker replied promptly. The golden-haired citizen commander had a formidable reputation as a tactical officer (indeed, she was widely regarded as something of a witch in that department), including the enthusiastic recommendation of her previous people's commissioner. Fortunately for Foraker, Citizen Commissioner Jourdain's report had also warned Honeker that when she became immersed in a problem, she often backslid into some rather prerevolutionary habits of speech. Viewed against her accomplishments, Honeker—like

Jourdain before him—was prepared to cut her some slack, and one of the things he most liked about her was that it never seemed to occur to her to cover her own posterior by hedging. If someone asked her a question, she answered it to the best of her ability and without equivocating, and that, unfortunately, was increasingly rare in the People's Navy. In his more honest moments, Honeker knew why that was, though he preferred not to think about it too closely.

"Our info on Micah is especially spotty," Foraker went on. "We *think* there's a light Manty task force—call it a couple of divisions of the wall—with escorts from the Grayson and Casca navies. That's what moved in and took it away from us, anyway, and I think it would be smart to assume they're still there until we prove differently."

"I agree," Honeker said firmly. He didn't know whether or not Tourville would have disputed that cautious note, but he didn't intend to find out, either. "And Adler?"

"We think we've got a better picture there, Sir," Foraker replied. She punched up data on her own terminal and consulted it to refresh her memory before she continued. "At our last count, their Adler picket was only a cruiser squadron and two or three divisions of tin cans. That's probably gone up some since, but given that we haven't counterattacked or raided at all in this entire sector for over six months, I doubt they've reinforced very heavily. They're strapped for ships, too, Citizen Commissioner. They have to be skimming hulls off from quiet areas to build up for their next offensive."

"Which is precisely why this operation is more important than its scale might seem to suggest," Tourville pointed out, waving his cigar like a smoldering baton. "Like I say, Citizen Commissioner—the bastards are getting too confident. They're taking it for granted that since we *haven't* counter-attacked them, we *won't*. But if we hit them hard a couple of times and disillusion them, they'll probably beef up the local picket forces. And *that* will suck at least light forces away from their eventual attack on Barnett—or attacks anywhere else, for that matter."

"I understand the intent of our orders, Citizen Admiral." Honeker's tone was a touch repressive, but Tourville only grinned, and the people's commissioner hid a mental sigh. Everyone in this briefing room knew that he, as the squadron's commissioner, was its true commander. A single word from him could "disappear" any of these officers, even Tourville, and they knew *that*, too. So why did he feel like a harassed scout master besieged by an entire troop of ten-year-olds? It wasn't supposed to be like this.

"All right," he said after a moment. "I assume, Citizen Rear Admiral, that you concur with Citizen Commander Foraker's recommendations?"

"Of course I do," Tourville replied cheerfully. "Shannon's got the right idea, Sir. Make our sweep, sneak in on Adler before they know we're there, and shoot us enough Manties to get their attention and draw some more picket ships into the area."

"When could we depart Barnett?" Honeker asked.

"Within six hours, Sir," Bogdanovich answered for his CO. "We're topped off with ammunition and spares now, and we're scheduled to tank for reactor mass within six hours. Judging from HQ's alert order, though, I doubt we'll be leaving for at least a few days. We're anticipating the arrival of BatRon Sixty-Two sometime in the next ninety-six hours. My understanding is that we won't be released for operations until they get here."

"So we've got some time for contingency planning," Honeker observed.

"Yes, Sir," Tourville agreed, "and with your concurrence, I intend to get started on that this afternoon."

"Good," Honeker said, and meant it. Bellicose as Tourville often appeared, he was meticulous in planning for every conceivable—and most *in*conceivable—contingencies. For all his aggressiveness, he calculated the odds finely before he committed to action, which was one reason Honeker was willing to put up with his whirlwind approach to command. The people's commissioner leaned back, then cocked an eyebrow as Bogdanovich twitched in his chair.

If Honeker hadn't known better (and he didn't), he would have sworn Foraker had just kicked the chief of staff under the table.

"Ah, there was one other point I wanted to raise, Citizen Rear Admiral," Bogdanovich said, glancing sideways at Foraker as he spoke.

"Yes?" Tourville invited.

"Well, it's just that I—that is, Citizen Commander Foraker and I—wondered if we could get HQ to agree to release some of the new missile pods to us?" There was a moment of silence, and Bogdanovich hurried on before anyone else could break it. "The thing is, Citizen Rear Admiral, that by now the Manties *must* be aware that we've got them. We know they've already been used closer to Trevor's Star, and we know HQ is planning to use them against any attack on Barnett. But what we *don't* know is whether or not the Allied units in our sector have been informed that we have them. If they haven't, the surprise factor could be decisive. And we *have* been assigned *Yarnowski* and *Simmons*, Citizen Admiral. Each of them could carry up to seventy pods and a complete set of reloads and still leave plenty of capacity for the rest of our requirements."

"Um." Tourville chewed his cigar, then glanced at Honeker. "Citizen Commissioner?"

"I don't know," Honeker said slowly, and plucked at his lower lip while he frowned in thought. Bogdanovich and Foraker were certainly right about the probable utility of the system, but asking HQ to let it out of the bag would really mean sticking his neck out. On the other hand, he decided, LePic and Theisman could always veto the suggestion. If they didn't, then any repercussions would be on their heads, not his.

"All right," he said finally. "I'll support you if you want to ask for them, at any rate. Just try to write a convincing proposal."

"Oh, I think we can manage that, Sir," Tourville assured him with a smile, then nodded to Foraker once more. "All

right, Shannon. Assume you've got your pods. Now sketch
me out an ops plan to make the best use of them."

"Yes, Sir." Foraker punched up fresh data, her long,
narrow face intent, and Honeker bit his lip against the
automatic urge to correct her. He'd seen her at work often
enough by now to realize that Jourdain had been right: her
reversion to the older, forbidden military courtesies simply
meant her brain was too thoroughly engaged on the
problem before it to leave any room for other considerations.

"First of all," the ops officer began, "we have to bear
in mind that Manty tech systems are still better than ours
across the board. On the other hand, they haven't been
in possession of Adler or Micah long enough to have
deployed their usual sensor platform network. Even if they
had been, their operational patterns around Trevor's Star
indicate their Sixth Fleet is short of platforms just now.
That, at least, is NavInt's interpretation of their increased
use of destroyers and light cruisers as perimeter pickets,
and it makes sense to me, too. If they don't have enough
sensor platforms, they'd have to cover the gaps with ships.
I also think it's a fairly safe bet that if they're short at
someplace as critical as Trevor's Star, they're probably even
shorter in the much lower priority systems in our operational area. If they do have a sensor bottleneck, it's probably
temporary, but until they get it fixed, it offers us a window
of opportunity."

The other members of the staff were leaning forward
as they listened raptly to Foraker and punched notes and
questions into their memo pads for later discussion. And,
for all his feeling that control of the squadron's affairs
somehow eluded him, Everard Honeker leaned forward
with them, for this was the reason he was willing to put
up with Tourville's posturing and defend him against the
occasional charges of having created a "personality cult."
Whatever faults the citizen rear admiral might have, he
was a fighter. In a People's Navy which had far too much
experience with desperate—and losing—defensive fights,

Tourville looked constantly for opportunities to attack. No wonder he'd wanted Foraker for his staff! The two of them were exactly alike in at least one respect, for where all too many of their fellows viewed the Manticorans' superior technology as a fatal disadvantage, Foraker and Tourville saw it as a challenge. They were more concerned with finding ways to exploit any opening *against* the Manties than with seeking ways to protect themselves *from* the Manties, and Honeker would tolerate anything short of outright treason to protect people who actually *wanted* to fight.

"Now," Foraker continued, replacing the star map with a detailed schematic of a hypothetical star system, "let's assume that this is our objective and that the Manties only have about half the sensor platforms they'd really need to cover its perimeter. If *I* were them, I'd put the platforms I did have here, here, and here." Volumes of space within the star system blossomed with tiny red speckles to indicate the areas covered by her theoretical sensors. "This pattern would make optimum *tactical* use of their platforms, but it leaves the system periphery vulnerable, so what I'd suggest would be—"

She went on talking, sketching out her proposed attack plan with bold red arrows, and Everard Honeker smiled in approval as he listened.

• Chapter Nine

GNS *Jason Alvarez's* flag briefing room was on the small
size, compared to that of a battlecruiser or ship of the wall,
but it was well equipped and large enough for Honor's
needs. A little more space between the back of her chair
and the compartment's forward bulkhead would have been
welcome, and inviting anyone in addition to her staff quickly
made it seem badly congested, but she'd had to work under
much less congenial conditions, and at least her chair was
comfortable.

"All right, people," she said now, rapping a knuckle lightly
on the long, narrow table which ran the length of the
compartment. "Let's settle down."

The others found their chairs and slid neatly into them.
Except—inevitably—for Carson Clinkscales, who managed
to trip over what appeared to be his own feet. The ensign
fell to his right, and his left arm, windmilling for balance, took
Lieutenant Commander McGinley's GSN cap off her head.
The heavy peaked cap catapulted across the conference table,
hit the polished surface, slid past Andreas Venizelos' reaching
hand with demonic precision, and struck a carafe of ice water
dead center. The unintentional missile had just enough kinetic
energy to knock the carafe over, and water exploded from it
as the top some steward had neglected to fasten properly
popped clear. Three different people clutched for the carafe,
but none reached it, and Captain Greentree gasped as the
container rolled off the table and an ice-cold fountain
inundated his lap.

The silence which followed was profound, and Clinkscales
stared in horror at the flag captain, waiting for the blast

of outrage which would reduce him to a grease stain on the spot. But the blast didn't come. Greentree simply looked down into his lap, then picked up the (now empty) carafe between thumb and index finger, and extended it gingerly to Lieutenant Mayhew. The intelligence officer took it without comment and carried it to the hatch for disposal while Venizelos and Howard Latham retrieved their electronic memo pads from the small lake on the table, and the flag captain plucked a handkerchief from his tunic pocket and dabbed at his drenched trousers.

"I—" Clinkscales blazed crimson and looked as if he would have preferred dying on the spot. "I-I'm sorry, Captain," he managed to get out. "I don't know— That is—" he swallowed and started around the table "—if you'd let me help—"

"That's quite all right, Mr. Clinkscales," Greentree said. "I know it was an accident, and I can deal with it myself, thank you."

Clinkscales' blush burned even darker, and Honor felt his humiliation. She was certain Greentree hadn't done it intentionally, but his refusal of the flag lieutenant's assistance had come just quickly enough to sound defensive—as if he didn't want the young man anywhere near him. She contemplated saying something herself, but for the life of her, she couldn't think of anything that wouldn't simply make things worse, and she looked up to meet the gaze of the only other person present who wasn't one of her staff officers. Alistair McKeon stood just inside the hatch, gray eyes twinkling as he surveyed the carnage. His wry amusement came clearly over her link to Nimitz, and it appealed to her own sense of the ridiculous. Embarrassing accident or not, no permanent damage had been done, and living with the consequences might actually do Clinkscales some good. The galaxy wasn't going to go around padding its sharp corners for him. Sooner or later he'd either have to stop having accidents or learn to cope with their aftermath gracefully—and without covering fire from his superiors—and so she simply leaned sideways to collect McGinley's cap from the carpet.

"I believe this is yours, Marcia?" she said, and the ops officer smiled at her, tucked it under her left arm, and pressed back against the bulkhead to let Clinkscales squeeze by her. The ensign's broad shoulders drooped miserably as she obviously got herself out of his way, but Honor noticed the gentle, unobtrusive pat of encouragement the lieutenant commander gave him as he passed.

Jasper Mayhew returned to the table with a fresh carafe and a towel. He placed the former on the table and handed the latter to Greentree, then settled back into his own chair with catlike composure as Honor rapped on the table top once more.

"As I was saying, let's settle down," she repeated calmly, and McKeon, as her second-in-command, took the chair facing hers from the far end of the table. Clinkscales sank into his own chair with unmistakable relief at having made it without further disaster, and she suppressed an urge to shake her head.

"Thank you for coming, Alistair," she went on instead, nodding to McKeon. He nodded back just as gravely as if accepting an invitation from a commodore were optional, and she glanced at Greentree. "The reason I wanted you and Thomas present is that we've received official notification that we'll be escorting Convoy JNMTC-Seventy-Six from Grayson to Treadway. I know we discussed this the other night, but we've been given real numbers and destinations to work with now, instead of guesstimates, and we've got some decisions to make. Marcia?"

She nodded to McGinley, and the ops officer leaned forward slightly in her chair.

"According to Command Central, Milady, we're looking at taking a total of twenty vessels from Yeltsin to Casca, then to Quest, Clairmont, Adler, Treadway, and finally home via Candor. All our merchies will be JNMTC units, so we should make fast passages, but we'll have a layover of at least thirty-six hours in Casca to transship cargo. We'll also be detaching one ship there and three more for Clairmont Station. The biggest delivery will be to Adler: two Marine transports and five support ships, but we'll simply detach those ships in passing and continue on to Treadway. We'll drop off three more ships there and pick up four empties headed back to Yeltsin, then spend at least four days at Candor unloading the other seven ships of the original convoy before departing for Yeltsin. Estimated time for the round trip is approximately two months."

She paused, inviting questions. There were none, and Honor nodded for her to continue.

"Obviously, our single greatest concern has to be the possibility of encountering Peep raiders," McGinley went on. "According to our latest intelligence, the People's Navy is in deep trouble on its southern flank. Unfortunately, that intelligence is less definite than I could wish, which leaves room for some differing interpretations. With your permission, Milady, I'll ask Jasper to address this point."

"Certainly. Jasper?"

The Grayson intelligence officer looked even younger than usual, but his blue eyes were serious as he returned his senior officers' combined gazes.

"First of all," he began, "I must stress that, as Commander McGinley's indicated, our intelligence is a lot softer than I'd prefer. We're fairly confident the Peeps haven't managed to scrape up the strength to hold Barnett against serious attack, but they have enough firepower there to prevent us from carrying out any manned deep penetrations or getting recon drones into the inner system, so all we can say with certainty is that our patrols haven't reported the arrival of any substantial number of ships of the wall.

"Our biggest problem is that, for the moment, *we* aren't anywhere near as strong in the sector as we could wish, either. The situation around Trevor's Star has drawn off most of the available Peep tonnage, but it's done the same thing for us, too. Given how many capital ships the final fighting there sent to the repair yards, quieter sectors—including ours—have been raided pretty hard to build up Admiral Kuzak's strength, and drawing in Eighth Fleet's designated units has stripped the cupboard still barer between Yeltsin and Barnett. What that means for us is that our pickets are all relatively light and much too shorthanded for aggressive reconnaissance of Peep-held systems, which means we have to pretty much guess at what's on the other side of the hill."

He paused for a moment to let that settle in, then continued.

"On the basis of the information we do have and the best estimates our analysts can come up with, Command Central feels we can anticipate that most local Peep pickets will be weak—probably no more than a screen of cruisers whose primary function is more to warn Barnett an attacking force is inbound than to mount any serious defense of their station. Command Central also feels Peep system COs will tend to be cautious, since they must be aware that we're planning an eventual move into their command areas in strength. While Central's latest update stops short of predicting that the enemy will adopt a purely defensive posture, it clearly anticipates a high degree of timidity on his part."

"I see." Honor leaned back and pursed her lips. She reached up to rub Nimitz's ears where the 'cat lay stretched across the top of her chair back and let her eyes rest on Mayhew's face. "Should I gather, Lieutenant, that you don't share that anticipation?"

"No, My Lady. I don't." Many a lieutenant would have waffled, but Mayhew shook his head firmly. "According to the Manty Office of Naval Intelligence's last download, the new system commander at Barnett is Admiral Thomas Theisman." Honor felt her eyebrows arch. This was the first she'd heard of that, and the news put a human face on the enemy, for she and Thomas Theisman had met, and she had a high respect for his ability and initiative. "I've studied Theisman's record," Mayhew went on, unaware of his commodore's thoughts, "and he doesn't fit the standard Peep profile. He's a chance-taker. I wouldn't call him rash, but he's proved he's willing to go against the odds when his own judgment tells him to. Sooner or later, that's almost certain to get him shot. He can't be right *all* the time, and the first time he blows an operation, he's done for. But so far he's always managed to deliver, and I don't see him changing his approach now."

"I see," Honor repeated. She rubbed the tip of her nose, then turned to Venizelos and McGinley. "Do you and Marcia agree with Jasper, Andy?"

"On balance, yes," Venizelos replied. "We differ a bit on the specific implications for our escort operation, but I think Jasper's read Theisman pretty well. I also discussed Theisman with Rear Admiral Yu." He paused, and Honor nodded. Like her, Venizelos had fought—and met—Thomas Theisman, but in his last operation as an officer of the People's Navy, Alfredo Yu had handpicked Theisman as his second-in-command. If anyone in Allied service might have insights into what made Theisman tick, Yu was the man.

"According to Admiral Yu," Venizelos said, "Admiral Theisman is a dangerous man. The Admiral described him to me as determined, intelligent, and calculating. He'll study a situation carefully and make his own assessment of it, and wherever possible, he'll act on *his* assessment, even if that requires some creative bending of his orders—which matches my own impression of the man. Frankly, I'm amazed he's lasted this long under the present regime, but I agree with Jasper that Command Central may be making a serious mistake if it expects him to stand passively on the defensive."

"So where do you and Jasper 'differ a bit'?"

"If I may, Milady, I'll take that one," McGinley said, and Honor nodded to her.

"The main difference between us isn't whether or not Theisman will act as offensively as his resources permit so much as it is a question of what resources he *has*. Bearing in mind how weak our own system pickets are in this region, Jasper is afraid that Theisman will launch a series of selective strikes against them. Assuming he actually has the strength for such a strategy, Andy and I certainly agree that it would represent his most effective option, but in light of the much greater threat Trevor's Star represents to the heart of the People's Republic, I can't see the People's Navy dispatching serious numbers of the wall to Barnett. They can't possibly assemble sufficient strength there to keep us from taking it whenever we get around to it, and they know it. Accordingly, I'd expect any reinforcements to consist of fairly light units, vessels which would be both expendable and better suited to screening and *commerce* raiding. Theisman would be forced to commit battlecruisers at the very least to have a realistic chance of taking any of the local systems away from us, but light and heavy cruisers or even destroyers could be used to pounce on our shipping. If I were him, that's precisely what I'd do to get the biggest return on my investment."

"Um." Honor rubbed her nose once more, then quirked an eyebrow at Mayhew.

"Jasper?"

"Commander McGinley's certainly got a point, My Lady," the lieutenant conceded, "but her conclusion rests on two assumptions. One is that the Peeps won't cut loose the battlecruisers needed to take out one of our system pickets, and the other is that the lighter forces available to them would willingly attack our shipping. In response to the first, we can only guess at exactly what higher command authority is likely to assign to Theisman. Yes, they've probably written Barnett off. I know ONI's concluded that, on the basis of available shipping, they can't do anything else, and the logic is compelling. But even if they decide Barnett is expendable, they may make a fight for it anyway. *I* certainly would, if only to compel us to commit the maximum strength against that system and away from operations around Trevor."

He paused, and Honor nodded noncommittally. Mayhew was sticking his neck out by disagreeing with the received wisdom handed down by better paid, higher ranking heads. It took a certain amount of courage—or ego—for a mere lieutenant to dispute ONI's view, but Mayhew's very lack of seniority might actually make it easier for him in at least one sense. He could disagree and offer alternative hypotheses all day long, but he lacked the rank to make any of his interpretations stick. Even if one of his seniors chose to act upon his advice, the ultimate responsibility (and blame) for the outcome would rest not on Mayhew, but on the senior officer in question.

None of which changed the fact that the strategy Mayhew had just sketched out was the same one which Honor would have adopted in the Peeps' place.

"In response to the second point, that lighter Peep units would willingly attack our shipping," the lieutenant resumed, "I'd simply point out that our local shipping patterns have been materially altered to consolidate our escort capability over the past months. We're sending out more ships per convoy, but the total number of *convoys*—and thus potential targets—has been cut in half, which means, theoretically, at least, that the available escort strength per convoy has been doubled. The Peeps may not know that yet, though anyone sent out to raid our shipping lanes will catch on in a hurry. But what if they already *realize* how our deployments are shifting? Command Central is sending us out to escort a single convoy, which means that there will be six heavy cruisers waiting for any raiders. That comes close to matching the strength available to more than a third of our local system pickets, so why go after a moving target? The enemy would have to spread his available strength widely to locate a convoy in hyper, even if he knew its exact schedule, and that very dispersal would mean he was unlikely to have enough combat power to engage its escort if he managed to find it at all. On the other hand, star systems don't dodge around. He knows exactly where they are, and if he does have battlecruisers available *and* chooses to operate them aggressively, he'd be like a spider in a web. If he managed to seize a system, it would be impossible to warn any ships already en route to it until they arrived . . . at which point his *concentrated* strength would be available to take out any escorts before he massacred the merchantmen.

Especially if he could suck them inside the hyper limit to keep them from simply translating out on him."

Honor frowned and rubbed her chin thoughtfully. She considered for several seconds, then lowered her hand to point a long index finger at McGinley.

"If I understand correctly, you disagree with Jasper not over what would constitute a rational Peep strategy but over Theisman's probable resources. Is that correct?"

"Essentially," McGinley agreed. "So far we don't have any reports of attacks on convoys in the area, so I'm also inclined to doubt that the Peeps have caught onto our new shipping patterns yet, but that's a minor point. If, in fact, they have the strength to punch out one of our pickets even temporarily, there's no question but that it would be the smart move on their part. Not only would they get the shot at incoming traffic that Jasper's just described, but they'd also have an excellent opportunity to inflict significant losses on the picket they attacked. I simply find it difficult to believe that they're willing to pour more capital ships down a rat hole for a system they can't hope to hold in the end. And even if they did send him any substantial rein-forcements, I question whether or not Theisman would dare risk them in some sort of unauthorized forward operation."

"Thomas Theisman might fool you, Marcia," Honor murmured. She rocked her chair back and forth for several thoughtful moments, then focused once more on McGinley.

"You may well be right about Barnett's resources," she said, "but I think Jasper has his finger on our worst potential danger. Whether it actually happens or not, we have to assume it's at least possible that the enemy will choose to attack our forward pickets rather than carry out search and destroy operations against convoys between star systems. How do we protect ourselves against both possibilities?"

"If we had a larger escort, I'd vote for the Sarnow Deployment," McGinley replied promptly, and Honor nodded once more.

Any commerce raider knew that the best chance to hit

a merchantman (or a convoy of them) was immediately after it translated from hyper- to normal-space, before its sensors had time to locate potential threats and while its velocity was at its lowest. Since the general volumes in which traffic was likely to make translation could be predicted with a fair degree of accuracy, placing a raider in position to hit merchantmen at their most vulnerable wasn't particularly difficult. Covering all probable target areas might require a goodly number of hulls, but their actual *placement* was straightforward.

By the same token, the best relative position from which to attack a convoy, whether in hyper- or n-space, was from directly ahead of it, where its velocity would carry it straight towards you. The execution of any effective evasion maneuver would require its ships to overcome a potentially enormous relative closing velocity, and no vast, lumbering merchantman, with its commercial grade inertial compensator and impellers, could match the acceleration and maneuverability of a warship. As a consequence, raiders preferred to get ahead of a convoy and let it come to them.

The classic defensive gambit was for the escort commander to place the majority of her strength ahead of her charges, so as to put her warships between them and the most probable axis of threat while one or two pickets watched the rear as a hedge against the lesser threat of a raider overtaking from astern. Against pirates, whose primary goal was to take prizes (and those prizes' cargoes) intact, that remained RMN convoy doctrine, but against *Peep* commerce raiders, the Navy had adopted the new strategy proposed by Vice Admiral Mark Sarnow. Instead of massing the escorts ahead, they were concentrated on the flanks and *astern* of the convoy, with relatively weak scouting elements deployed at least thirty to forty minutes of flight time ahead of the entire formation.

It made sense, given that Peeps, unlike pirates, were interested only in denying a convoy's cargo to the Alliance. They might *prefer* capturing it, but simply destroying it would do the job just as well, so from their perspective, it only made sense to open fire the moment they reached attack range of the merchies, which, in turn, made it imperative for the escorts to keep them *out* of range. The new doctrine placed the escorts' main fighting strength in a position which let them use their superior speed to intercept a threat coming in on any attack vector, and the forward scouting elements served to "sanitize" the convoy's projected course in order to prevent surprises. It also, of course, meant that the ships assigned to break trail were the most exposed units of the escort, but that couldn't be helped, and the scouts should have time to fall back on the main body of the escort before they could be overwhelmed in isolation.

That, at least, was the theory, and Honor's own experience suggested that it should work effectively. Unfortunately, as McGinley had just implied, her understrength squadron lacked the numbers to deploy multiple units ahead without unacceptably weakening the close-in escort. That meant that whoever she put out there was going to be dangerously exposed, with no one to watch his or her back.

She considered briefly, then looked at McKeon.

"Alistair?" she invited, and the heavyset captain leaned forward to brace his forearms on the table.

"I agree that the worst thing the Peeps could do from our perspective would be to punch out one of our system pickets. Commander McGinley may well be right that they don't have the strength to do it, but I think Lieutenant Mayhew is right about Theisman. As you may recall," he smiled wryly, "you and I have both had the pleasure of making his acquaintance. If he's got enough firepower to give him a realistic chance at a system raid, he'll go for it unless someone higher up the chain specifically orders him not to.

"At the same time, I don't think it matters a great deal to us which strategy he adopts. Commander McGinley is correct that a Sarnow Deployment will give us the best coverage against either possibility."

"And just who do we put on point?" Captain Greentree's

question could have been a challenge, worded as it was, but his tone was mild, and he'd cut to the heart of Honor's own concerns. "We don't have enough hulls to put as many as the Book calls for out in front—not unless we reduce our flank strength and defeat the entire point of the deployment," the flag captain went on. "If we had a few destroyers along things would be different; we could put two or three of them up front to cover one another's backs. As it is, though, we'd have to detail a single ship, and whoever we stick out there will be badly exposed. He'll be much too far ahead for us to cover him if he's attacked."

"True enough," McKeon agreed. "But our first responsibility is to the convoy. If it comes right down to it, any escort is expendable, and a Sarnow deployment will stretch the convoy's sensor envelope by a good nine light-minutes. Even those of us who don't have built in FTL coms have recon drones that do, and that means the picket will be able to see any bad guys and report them to the flagship long before they see the flagship. At worst, that should at least let us keep the merchies clear of them; at best, we'll have a pretty fair shot of sucking any weak raiding force into an ambush of our own."

"I don't disagree," Greentree said. "I'm simply asking who we put out in front."

"That's the easy part." McKeon grinned. "I'd say *Prince Adrian* is the only logical choice, wouldn't you?"

Greentree opened his mouth, then closed it, and Honor felt his irritation—not at McKeon, but at McKeon's logic. She not only felt it but understood it, for like Greentree, she would much prefer to take point herself. Position of maximum risk or no, it was also the one from which the escort would most probably have its first glimpse of any oncoming threat. Any good tactician hungered to be able to gauge the situation for herself, not through someone else's reports. Besides, she hated the thought of sending people into any danger she couldn't share with them. It was irrational, and a weakness she knew a flag officer had to learn to overcome, but that didn't make it any less real.

Yet, like Greentree, she knew McKeon was right. The entire point was to extend the squadron's sensor reach and trip any traps in the convoy's path, and if she couldn't be there herself—which she couldn't; her command responsibilities precluded exposing her flagship unnecessarily—McKeon was the best person for the job. Not only was he her second-in-command, but she trusted his judgment implicitly. And, perhaps just as importantly, he knew *her* well enough to be willing to *use* that judgment in a time-critical situation without waiting for permission.

"All right," she said. Her calm soprano gave no sign of the thoughts which had flowed through her mind, and she nodded crisply. "Alistair is right, Thomas. We'll put *Prince Adrian* on point." Greentree nodded, and she switched her gaze back to Venizelos. "From Marcia's original comments, I gather that we've received hard numbers on the convoy. Do we have an actual ship list yet?"

"There are still a couple of blanks, Ma'am," the chief of staff replied. "We should have them filled by fifteen-thirty, though. My understanding is that they're all present in Yeltsin but that Logistics Command is still deciding exactly which ships to load the last of the Samovar garrison's supplies aboard."

"Good. Howard—" she turned to her com officer "—once we have a complete list, I want you to contact the master of each ship on it. Invite him and his exec to a meeting here aboard *Alvarez* at, oh, call it nineteen hundred hours."

"Yes, My Lady."

"Marcia, between now and then I want you and Andy to rough out a Sarnow deployment for the squadron. Assume *Prince Adrian* will take point and assign *Magician* to watch the back door."

"Yes, Ma'am."

Honor sat for a long moment, rubbing her nose once more as she tried to decide if that was everything that needed saying. Then she looked at Mayhew.

"That was a good job of pointing out an alternate

interpretation of ONI's analyses, Jasper. Sometimes we forget to think about the person behind the rank on the other side." Greentree and McKeon nodded firmly, echoing her approval, and she felt the lieutenant's pleasure. Perhaps even more importantly, she also sensed the lack of resentment in Marcia McGinley's emotions. A lot of staff officers would have been angry with a junior who dared not only to disagree with her but actually to convince their commodore that he was right and she was wrong. It was good to know McGinley wasn't one of them.

Honor started to rise, officially bringing the meeting to a close, but then she stopped. There was one other point that needed to be dealt with, and she drew a deep breath and steeled her nerve.

"Carson?"

"Yes, My Lady?" The flag lieutenant seemed to quiver in his chair, as if it required a physical effort not to spring to his feet and snap to attention.

"I'll be inviting the convoy's skippers to join me for supper when they come aboard," she said. "Please get hold of my steward and see to the arrangements."

"Yes, My Lady!" the ensign said sharply, and the burst of determined enthusiasm which flooded from him over Honor's link to Nimitz was almost frightening.

But not, she reflected silently, *as frightening as the potential for disaster in letting Carson anywhere near a table covered with food. If he can make that much mess with a single pitcher of water, what* couldn't *he do with an entire formal dinner? But at least,* she told herself hopefully, *he'll have Mac to ride herd on him. So how bad can it be?*

The answer to her last question suggested itself to her, and she shuddered at the very thought.

• Chapter Ten

"Will you look at *that*," Yuri Bogdanovich murmured almost reverently. "It's actually working!"

"Your surprise is hardly becoming, Yuri," Citizen Rear Admiral Tourville chided from within a cloud of cigar smoke. "And now that I think about it, it displays an appalling lack of confidence in our operations officer."

"You're right, Citizen Rear Admiral." Bogdanovich turned from his contemplation of the main holo sphere to bow in Shannon Foraker's direction. "I'm still surprised, you understand," he went on, "but that's just because the Manties keep sneaking up on *us*. And may I say, Shannon, that it's a pleasure to be the ones doing the sneaking for a change!"

"Here, here!" Karen Lowe muttered, and a chorus of laughter—muted, and mostly a bit more nervous than its authors would care to have admitted—ran around the bridge.

People's Commissioner Honeker listened appreciatively. He heard the anxiety within it, but he also knew how rare *any* sign of levity at a time like this had become for the People's Navy. He wasn't immune to ambition of his own, and once the domestic situation had stabilized enough, he intended to pursue a civilian political career, where having a stint as commissioner to a successful officer like Tourville on his record was going to look very good. Yet in fairness to him, he was more impressed with the citizen rear admiral's ability to motivate people to fight than he was by his own career prospects.

"How much longer, Citizen Commander Foraker?" he asked quietly. Foraker tapped numbers into a keypad, then studied the results for a moment.

183

"Assuming I've estimated their sensor platform availability correctly *and* that they really put the ones they had where I'm predicting, Sir, and assuming NavInt's estimate of their passive sensor capability is close to accurate, they should be in a position to begin picking us up within the next seven and a half hours," she said. "Of course, we're not emitting a thing, which will make their job a lot harder. As far as active sensors are concerned, the only ones I'm picking up at the moment are a long, *long* way outside detection ranges, and they look like standard navigation radars—*civilian* radars—from local intrasystem traffic."

"No active military sensors at all?" Honeker couldn't quite keep the skepticism out of his voice, and Foraker shrugged.

"Sir, any star system's a mighty big fishpond, and our approach course was designed to stay well clear of the ecliptic to avoid blundering into any of the local traffic's sensor envelopes. Unless a starship already has a pretty good idea about where another ship is hiding, its active sensor reach is simply too short for any realistically useful sweeps. That's one of the things that makes the Manties' remotes such pains. Their sensor arrays, signal amplification, and dedicated software are better than any of our shipboard systems can come close to matching, and just to be on the safe side, they like to seed the things so densely and generate so much overlap that active sensors *can* pick up anyone who tries to sneak through. Which doesn't even mention the fact that an intact sensor net lets them shut down their mobile systems completely and rely on relayed data without revealing their own positions. But everything we've seen so far supports the theory that they're short on platforms, and we'll pick up any active sensor emissions long before they can get a useful return off of us."

Honeker's grunt was as much an apology for doubting her as an acceptance of her explanation, for she'd been very careful not to add, "I already *told* you that, dummy!" And the fact was that she *had* explained the entire plan in detail after she, Bogdanovich, and Lowe had worked out the final points.

Tourville's squadron was doing something which was virtually unheard of: moving deeper and deeper into an enemy-held system without a single scout deployed to probe its line of advance. Instead, all four battlecruisers and all of their attached units were gathered into the tightest possible formation and coasting ballistically towards an interception with Samovar . . . and so far, it seemed clear that no one had seen them at all.

It was always possible Bogdanovich and Foraker were wrong about that, Honeker mused. Manty stealth systems were better than those of the People's Navy, and it was at least possible that the entire Allied picket force was headed straight for *Count Tilly* and her consorts at this very moment. It seemed unlikely, however, for as Foraker had just pointed out, so far the squadron had yet to take a single active sensor hit, and only active sensors stood any realistic chance of picking them up.

"What the—?" Lieutenant Holden Singer frowned at his display, then made a tiny adjustment. His frown deepened, and he scratched his nose with a perplexed finger.

"What is it?" Commander Dillinger, HMS *Enchanter*'s executive officer, crossed the bridge to peer over Singer's shoulder.

"Not sure, Sir." Singer stopped scratching his nose and reached to one side, never taking his eyes from the display as he ran his fingers down a bank of touchpad controls with the precision of a blind concert pianist. The display shifted as the heavy cruiser's com lasers queried the other units tied into her tactical net for additional sensor data, and Singer made a disgusted sound. A single data code hung in the display's holo projection, but it wasn't the crisp, clear icon of a known starship. Instead, it was the weak, flickering amber of a possible, completely unidentified contact.

"Well?" Dillinger prompted, and Singer shook his head.

"Probably just a sensor ghost, Sir," he said, but he sounded unsure of his own conclusion.

"What kind of ghost?" Dillinger demanded.

"Sir, if I knew what it was, it wouldn't *be* a ghost," Singer pointed out, and Dillinger inhaled deeply and reminded himself that all tac officers were smartass hotdogs. He should know; he'd come up the tac officer career track himself.

"Then tell me what you *do* know," he said after a moment, speaking with such elaborate patience that Singer had the grace to blush.

"All I know for certain, Sir, is that something twanged the passives aboard one of my remotes about—" he checked the time "—eleven minutes ago. I don't know what it was, I didn't pick it up from here, and no one else in the net saw it at all. Battle Comp's calling it 'an anomalous electromagnetic spike,' which is the computers' way of saying they don't know what it was, either. What it *looked* like was a scrap of an encrypted burst transmission, but there doesn't seem to be anything out there to produce it."

"Is it inside our active envelope—assuming it's really there at all?" Dillinger asked.

"Can't say, Sir. All I've got is a bearing to where something *might* have been. I couldn't even begin to estimate the range. Assuming something really is out there, it's beyond our proximity warning radar, which means it's still at least a quarter million klicks out, but from the bearing on the 'anomalous spike,' it has to have originated in-system from our drone shell. That's all I can tell you for sure."

"I see." Dillinger rubbed his jaw for a moment. Given that none of *Enchanter's* enormously sensitive passive arrays had picked up anything, it seemed most likely that Singer's "ghost" was just that: an electronic glitch with no existence in real space. For it to be anything else would have required a starship to be coasting in-system under total EmCon, and that sort of maneuver took more balls than any Peep CO was likely to boast. Especially after the way Manticoran perimeter sensor platforms had repeatedly spotted incoming hostiles far short of the inner system. Still . . .

"Go active," he said.

Singer glanced up over his shoulder and raised an eyebrow. Commodore Yeargin had specifically instructed her orbiting units to maintain a passive sensor watch only. Active sensors were too short ranged to do much good, anyway, and their only practical function would have been to turn the emitting ships into brilliant electronic beacons for anyone who'd managed to make it past the limited number of platforms her understrength "task group" had been able to deploy. But her orders had included a proviso authorizing officers of the watch to make targeted, short-duration active sweeps if they felt they were required, and Dillinger nodded to Singer to get on with it.

"Aye, aye, Sir," the ops officer said, and reached for his console once more.

"Radar pulse!"

Shannon Foraker's harsh announcement cut through *Count Tilly's* flag bridge like a saw. Despite their confidence in their tac witch, Tourville and his staff (including People's Commissioner Honeker) had felt the tension ratcheting to almost unbearable heights as they swept closer and closer to Samovar. It seemed impossible that they could have gotten so close to a Manty force without being detected . . . unless the enemy's supply of sensor platforms was even smaller than Foraker had estimated.

"Strength?" Tourville snapped.

"Well above detection values," Foraker replied, never taking her eyes from her display as she worked her passive sensors. "They've got us . . . but I've got *them*, too!" She looked up at last and bared her teeth at her commanding officer. "I make it right on two-point-four million klicks, Sir—and I've got a good fix on whoever just pulsed us!"

"Set it up!" Tourville looked at Citizen Lieutenant Fraiser. "Pass the word," he told the com officer. "We launch in thirty seconds!"

✧   ✧   ✧

"My God!"

Holden Singer snapped upright in his chair, eyes wide. It took eight seconds for his radar pulse to reach *Count Tilly* and her consorts, and another eight seconds for it to return. During that time, the Peeps' approach speed had cut the range by over a million kilometers . . . and brought them well into missile range. It took the lieutenant another two seconds to realize what he was seeing and shout a warning, and it took Commander Dillinger another second and a half to order the General Quarters alarm sounded. In all, twenty seconds elapsed between the time Tourville passed his order to fire and the moment the atonal, two-toned howl of the alarm actually began to sound.

HMS *Enchanter*'s crew had barely begun to race to their battle stations when four battlecruisers, eight heavy cruisers, and six light cruisers, with a combined total of fifty-six missile pods on tow behind them, opened fire. Peep missiles were less efficient than those of the RMN, but in compensation, Peep warships mounted more tubes . . . and so did their missile pods.

By the time Singer's assistant tac officer flung herself into the chair beside his, over nine hundred missiles were in space and streaking for his ship.

"*Yessss!*"

Citizen Captain Bogdanovich's exultant, sibilant whisper said it all as Tourville and his staff watched their massive salvo stream towards the enemy. Even as the missiles went out, Tourville's engineers were bringing up his ships' impellers and sidewalls, for there was no longer any reason to hide. Unlike the Manties, Tourville's officers had known their drives and defensive systems would be needed, and they'd been at standby for over fifteen hours, but even with hot impeller nodes, they would need at least another thirteen minutes to bring their wedges up.

Yet that still put them far ahead of the Manties, for the Manties *hadn't* known this was coming. Their missile-defense fire control started to come on-line, blossoming on Shannon Foraker's display in bursts of light, but their passive defenses could never be brought up in time. And against the hurricane of fire coming at them, all their radar and lidar could really do was provide targeting beacons for her missiles' onboard seekers.

Commodore Frances Yeargin hurled herself onto her flag bridge almost before the lift doors opened. She hadn't waited to don her skinsuit; she came charging out of the lift in shirt sleeves, without even her tunic . . . just in time to see the first laser heads detonate in the depths of her visual display.

Lester Tourville stared into the master plot, unable even now to truly believe what it showed. A *Manty* task group had been caught totally unprepared, and that wasn't supposed to happen. But it had, and Shannon's plan had taken merciless advantage of the Manties' fatal over-confidence. He watched targeting codes blossom and change as the missiles reported back over their telemetry links. They were on their own, but Foraker had told them precisely what to look for, and the steady procession of fire control systems coming on-line before them beckoned to their homing sensors. The massive flight of missiles began to spread and disperse, apportioning itself among the victims in its path.

It wasn't a perfect distribution, a corner of his brain noted. One or two of those ships were going to get off with no more than a dozen or so birds, while others were going to be attacked by scores of them, but it didn't really matter. Shannon was already reprogramming the missiles waiting in her broadside tubes, and even as Tourville watched, a second salvo—much smaller than the first, but carefully targeted on the handful of Manties who might survive the first one—spat from his ships.

For all intents and purposes, surprise was total. Commodore Yeargin's crews were still scrambling frantically to their stations when the first wave came in. Of her six heavy cruisers, two never got their point defense on-line at all. Three more managed—somehow—to bring their laser clusters up under computer control, but only *Enchanter* got off a single salvo of counter-missiles. Not that it made much difference. One hundred and six incoming missiles were picked off before they reached attack range; the other eight hundred and sixty-two raced in to twenty-thousand kilometers and detonated in rippling succession.

Nuclear explosions pocked space, each one generating a thicket of bomb-pumped X-ray lasers. It wasn't even a massacre, for there was nothing—absolutely *nothing*— between those lasers and their targets. It took less than four seconds for all eight hundred-plus warheads to attack. Sixteen seconds later, Shannon Foraker's second salvo streaked down on the stunned, mangled survivors, and when the last of *them* detonated, the Manticoran Alliance had lost six RMN heavy cruisers, three RMN and seven GSN light cruisers, and nine destroyers . . . without getting a single shot off at their attackers.

Commander Jessica Dorcett sat frozen in her command chair, staring with numb incomprehension at the impossible tactical imagery. Hers was the senior ship of the destroyer division assigned to cover the main processing platform of the Adler System's asteroid extraction industry. The platform's Peep-built technology wasn't much by Manticoran standards, but it was still an important facility, and it was presently over fifty light-minutes from Samovar, well away from the course the enemy must have followed on his way in-system. Which meant that Dorcett's three ships had survived . . . and that she was now the system's senior officer. It was up to her to decide what had to be done, but what in God's name *could* she do?

The task group was gone. Only her own division remained, and it would be less than useless against the force decelerating towards the fresh wreckage orbiting Samovar. She had just witnessed the most crushing, one-sided defeat in the history of the Royal Manticoran Navy, and there was nothing at all she could do about it.

A dull ache told her her teeth were clamped in a deathlike rictus, and she sucked in an enormous breath and made her jaw relax. Then she shook herself, like a dog throwing water from its coat, and turned to her exec. Lieutenant Commander Dreyfus was still staring at the plot, his normally dark face pale, and Dorcett cleared her throat loudly.

Dreyfus twitched as if she'd stuck a pin into him, then closed his eyes for just a moment. When he opened them again, the shock had been dragged under a ruthless pretense of control, and he met his captain's gaze squarely.

"Pass the word. We'll hyper out to Clairmont ourselves. *Rondeau* and *Balladeer* will head for Quest and Treadway respectively."

"But—" Dreyfus paused. "That won't leave anyone to picket the system and keep an eye on them, Ma'am," he pointed out quietly.

"We don't have that luxury." Dorcett's tone was as bleak as her expression. "I don't know what the schedule was, but I do know GHQ's already detailed reinforcements for this system. The warships will probably be coming in in ones and twos, which is bad enough, but Logistics Command has supply ships and troop transports in the pipeline, as well. Individual warships won't stand a chance against a force that size, but at least they may have the speed to run for it. Transports won't . . . but Logistics Command is bound to stage them through Clairmont, Quest, or Treadway. Which means we have to catch them in one of those systems and warn them off in time. Besides—" she managed a death's head grin "—we're all there is. Someone's got to alert the other local pickets about what's happened here, and the only people who can do that are us."

"Yes, Ma'am." Dreyfus beckoned to the com officer, and

Dorcett heard the urgent, low-pitched murmur of his voice as he passed her orders on. She knew she should be listening to be sure he'd gotten those orders right, but they'd served together for over a T-year. He wasn't the sort to make mistakes, and even if he had been, it was physically impossible for her to look away from her display and the icons of the Peep warships settling into orbit around Samovar.

Compared to the tonnages routinely destroyed when walls of battle clashed, the loss of Commodore Yeargin's task group would hardly be noticed, but Dorcett knew tonnage was the least of what had been lost here. Even the personnel casualties, terrible as they must have been, were secondary to what she'd just seen. It was the speed—the brutal, overwhelming power and efficiency—with which the task group had been killed that mattered. That was what was going to stick in the craws of the Alliance and, especially, the Manticoran Navy.

This wasn't the first victory the Peeps had won, but its totality put it in a category all its own. A category the RMN had believed was reserved for *it*, not for the clumsy, outclassed stumblebums of the People's Navy.

Well, Dorcett told herself grimly, *we were wrong. And from the salvo density, they had to have been using missile pods, too. They outthought us, they outplanned us,* and *they outshot us, and if they can do that here, then where* else *can they pull it off?*

She didn't know. The only two things she *did* know were that it was her job to spread the warning before more ships sailed into the trap this system had just become . . . and that whatever else happened in her career, she and every officer aboard her three ships would always be known as the people who'd watched the worst disaster in Manticoran naval history and done nothing to prevent it. It wasn't their fault. There was nothing they *could* have done. But that wouldn't matter, and she knew it.

"*Rondeau* and *Balladeer* are ready to pull out, Ma'am,"

Lieutenant Commander Dreyfus reported quietly, and Dorcett nodded.

"Very well, Arnie. Send the self-destruct code to the sensor platforms, then get us moving," she said.

• Chapter Eleven

At his age, Howard Clinkscales was out of the habit of feeling ill at ease in public. He'd begun his career as a Sword armsman recruit—not even an officer cadet, but an enlisted man—sixty-seven T-years ago and climbed to the rank of brigadier in palace security by age thirty-six. By the time of the Mayhew Restoration, he'd been commanding general of Planetary Security, a post he'd held under Benjamin IX's father, as well, and an unofficial member of the royal family. Along the way, he'd dealt with street criminals, serial killers and other psychotics, assassination plots, and treason, and taken them all in stride.

Even more surprisingly, he'd also learned to take the monumental social changes of his home world in stride, which was something no one who'd known him before Grayson joined the Alliance would ever have predicted. He'd been almost eighty when the treaty was signed, and a more hidebound reactionary would have been hard to find. Not even his best friends would have called Clinkscales a brilliant man—he was no fool, certainly, and he liked to think he'd learned a *few* things in eight decades, but no one had ever considered him a genius—and that was one reason so many people had expected him to reject any sort of accommodation with the reforms rolling through the society he'd known since boyhood. But those people had overlooked the three qualities which had carried him so high from such humble beginnings: inexhaustible energy, an unyielding sense of duty, and an iron-bound integrity.

It was the last quality which had turned the trick in the end, for his was a *personal* integrity. Many people could be conscientiously honest in dealing with public responsibilities or other people; Clinkscales was one of those much rarer individuals whose integrity extended to himself, and that meant he could no more shut his eyes to the truth just because it was unpalatable than he could have flown without a counter-grav belt.

That was why Benjamin IX had appointed him as Honor Harrington's regent, for his sense of duty had been the Protector's insurance policy. It was unthinkable that Howard Clinkscales would do anything less than his best to serve his Steadholder and her steading, and the fact that the planet's other conservatives knew he shared their philosophical leanings made him uniquely valuable as Harrington Steading's regent. If *he* could do his duty and live with the changes he personally detested, then *they* could, as well— or that, at least, had been Benjamin's theory.

It hadn't quite worked out that way, however. Oh, Clinkscales' role as regent had undoubtedly had an impact on the more reasonable among Grayson's conservatives, but it hadn't prevented the true fanatics from plotting against Honor and the Mayhew reforms. Of course, realistically speaking it was unlikely that *anything* could have dissuaded people whose minds were that far gone, so expecting his appointment to slow *them* down had probably been wishful thinking, anyway. But that appointment *had* had one effect which Benjamin had never anticipated and would, in fact, have denied was possible. It hadn't precisely turned Clinkscales into a radical reformer (to be honest, the mind still boggled at the thought of him in that role), but he'd actually come to see the changes in his world as beneficial. And that was because his position had brought him into regular contact with Honor Harrington at the same time it required him to superintend the mountain range of details involved in creating the first new Grayson steading in over seventy-two T-years. Not only had he been forced to confront the reality of a woman whose capability, courage, and—perhaps most importantly of all—sense of duty at least matched his own, but he'd also been forced to actually work out the details of *implementing* the reforms as he labored on the blank canvas which was to become Harrington Steading.

It was a tribute to him that he could make such major adjustments to his thinking so late in life, although he didn't see it that way himself. As far as *he* was concerned, he was still a conservative trying to mitigate the more extreme demands of the reformers, but that was all right. He was actually quite a few strides in front of the curve, and Honor had been gently amused on more than one occasion by his irate reaction to "troublemakers" who tried to get in the way and slow things back down.

If anyone could have screwed up the nerve to ask him why he supported the changes, his answer would have been simple enough. It was his duty to his Steadholder. If pressed, he would have admitted (not without a choleric expression and a fearsome glower) that his support stemmed not simply from duty, but from *devotion* to a woman he'd come to respect deeply. What he would *not* have admitted was that he had come to view his Steadholder through a curiously mixed set of lenses, as a warrior, a leader, his personal liege lady . . . and also as one of his own daughters. He was *proud* of her, as proud as if she actually were his own child, and he would have killed anyone who dared to say so, for like so many people who care deeply, Howard Clinkscales went to great lengths to conceal his feelings from the world. Emotions had been dangerous chinks in a policeman's armor, and so the man who had become the commander-in-chief of a planet's security forces had learned to hide them, lest they be used against him. It was a habit he had never learned to break . . . but that didn't mean *he* was unaware of what he felt.

And that was part of the reason he felt uneasy at this particular public function, for his Steadholder should have been here for it, and his mental antennae insisted that the reasons she'd given him for departing again so quickly weren't her actual motives. Oh, all of them were true enough—he'd never known Honor Harrington to lie; in fact, he wasn't at all certain she knew *how* to—but they hadn't been the real cause for her decision, and that worried him. She was his Steadholder, and it was his job to know when something worried *her* and to deal with it. Besides, if the fanatics plotting against her under the late, unlamented Lord Burdette and Brother Marchant hadn't been enough to drive her off-planet, anything that *could* do the trick obviously needed seeing to.

But even that was only a partial explanation for his uneasiness, and he drew a deep breath and admitted the rest of it to himself as he watched the shuttle descend. He might have become more comfortable with the reforms around him, but at heart he was still an old-fashioned Grayson patriarch. He'd learned to admit that there were women in the galaxy, including quite a few homegrown Graysons, who were at least as capable as he was, but in the final analysis, that was an *intellectual* admission, not an emotional one. He had to have personal contact with a woman, actually see her demonstrate her abilities, before his emotions made the same connection. It was foolish of him, not to mention patronizing, and he knew it, yet it was nonetheless true. He did his best to overcome it, and much as it might affect his attitudes he managed to keep it from affecting his *actions*, but he'd come to the conclusion that it was too fundamental a part of his societal programming for him ever to be fully free of it. And that was a problem today, for the shuttle about to touch down contained a person his brain knew had to be one of the smartest, most capable individuals he was ever likely to meet . . . and she was a woman. The fact that she was also the mother of his Steadholder and thus, whether she knew it or not, one of the two or three hundred most important people on the entire planet, didn't help, and neither did where she had been born and raised.

Dr. Allison Chou Harrington was a native of Beowulf in the Sigma Draconis System, and Beowulf's society had a reputation for . . . liberal mores which would have curled a *Manticoran's* hair, much less a Grayson's. Clinkscales was fairly certain (or, at least, he *thought* he was) that that reputation had grown in the telling, but there was no denying that Beowulf was as famed for the many—and imaginative—marital and sexual arrangements of its citizens as it was for providing the human race's best medical researchers, and—

The shuttle touched down, and the opening hatch chopped off his thoughts. He watched the ramp extrude itself, then turned his head to smile wryly at Miranda LaFollet. She smiled back with a mixture of amusement and compassion, and the treecat sitting beside her bleeked a laugh of his own. Clinkscales was still getting to know Farragut, but he'd already concluded that his sense of humor was entirely too much like Nimitz's. Worse, Nimitz had spent forty years interacting with humans, which gave him a certain polish Farragut had yet to acquire, and the younger 'cat had quickly demonstrated a taste for practical jokes—usually of the low variety. But at least Miranda had spoken to him very firmly about the need to behave in public, and Clinkscales allowed himself to hope that her admonitions would have some effect.

He realized he'd allowed thoughts of Farragut to distract him when the band broke into the Harrington Anthem. Only a steadholder was greeted with the Steadholders' March, but any member of Lady Harrington's family was properly saluted with her steading's anthem, and a shouted command brought the honor guard to attention. The perfectly turned out members of the Harrington Guard formed two ruler-straight rows of green-on-green uniforms, flanking the path from the foot of the shuttle pad to the terminal escalator, and a very small figure paused in midstride as the music surprised her.

Clinkscales blinked as he saw Allison Harrington for the first time. He'd known she was shorter than her daughter, but he'd been unprepared for a person *this* tiny. Why, she was actually shorter than the majority of *Grayson* women, and the thought that she had produced the Steadholder who towered over virtually all her steaders—including one Howard Clinkscales—was hard to accept.

It was obvious no one had warned her to expect a formal welcome, and Clinkscales swore silently at himself for not attending to that detail himself. Of course, it was likely that the Steadholder wouldn't have arranged for so much formality if she'd been here. She still had difficulty thinking of herself *as* a steadholder, and she probably would have just hopped into an air car, flown over, and picked Dr. Harrington up without any of what she insisted upon calling "all this ridiculous hullabaloo." Clinkscales, unfortunately, couldn't do that without offering what might well have been construed as an insult, but he *could* have ensured that Dr. Harrington knew what was coming.

Yet it was too late for that, and her brief hesitation was over before it became obvious. She squared her shoulders and moved more sedately down the pad stairs, and Clinkscales and Miranda went to meet her. Miranda lacked the strength which allowed Lady Harrington to carry Nimitz on her shoulder, but Farragut seemed content enough to walk at her side, and he flirted his tail right regally while he padded along between her and Clinkscales as if the music and the honor guard were no more than *his* just due.

The welcoming party timed things almost perfectly, arriving at the foot of the stairs no more than a stride or two before Dr. Harrington stepped off the bottom tread. She looked up at her greeters, and almond eyes uncannily like her daughter's sparkled with impish delight.

"You must be Lord Clinkscales," she said, extending her hand to him, and dimpled as he bent to kiss it formally rather than shaking it.

"At your service, My Lady," he told her, and her dimples grew.

"'My Lady'?" she repeated. "Goodness, I see Honor was right. I *am* going to like it here!" Clinkscales' eyebrows arched, but she turned to Miranda before he could speak again. "And you're Miranda, I'm sure," she said, reaching out to shake the younger woman's hand. "And unless I'm mistaken," she went on, bending to hold her hand out to the treecat, "this is Farragut." The 'cat shook her hand in brisk, Nimitz-like fashion, and she laughed. "It *is* Farragut. Am I to assume that one of you two has had the sometimes questionable good fortune to be adopted?"

"I have, My Lady," Miranda admitted. She smiled as she spoke, but Dr. Harrington heard the softness—the persistent echo of wonder—in her voice and straightened. She reached out and rested a hand on Miranda's shoulder, squeezing gently.

"Then I'm very happy for you," she said.

"Thank you, My Lady."

Clinkscales listened to the exchange. Under the old-fashioned rules of his youth, it would have been most improper for Miranda, a mere female, to take the lead in greeting an important visitor. Of course, under the old rules, the visitor in question would almost certainly have been a man, not a woman, and the old rules didn't apply anymore, anyway. And just at the moment, he was happy that was the case, for it gave him an opportunity to stand back and size up Harrington's guest.

A single glance would have been enough to identify her as the Steadholder's mother. It was the eyes, especially, he thought, those huge, dark, almond eyes, yet there was more to it. Dr. Harrington's face had a delicate loveliness, a perfection of feature and proportion which was just sufficiently *im*perfect to prove it was natural, not the product of biosculpt. Lady Harrington shared the same features on an almost point-by-point basis, but what was delicate in *Doctor* Harrington was too bold, too strongly carved, for classical beauty in Lady Harrington. It was as if someone had taken all the undeniable strength in her mother's features and distilled it down, planing away the delicacy—the "softness"—to bare the falcon hiding beneath, yet the kinship was there for anyone to see.

But there were differences, as well. For one thing, Dr. Harrington was actually two years older than Clinkscales, and even now that was hard for his emotions to accept. He'd gotten used to the Steadholder's age, but at least she was still younger than he was. Her mother wasn't, despite her long dark hair, untouched by a single streak of white, and youthful, unlined complexion, and he suspected that this was one mental adjustment he was going to find it difficult to make. At least she *did* look older than her daughter, but the prolong process had originated on Beowulf, and Allison Harrington was one of the very first second-generation recipients. That meant she looked several years younger than Miranda, and the roguish sparkle in her eyes made Clinkscales acutely nervous.

He was being silly, he told himself firmly. Whatever she might look like, this woman was almost ninety T-years old! She was also an enormously respected doctor, one of the top two or three geneticists of the Star Kingdom of Manticore, *and* the mother of a steadholder. The *last* thing she was going to do was contemplate any action which might arouse the merest wisp of a potential scandal. Yet firmly as he lectured himself, he couldn't quite ignore those wickedly gleaming eyes . . . or the way she was dressed.

Howard Clinkscales had never seen the Steadholder in civilian Manticoran clothing. When not in uniform, she'd always dressed in Grayson styles here on Grayson, but her mother was another matter entirely. She wore a short-waisted, bolero-style jacket of a deep royal blue over a tailored blouse of cream-colored Old Earth silk which must have cost several hundred Manticoran dollars . . . and, for all its opacity, was deplorably thin. Her jewelry was simple but exquisite, its worked silver contrasting with her sandalwood complexion, and her elegantly styled slacks matched her jacket.

No Pre-Alliance Grayson woman would ever have been seen in public in garments which revealed her figure with such uncompromising frankness, and Clinkscales couldn't even console himself with the thought that it was a uniform. No one could have complained about Lady Harrington's RMN uniform (well, not *legitimately* . . . which hadn't prevented some of the real reactionaries from doing so anyway) when she wasn't responsible for its styling. But Doctor Harrington didn't have that excuse, and—

Now just one damned minute, Howard! he told himself sternly. *This woman doesn't* need *an "excuse"* . . . *and she wouldn't need one even if she* weren't *Lady Harrington's mother! There is absolutely nothing "indecent" about her appearance—except, perhaps, in your own fool mind—and even if there* were, *she has every possible right to dress according to Manticoran standards. If we're such a parochial, backward planet that we can't accept that, then the problem is ours, not hers!*

He inhaled deeply, feeling an odd sort of relaxation flow through him with the oxygen as he took himself to task. In a way, he was almost relieved that he'd let his spinal-reflex social programming get out of hand, because calling it to heel had helped settle his mind. Yet for all that, he couldn't *quite* stamp out the last, flickering glimmers of uneasiness.

It was her eyes, he thought again. It was the sparkle in those eyes so like and yet so unlike his Steadholder's. Grayson was a planet where female births outnumbered male by three to one, and where the only respectable female career for close to a thousand years had been that of wife and mother. That meant competition for mates had always been fierce, even with the Grayson practice of polygamy, and for all their decorous behavior, women had waged the battle between the sexes (and against their competitors) with a will. That was what worried Howard Clinkscales, for he'd seen exactly that same sparkle in countless female eyes over the years. Usually those eyes had been very young, looking forward to the glories of conquest with all the energy and passion of youth. But even though Allison Harrington's eyes were very young *looking,* they also held the confident assurance of long experience and a dangerously wicked sense of amusement.

Howard Clinkscales had no doubt that he would soon discover that Dr. Harrington was just as capable in her field as her daughter was in *hers,* but it was already obvious that she was *very* different from Lady Harrington in other ways. He was surprised to admit it, but a part of him was actually looking forward to watching her confront the conservatives. The rest of him cringed at the very thought, but that tiny inner part liked the twinkle in her eye, her obvious gusto for living, and her refusal to be pinned down and squeezed into anyone else's box.

It might turn out to be a rough ride, but he suddenly realized that he had no doubts at all about the outcome. There were two of them, after all, and between them, Doctor Harrington and the Steadholder clearly had the rest of the planet outnumbered.

"—and this is your office, My Lady," Miranda said, leading the way into the large, palatially furnished room.

Allison Harrington followed her and stopped, looking around and raising both eyebrows at the sheer luxury of its appointment. And not just in terms of comfort, either, she thought. The desk's built-in computer and communication interfaces were better even than those she had at home on Sphinx, but that wasn't really a surprise. Honor had promised her the best equipment, and she'd kept her word. The Doctor Jennifer Chou Genetic Clinic—Honor had chosen the name to honor her maternal grandmother— had the finest facilities Allison had ever seen. Her daughter had spared no expense, and Allison felt a quiet glow of pride in her. She knew Honor's personal fortune had grown to a point which made all of this easily affordable, but she wondered how many other people it would have occurred to to make the investment in the first place. It wasn't as if Honor were going to see any return on it, after all . . . except, of course, for the thousands of children who would grow up strong and healthy as a direct result of it.

"I hope you like it, My Lady," Miranda said, and Allison blinked, then gave her head a tiny shake as she realized she'd been standing there gathering wool. Miranda looked a little anxious, and Allison smiled.

"Oh, I *like* it all right!" she assured her guide. "Honor promised I would, and she's always been a truthful sort of girl." Her eyes danced at Miranda's expression as she referred to Honor as a "girl." Well, it wouldn't do these people a bit of harm to have someone take a little starch out of Honor's reputation. Allison knew her daughter well enough to know that too much deference would be suffocating to her.

Besides, she told herself cheerfully, *the girl's always taken life too seriously. It'll do her good if she gets back to find out I've made a spectacle of myself!*

She smothered a giggle at the thought. Like Honor, she hated the way she sounded when she giggled. Both of them were convinced it made them sound like schoolgirls, and Allison's small stature only made it worse. Not, she reflected complacently, that anyone who'd ever gotten a good look at her would mistake her for a child. That thought threatened another giggle attack, but she suppressed it firmly and waved a reassuring hand at Miranda as the Grayson regarded her anxiously.

Poor girl probably thinks I'm having some sort of attack! I wonder what she'd think if she knew I was planning *an attack, instead?*

Allison took several minutes to examine the office carefully, but only a part of her attention was on desks and coffee tables and credenzas. She was thinking about her sixty years in the Star Kingdom and rubbing gleeful mental hands together as she contemplated yet more worlds—literally—to conquer.

Allison Harrington knew perfectly well how the rest of the galaxy regarded those libertine Beowulfans. She sometimes wondered just how her home world had ended up as the uncontested holder of the Galaxy's Most Decadent Planet Title, given that Old Earth, for one, was every bit as sophisticated and "libertine" as Beowulf, but the universe worked in mysterious ways. Perhaps it was because of Sigma Draconis' unrivaled reputation in the life sciences. Beowulf's invention of the prolong process was only the most spectacular of its contributions to the health and longevity of the human race, which meant Dr. Harrington's home world had produced a direct impact on every human being anywhere, second only to that of Old Earth herself, so perhaps it was inevitable that natives of Beowulf should somehow acquire larger-than-life status in the eyes of outworlders. Which still didn't explain why everyone had fastened on the planet's sexual practices instead of, say, Sigma Draconis' systemwide passion for grav-ski polo!

But whatever the reasons, Allison had known she would be entering another world—figuratively, as well as literally—when she fell in love with a scholarship student at Semmelweiss University named Alfred Harrington. Alfred had hardly been an untutored, gawking yokel, of course. The Star Kingdom had been one of the wealthiest, most technically advanced interstellar powers, certainly of those outside the Solarian League, for centuries, and its capital planet was probably as sophisticated as Beowulf itself. But Alfred wasn't *from* the planet of Manticore; he was from Sphinx, and Sphinx was undoubtedly the most straitlaced of the three habitable worlds of the Manticore Binary System. He'd been almost painfully earnest in explaining that to her—not because he wanted her to change to satisfy his home world's sometimes parochial standards, but because he was on a military scholarship that committed him to a minimum of fifteen years naval service. He would have no choice but to return to the Star Kingdom to fulfill that commitment, so if she accepted his proposal of marriage, she was going to find herself confronting the society from which he sprang.

If he'd been one bit less earnest, she would have smiled, patted him on the head, and assured him that she was all grown up. As it was, she'd been too touched by his concern to let her amusement show, and she'd assured him with admirable gravity that she appreciated his warning and that, yes, she believed she *could* survive in the boondocks if she truly had to.

And, of course, things hadn't proven nearly as onerous as one might have feared from his descriptions. The fact was that Beowulfans were no more "libertine" than anyone else; they simply declined to pass judgment or declare that any single lifestyle, regardless of who sanctioned it, was the one true way, and Allison would never have accepted Alfred's proposal if she'd had any intention of pursuing a lifestyle which would distress him. Nor would she have accepted it if she'd believed he would expect her to squeeze herself into one which distressed *her*. That didn't prevent her from feeling that Sphinxians were much too sexually repressed, nor had it kept her from worrying—a lot—over Honor's total lack of a sex life prior to Paul Tankersley, but she'd never felt any actual temptation to be anything but monogamous.

Not that she'd exactly gone out of the way to make that fact public. The mere fact that she was from—*gasp!*—Beowulf had been enough to earn her sidelong glances from the more puritanical of Sphinx's populace, and her mischievous streak had been totally unable to overlook the possibilities that offered. After almost seventy years honing her skills, she could play a prude like a Stradivarius, and she took a devilish delight in doing so. It was so much *fun* to play to their prejudices and stereotypes and come as close as she possibly could to the edge without ever *quite* stepping over it. Besides, as a physician, she owed it to her critics. A little apoplexy from time to time elevated the pulse and improved the circulatory system.

Of course, she wouldn't dream of doing anything to embarrass Honor—well, not seriously, anyway. A *little* embarrassment would probably be good for her. Following Paul's death and Honor's duel with Pavel Young, Allison had finally found out about the episode at the Academy which had done Honor's self-image such crippling damage. She understood a lot of things which her own upbringing—and Honor's reticence—had prevented her from seeing at the time, but her daughter still seemed far too serious and emotionally detached. Paul had been dead for over five T-years after all, and deeply as he and Honor had loved one another, it was time she got on with her life. So if she needed something to shake her up a little, well, it was a mother's duty to look out for her daughter, wasn't it?

And if *Sphinx* had looked at her askance for being from Beowulf, she could just imagine how Honor's Graysons were going to approach her! She was pleased that Miranda, at least, seemed comfortable around her, because she'd already realized how critical Miranda was—despite her official title of "maid"—to the functioning of Harrington House and the entire steading. If someone that important to Honor *hadn't* been comfortable with her, Allison would have expended however much effort it took to put her at ease. As it was, she rather suspected she would find it easy to enlist Miranda as an ally and an accomplice when she began her assault on the *rest* of Grayson.

And, she thought almost dreamily, with Honor back in space, just think of all the time she'd have to do it right.

But that brought another point back to her mind, and she seated herself in the comfortable chair behind the desk and waved Miranda into the one facing her across the coffee table. Farragut flowed up into the Grayson woman's lap as soon as she was seated, and Allison smiled wryly.

"I remember when Honor first brought Nimitz home," she said. "You might not believe it to look at her now, but her growth spurt came late, and third-generation prolong slows things down even more. She was—oh, sixteen, I think, before she started shooting up, and when Nimitz first adopted her, he was almost as long as she was. But she insisted on carrying him *everywhere*. For a while, I thought his legs were going to atrophy completely!"

"Farragut isn't quite *that* bad, My Lady," Miranda said with a smile, rubbing his ears while he purred loudly.

"No, he isn't," Allison agreed. "Or not *yet*, anyway. Treecats are a shamelessly hedonistic lot, though, so watch yourself."

"I will, My Lady," Miranda promised with a smile, and Allison tipped her chair back.

"I'd like you to do me a favor, Miranda," she said. "Well, two of them, actually."

"Of course, My Lady. What are they?"

"The first is to cut back on the 'My Ladies,'" Allison said, and grinned impishly at Miranda's expression. "Oh, I'm not offended or anything. It's just that I've spent all my life as a commoner. I realize Honor's gone and changed all that as far as you folks here on Grayson are concerned, but I keep wondering who you're actually talking to!"

Miranda gazed at her for a moment, then leaned back in her own chair and crossed her legs, cradling Farragut against her chest.

"That's may be harder than you think, M—Doctor," she said finally. "Your daughter is a steadholder—the first *female* steadholder ever—and the modes of address for steadholders and their families are part of the bedrock of Grayson's formal etiquette. Of course, we've had to make some adaptations. Before Lady Harrington, the only proper address for a steadholder was 'My *Lord*,' so that had to change, but getting people to change the *rest* of it . . ." She shook her head. "Let's just say that Graysons can be a little stubborn, Doctor."

"If it won't sprain your tongue, you might try 'Allison' or even 'Alley,' at least when there's just the two of us and we're off-duty," Allison pointed out. Miranda colored slightly at her astringent tone, but then she smiled and Allison smiled back. "And I do believe I've heard a little something about Grayson stubbornness from Honor. Which," she added with some asperity, "is a case of the pot calling the kettle black! But I figure if you're not any stubborner than *she* is, and if we start gradually and work at it steadily, we should have even Graysons properly reprogrammed in, oh, a century or so."

Miranda surprised herself with a laugh, and Allison grinned at her. But then her grin faded, and she let her chair come upright to lean forward and rest her elbows on her new desk while she looked at Miranda intently.

"As for the second favor," she said in a much more serious voice, "I wonder if you could tell me why Honor left so much sooner than planned."

"I beg your pardon, M—Allison?"

"You did that very well," Allison complimented her.

"Did what?" Miranda asked.

"Sounded totally surprised by the question," Allison explained, and this time Miranda's blush was dark. "Aha! There *was* something, wasn't there?"

"Not really," Miranda said. "Or, at least, not anything she discussed with me."

"'Discussed'?" Allison repeated, and in that moment she sounded very like her daughter. They both had that habit of pouncing on the most important parts of any sentence, Miranda thought, and wondered exactly what she could— or, for that matter, *should*—say without violating her Steadholder's confidence. The fact that Lady Harrington had never actually said a word to her about it only made the decision harder, and she bent to press her cheek against Farragut's head while she considered it.

"My Lady," she said finally, in a formal tone, "I'm your daughter's personal maid. As much as Lord Clinkscales, or my brother Andrew, I have an obligation to respect and guard her confidence from anyone—even her mother."

The seriousness of her response widened Allison's eyes. It confirmed her already high opinion of Miranda's integrity, but it also suggested that there had, indeed, been a reason for Honor's sudden departure. She'd suspected there must have, for she knew how much Honor had looked forward to welcoming her to Grayson and personally showing her around the clinic. The fact that Honor hadn't written to warn her that she would be away was only another sign that whatever had happened must have come up suddenly, but as she gazed at Miranda's face, she realized that she wasn't going to discover what it had been from her daughter's maid.

"All right, Miranda," she said after several seconds. "I won't press you about it—and thank you for your loyalty to Honor." Miranda nodded slightly, the gesture thanks more for the promise not to push her than for the implicit compliment, and Allison nodded back, then stood.

"In the meantime, however," she said briskly, "I understand we're supposed to join Lord Clinkscales and his wives for dinner this evening?"

"Yes, M—Allison. And I hope you won't be offended, but I simply wouldn't dare address you by name in front of Lord Clinkscales." Miranda feigned a shiver of terror, and Allison laughed.

"Oh, don't worry about *that*, dear! I had something else in mind."

"Oh?" Miranda cocked her head as her guest's tone rang warning bells, and Allison smiled wickedly.

"Certainly. You see, I haven't had time to as much as try on a Grayson gown, so I'm going to have to choose something to wear from my Manticoran wardrobe, and I need advice." A sort of wary consternation crept into Miranda's expression, and Allison's smile grew broader and still more wicked. "I'm afraid styles are just a *bit* different back home," she went on in an artfully worried voice, "but I did manage to find a few formal gowns before I left. Do you think I should wear the backless one with the V-neckline, or the one slit to the hip?"

• Chapter Twelve

"Oh, stop moping, Mac! It's not like I'm abandoning you."

"Of course not, Milady." Senior Master Chief Steward James MacGuiness spoke with a most unusual lack of expression, and his formal choice of title was not lost upon his commodore.

Honor sighed mentally, eyeing herself in the bulkhead mirror as she adjusted her black beret. Nimitz sat on her desk, watching her preparations, and she felt his silent chuckle. He and MacGuiness were old and close friends, but the free-spirited treecat found the steward's periodic obsession with what he considered proper protocol hilarious. Neither Nimitz nor his person could ever doubt the depth of MacGuiness' attachment to Honor, but there *was* an undeniable edge of outraged professional jealousy in the steward's emotions at the moment. The real reason for his formality—the equivalent, for him, of a screaming tantrum—was his indignation over the notion that someone else's steward would be in charge of a dinner party *his* commodore was throwing. And, of course, the 'cat's link to Honor meant that she knew that as well as Nimitz did.

It'd be nice, sometimes, she reflected, *if Mac could just figure out that I'm not a child he has to keep an eye on all the time. I got along without him for forty years, after all, and I really can* take care of myself! She felt a stir—small but stubborn— of guilt at the thought and grimaced at her mirrored image. *All right, so I wouldn't want to take care of myself, but honestly! There are times I could cheerfully strangle him.*

"Look," she said finally, turning to face him. "There are two reasons you're not coming. First, seating's too limited

211

on the flight over to fit you in. Second, and more to the point, we'll be going aboard *Prince Adrian* as Captain McKeon's guests, and if I tried to bring you in to supervise, *his* steward would be just as ticked off as you'd be in his place. And I might point out that I'm only going to be gone for about eighteen hours. Whether you believe it or not, Mac, I *am* capable of looking after myself for that long!"

Her dark brown eyes held his, touched with a twinkle but stern, until his gaze dropped. He looked down at his toes for a moment, then cleared his throat.

"Yes, Ma'am. I, um, didn't mean to suggest you weren't."

"Oh yes you did," Honor retorted, the twinkle in her eyes more pronounced, and he grinned sheepishly. "That's better!" She punched him lightly on the shoulder, then scooped up Nimitz. "Now, having just informed you that I can manage on my own, am I presentable enough to avoid embarrassing you in public?"

"You look just fine, Ma'am," MacGuiness assured her, but he also reached out to twitch her tunic collar a bit more perfectly into position and brushed an imaginary speck of lint from her 'catless shoulder. It was Honor's turn to grin, and she shook her head as he stepped back. Then she led the way into her day cabin and ran a critical eye over the trio of armsmen who would accompany her aboard *Prince Adrian*.

As expected, they were perfectly turned out. Andrew LaFollet and James Candless had been with Honor ever since her formal investiture as Steadholder Harrington, and although Robert Whitman had become the third man of her regular security detail little more than a year and a half ago, following Eddy Howard's death in HMS *Wayfarer's* final battle, LaFollet had hand-picked him for the slot. Whitman was well aware of that fact, and, if possible, he was even more brightly shined and sharply creased than either of his seniors, but all three of them would sooner be gnawed to death by Grayson neorats than let their appearance embarrass their Steadholder, and she nodded in satisfaction.

"Very nice, gentlemen," she complimented them. "Even you, Jamie. I don't think I'd be ashamed to be seen in public with any of you."

"Thank you, My Lady. We did try," LaFollet replied with straight-faced, exquisite politeness, and she chuckled.

"I'm sure you did. Got the package, Bob?"

"Yes, My Lady." Whitman held up a small, brightly wrapped box, and she nodded once more.

"In that case, gentlemen, let's be about it," she said.

The other pinnace passengers were waiting in Boat Bay Two when she arrived. At Honor's request, *Alvarez* was skipping formal honors, so there was no official side party, but Captain Greentree had come down to see them off.

"We won't be gone all that long, Thomas," she told him, shaking his hand.

"Of course not," he replied. "Anyway, I imagine I can mind the store for a few hours without you, My Lady."

"I imagine you can," she agreed. "Even if I am stealing your exec."

"That may make it a little harder, but I'm sure I'll survive," Greentree said dryly, and Commander Marchant smiled. He'd become much more comfortable with Honor in the last five T-weeks, as he and Greentree worked with her and her staff. Greentree's role as Honor's tactical deputy placed an even larger than usual share of the responsibility for managing *Alvarez* on Marchant's shoulders, and with Honor's strong approval, the flag captain had deliberately involved him in as many staff meetings as possible, as well. If anything happened to Greentree, Marchant would inherit his squadron responsibilities along with command of the flagship, and it was highly unlikely that there would be time for Honor to explain her policies or operational postures to her new flag captain if that happened. She'd been pleased by Greentree's determination to keep Marchant clearly in the picture in order to minimize the chance for confusion in such a catastrophic event, and Marchant's enforced contact with her had also given her the opportunity to evaluate his skills. She was pleased by what she'd seen . . . and also by the opportunity it had given her to make it clear that she didn't hold his distant relative's treason against him. He'd responded by developing not only a sure grasp of the squadron's operations but a strong personal sense of loyalty to her, as well.

"I'll try to have him home before he turns into a pumpkin," she promised Greentree now, and released his hand. Then she turned to the personnel tube and reached for the grab bar. LaFollet and her other armsmen followed immediately behind her, and were trailed in turn by Andreas Venizelos and the other members of her party, in descending order of seniority.

She swam down the tube, then swung herself gracefully into the pinnace's internal gravity and nodded to the burly, battered-looking flight engineer.

"Good morning, Senior Chief," she greeted him.

"Morning, Ma'am," Senior Chief Harkness rumbled back. "Welcome aboard."

"Thank you," she said, and twitched the hem of her tunic straight as she headed down the aisle to her seat. Horace Harkness was more than a little senior for his present duty, but she'd known he'd be here, given who was on the flight deck.

She set Nimitz in the seat beside her and strapped herself in, then looked back over her shoulder at the rest of her party. There were quite a few of them, and Honor allowed herself a rare, lazy smile which not even Nimitz could have bettered. *Poor Alistair,* she gloated. *If I've managed even half as well as I think I have, he doesn't have a clue what's really coming!* But then her smile faded a bit. There was a downside to her arrangements, after all, for the news she had for McKeon was going to make things harder for *her* down the road. She knew it, yet that inconvenience paled beside her anticipation of his expression when she told him. Besides, he had it coming.

She chuckled at the thought while she watched the others settle into the truncated passenger compartment. As she'd told MacGuiness, seating was limited, for the pinnace was heavily loaded with cargo—in this case, consigned to *Prince Adrian's* engineer. One of the cruiser's air scrubbers had failed, reducing her life-support capacity by ten percent, and although McKeon's ship had enough spares to rebuild the scrubber from scratch, if necessary, the job would take over a week without yard support. No one looked forward to the amount of sheer grunt work involved, but that was a relatively minor concern beside the lost capacity the scrubber represented. Taking it off-line had reduced *Prince Adrian's* environmental safety margin by thirty-three percent, and no starship skipper wanted to operate with that little reserve for an entire week if it could be helped.

And as it happened, this time it *could* be helped. *Prince Adrian* carried sufficient spare parts to *repair* the scrubber, but the newer, bigger *Alvarez* turned out to have three complete backup *scrubbers* tucked away in her capacious Engineering spaces. Exactly where *Alvarez's* chief engineer had acquired the third one (which put her above establishment) was something of a mystery, and Lieutenant Commander Sinkowitz had been a bit vague when discussing the subject, but Honor was used to the way odds and ends of extra equipment had a habit of turning up aboard ship. *Alvarez's* higher-volume scrubbers weren't exact matches for *Prince Adrian's*, but they were close enough that one of them could be adapted to replace the failed unit. Swapping them out would save at least eight days and a lot of sweat, and Greentree had offered to trade McKeon the complete scrubber for the spare parts the Manticoran ship would have used for repairs.

McKeon had been grateful for Greentree's offer, and local hyper-space conditions had made the transfer practical, although the transport window would be brief. They were just over five days out from Clairmont, and they happened to be under impeller drive at the moment, transiting between two grav waves, which made small craft traffic practical. But the transition to the grav wave which would carry the convoy the rest of the way to its current destination would take only another two hours, after which the ships would be required to reconfigure their drives from impeller mode to Warshawski sails. Since nothing smaller than a starship mounted Warshawski sails, no small craft would be able to move between ships again after that until the convoy reentered n-space.

The Grayson and Manticoran navies shared Edward Saganami's dictum that time, as the single absolutely irreplaceable commodity any fleet possessed, was never to be wasted. Greentree and McKeon had set briskly to work to transship their engineering stores within the window they'd been offered, and when Honor had heard about it, she'd taken the opportunity to transship herself and several members of her staff, as well. Discussions with her staffers over the past two days had led her to approve a few small but significant alterations to the squadron's tactical planning, and she wanted to sit down with her second-in-command to discuss them in person. Even if she hadn't been a firm believer in face-to-face discussion, the com lag imposed by *Prince Adrian's* lead position would have made any sort of electronic conference impractical. And while she supposed she *could* have waited until they reached Adler, she had her own ulterior motive for paying a visit to *Prince Adrian* right now, instead. Besides, as much as she and Greentree had grown to like one another, she suspected her flag captain would feel a certain relief to have her out from underfoot for a few hours.

She was impressed by how swiftly and smoothly *Alvarez's* boat bay officer had coordinated the transfer, but the scrubber was big enough (and awkwardly enough shaped) that he'd been forced to close off the after two-thirds of the pinnace's modular interior to free up the cargo space to accommodate it. That had also required him to remove the seating which usually occupied that space, of course, and accounted for the cramped personnel area which had been Honor's excuse to leave MacGuiness behind.

Even without the steward, seats were at a premium. In addition to the precious scrubber unit, Sinkowitz was sending along a half dozen of his own people to assist Lieutenant Commander Palliser, *Prince Adrian*'s chief engineer, in the job of installing it. That used up a third of the available places, and Honor had quickly filled the rest. Besides her armsmen, Commander Marchant, and Venizelos, she was bringing along Fritz Montoya, Marcia McGinley, Jasper Mayhew, Anson Lethridge, and Scotty Tremaine, and she'd added Carson Clinkscales almost as an afterthought. Her flag lieutenant's performance had improved markedly over the past three weeks. He remained an accident looking for a place to happen, but he was learning to anticipate and minimize disasters . . . and to cope with the embarrassment when they happened anyway. Yet that was when he was among superiors he'd come to know, and she'd decided it would do him good to spend a few hours with strangers. His confidence had grown steadily aboard *Alvarez*, and if his improved efficiency survived the visit to a new environment, it would do his overall self-image a world of good.

Besides, when it came to the ostensible purpose of her visit, Carson's inclusion was at least as logical as Montoya's. After all, there was no practical reason for the squadron's senior medical officer to sit in on a discussion of tactics . . . even if he *did* happen to be an old personal friend of *Prince Adrian*'s CO.

The last of the passengers found a seat, and Harkness sealed the hatch. He consulted the telltales carefully, then spoke into the boom mike of his headset.

"All secure aft," he announced to the cockpit.

"Thank you, Chief," Scotty Tremaine's voice replied. "Disengaging tube and umbilicals now."

The pinnace's hull transmitted indistinct thuds and bangs to its passengers as Tremaine unhooked from *Alvarez*'s systems, and Harkness watched his readouts.

"Green board," he informed Tremaine after a moment. "Clear to undock."

"Undocking," Tremaine said crisply, and the mechanical docking arms retracted as Honor's electronics officer drifted the pinnace free of the bay on reaction thrusters.

Honor watched through the view port, smiling at her reflection in the armorplast as the brilliantly illuminated boat bay slid away from her. At least fitting Scotty aboard hadn't been a problem. He'd made it respectfully but firmly clear at a very early date that staff officer or no, he would permit no one else to serve as Honor's small craft pilot. Given protocol's dictate that Honor's seniority meant she couldn't fly herself, she was more than willing to let Tremaine have his way, since he happened to be one of the five or six best natural pilots she'd ever seen. But he and Harkness came as a matched set, so letting him onto the flight deck had also made it inevitable that the senior chief would be aboard as her flight engineer. Precisely how Harkness managed to manipulate BuPers in order to turn up wherever Tremaine went remained one of the unexplained mysteries of the Royal Manticoran Navy, and Honor wasn't about to attempt to get to the bottom of it, either. They were far too useful a pair for her to risk jinxing the magic.

The pinnace cleared the bay, and *Alvarez* dropped her impeller wedge long enough for a stronger kick from the pinnace's thrusters to carry it beyond its own wedge's safety perimeter. Tremaine brought his drive up quickly and smoothly, transitioning from thrusters to impellers, and the pinnace accelerated away from the flagship at well over four hundred gravities. *Alvarez*'s wedge snapped back up behind her, and Honor leaned back in her seat as Tremaine steadied down to overtake *Prince Adrian*.

The flight would require the better part of the available two hours, for a pinnace's particle shielding limited its top speed to little more than 22,500 KPS more than a merchantman could pull here, and McKeon's ship was almost nine full light-minutes ahead of *Alvarez*. Deep down inside, a part of Honor still resented the fact that she'd had to put someone else in that exposed position, but she'd had plenty of time to learn to accept it. Besides, she knew her resentment was silly. It was her job to command the squadron, just as it was Alistair's job to take the point position, and that was that.

Now she leaned back in her comfortable seat, one hand rubbing Nimitz's ears while the 'cat purred contentedly in her lap, and watched the eerie, beautiful depths of hyper space flicker beyond her view port's thick armorplast.

"So what did you think of my girls' and boys' ideas?" Honor asked, raising an eyebrow at her host as the lift carried them smoothly up-ship towards his dining cabin. *Prince Adrian*'s design was over sixty years old, one consequence of which was that her lifts were more cramped than those of newer ships, and Honor's staffers and McKeon's exec had decided with silent tact to let their seniors have the first car to themselves. Well, to themselves and Honor's armsmen, which was as close to "to herself" as she was likely to come ever again.

"Impressive. Very impressive," McKeon replied. "That's some particularly nice work on the EW side from Scotty, and your McGinley's done an excellent job integrating his deception plans with the extra reach of our new passive systems, too. Of course," he added in an elaborately casual tone, "we won't be able to make maximum use of either of those until we get our hands on some of the new missile pods."

"New pods?" Honor's brows came back down—not in a frown, but rather in the *absence* of one—and her voice was cool. "What new pods would those be?"

"The low-image, top secret, burn-before-reading-classified pods with the new long-ranged, multiengined missiles," McKeon replied patiently. "You know—the ones you helped write the final specs on while you were at the WDB? Those pods."

"Oh," Honor said expressionlessly. "*Those* pods. And just how, Captain McKeon, do you happen to know 'those pods' even exist, much less who wrote the specs?"

"I'm a captain of the list," McKeon explained. "But back in my lowly days as a mere commander, I just happen to have been assigned to field-testing the original FTL drones' utility for light units back before the war. Playing test bed was my first big job with *Madrigal*, remember? And I'm still tapped into BuWeaps and BuShips. As a matter of fact, I'm still on Admiral Adcock's short list for operator input."

"His 'short list'?" Honor repeated. "I didn't know he had one."

"He doesn't, officially. But the Admiral's always been a little leery of giving the back room types too free a rein. He likes to run their concepts by line officers he's worked with before and whose judgment he trusts. Nobody gets a peek unless they're cleared to whatever classification level a given proposal's been assigned, but we're outside the official loop. Which means—since no one with the WDB will ever see our reports—that we can speak frankly without worrying about retaliation."

"I see."

Honor gazed at McKeon thoughtfully. Vice Admiral of the Green Jonas Adcock, the Bureau of Weapons' commanding officer, was one of the RMN's characters. He was also one of the Navy's very few senior officers who had never received prolong, for he and his family had immigrated to the Star Kingdom from Maslow, a planet as technically backward as Pre-Alliance Grayson. Adcock had been too old to accept prolong when he arrived, but there hadn't been anything wrong with his brain. He'd graduated eighth in his Academy class, despite not having encountered a modern educational system until he was nineteen T-years old, and his career had been distinguished. Now, at an age of just over a hundred and fourteen, he was far too physically frail ever to hold a spacegoing command again, but there was still nothing wrong with his brain. He'd taken over BuWeaps eleven years before, just in time for the war, and he'd been an aggressive dynamo ever since. Indeed, he was probably the largest single reason that rationalized versions of the *jeune école's* proposals were beginning to come off the drawing boards as useable hardware.

Honor had enjoyed several far-ranging discussions with him while she'd been assigned to the Weapons Development Board, and she'd been impressed by his ability to think outside the boxes. She also liked and respected him, and, looking back with the advantage of what McKeon had just said, she realized he'd picked her brain on current operational problems even more thoroughly than she'd realized at the time. But he'd never suggested that he maintained an unofficial network of evaluators.

On the other hand, she'd been a member of the Board herself during their talks, and from what McKeon was saying, the admiral had taken pains to keep the WDB's members from realizing that he was using line officers to critique their proposals before he signed off on them. Which, she admitted to herself, was probably wise of him, given the egos of some of the officers who'd served on the Board. Sonja Hemphill came to mind, for "Horrible Hemphill" would have been furious to find that *her* proposals were being independently evaluated (or, as she would no doubt have phrased it, "second-guessed") by her juniors, no matter how experienced those juniors might be. Honor wasn't certain that Hemphill would have taken overt revenge upon any junior officer rash enough to object to one of her pet projects, but the *jeune école's* leader would never—ever—have *forgiven* the officer in question. And other officers Honor had known most certainly would have punished any outside, unofficial evaluator who disagreed with them.

"Were you cleared to tell *me* about this?" she asked after a moment, and McKeon shrugged.

"He never told me not to, and I'll be very surprised if you don't start hearing from him yourself, now that you're off the Board. From what he said to me before *Adrian* pulled out of Manticore for Yeltsin, you really impressed him. In fact—" McKeon grinned "—he sounded a mite perplexed over how you landed on the Board in the first place. He's fond of mangling an old cliché: 'Those who can, fight; those who can't, get assigned to the WDB to figure out ways to handicap those who can.'"

"Am I to understand," Honor said, once she was certain she could keep her voice steady, "that he regards the WDB as somewhat less than effective?"

"Oh, no! Not the *Board*," McKeon assured her. "Only the officers who keep getting *assigned* to it. But you, of course, are the exception that proves the rule."

"Of course." Honor regarded him sternly for several seconds, then shook her head. "He should never have encouraged you," she observed. "You were quite bad enough *before* you had friends in high places."

"Like you, Your Ladyship?" McKeon's obsequious tone would have fooled anyone who didn't know him. Andrew LaFollet and James Candless, who'd been with Honor long enough to realize that McKeon was one of her two or three closest friends, were sufficiently accustomed to his sense of humor to take it in stride. Whitman, however, had never met the captain before, and Honor felt her newest armsman's immediate, instinctive flash of anger at McKeon's familiarity. But she also felt him get that anger under control almost instantly as he took his cue from his fellow armsmen and Honor herself, and she smiled at him before she glanced back at McKeon and grimaced.

"Maybe in Yeltsin," she told him, only half humorously, "but it might not be very smart to let too many people back in the Star Kingdom know we're friends. I haven't been entirely rehabilitated yet, you know."

"Close enough," McKeon said, and his voice was suddenly serious. "*Some* idiots will always listen to assholes like Houseman or the Youngs, but the people whose brains still work are starting to figure out that your personal enemies are a batch of—"

He bit off whatever he'd been about to say, but his expression was so disgusted—and angry—that Honor reached out and rested a hand on his shoulder.

"You're probably not the most unprejudiced judge of them," she replied in a tone whose lightness fooled neither of them, "but *I* like your evaluation. And Nimitz certainly agrees with you."

"An excellent judge of men—and women—is Nimitz," McKeon observed. "I always said so."

"He just likes you because you slip him celery."

"Why not? How could anyone who doesn't recognize a deeply sincere bribery attempt when he sees one possibly be a good judge of character?" McKeon grinned at her, and she shook her head sadly.

"And to think," she sighed, "that the Lords of the Admiralty saw fit to make someone of your dubious moral character a Queen's officer."

"But of course, Milady!" McKeon said, grinning even more broadly as the lift came to a halt. "Surely you didn't think Nimitz was where I *started* bribing people, did you?"

The lift doors slid open, and Honor and McKeon headed down the passage, walking side by side and laughing while her armsmen brought up the rear.

• Chapter Thirteen

Citizen Admiral Theisman walked silently into the War Room and stood watching the incoming green dot decelerate towards Enki. It was late arriving—System Control had expected it over a week ago—but delayed arrivals weren't all that unusual. Of course, an entire week was a bit excessive. In fact, a regular Navy captain who turned up that late could expect his superiors to devote several unpleasant minutes to discussing exactly why he'd been so casual about his movement orders. But no one was likely to raise any such question with the captain of this ship.

Warner Caslet had the acutely developed antennae of any staff officer, and he turned his head as he sensed Theisman's arrival. He stood quickly and crossed to the citizen admiral, and Theisman nodded to him.

"Warner."

"Citizen Admiral." Caslet didn't ask what brought Theisman here. He simply turned back to the huge display, standing at his admiral's side with his own hands folded behind him, to watch the green bead. It barely seemed to move across the twenty-five meter holo sphere, but its velocity was almost twelve thousand kilometers per second, and it drew steadily closer to the larger blue icon that indicated Enki's position.

"ETA?" Theisman asked after a moment, his tone conversational.

"Approximately fifty minutes, Citizen Admiral. She'll reach Enki in about forty minutes, but it'll take a little longer to settle her into the designated orbit."

Theisman nodded without comment. Normally, Traffic Control for a system as busy as Barnett assigned parking orbits to ships on a "first available" basis. Far though the system had fallen from its glory days as the Republic's launch pad to conquest, there was more than enough traffic to make its management a full-time job, and controllers hated VIP ships which required special treatment. But no one was going to complain, even if Traffic Control *was* required to clear all other ships from the newcomer's assigned orbit *and* a security bubble five thousand kilometers across.

Of course, Theisman thought mordantly, *only an idiot would think five k-klicks actually provided any advantage. Oh, it might help against a boarding action or keep some demented crew of kamikazes from physically ramming you, but five thousand kilometers wouldn't mean diddly against a graser or an impeller-drive missile. Hell, for that matter, at five k-klicks a laser head would* start out *inside its attack range!*

Not that I *harbor any such designs, of course.*

He added the last thought quickly, and then smiled with wry bitterness. He was getting even jumpier than he'd realized. Not even StateSec had yet figured out a way to bug a man's thoughts.

Someone's heels clicked on the floor behind him, and he turned to nod to Dennis LePic. The people's commissioner nodded back and glanced at the display. Over the course of his lengthy assignment to Theisman, LePic had acquired a certain familiarity with Navy hardware. He still didn't know a thing about how the vast majority of it worked, and he continued to require expert explanations of many of the data codes attached to the various icons, but he knew enough to pick out the newly arrived dot and the ship's name displayed beside it.

"I see Citizen Committeewoman Ransom has arrived," he remarked.

"Or, to be more precise, that she *will* arrive in the next, ah, thirty-six minutes," Theisman replied with a glance at his chrono. "Not counting however long it takes *Tepes* to maneuver into her final orbit, of course."

"Of course," LePic agreed, and turned his head to give Theisman a smile that held genuine warmth. The citizen admiral's comment could have been a thinly disguised sneer—an implication that LePic was so ignorant that he needed extra explanations—but both he and Theisman knew it wasn't. That, in fact, the precision of Theisman's correction had been a sort of shared joke . . . and evidence that they were comfortable enough with one another for the citizen admiral to risk what might have been misconstrued as insult by another commissioner.

Of course, it helped that LePic understood not only that most of the Navy's officers resented the Committee of Public Safety's spies but the *reasons* they were resented. If he'd been a regular officer, *he* would have resented the people's commissioners' interference, and especially the fact that political appointees with little or no military training were empowered to overrule him. That was the reason he made it a point not to interfere in Theisman's professional decisions any more than he absolutely had to.

In turn, the citizen admiral recognized a reasonable man and went out of his way to maintain as friendly a relationship as any officer was likely to manage with any commissioner. Over the last couple of years, LePic had come to suspect how Theisman and Citizen Captain Hathaway had put one over on him in the closing stages of the Fourth Battle of Yeltsin. But no one higher up had commented on it, their actions had probably saved his life as well as their own, and whatever had happened at Yeltsin, Theisman had fought stubbornly, courageously, and well at Seabring. Under the circumstances, LePic had decided to forgive the citizen admiral.

He'd also kept a closer eye on Theisman since, and along the way mutual respect had turned into something much more like friendship than LePic had any intention of admitting to his own superiors. Or, for that matter, to Theisman. Whether he liked the man or not, it was LePic's job to exert civilian control over the citizen admiral and watch for any signs of unreliability, and the people's commissioner was a man who believed both in the importance of his job and in the ultimate objectives of the Committee of Public Safety. He didn't have to like everything StateSec did under the harsh, short-term imperatives of revolutionary survival, and many of the SS's excesses disturbed him deeply, but he continued to believe. That might be growing harder to do than it once had been, but what would he have left if he ever *stopped* believing?

Dennis LePic was unprepared to answer that question, yet it was one reason he was so often frustrated by Theisman's dislike—no, be honest: his *contempt*—for politics. The Republic needed men and women like Theisman desperately. It needed them for their skill in battle and perhaps even more as counterweights, both against the reactionary elements which hungered for a return of the old regime and against the revolutionary extremists who let their zeal carry them into excess. It was LePic's duty to report Theisman's lack of revolutionary ardor, but he was uneasily aware that he'd kept his estimate of the full depth of the citizen admiral's disaffection to himself. He really shouldn't have done that, but he felt certain Theisman's loyalty to the Republic and to his own oath of allegiance would continue to overcome his lack of political awareness. It always had so far, at any rate.

Theisman returned LePic's smile with the same edge of warmth. He was unaware of the thoughts passing through the other's mind, but he'd had ample opportunity to see how much better off than many of his peers he was. He would never trust their unspoken partnership to carry LePic into any action which transgressed his own principles, but he was honestly and deeply grateful that at least he didn't have to watch his back against one of the people's commissioners who combined the suspicion of a paranoiac with the conviction that revolutionary fervor made him a better judge of strategy and operations than thirty years of naval experience. Besides, their quasifriendship meant he could actually take the risk of teasing LePic gently from time to time.

At least as long as I don't make the mistake of rubbing his face in something my staff and I shouldn't be doing . . . like Megan's warning me Ransom was coming. There's a limit to what he can ignore.

"Have we heard anything from Citizen Committee-woman Ransom?" LePic asked after a moment. Even he found the title a bit cumbersome, but he got it out gamely.

"I don't believe so, Sir," Theisman replied, and raised an eyebrow at his ops officer. "Have we heard anything from *Tepes*, Warner?"

"Only routine contact with System Control, Citizen Admiral," Caslet said.

"I see. Thank you, Citizen Commander." LePic nodded gravely to Caslet. He'd entertained some doubts about the citizen commander originally, yet Caslet had proven himself to LePic's satisfaction since arriving on Theisman's staff. It was a pity he was under a cloud with higher authority, but LePic was doing his best to rehabilitate him in his confidential reports. Of course, one had to do that sort of thing slowly and carefully.

The people's commissioner turned back to the plot, watching the battlecruiser move slowly nearer, and hid a sigh as he evaluated the mood of the others in the War Room. It was difficult to get a true read on the emotions behind an experienced officer's professional mien, but LePic had gotten ample practice over the last six years, and what he sensed disappointed him. He was too self-honest to pretend it wasn't inevitable, yet it saddened him that the Republic's officers should feel near universal distaste—if not overt dread and hatred—for a member of the Committee of Public Safety itself.

She was shorter than he'd thought.

Theisman felt a flicker of surprise at the prosaic nature of his own observation as Cordelia Ransom stepped into his office. It seemed so . . . inappropriate, somehow, to think about a thing like that at a time like this. Yet it was true, and as he rose to greet her, it occurred to him that his surprise might say something significant about her. Her HD appearances had led him to expect someone at least ten centimeters taller, and it must have taken careful camera work and editing to create that impression. That sort of trick wasn't complicated, but it didn't happen by accident, and he wondered why it was important to her.

Her eyes were as blue as his own, though darker. They were also much colder and flatter than they appeared on HD, but that, at least, was no surprise. Unfortunately. Different personalities sought power for different reasons, and it gave him very little satisfaction to realize he'd been right about what had driven Ransom to seek it, but he could hardly call it a surprise.

Two hulking bodyguards in civilian clothing, not SS uniform, followed her into the office. Theisman was willing to bet they'd been picked more for mass than brainpower, and they radiated the focus and ferocity of well-trained Rottweilers. Their eyes swept the room like targeting lasers, and one of them crossed wordlessly to the door to the attached executive head. He opened it and gave the spotless bathroom a quick look, then closed the door and returned to join his fellow. They stationed themselves on either side of the door, each with one hand slightly cocked, as if ready to dart inside his unsealed tunic at a moment's notice, and an utterly incurious expression.

"Citizen Committeewoman," Theisman said, reaching out to take her hand as her guards settled into place. "Welcome to the Barnett System. I trust you'll enjoy your visit."

"Thank you, Citizen Admiral," she replied. Her small hand felt inappropriately warm and delicate for the spokeswoman for the Committee of Public Safety's terrorism. Theisman's subconscious had expected it to feel cold and clawlike, but it didn't, and she smiled at him. Which, if she was trying to charm him, was a mistake. She was an attractive woman in many ways, yet coupled with those flat blue eyes, the small, white teeth her smile exposed made Theisman think of a Thalassian neoshark.

"Please, call me 'Citizen Secretary,'" she added. "I'm here

in my role as Secretary of Public Information, after all, not
on some sort of formal fact-finding mission, and it's so much
less awkward sounding than 'Citizen Committeewoman,'
don't you think?"

*And you can believe as much of that "not on some sort
of fact-finding mission" as you like, Thomas my boy,*
Theisman thought sardonically.

"As you wish, Citizen Secretary," was all he said, and
something like amusement glittered in those cold eyes as
she gave his hand one last squeeze and released it.

"Thank you," she said, and glanced around the office.
A raised eyebrow was her only comment on its somewhat
worn opulence, and she allowed herself a gracious air as
she settled into the chair Theisman indicated. She leaned
back and crossed her legs, and he took a facing chair rather
than returning to the one behind his desk. It wouldn't do
to do anything that could be construed as an effort to assert
his own authority, after all.

"Would you care for some refreshment, Citizen Secretary? I hope you'll join Citizen Commissioner LePic, the
senior members of my staff, and myself for supper shortly,
but if you'd care for anything in the meantime . . . ?"

"No, thank you, Citizen Admiral. I appreciate the offer,
but I'm fine."

"As you wish," he repeated, settling back in his own chair
with a politely attentive expression, and more amusement
flickered in her eyes. His expectant silence was its own form
of defensive social judo. It was courteous enough, but keeping
his mouth shut was also the best way of making certain he
kept his foot out of it, and this was one conversation in which
even a minor *faux pas* could have major consequences. She
seemed to enjoy his wariness, and she let the silence linger
for several seconds before she spoke again.

"I suppose you're wondering exactly what I'm here for,
Citizen Admiral," she said at last, and he gave a small shrug.

"I assume that you'll tell me anything I need to know
in order to meet your needs, Citizen Secretary," he replied.

"Indeed I will," she said. Then she cocked her head to

one side. "Tell me, Citizen Admiral. Were you surprised when I asked to meet you alone?"

Theisman considered pointing out that they were not, in fact, alone, but she clearly regarded her bodyguards as mobile pieces of furniture, not people. He also considered playing fat, dumb, and happy, but not very seriously. A man with no brains didn't make it to the rank of full admiral, even in the PRH, and trying to pretend otherwise— especially with this woman—would be not only stupid but dangerous.

"Actually," he admitted, "I *was* a bit surprised. I'm simply the system's military commander under Citizen Commissioner LePic's direction, and I suppose I assumed that you'd want to speak to him, as well."

"I do," she told him, "and I will. But that will be largely as a member of the Committee, and I wanted to speak to *you* as head of Public Information. That's the main reason I've come all the way out here, and I need your advice as well as your assistance."

"*My* advice, Ma'am?" An edge of genuine surprise leaked into Theisman's tone before he could stop it, and her eyes gleamed.

"As I'm sure you're aware, Citizen Admiral, we've been on the defensive virtually since this war began. Not that it's the fault of our heroic Navy and Marines, of course," she said, and paused, smiling another of those thin smiles. But Theisman only waited, refusing to rise to the bait, if bait was what it was, and she went on after a few seconds.

"The corrupt, imperialistic ambitions and incompetence of the Legislaturalist oppressors combined to betray the Republic on both the domestic and the military fronts," she said. "Domestically, they systematically impoverished the People for their own greedy ends and to support the machinery of oppression needed to suppress resistance to their ruthless exploitation of the People. Militarily, their criminal overconfidence led them into the initial disasters on the frontier which squandered our original numerical superiority and allowed the enemy to throw our courageous fighting forces back in disarray. Would you agree with that analysis, Citizen Admiral?"

"I'm scarcely the best person to ask about domestic affairs, Ma'am," Theisman replied after a moment. "As you may know, I was raised in a crèche, and I went straight into the Navy out of high school, so I never really worked in the civilian sector and I have no close family. In a sense, I suppose, you might say I've always been in the service of the state one way or another, without much of a personal experience basis from which to evaluate conditions in civilian society. And I haven't been back to Haven—except on Navy business—in fifteen T-years, which, I'm sorry to say, hasn't given me the opportunity to see how conditions have changed since the coup."

"I see." Ransom steepled her fingers under her chin and arched her eyebrows. Apparently she'd decided to be amused by Theisman's carefully phrased evasions, for which he was grateful, but she wasn't prepared to let him completely off the hook. "I don't suppose I ever really realized how, um, *sheltered* a naval career could be—in a social sense, I mean," she said slowly. "But perhaps it's just as well. It should give you an even greater insight into the military aspects of my analysis, shouldn't it?"

"I'd certainly hope so, Citizen Secretary!" Theisman responded vigorously in his relief at having gotten out of perjuring himself over his own opinion on the relative oppressiveness of the Legislaturalists and the Committee of Public Safety.

"Good! Then tell me how *you* think we got into this mess," Ransom invited, and she sounded so sincerely curious that Theisman almost answered her candidly. But even as he opened his mouth, that cold flatness in her eyes hit him like a splash of ice water. This woman was even more dangerous than he'd thought, he realized. He *knew* how perilous answering her honestly could—would—be, yet she'd almost sucked him into doing just that. And she'd made it look so *easy*.

"Well, Ma'am," he said after the briefest of pauses, "I'm

not as gifted with words as you are, so I hope you'll forgive me if I speak bluntly?" He paused once more until she nodded, then went on. "In that case, Citizen Secretary, and speaking bluntly, the military 'mess' we're in is so deep that picking a single cause—or even the most important *group* of causes—for it is extremely difficult. Certainly our prewar officers' planning and their faulty execution of the war's opening operations are major factors. As you yourself suggested, we began the war with a substantial numerical advantage which was frittered away in the opening battles. That was compounded by the Manties' superior weapon systems, and I'd have to say that the failure to recognize our technological inferiority and delay operations until we'd attained at least parity was the direct responsibility of the prewar government and officer corps. Our intelligence services obviously came up short, as well, given their failure to correctly project the Manties' initial deployments . . . not to mention their failure to detect and prevent the Harris Assassination."

He paused again, lips pursed as if to consider what he'd said, then shrugged.

"I suppose what I'm trying to say, Citizen Secretary, is that our present military difficulties are the product of everything that preceded them, and that the disastrous way the war opened, plus the confusion engendered by the Harris Assassination, paved the way for everything else. So, yes, on that basis I'd have to agree that incompetence and stupidity on the part of the old officer corps and our political leadership are to blame."

"I see," Ransom repeated, and Theisman held his breath, for his final sentence had come much closer to candor than he'd intended. The old officer corps *had* blundered badly in the opening phases of the war, but the People's Navy had suffered its heaviest losses only after the Legislaturalist admirals had been massacred or driven into exile. It had been the confusion and fear as the purges began which allowed the Manties to *really* cut the Fleet to pieces, and those things were hardly the fault of the Legislaturalists, most of whom had been dead at the time. But, then again, he hadn't laid the blame on the *prewar* political leadership, and he devoutly hoped that Ransom wouldn't notice.

Apparently, she didn't. She sat there, gazing at him while she considered what he'd said, then nodded and leaned slightly forward.

"I'm glad to see that you have a realistic grasp of how we got where we are, Citizen Admiral," she said. "It encourages me to believe that you also understand what we have to do to dig ourselves out of our current difficulties."

"I can think of several things I'd like to see done from a military perspective," Theisman said cautiously. "Not all of them are possible, of course, particularly in light of our heavy losses to date. But I'm not really qualified to offer advice on economic or social policies, Ma'am, and I'm afraid I'd feel presumptuous if I made the effort."

"It's good to meet someone who recognizes the limitations of his own experience," Ransom replied so smoothly that her silken tone almost—*almost*—concealed the dagger at its heart. Theisman felt a moment of fear, but then she smiled and sat back once more, and he relaxed in relief. "I think, though, Citizen Admiral, that I can show you how your command here in Barnett can have a direct impact on those social and economic questions. And, of course, on the direct, immediate military conduct of the war."

"I'm certainly prepared to do anything I can to serve the Republic, Ma'am."

"I'm sure you are, Citizen Admiral. I'm sure you are." Ransom ran one hand over her golden hair, and when she resumed, her voice had taken on a seriousness—an earnestness—which Theisman hadn't really been prepared to hear from her.

"Basically, it comes down to morale," she said. "I'm not going to suggest that morale can overcome enormous material odds. All the courage and determination in the universe won't mystically enable a mob armed with rocks to overcome trained infantry in battle armor, and you wouldn't believe me if I told you it could, now would you?"

"Probably not, Ma'am," Theisman admitted, bemused by the shift in her emphasis and intensity.

"Of course not. But if you want to arm people with something better than rocks, you have to buy or build their weapons. And if you want them to use those weapons properly, you have to motivate them. You have to convince your civilians that their military will use the weapons they're given effectively if you expect those civilians to dig in and build the weapons in the first place. And you have to convince your military personnel that they can *win* if you expect them to risk their lives. Correct?"

"I certainly can't argue with any of that, Citizen Secretary."

"Good! Because you, Citizen Admiral, are one of the unfortunately few flag officers who have actually done that—won battles, I mean—and that's why I'm here. It's vital for Public Information to get the message that we have admirals who *can* win across to the civilians. And it's almost equally important to show both the civilians and our military how vital it is to hold systems like Barnett. That's why my technical people will be shooting a great deal of footage over the next few weeks. I'll assume responsibility, in conjunction with Citizen Commissioner LePic, for any censorship which may be required by operational security concerns, so please instruct your officers to cooperate by answering questions as fully as possible in terms laymen can understand."

"I'll be happy to instruct them to cooperate with you, Ma'am," Theisman said. "But if the footage you shoot is for public broadcast, I'd like to have some input into the security concerns you just mentioned. I'm sure the Manties watch our media as closely as we watch theirs, and I'd hate to give them any clues as to our dispositions here."

"Of course we'll consult you in that regard," Ransom assured him. "The main thing, though, is to be certain that the entire operation is properly handled. Information is another weapon, Citizen Admiral. It must be deployed and managed in such a way as to have the maximum possible effect, and that's why I decided to come to Barnett in person. Obviously, I have a great many responsibilities to the Committee and the Republic over and above those of the Ministry of Public Information. But to be completely honest, I feel Public Information is the most important job I have. That's why I'm here, and I hope I can count on you and your people to help me with my job."

"Of course, Citizen Secretary. I'll be delighted to assist however I can, and I'm certain I speak for every officer here in Barnett," Theisman assured her. *We'd better, anyway, if we want to avoid firing squads*, he added silently, and smiled at her.

"Thank you, Citizen Admiral. I appreciate that." Ransom returned his smile with interest. "And I assure you that Public Information will make the best possible use of our time here," she added.

• Chapter Fourteen

"All right, Commander. What's so damned urgent?"

Vice Admiral of the Red Dame Madeleine Sorbanne wasted no time on pleasantries, and her expression, as brusque as her tone, made it clear she had better things to waste her time on than courtesy calls from newly arriving starship captains who refused to take her yeoman's "no" for an answer. The petite admiral had only half-risen to offer a perfunctory handshake, and she flopped back into the chair behind her desk even as she spoke. That desk, unusually littered with data chips and folders of hardcopy, lacked the spartan neatness that was the RMN's ideal, and Sorbanne's short, white-stranded mahogany-red hair looked as if she were in the habit of running her fingers through it while she fretted.

Well, Dame Madeleine had plenty of excuses for her desk's untidiness . . . and any fretting she happened to be doing, Jessica Dorcett reminded herself. As the senior officer on Clairmont Station, Sorbanne had seen half her capital ship strength siphoned off to build up Eighth Fleet, but no one had bothered to reduce her command area or responsibilities to reflect her lower strength. And with all the comings and goings leading up to Earl White Haven's eventual advance on Barnett, the bustling confusion of Clairmont's local and through traffic must be enough to try the patience of a saint. Of course, no one had ever nominated Dame Madeleine for canonization, and Dorcett's request for an immediate personal meeting had clearly ticked her off.

"I'm sorry to interrupt your schedule, Ma'am," the commander said now. She ignored the admiral's gestured

237

invitation to take a seat of her own, choosing to remain standing at parade rest instead, and saw Sorbanne's eyebrows rise in surprise. "Under the circumstances, however, I thought that I should make my report directly to you."

"What report?" Some of the irritation faded from Sorbanne's tone. Her reputation for irascibility was exceeded only by her reputation for competence, and crispness diluted her testiness as Dorcett's strained expression began to register fully. The commander hesitated just a moment, then drew a deep breath and took the plunge.

"Admiral, we've lost Adler," she said, and Sorbanne's chair snapped suddenly upright. The admiral leaned forward, and her high-cheekboned face lost all expression, as if Dorcett had cast a magic spell.

"How?" she asked harshly, and the commander shook her head.

"I don't have all the details—*Windsong* was too far out for good tactical imagery—but I'm afraid the bare bones were pretty clear. We screwed up, Ma'am, and whoever planned the Peeps' attack had the guts and the smarts to take advantage of it." Dorcett didn't like saying that, yet it had to be said, and her own anger—and shame—made her voice come out flat.

"Explain." Sorbanne sounded as if she were regaining her mental balance, and Dorcett wondered how much of that was real and how much was acting ability.

"Commodore Yeargin had too few sensor platforms for complete coverage, Ma'am, so she placed what she did have to cover the most obvious approach vectors. Then she put her main force into Samovar orbit . . . and aside from detaching my destroyer division to cover the main asteroid processing node, she posted no pickets at all." Despite iron self-control, Sorbanne winced, and Dorcett went grimly on. "The Peeps came in from above the system ecliptic, which let them skirt the Commodore's platforms and avoid my command's sensor envelope entirely. And they also came in ballistic."

"*Peeps* came in ballistic?" Sorbanne repeated carefully, and Dorcett nodded.

"Yes, Ma'am. They must have. Either that, or their stealth systems have achieved a much higher degree of improvement than ONI's been projecting. Even on the course they followed, they should have passed close enough to at least one of our sensor platforms for active impellers to've been detected."

"They came in powered down all the way to attack range?" Sorbanne still seemed to be having trouble with the concept, and Dorcett nodded again.

"Yes, Ma'am. And I'm afraid that isn't all." Sorbanne eyed her narrowly and made a "tell me more" gesture, and Dorcett sighed. "They used missile pods, Admiral," she said quietly.

"Shit." The soft, whispered expletive was almost a prayer, and Sorbanne closed her eyes. She sat that way for several seconds, then opened them and looked at Dorcett once more. "What's the Peep strength in the system?"

"I'm not certain, Ma'am. As I say, we were too far out for really good scans, but my best estimate is four battle-cruisers, six to eight heavy cruisers, and half a dozen light cruisers. My tac officer and I saw no destroyers, but I can't guarantee there weren't any."

Sorbanne winced again, this time at the disparity in weight of broadside Dorcett's estimate suggested, especially if the Peeps had, indeed, used missile pods.

"How bad were Commodore Yeargin's losses?" she asked after a moment.

"Ma'am, I—" Dorcett stopped and swallowed. "I'm sorry, Admiral. I must have been . . . unclear." She inhaled, then went on very flatly. "Aside from my division, the task group's losses were total, Dame Madeleine. I'm . . . the senior surviving officer."

Sorbanne didn't say a word. She only sat there for endless, aching seconds, staring at Dorcett while her mind raced. The news that the Peeps had finally deployed missile pods was unwelcome and frightening, but hardly unexpected. Every thinking officer had known the enemy had to be working at full stretch to overcome the huge advantage the Allies' pod monopoly had conferred upon them. But having the long-awaited weapons employed so competently and to such crushing effect by the despised Peeps . . . that *was* unexpected. And the moral shock was far more than merely frightening.

Madeleine Sorbanne leaned slowly back in her chair once more, still staring at Dorcett, but she wasn't really seeing the commander. She was seeing another woman's face and thinking about Frances Yeargin and her command. *Yeargin always was an arrogant, overconfident bitch,* she thought slowly, remembering the dead commodore and her oft expressed contempt for the People's Navy. *Damn it, she* knew *she was short of platforms! The woman should have had at least* some *pickets out, for God's sake! What the hell did she think she was* stationed *there for?*

But what Yeargin had been thinking was immaterial now. Rightly or wrongly, the future was going to condemn her even more harshly than Sorbanne did now, for never in its entire history, had the RMN suffered a disaster like this . . . until now. An entire generation of analysts would examine every tiny facet of the Battle of Adler, apportioning blame and assigning guilt with twenty-twenty hindsight and the fine ruthlessness of people who'd never been there, and that was just as immaterial right now as what Yeargin had been thinking. What mattered was that her entire command was gone, wiped out. Blotted away. And if the Peeps had used missile pods with the advantages of surprise and short range, casualties must have been massive, for no one would have been suited up and very few people would have gotten off in life pods before their ships died.

Pain twisted deep inside her at the thought of all the dead, but then another thought hit her, and her eyes dropped back into intent focus.

"If you're the surviving SO, then who's picketing the system, Commander?"

"No one, Ma'am. I only had three ships: *Windsong, Rondeau,* and *Balladeer.* Under the circumstances, I judged that my immediate duty was to use all three of them to spread the word as quickly as possible, so I brought *Windsong* here and sent the other two to Quest and Treadway."

"I see." Something in the vice admiral's almost mechanical reply gripped Dorcett's attention by the throat, and her hands clenched behind her. She tried to keep her expression neutral, but she knew she'd failed when Sorbanne shook her head.

"It's not your fault, Commander." She sighed, reaching up to pinch the bridge of her nose hard. "You reasoned that your command would be best employed in alerting other station commanders before more ships were dispatched to Adler than in dodging around the system trying to avoid Peep pursuers, correct?" She lowered her hand, gazing at Dorcett, and the commander nodded. "That was the proper and logical judgment, and my report to the Admiralty will endorse it as such. But you're too late."

"Too late, Ma'am?" Cold, intuitive despair burned in Dorcett's belly even as she repeated the admiral's words, and Sorbanne nodded.

"Seventeen merchantmen and their escorts sailed from Clairmont just over five days ago, Commander Dorcett. They should arrive in Adler within the next twelve hours, and with no pickets to warn them—"

She shrugged, and Jessica Dorcett closed her eyes in horrified understanding . . . and guilt.

Alistair McKeon sat at the head of his dining cabin table and watched his guests. They'd pretty much come to the end of their comfortable, tasty dinner; now they were working on the last few morsels while they engaged in a dozen separate conversations and sampled their wine, and McKeon allowed himself the mild, self-congratulatory glow a successful host deserved.

Honor sat to his right, as his guest of honor, and Commander Taylor Gillespie, *Prince Adrian's* executive officer, faced her across the table. Lieutenant Commander

Geraldine Metcalf, McKeon's tactical officer, sat to Gillespie's right, facing Nimitz, and Honor's officers and Surgeon Lieutenant Enrico Walker, *Prince Adrian's* doctor, occupied the rest of the chairs around the table. James Candless shared the watch outside the hatch to McKeon's quarters with the Marine sentry while Andrew LaFollet and Robert Whitman stood against the bulkheads, courteously unobtrusive but nonetheless an alert reminder that CruRon Eighteen's commodore was also a great feudal lady.

Some RMN officers, McKeon knew, would have found Honor's title and status either ridiculous or irritating. A certain percentage of Manticorans—mostly civilians, but including a number of Queen's officers who should know better—had never bothered to amend their mental images of the Yeltsin System. They still looked down on Grayson (and its navy) as some sort of comic opera, technically backward vest-pocket principality of religious fanatics with delusions of grandeur, and their contempt extended itself to the planet's aristocratic titles and those who held them. And however much most of the RMN's officers might respect Honor's achievements, there would always be those souls who would denigrate her reputation, whether out of jealousy, resentment, or the genuine belief that she owed it all to luck.

God knows there're enough idiots like Jurgens and Lemaitre, he reflected. *They actually buy the theory that she's some sort of loose warhead—that her casualties and the ships she's lost or had damaged only happened because she was too reckless to think before she went charging in! The fact that no other skipper could have brought* anyone *home doesn't mean squat to them. And, of course, there are always the Housemans and the Youngs. It doesn't matter* what *she accomplishes as far as they're concerned.* He reached for his own wineglass as he watched Honor turn her head to address Walker across Nimitz, and hid a mental smile. *Well, screw them. We* know *how good she is, and so does the Admiralty.*

Honor paused in her conversation with Walker, as if she felt McKeon's eyes upon her. She turned to smile at him, and he made a small, semisaluting gesture with his glass. She opened her mouth as if to speak, then hesitated, eyes refocusing as she gazed over his shoulder. McKeon looked a question at her, but she said nothing, so he half-turned in his chair to look in the same direction and felt his eyebrows arch in surprise.

Alex Maybach, McKeon's personal steward, hovered over two junior stewards as they wheeled an enormous confectionery monstrosity through the pantry hatch. The cake was at least a meter long, baked in a stylized shape obviously intended to represent *Prince Adrian*, and blazed from end to end with burning candles, and a corner of his surprised brain wondered how Maybach could possibly have kept the thing hidden from him.

He was still wondering when someone gave the signal and the entire dining cabin burst into what a particularly charitable observer might have called singing. McKeon wheeled back to his guests, trying to glare while those of them with sufficient seniority grinned like loons and those too junior for such levity did their best to maintain straight faces, and Nimitz's clear "Bleek!" of delight cut through the chorus.

"—birrrthday to yoouuu!"

The song came to a merciful close in a burst of applause, and McKeon shook his head at Honor.

"How did you manage it?" he demanded under cover of the general hilarity. It never occurred to him to doubt that she was behind it. His own officers might have been willing to ambush him in the wardroom, but none of them would have had the nerve to try the same thing in his own quarters. Yet not even she could have planned this without using the com to arrange things, for until the scrubber unit failed, she'd had no way to know she would be aboard at the proper time. So how had she kept him from realizing that she was in communication with his people while she set it up?

"You remember that long parts list and technical data file Commander Sinkowitz downloaded to your Engineering

Department?" she asked with a lurking smile, and he nodded. "Well, I got him to hide a personal message to Commander Palliser in it, and Palliser relayed it to Alex. Surely you didn't think we were going to let you get away without inflicting *some* sort of party on you!"

"I could hope," he mock-growled, and she laughed, then held out her hand to him. The background noise faded as he gripped it, and she glanced at the others, then looked back at him.

"Happy birthday, Captain, and best wishes from all of us," she said simply. Someone started to clap again, but she raised her left hand in a silence-restoring gesture and went on. "I'm certain your ship's company has its own gift for you—it *better* have one if it knows what's good for it!— but I brought along a little something of my own."

She released McKeon's hand and reached out towards Robert Whitman. The armsman took three crisp strides forward and drew a small, gaily wrapped package from his tunic pocket. He handed it to his Steadholder with military precision, then came to attention at her shoulder. Andrew LaFollet braced simultaneously to attention against the bulkhead behind her, and the general air of festivity abruptly focused into something much more intense as Honor extended the package to McKeon.

He took it from her slowly, his expression a silent question, but she merely shook her head and gestured for him to unwrap it. Her armsmen's formality and her own change of demeanor made McKeon's nerves tingle, and he untied the ribbon and quickly ripped away the wrapping to reveal the simple black box under it. He glanced back up at Honor, then opened the box slowly and inhaled sharply. Its velvet-lined interior held a pair of RMN collar badges, but instead of the single gold planet of a captain of the list, each of them bore a *pair* of planets, identical to the ones on Honor's collar. He stared at them for a dozen heartbeats, then shook himself and met Honor's gravely smiling eyes.

"Congratulations, Alistair," she said. "It won't be official until we return to Yeltsin, and I know it's supposed to be bad luck to let the cat out of the bag early. But the Admiralty sent out confirmation just before we sailed, and High Admiral Matthews knew I'd want to be the one to tell you, so he passed me the word. When you suffered your Environmental casualty, I decided your birthday was the perfect time to tell you."

No one else said a thing, and as McKeon felt the curiosity hovering in the cabin like an extra presence he realized that she hadn't told anyone else, either. Only her armsmen and—he looked past her at the smile on Andreas Venizelos' face—her chief of staff had known, and he swallowed hard, then turned his wrist so the others could see into the box. There was a moment of intense silence, and then the applause began.

"Congratulations, Skipper!" Commander Gillespie snatched up his glass, raising it to his captain, and other glasses rose around the table. "Hey, if they're kicking you upstairs, does this mean *I* get command of the *Adrian*?" Gillespie demanded.

"Not unless BuPers is *really* desperate!" McKeon growled back. Gillespie laughed, and McKeon reached into the box to brush one collar pin with a fingertip. "Me, a commodore?" He shook his head wonderingly, and Honor laid a hand gently on his arm.

"You deserve it," she said, quietly but firmly, "and I'm glad for you. Of course, this will make you awfully senior to command a heavy cruiser division, so I'll probably lose you, but I'm still glad. And given the way Eighth Fleet's expanding, Admiral White Haven will probably find something for you to do without sending you home."

"I—" McKeon paused, unable to decide exactly what he'd meant to say, then reached down to put his own hand over the one on his forearm. "Thank you," he said, equally quietly. "That means a lot, coming from you."

She didn't reply, only squeezed his arm for a moment, then sat back with a smile, and he cleared his throat.

"All right, you lot! That's enough racket!" He shook his head sternly at his unrepentant juniors. "This is no way for the senior officers of a Queen's ship—or their allies!—to carry on. Not only have you demonstrated unruliness and a severe case of lèse majesté, but a total ignorance of proper birthday party protocol!" He swept them all with twinkling gray eyes, then pointed at the candle strewn cake. "The guest of honor is supposed to blow out his candles to *begin* the celebration, and unless you people get your priorities straightened back out, I won't share my cake with *any* of you!"

It was early the next morning by *Prince Adrian's* clocks when Convoy JNMTC–76 reached its next port of call. Honor had enjoyed her visit to McKeon's ship, and especially the success of her surprise party. Organizing it on such short notice without tipping off an alert skipper like McKeon had been much more complicated than her casual explanation might have suggested, and she felt rather smug at how well she'd pulled it off. But the truth was that she'd become even more spoiled than she'd realized. Alex Maybach had done his best, but she'd missed MacGuiness' unobtrusive services when she turned in after the party. She'd especially missed the rich cocoa that magically appeared just as she was getting ready for bed, regardless of how late that happened to be, and she was rather looking forward to getting "home" again once the convoy reentered normal-space and Scotty could chauffeur her back to *Alvarez*.

At the moment, however, she stood with Venizelos on *Prince Adrian's* command deck, Nimitz on her shoulder, and watched McKeon's crew prepare for translation out of hyper. Andrew LaFollet had found a corner into which to tuck himself, though he looked as if he were suffering from a touch of claustrophobia, and Honor didn't blame him. She really would have preferred to have at least McGinley present, as well, but there simply wasn't room to fit her ops officer onto the cramped bridge without getting in the way of *Prince Adrian's* command crew. Honor supposed she could have insisted on cramming Marcia in anyway. Some flag officers would have done so, at any rate, but without some overridingly important justification, Honor refused to crowd the people who *had* to be there to operate the ship, however inconvenient it was for her.

The *Prince Consort*-class ships like *Prince Adrian* were the product of a design philosophy which had been abandoned with the emergence of the later *Star Knights*. The *Prince Consorts'* original design was over sixty T-years old, dating back to the very first installment of the naval build-up Roger III had begun to counter the PRH's expansionism, and they hadn't been intended to function as flagships. Instead, in an effort to get as much firepower into space as quickly—and for as low a cost—as possible, BuShips' architects had chosen to omit a proper flag deck and all its support systems and used the freed mass to tuck an extra graser and an extra pair of missile launchers into each broadside. In fact, even their *regular* command decks had been built to unusually austere standards to help compensate for the increased armament and more magazine space. Instead of the extra, unused bridge volume BuShips normally allocated to new designs to provide room for the proliferation of control systems which always occurred, the *Prince Consorts* had been given just enough room for their original requirements. Which meant their bridges had become increasingly cramped as inevitable refits jammed in supplementary consoles and displays and panels anywhere a few cubic centimeters could be found for them.

The problem had been recognized at the time, but accepted as an unavoidable consequence of producing ships with maximum firepower for their cost and tonnage, and BuShips had projected a program which would have built the *Prince Consorts* in groups of seven and paired each group with a *Crusader*-class ship which *did* have a flag deck to make a full eight-ship squadron. Unfortunately, what had seemed like a good idea at the time had begun to look very different since the outbreak of the Navy's first serious shooting war in a hundred and twenty T-years.

The original *Crusader* building program had failed to allow for the unavoidable cycle of overhauls any warship required, with the result that at least twenty-five percent too few flagships had been allowed from the beginning, and Sir Edward Janacek's decision to cut funding for the *Crusaders* by over seventy percent during his first tenure as First Lord of the Admiralty had only made bad worse. But Janacek had viewed the Navy's proper role as anti-piracy patrols and defense of the Manticore Binary System itself. Anything more "aggressive" than that had clashed with his Conservative Party prejudice against "imperialist adventures" which were likely to "provoke" the People's Republic, and he'd regarded the deployment of cruiser squadrons to distant stations as the precursor to the gunboat diplomacy he rejected.

One way to hamstring such deployments was to cut down on the number of available flagships, which was precisely what he'd done, although he'd been careful to make the *Crusaders'* higher cost per unit his official reason. During his tenure, more than half the Navy's total cruisers had been tasked for solo operations chasing pirates on distant stations (for which no command ships were required), and most of the remainder had been concentrated in one spot and attached to Home Fleet, where only a limited number of flagships were needed. As a result, the implications of the shortage of *Crusaders* had gone largely unobserved at the time.

That, unfortunately, was no longer true. Janacek had been out of office for eleven T-years now, but the pernicious effects of his funding decisions lingered on. Numerically, the *Crown Princes* were the largest single class of heavy cruisers in the RMN's inventory, yet their lack of squadron command facilities severely limited their utility. The fact that the bigger, less numerous *Star Knights'* flag accommodations forced the Admiralty to keep tapping them for the detached command roles the *Crown Princes* couldn't fulfill properly also meant that the newer ships had suffered higher proportional losses. *Prince Adrian* and her sisters tended to stay tethered to task force and fleet formations, where someone else could provide the space for a commodore or admiral and her staff. That meant they were normally found in company with ships of the wall, whereas the *Star Knights*, exposed on frontier and convoy deployments without capital ship support, were much more likely to find themselves engaged with fast battlecruiser/cruiser-level raiding forces. And, of course, every *Star Knight* lost to enemy action or sent to the yard by battle damage reduced the supply of command ships by yet another unit.

There wasn't actually all that much to choose between the individual offensive power of the two classes, which—given the difference in their tonnages—only went to prove that even the *Star Knights'* design was less than perfect. Powerful as the *Star Knights* were, too little of their volume was allocated to offensive systems, in Honor's opinion, and too much was used on defense, probably as a reaction against the perceived shortcomings of their predecessors.

The newer class's more powerful sidewall generators, heavier armor, better electronic warfare capabilities, and more numerous point defense systems made them at least thirty percent tougher than the older *Prince Consorts*, and BuShips fully recognized the need for a better balance between offense and defense. Unfortunately, the need for cruiser flagships meant the yards were churning out *Star Knights* as quickly as they could—given the limited amounts of space which could be diverted from capital ship construction for *any* sort of cruiser—and that had significantly delayed introduction of the new *Edward Saganami*-class ships. The *Saganamis*, ten percent larger than the *Star Knights* and designed to take full advantage of the Navy's current battle experience and to incorporate the best balance of Grayson and Manticoran concepts, should have entered the construction pipeline over three T-years ago, but BuShips had decided it couldn't afford to divert building capacity to a new class (which, undoubtedly, would have its own share of production-oriented bugs to overcome) when the need for volume production was so acute. And so the *Star Knights* continued to be built to a basic design which was now eighteen years old. To be sure, their design had been on the cutting edge when it was finalized, and—like the *Prince Consorts*—they had been materially upgraded since, but even with as heavy a refit schedule as deployment pressures would permit, the class was losing its superiority over the Peeps.

In a way, Honor thought, standing to one side while she watched McKeon's bridge crew, *that illustrates the entire problem Earl White Haven and I . . . disagreed over.* (She was slightly—and pleasantly—surprised to feel only the smallest twinge as she thought about the earl.) *We've still got the tech edge on a ship-for-ship, ton-for-ton basis, but it's shrinking. We can't afford that, but unless we can somehow find a way to break the traditional building patterns, our advantage is going to continue to erode. It won't be anything dramatic or obvious in the short term, but in the* long *term . . .*

She gave herself a mental shake and commanded herself to stop woolgathering and pay attention as Lieutenant Commander Sarah DuChene, McKeon's astrogator, completed her final course adjustments and looked at her captain.

"Ready to translate in eight minutes, Sir."

"Very good. Communications, inform the flagship," McKeon said.

"Aye, aye, Sir. Transmitting now." Lieutenant Russell Sanko, *Prince Adrian's* com officer, depressed a key to send the stored burst transmission. "Transmission complete, Sir."

"Thank you. Very well, Sarah. The con is yours."

"Aye, aye, Sir. I have the con. Helm, prepare to translate on my command."

"Aye, aye, Ma'am. Standing by to translate," the cruiser's helmswoman replied.

Honor walked quietly over to stand beside McKeon's command chair, careful to stay out of his way but placed to watch his repeater plot more comfortably, and he looked up to give her a small smile. Then he turned to Lieutenant Commander Metcalf.

Honor nodded to herself as he and the tac officer began a quiet discussion. Unlike her flagship, *Prince Adrian* had no internal FTL transmitter. The technology hadn't existed when she was built, and finding room to retrofit the impeller node modifications required to project the gravity pulses upon which the system relied would have required complete rebuilding, not just a refit. Any ship could use its standard gravitic detectors to *read* an FTL message (assuming it knew what to look for), and *Prince Adrian's* recon drones, built to a more modern design than their mother ship and with enormously smaller impeller nodes, mounted less powerful transmitters for long-range reconnaissance missions. But the ship's onboard transmission capability was limited to light-speed, which meant that, since *Alvarez* was still nine light-minutes astern of *Prince Adrian* in hyper-space (which translated to an n-space distance of almost nine light-*days*), the message Sanko had transmitted would take approximately six minutes to reach the flagship—during which *Alvarez* and her charges would continue to advance through hyper at sixty percent of light-speed (which translated to an apparent velocity of 2,500 c in normal-space terms). The main body of Convoy JNMTC-76 would reach the point at which *Prince Adrian* had translated into n-space seven minutes after that, but rather than follow McKeon immediately out of hyper, the other ships would decelerate to zero and wait another two hours before beginning their own translations. The delay was designed to give *Prince Adrian* time to sort out her sensor picture and move far enough in-system to be sure no nasty surprises awaited them.

That precaution was almost certainly unnecessary here, and some convoy commanders would have skimped on it, but the safety of those ships and all the people and material aboard them was Honor's responsibility. Time wasn't in such short supply that she couldn't afford to spend a couple of hours insuring against even unlikely dangers, and McKeon's quiet double-checking of his tactical section's preparations with Metcalf showed that he shared her determination to do things right.

"Translation in one minute," DuChene announced, and Honor felt a shared, unstated tension grow about her. No hardened spacer ever admitted it, but no one really enjoyed the speed at which warships routinely made transit from hyper. *Prince Adrian* wasn't contemplating a true crash translation, but she'd translate on a steep enough gradient to make every stomach aboard queasy, and her crew knew it.

"Translating . . . *now!*" DuChene said crisply, and Honor grimaced and gripped her hands more tightly together behind her as the bottom dropped out of her midsection.

"Hmmm . . . ."

Citizen Commander Luchner, executive officer of PNS *Katana,* looked up at the soft, interested sound from his tactical section. Citizen Lieutenant Allworth was hardly in the same league as Citizen Rear Admiral Tourville's new tac witch—yet—but he was learning from her example. For that matter, so was Luchner. *Katana* had been part of the citizen rear admiral's task group for almost a year, and that task group had done well, by the People's Navy's standards, during that period. But Foraker, now . . . She'd brought something new, an almost innocently arrogant confidence, to the task group, and it seemed to be contagious.

Luchner hoped so, anyway, as he watched the citizen lieutenant make very slow and careful adjustments at his panel. Allworth's eyes were rapt, focused on his readouts with unusual intensity, yet that wasn't particularly noteworthy. The tac officer managed to find *something* to interest him on any given watch. But he seemed to be taking longer than usual to decide that he'd picked up some natural phenomenon, and Luchner walked over to stand beside him.

"What?" he asked quietly.

"Not sure, Citizen Exec." Allworth might be emulating Citizen Commander Foraker's professional competence, but he had no intention of imitating her occasional, dangerous lapses into counterrevolutionary forms of address. *Not until my reputation is as good as hers, anyway!* he thought absently. "It could be nothing . . . but then again, it *could* just be a hyper footprint."

"Where?" Luchner asked more sharply.

"About here, Citizen Exec," Allworth said, and a tiny icon appeared on his plot. It was a good nineteen light-minutes away along the periphery of the G0 primary's twenty-two-light-minute hyper limit, and Luchner frowned. That was too distant for *Katana's* onboard sensors to have detected, but Allworth continued speaking before he could object. "We've got it on our number eleven RD," he explained.

"And what, pray tell, is one of *our* recon drones doing over there?" Luchner asked.

"Citizen Captain Turner asked us to take that side of *Nuada's* zone, Citizen Exec," Allworth replied respectfully. "Her main gravitic array was already down, and now her secondary array's developed some sort of glitch. Her engineers have shut down most of her normal passive sensors while they try to sort things out, and she's relying solely on RDs until they can figure out what the problems are. But trying to cover her entire zone with drones would overload her telemetry section. Until she gets her sensor glitches straightened out, she can't cover more than two-thirds of her assigned area, so I told Citizen Captain Turner we'd take the rest for him."

Luchner frowned so darkly that Allworth had to fight an urge to quail. Not that the citizen exec doubted the explanation. *Katana* and *Nuada* had worked together to nab a pair of Manty destroyers and a single fast, independently routed freighter since the task group had taken Adler, and Turner's ship had lost two-thirds of her primary sensor suite during the pursuit of the second destroyer. Such equipment failures were less uncommon in the People's Navy than they ought to have been, especially when undertrained maintenance staffs were handed new systems to look after when they still hadn't fully mastered the old ones. Turner's engineers had promised then to fix whatever had gone wrong, but now it appeared *Nuada* had been even unluckier and lost her *secondaries*, as well. Luchner had no doubt that Turner's engineers would solve their problems—eventually—but he also knew it was going to take them longer than it should have.

Their shortcomings weren't really their fault, of course. Every line officer knew that rushing replacements—especially replacements drawn from the Dolists' ill-educated ranks—through the training schools in half of what prewar standards had established as the minimum time meant the newbies had to pick up their real training on the job.

Unfortunately, the political establishment didn't want to hear about that. Given the Navy's heavy losses in combat, the people's commissioners assigned to supervise the Admiralty's manpower programs had no choice but to find recruits anywhere they could and then push them through training as rapidly as possible. But they had their own heads to worry about, and admitting they were sending out insufficiently trained personnel might bring StateSec sniffing around *them*. Which meant that trying to defend *Nuada's* lack of progress to higher authority would probably be pointless. It probably also meant that Turner had asked Allworth—very indirectly and discreetly, of course—not to mention the breakdown to anyone else. And the reason *Nuada* had asked for help rather than trying to rely solely on her own recon drones to make up the difference was equally easy to understand. The *Mars*-class cruisers had given up almost a third of the telemetry capacity of the older *Swords* in part exchange for their superior electronic warfare capabilities, and *Nuada* simply couldn't operate sufficient drones to cover her entire zone of responsibility without the backup of her shipboard systems.

Luchner understood that, and he had no objection to helping to cover a colleague's ass. After all, it might be his posterior next time. No, his frown arose from another consideration, and he raised one eyebrow as he glowered down at the citizen lieutenant.

"I see. And did you, perhaps, inform myself or Citizen

Captain Zachary that *Katana* was assuming this additional responsibility?"

"Uh . . . no, Citizen Exec." Allworth blushed. "I guess I forgot."

"You 'forgot,' Luchner repeated, and Allworth's blush darkened. "It failed to occur to you that we might like to know about it? Or, for that matter, that the Citizen Captain and I are legally responsible for your actions?"

"Yes, Citizen Exec," Allworth admitted miserably. He obviously wanted to lower his eyes to his display to avoid his superior's stern expression, but he made himself meet Luchner's gaze. The citizen commander regarded him coldly for several more seconds, but beneath his baleful exterior, Luchner was pleased by the youngster's refusal to flinch, and, after a moment, he reached out and rested a hand on Allworth's shoulder.

"Citizen Commander Foraker is an outstanding tac officer," he said, and allowed himself a small smile. "You could do a lot worse for a model. But *do* try to stay in touch with the rest of the universe better than she does, Citizen Lieutenant. Do you read me?"

"Yes, Citizen Exec!"

"Good." Luchner gave the younger man's shoulder a squeeze. "Now tell me about this possible contact."

"It translated into n-space just outside the hyper limit eight minutes ago, Citizen Exec . . . assuming it *is* a contact. It's hard to be sure that far from the drone."

The citizen lieutenant paused, and Luchner nodded his comprehension. The PN's drones weren't as good as the Manties', with a maximum passive detection range of no more than twelve to fourteen light-minutes, depending on the strength of a target's emissions, and a maximum telemetry range of ten light-minutes. Because of that, they were normally deployed at ranges of no more than seven or eight light-minutes, which limited their mother ships' sensor reach to twenty light-minutes or so, but got the data on FTL sources (like the gravitic energy of an impeller wedge or a hyper translation) to the combat information center quickly. In this case, Allworth had deployed the drone at the very limit of the telemetry links to take up the slack for *Nuada*, but even so, the possible contact was near the edge of the drone's envelope.

"If it's headed for Samovar," Allworth went on, "the geometry of its vector is going to take it out of the drone's reach without its ever coming close enough for us to get any sort of a mass estimate from its impeller signature."

"Um." Luchner rubbed his chin for a moment. "Assume that it is a contact and that it's headed in-system. Who'd be in the best position to intercept?"

"Normally, I'd say *Nuada*, Citizen Exec, but the sensor snafu would make things tough for her. The contact's barely sixty-six million klicks from her, but its also smack in the middle of the area we're watching for her. Without her gravitic array, she probably hasn't picked up a thing, and if it's headed for Samovar, it's accelerating almost straight away from her. She could probably run down a merchant ship, but even if she cuts her pods loose, just about any kind of warship should have the accel to stay away from her with the kind of head start this one will have."

"Which means we probably can't intercept in the outer zone," Luchner observed. "Which leaves *Dirk*."

"Yes, Citizen Exec," Allworth confirmed, and Luchner frowned again as he digested the information.

Technically, what happened in *Nuada*'s zone was her responsibility. *Katana* had her own sector to look after, and if she horned into someone else's interception problem and things went wrong, Luchner—or, rather, Citizen Captain Zachary—would make a convenient scapegoat. But Luchner possessed information Citizen Captain Turner didn't have, and that imposed a responsibility that cut across technical lines of authority. Or it did in Citizen Admiral Tourville's command, anyway, and Luchner rubbed his chin gently as he made himself look at the situation through Tourville's eyes.

The task group had too few ships to set up complete coverage, so Shannon Foraker had created a layered ambush to cover most likely arrival vectors. Anything that came in somewhere else would probably escape, but anything that translated back into n-space on a logical course would find evasion a much tougher proposition. So far the task group had managed to run down everyone who'd arrived in Adler since the system's change in management, though *Nuada's* hardware glitches threatened to throw a spanner into the works now. Luchner hoped that wouldn't come home to haunt Turner and his crew, but he made himself set that thought aside while he considered how the intercept effort was most likely to develop.

Like *Katana*, PNS *Dirk*, the ship responsible for the middle interception zone in Turner's sector, was one of the older *Sword*-class ships. That was why the ops plan relegated her to the inner, less risky station and assigned the bigger *Nuada* to play the role of beater, closing in from three and a half light-minutes beyond the hyper limit to cut any target's retreat. The *Mars* class were expected to come as a nasty surprise to the Manties: almost as large as some of the PN's prewar battlecruisers, they took full advantage of the improved EW systems the Navy had acquired from its contacts in the Solarian League . . . and by reducing magazine space they'd also managed to pack in nearly twice the broadside of a *Sword*-class ship but gave up less than twenty gravities in maximum acceleration to do it.

But however powerful *Nuada* was, her hardware faults meant she didn't know what *Katana* had just discovered. Without that knowledge, she wouldn't leave her station to pursue the possible contact, which would leave *Dirk* to cope with whatever it was on her own, and that could be bad. Not only could she find herself outclassed in a single-ship action, if in fact the contact was a Manty warship, but unlike *Katana*, the ships in the inner zone relied on the outer pickets to pick up incoming traffic. That meant *Dirk* would have deployed neither RDs nor missile pods.

"What's the current com delay to *Nuada*?" he asked after a moment.

"Twenty-two minutes, Citizen Exec."

"And the range from the target to *Dirk*?"

"Approximately eighteen-point-three light-minutes."

Luchner nodded again, then walked back to the command chair at the center of the bridge. He leaned over without seating himself, punched a com key, and waited until the small screen flicked alight with the image of Citizen Captain Helen Zachary. A moment later, the screen divided neatly in half down the center as Citizen Commissioner Kuttner dropped into the circuit.

"Yes, Fred?" Zachary said.

"We've got a possible contact in *Nuada*'s sector, Citizen Captain," the exec replied. He summarized Allworth's report, then went on, "With your permission, Citizen Captain, I'd like to alert *Nuada* and *Dirk* for an Alpha Intercept. We're only fifteen light-minutes from *Dirk*, so our transmission should reach her long before a ship accelerating after translation enters her sensor range, and if *Nuada* cuts her pods loose and goes to max accel as soon as she gets the word, she should have a pretty fair chance of intercepting the bogey if it tries to break back out across the limit. But since she *will* have to leave her pods behind to have a shot, I'd also like to alert *Raiden* and *Claymore* to support her and *Dirk* in case this is a battlecruiser or something even heavier."

"Um." Zachary scratched the tip of her nose. "How much delay would we build in if we simply alerted Turner and let him handle it?" she asked. She and Luchner both already knew the answer to that; she was asking it only to be sure the answer was officially on record before they stuck their necks out.

"*Nuada*'s about twenty-two light-minutes from us and eighteen from *Dirk*," Luchner replied. "It would take Turner at least forty minutes from the moment we send him the alert to pass it on to *Dirk*, and another two minutes to hit *Raiden* and *Claymore*. If we pass the word to the others at the same time we inform *Nuada*, we'll cut a minimum of thirteen minutes off the time for every one of the other ships, but our current geometry will let us take a full nineteen minutes off the time for *Dirk*."

"That sounds to me like ample justification for sticking our oar in," Zachary said, and shifted her eyes to meet Kuttner's on her own com screen. "Citizen Commissioner?"

"I agree. And we should probably alert *Count Tilly*, as well."

"Yes, Sir," Luchner said respectfully, forbearing to mention that standing orders required *any* contact to be reported to the flagship. Kuttner ought to know that—he'd certainly been present often enough when it was discussed—but it could be unwise to remind people's commissioners of things they were supposed to know.

"Very well, Fred. See to it. And keep us informed of any further developments," Zachary said.

"Yes, Citizen Captain." Luchner killed the circuit and turned to the com officer of the watch. "Fire up your transmitter, Hannah," he said.

• Chapter Fifteen

"Still nothing from Commodore Yeargin?" Alistair McKeon asked. Forty minutes had passed since *Prince Adrian's* translation back into normal-space. She'd moved almost two and a quarter light-minutes deeper into the Adler System, her velocity was up to 21,400 KPS, and the silence of her com section had become more than merely puzzling a half-hour ago.

"No, Sir." Lieutenant Sanko's reply was tense, despite its professional crispness, and McKeon turned his head to look at Honor. His gray eyes were worried, and Honor felt Nimitz twitch his tail uneasily as the emotions of those around him seeped into him.

The tension on the cruiser's bridge had begun as little more than vague disquiet—a sort of itch no one knew how to scratch—at the absence of any challenge from the system pickets, but it had grown steadily as *Prince Adrian* continued to accelerate in-system at a constant four hundred gravities. She might not be capable of transmitting FTL herself, but the ships of Task Group Adler were, and Sarah DuChene's course had been plotted to emerge from hyper within the envelope of one of Commodore Yeargin's limited numbers of sensor platforms. As such, *Prince Adrian* should have been detected, identified, and reported to Yeargin's flagship via the platform's grav pulse transmitter . . . and she should have picked up an FTL challenge from *Enchanter* within ten minutes of arrival.

She hadn't, and Honor had done her best to look unworried as the minutes stretched out. There was almost certainly a simple explanation, she told herself. *Yeargin doesn't have all that many sensors, so maybe she decided to change the deployment of the ones she does have from the pattern we were told about. But if she were going to do that, why didn't she post a picket to cover the hole? We're right on the most logical approach from Clairmont. Surely she'd want to be certain it was covered, wouldn't she?*

For that matter, it was possible Yeargin *had* picked *Prince Adrian* up and simply saw no reason to challenge a ship her sensors had already identified. If that were the case, however, it displayed an appallingly casual approach to the security of her command area. *Honor* would never have assumed a contact was in fact what it seemed to be until she'd absolutely confirmed its identity, and she found the thought of a system commander who would make such an assumption distasteful. Yet there was only one way to find out what Yeargin thought she was doing, and that was to go see.

But cautiously, Honor told herself. Very *cautiously. Better to be paranoid and wrong than overconfident and dead.*

McKeon was obviously thinking along the same lines, for he had quietly instructed Geraldine Metcalf to launch a pair of recon drones down his projected track. The stealthed RDs would sweep the area ahead of the ship, and their small FTL transmitters would report whatever they found in near real-time. Drones weren't cheap. Even when they could be recovered, as these probably could, it cost thousands to overhaul and refurbish them for reuse. Despite that, McKeon hadn't even asked for her approval to cover his decision to use them, which said a great deal about his state of mind.

Not that Honor would have hesitated for a moment if he had asked. The one thing no captain could ever have enough of was information, and McKeon had none at all. Without a position fix on at least one of Yeargin's ships, Russ Sanko couldn't even align his com lasers on it, so there was little point trying to contact anyone closer than Samovar itself. In the absence of an FTL challenge, McKeon had, in fact, transmitted a light-speed message to the planet ten minutes after arriving in-system. Unfortunately, Samovar's current orbital position put it over a half light-hour from *Prince Adrian*, so assuming an instant response, they still wouldn't hear anything back for another ten minutes. And if one thing was likely, given the general slackness which seemed to be the rule here, it was that there would be a delay before any acknowledgment was sent, so—

A sharp tone sounded, and Honor looked up quickly. She turned towards the tactical station, forcing herself to move with much greater calm than she actually felt, and watched Lieutenant Commander Metcalf bend over the shoulder of one of her techs. The slightly built tac officer twirled a lock of sandy-blond hair around one finger and pursed her lips, dark eyes thoughtful as she studied the plot, then looked at Alistair McKeon.

"We've got a contact, Skipper. It looks—"

Another tone sounded, and she broke off to recheck the plot. Her pursed lips turned into a puzzled frown, and she tapped in a command of her own. Her eyebrows rose, then flattened as the computers obediently brought their enhancement capacity to bear, and her voice was more than professionally flat when she looked back up.

"Correction, Skipper. We've got at least *two* contacts—and they're both operating stealthed."

"Two?" McKeon cocked his head, and Metcalf nodded.

"Yes, Sir. The closer is pursuing us from astern, coming in from about one-seven-eight by zero-zero-four. CIC is calling this one Alpha One, and range is approximately five-point-nine light-minutes. It's on a direct pursuit course with an acceleration of five hundred and ten gravities, but present velocity is barely twelve hundred KPS. The other one, designated Alpha Two, is almost dead ahead—bearing zero-zero-three, zero-one-four, range about fifteen-point-eight light-minutes. Alpha Two is on an intercept heading at seven-six-five-zero KPS, accelerating at five hundred and twenty gravities."

"How in hell did Alpha One get that close before we spotted him?" McKeon demanded.

"At her current velocity and acceleration, she can't have been under power for more than six minutes, Sir, so there was nothing *to* detect on passives. According to CIC's analysis, her EW seems to be quite efficient, too, and we've been concentrating on the area ahead of us. Given the contact's EW activity, CIC did well to spot him this quickly. And we only saw Alpha Two because our Beta Drone is practically on top of him." Metcalf's tone was that of a professional trying hard to sound neither defensive nor exasperated, and McKeon raised a hand to acknowledge her point.

"What can you tell me about Alpha One now that we *do* see him?"

"All we've got so far is a fairly fuzzy impeller signature. I've never seen anything quite like this bird's EW, and we're still trying to get a good enough fix on his systems to get through them. My best guess would be that he's either a battlecruiser or a really big heavy cruiser, Skipper, but it's only a guess."

"Understood," McKeon said, and glanced at Honor. "Ahead and astern? Under stealth?" he half murmured, then shook his head and turned to his com section. "Still nothing from Commodore Yeargin?"

"Nothing, Sir," Lieutenant Sanko replied, and McKeon's frown deepened. He rubbed an eyebrow, then climbed out of his command chair and crossed to Honor's side.

"Something's out of whack here, Ma'am. Badly," he said softly.

"Agreed." Honor's voice was equally low, and she reached up to rub Nimitz's ears as the 'cat shifted uneasily on her shoulder. She let her eyes sweep the bridge, watching the officers who were very carefully *not* watching her confer with their captain. Their earlier uneasiness had become something much sharper—not yet fear, but more than anxiety—and it suffused her link with the treecat like smoke.

"They're maneuvering to intercept," she said, and her mind ticked quickly and urgently as McKeon nodded.

There was no reason for Commodore Yeargin's units to intercept *Prince Adrian* rather than challenging her by com unless for some reason they'd decided to assume she was hostile, and that was ridiculous. A wise system commander always assumed that anything not definitely identified as friendly was *potentially* hostile, but pulling pickets off station for a physical intercept opened holes through which other potential hostiles could penetrate your perimeter, so the first step was always to challenge the unknown unit. And what Metcalf had just said about Alpha One's EW worried her. If the contact had been using Allied systems, CIC's database should have recognized them. But if they weren't Allied technology, they *were* better than anything the Peeps were supposed to have, which—

"Additional unidentified contacts!" Metcalf's senior petty officer sang out. "*Two* unidentified contacts in close company!"

"Designate as Alpha Three and Four and give me a position!" Metcalf snapped.

"We've got them on the Alpha Drone, Ma'am. Bearing zero-one-one by zero-zero-four, range approximately eighteen light-minutes. Present velocity is two-five-zero-zero KPS, accelerating at five KPS squared. Whatever they are, they're running under stealth, too, Commander, and I don't think they're using Allied systems. We've got better reads on their impeller signatures than our EW would give up to a drone's sensors." The petty officer turned her head to meet her officer's eyes. "CIC's calling Alpha Three a definite heavy cruiser and Alpha Four a possible battlecruiser, Ma'am, but Four's EW looks a lot like Alpha One's and the ID is tentative. Whoever they are, they're on intercept courses."

"Captain, I—" Metcalf began, then broke off, one hand pressing her earbug more firmly into her ear while she listened intently. Her face paled, and she cleared her throat. "Captain, CIC has just reclassified our contacts as definite hostiles. I am redesignating them Bandits One through Four. Bandits One and Four are still indeterminate, but the other two are definitely using Peep EW."

McKeon whirled to her, but Honor didn't even feel surprise. Not really. In fact, she was astonished by how calm she felt, as if her instincts had realized that something like this had to be happening from the moment Commodore Yeargin had failed to challenge their arrival. She folded her hands behind her and gazed at Metcalf's plot for perhaps four more seconds, then turned her gaze to the tac officer.

"Thank you, Commander Metcalf," she said, and the calmness of her voice would have fooled anyone who didn't know her. She stood for another moment, rocking gently on the balls of her feet, then turned back to McKeon. "Captain McKeon," she said formally, "we must assume the enemy has taken the Adler System."

A ripple of shock flowed outward from her. Alistair McKeon's bridge officers were veterans. Even before CIC reclassified the unknowns as hostile, the same explanation for the lack of a challenge had to have been nibbling at the backs of their brains, however unlikely and however much they would have preferred to deny the possibility, yet hearing their squadron commander actually say it was still a shock.

"But why come after us *this* way?" Venizelos asked. "The stealth I can understand, at least on the ones ahead of us, but we must've been right on top of Bandit One when we made our alpha translation. He *had* to see our footprint and get a good mass estimate off our impeller signature, so why wait—what? Over thirty-five minutes?—to start chasing us? Especially if he's a battlecruiser?"

"I don't know, Andy," McKeon said, never taking his eyes from Honor's. "Somebody must have picked up our footprint and warned the bastards in front of us—*they* certainly don't have the sensor range for it. So maybe *that's* what Bandit One's been doing: waiting until he was sure his buddies had received his alert."

"Probably," Honor agreed. "Not that an explanation really helps at this point." She crossed to Sarah DuChene's console and touched the astrogator on the shoulder. "Excuse me, Commander. I need to borrow your panel," she said almost absently. DuChene gave her a startled look, then moved out of her way, and Honor slid into the emptied chair.

Her eyes were as intent as her whirring thoughts, and her long fingers flicked over the number pad with crisp assurance. Usually she worked slowly and carefully, double- and even triple-checking her calculations, but now concentration overcame her normal lack of confidence in her mathematical ability and her fingers flew. A series of complex vectors—some red, some green—flashed across DuChene's display in rapid succession, but no one spoke as she worked, despite the ticking seconds.

It's going to be tight. Probably too tight, but there's no other way, is there? she thought, still with that inexplicable inner calm, looking at the results of her efforts. She felt something very different—something harsh and ugly with fear—gibbering on the far side of that calm, but she refused to let it affect her as she gazed at the last of the evasion courses she'd tried.

Had *Prince Adrian* been operating solo, Honor would already have ordered her to begin accelerating straight "up" from the ecliptic on a course which would have given her an excellent chance—not a certainty, but a chance any bookmaker would have taken—of getting away clean from all of her enemies. But she cruiser *wasn't* operating solo, which meant that simply running away, however tempting, was an unacceptable option.

"Commander Metcalf," she said into the silence about her.

"Yes, Milady?"

"When will Bandit One cross the hyper limit at his present acceleration?"

"In approximately . . . seventy minutes, Milady," Metcalf replied, and Honor heard McKeon inhale sharply as his tac officer confirmed what Honor's own calculations had already told her. She sat quietly for a moment longer, then stood and nodded to DuChene.

"Thank you, Commander. I'm finished now," she said quietly, and another nod of her head drew McKeon back over to the captain's chair. She stood for several seconds, looking into her old friend's eyes, then sighed.

"I don't know why Bandit One delayed his pursuit so long, either," she said, "but it's certainly working for him. Do you suppose he's clairvoyant?"

"That's one explanation, at least." McKeon tried to match her feeble attempt at humor, but his eyes were worried. "He's going to be right on top of the convoy at the moment it makes transit."

"Exactly." Honor nodded and pinched the bridge of her nose. On its present course, Bandit One would cross the hyper limit within less than a minute of the moment Thomas Greentree brought the rest of the convoy out of hyper . . . and the convoy would emerge right in the heart of the Peep's missile envelope.

It was unlikely Greentree would have time to realize what was happening before the first broadsides arrived. The odds might be five-to-one in favor of the convoy escorts, but the overwhelming advantage of surprise would go a long way towards canceling that numerical edge even in a stand-up fight. And the Peep might not even choose to engage the escorts at all—might not even *see* them with all those fat, defenseless merchantmen and transports on his targeting display. There were almost a hundred thousand garrison troops and technicians aboard the personnel ships of JNMTC–76, and every one of them could die in a matter of seconds if Bandit One chose to ignore the escorts.

That could not be allowed to happen. It *must* not be allowed to, and Honor dared not assume the Peeps were any stupider than she was. Indeed, their presence here—and the ominous absence of Commodore Yeargin's command—was a clear indication that this batch of Peeps, at least, knew what it was about. Which was the reason why *Prince Adrian* couldn't simply run for it.

If *Prince Adrian* came to a heading which made it impossible for Bandit One to overhaul, the Peep might do one of several things. He might continue the pursuit anyway, however unlikely that he could overtake his prey, on the principle that someone else might head *Prince Adrian* off and force her to break back towards him. Or he might simply give up, decelerate, and return to his original station, leaving his consorts to deal with her. Or he *might* do what Honor would do in his place: head for the point at which *Prince Adrian* had made her alpha translation. Bandit One would have to consider the possibility that *Adrian* was a singleton, but a captain with imagination would also allow for the possibility that she wasn't. That she had, in fact, arrived as exactly what she was: the lead scout of a convoy which would follow her into normal-space shortly.

And that was why Honor had to throw away her best chance to avoid action.

"We can't let that happen, Alistair," she said, still quietly. "And I'm afraid I see only one way to guarantee that it doesn't."

"We make him chase us," McKeon said flatly.

"Yes." Honor reached out to the arm of his command chair and tapped a function key, throwing one of the evasion patterns she'd entered at DuChene's station onto McKeon's repeater plot. "If we alter course about thirty-five degrees to port and go to five hundred gravities for fifteen minutes, then break back for the limit in the same plane," she said, "we'll swing away from Two, Three, and Four. Two will still have a chance to overhaul us, but only if she's got some accel in reserve. But we'll be giving One a chance to cut the angle on us and bring us to action short of the limit. Not by much. I estimate we'll be in his engagement envelope for no more than twenty-five minutes. To get the shot, though, he'll have to conform to our movements . . . which should put the convoy's translation point outside his range on emergence."

"I see." McKeon studied the vectors on his plot, then cleared his throat. "I can't fault your logic, Ma'am," he said quietly, "and if he's the only one with a shot at us, he'd almost have to take it on the theory of a bird in the hand's being worth two in hyper. But suppose he doesn't?"

"If he doesn't, he doesn't," Honor replied, "but it's all we can do. Even if we turned immediately to engage him, we'd need over an hour just to decelerate to rest relative to Adler . . . and we'd be another forty-three million klicks further in-system. He'd certainly maintain his present course and acceleration until he was inside the hyper limit, and Bandit Two would have so much overtake by the time we started back *out*-system that he'd run right up our backside before we ever engaged Bandit One."

McKeon rubbed his chin for a moment, then decided not to ask what she intended to do if her proposed course took them into the clutches of yet another Peep—one which hadn't brought its drive up and so had no impeller signature to warn them it was waiting for them. She would have considered that just as he had, and—also as he had—come to the conclusion that there was nothing they could do about it if it happened.

"If I may, Ma'am," he said instead, "I'd suggest we also deploy an RD and program its grav transmitters to order Captain Greentree and the rest of the convoy to hyper back out immediately."

"Agreed." Honor nodded crisply and stepped back from his command chair. He smiled crookedly at her courtesy and seated himself.

"I wish you were still aboard *Alvarez*," he said very, very quietly, and then turned his chair to face Commander Gillespie.

"Very well, Tony," he said calmly. "Bring us to battle stations and come thirty-five degrees to port at five hundred gravities."

• Chapter Sixteen

"Well I'll be damned." Citizen Captain Helen Zachary leaned back in her command chair and gave the people's commissioner seated beside her a tight smile. "It looks as if we're about to have company, Citizen Commissioner."

"So I see." Timothy Kuttner nodded, but he also frowned, and the fingers of his right hand drummed a fretful tattoo on his helmet. Like everyone else on *Katana's* bridge, Kuttner wore his skinsuit, but rather than rack his helmet on his command chair in proper naval fashion, he had it in his lap. Zachary had tried to explain (tactfully) to him why that was a bad idea—the shock of a hit could easily throw an unsecured helmet clear across a compartment, with potentially fatal consequences for its owner—but Kuttner liked to play with the thing. And, Zachary admitted, she hadn't really tried all *that* hard to convince him not to. He wasn't as bad as some commissioners, but he was a lot worse than others, and at the moment his expression was the one she least liked: that of a man looking hard for some suggestion he could make to prove he was on top of the situation. She'd had sufficient experience of that expression's consequences in the past, and she turned her attention quickly to Citizen Lieutenant Allworth in an effort to preempt Kuttner.

"How long until she enters the bag, Tactical?"

"Roughly another twenty-three minutes, if present headings and decelerations remain constant, Citizen Captain," Allworth said promptly, and Zachary nodded. She pondered for a moment, still carefully not meeting Kuttner's gaze while she did so, then beckoned her exec over before she finally looked back at the people's commissioner.

270

"With your permission, Sir," she told him briskly, "I intend to go to full power in twenty-five minutes."

"But if you wait that long, especially towing missile pods, you won't be able to match vectors with him before he breaks past us, will you?" Kuttner sounded surprised, and Zachary suppressed a sigh.

"No, Sir," she said patiently. "But there's no real reason for us to do so. Her closing velocity will be only six thousand KPS when we go to our own maximum acceleration, and at that point she'll be too close to avoid us. She'll have no choice but to accept action, and while our own velocity will never match hers, we can certainly keep her in range until she crosses the limit . . . assuming she lasts that long."

Her eyes flicked to Luchner's face, but the exec's attentive expression gave no sign of the exasperation she knew he had to share. *Katana* had gone to five percent power the moment it became clear the Manty's maneuvers were going to bring the enemy ship back towards her. *Katana's* EW could hide that weak an impeller signature even from Manticoran sensors at anything over thirty light-seconds, and Zachary, Luchner, and Allworth had made an almost perfect estimate of the Manty's course. Unless she changed heading in the next twenty-three minutes, she would enter *Katana's* missile envelope, headed almost directly towards the Republican cruiser . . . and still a good half-hour's flight inside the hyper limit.

Under other circumstances, that would have made Zachary nervous. The citizen captain was no coward, but only a fool (which she also was not) would try to deny the combat edge Manticoran ships enjoyed. But *Katana* had powerful support ready to hand in the form of PNS *Nuada*, which would enter extreme engagement range barely ten minutes after *Katana* opened fire. More than that, the system defenders had been given ample time to identify their target. It was one of the older *Prince Consort*-class cruisers, not a more modern *Star Knight*, which meant she and *Katana* would be well matched.

Or would have been, Zachary thought with a sharklike smile, if not for the half-dozen missile pods trailing astern of her own ship.

"I realize you can keep him in *missile* range, Citizen Captain," Kuttner's somehow petulant voice cut into the citizen captain's thoughts, "but you won't be able to bring him into *energy* range. Are you sure that fighting such a long-range action is wise, given the, ah, *disparity* in our antimissile capabilities?"

Zachary bit back an injudiciously candid response, but it was hard. She thought—briefly, but with intense longing—of sudden pressure losses and helmets which bounced away from idiot commissioners who combined a sense of their own importance with just enough knowledge to make them dangerous. *My, but he'd look nice with his lungs oozing out of his nose,* she reflected, but she also made herself smile gravely.

"I understand your point, Citizen Commissioner," she said, "but the conditions are a bit atypical, and I'd like to keep them that way." Kuttner frowned in puzzled confusion, and Zachary reminded herself to keep things literal—and simple. "What I mean, Sir," she went on, "is that, at the moment, the enemy can have no idea we're here. If she did, she would have chosen a different heading, or at least already changed course."

The citizen captain paused politely, quirking one eyebrow to ask if he followed her logic. It could have been an insulting expression, and part of Zachary longed to make it just that, but it wasn't, and Kuttner nodded his comprehension.

"That being the case," Zachary resumed, "I prefer to keep her ignorant of our presence until it becomes impossible for her to avoid us. In order to do that, I intend to hold our acceleration down to something I'm positive our EW can hide until she's at least two minutes inside the range at which she could avoid action with us. You're quite correct that waiting that long will mean we'll be unable to match velocities with her before she crosses the hyper limit, and that we'll be unable to force her into range of our energy weapons. However, the only headings on which she can *avoid* our energy envelope will force her closer to *Nuada,* which will push her deeper into Citizen Captain Turner's missile envelope."

She paused once more, and Kuttner nodded again, this time more positively.

"And, of course," she finished up, "while it's true our antimissile defense hasn't yet caught up with the Manties', we *do* have the advantage of our pods. That means we can open the action with a salvo of eighty-four birds. I doubt she'll be expecting that kind of fire, and even if she is, it should saturate her point defense."

"I see." Kuttner frowned importantly for another moment, then nodded a final time. "Very well, Citizen Captain. I approve your plan."

"What's your best estimate of Bandit One's engagement time now, Gerry?" Alistair McKeon asked.

"I make it no more than eleven minutes from the time she can first range on us, Skipper," Lieutenant Commander Metcalf replied instantly. "She was late making her first turn." The tactical officer looked up at her captain. "I'm starting to think there's something wrong with her sensors, Sir. If her gravitics are unreliable, it might explain why she was slow starting after us. And if she has to wait for light-speed telemetry from an RD or sensor updates from other ships, it could also explain why she was late adjusting to our evasion."

"I see." McKeon rubbed his chin. "Any better read on her mass?"

"It's firming up some as the range drops, Skip, but whatever she's using for EW is a lot better than anything the Peeps are supposed to have. CIC still wants to call her a battlecruiser, but I think this may be one of those new heavy cruisers ONI warned us about. Unless she's red-lining her compensator—and I don't see any reason for her to take that kind of risk just to catch a single Manticoran cruiser—her accel's too high for a battlecruiser. If I had to bet money, I'd say Bandit Four's the same class, whatever it is."

"I see," McKeon repeated. He patted her lightly on the shoulder and turned back towards his own command chair, then paused. Honor stood beside that chair, hands clasped behind her. Her spine was ramrod straight, and her expression was composed, but she, Andreas Venizelos, and Andrew LaFollet, unlike anyone else on the command deck, wore no skinsuits, and McKeon's stomach muscles tightened once again at the sight.

He drew a deep breath and walked over to stand beside her, and she turned her head to regard him gravely.

"Eleven minutes," he said quietly.

"I heard," Honor replied, and took one hand from behind her to rub the tip of her nose. She glanced at the time readout in the corner of McKeon's command chair repeater plot, then gestured at the small icon that represented the convoy's projected arrival point.

"Ten minutes," she said softly, and McKeon nodded.

"Ten minutes," he agreed. "And Bandit One's not going to be able to range on them before they hyper back out."

"We also serve who run away," Honor replied with a small smile, and McKeon surprised them both with a genuine chuckle.

But his moment of humor was short lived, and his eyes returned to the plot as if drawn by magnetism. *Prince Adrian's* effort to lure Bandit One away from the convoy's translation point had worked, but it had also demonstrated just how much firepower the Peeps had deployed to ambush them. In addition to the four ships Metcalf had originally picked up, she and her recon drones had since located five more, including three destroyers, a light cruiser, and what could only be a battlecruiser. None of the additional units she'd picked up had any chance of over-hauling *Prince Adrian*, but their sheer numbers and the fact that they were *trying* to overtake her said ominous things about the person who'd set this ambush up. Whoever was in command over there had positioned his ships with such care that even with her early detection, *Prince Adrian* would have found it all but impossible to evade all of them.

Having done that, the enemy commander obviously intended to bring all the strength he could to bear. He wanted not equality or a simple advantage in firepower but a crushing superiority, and where many a CO would have given up and whistled his rearmost units back to their initial positions, this one had done nothing of the sort. The numbers said they would never catch *Prince Adrian*, but those numbers didn't include the possibility that the Manticoran ship might be damaged in the coming clash with Bandit One, now bearing down on her from starboard. If *Adrian* took heavy impeller damage or some other freak hit—or even if she was simply forced to turn sharply away from her opponent—one or more of the trailers might conceivably get into range to engage her yet. The odds against it were long, but this character was going to keep coming with everything he had for as long as there was the smallest conceivable chance that it might do him some good, and that was a most un-Peep-like attitude.

McKeon drew his eyes from the plot and looked back at his commodore, and his lips tightened. He hesitated a moment, and then leaned close to her.

"Honor, will you *please* get out of here and into a rescue suit?" he demanded in a voice pitched too low for anyone else to hear but still harsh with concern.

She gazed at him with dark, chocolate-brown eyes, and he felt his teeth trying to grind together at her calm expression and quizzically arched eyebrow. She reached up to rub Nimitz's ears, and the 'cat pressed against her fingers. McKeon needed no link to Nimitz to know the 'cat's deep, anxious purr urged Honor to take his advice, but she seemed as unmoved by Nimitz's advice as by McKeon's.

"I need to be here," she said mildly, and McKeon inhaled sharply. Part of him wanted to grab her by the scruff of the neck, haul her physically off the bridge, and hand her over to his Marines with orders to stuff her into a suit for her own good. The fact that any such attempt on his part would end in a swift and humiliating fiasco made it no less attractive . . . only impractical. Even assuming LaFollet didn't take his head off for laying hands on Steadholder Harrington, Honor herself could tie him up in a bow anytime she felt like it, and they both knew it. But commodore and steadholder or not, he wanted her off his command deck before they entered Bandit One's range, because neither she nor any other human member of her party had brought their skinsuits with them when they came over from *Alvarez.*

Navy and Marine skinsuits weren't something which could be ordered off the rack. They had to be very carefully fitted to their wearers—indeed, "fitted" was a barely adequate word, for in many respects they were custom built to suit the individual for whom they were intended. Other vacuum gear, like the heavy hardsuits that construction crews wore or the clumsy rescue suits which were part of any ship's lifesaving gear, could be worn by almost anyone but had limited utility. Hardsuits, for instance, were basically small, independent spacecraft designed for extended deep-space use or handling cargo in depressurized holds. They literally wouldn't fit into the internal spaces of a starship, and while rescue suits could be worn almost anywhere, they were little more than emergency environmental envelopes designed to be towed around by rescue crews.

In many respects, Honor and her party would have been better off aboard a civilian transport, for interstellar law required commercial ships to carry sufficient suits for all passengers. Sheer cost, not to mention the need for fitting time, made it impossible for liners to provide that many *skinsuits*, so passenger suits were a cross between a rescue suit and a skinsuit—almost a throwback to the clumsy suits of the early first-century Post Diaspora, though considerably less bulky. Even they would have been unsuitable for long-term wear, and their old-fashioned gloves lacked the miniaturized, biofeedback servomechs which made it possible for a skinsuited individual to thread a needle even in vacuum, but they were infinitely preferable to a rescue suit.

Unfortunately, *Prince Adrian*'s equipment list didn't include any of them. Rescue suits were provided for those cases in which people were temporarily separated from their personal equipment, but the Navy assumed naval personnel normally would keep their issue skinsuits to hand. Under the letter of the regs, Honor and her people should have brought their suits with them, however inconvenient the extra baggage would have been, since they'd intended to be aboard *Prince Adrian* for over twelve hours, but that regulation was routinely ignored. And so it was that of her entire party, only Nimitz, whose special skinsuit fitted neatly into a custom-designed carryall, was properly equipped for a warship at battle stations.

"Look," McKeon said now, still careful to keep his voice low, "you're not the only one who's going to die if we lose pressure here." He twitched his head at Venizelos and LaFollet, who were busy ignoring the conversation. *"They're* not suited up, either."

Something flickered in those dark brown eyes, and Honor turned to look at her subordinates. LaFollet seemed to feel her gaze, for he looked up and met it levelly, and her eyes flicked back to McKeon.

"You fight dirty," she said softly, an edge of steel in her voice, and he shrugged.

"So sue me."

She regarded him for several silent seconds, then cleared her throat.

"Andy, take Andrew and go below and join the others," she said crisply.

Venizelos turned quickly, and his expression indicated both that he'd anticipated her order and that he didn't much like it.

"I assume you'll be joining us, Milady," he said flatly. It wasn't a question, and Honor's lips thinned.

"You may assume whatever you wish to assume, Commander. But you'll do your assuming in the boat bay gallery in a rescue suit."

"With all due respect, Commodore Harrington, I believe my place is here," Venizelos replied. Honor's eyes hardened and she started to speak harshly, then paused and visibly got a grip on her temper.

"I understand that, Andy," she said much more quietly, "but there's nothing at all you can do here, and there's no point in both of us being pigheaded."

Despite the tension in the air, amusement flickered in Venizelos' eyes at the word "both," but he showed no sign of retreating.

"You're right there, Ma'am. That's why I feel you should join the rest of us in the boat bay."

"I'm sure you do," Honor replied evenly, "but there *is* a difference between us, you know." One of Venizelos' eyebrows arched, and she smiled with bleak humor. "You're a commander, and I'm a commodore. That means *I* can order *you* to go."

"I—" Venizelos began, but her raised hand cut him off in midbreath. It wasn't an arrogant gesture, or a dismissive one, yet its finality was impossible to disobey.

"I'm serious, Andy. Whatever Captain McKeon may believe, *I* need to be here. This ship is part of my squadron, and her current position is the result of my orders. But you *don't* need to be here, and you're going to the boat bay right now."

Venizelos' mouth set rebelliously, and he darted a look past her to McKeon, as if appealing to *Prince Adrian*'s CO for support. But McKeon only looked grimly at Honor's back, with the expression of a man who knew he'd lost the argument. The chief of staff hesitated a moment longer, but then his shoulders sagged and he nodded.

"Very well, Ma'am," he said heavily, and turned to punch for the lift. "Come on, Andrew," he said in that same, resigned tone, but the armsman shook his head.

"No, Sir," he said calmly. Venizelos' head turned, but the major wasn't looking at him. Instead, his gray eyes were locked with his Steadholder's, and he smiled ever so faintly. "Before you say anything, My Lady, I should remind you that this is one order you can't give."

"I beg your pardon?" Honor's tone was chill, but LaFollet refused to flinch.

"I'm your personal armsman, My Lady. Under Grayson law, you can't legally order me to leave you if I believe your life is in danger. If you attempt to, it is not only my right but my responsibility to refuse to obey."

"I'm not in the habit of tolerating insubordination, Major!" Honor said sharply, and LaFollet came to attention.

"I'm sorry you regard me as insubordinate, My Lady," he said. "If you wish to construe my actions in that light, you are fully entitled to dismiss me from your service upon our return to Grayson. In the meantime, I remain bound by my oath—not simply to you, but to the Conclave of Steadholders—to discharge my duty as your armsman."

Honor glared at him for a long, smoldering moment, but her tone was almost conversational when she spoke again.

"We're not on Grayson, Andrew. We're on a Queen's ship. Suppose I instruct Captain McKeon, as *Prince Adrian's* commanding officer, to order you below?"

"In that case, My Lady, I would, regretfully, be forced to refuse his orders," LaFollet said, and his tone, too, had changed, as if they both knew already how the argument was going to end yet shared some peculiar responsibility to carry the debate to its inevitable conclusion. And as Alistair McKeon watched them, he realized that more than misplaced pride or even LaFollet's sense of duty drove him. The Grayson's granite intransigence arose from a deep, intensely personal loyalty—in its own way, a deep and abiding love, though one without romance or sexuality— to the woman he served.

"You can't refuse." Honor's voice was gentler. "He's the captain of this ship."

"And I, My Lady, am your armsman," LaFollet replied, and this time he smiled.

Honor gazed at him a moment longer, then shook her head. "Remind me to have a long discussion with you when we get home, Major," she told him.

"Of course, My Lady," he said politely, and she smiled one of her crooked smiles. Then she pointed a long index finger at Venizelos.

"As for you, Commander, on your way!" she said, and to his own surprise, Venizelos chuckled. He, too, looked at LaFollet for a moment, and then he nodded and stepped into the lift. The doors closed behind him, and Honor turned, gave McKeon another of those smiles that combined intransigence and apology.

"Convoy translation in six minutes," Geraldine Metcalf announced into the silence.

"They'll enter the bag in another fourteen minutes, Citizen Captain," Citizen Lieutenant Allworth observed, and Helen Zachary nodded.

"You know, Skipper," Citizen Commander Luchner said, "there's something odd about this bird."

"Odd? What do you mean, Fred?"

"I'm not sure," the exec said slowly. He rubbed his upper lip with the side of an index finger for a moment, frowning in thought. "It's just that I can't figure out why he's made all his maneuvers in the same plane. I mean, if I were him, I'd have been looking for the least-time course out of here the instant I realized someone was waiting for me."

"What are you trying to say, Citizen Commander?" People's Commissioner Kuttner demanded.

"I'm not sure," Luchner repeated, hiding a flash of annoyance at Kuttner's intrusion into his conversation with his captain. The commissioner's tense, almost accusatory tone didn't help things a bit, the exec reflected, fighting to avoid the feeling that he had to defend himself against it.

"I believe what the Citizen Exec is pointing out, Sir," Zachary intervened, "is that the evasive action the enemy's initiated wasn't the most effective one available. Of course, it's entirely possible that whoever's in command over there simply made a less than optimum decision; that sort of thing can happen in any navy, after all. But it's part of Citizen Commander Luchner's duties to consider whether or not there could be some other reason for it—one which would make sense to us, too, if we only knew what it was."

"With all due respect, Citizen Captain," Kuttner said impatiently, "I don't see any mystery. He's detected the units pursuing him, but as you yourself pointed out to me, he doesn't know we're here, which means he's running for what he thinks is open space."

"Perhaps so," Zachary replied politely, "but it's never wise to get too locked into a single possible explanation, Sir." She was a bit surprised at herself. She'd entered the conversation only to divert Kuttner from Luchner and protect her exec; now she felt an odd compulsion to continue the argument, and she wasn't certain whether it arose simply out of her irritation at Kuttner's smug assurance or if Luchner's question had roused some instinctive suspicion of her own. "She may not know *we're* here, Citizen Commissioner," she went on, "but her course changes certainly make it clear that she's known *Nuada* was there from the beginning. In fact, I think it's most likely that she picked *Nuada* up before she realized anyone else was waiting for her."

"And?" Kuttner demanded impatiently when she paused.

"And her present course makes it impossible for her to avoid engaging *Nuada* . . . the ship she must have the best fix on," Zachary said slowly. She turned to Luchner and her eyes darkened. "That's it, isn't it, Fred?" she said. "That's what's bothering you. Why choose a course that gives the one ship she *has* to know about a shot at her?"

"Yes, Citizen Captain." Luchner's own eyes lit with sudden understanding. "That's exactly what it is! If he'd simply made a ninety degree alteration in any plane—or even turned at right angles in the *same* plane—he'd have scooted back out across the limit before *Nuada* could possibly catch him. He'd have avoided *all* of us, unless he happened to stumble over a ship lying doggo like we were. But as it is—"

"As it is, she's drawn the pursuit of the only ship who could have interdicted the volume in which she made her alpha translation," Zachary said flatly. Kuttner swiveled his head back and forth between the officers, his expression baffled, and Zachary leaned back with a sigh. "That's a very clever captain over there," she said. "Aside from the fact that she doesn't know *we're* out here, she's done everything exactly right."

"Would you mind explaining what you're talking about?" Kuttner snapped, and Zachary turned her head to look at him.

"If the Citizen Commander and I are correct, Sir, it's very simple. You see—"

"Hyper footprint!" Citizen Lieutenant Allworth barked. "Multiple hyper footprints bearing one-oh-six by oh-oh-three!"

GNS *Jason Alvarez* led Convoy JNMTC–76 back into n-space. Ship after ship emerged from hyper, each in turn spangling the emptiness with brilliant azure fire as Warshawski sails hundreds of kilometers in diameter bled transit energy. No sensor array within forty light-minutes could have missed that massive signature, and on the flag bridge of PNS *Count Tilly*, Lester Tourville swore with vile intensity as CIC reported.

Nor was he alone. Every Peep skipper in the Adler System realized what *Prince Adrian* had done, and their sulfurous reactions to the enormity of the prize they'd been sucked away from mirrored their admiral's. Aside from *Nuada* herself—and, of course, the hidden *Katana*—every ship which had been pursuing *Prince Adrian* swerved away to go after the convoy. Not because they had any realistic hope of intercepting it, but simply because they couldn't see that huge, glittering opportunity and *not* pursue it.

Captain Thomas Greentree stood at Lieutenant Commander Terracelli's shoulder, looking down at the tac officer's larger, more detailed plot. It would take a few minutes for *Alvarez*'s sensors to sort things out, but in the meantime—

"Sir!" Greentree's turned quickly at his com officer's sudden, uncharacteristic exclamation. He started to open his mouth, but Lieutenant Chavez went right on speaking. "We're picking up a Flash Priority transmission from Lady Harrington, Sir!"

"*Flash* Priority?" Greentree repeated. "What does it say?"

"I don't know yet, Sir. It's FTL and it's still coming in. I—"

Chavez broke off, his eyes going wide, and Greentree made himself clamp his mouth shut. There was no point badgering the com officer with questions he couldn't answer yet, and despite many improvements over the crude original systems, the FTL com's one real drawback remained its slow data transmission rate. It could shoot pulses across light-minutes virtually instantaneously, but the time required to generate each pulse meant a simple declarative sentence could take as much as two full minutes to transmit. Which, of course, was why code groups were used. It was almost like a revision to the ancient wet-navy days of signal flags, when a flag could stand for a single letter of the alphabet or an entire sentence from the fleet's code book, and—

"Orders from the Flag, Captain," Chavez said, and Greentree felt his jaw clench as he noted the com officer's shaken tone and jerked his head for him to continue.

"The convoy is to reenter hyper and return to Clairmont immediately," Chavez said, and now his voice was flat and utterly toneless. "You are to assume command, Sir . . . and inform Admiral Sorbanne at Clairmont that the enemy has taken the Adler System."

"*I'm* to assume command?" Greentree heard his own voice asking the question before he could stop it, and Chavez nodded.

"Yes, Sir. And return to Clairmont with the convoy. Immediately."

"But what about Lady Harrington?" Terracelli blurted. Greentree turned to glare at him, but his heart wasn't in it, for the tac officer's question burned in his own mind.

"I—" Chavez paused and looked back down at his display where more clusters of alphanumeric characters had continued forming even as he spoke. His eyes flicked over them, and then he swallowed. "*Prince Adrian* is drawing the Peeps into pursuing her, Captain," he said in that same flat voice. "She will proceed independently to rejoin the squadron at Clairmont. And—" his tonelessness wavered, and he looked back up to meet Greentree's eyes "—the order to hyper back out is repeated, Sir. Twice."

Greentree stepped quickly to the lieutenant's side and gazed down at the display, and his lips were a thin, tight line. Chavez was right, and the captain's lips thinned still further as one final sentence spelled itself out very slowly, letter by letter.

"These orders are nondiscretionary, Thomas," it said, and his fists clenched. He looked up, meeting Chavez's eyes, and for just an instant he hovered on the brink of ordering the com officer to delete that final sentence from the message log. But he was a naval officer. However much his instincts might scream to go to Lady Harrington's assistance, he was a naval officer, responsible not just for himself but for all the ships of the squadron and all the merchantmen under their escort, and he had his orders.

"Sir," Lieutenant Commander Terracelli said into the silence, "I'm picking up incoming impeller signatures."

"How many?"

"At least five, Sir. Two are probably battlecruisers."

"How long?"

"Minimum of thirty-one minutes to extreme missile range for the closest, Sir."

"Thank you."

Greentree turned away, walked slowly back to his command chair, and lowered himself into it. Thirty-one minutes. It was plenty of time for the convoy to make its escape. Once back across into hyper, the grav wave they'd ridden to Adler would let them accelerate at thousands of gravities, and all his merchantmen were JNMTC ships. By the time the first Peep could translate in pursuit, they'd be too far down range for the Peeps even to track them, far less fire on them. All he had to do was abandon his commodore.

But he really had no choice, did he? He closed his eyes for a moment, then opened them and looked back at Chavez.

"General signal, Com," he rasped. "The convoy will reenter hyper in two minutes. Adrian," he didn't even look at his astrogator, "plot our course back to Clairmont and pass it to Lieutenant Chavez for transmission to all units. *Santander* will take point."

"There they go," Luchner said bitterly, and Zachary nodded in silent agreement. She shared his bitterness—a bitterness made all the worse because they'd figured out what was coming before it actually happened—but she also felt an unwilling professional admiration for the Manty cruiser skipper who'd sucked *Nuada* out of position to do anything about it. Not that she intended to let that stop her from destroying her opponent.

She watched the impeller signatures of the convoy vanish and raised her voice.

"How long were they in n-space, Tactical?"

"Approximately nine minutes, Citizen Captain, but their initial translation required over three minutes."

"Thank you," Zachary said absently, and looked at Luchner. "Not bad at all for a convoy that size, was it Fred?" Luchner shook his head, and she smiled thinly. "Well, now that they've put one over on *us*, let's just see if we can't give Ms. Cruiser a little surprise of her own. Pass the word to Engineering. I want maximum military power in four minutes."

• Chapter Seventeen

Honor managed to keep the exultation out of her expression, yet she felt as if the entire universe had just been lifted from her shoulders. An echo of her own enormous relief flowed into her from the rest of *Prince Adrian*'s bridge crew as the convoy blinked safely back into hyperspace, and she turned her head to exchange a satisfied look with McKeon. Now all they had to do was deal with the one enemy between them and escape, and while anything could happen in a deep space engagement, Honor was more than willing to take her chances in an eleven-minute, maximum range running engagement with a Peep. The Allies' advantages in missile combat remained overwhelming, and even if that really was a battlecruiser over there, it wouldn't have the time or the firepower to—

An alarm buzzed harshly, and her head snapped around to the tactical station as a brilliant red icon glared in Metcalf's main display, thirty degrees off *Prince Adrian*'s port bow but accelerating to cross her base course

"New unidentified contact!" Surprise sharpened the tac officer's voice. "Designate this contact Bandit Ten. She must've been holding her accel down to hide from us," Metcalf continued, but then her tone changed as initial surprise gave way to puzzlement. "Skipper, CIC calls it a *Sword*-class cruiser from its impeller signature and emissions fingerprint, but there's something wrong with the drive numbers."

"What d'you mean, 'wrong'?" McKeon demanded.

"She's not accelerating nearly fast enough for the amount of energy she's radiating," Metcalf replied. "She should be

286

turning up at least five KPS-squared with that strong a drive signature, and she's barely making a good four and a quarter."

McKeon frowned, but he had much more to worry about than an unexplained drive ambiguity, and he shook that concern aside to concentrate on more pressing ones.

"Assume constant accelerations and headings and project time to missile range and our time to the hyper limit," he said crisply.

"Aye, aye, Sir." Metcalf's hands danced across her panel while McKeon frowned down at his plot. Honor frowned at it, as well, but she also gnawed the inside of her lip, for she could think of at least one all too likely reason for the Peep's low acceleration.

"On the assumptions you specified, Skipper, we're thirty-one minutes from the limit," Metcalf reported after several seconds. "The missile geometry will give Bandit Ten a maximum powered engagement range of just under eight million klicks, and we'll enter her envelope in seventeen and a half minutes. Assuming our course and accel remain constant, but she alters to maximize her engagement time, she can stay with us all the way to the limit—call it thirteen-point-five minutes from the time she opens fire."

"Can we avoid her?"

"Negative, Sir. We can reduce her engagement window, but we can't stay out of her reach. And she's positioned herself just about perfectly, Skip. With her coming in high from the left and Bandit One coming in from starboard and low, she's got us boxed. The further away from *her* we stay, the closer we come to Bandit One. As it is, we'll be in range of both of them simultaneously for at least eleven minutes."

"I see." McKeon rubbed his jaw, then punched numbers into his plot. He considered them briefly, tried another combination, and looked up at Honor. "Gerry's right, Ma'am," he said quietly. "We're between Scylla and Charybdis. I can reduce Bandit Ten's engagement window to a maximum of ten minutes, but only if I *increase* Bandit

One's to a minimum of fifteen. Or I can leave Bandit One at eleven minutes and accept the thirteen-plus-minute engagement from Bandit Ten."

Honor nodded and gripped her hands together behind her. She pursed her lips for a moment, then sighed.

"You do realize the most likely explanation for Bandit Ten's low observed accel, of course," she said.

"Missile pods," McKeon replied grimly.

"Probably," Honor agreed. She gazed at her old friend for several seconds, but she said nothing more. She might be the commodore of CruRon Eighteen, but Alistair McKeon was the captain of HMS *Prince Adrian*. The responsibility for what happened to his ship was his, and so was the decision on how he fought her. Honor was as aware as McKeon that many flag officers would have refused to admit that in their own desperate need to *do* something, but this was no squadron-level decision, for there *was* no squadron. There was only *Prince Adrian*, on her own in a single-ship engagement, and even if she hadn't been, Honor had complete faith in Alistair McKeon's judgment. She would not insult him by interfering with his orders or second-guessing his decisions, and she saw a flicker of gratitude in his eyes before he turned back to his officers.

"Chief Harris, roll us a hundred degrees to starboard but maintain heading and acceleration," he told his helmsman crisply, and then swiveled his chair to face Metcalf. "From his accel, Bandit Ten is probably towing missile pods, Gerry, but Bandit One's accel has been too high for that all along. We could cut Ten's engagement time by altering course to starboard and diving away from him, but there's not much point. Ten minutes or thirteen, he's still going to get his initial salvo off, and there's nothing we can do about it, but Bandit One's probably got more *sustained* missile capacity. So we'll stay low, take Ten's best punch, and keep as far from One as we can for as long as we can."

"Understood, Sir," Metcalf replied tensely.

❖   ❖   ❖

"Well, she's made up her mind," Helen Zachary said softly. The Manticoran cruiser had rolled ship, turning the belly of her wedge to *Katana*, and her EW had come on-line. With the enemy accelerating steadily towards *Katana*, the theoretical maximum powered range of the bigger, more powerful missiles in Zachary's pods was on the order of eight and a half million kilometers, but the Manty's ECM and decoys would reduce their *effective* range to barely seven million. That should still be enough, however.

"What do you mean, 'made up her mind'?" Kuttner demanded. "He hasn't done a thing except bring up his EW. He certainly hasn't altered course!"

"No, she hasn't," Zachary agreed. "And she's not going to. Her original heading will expose her to a total of just under twenty-five minutes of fire: thirteen and a half from us, and eleven from *Nuada*. Any course alteration would decrease the engagement window for one of us, but only by *increasing* it for the other. She's playing the odds, but notice the fact that she's rolled ship away from us."

"So what?" Kuttner asked, and Zachary managed not to sigh.

"By rolling her port sidewall away from us, Sir, she rolls it *towards* Citizen Captain Turner. It doesn't give him a very good shot, but it gives him a better one than it gives us, and she's also staying low, keeping the belly of her wedge towards us. In other words, she's more worried about protecting herself from our fire than *Nuada*'s, which suggests she's figured out we're towing pods." Zachary shook her head. "I told you that was a sharp customer over there, Citizen Commissioner."

Seconds dragged on *Prince Adrian*'s bridge even as the digital time displays raced downward. There was no brilliant, last-minute maneuver this time. The elements of the equation were brutally clear, and most of *Prince Adrian*'s officers had seen Allied missile pods in action. They knew what was coming, and the only real question was how many missiles Bandit Ten had available. Oh, it also mattered how good they were, and when the Peeps would choose to fire them, but if Bandit Ten had enough of them, quality and timing became secondary. Even under ideal conditions, EW could expect to fool only so many missiles. Those that got through would have to be intercepted by active defenses, and there was, quite simply, an absolute upper limit to the number of targets *Prince Adrian's* defensive fire control and weapons could handle before they became saturated. And without her squadron mates to lend their weight to her defensive fire, that number was lower than Alistair McKeon or Honor Harrington wanted to think about.

"Coming into our maximum missile range in fifteen seconds," Metcalf announced finally, her voice taut with the professional calm of her training.

"Engage as specified," McKeon replied firmly.

"Hostile launch!" Citizen Lieutenant Allworth sang out. "Multiple launches. Estimate sixteen inbound."

"This soon? How can they possibly expect to hit us at this range?" Kuttner forgot to sound officious in his genuine bafflement, and Zachary smiled humorlessly.

"They're not shooting at *Katana*, Citizen Commissioner, and those aren't laser heads." Kuttner stared at her, and her nostrils flared. "They're old-fashioned nukes, Sir, going for proximity soft kills on the pods." She looked away from the commissioner and considered her tactical display. The Manticoran warheads sped towards her command, and if she was right about their warheads and targeting, they would detonate well astern of *Katana*—far enough out to be a difficult point defense solution, yet close enough to burn out the electronics of her missile pods. But they would take time to arrive, and she refused to allow their threat to spook her into a premature launch of her own missiles.

"Citizen Lieutenant Allworth," she said crisply.

"Yes, Citizen Captain?"

"You will flush your pods in . . . one hundred and forty seconds from now."

✧   ✧   ✧

Honor watched *Prince Adrian*'s first salvo sweep towards the enemy. A second followed fifteen seconds later, and a third. A fourth, and still the Peep made no reply. Ten broadsides were in space—a hundred and sixty missiles—without drawing a single answering shot, and she felt the rising hope of some of McKeon's officers. But she didn't share their elation . . . and neither did McKeon. They looked at one another, and Honor didn't need Nimitz to know what McKeon was thinking.

The captain had hoped an early launch on his part might shake his enemy's nerve, push her into an early launch of her own, while her accuracy would be at its lowest. But the Peep commander had refused the bait, which left only the meager hope that she might wait too *long*, let the missiles of *Prince Adrian*'s first broadside get in close to her pods and cripple them before they could—

"Missile separation!" Geraldine Metcalf announced flatly, and Honor's nails cut into her palms as her hands fisted behind her. "Multiple missile separations," Metcalf went on. "Estimate eighty-plus inbound."

"Damn," Alistair McKeon said almost mildly.

Eighty-four missiles howled towards HMS *Prince Adrian*. That was little more than half the total she had already fired, but there was an enormous difference between ten separate sixteen-missile broadsides, separated in time and space so that each offered the missile defense crews its own fire solution problem, and a single, massive deluge. It was a grim equation the People's Navy had faced all too often since the war's opening battles. Now it was the turn of the Royal Manticoran Navy, and Geraldine Metcalf and her assistants did their best as the tide of destruction roared down on them.

Jammers snarled, fighting to blind the incoming missiles' homing systems, and decoys sang to them, tempting them astray. But the People's Republic's new Solarian League-upgraded missiles were far more dangerous than the ones with which the PN had begun the war. Their sensors were more sophisticated, the capability of their targeting discrimination software had been increased by a factor of three, and the RMN's lack of data on them made Metcalf's ECM much less effective than projected. Barely a quarter of the birds in that massive salvo were blinded, and only a handful more succumbed to the decoys' seduction. Fifty-seven of them burned straight through the cruiser's best EW efforts, and countermissiles zipped out to meet them. The bloodred icons began to vanish from Metcalf's plot with mechanical precision, but they died too slowly. Thirty-five broke through the countermissile envelope, and last-ditch laser clusters trained onto them, firing desperately, trying to kill them before they reached attack range.

The lasers got nineteen. Only sixteen missiles, less than twenty percent of the original broadside, survived to reach attack range, but it was enough. The cruiser writhed in desperate evasion attempts, and she managed to avoid some of them, but they came driving in, with ample time and power remaining on their drives to execute their terminal attack maneuvers, and she couldn't avoid them all.

Four of the sixteen laser heads wasted themselves against the floor of *Prince Adrian's* impeller wedge as she spun on her axis to interpose it, and three more overshot her and clawed equally uselessly at her wedge's roof. Of the other nine, five detonated to port and "above" the cruiser, and like the missiles in Manticoran missile pods, those in *Katana's* pods were as powerful as anything a super-dreadnought might have carried. *Prince Adrian* bucked as clusters of bomb-pumped lasers slashed arrogantly through her sidewall to savage her hull. Armor splintered, internal bulkheads shattered, two missile tubes, a graser, three laser clusters, and her number three radar array were smashed, and thirty-two members of her crew died as the energy blew into her hull, but the sidewall and the antiradiation fields inside it had blunted and attenuated those lasers.

But there *was* no sidewall to protect against the four laser heads which exploded directly ahead of her. Their clustered fury ripped straight down the throat of her wedge, and damage alarms shrieked as transfer energy slammed into her, tearing alloy like tissue and slaughtering her people. Power levels fluctuated madly, spikes surging through the systems in the forward portion of the ship too quickly for circuit breakers to function, and massive secondary explosions followed in their wake. Honor was thrown to her knees as a giant's fist shook McKeon's ship, like a terrier shaking a rat, and the bridge displays flickered, died, and then came back up.

"Damage report!" McKeon snapped, but there was no response. He stabbed at the com buttons on his chair arm, plugging directly into Damage Control Central. "Damage report!" he repeated, but *still* there was no answer, and he punched another combination, this one direct to Commander Gillespie's com. "Taylor, I need a damage report!"

"The Exec's dead, Skipper," someone gasped over the intercom after a seeming eternity. "DCC's gone. We're . . . all . . . dead . . . down . . . ."

The voice died, and McKeon closed his eyes in anguish.

"Good hits on Bandit Ten!" Metcalf announced. "We got at least four in on the bastards, Sir!"

"Negative function on all forward point defense!" someone else barked. "We've lost Lidar One and Two! Grav Three's down!"

"Switch to Lidar Five!" Metcalf replied, and one of her assistants acknowledged the order, but the tide of disaster rolled on over her voice. Without Damage Control Central the reports came in piecemeal . . . but they came.

"Graser One is down. Heavy casualties on Graser Three and Five and in Missile Five. No contact with Missile Seven. Magazine One is out of the feed queue."

"What about Impeller One?" McKeon demanded of the helmsman, abandoning his efforts to get through to anyone in Engineering.

"Sir, Impeller One doesn't answer," Chief Harris replied tautly. "Our accel's down to two hundred gravities and dropping."

"Sidewall Generators One, Three, Five, and Seven are off-line. We're losing the port sidewall, Captain!"

"Sir, Bandit One has opened fire. Twenty-four missiles inbound. Impact in one-seven-three seconds."

"Bandit Ten is altering course and increasing acceleration. Closing at five-point-three KPS-squared!"

Prince Adrian shuddered again, twisting about her iron bones as fresh energy smashed into her.

"Direct hit on CIC!" a voice shouted over the com. "We're losing con—"

The voice chopped off in midsyllable. Smoke gouted from the main ventilation trunk before it slammed shut, and more damage alarms snarled.

"Bridge, this is Juno in Fusion Two!" The voice of Lieutenant Juno, *Prince Adrian's* junior engineering officer, came from the intercom. "I'm setting up here for damage control, but it doesn't look good."

"Status of Impeller One?" McKeon demanded.

"Gone, Sir," Juno said harshly. "We may have four or five beta nodes left, if I can get them back on-line, but that's it."

McKeon's face clenched. With her forward alpha nodes gone, *Prince Adrian* had lost her Warshawski sails . . . and Adler lay squarely in the heart of a hyper-space gravity wave, where only sails would permit a ship to maneuver. That single, devastating salvo from *Katana* had doomed his ship, and McKeon knew it.

"Helm, bring us forty degrees to port!" he snarled, and his gaze locked with Metcalf's across the bridge as Harris acknowledged. "We're going down Ten's throat, Gerry. Hit the bastard with everything you've got!"

"Aye, aye, Sir." Metcalf hunched over her panel, fighting the destruction of her sensors and fire control systems as much as the enemy, and the ship bucked as still more missiles smashed through her crippled defenses to blot away weapons and the people who crewed them.

Honor dragged herself to her feet, Nimitz clinging to her shoulder. She felt blood dribbling down her chin from where she'd bitten her lip in her fall, but it was a distant awareness, one that belonged to someone else, far, far away, and she swept her eyes over the glaring crimson damage lights on McKeon's displays. She opened her mouth, then staggered and clung to the command chair's back as *Prince Adrian* heaved in fresh agony. She almost fell again, but she stayed upright somehow and grabbed McKeon's shoulder.

"Surrender, Alistair." She didn't raise her voice, yet its very calmness cut through the combat chatter and damage reports and the howl of alarms like a knife, and McKeon stared at her.

"But—" he began, but she shook her head and squeezed his shoulder hard.

"Surrender," she repeated. "That's an order."

Still McKeon stared at her, and she understood his agonized hesitation. His shame. In the five hundred-T-year history of the Royal Manticoran Navy, only thirty-two Queen's ships had ever surrendered to an enemy.

"I said *surrender*, Captain!" she said more sharply. "We got the convoy out, but your entire forward impeller room's gone. Now surrender your ship before any more of our people die for *nothing!*"

"I—" McKeon closed his eyes, then shook himself and nodded. "Helm, turn us away from the enemy and kill your accel," he said in a voice like hammered iron. "Commander Metcalf, jettison every FTL-equipped drone with a locked in self-destruct command, then purge the computers and instruct all hands to destroy classified equipment and material. Lieutenant Sanko, hail Bandit Ten. Inform her captain we surrender."

• Chapter Eighteen

"*Who* did you say?" Lester Tourville stared at the face on his com, certain he'd misunderstood, but Citizen Captain Bogdanovich nodded vigorously.

"There's no mistake, Citizen Admiral. May I play Citizen Captain Zachary's message for you?"

Tourville nodded, and the time and date header for a burst transmission message addressed to the chief of staff replaced Bogdanovich's image. The header disappeared in turn, and a slim, severe-faced woman appeared. The name patch on the left breast of her skinsuit said "ZACHARY, HELEN G," and her dark eyes seemed to hold an echo of the astonishment Tourville himself had just experienced. She looked out of the screen for a moment, then cleared her throat.

"Citizen Captain Bogdanovich," she said formally, "I have to report that PNS *Katana*, under my command, and PNS *Nuada*, Citizen Captain Wallace Turner, commanding, have engaged the Manticoran heavy cruiser *Prince Adrian*. After a long range exchange in which I was able to take maximum advantage of my towed missile pods, *Prince Adrian* was compelled to surrender. *Katana* suffered moderate damage, including twenty-one casualties, seven of them fatal, but *Nuada* sustained no damage, and my executive officer's preliminary survey indicates that *Prince Adrian*'s casualties were at least six times our own. We are examining the prize, but her crew's destruction of classified equipment seems to have been thorough, and the heavy damage we ourselves inflicted includes the destruction of her forward impeller room. My present impression is that repair will be impossible out of our available resources, and I'm afraid we'll have to destroy her rather than take her with us when we withdraw from the system."

She paused for a moment, as if drawing a mental breath, and went on in an almost mechanical voice.

"Among the prisoners we've so far identified are *Prince Adrian's* commander, Captain Alistair McKeon, RMN, and the commander of the escort squadron attached to the convoy which evaded our attack, Commodore Honor Harrington. We also have several of Commodore Harrington's staff officers in custody." She paused again, almost as if she found what she'd just said impossible to believe, and then her shoulders twitched in the tiniest of shrugs.

"Unless instructed otherwise, I intend to leave Citizen Captain Turner and his ship to complete the task of securing *Prince Adrian* and take my own command to rendezvous with the flagship in order to transfer my commissioned prisoners aboard as quickly as possible. I will continue my survey of my own damages en route to you, and hope to be able to give you a complete report on them upon my arrival. Citizen Commissioner Kuttner has been informed of my intentions and endorsed them. Zachary, clear."

The screen blanked briefly once more, and Bogdanovich's image reappeared. The chief of staff's eyes sparkled, and Tourville felt a huge grin spread across his face. He knew his excitement and delight were out of keeping with the addition of a mere heavy cruiser to the eleven prizes his ships had already taken in Adler—even if the cruiser in question did belong to the navy which had kicked the PN's butt regularly for six years now—but he didn't really care.

"Harrington," he murmured. "*Harrington*, by God!"

"Yes, Sir! I mean, yes, Citizen Rear Admiral!"

Bogdanovich returned his grin with interest, and Tourville tipped his chair back and crossed his legs. His smile turned almost dreamy, and he drew a cigar from his breast pocket. Affectation or not, there would never be a more appropriate moment for one.

Harrington, he thought. *First Adler, and now* Harrington!

He unwrapped the cigar, nipped its end off with strong,

white teeth, then lit it with finicky precision while his mind considered what Public Information would do with *this* bit of news. A mere commodore shouldn't have been all that big a catch, especially not against the galaxy of Republican vice admirals and admirals the Manties had bagged. But there was nothing "mere" about this particular commodore. Honor Harrington was one of the bogeymen of the People's Navy. She'd come to epitomize the vast gulf between the capabilities of the RMN and the People's Navy, and Tourville savored the sense of having taken a large first step to bridge that gulf. For all its small scale, his success at Adler was the most one-sided defeat the Manties had suffered in five hundred T-years, and their people would realize that just as clearly as Tourville did. That was probably already more than Citizen Admiral Theisman had dared hope for when he sent Tourville out, but now, as an unexpected bonus, ships under his command had also captured *Harrington.*

He allowed himself to consider the consequences of his triumph for several more seconds, but then he blew a cloud of smoke and made himself come back to ground. There was a certain danger bound up in his success, he reflected. For one thing, it was damned likely to get him promoted, and that was bad. He'd prospered so far by avoiding the higher rank which would take him away from the inde- pendent commands he loved, on the one hand, and expose him to the risk of being made an example for failure that went with fleet command, on the other. But if Public Information poured it on too thick and heavy, the Navy would have little choice but to offer him promotion, and he could hardly escape it once it had been offered.

Any navy, even one whose high command languished in the grip of revolutionary fervor, had a simple rule where officers who refused promotion—and thus indicated they were unprepared to accept the responsibility which went with it—were concerned. They were never again asked to accept it. In fact, they were never employed in responsible positions again . . . and only in the most extraordinary of conditions were they ever employed in *any* capacity. And while he was hardly alone in looking for ways to avoid the role of StateSec's scapegoat, people who refused promotion, especially in a navy fighting for its life, were likely to find their professional colleagues actively assisting the SS in getting rid of them.

He frowned at the thought and made a mental note to be certain that his reports gave full credit for Harrington's capture to Zachary and Turner. The *Fleet* would know he'd been in command, and his modesty would stand him in excellent stead with his peers, but with a little bit of luck— *well*, he admitted, *probably it'll take a lot of luck, but it's worth trying for*—the official record would steer any promotion towards Zachary and Turner. *And*, he reflected, *both of them certainly deserve it. Luck may have played a big part in their pulling this off, but luck always plays a part. God knows Harrington's been shot through with luck to manage all she has!*

He nodded and took his cigar from his mouth. He held it in front of himself, studying the glowing tip with a frown, and let his mind replay Zachary's message. He was certain the citizen captain would have told him if Harrington had been injured in the battle, and he was glad she hadn't been. Much as news of her capture pleased him, Tourville was not one of the Republican officers who hated her for what she'd done to their Navy. Indeed, that was one reason the thought of capturing her pleased him so. She was a foe he could respect, one worthy of his steel, and he looked forward to meeting her. *And*, he told himself with a mental chuckle, *I especially look forward to being the first senior Republican officer to meet her when he's not her prisoner!*

But the fact that he did respect her, as much as her own military record or her political importance, made it even more important that she be treated with the courtesy her rank and achievements had earned. The Republic's reputation for proper treatment of prisoners of war had not been an admirable one even under the Legislaturalists. Lester Tourville was one of the officers who felt both shamed by and bitter over that, and the Republic's record had gotten even worse under the new regime. State Security now had primary authority for the management of prisoners, both military and political, and the Navy fought a continuous, clandestine war to keep its POWs out of StateSec's clutches. Unfortunately, the Navy won only the battles the SS chose to let it win, and even those victories were usually no more than the result of StateSec's decision to let the Navy come up with the personnel required to run its own POW camps while the SS concentrated on more important (and politically sensitive) prisons.

It was possible, even probable, that StateSec would demand that Harrington be turned over to it, Tourville realized, and his smile vanished into a bleak nonexpression. Not only did she deserve better, but unlike StateSec's thugs, Tourville and every other member of the People's Navy had a direct interest in the proper treatment of captured Allied personnel. There were many more PN officers and ratings in Allied hands than the reverse, and if the Manties decided to retaliate for the mistreatment of *their* personnel, it wouldn't be State Security who paid the price.

The citizen rear admiral cocked his chair back again and gazed thoughtfully at his com. He noted Bogdanovich's expression, the puzzlement in the chief of staff's eyes as he sensed his admiral's change of mood without grasping all the reasons for it. But Bogdanovich was secondary to Tourville's thoughts at the moment. There were aspects to this situation which he'd overlooked in his immediate exultation, and his mind began to click as he considered how best to deal with the repercussions looming up down the road.

Could he enlist Everard Honeker's aid? He certainly couldn't explain his reasoning to the people's commissioner on the record, but Honeker had been his political watchdog long enough for them to develop a certain mutual understanding. And Honeker would reap his own share of the credit for Harrington's capture, which might just incline him to listen to what Tourville had to say. Properly speaking,

Honeker himself belonged to the Office of State Security, which could reasonably be expected to hold his institutional loyalty, but he was also at least a quasi-officer who'd been exposed to the realities of naval service. More to the point, perhaps, he wasn't an idiot like too many other commissioners. Although he certainly wasn't about to admit it, he seemed to understand that a navy which expected to win wars simply could not ignore operational realities in favor of subservience to every jot and tittle of revolutionary doctrine, however asinine. He'd certainly shown himself willing to look the other way from time to time in the interest of rationality and efficiency, but could Tourville convince him to lend his support to keeping Harrington in Navy hands rather than turning her over to the SS?

The one thing the citizen rear admiral couldn't do was appeal to Honeker solely on the basis of moral obligations and the honor of the Fleet. Not because Honeker wouldn't understand the appeal was seriously meant, but because the people's commissioner—like *any* people's commissioner—came with a preprogrammed rejection of anything that smacked of the old regime's prerevolutionary concepts. It was, after all, an imperishable article of faith with them that the Legislaturalist regime had collapsed under the weight of its own corrupt decadence, and that the Committee of Public Safety was engaged in a revolutionary fight to the death against the forces of reactionism, aristocracy, elitism, and entrenched plutocratic interests. The values of those opponents of justice and progress were only lies, invented to manipulate the masses, and so had to be cast aside as the posturing of the greedy elite, which had conspired throughout history to oppress and debase the People. As Citizen Committeewoman Ransom herself was fond of putting it, "Honor is a word plutocrats use when they want someone killed."

Tourville had come to suspect Honeker subscribed more deeply to the decadent values Ransom despised than he was prepared to admit, but the people's commissioner was like a man from an intensely religious family who still attended church regularly without ever admitting to himself that he'd secretly become an agnostic. Whatever might go on in the depths of his mind, he would never openly contest orthodox doctrine, and so Tourville would have to base his argument, overtly, at least, on an analysis of solid, tangible, and *immediate* advantage and disadvantage. Even though that agnostic part of Honeker might actually hear the moral argument, he had to give the commissioner something else which they could both pretend was the real reason for his support.

The best bet is the Deneb Accords, Tourville told himself. *God knows StateSec's violated them often enough, but they're still the official basis for the treatment of captured personnel, and they explicitly charge their signatories' militaries with seeing to it that military POWs are properly treated. And the Solarian League's accepted responsibility for monitoring the treatment of both sides' prisoners in this war. StateSec may have managed to fob off the League's investigators so far, but what if I make the point to Honeker that Harrington's going to be an especially high-profile prisoner? The Manties aren't going to accept any "sloppy record keeping" excuses if she disappears, and she's also a steadholder. Even those idiots the League sends out here will have to get off their asses and really look at the situation if we "misplace" a head of state! And I could argue that naval efficiency will suffer if our people expect the other side to violate the Accords and that mistreating— No, better stay away from the idea of mistreating. He's likely to get defensive if I suggest that I expect the SS to abuse prisoners, even if we do both know that's precisely what happens. Let's say that if our treatment of Harrington violates the letter of the law as laid down by the Accords, a politically reactionary regime like the Star Kingdom is likely to retaliate, and our people know it.*

He frowned down at his cigar for several more seconds, running over possible ways to phrase his argument. He needed to polish it up a bit, pick out exactly the right words . . . and think of some way to catch Honeker in an area where any bugs would be less effective before he sprang those words on the people's commissioner. Fortunately, he had several hours yet before *Katana* could possibly deliver her prisoners to *Count Tilly*.

He refocused on Bogdanovich's face at last and smiled.

"That's wonderful news, Yuri," he said. "Please inform Citizen Commissioner Honeker immediately, then make arrangements to receive Commodore Harrington and the other senior prisoners with proper military courtesies. From what I've heard, she's always been careful to treat *her* prisoners properly, and I intend to return the compliment."

"Yes, Citizen Rear Admiral."

"Oh, and that reminds me. Pass the word to Shannon, as well. I'm sure she'll want to pay her own respects to Commodore Harrington."

"I'll see to it, Citizen Rear Admiral."

"Thank you. And let me know—oh, forty-five minutes before we rendezvous with *Katana*."

"Yes, Citizen Rear Admiral."

"Thank you," Tourville repeated, and cut the circuit. His cigar had gone out, and he relit it, puffing reflectively while he rocked his chair gently back and forth.

Now exactly how, he wondered, should he go about luring Honeker into lending him his support?

"Citizen Captain Zachary extends her compliments and asks you and your officers to accompany me to the boat bay for transfer to the flagship, Commodore."

Honor turned at the sound of Citizen Commander Luchner's voice. She hadn't heard the hatch open, and a part of her wondered how much her crushing despair had to do with her inattentiveness. She knew her lack of expression was all the proof anyone could need of how utterly defeated she felt, but it was also the best she could manage, and she nodded to *Katana*'s executive officer.

"Thank you, Citizen Commander." She was distantly amazed by the sound of her own voice. It came out a bit hoarse, as if it were something whose exact management she had forgotten, yet aside from that it sounded so natural—so *normal*—that she felt certain it must really belong to someone else pretending to be her. She brushed her foolish notion aside and cleared her throat. It didn't seem to help a lot.

"Please convey my gratitude to your commanding officer. You and your personnel have taken good care of our people . . . especially the wounded. I appreciate it."

Luchner started to reply, then stopped. There was very little he could say, after all, and he settled for a polite nod and stepped aside to wave Honor through the hatch.

She obeyed the gesture, and every step seemed to jar through her. The spring had gone out of her stride, replaced by a brutal, flat-footed weariness which had nothing to do with her physical state. Or, rather, it was a weariness heaped atop her bodily fatigue, and she suspected it would weigh down upon her long after she'd recovered physically.

Alistair McKeon walked at her side, and she felt his agony—his shame—burning even more cruelly than her own. She longed to comfort him, yet there was no realistic comfort to be offered, and even if there had been, McKeon was in no state to accept it. He was like a parent, mourning the death of a child and blaming himself for it, and the fact that none of it was his fault meant nothing to him at this moment.

Nor was Alistair the only person whose emotions lashed at her, for Andrew LaFollet followed close behind her. His utterly emotionless expression might conceal it from everyone else, but Honor felt every nuance of his frantic sense of helplessness . . . and failure. Echoes of those same emotions snarled in the back of her brain from James Candless and Robert Whitman, as well, for they were Grayson armsmen who could no longer protect the woman they were sworn to guard, and their desperate concern for her threatened to be more than she could bear.

She wanted to scream at them, to command them to stop. To beg them to protect her from their emotions, at least, since they could no longer protect her from anything else. But even if there'd been any hope that they could obey such an order, she had no right to give it, for the feelings whose echoes gouged away bits and pieces of her soul sprang from who and what her armsmen were. It was their devotion to her which made them so frantic, and how could she add to their distress by telling them how *their* misery tormented *her?*

She couldn't, of course. In fact, she'd done all she could by identifying them to their captors as Grayson Marines. She'd recognized McKeon's astonishment when she informed Luchner that LaFollet was a Marine colonel and that Candless and Whitman were both Marine lieutenants, but he'd said nothing. She knew he'd assumed she was lying in order to keep Candless and Whitman from being separated from her when the prisoners were segregated into commissioned and enlisted ranks, but he was only half right. That *was* the reason she'd identified them as Marines, but she hadn't lied.

The Grayson word "armsman" was a term with a multiplicity of uses. It was used for most police personnel, but it had a very special meaning where a steadholder's retainers were concerned. The "Harrington Steadholder's Guard" was actually two separate bodies, one within the other. The smaller of the two—properly known as the Steadholder's *Own* Guard—consisted of only fifty men, because the Grayson Constitution limited any steadholder to a maximum of fifty *personal* armsmen. The Harrington Steadholder's Guard as a whole *contained* the Steadholder's Own, who held commissions in both, plus every other uniformed member of Harrington Steading's police force. *All* of its members—to the confusion of foreigners—were called "armsmen," but there were significant differences between their duties. The Steadholder's Own provided Honor's personal security detachment—a function in which the rest of the Guard assisted as required—and replacements for the Steadholder's Own were normally drawn from the rest of the Guard, as well. But she could never have more than fifty personal armsmen, for Benjamin the Great hadn't spent fourteen years fighting one of the most bitter civil wars in human history just so his son or grandson could do it all over again. The steadholders' armies of personal retainers had provided the core of trained troops for both sides in the civil war, and so Benjamin's Constitution had set an absolute ceiling on the personal legions his steadholders could thenceforth raise. And he'd taken one more precautionary step by granting every armsman an officer's commission in the Grayson Army, as well.

His intent had been simple. If all armsmen belonged to the Army, then—in theory at least—a Protector could summon the armsmen of a recalcitrant steadholder to active Army service, thus depriving him even of the fifty personal retainers he was allowed. The fact that a steadholder who was allowed only fifty armsmen would tend to recruit the very best he could find also meant that the supply of backup officers they represented would be of high caliber if they were ever actually needed, which was an additional benefit, but everyone knew it had also been a secondary one from Benjamin's viewpoint.

Unfortunately for his plan, however, the Planetary High Court of a later (and weaker) Protector had observed that armsmen received their Army commissions *because* they were armsmen . . . and that they became armsmen in the first place on the basis of the oaths of loyalty they'd sworn to their steadholders. In the court's view, that meant their first responsibility was to the steadholders they served, not the Army. As such, they could be called to active Army service only with the consent of their liege lords, which no steadholder engaged in a face-off against the Protector was likely to grant.

That had blown Benjamin's intentions out from under his descendants, but the constitutional provisions remained. And since Grayson Marines were simply Army troops assigned to shipboard duty, and since LaFollet, Candless, and Whitman *did* hold Army commissions, they were indeed technically Marine officers. It was a fragile assertion, resting entirely on the peculiarities of Grayson's domestic laws, but it was an honest one, and the fact that the personnel records for Honor's armsmen had all been left in her personal files aboard *Alvarez* meant there was no documentary evidence to challenge it.

Yet any satisfaction Honor had felt when Luchner accepted them as Marines had been no more than a brief flicker in the blackness which had engulfed her, dwarfed by the defeat and failure which filled the men and women about her. In many cases it was accompanied by an enormous sense of gratitude at having survived, as well, but for most even that relief was flawed. In a way, having been spared death or injury became another source of shame, for the survivors felt guilty for *being* grateful, as if that very human reaction were somehow despicable, and that, too, beat in upon Honor through Nimitz.

She closed her eyes, tasting the bitter flavor of her officers' inner darkness, and hugged the 'cat to her chest. Like most of the captured officers following her towards *Katana*'s boat bay, he still wore his skinsuit. It made him much too heavy to ride in his usual place on her shoulder, but she had deliberately chosen to leave him in it, and her arms tightened about him as she faced the reason she had.

A dark and terrible—and intensely personal—fear snarled deep inside her. She'd done her best to drive it out of her forebrain, to ignore it or at least to so occupy herself with her duties that she could *pretend* she'd ignored it, but all her efforts had been a lie. The fear only laughed at efforts to suppress it. It jeered and whispered to her, mocking her, and her inability to set it aside as her intellect insisted she ought only made her ashamed of the weakness she could not master.

But worst of all, the same intellect which told her it was her duty to defeat her fear knew that fear was valid, for it was the fear of separation. The fear that her captors would dismiss Nimitz as no more than a curious, alien pet—an animal—and separate her from him. Or, still worse, that they would class him as a *dangerous* alien animal. The consequences of any such decision terrified her so deeply that she dared not let herself face them fully, yet neither dared she ignore them. And so she'd left him in his suit, hoping his obvious training in its use would emphasize his intelligence and make it clear he was far more than a "mere animal" when the time came for her to defend him as such. And, she admitted, the suit's gloves hid the murderous, centimeter-long scimitars of his claws. None of her captors had ever seen Nimitz in action, and if she could just conceal the lethality of his natural weapons until she'd had a chance to fix his intelligence and self-control firmly in their minds, perhaps she could protect him.

Perhaps . . . and perhaps not. But if she couldn't, if someone tried to separate them or to injure Nimitz, if—

She clenched her jaw and jerked free of the choking panic as it tried to build within her once more. She had other responsibilities, duties she must somehow discharge, and she felt Nimitz reach up to stroke her face with a gentle true-hand. He felt her dread, and she knew he understood its source, for she felt his answering fear. In fact, the two of them were trapped in a feedback loop in which their shared fear fed upon itself and grew strong. But she also felt his support, his love and fierce rejection of her conscience's efforts to punish her for the way her thoughts seemed to waver and flow like water when she should be concentrating on her duty to the people her orders had brought to this.

But he was wrong. She did have those other responsibilities, and somehow she forced her shoulders to straighten and her head to rise as the procession of prisoners reached the boat bay gallery. Expressionless Peep Marines lined the bulkheads, pulse rifles at port arms, not overtly threatening but instantly ready, and Honor's lips quirked bitterly. She'd seen her own Marines in similar poses, alert eyes watchful as surrendered *Peep* personnel passed into captivity. Now it was her turn, and that wasn't supposed to happen. The Royal Navy was supposed to take its enemies prisoner, not be captured *by* them, and not even the fact that *Prince Adrian's* sacrifice had saved the rest of the convoy could assuage Honor's shame at having failed her Queen.

Citizen Commander Luchner extended his hand to her, and she gripped it firmly. Somehow she managed to dredge up a caricature of a smile for him, and the shamed part of her sneered at the paucity of her efforts. Whatever else had happened, Luchner and his CO had, indeed, treated their prisoners well. He deserved more than a corpse grin from her for his efforts, yet it was the best she could offer, and she hoped he understood.

He stood aside once more, and the Marines split Honor and her officers up into pinnace-sized groups. They swam down the boarding tubes to the small craft, once more watched by the silent Marines, and took their seats. Then the pinnaces undocked, turning on reaction thrusters to exit the bay in a long line, and Honor leaned back in the inappropriately comfortable chair and closed her eyes, alone once more with her despair.

Citizen Rear Admiral Tourville turned from his conversation with Citizen Captain Hewitt, his flag captain, as the boat bay tractors deposited the lead pinnace in the docking buffers. Mechanical docking arms locked, the boarding tube and umbilical connections ran out to the small craft, and Tourville inhaled deeply.

He'd done his best with Honeker, and to be honest, he'd wrought a bit better than he'd hoped. They'd discussed the situation quietly in a corner of *Count Tilly's* gym under cover of the background noise from a basketball game. Neither of them had commented on *why* Tourville had chosen that particular difficult-to-bug spot, but that in itself had told him Honeker understood his reasons for inviting the people's commissioner there.

And, as he'd hoped, Honeker had been sympathetic. In fact, Tourville suspected Honeker had been almost as responsive to the citizen admiral's concern over the honor and moral responsibilities of the Fleet as to the more "practical" implications of the way they treated their prisoners. Yet there were limits on how far the commissioner was prepared to go. In effect, he'd agreed—without ever specifically saying it in so many words—to defer to Tourville's treatment of Harrington and her personnel. The matter, he'd said, was "appropriately a responsibility of the military." That was a phrase more than one people's commissioner had used to dump a difficult decision on the Navy without giving up the right to hold the Navy accountable for any adverse consequences, but this time Tourville was glad to hear it, for it freed him to act as he saw fit.

But at a price. In allowing "the military" to take responsibility, Honeker had been forced to disassociate himself from Tourville's decisions, and so he was conspicuously absent as the surrendered Manticoran personnel arrived aboard *Count Tilly*. For him to avoid interfering with Tourville's actions, he also had to distance himself from them. In turn, that would limit his ability to support Tourville against higher authority—assuming he had any inclination to do so—down the road.

The boarding tube's inboard hatch opened, and Tourville clasped his hands behind him and waited. No more than fifteen or twenty seconds passed before the first person—a tall, athletic woman—swam down the tube. Unlike almost all of the other prisoners, she was in uniform, not a skinsuit, and she moved gracefully, despite the sixty-centimeter-long creature she clasped to her chest with one arm. Her free hand reached up for the grab bar at the inboard end of the tube, and she swung herself across the interface into *Count Tilly*'s shipboard gravity and stepped forward, clearing the way for those behind her.

She stood tall and erect, her shoulders squared and her chin high, and her strongly carved, triangular face was almost inhumanly calm, yet Tourville hid a wince at the bleak pain in her almondine eyes. Those eyes moved over the officers—and Marine guards—assembled in the boat bay gallery. They swept across Tourville himself and locked on Citizen Captain Hewitt, and she came to attention as she turned to face him.

"Commodore Harrington, Royal Manticoran Navy," she said. Her soprano was sweet and soft . . . and as leached of all emotion as her face.

"Citizen Captain Alfred Hewitt, PNS *Count Tilly*," Hewitt replied. He didn't add any stupid formulae about welcoming her aboard. He simply held out his hand.

Honor stared down at it for a moment, then took it. He squeezed more firmly than she'd expected, and she saw an odd mixture of triumph and sympathy in his face. She knew that expression; it was just that she'd never seen it on someone *else's* face.

"Commodore Harrington," Hewitt went on formally, "allow me to present Citizen Rear Admiral Tourville."

"Citizen Rear Admiral." Honor turned to Tourville just as Alistair McKeon swung out of the tube. She heard McKeon and Hewitt beginning the same formal exchange, but her attention was on Tourville, and she felt a first, small stir of hope as tendrils of his emotions reached out to her. The Peep admiral's feelings were too complex for easy analysis. A sense of triumph and professional pride predominated, yet she tasted both sympathy and a determination to act honorably under them as he offered his hand in turn.

"Commodore Harrington." Tourville looked into his prisoner's eyes, trying to get a feel for the woman behind them, and she met his searching gaze without flinching. "I was sorry to hear your casualties were so high," he said. "I promise our medical personnel will treat your wounded as if they were our own . . . and that you and all your people will be treated with the courtesy of your rank."

"Thank you, Sir." Honor saw his eyes flicker and wanted to kick herself for forgetting that only people's commissioners were addressed as "Sir" or "Ma'am" aboard Peep ships. But then she realized there *was* no commissioner present, and a faint sense of curiosity nibbled at her shell of despair.

"You're welcome," Tourville replied after a moment, and then gave her a small, fleeting smile. "It's only fair, after

all, given your own record with those of *our* people who've,
ah, found themselves your guests, shall we say?" She blinked
in surprise, and he gave another, more natural smile. "In
fact, I believe that my operations officer, Citizen Commander Foraker, spent some time aboard your last flagship,"
he added.

"*Shannon* Foraker?" Honor said, and he nodded.

"Indeed. I've spoken with her at some length, Commodore. And while nothing can ever be guaranteed in
wartime, I hope you and your personnel will find your
treatment in our hands as humane and proper as Citizen
Commander Foraker found her treatment in yours."
Tourville's voice—and emotions—were sincere, yet there
was an edge of warning in his tone, and Honor understood
the unspoken message behind it. But then he looked
directly into her eyes. "In particular, Commodore, I'm glad
the Citizen Commander was able to give me some additional background on your, um, *companion*." He gestured
at Nimitz, never unlocking his gaze from Honor's. "I
understand you have a unique sort of bond with him, and
Citizen Commander Foraker assures me he's far more
intelligent than one might normally assume from his small
size. Under the circumstances, I've given instructions that
he's to remain with you, so long as he behaves himself, for
the duration of your stay aboard *Count Tilly*. Of course, I
will also have to hold you responsible for ensuring that
he *does* behave, and I trust you—and he—will see to it
that I have no cause to regret my decision."

"Thank you, Citizen Rear Admiral," Honor said quietly.
"Thank you very much. And you have my word Nimitz and
I will give you no cause to regret your generosity."

Tourville made a small, dismissive gesture, waving aside
her thanks, and turned to Alistair McKeon, but Honor felt
Nimitz relax in her arms as he sensed the sincerity of the
citizen rear admiral's offer. The easing of the 'cat's tension
damped the feedback effect, and she felt her muscles
unknotting, yet her own reaction was more guarded than
his. Treecats concentrated on the here-and-now, operating

on a "sufficient unto the day" basis that put aside threats and problems which were not immediate. And because 'cats operated that way, Nimitz, despite his empathic sense, had missed the subtle subtext of Tourville's last sentence. His assurance that Nimitz and Honor would remain together "for the duration of your stay" aboard his flagship was both a promise . . . and a warning that he could guarantee nothing once they *left* the battlecruiser.

The future yawned before her, dark and threatening, and already something inside her had begun to recognize the crushing effect helplessness could exert on a personality accustomed to controlling its own destiny and taking responsibility for its own actions. But there was nothing she could do about that, and so she drew a deep mental breath, stepped back from the things she couldn't change, and tried to take a page from Nimitz's book.

One day at a time, she thought. *That's how I have to take it: one day at a time.*

Yet even as she told herself that, and knew it was true, she felt the dangerous void of her powerless future waiting to suck her under, and she was afraid.

• Chapter Nineteen

Vice Admiral Sorbanne walked around the end of her desk and extended her hand to her visitor. One look at that desk was enough to tell anyone the responsibilities of Clairmont Station's CO had become more pressing, not less, with Adler's fall, but her famed irascibility was in abeyance, and her expression was compassionate.

"Captain Greentree," she said quietly, and waved at the chairs clustered around her office coffee table. "Please, have a seat."

"Thank you, Dame Madeleine."

The Grayson officer had come by for a courtesy visit before he took what was left of Honor Harrington's squadron back to Yeltsin's Star, and he looked terrible. His face was gaunt, dark, bruised-looking shadows underlay his eyes, and his chunky body seemed to have shrunk. Even his uniform seemed to have become too big. It hung upon him—immaculately tailored and arranged, yet somehow subliminally unkempt—and although he obeyed her invitation to sit, it was as if the chair's comfort were an enemy he must resist. He sat bolt upright, feet together, clasping his peaked cap in his lap, and Sorbanne could actually feel the tension radiating from him.

She took her own chair and decided not to buzz for the coffee tray after all. This man was in no mood for refreshments, and while she had no doubt he would be polite, offering them would be almost insulting, a trivialization of his burning concern.

"I'm certain you realize why I asked you to visit me, Captain," she said instead. She'd tried to keep the formal

314

note out of her tone, but she'd also failed, and she saw Greentree's face clench as he heard it. "I'm afraid the news isn't good," she went on, saying what had to be said, however little either of them wished to hear it. "Even with the most generous allowance for a slow passage, *Prince Adrian* should have reached Clairmont two days ago. I'm afraid that, as of thirteen hundred hours local time today, she will be listed as officially overdue . . . and presumed lost."

"I—" Greentree started to speak, then stopped, staring down at the cap in his lap, and his knuckles whitened as his hands locked upon it. He drew a deep breath, and Sorbanne leaned across the coffee table to touch him lightly on the knee.

"It's not your fault, Captain," she said gently. "You did precisely what you ought to have done—precisely what Lady Harrington *wanted* you to do. And my staff and I have analyzed your sensor records of the tactical situation which obtained in Adler at the time you made translation into n-space. Even if you'd gone immediately to her assistance, it would have had no bearing on whatever happened to *Prince Adrian*."

"But I could have *tried*." The anguished whisper was so faint Sorbanne doubted Greentree even realized he'd spoken aloud, but she decided to pretend the words had been meant for her.

"Of course you could have tried," she said so sharply that he looked up in surprise. "People can *always* try, Captain, but sometimes a naval officer has to know when *not* to try. When trying is the easy way out for her, or her reputation, or her conscience, but only at the cost of failing in her *duty*. I'm certain any number of idiots who weren't there are going to tell you you should have rushed in to rescue Lady Harrington no matter what she'd ordered you to do. No doubt you could have saved yourself all the pain those accusations are going to cause you if you *had* tried. But you and I both know, however much it hurts to admit it, *that it would have been the wrong decision*."

She held his eyes, her expression fierce.

"Even if Lady Harrington hadn't specifically ordered you to hyper out, you could never have gotten into support range of *Prince Adrian*. She was much too far away for you to reach before she either crossed the hyper limit and escaped on her own or was forced into action. In either case, there was nothing you could do to affect what happened to her. If you'd tried, you would have risked what probably happened to her—running into someone lying doggo in your path—and your primary responsibility, both under Lady Harrington's direct orders and as the squadron's flag captain, was to the convoy under your escort. You're going to hear enough people second guess you, Captain. We're both adults. We know that's going to happen, and we both know some of the people doing it are going to be unfair and cruel. Don't *you* start doing it, as well."

"But what am I going to tell Grayson?" Greentree asked wretchedly. "I lost the *Steadholder*, Admiral!"

"*You* didn't lose anyone, Captain!" Sorbanne half-snapped. "Lady Harrington did her duty, just as you did yours. She *chose* to wear that uniform, to assume the risks that go with command of a squadron in time of war. And she also *chose* to order *Prince Adrian* to draw the enemy away from the convoy."

"I know," Greentree said after a moment. "I suppose I even know you're right, and I appreciate your kindness in telling me so. Someday, I'm sure, what you've said will come to mean a great deal to me. But right now—right this minute, Dame Madeleine—all I can think of is all those people on Grayson. Not because they'll blame *me* for it, but because they've lost her. Because we've *all* lost her. It just . . . doesn't seem possible."

"I know," Sorbanne sighed. She leaned back, running her fingers through her short hair, and managed a bleak smile. "It always seems that way with the really good ones, doesn't it? They're not like *us*. They're invincible, some-how—immortal. The magic will keep them safe, bring them back to us, because it has to. Because they're too important

for us to lose. But the truth is that they *aren't* invincible
. . . or immortal. No one is, and when they go down, the
rest of us have to find some way to take up the slack."

"I don't think we can 'take up the slack' this time,"
Greentree said soberly. "We'll do our best, Admiral, and
we'll survive." He returned her bleak smile. "We're
Graysons, and Graysons know a thing or two about surviving. But find someone else who can fill her shoes? Be
what she was?" He shook his head. "We'll be a poorer
planet for having lost her, Dame Madeleine, and those of
us who knew her will always wonder what we might have
managed to do or become if we *hadn't* lost her."

"Maybe living up to what you think she would have
expected of you will actually inspire you to accomplish even
more," Sorbanne suggested gently. "A woman could have
a worse legacy than that. And don't automatically assume
you've 'lost her,' either. All we know right now is that *Prince
Adrian* is overdue. Of course we have to allow for the worst,
but there are almost always survivors, even when ships are
lost in action, and from what I know of Lady Harrington,
she had—has—the moral courage to accept responsibility
for ordering a Queen's ship to surrender. I don't think she
would've let *Prince Adrian* fight to the death if it was
obvious she couldn't win—not when she had to know you'd
gotten the convoy out. I'd say the odds are at least even
that she's alive and a prisoner."

"You're probably right, Ma'am," Greentree replied, "and
I hope you are. But the Peeps don't have a very good record
for treating POWs properly, and if I were the Committee
of Public Safety, Lady Harrington is one officer I wouldn't
be in any hurry to exchange. I hate thinking of her in their
hands—not as much as I do the thought that she may be
dead, but I still hate it. And given how long this war looks
like lasting, it may be years—even decades—before we get
her back."

"There, I'm afraid, I can't argue with you," Sorbanne
admitted with another sigh, "but years are better than never,
Captain."

"Yes, Ma'am," Greentree said softly. "They are."

He gazed down at his cap again for several long seconds, then stood and tucked it under his left arm.

"Thank you, Admiral Sorbanne," he said, holding out his right hand as she rose in turn. "I appreciate your taking the time to tell me personally, and your advice." He managed a smile that would have looked almost natural on a less harrowed face. "I suppose from my whining it must sound as if we Graysons have forgotten Lady Harrington is also a Manticoran, Ma'am, but we haven't. We know how badly your navy is going to miss her, as well."

"We are that, Captain," Sorbanne agreed, squeezing his hand firmly. "I'll say good-bye now," she continued. "You have to be getting back to Yeltsin, and I've got things to organize here. For your private information, I'm putting together a reconnaissance in force for Adler. We'll be sending in a dozen battlecruisers and cruisers with a superdreadnought division in support, so unless they've reinforced mighty heavily, we should kick their asses clear back to Barnett or wherever else they came from."

"I wish we could come along, Ma'am."

"I know you do, and I wish you could, too, but—" Sorbanne shrugged, and Greentree nodded and released her hand. She returned his nod, and he turned and headed for the office door, but her raised voice stopped him just before he left.

"One thing, Captain," she said quietly, and he turned back to face her. "From what I've seen of you, you're a man who believes in doing his duty, however unpleasant it may be," she told him, "but I've taken the liberty of sending a dispatch boat to Yeltsin. It left two hours ago, with the news of Lady Harrington's presumed loss."

"I see." Greentree gazed at her for a moment, then exhaled heavily. "I understand, Dame Madeleine, and though I probably shouldn't be, I'm grateful."

"I won't say you're welcome," Sorbanne said, "because I wish *no one* had to tell your people she's missing, but—"

She shrugged again, and Greentree bobbed his head.

"I'll be going, then, Ma'am," he said.

A moment later the door slid shut behind him, and Madeleine Sorbanne stood gazing at it for several seconds before she drew a deep breath and nodded sharply to it.

"Good luck, Captain," she said softly, and then she squared her shoulders and walked back to the chair behind her desk and the responsibilities that went with it.

Thirty minutes later, a lift aboard GNS *Jason Alvarez* came to a halt and Thomas Greentree drew a deep breath and stepped out. He made himself walk as closely to normally as he could, yet he knew his face was like stone. He couldn't help that. Indeed, he wasn't even certain he wanted to, for what he was about to do was almost a rehearsal—on a very personal and painful level—of what would await him when he returned to Yeltsin's Star, and his expression simply matched the heart which lay like frozen granite in his chest.

He turned a bend, and his eyes flinched from the green-uniformed man standing outside Lady Harrington's quarters. Normally, that duty belonged to James Candless or Robert Whitman, as the junior members of her regular three-man travel detail. When she was . . . away, however, someone else was responsible for guarding the sanctity of her quarters. As Andrew LaFollet's second-in-command, Simon Mattingly was too senior for that duty, but someone had to make out the assignment roster, and in LaFollet's absence that person was Corporal Mattingly. He could station anyone he wanted here, and he stood as straight as a spear, his shoulders square, buttons and brightwork shining like tiny, polished suns. He even wore the knotted golden aigulette with the Harrington arms which a steadholder's personal armsmen wore only on the most formal of occasions, and Greentree's jaw clenched.

He understood the silent armsman's unspoken message. The corporal's presence was no mere formality; it was an everyday duty. And the Steadholder wasn't gone; she was merely absent, and when she returned, she would find her liegemen *doing* their duty. However long it took, however long he had to wait, Simon Mattingly would stand watch for her, and in so doing he would somehow *keep* her from being gone.

The captain came to a halt, and Mattingly snapped to attention.

"May I help you, Captain?" he asked crisply.

"Yes, Corporal. I wanted to speak to Steward MacGuiness."

"Just a moment, Sir."

Mattingly pressed the com button and waited. Several seconds ticked past—a far longer wait than normal—before a voice Greentree almost didn't recognize responded.

"Yes?" The one-word response came heavy and dull, dropping from the intercom like a stone, and Mattingly's eyes flicked briefly to the captain.

"Captain Greentree would like to speak to you, Mac," he said quietly. There was another moment of silence, and then the hatch slid open.

Mattingly said nothing more. He simply braced back to attention, and Greentree stepped past him into Lady Harrington's quarters. MacGuiness stood just inside the hatch opening into his pantry, and if his eyes were suspiciously swollen, Thomas Greentree was not about to comment on the fact. Unlike Mattingly, the steward's shoulders slumped, and for the first time in Greentree's experience, he looked his chronological age. His arms hung awkwardly at his sides, as if the capable hands at their ends had somehow forgotten their utility; the lines prolong had kept age from etching into his face showed now, drawn deep by grief and worry; and the captain could actually feel the strength with which he made himself hope, made himself cling to the belief that there was some sort of news, as if by hoping hard enough he could make it so.

"Good morning, Sir," he said huskily, trying to smile a welcome. "Would you care for some refreshment? I'm—" His voice broke, and he cleared his throat. "I'm sure the

Commodore would want—"

His hands clenched and his voice died, and Greentree felt a deep, irrational flare of guilt. It was his expression which had cut MacGuiness off, and he knew it. He saw it in the way the steward's face tightened, the way his shoulders hunched as if to fend off some dreaded blow. But there was no way to spare him, and the captain inhaled sharply.

"Admiral Sorbanne has made it official," he said, trying to find kindness by being brutally brief. "As of this afternoon, *Prince Adrian* is officially overdue and presumed lost." MacGuiness' face went white, and Greentree reached out to rest his right hand on the older man's shoulder. "I'm sorry, MacGuiness," he said much more softly. "At the moment Lady Harrington is only missing. Until we get some report from the Peeps or from the League inspectors, that's all we know. I—" He paused and squeezed the steward's shoulder. "I wanted you to hear it from me, not the rumor mill."

"Thank you, Sir." It came out in a whisper, and MacGuiness blinked hard as he looked around the empty cabin. "It doesn't seem—" he began, then stopped, clenched his jaw, and turned his head away, concealing his face from the captain. "Thank you for telling me, Sir," he said in a strangely breathless voice. "If you'll excuse me, I . . . I've got some things I have to take care—"

He pulled away from the hand on his shoulder and walked quickly into Lady Harrington's sleeping cabin. The hatch closed behind him, and Greentree gazed at it for several silent seconds, then sighed and turned back to the hatch. He was certain Mattingly must have guessed the reason for his visit to MacGuiness, but that wasn't going to spare Greentree the task of telling him, as well. Of being the official spokesman for the news none of Lady Harrington's people wanted to hear.

Behind him, in Honor Harrington's sleeping cabin, James MacGuiness sat in a chair, staring up at the gemmed scabbard of the Harrington Sword above the crystal cabinet which held the Star of Grayson and the Harrington Key.

He made no sound, and his body never moved, and the tears sliding down his face fell as silently as rain.

Honor sighed, looked up from the book she'd been pretending to read for the last hour or so, and rubbed her eyes wearily. She sat for a moment longer, then laid the book aside, swung her long legs off the narrow bunk, crossed to the center of the single large compartment she shared with Marcia McGinley, Geraldine Metcalf, and Sarah DuChene, and began a series of stretching exercises.

McGinley looked up from the chess problem she was currently working through. She watched Honor for a moment without speaking, then glanced at DuChene and raised an eyebrow. The astrogator nodded in answer to the unvoiced question, and the two of them rose to join Honor. She moved aside to give them a little more space, and the three of them circled about one another in the strangely graceful almost-dance the limited deck space enforced upon their exercises while Metcalf watched them from her own bed. There was no room for her to join them until one of them sat down, and she waited patiently, but Nimitz was unprepared to see a perfectly good—and stationary lap— go to waste. He launched himself from the foot of Honor's bed to Metcalf's, and the tac officer chuckled as he sprawled across her legs and turned his belly fur up to be petted.

Honor watched the others from the corners of her eyes as she exercised and wished longingly for even a little more space. There wasn't really enough room for her to have gone through her training katas properly even if she'd been alone. With the others crowding in on her, she probably would have inflicted serious bodily injury on someone if she'd tried. Yet for all the inconvenience of being squeezed so tightly together, the part of her which eroded a little further every day under the dead weight of her helplessness was grateful the others were present. Not that any of them *wanted* to be here, but at least she and Nimitz didn't have to face the added burden of isolation which proper military courtesy would have imposed upon them in a larger vessel.

Despite the vast gulf between Honor's rank and theirs, McGinley, Metcalf, and DuChene were the next most senior female POWs, and it was impossible for the Peeps to offer any of their prisoners—even Honor—private quarters. Citizen Captain Bogdanovich had apologized on Citizen Rear Admiral Tourville's behalf for crowding the four of them together, but *Count Tilly* was only a battle-cruiser. There was only so much space to go around, and however spartan, the compartment—intended by the ship's designers to provide berthing space for six junior officers— was preferable to a cell in the brig.

At first, Metcalf and DuChene had been more than a little uncomfortable at being thrown in with Honor . . . and Nimitz, of course. They'd seemed to feel it was somehow their fault that she'd been denied the privacy they were convinced she deserved, and the difference in their ranks had only made things worse. She'd done her best to disabuse them of the notion that they were to blame for anything that had happened, and McGinley's presence had helped. Neither Metcalf nor DuChene had ever served with Honor before. Aside from the brief contacts they'd had during her visits aboard *Prince Adrian*, they'd been total strangers, but McGinley, as Honor's operations officer, offered a sort of bridge. She held the same rank as the other two, yet she was also comfortable with her role as the second most important member of Honor's staff, and her existing working relationship with Honor had gradually extended itself to Metcalf and DuChene. Nothing could make their situation anything other than irregular and awkward, but the others had settled down after the first few days.

The difference in their ranks remained, of course, even in their new and strained circumstances. Honor was not simply their superior but their CO, the senior officer of all the Allied POWs, which required her to remain aloof from the others. She could never hope to be "one of the girls," but they'd fallen into an almost comfortable relation-ship, and Honor was glad, for she was self-honest enough to admit that in her current situation she needed any sense of stability she could get. Her contact with the other POWs was virtually nonexistent, and a sense of being disconnected—of never knowing exactly what was happening to people for whom she still felt responsible—added to the gnawing fear of the future which continued to eat at her.

Nimitz, on the other hand, seemed almost content . . . but appearances were deceiving. He couldn't hide his sense of being trapped from Honor, although his cheerful opportunism would have fooled anyone who lacked her link to his emotions. He'd gotten to know McGinley well aboard *Alvarez*; now he imposed shamelessly upon her for petting and grooming. In fact, he'd deigned to accept the ministrations of all three of Honor's junior officers. She might almost have felt abandoned if she hadn't realized how he'd turned petting or playing with him into a sort of occupational therapy for them . . . and if his willingness to luxuriate unabashedly in their attentions hadn't been such a major factor in overcoming Metcalf's and DuChene's original discomfort.

Besides, watching Nimitz manipulate the others out of *their* depression helped distract Honor from her own. And her fellow prisoners weren't the only people the 'cat had charmed. Indeed, Shannon Foraker visited Honor—and Nimitz—so regularly that Honor worried about her. Too much familiarity with a Manticoran officer was likely to cause a *Peep* officer serious trouble, and she felt a little guilty for not having hinted to Foraker that she might want to keep her distance. But the truth was that she was too grateful for the citizen commander's visits to discourage her, and Tourville had decided to use his ops officer as his official liaison with Honor.

Foraker was certainly a good choice, if his object was to be sure he'd picked someone he could trust to see to it that his prisoners were properly treated, but Honor had come to suspect the citizen rear admiral of an additional motive. Despite her promotion, the ops officer hadn't changed much since Honor had met her in Silesia, and she clearly wanted to repay Honor for how well she'd been treated aboard HMS *Wayfarer*. But what superiors in most navies might have seen as an honorable intention on her part could be extremely dangerous to an officer in the present People's Navy, and that, Honor suspected, was the real reason Tourville had made her his liaison. Since she'd been *ordered* to see to the prisoners' well-being, her superiors could hardly come down on her for being conscientious in the discharge of her duties.

It was unlikely the ops officer realized what Tourville was up to (always assuming, of course, that *Honor* had figured it out properly), but that blind spot was part of her charm. She had an almost childlike innocence. Not foolishness or stupidity, but a refusal—or perhaps an outright inability—to let her personal relationships be dictated by the ideologically-fired pressures swirling through the People's Navy. She seemed to possess absolutely none of the constructive paranoia which helped guide many of her fellows through the minefields about them, and the thought of what might have become of her if her skill and talents had made her one bit less valuable to her superiors was enough to send a chill down Honor's spine. No doubt it was silly of her to worry herself over what could happen to an officer in an enemy navy, especially when those very talents made the officer in question uniquely dangerous to her own side, but it was hard to remember that when Foraker made a point of reminding *Count Tilly*'s cooks of Honor's special dietary needs or stopped by on her limited off-duty time to play chess with McGinley, or feed Nimitz celery, or give Metcalf the painting supplies which had been recovered from her quarters aboard *Prince Adrian*.

And however little awareness Foraker seemed to have of potential risks to *her*, she clearly recognized Honor's greatest worry, and she'd set out to do something about it. She'd not only brought other Peeps to meet Nimitz—whose charm could be relied upon to loosen up the stiffest courtesy call—but she'd also "borrowed" the 'cat several times. Officially, she was taking Nimitz out for exercise;

actually, she was introducing him to as many people as possible aboard *Count Tilly* with the obvious intention of convincing them he represented no danger to them.

Honor was immensely grateful for Foraker's efforts, although she would have felt more optimistic about their success if she hadn't discovered that Tourville, at least, knew Nimitz *was* a danger. The citizen rear admiral had taken to inviting her, McKeon, and "Colonel" LaFollet, as the three highest ranking POWs, to dine with his officers on a semiregular basis. Honor was grateful for the opportunity to see the others, although she knew those dinners were hard on LaFollet, but they had also offered Tourville the chance to "let slip" that the Peeps' Naval Intelligence had assembled a file on her.

She'd been startled at first, though a little consideration had told her she shouldn't have been. After all, she routinely saw the files ONI compiled on Peep officers whom the RMN had decided were important enough to keep tabs on. She simply hadn't considered that the People's Navy might see *her* in that light. But they did . . . and as part of her file, they'd included full details of her career on Grayson. From Tourville's deliberately casual remarks, it was obvious those details included clips from the gory Planetary Security video of her and Nimitz foiling the attempt to assassinate Protector Benjamin's family. No one who'd seen that footage could ever make the mistake of underestimating Nimitz's lethality, and while Tourville clearly didn't feel threatened by him, she rather doubted that everyone else who had the rank to see it would share his equanimity.

From that viewpoint, at least, the existence of her file made it far more likely she and Nimitz *would* be separated. Indeed, had she been a Peep, she suspected she would have argued against allowing any prisoner to retain a "pet" she knew had killed people. Admitting that did absolutely nothing to make her feel confident, and she was shocked when she first realized how deeply her future's looming uncertainties were affecting her.

It wasn't a sort of pressure she'd ever before faced, and it was one she was uniquely unsuited to handle. It would, she'd realized slowly, have been impossible to *design* a situation which could have turned the normal mainstays of her personality more cruelly against her. The very act of ordering *Prince Adrian's* surrender had turned her sense of duty and responsibility to her Queen and her Navy into a source of guilt, not strength. The matching sense of duty to her personnel—the sense of mutual obligation and responsibility which existed between any officer and those under her orders—had become another vicious goad, for there was no way she could discharge it. She did her best as their representative, and the decency of officers like Tourville and Foraker had prevented their captors from abusing her people . . . so far. But that was the point, wasn't it? She had no *power* to protect her personnel if—no, *when*—Tourville was replaced by someone else. And above and beyond all those grinding concerns was her bond with Nimitz. What had been the single most important cornerstone of her life for over forty years, the wellspring of stability and love to which she had been able to turn even in her darkest moments, was now the greatest threat she'd ever faced. She could lose Nimitz. He could be taken from her— even killed—at the whim of any Peep Navy or Marine officer, any State Security thug, even a simple prison camp guard. There was *nothing she could do* to protect him from any of those people, and the desperation that woke within her could only be concealed from her subordinates, for it could not be dispelled.

And because she couldn't dispel her desperation—or her terror—they only grew, like sources of infection which could not be lanced and cleaned. The dark cores of fear grew deeper and stronger, eating into her reserves of strength and undermining her sense of self, and all she could do was try to ignore them. To avoid thinking about them. To pretend they weren't there . . . when she knew perfectly well that they were.

It was destroying her. She knew it was, felt her growing fragility as the poison of helplessness ate away bits and pieces of her, and she hated it. *Hated* it. Not just for what it was doing to her, but even more because of what it was *preventing* her from doing for the people she'd brought to this with her.

She suspected that only McKeon and LaFollet—and possibly McGinley—realized how she was eroding from the core out. She hoped no one else did, anyway. It was bad enough that the people closest to her should be forced to deal with her failures and her preoccupation with her private terrors when they had fears and worries of their own and a right to her support in coping with them. But—

A soft chime sounded, and Honor looked up gratefully, thankful to be pulled from the ever tightening spiral of her self-condemnation, as the compartment hatch slid open. Shannon Foraker stood in the doorway, and Honor started to smile in welcome. But her smile died stillborn as Foraker's expression registered, and she sensed McGinley and DuChene slowing, then stopping, in their exercises behind her.

"Yes, Citizen Commander?" she said, and as always, the steadiness of her voice surprised her. It should sound as frayed and stretched as she felt, quivering like an over-stressed cable.

"Citizen Admiral Tourville sent me to extend his compliments to you and inform you that we've received new orders, Commodore." If Honor's voice sounded unnaturally natural in her own ears, Foraker's came out with an equally unnatural flatness. Even the words sounded wrong somehow, as if they'd been written for her by someone else, and that, Honor realized, was because they *had*. Foraker was the messenger, but the *message* was from Tourville, and the citizen commander paused to clear her throat before she continued.

"The dispatch boat has returned from Barnett," she went on, looking straight into Honor's eyes. "Citizen Admiral Tourville's dispatches were intended for Citizen Admiral

Theisman, the system CO, and his commissioner, but Citizen Ransom of the Committee of Public Safety is currently in the system and she was, of course, shown the message."

Honor felt her breathing pause. She'd felt a momentary stir of hope at the name Theisman, for she and the citizen admiral had met, and enemy though he was, he was also a man of integrity and courage. But Cordelia Ransom's name brought any sense of hope crashing down, and she fought to keep the dread out of her expression as she made herself meet Foraker's level gaze.

"Most of your enlisted personnel and junior officers will be transported directly to a Navy holding facility in the Tarragon System," Foraker told her. "You, however, with your senior officers and some of your more senior petty officers, will be returning to Barnett with us aboard *Count Tilly*."

The citizen commander paused once more, as if she wanted to find some way—any way—to avoid completing her message. But there wasn't one, and her voice was even flatter when she continued.

"Citizen Ransom has instructed Citizen Admiral Tourville personally to conduct you to Barnett, Commodore. According to her message, she wishes to interview you in person before determining the precise disposition of your case."

"I see." Honor's soprano didn't even waver. It was as if she stood to one side, watching a stranger use her body and her voice. She'd seen ONI's briefings on the Committee of Public Safety and its members. She knew Cordelia Ransom's record, and knowing it, she couldn't lie to herself about the reasons Ransom might wish to "interview" her . . . or what sort of "disposition" Ransom would make of her. Yet in a strange sort of way, she realized distantly, she was almost relieved. At least now she could no longer torment herself with false hopes.

She heard Nimitz's feet thump as he jumped down from Metcalf's lap and crossed the deck to her. She bent without looking away from Foraker and scooped him up, hugging him to her breasts so fiercely she was surprised he didn't squeal in pain, and the universe seemed to have stopped about her. There was only Foraker, the misery in her eyes confirming the fact that she shared Honor's own estimate of what her future held, and the living, infinitely precious warmth of the treecat in her arms.

But then she realized she was wrong. There was one more thing which, even now, she could not evade. There was duty. Duty to her Queen, whom she could not disgrace by showing weakness. Duty to her people, whom she could not fail by collapsing at the moment when they would need her most. And finally, there was duty to herself. The duty to gather whatever fragments of her frayed and eroded strength remained and meet whatever came with at least a pretense of dignity.

"Thank you, Shannon. And please extend my thanks to Citizen Admiral Tourville, both for informing me and for all his many kindnesses," Lady Dame Honor Harrington said serenely, and she smiled.

• Chapter Twenty

Hamish Alexander felt as if someone had punched him in the belly.

He sank into a chair, never taking his eyes from Nathan Robards' face, and his palatial cabin aboard GNS *Benjamin the Great* was very quiet, the only sound the patient, rhythmic ticking of an antique clock. The Duke of Cromarty had given him that clock, a corner of his brain reflected, as if searching for something—anything—to distract itself. But now its small, precise ticks only emphasized the stillness around him, as if his superdreadnought flagship itself could not believe what his flag lieutenant had just said.

"Presumed lost?" he repeated finally, and even to his own ears, the words sounded as if they belonged to someone who thought he could make the truth untrue simply by closing his eyes and wishing hard enough.

"Yes, My Lord," the young Grayson said. "I have Admiral Sorbanne's message here." He offered White Haven the electronic message board under his arm as if he were anxious to be rid of it, but the earl shook his head.

"Later." His voice was husky, and he looked down at his hands and swallowed. "I'll view it later, Nathan," he managed more naturally. "Just give me the high points."

"Admiral Sorbanne's preliminary report is short on details, My Lord," Robards said respectfully, but White Haven only nodded impatiently, and the flag lieutenant put the message board back under his arm unhappily and straightened his spine, coming to a sort of abbreviated parade rest.

"As Dame Madeleine had already reported," he said, "the Peeps have secured at least temporary control of the Adler

331

System after destroying Commodore Yeargin's task group, but Lady—" Robards paused, as if his own report had taken him by surprise. Then he coughed into a fist and continued in a voice of determined normality.

"Lady Harrington was unaware of those facts, and so had no reason to anticipate a hostile presence there. For reasons which aren't quite clear from Admiral Sorbanne's report, she was visiting Captain McKeon's ship, which was running point for the convoy. At some point between *Prince Adrian's* n-space translation and that of the convoy's main body, Lady Harrington became aware of the Peeps' presence and ordered Captain McKeon to draw the enemy away from the convoy's translation point. She also ordered Captain Greentree to hyper back out with the convoy. Her intention was to proceed independently to Clairmont, and when last seen, *Prince Adrian* appeared to be clear of all pursuit, aside from a single enemy cruiser or battlecruiser which should have been capable of forcing only of a brief passing engagement. But—"

Robards stopped and stood for a second longer. Then his shoulders slumped ever so minutely and his eyes to met his admiral's.

"That's all we know, My Lord," he said quietly. "As of the dispatch boat's departure from Clairmont, *Prince Adrian* was fifty hours overdue. Admiral Sorbanne has now officially listed her as presumed lost."

"I see." White Haven stared down at his desk, and his nostrils flared as he inhaled deeply. "Thank you, Nathan," he said. "Leave Dame Madeleine's message. I'll view it later."

"Yes, My Lord."

The message board clicked as Robards set it on the corner of the desk. Then the flag lieutenant withdrew, and the hatch closed noiselessly behind him. Silence filled the day cabin, broken only by the soft, meticulous ticking of the clock, and the earl sat very, very still.

How many ships, over the years, had been listed as "overdue and presumed lost" only to turn up eventually?

There must have been many. There *had* to have been. But at this moment, he couldn't think of the names of any, and somehow he knew *Prince Adrian* would not be one of them.

How did it happen? he wondered. *She was too* good *to let the Peeps catch her this way—and so was McKeon. So what in God's name* happened?

The missile pods. That had to be it. The very pods she'd warned him the Peeps were beginning to deploy. They couldn't have come from the ship she'd known about, either. She was too careful. Towed pods would have reduced its acceleration rate, and she would never have missed something like that. She would have wondered why it was accelerating so slowly, and the earl knew she would have drawn the correct conclusion.

He rose and folded his hands behind him to pace back and forth, frowning down at the decksole while his brain considered the possibilities.

Someone was lying doggo, he decided. *Had to be it— the one thing no one can ever really guard against. God, what were the* odds *of something like that?*

But it made sense. A ship she didn't know about, hiding in front of her, loaded with missile pods and waiting until it became impossible for her to evade. White Haven closed his eyes in pain, picturing the moment of awareness, the instant in which she must have realized what was happening . . . and that there was no way to avoid it. And then the carnage the earl had seen too many times—unleashed *himself* too many times—as the wave of laser heads crashed down on *Prince Adrian* like a Sphinx tidal bore.

He turned, facing the huge painting of Benjamin IV on the bulkhead behind his desk, and his face was etched with pain. *Overdue and presumed lost*. The officialese replayed itself mockingly in his mind, and his fists clenched behind him as he wondered if she were alive or dead. Even if she were alive, she was a prisoner now. She had to be.

He remembered his conversation with High Admiral Matthews, the questions about himself and his feelings which he'd faced then. He never had answered them. He'd put them aside, refused to think about them, and now . . . Now it was all too likely he never *would* know the answers. Yet as he stared into the hazel eyes of the bulkhead portrait, he also knew he would always feel a dark, personal responsibility for what had happened. She never would have been sent to Adler if she hadn't reported back for duty early, and if not for whatever he'd given away that night in her library, she wouldn't have reported early. And so, in a way no one else would ever know, it was *his* fault.

He never knew exactly how long he stood staring into the face of the long-dead protector for whom his flagship was named, but finally he drew a deep, painful breath and shook himself.

There was no reason to assume she was dead, he told his conscience. She'd already demonstrated an uncanny ability to survive, and there were almost always *some* survivors from any ship. Until—and unless—her death was positively confirmed, she *would* survive in his mind. She had to.

He turned from the portrait and sat once more behind his desk. He started to reach for the message board Robards had left, but then he drew his hand back. That, too, could wait, his brain insisted firmly, and he turned back to his terminal and the reams of reports awaiting him. He'd never thought the endless, bureaucratic details of activating a fleet command could be welcome, but today they were, and he dove into them like a man seeking refuge from demons.

Thomas Theisman's dark green tunic was flung untidily across the back of a chair, his stocking feet rested on a beaten copper coffee table, the neck of his blouse had been dragged untidily open, and he stared moodily into his glass. Not even a citizen admiral could afford the prices Old Earth whiskey brought in the PRH these days, and Theisman seldom drank. He certainly wasn't enough of a drinker to have built up his own supply of liquor, but his logistics officer had managed to turn up a brand of imitation Old Earth whiskey bottled right here in Barnett. Drinker or

no, Theisman suspected this was a pretty poor imitation—
a conclusion he'd reached when the first glass cauterized
his taste buds. The copious quantity he'd consumed since
churned in his stomach with a virulence which had done
nothing to change his judgment of its quality, but at least
it was having the desired effect of anesthetizing his brain,
and he poured more of the amber liquid over the ice in
his glass while he cursed the bitch goddess of coincidence.

Cordelia Ransom had been in the Barnett System for
ten days before the dispatch boat from Tourville arrived,
and he'd let himself begin to feel a glimmer of hope. Her
HD crews were everywhere, intruding into everything,
getting under everyone's feet, and generally playing havoc
with the efficiency of his command. Even his enlisted
personnel had been uneasy at having Public Information
crawling all over them, and his intelligence staffers had run
themselves frantic trying to guard against potential security
breaches.

It must have been nice, he'd thought, to have lived before
the Warshawski sail had made true interstellar communication
possible once more. Today it might take dispatch boats weeks
or even months to complete their voyages, but, unfortunately,
they always did seem to get there in the end. The great news
agencies like United Faxes Intragalactic, Reuters of Beowulf,
and the Interstellar News Service—all headquartered in the
Solarian League—were bad enough, but at least restricted
access and alert security could limit the damage they did. Not
that any measures could be absolutely counted upon, and the
League's official insistence on "freedom of the press" made
it even harder. Their correspondents seemed to think their
press passes made them gods, and DuQuesne Base's Marine
security types had grabbed a pair of stringers—one with UFI
and the other with INS—trying to sneak aboard a freight
shuttle with the evident intention of getting onboard interviews
from the crew of the superdreadnought for which it was
bound.

All in all, however, Theisman felt reasonably confident
of his ability to protect operational security from outsiders;

it was his own propagandists he feared. God knew NavInt and StateSec spent enough time—and money—paying neutral agents for recordings of the Manties' domestic news and information broadcasts. Those broadcasts were weeks or even months old by the time they reached the analysts, yet the intelligence types always managed to glean at least some useful information from them, if only by helping to fill in background. He had to assume the Alliance returned the compliment where the Republic was concerned, which meant a single wrong word in a propaganda broadcast could blow secrets the Navy had spent months hiding, and all because some Public Information writer who neither understood nor cared about operational realities wanted a good sound bite.

But for all the monumental pain in the ass Ransom's presence had been, his own contacts with her had encouraged him to hope that perhaps he *hadn't* been set up to be the scapegoat when Barnett fell. He couldn't be certain, of course. Whatever else she might be, Cordelia Ransom would have made a wonderful poker player, but she'd spent too much time with him and recorded too much footage of interviews with him for him to believe she intended simply to write him off along with Barnett, and the scripts from which his interviewers worked had reinforced that hope. Much of the propaganda content had been too blatant (and strident) for his taste, but the HD clips were clearly designed to present one Thomas Theisman in the most heroic light possible. Surely PubIn wouldn't invest so much time—and the personal attention of its director— in building up someone it intended to toss aside. After all, the loss of a public hero couldn't help but hurt civilian morale, could it? Especially when the Secretary of Public Information had personally presented that hero as the Republic's champion.

The thought of being made the Committee of Public Safety's paladin had been hard for Theisman to stomach, yet if that was the price of survival, he'd been willing— even relieved—to pay it. But even as he'd begun to think

Ransom's interest in him might spell salvation, coincidence had been waiting to put yet another stain upon his conscience. For if Ransom hadn't been in Barnett to make specials portraying Thomas Theisman as a hero, she never would have seen Tourville's dispatch.

The citizen admiral growled a curse and threw back another long swallow. The alcohol burned going down and seemed to explode in his stomach, but he appeared to have reached the limit of the solace it could offer, and he leaned back in his chair with a sigh.

He wasn't certain how Tourville had gotten his people's commissioner to sign off on his plan for dealing with his prisoners, but it had been obvious from the dispatch that the fix was in. Tourville had intended to send all of his prisoners, including the officers, to the Navy's facility in Tarragon. The prison camps there were hardly luxury hotels, but unlike the SS, the Navy had a strong vested interest in treating captured Allied military personnel decently. More than that, the Solarian League's Prisoner of War Commission, which monitored the belligerents for compliance with the provisions of the Deneb Accords, maintained an office in Tarragon and compiled lists of all incoming prisoners. That meant the Star Kingdom would have been informed within weeks of *Prince Adrian's* fate . . . and that Honor Harrington would have been safe. Nothing could have protected her against the *possibility* that StateSec would demand she be turned over, but the SS had so far followed a policy of leaving POWs in military hands once they got there in the first place. Tourville and Theisman could at least have hoped they would adhere to the same policy in Harrington's case, and even if they hadn't wanted to, her location would have been a matter of public record, and her prominence would have added another layer of protection. Surely not even the SS would be stupid enough to mistreat her in the full glare of publicity. Think what propaganda opportunities *that* would have offered the Alliance!

But Ransom's presence had derailed Tourville's efforts,

and her own orders had sent a chill down Theisman's spine. She'd overridden Tourville's plan to send all of his prisoners to Tarragon and insisted that all senior officers and a sampling of senior petty officers be delivered to Barnett, instead. That much had probably been inevitable, once she'd learned of Harrington's capture, but what frightened Theisman was the order to suppress all mention of that capture. No one—not the League inspectors, not the Manties, not even the Navy at large—*no one* was to be told Harrington was now a prisoner, and an order like that sounded ominous alarms for any citizen of the PRH.

The Legislaturalists' old prewar Office of Internal Security had been frightening enough. The formality of trials had been an irritating nuisance which InSec had felt no particular need to burden itself with, and everyone had heard whispered tales of someone who had been made to disappear by InSec, or the Mental Hygiene Police, or one of their countless sister agencies. But State Security was worse. No one needed whispered reports now, for StateSec *wanted* its citizens to know about arrests and punishments. And trials were no longer irritating nuisances; they had become golden opportunities for propaganda and tools to legitimize SS atrocities. Yet the first stage in the process remained unchanged. Show trials might come later, but until StateSec decided how it wanted to deal with any given individual, that person was made to vanish. He could always be produced later if a trial seemed desirable . . . and if it was more convenient to avoid that in his case, it was a simple matter for his disappearance to become permanent.

Theisman couldn't believe Ransom intended for that to happen to Harrington, for he was certain she saw the disadvantages too clearly. He'd told himself that firmly, almost desperately, and he knew that was because deep down inside he was far less certain than he wanted to be. Too many stupid things had already been done in the name of the revolution and "the People's war." Too much blood had already been spilled simply because it could be. And he didn't want that to happen to Honor Harrington.

He took another, smaller sip of his drink, closed his eyes, and pressed the cold glass to his forehead while whiskey fumes sent strands of thought he might never have dared to face without the drink pirouetting through his brain.

He respected Harrington. More, he owed her his own life, and the lives of the crew she had allowed him to surrender when she'd had every possible reason simply to blow them out of space and be done with it, and she'd continued to show compassion to her enemies since. Warner Caslet had been returned to the Republic because Harrington had felt the Star Kingdom owed him and his crew a debt. Citizen Captain Stephen Holtz and the forty-six survivors of PNS *Achmed* had lived only because Harrington had sent her pinnaces to take them off the dead hulk of their vessel when she hadn't known if the remaining life support of her own crippled ship would keep even her own survivors alive. And she had arranged for *them* to be repatriated along with Caslet and his people.

The People's Navy owed her a debt of honor, and Thomas Theisman owed her a personal debt, both of which simply reinforced the argument of reciprocity. Honor Harrington was, quite simply, a person whom the Republic *must* treat with dignity and respect if it expected its own personnel to be properly treated. And the thought—

The admittance chime sounded, and he grunted in irritation. He set his glass aside and pressed the stud on the arm of his chair.

"Yes?" he growled.

"I'd like to speak to you, Citizen Admiral," someone said, and Theisman jerked upright as he recognized Cordelia Ransom's voice. Time seemed to stop—a single instant stretching itself out towards eternity—and in that crystalline suspension, he realized how incredibly stupid he'd been to get drunk when Cordelia Ransom was anywhere in the same star system.

But then the instant shattered, and self-preservation tamed his flood of panic. Stupid he might be, but kicking himself wouldn't save him from the consequences. *That* was going to take action, and he shook himself violently and shoved up out of his chair.

"Uh, just a moment, Citizen Secretary!" he got out, and his feet fumbled their ways into his boots while he resealed his blouse's collar, then reached for the inhaler beside the whiskey bottle. He hated the damned thing, and he seldom drank heavily enough to need it, but he'd learned the hard way to keep it handy when he did drink. Up till this moment, he'd thought that disastrous evening in his third year at the Academy would retain a pure and unsullied prominence as the worst drunken night in his life. Now he knew better, and he raised the inhaler, pressed the button, and breathed in deeply.

The sudden, hacking cough which doubled him over took his body by surprise. His mind had known it was coming, but not the rest of him, and his skull seemed to expand hugely. For an instant he thought he was dying—then he only *wished* he were. But at least the damned thing had the desired effect. His stomach felt even more upset than before, but his brain cleared—mostly—and the room stopped trying to polka about him.

He gave himself another shake, shoved the inhaler into the pocket of his trousers, and snatched his tunic up from the other chair. He started to pull it back on, then changed his mind. He was in his personal quarters, after all, and Ransom hadn't warned him she was coming. Under the circumstances, he refused to greet her in full uniform like some neorabbit scurrying to present the best possible appearance to a hunter.

He settled for hanging the tunic more neatly on a coat tree, drew a deep breath, and pressed the admittance button.

The door slid open, and Cordelia Ransom stepped through it, trailed—as always—by her hulking bodyguards. Actually, Theisman realized as he looked more closely, this was a different pair from the one which had accompanied her to his office that first day. Not that it seemed to matter. They obviously came in interchangeable matched sets.

"Good evening, Citizen Secretary," he said. "I wasn't expecting you."

"I realize that, Citizen Admiral," she replied, and cocked her head. Her blue eyes rested for a moment on his tunic, then flicked to the whiskey bottle and glass on the coffee table. "I apologize for disturbing you without prior notice, but there were a few points I wanted to discuss with you. In private."

"Indeed?" Theisman said politely. The inhaler had left him with a throbbing headache, but the pain seemed to help clear his thoughts, and he let his own eyes flick to her bodyguards. The hint was wasted. The concept of private discussions obviously didn't extend to excluding them, and Theisman was struck by a sudden insight. He wondered if the residual clash between the inhaler's contents and the fuzzy remnants of his inebriation had somehow freed him to make the association, but once made, it was so blindingly obvious he wondered how he could possibly have missed it before. Those guards' presence had nothing at all to do with any genuine feeling of danger on Ransom's part. They were present simply because she was important enough that she could have them. They were an expression of her power and importance, a totem or trophy she was unprepared to dispense with.

"Indeed," she replied, oblivious to the thoughts flickering through his mind, and he stepped aside and waved to invite her to select a chair.

"I was just having a drink to unwind," he said. "May I offer you one, as well?"

"No, thank you. Please feel free to refresh your own glass, though."

"Not just now, thanks," Theisman told her, and waited until she'd seated herself before he sat facing her. "How can I help you, Citizen Secretary?" he asked in a courteous tone while the bodyguards stationed themselves behind her.

"I wanted to discuss Citizen Rear Admiral Tourville's actions," she replied, and he felt a fresh stab of alarm, for her voice was cold and the flatness was back in her eyes.

"In what respect, Ma'am?" His whiskey-abused stomach knotted, yet he managed to keep the wariness out of his voice and expression. But it was hard, and Ransom's next words made it even harder.

"I'm not at all happy about his obvious attempt to consign his prisoners to military custody," she said.

"I'm not certain I follow your reasoning, Citizen Secretary," Theisman said as calmly as he could. "His prisoners are already *in* military custody, and he did report their capture and seek confirmation of his intention to transfer them direct to Tarragon."

"Don't play games with me, Citizen Admiral." Ransom's voice was colder still, and she smiled thinly. "Loyalty to one's subordinates is an admirable quality, but you know what I mean. This Harrington is scarcely an ordinary prisoner of war, and you and Tourville both know it. Her capture is a political factor of the first importance. As such, her disposition is a political, not a military, decision!"

"But, Citizen Secretary," Theisman tried, "under the Deneb Accords—"

"I'm not *interested* in the Deneb Accords!" Ransom snapped. She leaned forward and glared at Theisman. "The Deneb Accords were signed by the Legislaturalists, not the representatives of the People, and the People aren't bound by archaic remnants of the plutocratic past—not when they're locked in a fight to the death with *other* plutocratic elitists! This is a war of ideologies, and there can be no compromise between them. Why can't military officers *realize* that? This isn't another one of your 'warrior' clique's wars against 'honorable enemies' or 'fellow officers,' Citizen Admiral! It's a *class* war, a revolutionary struggle in which the sole acceptable outcome is not just the defeat but the *annihilation* of our enemies, because if we fail to wipe them out this time, they'll surely crush us and reimpose their exploitative rule once more. The one thing—the *only* thing—that matters is *winning*, and only people who have the political vision and willpower to admit that offer any chance of survival. Well, the Committee of Public Safety *has* that vision, and we refuse to throw away any tool or option which can help us win just because of some useless scrap of paper *we* never signed!"

Thomas Theisman wondered if the inhaler had actually worked after all, for her fervor sounded completely genuine. But that was ridiculous . . . wasn't it? What she'd just said was entirely in line with the Republic's official propaganda line, yet surely the woman responsible for presenting that line had to know better than to believe it herself!

"I can't disagree in theory, Citizen Secretary," he said carefully, "but I feel there are some practical consequences—tactical ones, not matters of fundamental principle—which must also be considered."

Ransom's mouth tightened ominously, but she didn't interrupt, and he kneaded his throbbing temple with one hand and went on even more cautiously.

"Specifically, Ma'am, it seems to me that the rank and file of the Manticoran Navy actually believe in the system for which they're fighting, and they see the Deneb Accords as an important part of that system. If we violate—"

"Nonsense!" Ransom broke in impatiently. "Oh, no doubt many of the enemy's prewar professionals do believe that drivel. After all, they're mercenaries who were stupid enough—or brainwashed or greedy enough—to *volunteer* to serve their imperialist exploiters for pay! But since the war started, their navy's been forced to recruit from the masses of the People. As the fighting goes on, more and more of their total manpower will have to be conscripted, just as ours is, and the conscripts *won't* believe the elitists' lies. They'll realize they're being sacrificed in a war against their own kind for the profit of their natural enemies, and when they do, they'll turn on their overlords just as we turned on ours!"

Theisman flinched. He couldn't help himself, for he'd just discovered a terrifying secret: Cordelia Ransom actually believed her own propaganda.

He sat very still, wishing he'd picked any other night to get drunk, and made himself draw a deep mental breath. *She can't* really *believe it*, he argued with himself. *Or can she? Is it really possible that she actually* believes *what she tells the Proles?*

No, he decided. She was a master at manipulating the Mob, and she'd shifted ground too quickly in the early days, changed course too rapidly in response to the Mob's unformed, changeful urges and desires. She'd been too successful at running in front of it, trying to anticipate its next lunge, to be a true ideologue.

But that only tells you what she was, *Thomas. She's had years since then—years to put her own imprint on what the Mob wants. She's not really anticipating its direction anymore; she's* shaping *that direction.*

His roiled stomach clenched at that thought, yet there was a fundamental conflict between the images of the cynical manipulator he was certain she was and the passionate ideologist who could believe the line she'd just spouted. The woman who dragged bodyguards everywhere to prove how important she was and whose propaganda ministry shaped and forged its lies to support any claim the Committee cared to make made an even more unlikely paladin of the proletariat than Thomas Theisman did. She *had* to know she was lying, or she couldn't have done it so consistently and well.

But there was another possibility, one almost as frightening as it was probable. After so long in a position of unchecked power, after so many years of being able to make the official truth over into whatever image she pleased, could it be that she'd lost the ability to recognize the *actual* truth? Theisman had known officers from powerful Legislaturalist families who'd fallen prey to a similar blindness. They'd known the situations described in their reports to the Admiralty bore only casual relationships to the truth, yet given their family positions, no one had dared to challenge those reports. And over the years, they'd come to operate on two separate levels: one in which they lied to their superiors to protect their private little empires, and another in which they genuinely believed they could make something true simply by *saying* that it was so.

Who in the People's Republic could tell Cordelia Ransom she was wrong? She had no peers, aside from Rob Pierre and Oscar Saint-Just, and the whole suppressive force of the Office of State Security stood behind her. It was *high treason* to question the gospel as preached by Public Information, for God's sake!

The madness went even deeper than he'd suspected, he thought shakenly. At least one member of the triumvirate which ruled his star nation had come to see its enemies through the distorting prisms of her own invention, and she was actually making decisions—decisions which could mean the life or death of the Republic—on that basis!

"I can't speak for every officer in the Navy, Citizen Secretary," he said after a pause he hoped hadn't stretched dangerously long, "but I *can* speak for myself when I say that I've never doubted that military policy must be subject to civilian control."

He chose his words with exquisite care. He had never been in more danger in his life, and he knew it. But somehow someone had to shake Ransom back into accepting a policy which contained some vestige of reason, and he seemed to be the only spokesman available. His nausea and pounding head didn't help, and his palms felt clammy, yet fear gave his thoughts a razor sharpness as he continued.

"My concern with the observance of the Deneb Accords stems from my own reading of the attitude of the Solarian League's inspectors and, if you'll pardon my saying so, of the relevant political direction I have, in fact, received." All of which, he reflected, was true enough, although not in the way Ransom had in mind.

"What 'relevant political direction'?" Ransom demanded suspiciously.

"Public Information's official statements have always emphasized that the PRH will treat its prisoners 'properly,' a definition which most star nations apply to actions in keeping with the provisions of the Deneb Accords. It was never specifically stated that we would act within those limitations, but that certainly appeared to be implied, and I do know that several Solarian League representatives with whom I've spoken attached that interpretation to our statements. And while I realize disinformation has a critical role to play in wartime, I've received no directives to suggest our intention in this case was to mislead. Under the circumstances, the only conclusion I felt I could draw was that I was, indeed, to consider the Accords binding upon my actions and those of my subordinates. I certainly wasn't prepared to risk conflicts with the Committee's apparent intentions by instructing my officers to adopt any other position."

"I see." Ransom leaned back in her chair, crossed her legs, and cocked her head once more. "I hadn't thought of it in those terms, Citizen Admiral," she said after a moment, in much less chilling tones. "You raise a point which the Committee clearly hasn't considered in sufficient detail. A coherent, top-down announcement will be required if we expect our commanders to know just what policy is, won't it?" She pursed her lips, then nodded slowly. "Yes, I can see that. In fact, I wonder why I hadn't seen it already? We've certainly recognized the need to clearly enunciate other policy changes. I see Secretary Saint-Just and I obviously have to sit down and thrash this one out, as well, in order to promulgate the proper directives."

"I'm sure the Committee will make the right decision, Ma'am." *At least, I hope to* hell *Pierre and Saint-Just will overrule you, anyway!* "May I make an interim suggestion to govern our actions in the meantime, however?"

"Certainly," Ransom said almost graciously.

"Thank you." Theisman carefully refrained from wiping his brow and tried to sound reasonable and confident but nonconfrontational, with no sign of the agonizing care with which he chose his words. "On a purely pragmatic level, I think it would pay us to apply the Accords to the general population of POWs without requiring—or allowing—local military commanders to make decisions to the contrary without specific directions from above." He raised a deprecating hand as she opened her mouth. "I'm not suggesting that political decisions won't have to be made in some individual cases, but I see three major advantages in relying on the Accords in *most* cases.

"One is that the military requires some general policy upon which to base its actions. I realize our commissioners will be available to advise us, but without such a general policy, we'll find ourselves in a position in which every system, fleet, task force, and squadron commander and his commissioner will have to set their own individual policies. I'm afraid the only possible outcome of that could be chaos. If, on the other hand, we continue to use the Accords as a primary guide, local commanders can make their decisions on that basis to ensure consistent dispositions of captured personnel. Where deviations from that policy are properly indicated, appropriate political direction can always be transmitted to the commanders in question at a later time."

He paused until Ransom nodded grudgingly. "And the other advantages?" she asked.

"The second one," Theisman said, "is the propaganda opportunities adherence to the Accords would provide—and, conversely, the *dangers* which might arise from an official, wholesale abandonment of them. The Accords are important to the decision-making segments of both the Alliance and the Solarian League. Without admitting that those decision-makers are the legitimate representatives of the People—" *but without admitting that they* aren't, *either!* "—we can't deny the objective reality that they *are* making the decisions at this moment. Among those decisions are the ones under which we're receiving clandestine support from certain elements within the League. If we denounce the Accords, those supporting the war against us will certainly attempt to portray us in the worst possible light for domestic consumption, which could have the twin effects of stiffening the Manties' wills *and* providing them with additional leverage with which to attempt to cut off the aid we're receiving from the League.

"If, on the other hand, we continue to abide by the Accords' stipulations, we can present ourselves as the natural allies of the people of the Star Kingdom. Remember that only about twenty percent of captured enemy personnel are officers, Citizen Secretary, and not even all of them come from the aristocracy or plutocracy. Put another way, at least eighty percent of the prisoners who profit from our observance of the Accords will come from the other classes of Manticoran society. By emphasizing that we treat our prisoners as the Accords provide, we'll reassure our natural allies among the enemy's population that we'll treat *them* well if they surrender . . . or come over to our side."

"Um." Ransom rubbed her nose for a moment, eyes hooded and thoughtful, then nodded slowly. "There's certainly something to that, Citizen Admiral," she conceded. "Of course, if we make that our official position, we'll have to be very selective in the instances in which we *don't* comply with all of the Accords' ridiculous provisions. If we're not, Manty propagandists will certainly fasten on the individual cases in which we make other . . . dispositions as proof that we're lying."

"That may be so, Ma'am." *Of course it is, you twit! That's why I suggested it*, Theisman thought, but no sign of it showed on his face. "I'm simply offering you my own perspective on the matter."

"I understand that, Citizen Admiral. But you said there was a third advantage?"

"Yes, Ma'am. Put simply, it's a question of reciprocity. If we treat *their* captured personnel well, we have a basis for demanding that they treat *our* people well. In effect, they'll have to treat their prisoners at least as well as we treat ours or find themselves losing ground in the propaganda war, and I think that's worthwhile for two reasons. First, I feel we have a moral responsibility to see to it that the personnel fighting the People's war are treated as well as possible under all circumstances, including their capture by the enemy. Second, our Navy's morale will be stronger if our personnel feel they'll be well treated in the event that they fall into enemy hands."

He started to list yet another reason to hope for reciprocal good treatment of POWs, but stopped himself in time. Pointing out to the Secretary of Public Information that the Manties had so far captured ten or fifteen times as many

Republican personnel as the PRH had captured of them wouldn't be the smartest thing he could possibly do.

"I see," Ransom said again. She propped her elbows on the arms of her chair and steepled her fingers under her chin, regarding Theisman through opaque eyes, and he looked back steadily, trying to ignore the churning of his stomach. "I must say, Citizen Admiral," she went on after several silent moments, "that I'm impressed by the reasoning behind your arguments. It's a pity you've been so, ah, *apolitical* previously. We could make use of a flag officer with your insights."

"I've been apolitical because I don't feel suited to a political career," Theisman said with a generous ten thousand percent understatement.

"I'm not so certain of that," Ransom mused. "You certainly seem to have a keen grasp of the propaganda aspects of the situation!"

"I'm flattered that you think so, Ma'am, but I'm not sure I can agree," Theisman replied. He was very careful not to add that the fact that she thought he had "a keen grasp" of anything to do with the present situation said a lot about the faultiness of her own grasp of it. "Actually, I'm sure that if you consider it you'll realize my observations all relate to what I see as the military implications of our policy on the Accords. I'm concerned with things like not jeopardizing our contact with the Solarian League's technical experts, or strengthening the enemy's will to fight or weakening our own. I'm afraid that beyond that point, my grasp of the overall political and economic dimensions of the war are limited. Remember our discussion on the day you arrived her? My entire adult life and career have been within the military community, not society at large, and I feel very strongly that I should stay with the trade I know best in a war like this."

"Perhaps you're right," Ransom said. "Frankly, in light of your record in the field, we might be unwise to try moving you back to the capital system. The war effort requires political direction for success, but it also requires officers capable of translating that direction into successful action on the battlefield."

Theisman gave a nod that was half bow but said nothing, and she lowered her hands to run them up and down the chair arms.

"You've given me quite a bit to think about, Citizen Admiral," she said. "I may have been hasty in dismissing the Accords as useless. Mind you, I still see no reason we should consider ourselves bound by obsolete agreements drafted by our class enemies if it's to our advantage to discard them, but you've certainly gotten me to think about the unwisdom of doing so without careful consideration of the consequences."

Theisman nodded again. His stomach was a solid knot as tension combined with too much cheap whiskey, and the strain of keeping it out of his voice and expression made him want to throw up. But it looked as if his effort had been worthwhile, and he tried very hard not to think about all the other ways someone like Ransom could produce disasters . . . or atrocities.

"At any rate," she said more briskly, pushing up out of her chair, "this is clearly not the time to unilaterally denounce them." The relief Theisman felt at those words made his knees so weak he had trouble standing to match her movement, but she wasn't done. "And for the instances in which violating them is indicated," she added, "we'll have to be careful in our justifications—you're certainly right about that, Citizen Admiral."

It was fortunate for Thomas Theisman that she was turning toward the door as she spoke, for it meant she missed the flash of pure horror which flickered across his face despite all he could do.

"Yes," she went on thoughtfully as he made himself escort her courteously to the door, "this is going to take some thought. Perhaps what we should do is centralize *all* POW decisions. We could adopt a policy under which the names of captured personnel are provided to the League inspectors only from central HQs. For that matter, we could restrict the inspectors' contacts and unescorted movements to the planets where we put those HQs, couldn't we?" Her voice brightened. "Of course we could! We can take the position that it's a matter of our own military security and that doing things in an orderly, organized fashion will actually make it easier for us to assure our POWs receive proper care. We'll even be telling the truth! Of course," she flashed another of those icy, hungry smiles, "it will also mean we'll never have to admit ever having even seen the . . . inconvenient prisoners. What a pity we didn't think of all this before! It certainly would have simplified the present situation."

Theisman swallowed bile as the Secretary of Public Information paused at the door to shake his hand warmly.

"Thank you *very* much, Citizen Admiral!" she said enthusiastically. "You've been a tremendous help to the war effort. If you have any other valuable ideas, *please* share them with me!"

She gave his hand another squeeze, smiled brightly, and left, and Thomas Theisman barely made it to the head before he vomited.

• Chapter Twenty-One

The guards aboard the shuttle wore the black tunics and red trousers of State Security, not Navy green and gray or the brown and gray of the People's Marines, and there were more of them. In fact, there was as many guards as there were prisoners, each of them with a flechette gun and the expression of someone who would enjoy using it.

Honor sat straight and still, with Nimitz a stiff, motionless weight in her lap, and tried to hide behind an assumed calm as hard, hostile eyes bored into her back. It wasn't easy, and her mask had slipped when the SS guards arrived to replace the naval escort she'd expected. Nor had the prisoners remained together for their trip planet-side, for this shuttle held only her own staffers and the more senior of *Prince Adrian's* commissioned personnel. The rest of McKeon's officers and the senior noncoms Tourville had been ordered to deliver to Barnett were in a second shuttle, following behind this one, and a corner of her brain wondered if they would be reunited after landing.

She didn't know, but she almost hoped not, for they would be better off as far as possible from whatever the Peeps planned for her. She knew that now, for the emotions whipping through the shuttle roared and echoed within her, and she understood exactly why Nimitz was such a knot of tension. The anxiety and fear of her fellow prisoners, their helpless ignorance as they waited to discover what their futures were, would have been bad enough, but she also felt the emotions—and anticipation—of the StateSec thugs.

And thugs they were, she thought grimly, fighting to hold onto her stability and maintain her pretense of calm while the fear of others fed her own. Manticore's intelligence agencies had analyzed State Security and its role in maintaining the Committee of Public Safety in power, and Honor had seen ONI's reports. For the most part, Admiral Givens' analysts had been more concerned with StateSec's impact on the operations of the People's Navy than with how it functioned within civilian society, but even ONI's summary reports had noted that the SS had recruited its members not just from the elements which had been the most disaffected under the old regime but from the now defunct Office of Internal Security, as well. InSec's enforcers and executioners had been professionals, not ideologues. They'd been willing enough to shift allegiance to the new regime and teach *its* minions their trade, and their new colleagues had learned their lessons well. In fact, they'd learned to surpass their instructors, for they'd had lots of practice.

One reason for the Legislaturalists' fall was that their repression had been . . . uneven. One week they might make dozens of troublemakers disappear; the next, the government might grant a general amnesty to curry favor with the Dolists. But unevenness was a mistake the Committee of Public Safety had no intention of making. Cordelia Ransom herself had proclaimed, "Extremism in the defense of the People is the first responsibility of the State," and not a day passed without StateSec's doing its best to live up to that instruction. Even the official Peep news channels made no bones about State Security's deliberate use of terror against "enemies of the People"— who, after all, deserved whatever they got.

Honor hadn't questioned the accuracy of those ONI reports, yet neither had she thought their implications through. If she had, she would have realized what sort of people were required to embrace that sort of action.

She realized now. She couldn't help it, for their emotions beat in upon her like jeering demons, whispering male-volently in the back of her mind. The red fangs of hunger radiated from some of them, jagged with the need to prove their own power by grinding others under their heels. There was a sickness in that appetite for cruelty, one that turned Honor's stomach, yet there was worse, as well, for some of the guards standing behind her felt no hunger. They felt *nothing* when they looked at Honor and the other prisoners. She and her people might have been so many insects for all the emotion *those* guards would feel if the order were given to murder them all, and the deadness of their feelings carried a charnel reek more horrible than the most savage sadism. They were no longer human themselves. They had become automatons, and whether they'd been drawn to State Security because they'd always been sociopaths, or whether they had been dehumanized *into* sociopaths mattered not at all. When their gazes rested upon her, she felt the chill anticipation coiling behind their eyes. All the shuttle guards knew what had been planned for Honor, and she didn't have to be told what it was to know it had nothing at all to do with the Deneb Accords. The fierce delight of the haters told her that. Yet the other ones, the dead ones, were even more frightening, for they waited with the cold-eyed patience of pythons. There was little eagerness in *their* emotions, but neither was there any hesitation . . . and there was no pity at all.

The shuttle buffeted gently as it entered atmosphere, and Honor closed her eyes, resting her hands on Nimitz's warm softness. She wasted no effort hoping for the best. Not any longer.

Thomas Theisman glanced at Citizen Rear Admiral Tourville from the corner of one eye. Ransom had summoned Tourville, Honeker, Bogdanovich, and Foraker to face her even before she'd ordered Harrington and the other prisoners brought down from orbit. Theisman had been excluded from that meeting, but the normally fiery Tourville had emerged from the hour-long session white-faced and taut, and Honeker had looked equally shaken. Theisman hadn't been able to decide how much of Tourville's tension had been fear and how much fury, but he'd entertained no such doubts where Honeker was concerned, for the People's Commissioner had looked outright terrified.

Bogdanovich and Foraker had been at least as pale as their superiors, but there'd been a subtle difference between the two of them. The stone-faced chief of staff was clearly frightened, though he had it under better control than Honeker did. The ops officer, on the other hand, looked like a woman who wanted to strangle people with her bare hands. For all her fabled lack of social graces, Shannon Foraker was no fool, and she clearly had herself under iron self-control, but her long, narrow face's utter lack of expression only made the murderous fire in her blue eyes more obvious.

And now it was time for the macabre circus to play itself out, and Theisman spared a thought for Warner Caslet as the shuttle settled onto its pad. Caslet had been even more upset by Harrington's probable fate than Theisman himself. Indeed, he'd been angry enough to storm into Theisman's office and protest it openly in front of Dennis LePic . . . and in language no commissioner could possibly overlook. Yet LePic *had* overlooked it. He must have, for Caslet hadn't been arrested, and Theisman had done his best to protect his ops officer by ordering him out on an inspection tour of the system's perimeter sensor platforms. *It's not much,* he told himself bitterly, *but the way things are going, just keeping* Warner *out of StateSec's clutches has to count as a major victory!*

The shuttle grounded and opened its hatch, and Theisman realized StateSec had already taken over custody of the prisoners. The uniforms of the disembarking guards were unmistakable, and the shuttle bore the hull number of PNS *Tepes.* More than that, the guards who surrounded the pad were also SS, without a single Marine or Navy uniform in sight. There were a lot of them, too, and they were armed to the teeth. Then again, the SS was *always* armed to the teeth. Its troopers never went anywhere except in pairs, and they never went anywhere unarmed . . . which said a great deal about their paranoia, how they were regarded by the People they nominally protected, or perhaps both. Theisman's lip wanted to curl in contempt, but there was no room for contempt today. Not when he was afraid he knew why those guards were present in such strength.

He glanced across the terminal to where Ransom stood in casual conversation with Citizen Captain Vladovich, *Tepes'* captain. Vladovich's presence was one more thing to rasp Theisman's raw nerves, for the man should never have been promoted to his present rank. Theisman knew that from personal experience, for he'd sat on the last prewar promotion board that had rejected Vladovich's promotion to lieutenant commander . . . for the seventeenth time. The man had spent over twenty-six T-years as a lieutenant. Even in a navy in which Legislaturalist connections were required for promotion above captain, almost three decades in grade should have given the man a hint that he was in a dead-end career. And he had been. His undeniable ambition, drive, and experience had made him just too valuable to be ordered to retire, but the nasty stripe of sadism running through his personality had put any promotion to higher rank out of the question. He took too much delight in tormenting those junior to him, always in ways which didn't—quite—violate the letter of the regulations. That was something the Legislaturalists were prepared to tolerate only in one of their own, and much as Theisman himself had resented the Legislaturalist stranglehold on the senior rank ladder, he'd been more than happy that Vladovich would never climb it. Of course, Vladovich had never understood the true reason for his lack of promotion. He'd convinced himself it was due *solely* to the fact that he wasn't a Legislaturalist. Indeed, he'd actually come to believe—not simply claim, but genuinely believe—that he was the subject of a vendetta, a deliberate plot to exclude him from higher rank lest his capability and skill embarrass the Legislaturalists about him.

Under the old regime, that had been merely pathetic. Under the new, it made him a natural for service in the SS's paramilitary arms. For all his flaws, he did have a firm basic grasp of naval realities, and his ardor in rooting out and destroying "enemies of the People" was legendary. Unfortunately, he seemed to have learned nothing at all about the responsibilities of command. He was rumored to be unpopular, even with other StateSec personnel, and from reports, he ran *Tepes* as if the ship were his personal property and her crew (aside from his favorites) were his serfs. No doubt he was always careful to cloak his attitude in the proper platitudes about service to the People, but his particularly nasty type of favoritism and the way he played one faction of his crew off against another turned Theisman's stomach. And it was incredibly stupid, as well. Vladovich probably believed there was no chance his command would be called to battle like a normal fleet unit, but if it ever happened, he was going to find himself wielding a grievously flawed weapon, Theisman thought grimly. A crew whose own captain set its members at one another's throats would go into battle with both hands tied behind its back, crippled by lack of cohesion, and Vladovich didn't even seem to realize it.

But at the moment he looked every inch a battlecruiser's captain—allowing for the black-and-red State Security uniform—as Ransom chatted with him, apparently oblivious to the HD crew recording every instant of the day. Her back was turned to the windows—and the shuttle pad beyond them—in an elaborate show of disinterest, and Theisman clenched his jaw. Such obvious theatrics would have been amusing in someone with less power; in Cordelia Ransom they were terrifying. For she *wasn't* someone without power, and there was a message in her body language. She would not have made her contempt for the prisoners being brought to her so blatant—not with the cameras running—if she'd had any intention of treating them with respect, and Vladovich's smile of anticipation only confirmed the citizen admiral's dread.

He turned away from the two of them, gazing back out the window as the captured Manticoran and Grayson personnel emerged from the shuttle and were prodded roughly into a single file. Their guards marched them across the pad's ceramacrete apron and up the escalator to the terminal, and Theisman's eyes narrowed as he recognized the woman at the head of the line. He would have known that tall, athletic figure even without the cream-and-gray 'cat in her arms, and he inhaled deeply as he recognized the broad-shouldered senior captain immediately behind her. Alistair McKeon. Another Manticoran Thomas Theisman knew, and one whose good opinion he valued. What would McKeon think of him after today? It wasn't Theisman's fault, and he knew it, and part of him felt a fresh, terrible spasm of anger—this one directed as much at Harrington and McKeon as at Ransom. It was irrational, and he knew that, too, but still he felt it. They were going to judge him, just as he would have judged them if the roles had been reversed. And, as he would have, they would feel only contempt for him, for unlike him, they had never found themselves trapped between duty to themselves and duty to a star nation which had fallen into the grip of maniacs.

That was why he felt that dreadful flash of anger. Because however deeply his impotence shamed him, it was real. Because he longed to be worthy of their respect, and could not be. And because he knew there was no point even attempting to defy Ransom. Defiance could achieve nothing beyond dooming him beside Harrington, and even though a tired, angry part of him insisted he could do far worse than die in such company, the rest of him knew better. Impotent as he might be in this moment, it was his duty to remain alive and do what he could—*anything* he could— to mitigate the excesses of the madmen.

He knew that now, and a cold corner of his brain wondered why so few repressive regimes seemed to realize that they themselves created the rebels who must ultimately destroy them. How could someone like a Cordelia Ransom or a Rob Pierre, after taking advantage of that very blindness in the Legislaturalists, fail to recognize it in themselves?

The line of prisoners reached the top of the escalator, and Theisman's thoughts chopped off as one of the guards

turned Harrington towards the large VIP lounge in which
Ransom and her court—willing and unwilling—waited. The
SS trooper used the butt of his flechette gun, none too
gently, to direct his prisoner, and they were close enough
now for Theisman to see and recognize the snarl on Alistair
McKeon's face as the gun butt smacked Harrington's
shoulder. But strong as it was, McKeon's obvious anger was
less frightening than the utter lack of expression of the
green-uniformed man beside him. The cut of his uniform
labeled him a Grayson, which made him one of the
"Marines" who were obviously Harrington's armsmen . . .
and no doubt explained the dangerous tension churning
within him. Theisman had seen that sort of nonexpression
before. He knew what it meant, and the helpless spectator
trapped within him begged the auburn-haired Grayson not
to lose control. Surrounded by so many heavily armed
guards, the consequences of a berserk attack could only
be a massacre.

A growled command brought the prisoners to a halt and,
for the first time, Theisman forced himself to meet Honor
Harrington's eyes.

If possible, she looked worse than he'd dreaded, and he
bit his lip painfully. Her face was even more expressionless
than her armsman's. The only times he'd seen her before
in person had been during and immediately after the
Republic's first disastrous Yeltsin operation. Her left eye
had been covered by an eye patch then, and the entire side
of her face had been crippled from her wounds, yet even
so, it had been more expressive than today. Now it showed
nothing—not fear, not hope, not defiance, not even
curiosity. But it was only a mask, and a poor one, at that,
and Theisman was shocked by what hid behind it. He'd
been prepared for anger, for contempt, even for hatred;
what he saw was fear. Worse than fear, it was terror, and
with it came desperation.

He tasted blood as his teeth sank into his lip with
involuntary strength. In her situation, he knew *he* would
have been afraid, yet he hadn't expected Harrington to show

it so clearly. But then he saw the way her arms cradled her treecat, the hopeless protectiveness of her body language, and he understood.

"So." The single, flat word jerked his eyes away from her. Cordelia Ransom had turned from her conversation with Vladovich to regard the prisoners, and her blue eyes were as contemptuous as her voice. Her lip curled as she swept her gaze across the line of prisoners, and then she sniffed disdainfully. The dismissive sound carried clearly in the silence of the lounge, and Theisman saw more than one POW stiffen angrily.

"And who might these be, Citizen Major?" Ransom asked the senior SS guard.

"Enemies of the People, Citizen Committeewoman!" the major barked.

"Indeed?"

Ransom walked slowly down the line. But no, Theisman reflected, "walk" was scarcely the word. She swaggered down the line. She *strutted*, and he was suddenly ashamed of the image she projected. Didn't she even begin to realize how shallow and petty—how *stupid*—she made herself look? Or how her contempt could affect the members of the *Republic's* Navy? Whatever else her prisoners were, they had fought openly and with skill for their own star nations, just as Theisman had fought for his, and when Ransom spat upon *their* courage and *their* dedication, she spat upon his. And what had *she* done to earn the right to treat them with contempt? What enemies had *she* faced in combat? Even as an insurrectionist before the coup, she'd been a terrorist—a bomber and assassin; a murderer, not a warrior. Perhaps she didn't see it that way, but that couldn't change the reality. And because it couldn't, her theatrical contempt belittled *her*, not them, whether she could see it or not, and her own HD crews were recording it all. All too soon it would be broadcast all over the People's Republic, and after that it would just as surely find its way onto the airwaves of the Manticoran Alliance and the Solarian League, and he ground his teeth at the thought.

But there was nothing he could do except stand there, his own face like stone, and watch as Ransom stopped in front of McKeon.

"And you are?" she asked him coldly, as if he were the senior officer present. For an instant he said nothing, and his gaze flicked to where Harrington stood at his side. She didn't look back at him, but she nodded—ever so slightly— and he inhaled sharply.

"Captain Alistair McKeon, Royal Manticoran Navy," he grated in tones of hammered iron. His gray eyes glittered with anger, but Ransom only sniffed again and swaggered down the entire length of the line. Then she returned to her original position, and the HD crew shifted around to get her profile as she pointed at Harrington.

"What's that animal doing here, Citizen Major?" she demanded.

"It belongs to the prisoner, Citizen Committeewoman."

"And why hasn't it been removed?" Ransom's voice was softer, almost silky, and her lip curled in a hungry smile as she watched her victim's eyes. Not a muscle twitched in Harrington's face, but Theisman sensed the way her muscles coiled still tighter as Ransom savored her power like some rare vintage.

"We were instructed not to remove it, Citizen Committeewoman," the SS major told her. "Its owner is the senior prisoner, and we were instructed to allow her to keep it."

"What?" Ransom looked at Tourville, and arctic ice glittered in her blue eyes. There was more than triumph in her expression now, and Theisman's heart sank, for he was suddenly certain what was coming. She was going to pay Tourville off for his efforts to protect Harrington by taking the treecat away and having it destroyed in front of the cameras, he thought sickly. He was sure of it . . . but he was also wrong, for his suspicions fell short of what Ransom actually intended.

"Did I hear you identify this woman as the senior *military* prisoner, Citizen Major?" she asked softly.

"Yes, Citizen Committeewoman!"

"Then there's been some mistake," Ransom informed him, eyes still locked on Tourville's white face. "This woman isn't a military prisoner at all."

"I beg your pardon, Citizen Committeewoman?" the citizen major said, and if anything had been needed to prove his entire conversation with Ransom was a cruel charade, his tone supplied it. The words were right, but there was absolutely no surprise in his voice, and Theisman tensed as several of the citizen major's troopers shifted position ever so slightly behind the prisoners.

"Of course not," Ransom said coldly. "This woman is Honor Harrington, Citizen Major. I double-checked the records just this morning, and there's a civilian arrest order out for her. One which predates the outbreak of hostilities." Even Harrington twitched in surprise at that, and Ransom grinned viciously.

"Honor Harrington," she said very precisely, "was arraigned for murder following her deliberate, unprovoked destruction of the unarmed Republican freighter *Sirius* in the Basilisk System eleven years ago, Citizen Major. She was offered the opportunity to defend herself in court, but she rejected it and her plutocratic masters refused to surrender her for trial, which left the Ministry of Justice no choice but to order her tried in absentia. She was, of course, convicted . . . and the sentence was death."

She stared into Tourville's eyes, and the citizen rear admiral's fists clenched. His own eyes whipped to Harrington for a moment, then back to Ransom. Theisman felt his fury and agonized shame and willed him desperately to keep his mouth shut, but Tourville had been goaded too far.

"Citizen Committeewoman, I must protest!" he grated. "Commodore Harrington is a naval officer. As such, she—"

"She is *not* a naval officer!" Ransom's voice cracked like a whip. "She is a convicted *murderer*, Citizen Rear Admiral, and you would do well to remember that!"

"But—"

"Be careful, Citizen Rear Admiral. Be *very* careful."

Ransom's voice was suddenly soft, and Honeker surprised Theisman by reaching out and gripping Tourville's elbow. He hadn't thought the people's commissioner had that much courage—or concern for Tourville—but the pressure of his fingers seemed to remind the citizen rear admiral he wasn't the only one in Ransom's sights. Bogdanovich and Foraker were in as much danger as he, with less seniority to protect them, and he clamped his jaw shut.

Ransom watched him for several seconds, then nodded slightly.

"Better," she said, and turned back to the senior guard, dismissing Tourville as beneath her attention. "Now, Citizen Major," she said. "Since the warrant for this woman's arrest and execution is a civilian order, she's hardly a matter of concern for the military, is she? Whatever unhappy events may subsequently have transpired between the People Republic and the Star Kingdom of Manticore—" her tone made the last four words into expletives "—can have no bearing on the decisions of the civilian judiciary in time of peace, nor can a naval uniform be permitted to shield its wearer from the prewar verdict of a civil court. I believe Section Twenty-Seven, Subsection Forty-One of the Deneb Accords addresses that very point." She darted a swift glance at Theisman, who managed—somehow—to keep his hatred from his expression.

"In fact," she went on, "Section Twenty-Seven specifically states that the military status of individuals is nullified if they've been convicted of a civil crime *before the commencement of hostilities* . . . which means this woman isn't a military prisoner at all. So it's fortunate you and your people, as representatives of the People's civilian legal system, are here to take charge of her, isn't it, now?"

"Yes, Citizen Committeewoman!" The citizen major snapped to attention and saluted. "What are your orders?"

Thomas Theisman's teeth ground helplessly as Ransom smiled at the SS thug, for he knew what she was going to say. And it was his fault, he thought bitterly. No doubt she would have found a way to do what she wanted anyway, but *he* was the one who'd argued for observing the forms of the Deneb Accords, and the most sickening thing of all was that she'd cited them correctly. Section Twenty-Seven, Subsection Forty-One had been inserted after the Kersey Association's war against the Manitoban Republic. The Kerseyites' so-called government had put several dozen convicted Manitoban murderers into uniform for "special operations" against their home world and then claimed their status as prisoners of war protected them, if captured, from the execution of their sentences. Of course, the Kersey Association had been little more than organized pirates and murderers themselves, but their abuse of the Accords had led to their postwar modification in an effort to close the loophole the Kerseyites had exploited. And now *another* band of murderers was going to use that modification for its own twisted purposes, Theisman thought sickly, and the legal farce of that prewar "trial" would make it all technically legal.

"You will take her into custody for transfer to *Tepes*, Citizen Major." Ransom spoke to the SS officer, but her cold, triumphant eyes never left Harrington's face. "You will place her in close confinement aboard ship for transport to the State Security prison facility in the Cerberus System, where you will deliver her to the warden of Camp Charon for execution."

It was all a nightmare. It wasn't real, a part of Honor's mind insisted. It couldn't be happening. But the rest of her knew it *could* happen, and that it was. Her eyes flicked to Thomas Theisman's face as Ransom called her a murderer, and the helpless shame she saw there was the final straw. Ransom's cold, cruel delight in pronouncing her fate fed into her through Nimitz, like a knife twisting slowly and gloatingly in a wound, but it was Theisman's despair which made it all real by stripping away any pretense of hope.

She'd all but forgotten that so-called conviction. Everyone had known it was a propaganda ploy, an attempt by the Legislaturalists to convince their own subjects and the

Solarian League that they were the innocent victim of *Manticoran* aggression. What else could they have done? If they *hadn't* maintained that *Sirius* was an "unarmed freighter," they would have had to admit they'd sent a seven-and-a-half-million-ton Q-ship on a deliberate violation of Manticoran territory. But the entire thing had been so absurd that she'd never believed anyone could possibly take it seriously—especially at *this* late date.

But as Ransom's vindictive triumph flowed into her like venom, Honor realized it didn't really matter. Ransom wanted Honor dead, and not just because of what Honor had done to the People's Navy. No, there was something dark and poisonous—something *personal*—in her hatred, and even through her own despair, Honor realized what it was.

Fear. Ransom was *afraid* of her, as if she personified every threat to Ransom's own position. In the other woman's mind, Honor was the embodiment of the Alliance's military threat to the Republic, and hence to Ransom herself. Yet the committeewoman's hatred went even deeper than that should explain, and as Ransom glanced back at Tourville, Honor understood. The citizen rear admiral's efforts to protect her had only turned her into yet another threat: the threat that the Republic's own military would turn upon the Committee of Public Safety.

There'd been rumors enough of mounting unrest in the Haven System, where lunatic factions in the Nouveau Paris Mob had mounted at least one coup attempt. The Navy had put that down—somewhat to the surprise of ONI—but what if the military *didn't* put down the next one? What if it began to think for itself, to make its own policies and resist the Committee's? That was the only way a person like Ransom could possibly interpret Tourville's actions—as the first move in some plot to overthrow the Committee's authority—because it would never occur to her that the citizen rear admiral had acted out of a sense of decency. Cordelia Ransom couldn't conceive of viewing her enemies as honorable opponents who deserved to be honorably treated, and so she assumed that, just as she would have been, Tourville must be playing some Byzantine game in which Honor was only one more marker on the board.

If that was the case, then he must be crushed, in a way which would teach the rest of the military not to cross swords with the Committee of Public Safety or its members, and if Ransom could use the same opportunity to have Honor killed, so much the better.

Those thoughts flickered through her brain in a heartbeat, but she seemed paralyzed, unable to react or move or speak. Ransom turned her triumphant smile back from Tourville to her victim, and Honor didn't even twitch. She couldn't, but a dangerous ripple of movement ran down the line of prisoners. Ransom noted it, and her smile would have frozen helium as the glanced back at the SS major and pointed at Nimitz.

"In the meantime, Citizen Major, take that creature outside and destroy it. Immediately," she said softly.

"Yes, Citizen Committeewoman!"

The citizen major saluted again, then gestured to two of his troopers.

"You heard the Citizen Committeewoman," he growled. "See to it."

"Yes, Citizen Major!"

The two guards started towards Honor, and something snapped inside her. Resistance was worse than futile, for if *she* resisted, at least some of her people would do the same, and they were surrounded by armed guards. She'd known that would be the case, and she'd told herself she must endure whatever happened to her or Nimitz. She could not—*must* not—let any useless gesture on her part spark a massacre of the men and women for whom she was responsible, and she'd ordered herself not to make one.

But that was an order she could not obey. In that instant, her link with Nimitz was suddenly deeper and stronger than ever before. They were no longer two beings, and their single identity had no doubts . . . and only one objective.

The guards had been briefed on Ransom's intentions

and warned to expect trouble, but Honor's passivity had lulled them. Or perhaps her heavy-grav reflexes were simply too fast for them. Whatever the reason, they were too slow, even forewarned, as she rose on her toes and her up-sweeping arms launched Nimitz like a falconer with a hawk.

The treecat was a cream-and-gray blur, arcing sinuously over the guards' heads, and the ripping canvas snarl of his war cry was the only warning the citizen major had. The SS man shrieked in agony as six sets of scimitar claws reduced his face to ruin, and his shriek died in a hideous gurgle as one last slash severed his jugular. But he was only an intermediate step for Nimitz—a launching pad from which to redirect his trajectory, not his true objective— and he leapt from his first victim to hit another SS guard in the chest. The fresh target screamed, clutching uselessly at the six-limbed demon that hissed and snarled as it swarmed up him, claws savaging his belly and chest, and then sprang from his shoulders in a leap that carried him straight at Cordelia Ransom.

The first flechette gun butt slammed into Honor even before Nimitz hit the citizen major, but she'd sensed it coming and rode the force of the blow. She let it smash her aside, taking her out of the path of a second guard's swing, and her feet shot up as her back hit the floor. Both heels thudded into a man's belly, and she rolled frantically to avoid two more. She came up on one knee, and her left fist lashed out in a savage thrust to an unprotected groin. The stricken guard doubled forward as she came upright once more, and the heel of her right hand exploded into his face. It smashed his nose, driving shattered bone and cartilage up into his brain, and her left hand snatched for his flechette gun as he went down.

She never touched it. Another gun butt came down, and this time its owner made no mistake. It struck cleanly at the base of the neck, driving her back to the floor, stunned and unable to move, and two more slammed into her kidneys and ribs while shouts and orders and the sounds of blows erupted around her through the shrieks of Nimitz's second victim.

She couldn't even turn her head, but she caught glimpses of the chaos. She saw McKeon take down one guard with a smashed kneecap, then go down himself under battering gun butts. Andrew LaFollet was a madman. He spun like a cat, catching one SS trooper completely off guard, and his fist crushed the man's larynx like a hammer. Two more came at him, and he went into them in a blur of fists, elbows, and flying feet. Both of them went down, one with a broken neck, and he hurled himself at the woman who'd just smashed Honor in the ribs and was raising her weapon for yet another stroke.

Another guard's flechette gun came at him from the side, crunching into him so hard it lifted his toes into the air. A second gun butt crashed down, and he crumpled across Honor's legs just as Andreas Venizelos and Marcia McGinley were tackled and buried under the weight of half a dozen SS troopers.

Most of the other POWs never had time to react before they were beaten to their knees, but Nimitz's war cry still wailed as another SS trooper came between him and Ransom. The new guard wasn't trying to intercept him—in fact, she tried desperately to get out of his way—but she was the last barrier blocking him from his prey, and he snarled as he ripped her throat out. She went down in a gush of blood, but killing her had delayed him an instant too long, and he screamed as a gun slammed into him at last.

Honor screamed with him, her face against the floor, as the agony of his wound ripped through her. It was as if *her* shoulder, her ribs, had broken under the savage blow, and her body spasmed, trying to curl around the injury someone else had suffered. She sensed the flechette gun rising again, knew it was about to come smashing down, and she bared her teeth as Nimitz snarled up at his killer.

The gun butt started down, but a pair of hands caught it in midstroke, shoving it aside so that it thudded into the floor instead. The SS man spat a curse and turned towards the Manticoran who'd interfered, then froze in confusion.

It hadn't been a Manticoran after all, and he gaped at Shannon Foraker as she thrust him further aside and wheeled to Ransom.

"If you kill the 'cat, she'll die!" The ops officer's shout cut through the confusion, and she stretched out a hand to the committeewoman. "They're linked!" she shouted. "Don't you understand? If you kill the 'cat, *she'll die, too!*"

Honor lay on the floor, still too stunned to move or think coherently, but her body twitched and jerked as Nimitz writhed in agony, and Ransom's eyes narrowed. She'd expected something like this—in fact, she'd planned for it—but she hadn't expected to come so close to death herself, and it had all been over so quickly she hadn't really had time to react. Now she did have time, and after-the-fact panic filled her as she looked at the half dozen bodies Nimitz, Honor, and LaFollet had left in their wake. She bared her teeth at the injured 'cat who'd tried so hard to kill her and so nearly succeeded, and started to order Foraker out of the way.

But then she made herself draw a deep breath. She closed her eyes while she forced herself back under control, and her voice was cold when she opened them once more.

"What do you mean?" she snapped.

"Just what I said . . . Ma'am." Foraker went to her knees beside Nimitz, taking a risk even most Sphinxians would never have dared, for even a crippled 'cat could inflict terrible wounds. "Treecats are empaths, and probably telepathic," she went on, making herself speak urgently but clearly. "They bond to their partners, and when they die, their partners either die or go catatonic."

"That's nonsense!" Ransom snarled.

"No it isn't," another voice said, and the committeewoman turned towards the source. Like every other Manticoran in the room, Fritz Montoya was on his knees now, with the muzzle of a flechette gun pressed against the back of his head, but his Medical Branch caduceus glittered on his collar.

"What do you mean?" Ransom repeated suspiciously.

"It's in the medical literature," Montoya lied in support of Foraker's preposterous claim. "Treecats' bonds with humans are uncommon, and we don't know as much about them as we'd like, but the consequences of a 'cat's death are well established. Catatonia is more common than death, but the mortality rate is well above forty percent."

Ransom's mouth twisted as if to spit, but once again she made herself stop and draw a deep breath. She was on the downslope of the adrenaline rush now, her belated terror turning into a sense of elation at her survival, and it was hard to think as she ran her mind back over the SS dossier on Harrington. She'd studied it carefully before she planned this afternoon's events, and her estimate of Harrington's reaction to the order to kill the 'cat had been right on the money. The problem was that there were too many blank spots in the file for her to know whether or not Foraker was right.

She growled a mental curse as she admitted that. The clips from Grayson news broadcasts were their best source of information on treecats, for Harrington was a planetary heroine. She was always good copy on her adopted planet, and her bond to the beast was endlessly fascinating to her public. Unfortunately, the Graysons actually knew very little about how it all worked. Their coverage had warned Ransom that the animal was both dangerous and more intelligent than most people would have guessed, just as it had told her the best way to hurt Harrington would be to take it away from her and kill it, but she had no information at all on the actual nature of the bond between them.

Her eyes moved to Harrington, still twitching on the floor, and narrowed. The way she lay, half-turned on one side and curled around, mimicked the posture of the 'cat. Indeed, allowing for the fact that the animal had six limbs and Harrington had only four, it was virtually identical. But she wasn't even conscious. She couldn't have adopted that posture *deliberately*, and that argued for at least the possibility that Foraker had it right.

On the other hand, Foraker felt she owed Harrington something. Was she gutsy enough—and stupid enough—to risk spinning such a lie to protect the Manticoran?

"Just how did *you* happen to come by this knowledge, Citizen Commander?" the committeewoman asked after a long, fulminating moment.

"Citizen Rear Admiral Tourville assigned me as liaison to the prisoners aboard *Count Tilly*," Foraker replied without hesitation. "In the course of those duties, I asked Doctor Montoya about any possible specialized health needs they might have. Under the circumstances, he felt it best to alert me to the nature of Commo—of the prisoner's bond with the 'cat."

"I see," Ransom said very slowly. A part of her was certain Foraker was lying, but only a part, and the Manty surgeon had supported the ops officer quickly and smoothly enough. She wanted that disgusting beast *dead*, but what if Foraker and Montoya were telling the truth? Her plans for recording the details of Harrington's execution would go into the crapper if she had the 'cat killed and Harrington actually did die or go catatonic.

She thought furiously for several more seconds, and then she smiled. It was a chill smile, and an ugly one, and Thomas Theisman shivered as he saw it.

"Very well, Doctor Montoya," she said coldly, "you're now in charge of keeping the animal alive." She nodded for the doctor's guard to withdraw the flechette muzzle from the back of his head, and Montoya hurried over to kneel beside Foraker. "Do your best," Ransom told him. "I want it healthy when the prisoner goes to the scaffold."

Her smile turned even colder as she pictured Harrington's reaction to seeing the animal in a cage, knowing that the instant *she* was dead, her precious "Nimitz" would follow, and she turned to the massively muscled female SS captain who had been the major's second-in-command.

"As far as the rest of these . . . people are concerned, Citizen Captain . . . de Sangro," she said, reading the nameplate on her chest, "their actions here were clearly unprovoked." A wave of her hand took in the groaning SS wounded—and the bodies of those who would never groan again. "Even under the Deneb Accords, a prisoner of war who attacks our personnel except in the course of an escape attempt or in direct self-defense forfeits the standard protections accorded to captured military personnel."

She turned to smile at Theisman, who clenched his jaw as yet again she cited the letter of the Accords correctly in order to pervert their intent.

"The Accords don't give us the right to execute them for their actions—which, of course, we would never choose to do, anyway," she told the StateSec officer piously for the benefit of the watching cameras. "In light of their murderous, unprovoked assault on our personnel, however, a more secure disposition is clearly in order in their case. Under my authority as a member of the Committee of Public Safety, I instruct you to take charge of them in the name of the Office of State Security for transport to and imprisonment at Camp Charon. They can be shipped out on the same transport as their ex-commander."

"Of course, Citizen Committeewoman!" the citizen captain barked, snapping one hand to her cap brim in salute, and Theisman felt physically ill with impotent rage.

He shouldn't have been surprised, he told himself, but he was. Even now he was. It was amazing how a lifetime of expecting at least semicivilized behavior out of one's superiors could prevent one from seeing something like this coming, he thought almost calmly, but in retrospect, it should have been manifest from the first. Of *course* Ransom had played out her cruel game. The committeewoman hadn't had to be a genius to figure out how Harrington was likely to react to the death sentence of her treecat. Even a casual perusal of her dossier would have made *that* obvious. The reaction of her officers when the SS clubbed her to the floor had been equally predictable, and Ransom had relied on it to provide the pretext to send every one of them off to Cerberus with Harrington.

Of course she had, and malice and triumph mingled in her smile as she turned back to Tourville.

"As for you, Citizen Rear Admiral," she said, "I believe you ought to return to Haven with me. What's happened here raises serious questions as to the quality of your judgment where these prisoners are concerned. I think you should drop by the Admiralty for a discussion of proper procedure for dealing with captured enemy personnel."

Tourville said nothing. He met her gaze levelly, refusing to flinch, but that was all right with Ransom. She was willing to allow him his bravado. In fact, it would make the final outcome even more satisfactory.

"In fact," she went on, "I believe you should bring along your entire staff—and Citizen Commissioner Honeker." She glanced at Theisman. "Citizen Rear Admiral Tourville and his flagship will escort *Tepes* to the Cerberus System, Citizen Admiral," she told him. "Please have orders to that effect cut immediately."

"Yes, Citizen Committeewoman." Theisman managed to keep his voice more nearly normal than Tourville had been able to, but it was hard. And the fact that he'd succeeded made him feel contaminated.

"Then I think we're done," Ransom said brightly, and nodded to de Sangro. "See to having these—" she waved disdainfully at the battered, kneeling prisoners "—taken aboard ship, Citizen Captain. I'm sure we can find proper accommodations for them."

"At once, Citizen Committeewoman!"

The citizen captain saluted again, then jerked her head at her detail, and gun butts urged the prisoners back to their feet and out of the lounge. Those who couldn't walk were dragged, and as Thomas Theisman watched them go, he knew he would never feel clean again.

• Chapter Twenty-Two

Pain.

A roaring sea of pain sent fiery combers flaring through her brain to shatter her thoughts like explosions of foam, and she locked her teeth against a moan of anguish. Her mind refused to function, yet even so she knew only a tiny portion of the crippling pain was truly her own. She felt bruised and cruelly battered where the gun butts had smashed into her, but the agony of broken bones and torn muscle tissue was someone else's, and her soul cried out as the waves of hurt crashed over her from Nimitz.

She opened her eyes and blinked foggily, trying to resolve what she saw into a coherent image. It took her several long, dragging seconds to realize that she was slumped forward and sideways against the safety straps of a shuttle seat, staring down at the deck, and still more seconds oozed away before she could decide what to do about it.

She struggled upright in her seat, the effort made awkward by the handcuffs locking her wrists behind her, and her vision blurred once more as the surges of Nimitz's pain filled her eyes with tears. The strange, deeper fusion which had possessed them both in the moment of their despair still gripped her, and her vision was oddly doubled. It wasn't just the effects of the blows she'd taken after all, she realized, for while part of her saw the deck and the shuttle's forward bulkhead, less than a meter in front of her, another part looked up through Nimitz's eyes at Fritz Montoya as the doctor bent urgently over him. The touch of Montoya's hands was gentle, yet each contact sent fresh agony ripping through them both, and the part of them which was still Honor hoped desperately that Fritz knew what he was doing. But he was trained in human physiology, not Sphinxian, and she tried to strangle at birth her dread of his potential ignorance, before the half of them which was Nimitz detected it.

She blinked again, gritted her teeth, and fought the duality of her senses. It was hard—hard—for every fiber of her being cried out to be with Nimitz. To share his pain in hopes of somehow easing it, and to prove to him he was not alone. Yet the maelstrom of pain and fear and need—not just hers and Nimitz's, but beating in from all the other prisoners in the shuttle, as well—sucked at her too strongly, crippling her ability to think, and she knew Nimitz was too lost in his own pain even to realize she was there. And so she battled to separate herself from him, to become herself once more.

She succeeded, and her success sent a flash of shame through her, as if she had somehow abandoned the 'cat. The need to go to him physically sent her wrists turning against their manacles, muscles straining to break free of them as if she thought she could somehow reach him if only she were unchained, but it was useless. She merely bruised herself, and even if she'd been unfettered, the SS guards would simply have clubbed her down once more if she tried to get to him. Her memory of events in the terminal lounge was chaotic, but she knew that much, and she set her teeth and fought for self-mastery.

At least the pain stabbing into her proved Nimitz was alive. She wanted to sob in relief at the knowledge, yet she couldn't understand why he was. She and the 'cat had recognized the gloating pleasure dancing behind Ransom's order to kill him. It was that pleasure, the certainty that Ransom truly meant it, which had spurred them to action, for they'd known they had nothing to lose. But somehow, for some reason, Nimitz was still alive, and she slowly exerted control over the pain and the confusing mental echoes of that closer union with the 'cat and made herself consider how that could be true.

Vague memories flickered, just beyond her grasp. She remembered launching Nimitz at Ransom clearly enough, and her own brief fight before the guards battered her to the floor, but everything else was foggy and unclear. She recalled a brief image of LaFollet, fighting to reach her side, and one of McKeon being beaten to his knees, and she bit her lip as she realized how dearly her defiance might have cost the others. But nothing suggested a reason for Nimitz to still be alive, unless . . .

She frowned as the faint echo of a voice threaded itself through her memories. She couldn't quite summon the words back to her, but she recognized the voice. It belonged to Shannon Foraker, and if she couldn't recall the words, their urgency came back to her clearly. Somehow Shannon must have convinced Ransom not to kill Nimitz on the spot, but how? And at what cost to herself?

Honor had no answers to those questions, and she turned her head, looking for someone else to ask them of. But there was no one beside her. She was alone in the front row of seats in which her body had been dumped, and she started to turn to look behind her, only to gasp in pain as a hand twisted cruelly in her hair. It kept her from turning, forced her to stare directly in front of her, and she locked her teeth still harder, cutting off any other sign of how much it hurt, as her tormentor spoke.

"You just stay where the hell you are, *chica*." It was the SS captain who'd taken over the detail, and her accent was tantalizingly familiar. It took Honor a few seconds to realize that she'd heard it before, from Tomas Ramirez and other refugees from the Peeps' conquest of San Martin, the inhabited planet of Trevor's Star, and she wondered how the woman behind her felt now that her home world had been conquered in turn by the Alliance. At the moment, however, the origin of her accent meant far less to Honor than the sneering pleasure in her voice. "You don't talk, you don't turn your head, you don't do *anything* unless someone tells you to. You got that?"

Honor said nothing, and the hand in her hair turned its wrist, actually lifting her a few millimeters out of the seat by her scalp. San Martin's gravity was much heavier even than Sphinx's, and Honor bit her lip hard as the guard demonstrated the strength her birth world had given her. Honor had never imagined that simply pulling someone's hair could *hurt* that much, and the SS thug's voice went colder and harsher.

"I asked if you *got* that, *chica!*" she snapped.

"Yes." Honor made herself say the one word in the flattest voice she could, and managed—somehow—not to gasp in relief as the other woman snickered and released her hair with a contemptuous flicking motion. The pulsing of Nimitz's pain fogged Honor's ability to read the emotions of others, but she didn't need it to recognize the other's vicious satisfaction . . . and anticipation. This wasn't one of the cold, emotionless ones, Honor realized. This was one of the ones who enjoyed her work.

"Good. You're gonna have enough fun on the trip to Hell anyway, *chica*. Believe me—you *don't* want to borrow any more," the woman said.

Honor heard the soft brush of uniform fabric on upholstery as her tormentor leaned back in the seat behind her. Even without looking, Honor knew there was no one else in that row, either. Her captors had used it like some sort of moat, cutting her off from the support of her officers by physically separating her from them, and she knew it was only the first step.

Ransom's intentions were clear enough. Over the years, the PRH's security forces had discovered that it was much more effective to "disappear" troublemakers. It was a tactic InSec had used often enough against opponents of the Legislaturalist regime, and StateSec had brought it to a new, all-pervasive height. And it worked, she thought grimly, for there was an infinitely greater terror in knowing people you cared for could simply vanish. Death was terrible, yet it was an end, a conclusion. Disappearance was simply the doorway to ignorance and the cruelest emotion of all: hope that the one you loved still lived . . . somewhere. Which was what made it so effective—the ripple effect of a single "disappeared" individual could keep a dozen others in line in hopes that their submission would buy the life and eventual return of the person they loved.

But her case was different, for Ransom had orchestrated that entire confrontation before the cameras to officially justify Honor's execution. No doubt she could change her mind about going public later—the Secretary of Public Information could kill any story she wanted to, after all—but Honor didn't believe she would. She wanted her enemies, foreign and domestic, real or imagined, to *know* what had happened to Honor, and that meant Honor's death would be a special feature on the evening news. She could picture the solemn warnings about "violent content" and "viewer discretion," for they always preceded the broadcast imagery of "enemies of the People" paying for their crimes. Indeed, she was almost surprised, in a distant way, that she hadn't already been shot. There had to be countless convenient spots here in the Barnett System where a minor detail like that could be dealt with, so why send her all the way out to Camp Charon?

It was pointless to wonder about such details, but she couldn't stop herself. There was a sort of dreadful fascination to contemplating her own cold-blooded murder, and she wondered if perhaps Ransom had chosen Camp Charon for her execution in order to confirm the facility's existence. If so, the event would mark a major change in a policy InSec had established decades earlier and StateSec had maintained since, and one of those detached corners of her brain wondered if she should be flattered to be the catalyst for it.

For seventy-odd years, the Legislaturalists and then the Committee of Public Safety had steadfastly denied that there was any such planet as Hades or place as Camp Charon. Their existence was no more than a vicious rumor circulated by opponents of the regime, with no foundation in fact. Indeed, the Legislaturalists' denials had been so consistent that the Star Kingdom's intelligence agencies had almost been prepared to believe them. After all, as more than one analyst had pointed out, *rumors* of such a prison planet would be almost as effective as the reality for controlling the Peep population, and feeding the rumor mill would also be far cheaper than actually creating a Camp Charon.

But the consensus had been that the camp was real, and over the years a few dozen once-"disappeared" enemies had been "rehabilitated" amid rumors they'd been held there. And their fragmentary descriptions fitted together to paint a picture of the planet officially named Hades but called "Hell" by anyone who had ever been sent there. No one outside the PRH's security forces knew where it was, but all reports agreed escape was impossible, and stories abounded that the most recalcitrant military and political prisoners the Republic had taken in seventy T-years had been dispatched to its surface.

And now Ransom intended to use the occasion of Honor's execution to confirm the place's existence. For a moment, the thought that Ransom felt so threatened—that she believed the Committee of Public Safety's control was so fragile—that she wanted to be certain her enemies knew the iron fist really existed, that all the rumors of the suppressive power of StateSec were founded on fact, woke a distant stir of hope within Honor. It was like proof that there was a chink in the enemy's armor.

But any elation died even more quickly than it had come. Whatever all of this might imply about the ultimate fate of the People's Republic and the outcome of the war, Honor Harrington would not be around to see it happen, and she felt the hopelessness of her future crash in on her once more while she stared at the bulkhead. She knew she was *supposed* to feel hopeless—that the female thug behind her had deliberately driven that feeling home as the first step in crushing her spirit—but knowing that and being able to resist it were two different things. Her

memory replayed the exact words of Cordelia Ransom's
sentence of death again and again, like a defective
recording, as if, she thought, something inside her were
determined to grind home the lesson that she and Nimitz
had no future. It was a stupid thought, yet she couldn't
shake it off, and she wasn't certain she even wanted to,
for somehow the act of admitting what awaited her left
her feeling washed out and clear. Perhaps it was the
confirmation, she thought. Perhaps actually hearing herself
condemned had resolved the uncertainty and extinguished
the last tormenting embers some stubborn scrap of hope
had kept alive.

In its own way, there was a mercy in that. If there was
no longer any hope, then neither was there any reason to
act as if there were, and she felt the comfort of apathy
reaching out to her. She could let go of her dignity, she
thought almost dreamily. She could abandon the pretense
of pride and courage, for clinging to those qualities would
only challenge her captors to crush them, and surely they
had no real significance to a dead woman. Why try to
maintain the mask, play the role of the Queen's officer
facing adversity with fortitude?

Just let go, an inner voice urged. *They're going to do
their best to break you—you've already seen that much—
so why not let them? Why put yourself through what
trying to stop them will cost you? Go along with them,
play whatever part they insist you play. It won't mean
anything. It would only mean something if you had a*
choice. *If there were any option that would let it make
a difference, and there isn't one.*

It was insidious, that voice, and tempting, and a coldly
rational core of her knew it was even right. There was no
logical reason to subject herself to what her captors would
do if she defied them—not when she was going to die in
the end, anyway. But there *were* reasons, she realized,
thoughts still wandering with that odd, crystal clarity. Not
logical ones, no, but reasons which were no less important
because they were *il*logical.

In the end, no one except the Peeps would know what she did and how she did it, nor would the way she conducted herself mean a thing to anyone . . . except her. That was the crux of it. How she faced her captors and her death mattered to *her*, and if she was going to die, and if Nimitz was going to die with her, they must do so on their feet. Not because she was a Queen's officer. Not even because she owed her people an example. She was, and she did, and that was important, but that identity and that debt were simply part and parcel of who she was. In the ultimate analysis, they mattered only because they mattered to *her*, not because of what anyone else might think. No. The real reason for refusing to surrender was that she and Nimitz owed *themselves* that final dignity, that last defiance of the people like the woman behind her who would do anything in their power to take it from them. Resisting their enemies would invite those enemies to fill whatever time she and her beloved friend had left with brutality and humiliation, yet even as she faced that, she also felt a subtle strength flowing back into her.

It wasn't like the strength she'd summoned when she took a ship into combat, or like the courage she donned like armor when she led her people to what she expected to be their deaths. As she faced herself in that moment of odd clarity, she realized that the strength she'd summoned on those other occasions had always held an edge of . . . not *bravado*, but something like it. Something that was real enough, but intended for others, not for *her*. In a way, it was a gift, a power which came to her from outside to permit her to carry her people with her when there was nothing else. A confluence of duty and responsibility, of the determination to do her job because others depended upon her, because she'd sworn an oath to do it and would die before she broke that promise, and because the rules required her to play the game out to the final throw. And behind that intersection of duty, determination, and the needs of others was tradition, the example of the Star Kingdom's great captains, who served as model, inspiration, and challenge in one. How many times had she reached out to share the mantle of Edward Saganami or Travis Webster or Ellen D'Orville without even realizing that was what she was doing?

But the strength she felt now had nothing to do with those external sources or the need to do her duty for the sake of others. For the first time in her memory, she stood in a place where none of those things mattered. No, that wasn't right. They *mattered*, but they'd become secondary, subordinate to her duty to *herself* and to Nimitz, and their support had become secondary as well. What she felt now was *her* strength—hers and Nimitz's—and the desperation faded from her eyes as that awareness flowed into her.

How odd, she thought. She'd had to come to this point, to realize everything she was and all she might yet have become were going to end, to be blotted out, to find the true strength hidden at her core. But she'd found it now, and as she looked at it with clear mental eyes, she realized *this* strength had no end. It might fade, might be driven out of her for a time. Indeed, it could be suppressed and overborne again and again, but it would always return, for it was her and she was it. She was too self-honest and too much the realist to lie to herself. Given enough time and determination, experts like the creatures who worked for State Security could destroy anyone, yet in its own way, that was the point. They could *destroy* her. With the right drugs, the right abuse and pressures, they could smash her, even reprogram her into someone else entirely. But that was simply another form of execution, and so long as she lived—so long as a trace of the person she was and had always been remained—so would the strength which filled her now. In that sense, no one could take it from her; she could only surrender it herself.

Commodore Lady Dame Honor Harrington sat in the shuttle seat, face and body bruised and aching, hands chained behind her while Nimitz's anguish pulsed through her and her calm expression was no longer merely a mask to deceive her enemies.

"You can go in now, Citizen Commander."

"Thank you." Warner Caslet's curtness wasn't directed at the yeoman outside Citizen Admiral Theisman's office. In fact, he rather regretted speaking so sharply to Citizen Chief Maynard, and he knew it was dangerous, as well, but he couldn't help it. He was too angry to give such thoughts the weight they should have held . . . and that, of course, was what *made* his sharpness dangerous.

He stepped into Theisman's office and paused as he saw Dennis LePic standing at one end of the citizen admiral's desk. It was only a brief pause, and then his feet carried him across the carpet to face his superiors. The sight of the people's commissioner sent a splash of cold water through him, as if reiterating all the reasons he already knew he must conceal his anger, yet it also made that anger still worse. Not because he blamed LePic, personally, for what had happened, but because LePic, for all his efforts to be a decent human being, had voluntarily associated himself with the people he *did* blame.

And so did you, *in a way, didn't you, Warner?* his brain sneered. *You could have been heroic and defied the new regime. You could have refused to sully your hands or compromise your principles and honor, couldn't you? They would have shot you for it, but you could have done it . . . and you didn't. So don't be so damned holier-than-thou about a man like LePic.*

"You sent for me, Citizen Admiral?" he asked, trying to bury the echoes of anger in crispness, and Theisman nodded.

Something had changed in the citizen admiral's face. There were no new lines on it, yet it seemed as if Theisman had aged years in the space of hours. And as he saw the change in his commander, Caslet realized that what had happened to the prisoners must have been worse even than had been reported to him. Or perhaps it hadn't been. Perhaps Theisman had simply been too close, seen the events—and their implications—too clearly.

"I'm afraid I did, Warner," Theisman said after a moment.

"No doubt you've heard about the . . . disgraceful events of this morning."

He asked the question of Caslet, but he glanced at LePic as he spoke. The people's commissioner said nothing, yet something flickered in his eyes. His lips tightened and his nostrils flared, but then he gave a brief, unwilling nod, as if to endorse Theisman's adjective. It was a small thing, yet its significance struck Caslet like a shout, for it ranged the people's commissioner—for the moment at least—alongside the military officers upon whom he was supposed to spy.

"Yes, Citizen Admiral. I did." The citizen commander spoke quietly, and not just because he, too, agreed with Theisman's choice of adjectives. There'd been no discussion of the citizen admiral's reasons for sending him on the inspection trip from which he'd just returned, but he'd guessed what they were, and he was torn between gratitude and a sense that he'd somehow been absent from his post. That he'd evaded his responsibility to be present when Honor Harrington faced Cordelia Ransom.

"Well, I'm afraid there are going to be some repercussions from them," Theisman told him, and glanced at LePic again, as if he was considering just how open he could be. Well, Caslet could understand that. Temporary ally or no, there was a limit to the frankness Theisman dared risk in front of the commissioner. He saw the same thoughts flicker across his CO's face, but then the citizen admiral tossed his head like a horse shaking off flies—or a bull preparing to charge.

"In particular," he said, "Citizen Committeewoman Ransom feels the military has failed to properly embrace the realities of total war against our class enemies. She believes too many of our officers continue to cling to outmoded, elitist concepts of so-called 'honor.' While such a carryover may be understandable in the abstract, she feels the time has come to break such habits of thought, which create a dangerous sense of sympathy for the enemies of the People who are currently attempting to undermine our will to fight as part and parcel of their efforts to defeat and destroy the Republic."

Despite his own anger, Caslet's eyes widened at the sheer vitriol of Theisman's tone, and his gaze darted to LePic. No one could have faulted the citizen admiral's *words*, but the voice which had delivered them shouted a contempt and disgust which cut at least as deep as Caslet's own. The people's commissioner shifted unhappily, yet he said nothing. And that, Caslet realized, was because he was less unhappy with Theisman's tone than with the fact that he knew it was justified.

"In light of her conclusions," the citizen admiral went on in that same voice of supercooled acid, "the Citizen Committeewoman considers that her duty as a member of the Committee of Public Safety requires her to begin addressing the officer corps' failings. Accordingly, she's decided that although the prisoners are now in the custody of the Office of State Security, a delegation of military officers should be temporarily attached to State Security to observe the manner in which such enemies of the People are properly treated. For this purpose, she has instructed me to detach the *Count Tilly* to escort *Tepes* to Cerberus so that Citizen Rear Admiral Tourville and his staff can form the core of that delegation. In addition—" Theisman's eyes narrowed and bored into Caslet's like twin laser mounts "—she has specifically requested *your* presence."

"*My* presence, Citizen Admiral?" Caslet's surprise was genuine, and he blinked as Theisman nodded in confirmation. "Did the Citizen Committeewoman explain why she wishes me to accompany her?"

"No," Theisman replied, but his flat voice said he suspected the reason. And after a few seconds' thought, Caslet realized *he* did, as well.

Of course. The reports he'd already heard had warned him that Shannon's lack of caution had finally landed her in the disaster he'd tried so hard to protect her from, and it was unlikely someone like Ransom would have failed to check Shannon's record. After all, how could she have risen to her present rank without StateSec's detecting her unreliability unless her naval superiors had covered for her? And if Ransom had checked, she knew Caslet had not only been Shannon's CO but also recommended her promotion—twice. Another check would have revealed his own absence on his "inspection trip," and while there was no official reason for her to question his orders from Theisman, she wouldn't have hesitated to add two plus two. In light of the connection between him and Shannon, that was all she would have required, and she wasn't the sort to commit excesses by halves. If Caslet could have tolerated an officer like Shannon under his command, then no doubt he, too, harbored dangerous elitist sympathies. And it was entirely possible that Ransom also saw this as a way to slap Theisman's hand for sending Caslet away in the first place. She could hardly have Navy officers sticking together to protect one another from their so-called government, now could she?

The bitterness of his own thoughts frightened Caslet, for it took him towards a destination he was afraid to reach, and he deliberately refused to look too closely at it.

"I see," he said after another brief pause. "When are we scheduled to leave, Citizen Admiral?"

"The Citizen Committeewoman intends to depart for the Cerberus System at nineteen-thirty hours this evening," Theisman said. "Can you be packed by then?"

"Of course, Citizen Admiral. Will Citizen Lieutenant Commander Ito assume my duties in my absence?"

"I expect so, yes."

"In that case, I should confer with him before I go aboard *Count Tilly* and be sure he's up to speed on everything you, Citizen Commissioner LePic, and I have discussed," Caslet began, then paused, eyebrows rising, as Theisman's expression registered.

"You do need to discuss matters with Ito," the citizen admiral sighed, "but you won't be going aboard *Count Tilly*."

"I won't, Citizen Admiral?"

"No, Citizen Commander. Citizen Committeewoman Ransom has requested that you be temporarily attached to *her* staff to serve as military liaison to the prisoners until their formal delivery to Cerberus."

"To serve as—?" Caslet began before he could stop himself, and then clamped his jaw, chopping off the question, while his hands fisted at his sides.

"With all due respect, Citizen Admiral, I don't feel I'm the best choice for that duty," he said after several tense seconds, and his eyes met Theisman's pleadingly. "I don't have any security experience, and I've never even been attached to Naval Intelligence, much less State Security. Surely there are other officers better qualified for dealing with captured enemy personnel."

Theisman didn't look away, but he shook his head. Not to reject Caslet's estimate of his experience or qualifications, but gently, and the citizen commander's gaze switched to LePic. The People's commissioner met it steadily, then sighed.

"I'm afraid Citizen Committeewoman Ransom insisted, Citizen Commander," he said. His tone was less corrosive than Theisman's, but its quiet anger—and sympathy—cut even deeper coming from him. Not just because he was a direct representative of the Committee of Public Safety on which Ransom served, but because he'd *chosen* to be one, and as Caslet heard the commissioner's disapproval, he wondered if Ransom even began to recognize how much potential harm she'd inflicted upon her own cause that morning.

But whatever damage she might have done for the future, it wasn't going to save Warner Caslet from her vengeance in the present, he realized.

"I understand, Sir," he told LePic heavily, and the People's commissioner's unhappy expression actually made Caslet feel oddly sympathetic for him. "I can be ready to brief Ito by thirteen hundred, Citizen Admiral," he went on. "Two or three hours should be ample time. Will you be able to sit in with us?"

"I intend to," Theisman agreed, and stood behind his desk, holding out his right hand. Caslet straightened his back and reached out to shake his CO's hand firmly, and Theisman gave him a smile which held both sadness and warning.

"In the meantime," he said, "you'd better go and see to your packing. Citizen Chief Maynard is already working on your orders, and he should have everything tied up by the time you and I meet with Ito."

"Yes, Citizen Admiral." Caslet gave Theisman's hand a final squeeze, nodded respectfully to LePic, and turned for the door. It opened before him, and he started to step through, only to pause and look back as Theisman cleared his throat.

"Ito will do just fine while you're away, but Citizen Commissioner LePic and I expect you back as soon as possible, Warner," the citizen admiral said. "I expect the military situation to start heating up in the next few weeks, and given how much the Citizen Commissioner and I will need your talents if it does, we've asked the Citizen Committeewoman to expedite your return."

Caslet's hazel eyes widened, then softened as LePic nodded. If he was in as much trouble with Ransom as he feared, his superiors had run serious risks in making any such request of her. It was the kind of risk he might have expected a man like Theisman to run, but the fact that LePic had signed off on it as well put a surprised lump in his throat, and he had to swallow hard before he could reply.

"Thank you, Citizen Admiral. I appreciate that vote of confidence. From both of you," he said finally, his voice just a bit husky.

"It's no more than you deserve, Citizen Commander," LePic said.

"I appreciate it anyway, Sir. And I'll try to get back just as quickly as I can."

"I'm sure you will, Warner," Theisman said quietly. "Godspeed."

"Thank you, Citizen Admiral."

Caslet gazed into his CO's eyes one last time, nodded, and stepped through the waiting door. It slid noiselessly shut behind him, and Thomas Theisman and Dennis LePic looked at one another in silence.

• Chapter Twenty-Three

The yard which built PNS *Tepes* had altered her basic design to better fit her to her role in State Security's private navy. The most important of those changes was obvious to Warner Caslet as his cutter approached the ship, for *Tepes* had three fewer grasers and one less missile tube in each broadside than the original plans for the *Warlord* class had specified, and the tonnage saved had been expended in providing life support for a double-sized "Marine" contingent and two additional— and very large—boat bays.

The alterations gave the battlecruiser a superdread-nought's small-craft capacity, which seemed excessive until the tractors drew his cutter into one of those cavernous bays and he saw what was already docked there. No less than three outsized heavy-lift assault shuttles, each better than half again the size of a pinnace and up-armored and gunned to match, hung in the docking buffers, and his mouth twisted as he gazed at them.

This ship would never be attached to any normal task force of the People's Navy, which meant those shuttles would never be used against the PRH's enemies. They were to be used against *the Committee of Public Safety's* enemies, which wasn't quite the same thing. Their purpose was to land assault forces on the Republic's own planets in order to take them away from the Republic's own citizens, and he wished he could believe their presence represented simple paranoia. But it didn't. Whatever one might think of the Committee or State Security, the fact that they had real—and violently inclined—enemies was indisputable, and the thought added still more weight to his bleak depression.

Things didn't get any better when the boat bay officer greeted him. In another divergence from naval practice, no one requested formal permission to board a StateSec ship. Instead, it was just one more papers check, with armed guards waiting to shoot down anyone foolish enough to try to sneak aboard with forged ID. Logically, Caslet had to admit that as long as the bay officers kept track of who was aboard and who wasn't, the tradition of formal arrivals and departures was merely that—a tradition. But that didn't keep him from feeling it ought to be honored, and the arrogant-eyed guards and the boat bay officer's leisurely manner grated on his nerves. Not that the lieutenant in question seemed to care particularly if Caslet had a low opinion of him and his ship. Like everyone else in *Tepes'* company, he was State Security, not Navy, and his lip curled as he surveyed the new arrival. Caslet might be two ranks senior to him, but they were only Navy ranks. Besides, the rumor mill had been at work for over six hours now, and the SS officer knew Caslet was on Citizen Committeewoman Ransom's shit list. Added up, those factors made Caslet an object for contempt, not respect.

"You Caslet?" he demanded, extending an imperious hand for the newcomer's ID.

The question came out in a voice somewhere between surly and bored, with more than a dash of insolence, and Caslet turned slowly to face him. There was no point in reacting to the insult, but the other man's tone had kicked the embers of his earlier anger back into full flame. He was on thin enough ice without confrontations with the SS, and sanity and self-preservation told him to let it pass. Yet there was something almost liberating in knowing how much trouble he was already in. In a way, it left him with the sense of having nothing to lose, and he set his carryall on the deck and turned ice-cold hazel eyes on the StateSec man, ignoring the outstretched hand.

The boat bay officer flushed as that chill gaze considered him from head to boot heels with boundless contempt, and Caslet's lips twitched in what might have been called a smile if it hadn't bared quite so many teeth.

"Yes, I'm *Citizen Commander* Caslet. And you are?"

His voice was colder than his eyes, with a scalpel's edge, and he was furious enough—and felt reckless enough—to let that edge bite deep. The SS officer started a quick, angry response, then paused. He'd seen his share of desperate men and women, and the icy glitter in Caslet's eye worried him. There was too much anger and not enough panic in it. The rumor mill might have this man on a one-way ticket to ruin, but *he* seemed unaware of it . . . and the rumor mill had been known to be wrong. It probably wasn't, but if it was, Caslet was likely to emerge in a stronger position, not a weaker one. He was already the staff operations officer for the second most important naval command in the Republic, after all. If he returned to that post unscathed, he'd have access to very highly-placed ears, and as the SS officer looked into those icy eyes, it suddenly struck him that this particular Navy officer wouldn't turn out to be the sort to forgive and forget.

"Citizen Lieutenant Janseci, Citizen Commander," he replied much more crisply. Caslet nodded curtly, and Janseci braced to almost-attention. He considered actually saluting, but that would have been too obvious an admission that he should have done so at the beginning . . . and that Caslet had intimidated him. "I need to check your ID, Citizen Commander," he added almost apologetically.

Caslet reached slowly inside his tunic for his ID folio. He passed it to Janseci and felt an inner amusement, harsh as lye, as the armed guards in the background *did* come to attention. And all for a mere naval officer. How flattering.

The boat bay officer examined his ID quickly, then closed the folio and handed it back to Caslet. The citizen commander gazed down at it, his eyes still cold, for perhaps three seconds. Then he reached out, took it, and slid it back into his tunic.

"Well, Citizen Lieutenant Janseci," he said after a moment, "does anyone happen to know where, exactly, I'm supposed to go?"

"Yes, Citizen Commander. Your guide is on his way here now, and I expect—" Janseci broke off and raised a hand, beckoning to a petty officer who'd just stepped out of one of the two lifts serving the outsized boat bay. "Here he is now," he told Caslet with a sense of relief. "Citizen Chief Thomas will escort you to your quarters."

"Thank you," Caslet said, his tone now cool but correct, and turned away as the petty officer arrived and saluted.

"Citizen Commander Caslet?" Caslet returned the salute and admitted his identity. "If you'll come with me, Citizen Commander, we'll get you squared away," Thomas said, and gathered up two of the three bags the cutter crew had towed through the access tube while Janseci and Caslet were concentrating on one another.

"Thank you, Citizen Chief," Caslet said, much more warmly than he'd spoken to Janseci. He scooped up the third bag, slung his carryall's strap over a shoulder, and followed Thomas towards the lift, wondering what the citizen chief was doing aboard *Tepes*. Unlike Janseci, Thomas carried himself like someone who'd served in the real Navy and done it well, and Caslet couldn't imagine what could have tempted someone to transfer from that to . . . this.

He didn't ask, however. Partly because it was none of his business, and partly because he was half afraid of what he might hear. Good, fundamentally honorable men like Dennis LePic had become People's commissioners—and, technically, high ranking officers in State Security—because they believed in what the Committee of Public Safety had promised, and Caslet could half-way understand that. He could even respect it, however mistaken he thought them, but he didn't want to be able to understand what could cause someone— *anyone*—to enlist with StateSec's field forces.

Although the quarters he'd been assigned were smaller than they would have been for someone of his rank aboard a Navy ship, at least they weren't a cell. In his current situation, that had to be considered a good sign, but he reminded himself not to indulge in too much optimism as he thanked Thomas and set about settling himself into them. He opened his various bags and stowed their contents with the quick efficiency of someone who'd spent the last twenty years of his life moving from one shipboard assignment to another and tried not think about the fact that the Cerberus System was over a hundred and sixty-eight light-years from Barnett. Even for a battlecruiser, the voyage would last almost a month each way, which would give Ransom plenty of time to decide he *should* be in a cell.

And if you don't get yourself squared away and at least pretend *to be a good little boy, that's exactly what she* will *decide, idiot! Either that, or she'll just decide not to bring you home from Hades at all.*

He grimaced sourly at the thought, but he knew it was true, and he made himself think of his present situation as a tactical problem while he tried to get a firm grip on his emotions. The captain of a warship learned to put emotions on hold in combat, and he found that same self-discipline helping now. Of course, he reflected, it was unfortunate that thinking of Cordelia Ransom and State Security as "the enemy" felt so natural. Not because it didn't work, but because every step down that mental path could only make his ultimate survival even more problematical, however much it helped in the short term.

He was almost finished unpacking when the com chimed. He stopped what he was doing and turned to look at it for a moment, and it chimed again. The thought of answering it and being drawn further into whatever was going to happen to him didn't exactly fill him with eagerness, but refusing to answer would have been not only useless but childish, so he pressed the answer key.

"Citizen Commander Caslet?" the black-and-red uniformed woman on the screen said crisply, and he nodded. "Good. I'm Citizen Commander Lowell, the XO. Citizen Captain Vladovich asked me to welcome you aboard."

"Thank you, Citizen Commander," Caslet said politely, though he suspected Vladovich had as little use for him as *he* had for the entire Office of State Security.

"In addition," Lowell went on, "I was asked to inform you that Citizen Committeewoman Ransom and Citizen

Captain Vladovich will interview the prisoners shortly as the first step in processing them, and you are requested to be present."

"Understood, Citizen Exec," Caslet replied. At least they were being polite so far. Of course, they could afford to be.

"In that case, Citizen Commander, Citizen Lieutenant Janseci—I believe you've met?—will escort you to the interview in approximately half an hour."

"Thank you," Caslet said again, and Lowell nodded courteously and cut the connection. He stood a moment longer, looking at the blank screen, then shook himself. "Janseci," he muttered. "Wonderful! I wonder if he's as happy about playing guide for me as I am to have him?"

The screen returned no answer, and he sighed, gave himself another shake, and returned to his unpacking.

"Well, well, well. Look what the cat dragged in!"

Honor refused to turn her head or even move her eyes to locate the man who'd spoken. Instead, she stood very still, looking straight ahead, and tried to keep her face from reflecting the sinking sensation in her belly as she looked down the bare, gray-painted passage. Humans were humans, wherever they were from or wherever they went. There were inevitably troublemakers in any group of them, and every warship had its brig to deal with that contingency. But *this* ship's brig was far larger than any Honor had ever seen, and the harsh lighting, dreary gray bulkheads, and strong smell of disinfectant could have been specifically designed to crush the soul of anyone consigned to it.

And no doubt they *were* designed to do that, she thought. This wasn't simply a facility to hold prisoners; it was the first stage in a process designed to reduce them to pliable, servile obedience . . . assuming they weren't simply disposed of, instead.

She drew a mental breath and refused to let that thought drag her under. Her mind was clearer now, for the sweeping waves of Nimitz's pain had retreated. She didn't know if that was because Montoya had managed to ease that pain or if it was simply a factor of the distance between them, and she was torn between gratitude for her returning mental clarity and anguish over the separation. But giving into the anguish wouldn't help her, she reminded herself, and clearheadedness might.

"Snotty bitch, isn't she?" the male voice commented when she simply stood silently, waiting. "I imagine we can fix that."

Someone snickered, but Citizen Captain de Sangro shook her head.

"None of that, Timmons. Committeewoman Ransom wants this one delivered intact. Any breakage'll come out of someone's skin, and it won't be mine."

"Hmpf!" the man called Timmons snorted, then hawked and spat on the deck. The gobbet of spittle landed two centimeters from Honor's foot, and the naval officer in her noted the act with distant disgust. That sort of behavior would never be tolerated, if only on hygienic grounds, aboard any Manticoran ship, but no one seemed to care here. "No breakage, huh? That takes a lot of the fun out of it, de Sangro."

"My heart bleeds for you," the captain said. "Look, I've got better things to do than flap my gums at you. Suppose you just sign for this *puta,* and I'll be on my way."

"Always in a friggin' hurry, aren't you?" Timmons chuckled. "All right, all right! Give me the damned board."

Honor stood motionless while Timmons scrawled a signature and offered his thumbprint to the memo board's scanner. Her face showed no emotion as she was signed for like some piece of cargo. Indeed, her expressionlessness might have been mistaken for passivity by anyone who'd never seen her in the *salle* working out at *coup de vitesse* or honing her swordsmanship. She harbored no illusions that any martial arts skills could save her from whatever was going to happen, but she hadn't acquired them solely for purposes of combat. She'd spent forty years learning to draw upon their discipline and focus at need . . . and she'd never before needed either of those qualities as much as she knew she needed them now.

"There y'go," Timmons said, handing the board back to de Sangro. "Signed, sealed, and *dee*livered. You have a nice day now, de Sangro."

"Asshole," de Sangro snorted, and waved the other two members of her detail back into the lift, leaving Honor with Timmons and *his* detail.

A second or two passed in silence, and then hands grabbed her upper arms and jerked her around. The motion was quick and brutal, designed to surprise and disorient her, but she relaxed into it, the same way she rode a sparring partner's attack in the *salle*, and it failed to do either. The lack of resistance threw the man behind her off center, instead, and he half-staggered, his hands tightening on her arms as he found himself holding on for balance. He growled a curse, and the right corner of her mouth twitched with a bitter almost-smile. It was a petty triumph, but knowing this was a battle where ultimate victory was impossible made every triumph, however small, important.

The turn brought her face to face with Timmons, and she didn't care much for what she saw. The man was at least a couple of centimeters taller than she was, with broad shoulders and a face that actually had a sort of rough handsomeness, and he wore the insignia of a first lieutenant in the People's Marines, which she assumed denoted the same rank for State Security ground forces, as well. His hair was neatly trimmed, his uniform was freshly pressed, and the teeth that showed when he smiled were strong and white, yet that immaculate appearance was only a mask, a false surface that failed utterly to conceal something very different.

Despite her self-control, Honor blinked in surprise as she realized what that something was . . . and why his mask failed to hide it from her. It was as if Timmons carried the stink of rotting blood around with him, and he did. But not in any physical sense. What she was sensing came from inside him, and her nostrils flared as she realized that even so far separated from Nimitz she could scarcely feel his pain, she was picking up someone else's emotions. That had never happened before. Or she didn't think it had, anyway, but she didn't really know, for she'd never *tried* to read another's emotions on the rare occasions when she and the 'cat had been physically separated. Was this something new? Or something she could have done any time she'd tried? And with her sense of Nimitz's presence so faint, was she reading Timmons through the 'cat at all . . . or on her own?

The moment of discovery distracted her, breaking her cocoon of expressionless calm ever so briefly, but Timmons didn't notice. His attention was on the memo board he'd accepted from de Sangro. He punched the page key several times, scanning the screens of data for at least five minutes. Then he looked up with another white-toothed smile, and Honor hid an inner shiver. Sphinxian life forms were immune to the Old Earth disease of hydrophobia, but if a hexapuma could have contracted that sickness, it might have smiled like that.

"We've got us a *special* prisoner here, boys and girls," he told his detail. "This here is Honor Harrington. I'm sure you've heard of her?" Unpleasant laughter answered, and he chuckled. "Thought you might have. 'Course, she's come down in the world a mite. Says here they're taking her to Camp Charon to stretch her neck a little. Pity."

The blood stink of his emotions was stronger now, and Honor's stomach churned, but she had her expression back under control, and her eyes looked straight through him. He didn't like that. She could feel it in him—the anger fusing with a sadism worse than anything she'd sensed from de Sangro—and knew her lack of response was dangerous. But there was nothing she could do that *wasn't* dangerous.

She waited for his fuming emotions to spill over, but they didn't, and she felt an even deeper shiver of fear as she realized that underneath that calm, smiling exterior Timmons actually enjoyed the boil of fury. The anger and taste for cruelty which filled him were like drugs, something which put an edge on his life, and the need to restrain them only made that edge sharper. It was as if the denial of immediate gratification refined or distilled them, making the anticipation of loosing them almost sweeter than the actual moment when he did.

"According to this," he went on in a voice whose calm drawl fooled neither him nor Honor, "some of her friends are coming along for the ride, but they're military. They'll be riding topside, and she'll be all alone down here. Kinda makes you feel sorry for her, doesn't it?"

The others sniggered again, and a corner of Honor's mind wondered distantly if this was part of an orchestrated game plan to break down a prisoner's resistance or if Timmons simply enjoyed playing to the gallery. It didn't really matter which, of course. The practical consequences would be the same either way.

"How come they're military and she isn't?" a guard with the single chevron of a corporal asked. "The uniforms look the same to me."

"Anybody can wear a uniform, dummy," Timmons said with an air of enormous patience. "But according to this—" he waved the memo board "—this particular enemy of the People is a mass murderer. We've got us a *civil* criminal here, people, and as we all know, the Deneb Accords don't apply to criminals sentenced by civilian courts. That means all that shit about treatment of military prisoners goes right out the lock."

"Well, hot damn," the corporal said.

"Get your mind out of the gutter, Hayman," Timmons scolded with a smile. "I'm shocked by the very *suggestion* that anyone in my detachment would take liberties with a prisoner in our custody! This may not be a military prisoner, but proper procedure will be observed at all times. Is that clear?"

"If you say so, Sir," Hayman replied, "but it sure seems like a waste."

"You never can tell," Timmons said soothingly. "She may get lonely and want a little company after she's been down here a while, and what happens between consenting adults—" He broke off with a shrug, and fresh, ugly amusement gusted about Honor.

"In the meantime, though," Timmons went on more briskly, "let's get her processed. You're in charge of that, Bergren." He handed the memo board to a short, powerfully built sergeant. "It says here she's got an artificial eye, and you know the rules on implants. Get Wade in here to shut it down; if he can't do that, call the surgeon."

"Yes, Sir. And the rest of it?"

"She's a condemned murderer, Citizen Sergeant, not a paying guest," Timmons half-sighed. "Standard procedures. Strip search, cavity search, haircut, disease check—you know the drill. And since the Committeewoman wants to be sure she arrives intact, better put her on suicide watch, too. In fact," he gave another of those bright smiles, "we'd better take full precautions. I want her searched—completely, if you get my meaning—every time her cell's opened. And that includes meals."

"Yes, Sir. I'll get right on it," Bergren promised, and reached up to grab the collar of Honor's tunic. "Come on, cell bait," he grunted, and jerked. He was short enough that his grip dragged her awkwardly downward, bending her forward and making her stagger after him. It was a humiliating experience, but she knew it was supposed to be . . . and that the humiliation was only beginning.

"Just a minute, Bergren," Timmons said.

The sergeant turned back to face the lieutenant, and his grip gave Honor no choice but to turn with him. He didn't release her or let her straighten, but Timmons walked over, put two fingers under her chin, and tipped her face up to his. It was a contemptuous gesture, as if she were a child, but she made herself move with the gentle pressure and caught his flash of disappointment as her lack of resistance deprived him of the opportunity to *force* her head up against Bergren's grip.

"One thing, cell bait," he told her. "Every so often, we get someone in here who figures, what the hell, he's got nothing to lose, and tries to get rowdy, and that memo board says you're from a heavy-grav planet. It also says you're some kind of fancy-assed fighter, and I guess you heard Citizen Captain de Sangro tell me they want you at Camp Charon intact. I s'pose you might think that means *you* can get frisky with us 'cause we can't kick your ass without upsetting Committeewoman Ransom. Well, if you're thinking that way, you go right ahead, but remember this. There's another twenty, thirty friends of yours topside, and every time you give anybody trouble, we'll just have to take it out on one of *them*, since we can't take it out on you."

He smiled again, gave her chin a mocking flick, and nodded to Bergren.

"Take her away and get to know her," he said.

"Well? Can you help him?"

Fritz Montoya looked up from the treecat on the bunk in front of him. He, McKeon, Venizelos, LaFollet, and Anson Lethridge, as the senior male officers, had been shoved into a single large, bare compartment. Aside from the half-dozen bunks and the bare-bones head facilities in one corner it could have been a cargo bay, and its barrenness felt makeshift and coldly impersonal. It wasn't much, but at least the extra bunk was a place to put Nimitz . . . for whatever good it was going to do. The rise and fall of the 'cat's ribs was barely perceptible, and his eyes were slits, with no sign of intelligence in them. Unconsciousness probably wasn't a good sign, Montoya thought, but at least it had let him handle the 'cat without twisting him with those hoarse, near-screams of pain.

"I don't know," the doctor admitted. "I don't know enough about treecats. As far as I know, no one off Sphinx does."

"But you have to know *something*," LaFollet half begged. The armsman knelt beside the bunk, one hand resting ever so gently on Nimitz's flank. His own cheek was brutally discolored and swollen where a gun butt had split it, he'd walked with a painful limp on their way to their present quarters, and Montoya suspected his left shoulder was at least dislocated, but the anguish in his voice was for the treecat, not himself.

"I know his right midribs are broken," Montoya said heavily, "and as nearly as I can tell, so are his right midshoulder and upper arm. The gun butt caught him from above, striking downward, and I'm pretty sure it broke both the scapula and the joint itself. I don't *think* it caught him squarely enough to damage his spine, but I can't be sure about that, and I don't know enough about treecat skeletons to be sure I could set the bones I *do* know are broken even under optimum conditions. From what I can tell—or guess—though, that shoulder socket's going to need surgical reconstruction, and I don't begin to have the facilities for that."

"Is—" LaFollet swallowed. "Are you saying he's going to die?" he asked in a steadier tone, and Montoya sighed.

"I'm saying I don't know, Andrew," he said much more gently. "There are some good signs. The biggest one is that there's no bleeding from the nose or mouth. Coupled with the fact that his breathing may be slow and shallow, but it's steady, that at least suggests none of the broken bone damaged his lungs, and I don't feel any distention in his midsection, either, which suggests that if there's any internal bleeding, it must be minor. If I can get my hands on something to use as splints, I can at least immobilize the broken limb and shoulder, which should—hopefully—prevent any further damage, but aside from that—" He paused and sighed again. "Aside from that, there's not really anything I can do, Andrew. Whether he makes it or not is going to depend on him a lot more than it will on me. At least treecats are tough."

"I understand," LaFollet half whispered, and stroked Nimitz's hip. "He's never quit at anything in his life, Doc," the armsman said softly. "He's not going to quit now."

"I hope not, but—"

The doctor broke off as the hatch opened and an arrogant-looking StateSec ground forces lieutenant strode through the hatch, followed by two men with flechette guns. The other captured officers shifted position, turning to face the intruders with a sort of instinctive solidarity, and the lieutenant snorted contemptuously.

"On your feet!" he barked. "Citizen Committeewoman Ransom wants to see you!"

"I'm afraid that's out of the question." Montoya's cool, firm command voice would have surprised anyone who'd never seen him doing emergency surgery while direct hits shook his sickbay around him. Even the lieutenant seemed nonplused for a moment, but he recovered quickly.

"I see we've got a *comedian* aboard," he observed to his gun-toters. They snickered, but his voice was cold as he leaned closer to Montoya. "You don't make the rules here, Manty. *We* do—and when we say jump, you fucking well jump!"

"Committeewoman Ransom ordered me to keep this 'cat alive," Montoya said, and his voice was even colder than the lieutenant's. "I suggest you find out whether or not she meant that before you drag me away from him."

The lieutenant rocked back on his heels, his expression suddenly thoughtful. He hesitated a moment, then looked at one of the other guards.

"Com the Citizen Captain," he said. "Find out if they want the doctor, or if he should stay here with the animal."

"Yes, Citizen Lieutenant!" The trooper saluted and stepped back out into the passage. He was gone for several minutes that felt like hours, then he returned and saluted again. "The Citizen Captain says to leave the doctor here but bring the rest of them," he reported.

"All right." The lieutenant jerked his head at McKeon and pointed at the hatch. "You heard him, Manty. Get your sorry asses in gear."

The prisoners stood without moving, looking at McKeon. The lieutenant's mouth tightened, and he took a step towards the captain, only to pause as McKeon gave him a contemptuous glance.

"There's a limit to how many times you can butt stroke

us before one of us gets his hands on you, Peep." McKeon's deep voice was as cold as his eyes, and the lieutenant hesitated. Then he shook himself with a sneer.

"You're probably right, Manty. So why don't we just start shooting you, instead?"

"Because your balls are even smaller than your brain and you need orders in triplicate before you can take a shit," McKeon said disdainfully, and smiled a thin smile as the lieutenant flushed. But he knew better than to push too far, and he nodded to the others and said, "Let's go, gentlemen. We've been invited to meet with Ms. Ransom."

Warner Caslet wished he were somewhere—anywhere—else as Citizen Lieutenant Janseci led him into *Tepes'* enlisted gym. Exercise equipment edged the basketball court at one end of the compartment like the stranded bones of long-dead dinosaurs, and a dozen heavily armed State Security troopers stood along the court's other edge. Cordelia Ransom and Citizen Captain Vladovich sat behind a table which had been hastily draped with the PRH's flag, and Ransom's inevitable bodyguards stood behind her. A pair of HD camera teams had been strategically located to ensure that no nuance of the impending drama evaded their lenses, and the entire scene seemed to radiate a ghoulish unreality. He supposed the need for space made the gym's use inevitable—it was one of the few shipboard areas which could provide the amount of room Ransom had evidently decided she required—but the backdrop of exercise machines, racks of basketballs, volleyballs, and all the other cheerful items of play and exercise struck him as incredibly out of place.

Not that anyone cared how it struck Warner Caslet. Janseci ushered him across to the table, and Ransom looked over her shoulder at him for a moment. Her blue eyes were cold, but mindful of the watching cameras, she said nothing and simply pointed at an empty chair set well to one side, away from her and Vladovich. The sense of outraged defiance which had fueled Caslet's confrontation with

Janseci was sucked away by the chill in those eyes, for there was a universe of difference between an arrogant junior officer and the woman who stood third—or second—on the Committee of Public Safety.

He sank into the chair and sat silently as the sound of approaching feet warned him the Allied prisoners were approaching. He turned his head towards the sounds, and his jaw clenched as the captives were herded in. There was less use of gun butts this time, but the battered prisoners showed plenty of evidence of earlier mistreatment. A few found it difficult to stand up straight or even walk, and his jaw clamped still tighter as Geraldine Metcalf swayed for balance. The tac officer's left eye was swollen completely shut, the eyebrow above it scabbed with clotted blood where a flechette gun's butt plate had split it, and her right eye blinked in obvious disorientation. Marcia McGinley stood beside her, badly bruised herself but lending an arm to keep her friend upright.

There were others, some of whom Caslet had come to know well aboard HMS *Wayfarer*. Pain twisted deep within him as he saw Scotty Tremaine, Andrew LaFollet, and James Candless being shoved roughly through the hatch, and pain was joined by the dull burn of shame as the three of them recognized *him*. He made himself meet their eyes, hoping they would recognize his isolation for what it was, but their expressions revealed nothing and he made himself look at the other prisoners. There were twenty-five of them, including *Prince Adrian's* five senior surviving bridge officers, five members of Honor Harrington's staff, her three armsmen, two or three officers he couldn't identify, and nine petty officers. He recognized one of the noncoms, as well, for Horace Harkness' battered prizefighter's face was impossible to forget, but he wondered why the petty officers had been singled out for transport to Barnett when commissioned personnel senior to them had been sent to the Navy's Tarragon facility. From their expressions, they wondered the same thing, but they stood motionlessly with their officers to find out.

Silence stretched across the gym as Ransom sat back in her chair to regard the prisoners sternly. Caslet noticed one of the HD crews shifting position to catch her in profile— the better to capture her steely gaze, no doubt—but *she* seemed unaware of it as the seconds trickled away. Then she cleared her throat.

"You . . . people," she said with cold disdain, "are our prisoners. The uniforms you wear are sufficient to identify you as enemies of the People, but the People's Republic would have shown you the courtesies due to captured military personnel had you not demonstrated your true character by your conduct on Enki. Since you saw fit to assault our personnel, *killing* four of them in the process, you have forfeited whatever protections your military status might have earned you. Let that be clearly understood."

She paused, and the silence was different this time. It weighed in with a colder, more ominous pressure, for it was obvious her opening remarks had been intended to set the stage for something, and no one knew what.

"You are currently bound for Camp Charon on the planet Hades," she resumed after a small eternity, and showed an icy smile. "I'm sure all of you have heard stories about Camp Charon, and I assure you that all of them were true. I don't imagine any of you will enjoy your stay there . . . and it's going to be a very *long* one."

Her voice was cruel with pleasure, but she had more in mind than merely mocking helpless people, and Caslet wondered what it was.

"The People's Republic, however, recognizes that some of you—perhaps even many of you—have been misled by your own corrupt, elitist rulers. The citizens of plutocratic states are never consulted when their overlords choose to wage war, after all, and as the champion of the People in their struggle against plutocracy, it is one of the Committee of Public Safety's responsibilities to extend the hand of companionship to other victims of imperialist regimes. As the representative of the Committee, it therefore becomes my task to offer you the opportunity to separate yourself from the leaders who have lied to you and used you for their own self-seeking ends."

She stopped speaking for a moment, and the quality of silence had changed yet again. Most of the prisoners stared at her in frank incredulity, unable to believe she could possibly be serious, and Caslet shared their astonishment. Like most citizens of the Republic, he'd seen the confessions of "war crimes" from captured Allied personnel, and he'd never believed a one of them. Most of the self-confessed "war criminals" had come across heavily and woodenly, obviously repeating words someone else had scripted for them. Some had mumbled and stumbled their way through their "confessions" with the muzziness of the drugged, and others had stared into the cameras with terror-cored eyes, babbling anything they thought their captors wanted to hear. True, a few had sounded far more natural than that, but Caslet figured there were probably a few weasels in any body of men and women, and it wouldn't take much of a weasel streak to convince someone that cooperation was infinitely preferable to the things StateSec could do to a person.

But he couldn't believe Ransom would ask for volunteer traitors in front of her own cameras! Whatever the Proles might believe, she, at least, had to know how those other statements had been coerced out of the people who'd made them, and she was far stupider than he'd believed if she thought anyone who'd served under Honor Harrington would crumble *this* easily.

He sat motionless, watching the POWs stare back at Ransom and Vladovich. From where he sat, he could see Ransom's face clearly, and he noted her clenched jaw and the dots of red on her cheeks. Surely she hadn't actually expected them to cave in, had she?

"Let me make this clear to you," she said after another long pause, her voice flat and deadly. "The People's Republic is prepared to be merciful to those of you who, recognizing the criminal purposes to which you and your companions have been put, wish to free yourself of your shackles. Perhaps some remnant of the brainwashing to which your leaders have subjected you causes you to feel that it would be dishonorable to 'defect to the other side.' But you would *not* be defecting. Instead, you would be returning to your true side—the side of the People in their just struggle against their oppressors. Think carefully before you reject this offer. It will not be made again, however much conditions at Camp Charon may make you wish you'd accepted it."

She leaned forward, forearms planted on the table, and ran cold, burning blue eyes down the line of prisoners. Her posture made her look like some sort of golden-haired predator, crouched to spring, and one or two POWs shifted uncomfortably under her hungry glare. But no one spoke, and, finally, she inhaled sharply and sat back once more.

"Very well. You've made your choice. I doubt you'll enjoy it. Citizen Captain de Sangro, remove the prisoners."

"Yes, Citizen Committeewoman!" The SS captain snapped to attention, then jerked her head at her troopers. "You heard the Committeewoman. Let's get this elitist scum back to its cages!"

"Just a moment!" Heads swung as a single voice spoke from the prisoners. A broad-shouldered officer Caslet didn't know, his dark hair lightly streaked with silver, stepped forward, ignoring the dangerous looks the guards gave him, and Ransom cocked her head.

"And you are?" she asked disdainfully.

"Captain Alistair McKeon," the unknown officer said flatly.

"You wish to join the People in their fight against their oppressors?" Ransom's voice dripped sarcasm, but McKeon ignored the question.

"As the senior Queen's officer present," he said, still in that flat, biting tone, "I formally protest the abuse and mistreatment of my personnel. And I demand to see Commodore Harrington—at once!"

"A 'Queen's officer' has no standing *here!*" Ransom

snapped. "Nor am I impressed by your protests or *demands*. The only rights you have are those the People choose to *give* you, and at the moment, I see no reason to give you any at all. As for the woman you call 'Commodore Harrington,' you'll see her again—at her hanging!"

"Under the Deneb Accords—" McKeon began, and Ransom surged to her feet.

"Citizen Captain de Sangro!" she barked, and a gun butt slammed into McKeon's mouth. He went down, spitting blood and broken teeth, and Venizelos stepped forward angrily, but Anson Lethridge and Scotty Tremaine grabbed him. Surgeon Lieutenant Walker knelt beside his captain, and the look he gave the man who'd clubbed McKeon made the trooper step back involuntarily. Ransom watched contemptuously as Walker examined McKeon, then helped him back to his feet. McKeon swayed, leaning on his ship's doctor, and dragged the back of one hand across his smashed mouth. He gazed down at the blood on it almost dispassionately, then looked straight at Cordelia Ransom.

"I hope your cameras caught that." The words came out slurred and thick, but understandable. "It should be an important exhibit at your trial after the war."

Ransom paled, and for an instant, Caslet was afraid she was going to have the Manticoran killed on the spot. But then she inhaled deeply and shook herself.

"If there are any postwar trials, they won't be mine," she said icily. "And *you* won't be around to see them. Citizen Captain de Sangro!"

She jerked her head at the hatch, and de Sangro barked fresh orders.

The guards began shoving the prisoners towards the hatch, and Caslet sat back in his chair with a sense of sick, weary defeat. The "interview" had been shorter than he'd feared and, despite what had happened to McKeon, less ugly. But it had also been a parody of all he'd been taught to believe in, and—

"Wait a minute. *Wait a minute!*"

Caslet's head snapped back up, and Ransom wheeled

from her conversation with Vladovich as the rumbling voice cut the air. Senior Chief Harkness stood stubbornly in place, not so much resisting the SS trooper who was trying to drag him away as simply ignoring his efforts. The senior chief stood like an oak tree, but his battered face wore an expression of panic Caslet had never expected to see.

"Wait a minute!" he shouted again. "I ain't no hero— and I damned well didn't lose anything at this Camp Charon!"

"Senior Chief!" Venizelos barked. "What do you thin—"

The commander's shout died in a grunt of anguish as a gun butt slammed into his belly. Harkness didn't even turn his head, for his eyes were locked on Ransom with desperate intensity.

"Look, Ma'am—Ms. Committeewoman or whatever you are—I've been in the Navy for damned near fifty T-years. I didn't volunteer for any damned war, but it was my job, see? Or they *told* me it was, anyway, and it was the only job I knew. But this war ain't putting any extra money in *my* credit account, and I don't want to rot in prison for some rich son-of-a-bitch's fight!"

"No, Harkness!" Scotty Tremaine stared at the senior chief, his face twisted in horrified disbelief, and his outburst bought *him* a gun butt, as well. He went down, retching, and this time Harkness did look back.

"I'm sorry, Sir," he said hoarsely, "but you're an officer. Maybe you think you've got to go down in flames. Me, I'm only a petty officer, and you know how many times I got busted before I ever made chief." He shook his head and turned back to Ransom, his expression a blend of shame, fear, and desperation. "If you're offering transfers, Ma'am, I'll surely take one!" he blurted.

• Chapter Twenty-Four

"She *what?*"

Rob Pierre stared at his com screen in angry disbelief, and the man on it swallowed hard. He wore the lapel pin of the Ministry of Public Information and a nameplate which said L. BOARDMAN, SECOND DEPUTY DIRECTOR OF INFORMATION, and his lack of enthusiasm for this conversation was obvious.

"I could send you the chips, Citizen Chairman," his words tripped over themselves with the haste of an underling desperate to avoid blame. "I mean, I don't know all *that* much, Sir, and they make it all much clearer than *I* possibly could, so—"

"Shut up."

Pierre's frozen helium tone cut Boardman off in mid-blither, and he clamped his mouth shut. The Chairman of the Committee of Public Safety glared at him, dark eyes deadly, then made himself relax . . . some. The bureaucrat's terror underscored the vast gulf between them in a way which made him feel distantly ashamed. He could have the other man destroyed—literally or figuratively, as the mood took him—on a whim, and both of them knew it. That sort of power was dangerous, Pierre reminded himself. There was a corrosiveness to it he must guard against constantly, yet for all his wariness, the corrosion tasted sweet, as well. Surely he could indulge himself in it just a little . . . couldn't he? When the entire galaxy seemed hell-bent on exploding in his face, where was the harm in proving there were at least some irritations he could crush with a word?

411

He inhaled deeply and cleared his throat, then leaned closer to his pickup.

"Of course I'll want to view the chips," he said, in a tone whose enormous patience added the word "idiot!" without actually quite saying it. "Until I *do*, however, just give me the salient points. *Now.*"

"Yes, Sir!" Boardman seemed to come to attention in his chair. His hands were outside the field of his pickup, but his shoulders twitched as he fumbled at his desktop for a moment. Then paper rustled as he found the hardcopy notes he'd jotted down.

"Uh, let's see," he muttered, dabbing sweat from his forehead as he scanned them. "Oh. All right, Citizen Chairman." He looked back at the pickup and dredged up a sickly smile. "According to Citizen Mancuso, my assistant, Citizen Rear Admiral Tourville—" he peered back at his notes. "That's right, Citizen Rear Admiral *Lester* Tourville, captured several Manty ships, including a cruiser with Honor Harrington on board."

He paused, regarding his own handwriting as if he expected it to change if he took his eyes off it. Or, Pierre thought, as if he couldn't believe what he'd just said. Which was reasonable enough, given how regularly Harrington had kicked the asses of any PRH naval officers unfortunate enough to encounter her. But the pause stretched out long enough to become a fresh source of irritation, and Pierre cleared his throat with a sharp, explosive sound that snatched Boardman out of whatever reverie had possessed him.

"Uh, excuse me, Citizen Chairman!" he said quickly. "As I say, Citizen Rear Admiral Tourville captured Harrington and sent word back to the Barnett System, where Citizen Secretary Ransom was informed of it. The propaganda aspects of the event were obvious to her, of course, and she directed Tourville to return Harrington to Barnett."

"I understood that part of it!" Pierre snapped. "What I want to know is what the *hell* she thought she was doing *after* that!"

Boardman cringed, his eyes sick with panic. Internal clashes between members of the Committee were rare—publicly, at least—but when they happened, the disappearance of one of the disputants normally followed, and Rob Pierre was usually careful to avoid anything which could be construed as public condemnation of any of his fellows. Not because he didn't get angry, but because someone with his power dared not *show* that anger. If he made a clash public, then his position as head of the Committee would give him no *choice* but to eliminate whoever had angered him, for any lesser action would undermine his own authority and position.

Boardman knew that . . . and he also knew that, as one of Cordelia Ransom's senior assistants, any fallout from Pierre's fury at her could scarcely be beneficial for *him*. Of course, if he failed to shore up his patron's position and she survived, she would certainly learn of his lack of support . . . with equally fatal results. But at the moment, Ransom was light-years away, whereas Rob Pierre was barely sixty floors up in the same building, and the bureaucrat made himself meet the Citizen Chairman's eyes.

"I'm not certain of all she had in mind, Sir," he said with surprising firmness. "I wasn't there, and I haven't had time to view the chips yet. From the synopsis I was given, however, she remembered that the old regime's courts had sentenced Harrington to death before the war, and, well . . ." He paused and drew another deep breath. "She's decided to personally take her to Camp Charon for execution of sentence, Sir," he said.

"Can we stop her?" Esther McQueen demanded harshly. She and Oscar Saint-Just sat facing Rob Pierre's enormous desk, and her green eyes flamed. She'd started getting her teeth into her new job, and, along the way, she'd found the Ministry of War was in even worse shape than she'd thought from out at the sharp end of the stick. The problems she'd already discovered bore an overwhelming resemblance to the Augean Stables, and she did *not* need this kind of gratuitous insanity to make her task still harder.

"I don't see how," Saint-Just answered her in a flat voice. "Theisman's dispatch boat didn't even leave for Haven until three days after Cordelia departed for Cerberus. By now, she's less than six days from the system, and it would take *seven* days for any dispatch of ours to get there."

"We could at least *try!*" McQueen snapped. "Surely not even Ransom will have Harrington hanged the day she gets there!"

"I'm afraid you've missed the point, Citizen Admiral," Pierre said heavily. "Even if I could get word to her in time, we can't afford to countermand her."

"Why not?" McQueen managed to soften her tone at the last minute, but despite all her formidable self-control her frustration was evident, and Pierre sighed, wishing he could pretend her reaction was out of line.

"Because she's already dumped her 'interview' with Harrington into the broadcast stream," Saint-Just answered for him. "Our own people already know about it, and by now the Solarian League newsies must have sent reports to their bureau offices in Alliance space, and I'm sure you can imagine how the 'faxes will play up something like *this*. And even if the League correspondents didn't touch it for some reason, the spies monitoring our broadcasts for the Alliance have to have the same information. And that, of course, means that if it hasn't already reached Manticore, it will shortly . . . and that we can't change tacks without looking like *complete* fools."

McQueen stared at him for several seconds, then looked at Pierre, who nodded heavily. The new Secretary of War sat very still for a moment, then made herself speak in the calmest tone she could manage.

"Citizen Chairman, this must be thought through very carefully. In and of herself, purely as a naval officer, Harrington isn't that significant. I don't deny her ability or the damage she's done to us. In fact, I'll admit that, enemy or not, she's one of the best in the business. Tacticians like her come along possibly half a dozen times in a generation—if you're lucky—but bottom line, from a purely military perspective, she's just one more admiral— or commodore, depending on which navy she's serving in at the moment.

"But Citizen Committeewoman Ransom is making a very, *very* serious error if she regards Harrington solely as a naval officer. The Star Kingdom of Manticore sees this woman as one of its two or three greatest war heroes. The Protectorate of Grayson sees her not only as a hero, but as one of its great nobles. And our own Navy sees her as perhaps *the* outstanding junior flag officer on the other side. I'm sure the Fleet, and at least some segments of our own civilian public, will feel both relief and triumph to know she's been removed from play. But putting her in a prison camp will do that. We don't *have* to kill her . . . and her execution on what I hope you'll pardon me for charac- terizing as trumped up charges, will have consequences far beyond the loss of her abilities to the Allied military— or any short-term propaganda advantage for our own side. We'll turn her into a *martyr*, Sir, and that will make her ten times—a hundred times!—as dangerous as she ever was alive. And even if we completely disregard the effect her execution will have on the other side, think about what it will mean to our *own* people. The Manties will never forgive us for this—*never*—and with all due respect to Citizen Saint-Just, it's not StateSec personnel who'll be falling into their hands. It's the Navy and the Marines, and our fighting forces will know that *they're* the ones who will pay the price for this. Not only will that inevitably make them anxious over their own fates if they should face capture, but it will drive an equally inevitable wedge between them and State Security, because rightly or wrongly, *that's* who they'll blame for carrying out the execution."

She'd watched the two men's faces while she spoke, but the anger she'd more than half expected to awaken failed to appear. Actually, she couldn't remember ever having seen *any* emotion on Saint-Just's face, and Pierre's expression was more one of exhausted agreement than anger. But the chairman shook his head when she finished. He leaned back in his chair, one hand on his blotter while the other massaged his eyes, and his voice was heavy.

"I can't fault your analysis," he said. "But even if Harrington does become more dangerous to us as a martyr, we can't afford to overrule Cordelia. Not publicly." He lowered his raised hand, and his dark gaze pinned McQueen to her chair. "She's wrong. I know this entire idea is stupid, and so do you, and so does Oscar, *but she's already gone public.* If I overrule her now, I'll have to do *that* publicly, and I can't. Not this soon after the Leveler business. Not when she's one of the Committee's original members and the head of Public Information. We simply cannot afford a public disagreement at this time—not when God knows who is waiting to use any rupture at the top against us. No, Citizen Admiral," he shook his head wearily, "however steep the price of letting her proceed may be, it's lower than the cost of stopping her."

McQueen sat back and closed her mouth against the protests still burning on her tongue. Fury and disgust, as much as logic, fed her outrage, but it didn't take a hyper physicist to realize the decision had been made even before she was informed of what had happened. Pierre and Saint-Just were being as stupid as Ransom, at least in the longer term, she thought bitterly, but trying to convince them of that would only undermine her own new and fragile position. So far, her protests seemed to have struck a chord of agreement with them. They couldn't deny the validity of the points she'd made; it was just that they felt the risk of an open break with Ransom outweighed the ones she'd enumerated. They were wrong, but if she wanted to retain whatever respect she'd earned by stating her position, she had to abandon the argument before their present regretful decision to overrule her turned into something uglier.

"Very well, Citizen Chairman," she sighed finally. "I still think this is a serious mistake, but the decision is ultimately a political one. If you and Citizen Committeeman Saint-Just both feel it would be . . . inadvisable to override Citizen Committeewoman Ransom, the judgment is yours to make."

"Thank you, Citizen Admiral." Pierre sounded genuinely grateful, and McQueen wondered what for. He was chairman of the Committee. He and Saint-Just could damned well do anything they liked, with or without her approval . . . for now, at least. "I'm very much afraid your analysis of our own military's reaction is likely to be accurate," he went on, "and we're going to need all the help we can get in blunting the worst of it. To that end, I would appreciate any insight you can give Citizen Boardman." McQueen raised an eyebrow, and Pierre smiled wryly. "Citizen Boardman will be writing the official release from the Committee and the rough draft for a communiqué to our own armed forces, but I don't have, um, the liveliest respect for his abilities, shall we say? Especially where the military are concerned, he's going to need all the help he can get to make *this* look good."

"Citizen Chairman," McQueen said frankly, "I don't think we *can* make this look 'good' from the Navy's perspective. The best we can hope for is to make it look less *bad*, but I'm certainly prepared to give Citizen Boardman whatever help I can."

"Thank you," Pierre said again, and McQueen took her cue from his tone. She stood and nodded to the others with exactly the right blend of deference and a sense of her own value to them, then walked out the door and headed for the elevators, and it took all her willpower to keep her stride from revealing the anger still boiling within her.

But at least it wasn't my *decision,* she reminded herself. *I really did argue against it—and not solely out of expediency, either. Funny. For the first time in years, I can honestly say "my hands are clean" . . . and it doesn't change a damned thing.*

She punched for an elevator car, then folded her arms while she waited for it.

On the other hand, there may actually be a silver lining to all this, she mused. *Not immediately, no, but the execution was Ransom's idea, and Pierre and Saint-Just refused to override her, now didn't they? And the officer corps is going to know that as well as I do. For that matter, the Manties will know it, too. That could just make the whole thing a card worth playing when the time comes. After all, I'll be acting out of moral outrage over the excesses of State Security and the Committee, won't I? Of course I will.*

The elevator doors opened, and Esther McQueen's lip curled in a bitterly sardonic smile as she stepped through them.

Miranda LaFollet sat on the shaded bench and watched the children play. Farragut lay sprawled on his belly on the bench beside her, his chin resting companionably on her thigh, and she smiled down at him and reached out to stroke the magical softness of his spine. His gentle purr buzzed in her ear, and he arched his back ever so slightly, and even that tiny response made the wonder and amazement of him brand-new all over again. She couldn't imagine anything she could possibly have done to deserve his love or the magic of her bond with him. He was her companion, her champion, and her closest friend, all in one, and already the mere thought of a life without him in it had become impossible to conceive of. It simply couldn't happen, and she was unspeakably grateful to—

Her thought chopped off, and her gray eyes went dark. It always happened that way. She managed to put the thought out of her mind by concentrating on the things that had to be done—the simple, daily duties which could consume so much of her time—and then something would happen, and the darkness would return with abrupt, brutal power.

She looked back out at the other 'cats, and familiar worry

twisted deep within her. Samantha and Hera lay stretched out along separate limbs of an Old Earth oak tree, the very tips of their prehensile tails twitching as they guarded the kittens and watched Cassandra and Andromeda stalk their brothers through the underbrush under Artemis' tutelage. From here, everything looked completely normal, but Miranda had been there when James MacGuiness returned to Grayson. She'd watched him face Samantha, and she'd held Farragut in her own arms, feeling his tension as MacGuiness explained what had happened to Samantha's mate.

If anyone present had ever doubted treecats understood English, they would never doubt again. Samantha had been tense and ill at ease from the moment MacGuiness walked in, clearly sensing his own emotional turmoil—not that anyone would have needed an empathic sense for that. His worn, exhausted face had shouted it to the universe, and he'd gone down on his knees to face Samantha. The 'cat had sat fully upright, green eyes meeting his, and he'd told her.

Miranda would never forget that moment. She'd already heard the news herself, knew her brother, as well as her Steadholder, was missing. Yet she had all the rest of her huge, loving family . . . and Farragut. Terrible as the news had been, she'd had people who cared and duties to distract her from it. But Samantha had lost her adopted person barely twenty T-months before. Now her mate and *his* person had disappeared, as well, and the desolation in her eyes had twisted Miranda's heart. The other 'cats had converged upon her—even Farragut—surrounding her with the physical warmth of their bodies even as they lent her the deeper, inner warmth of their presence, yet empath and telepath or no, she had been as alone in that moment as any human.

In some ways, the endless days which had passed since then had been a blessing, for they had blunted the immediacy of their knowledge. Time might not heal all wounds, but no one—'cat or human—could sustain the anguish of the moment of loss indefinitely, and like Miranda, Samantha had her family. She had the rest of the clan she and Nimitz had brought to Grayson, and her children, and she'd buried herself in them as desperately as Miranda had turned to *her* family. And the 'cats hadn't forgotten MacGuiness. It was as if they understood—as no doubt they did—that he, too, needed his "family" at a time like this, and one of the adults was perpetually bringing him a kitten to rock to sleep or some other problem which required his attention. They watched over him as attentively as they guarded Samantha's children, and Miranda saw to it that the Harrington House staff did the same. None of Lady Harrington's people would ever *admit* that was what they were doing, of course, but the truth was that they were almost as attached to MacGuiness as they were to the Steadholder, and somehow watching over him was like a promise to Lady Harrington that her household and her steading would be ready when she returned.

Farragut stirred, raising his head from her lap. Miranda turned her head to see what had caught his attention, and a wry smile twitched her lips as the newest citizen of Harrington Steading walked down the path towards her. In some respects, there could not have been a worse time for Doctor Harrington to arrive on Grayson, but Miranda was devoutly grateful that she was here.

She had dived into the task of organizing the clinic with an energy every bit as formidable as her daughter's, and the results had been impressive. Manticoran physicians had flooded into Grayson over the past few years. Almost a third of them had been women, and the huge gap between modern medicine and that of Pre-Alliance Grayson had gone a long way towards demolishing any reservations about female doctors. It was difficult for any physician to argue that women must be less competent than men when the medical knowledge of the women in question was at least a century in advance of their own. Of course, *nothing* was impossible for the sufficiently bigoted. A certain percentage of the most conservative Grayson doctors had managed to maintain their prejudices, but they were a distinct minority. Despite that, however, some members of the Grayson medical profession—and not all of them bigots, by any means—had been prepared to assume that Dr. Harrington's relationship to the Steadholder, more than her own abilities, helped explain her selection to head the clinic.

So far, the longest anyone had managed to hang onto that assumption after meeting her was less than twenty minutes, and it didn't matter whether they'd come to consult her on an administrative matter or a medical one. She'd been trained at the finest medical university and best teaching hospitals in the known galaxy; she had sixty-five T-years of experience to draw upon and an energy and enthusiasm anyone a quarter of her age might have envied; and—like her daughter—she was simply incapable of offering less than her very best. She didn't even have to try to impress her critics; she simply had to be herself.

Unfortunately—or perhaps fortunately; Miranda's mental jury was still undecided—the differences between her background and her daughter's had quickly become apparent. In fact, a disinterested observer might have been pardoned for wondering whether or not Grayson society would find Doctor Harrington's impact survivable.

Miranda was certain there wasn't a malicious bone in Allison Harrington's body, but that didn't make her sense of humor a bit less wicked, and she was only too obviously aware of how Grayson's conservative elements must feel about Beowulf's reputation. That first night's dinner with the Clinkscales had made *that* abundantly clear, for she really had turned up in a smoke-gray backless gown of thin—*very* thin—neoworm silk from Naismith with a deeply plunging neckline. The simplicity of its styling had been almost brutal, but the opaque fabric had clung and flowed like the smoke it so resembled, outlining her body so frankly that, for the first few seconds, Miranda had feared for the Regent's health. He was no longer a young man, after all, and that gown's potential impact on his blood pressure had been enough to worry anyone. But he'd clearly taken Dr. Harrington's measure more accurately at their first meeting than Miranda had expected, and he'd evinced neither confusion, consternation, nor outrage. In fact, he'd actually smiled as he bent over her hand to welcome her with exquisite formality, then escorted her to the dinner table to introduce his wives.

Miranda didn't know whether or not he'd warned them ahead of time. She tended to doubt it, but over the past several years, all three of them had demonstrated a flexibility which she was certain would once have astonished their husband. Their response to Allison's gown had taken the form of appreciation of its fabric and simplicity of design, and they'd plunged into a comparison of Grayson and Manticoran styles. Rather to Miranda's amazement, Allison had jumped right into it with them, eyes sparkling with delight, and Miranda had realized something she hadn't really expected.

Allison Harrington was vain. Oh, not in a negative sense, but she was certainly well aware of her own attractiveness, and her love for "dressing up" was at least as deep as any Grayson woman's. Somehow Miranda had assumed Lady Harrington was typical of all Manticoran women. Certainly the Steadholder took pains with her appearance, and certainly she enjoyed knowing she looked her best, but that had always been secondary for her. And, in a sense, it was secondary for her mother, as well. Professionally, working to organize the clinic and begin the enormous task of mapping the genomes of every citizen of Harrington Steading, she was as efficient and ruthlessly disciplined as the Steadholder, and she couldn't have cared less what she looked like. But once she left the clinic behind, she took an almost childlike glee in clothes, jewelry, cosmetics . . . all those things her daughter seemed all but totally indifferent to.

That glee was accompanied by a merciless delight in puncturing the overinflated and hypercritical, and the combination of her beauty, her undisputed stature as the best geneticist ever to visit Miranda's planet, her sense of humor, and her Beowulf rearing made her a lethal weapon on Grayson. Traditionalists who had already been outraged by "that foreign woman" were sitting targets for the foreign woman's *mother*. She was poised, confident, and—unlike her daughter—she *loved* parties, dinners, and balls. She reveled in them with unfeigned, almost giddy delight, and where the Steadholder had felt out of place and ridiculous when she first began easing her way into "proper" Grayson female attire, Allison, aided and abetted by the Regent's wives and—especially—Catherine Mayhew, had plunged into the most extravagant fashions she could find. Very few *Graysons* could have worn the clothes she chose, but she was clearly a law unto herself, and her almond-eyed beauty and devastating charm made all things possible.

It must have been tempting for the members of the old guard to write her off as a frivolous ninny from a loose-living and licentious society, but anyone who made the fatal error of allowing her youthful exterior to draw them into underestimating her never got a chance to recover. It was obvious she missed—and loved—her husband deeply, but she'd also spent seventy-plus T-years delighting in her ability to attract the male of the species. So far she'd been careful to avoid doing anything which could embarrass her daughter, although Miranda suspected that that was *only* because it might embarrass Lady Harrington. But she most certainly *would* trade shamelessly on Beowulf's reputation to lure the social vultures into false positions expressly so that she could cut them off at the knees. Miranda had only had to watch her at a single party to realize where her daughter's ruthless tactical instincts had come from.

But there hadn't really been time for Allison to scandalize Grayson properly before the parties were brought to a shattering halt by the news of the Steadholder's loss. A cloud had descended on all of Harrington Steading, yet it was centered on Harrington House and the people who knew her best. Lord Clinkscales had immediately dispatched the *Tankersley* to Manticore to transport Lady Harrington's father to Grayson, and Protector Benjamin and his entire family had prepared to comfort Allison in his absence. Yet it hadn't worked out as they'd expected, for they'd discovered that at the heart of her, when all the jokes and fashions and poses were left behind, there was a vast, personal serenity and a bottomless strength. She'd drawn deeply upon it when her daughter was reported missing, and somehow she'd extended it to all of Lady Harrington's people. What the Steadholder had laughingly called her inner circle—MacGuiness, Miranda, and Howard Clinkscales—had found themselves especially in need of her serenity, and she shared it with them willingly. She had been on Grayson for barely two months, yet already Miranda could scarcely imagine Harrington House without her. More to the point, perhaps, she had no *desire* to imagine it without her.

Now she watched Allison approach, and her wry smile deepened. As the human "grandmother" of Samantha's children, Dr. Harrington kept close track of the kittens' doings. For that matter, she had a keen interest in all the 'cats who'd moved to Grayson. Miranda wondered if part of that was because they were a thread connecting her to her daughter, but whatever its basis, her interest was deep and genuine. Miranda made it a point to keep her up to date on anything interesting or amusing—especially now— and she knew the elaborate practical joke Farragut and Hood had perpetrated on the head gardener that morning would amuse her deeply.

But then Miranda's smile faded, for there was something wrong. It took her several endless seconds to realize what it was, and when she did, she snapped up from the bench in formless dread. She'd never seen Allison Harrington walk like that. The bustle and energy, all the gusto that was so much a part of her, had vanished, and she moved with a leaden, mechanical stride. It was as if her legs kept moving only because they had no choice, or as if their owner neither knew nor cared where she was going and would continue to walk blindly until she came up against some obstacle that stopped her dead.

Miranda darted a look down at Farragut. The 'cat's eyes were fixed on Allison, and his ears were flat to his skull while the ghost of a low, soft snarl rumbled in his throat. He felt his person's gaze upon him and looked up briefly, his green eyes dark, then returned his unwinking attention to Allison. Miranda looked around, confused, trying to grasp what was happening, and her stomach tightened as every adult 'cat began to appear as if by magic. They blended out of the shrubbery, came bounding from limb to limb, dashed up paths, and all of them—every single one of them—had his or her eyes fixed with urgent intensity upon the Steadholder's mother.

That slow, dead stride brought her close, and Miranda reached out, fighting a sense of formless dread. She wondered, in a corner of her mind, how much of that was instinctive reaction to the way Allison moved and how much, if any, was a resonance from the 'cats. What sort of feedback might a human expect from *nine* adult, desperately worried 'cats? But it was a distant thought, lost and unimportant, and she put her hand on Allison's shoulder.

"My Lady?" She heard the fear in her own voice, though she still had no idea what its source might be. Her touch stopped Allison, but for a moment Miranda thought she hadn't heard her . . . or that she was so lost in her own pain that she would ignore her. But then Allison looked up, and Miranda's formless fear rose suddenly in her throat, choking her, as the utter desolation of those almond eyes tore at her.

"What is it, My Lady?" she demanded, the words coming harsh and quick, and Allison reached up to cover the hand on her shoulder.

"Miranda," she said in a dead, lusterless voice Miranda barely recognized.

"What is it, My Lady?" she repeated more gently, and Allison's mouth quivered.

"I just—" She stopped and swallowed. "It was the HD," she said finally. "I-I just saw a news report. A League bureau feed from . . . from the Peeps, and . . ." Her voice died, and she simply stood there, staring up at Miranda with those huge, stricken eyes.

"What sort of feed?" Miranda asked as she might have asked a child, and her fear became terror as Allison Harrington's face crumpled at last.

• Chapter Twenty-Five

Scotty Tremaine finished his isometrics and wiped sweat from his face with one of the scratchy hand towels their guards had furnished. It wasn't much use for its designed function—it was about as absorbent as a sheet of plasti-wrap—but he supposed he should be grateful they'd given his people even that much. They certainly hadn't provided anything else!

State Security had seen no reason to bring along their prisoners' baggage, and, like everyone else, Scotty had only the uniform he'd been wearing when they'd first been dragged in to face Cordelia Ransom. Modern synthetic fabrics were tough and durable, but even so, there was a limit to how much wear one set of garments could absorb. Their guards had offered bright orange jumpsuits to replace them, but without success, for every one of their prisoners knew the offer hadn't been made out of kindness. Those jump suits would have separated them from what and who they were, reduced them from naval officers to so many hopeless, indistinguishable captives. Their uniforms might be becoming worn and tattered, and they might have to take turns washing them out by hand in the compartment's single lavatory, but none of his people had fallen for the offer.

His mouth tightened, and he wiped his face again, using the towel to hide his expression from the others as he remembered the one person who *had* accepted an offer from the Peeps. The pain of that cut deep—deeper than he'd ever imagined it could. Deeper, he sometimes thought, even than hearing that sadistic piece of human garbage sentence Lady Harrington to death. In the cosmic scale of events, Horace Harkness' defection probably didn't mean all that much. Its effect on the war would be minuscule, and as sources of anguish went, it shouldn't even come close to knowing that the woman Tremaine respected most in all the galaxy was going to die. He knew all that. But he also knew that what should be true and what *was* true were very different things.

He lowered the towel and sat on his bunk, staring at the featureless bulkhead, and despite anything he could do, his mind insisted on returning to his first deployment to Basilisk Station. He'd been almost as young as Carson Clinkscales and, hard as he tried to hide it, uncertain and afraid, but Harkness had taken him in hand. He'd taught a junior officer to *be* an officer—not by telling him what to do, but by *showing* him. By testing and pushing him, yes, but in the immemorial tradition not simply of the Queen's Navy but of *all* navies. No doubt grizzled boatswains had taken young Carthaginian landlubbers in hand and made officers of them for the Punic Wars, Scotty thought, for that was a senior noncom's job. Whatever else their duties might include, *they* were the true keepers of the tribal wisdom, the elders responsible for setting each new generation's feet upon the trail, and Horace Harkness had done that for Scotty Tremaine.

But he hadn't stopped there, and Scotty's eyes burned as he remembered all the other things he and Harkness had done together. Other than a single year when he'd been reassigned from the heavy cruiser *Fearless* to Captain McKeon's *Troubadour* before the First Battle of Yeltsin, he and the senior chief had *always* been together. They'd served in *Prince Adrian*, and gone through Third Yeltsin together aboard her, and they'd been at the first two battles of Nightingale, as well. And when Scotty had transferred to HMS *Wayfarer*, Harkness had followed him, and the two of them had saved one another's lives . . . and those of every other survivor of the crippled Q-ship's crew. He'd never been able to define their relationship—it hadn't been something that *required* definition—yet it had always been there, and deep inside, Scotty Tremaine had known he could never truly lose hope, however desperate the situation or however impossible the odds, as long as he had Harkness by his side.

And now he didn't, and it was as if some fundamental principle of physics had violated itself. One of the unwavering certainties of his life had crumbled in his hand, and that deeply wounded part of him wanted to scream at the universe for betraying him so. Only it wasn't the *universe* which had done it, and tantrums would change nothing.

He drew a deep breath and held it, mourning the death of the man Horace Harkness once had been, and once more forced himself to set his grief aside. It would return. He knew that, but he was also the senior officer in this compartment. It was his job to lead—to set an example—and he remembered the lessons Harkness had taught him before the final betrayal, and the need to live up to those lessons had taken on a strange, added urgency. It was almost as if as long as *he* honored them, in some perverse way it would mean Harkness hadn't fallen. And it was what Lady Harrington would have expected of him—and Captain McKeon. There were some people it was simply unthinkable to fail, and Scotty wondered if McKeon or Lady Harrington would ever know that it was the impossibility of allowing himself to come up short against *their* standards, not courage or dedication or patriotism, which truly kept him from admitting his despair to Clinkscales or Mayhew or Jamie Candless and Robert Whitman.

And, he admitted, pushing himself to his feet once more, it was Horace Harkness, as well. He'd learned the senior chief's lessons too well to abandon them now, whatever might have happened aboard *Tepes*.

James Candless watched Lieutenant Commander Tremaine cross the compartment to Ensign Clinkscales. Despite his own official status as a Marine officer, Candless felt out of place confined with these officers, and he knew Whitman felt the same. But he also knew that the true reason they felt so adrift and anchorless was that the central focus of their lives had been taken from them. They were Grayson armsmen, and their Steadholder was imprisoned and condemned to die, and they were still alive.

That was the shame they both bore, Candless thought as Tremaine lowered himself to sit beside Clinkscales and speak quietly and encouragingly to the ensign. They should have died before they allowed anyone to lay hands on the Steadholder, and they hadn't. They hadn't been present when the Peeps sentenced her to death, and the officers who had been there hadn't wanted to tell them what had happened, but they knew. It wasn't their fault, yet that changed nothing. The Steadholder had been beaten and clubbed to the floor. Nimitz had been crippled and half-killed. And the woman they were sworn to protect had been dragged off, alone in the hands of people who hated her.

Candless gritted his teeth and closed his eyes as he fought the agony of failure. He knew Whitman shared it, yet not even Whitman knew the full depth of his own despair. For six years Candless had watched the Steadholder's back, he and Major LaFollet. For six *years*, always in their proper place, guarding her against her enemies and, when the need arose, against herself—against her own courage and need to risk herself for others. And now she was alone, Tester only knew where, enduring Tester only knew what abuse and knowing she would die, and Jamie Candless would be denied even the right to die by her side.

He opened his eyes once more, watching Tremaine and Clinkscales, seeing the new maturity in the ensign's face and recognizing the way in which facing his own helplessness had burned away Clinkscales' youthful uncertainty. He turned his head to glance at Whitman, washing his uniform by hand in the lavatory, and then at Lieutenant Mayhew, sitting in one corner and playing chess against Surgeon Lieutenant Walker on a board which existed only in their minds. They were going on, all of them, because they refused to give up, but for how much longer would that be true? Even if they'd known the voyage time to Hades, they had no chrono, no calendar, no way to tell how long they'd already been aboard. But they knew they would arrive eventually, and what then? What would happen when the Steadholder was dead, and they were only so many more nameless, forgotten inmates in a planet-sized prison?

He didn't know the answers to those questions, but it didn't really matter, for those answers wouldn't apply to him. He could no more save the Steadholder than he could somehow capture this entire ship, but one thing he could do, and the decision had come surprisingly easily to someone who'd never realized he harbored a strand of the berserker. They wouldn't let him die with the Steadholder . . . but sooner or later, somewhere, sometime, his chance would come. Not immediately. He refused to act hastily, for it was important he succeed, and he was determined that he would. At least one of them. At least one of the bastards in their black and red uniforms before he *made* them kill him—that was all he asked for . . . and all in the universe he would ever want again.

"All right, cell bait. Get dressed!" The sneering female guard threw the orange jumpsuit at Honor with one hand and stood back, peeling the thin plastic glove from her other hand.

Honor caught the scratchy fabric without even looking, staring straight in front of her as she had ever since the two guards entered her cell for the regular postmeal "suicide watch search." There were always two of them for the degrading ritual. Usually, as today, the second was Sergeant Bergren, who took special delight in any opportunity to humiliate her, but if it hadn't been him it would have been Hayman, or perhaps Timmons himself, for the second guard was *always* male. That was part of the degradation.

Even State Security had rules. Its personnel might ignore or violate them, but the official procedures existed, and— on paper, at least—they looked almost reasonable. But

Timmons and his detail of two-legged animals understood how twisting those procedures without—quite—technically violating them only allowed even more scope to humiliate and debase anyone unfortunate enough to fall into their power. The letter of the regulations said strip searches and cavity searches of prisoners could be carried out only by security personnel of the same sex, and Timmons insisted that his thugs abide by that. But the regs also stipulated that a minimum of two guards must be present any time a priority prisoner was subjected to searches . . . and that *second* guard was always male.

Honor understood what Timmons expected that to do to her. Once he might even have been right to expect it, too. But not now. The years when the shadow of Pavel Young had blighted her life were long over, for she'd come to grips with its poison. The days she'd spent working out with men had helped put it behind her, but what had truly forced the poison from her system had been Paul Tankersley's love, and she drew the memory of that love about her now, like armor. The animal behind the leering eyes gloating over her naked humiliation might be *male*, but whatever else he was, Honor would never call him a *man*, and the bottomless contempt she felt for him—and for all her captors—fused with her memories of Paul and her own refusal to let such creatures defeat her. It was that fusion of strengths, each potent in its own right and yet so much more than the sum of their parts when all of them flowed together, which let her catch the jumpsuit without even a change of expression or the flicker of an eyelid.

She started to put it on, gazing at the blank bulkhead as she ignored her guards, and under their surface delight in mocking and humiliating her, she sensed their deeper bafflement and anger. She confused them, for with no way to know the true wellsprings of her strength, they couldn't understand it. They couldn't grasp what allowed her to maintain her maddening lack of response, but they knew that it wasn't the same thing as *passivity*. That *this* prisoner chose to ignore them as a form of defiance, not escape or surrender. Whatever the source of her inner toughness, it allowed her to elude them in a deep, fundamental way no one else had ever achieved, and they hated her for it.

Honor understood their confusion. All their experience told them their abuse and systematic denial of her humanity should have broken her. It should have brought her defiance crashing down, for it always had before, and on the surface of things, she knew, it should have done so *this* time, as well.

Her grim, featureless cell had no mirror, but she didn't need one to know what she looked like. Their precious regulations proscribed any sort of cybernetic prostheses or bioenhancement for prisoners, and one of their techs had disabled her artificial eye . . . and the synthetic nerves in the left side of her face. It had been a gratuitous insult, a gloating deprivation which served no useful purpose. Certainly there had been no possible way in which her eye or facial nerves could be considered a "security risk"! But that hadn't prevented them from doing it, and the relative crudity of their tech base had prevented them from simply shutting her implants down. With neither the access codes nor the technology to derive them, they'd taken a brute force approach and simply burned them out, blinding her left eye and reducing half her face to dead, numb immobility. Honor suspected the damage was irreparable and that complete replacement would be required . . . or would have been, if she'd been going to live long enough to receive it.

Nor had their petty cruelties stopped there. They'd shaved her head under the guise of "hygiene," cutting away the braids she'd spent so many years growing. But there, at least, their efforts to dehumanize her had hit a pothole that actually amused her, for they seemed unaware that she'd cut her own hair almost that short for the better part of thirty years for the sake of convenience. Whatever they might have hoped, the loss of her braids was scarcely likely to cause her resistance to crumble.

Yet for all that her spirit remained unbroken, she also

knew, mirror or no, that her confinement was gradually grinding her away. Timmons seemed unaware of her enhanced metabolism or its need for fuel. She didn't know if that was true or if he simply wanted her to beg for the additional food she required, and it didn't really matter. She'd long since decided she would die before asking *him* for anything.

The living side of her face had grown gaunt, and her muscle tone was slowly rotting under the impact of poor diet and lack of exercise. She knew Cordelia Ransom had wanted her in good shape for the cameras when they hanged her, and she took a certain grim, perverse satisfaction in knowing what Ransom would actually get. Yet inside, where she guarded the walls of her spirit's fortress, she knew she was growing dangerously detached. She had no clear idea how long she'd been in this cell where the light and the temperature never changed, where there was nothing to read or do, where no distraction was ever offered except for her meals and the mocking humiliation of the guards. No doubt they were drawing close to their destination and her execution, yet somehow that hardly seemed to matter. She hadn't spoken a word to her captors in the entire time she'd been here—however long that had been—and she sometimes thought, in the drifting stillness of her thoughts when she was alone, that perhaps she had forgotten *how* to speak. In an odd sort of way, she'd become a mute, withdrawing from the parts of her brain which engaged others in conversation in order to buttress the vital areas of her core. There was a sense of diminution in that loss of speech, a sense of yet another anchor to the world about her fraying its cable, and she knew it was only one facet of her own deliberate internal disconnection from the sadists who controlled her physical existence.

But there was one other anchor, one her guards knew nothing about, which she knew would never fail her. It was faint, reduced by distance to a shadow of what it once had been, yet it was there, and because it was, she knew that Nimitz was still alive.

She clung to that anchor, not as a drowning woman to a spar, but as a lover to her beloved, for she felt his pain—physical, continuing still, and spiritual as *he* sensed *her* pain and could not heal it—and she knew that now, as never before, they needed one another. And that one blessing, at least, they had, for none of the sadistic, hating creatures aboard PNS *Tepes* ever guessed their link still existed, that they fed one another over it. Not with hope, for there *was* no hope, but with something more important. With love. With the absolute assurance that they would *always* be there for one another, that neither of them would be allowed to go down into the dark alone, whatever the Peeps intended.

And that was the final leg of her strength, the one Lieutenant Timmons and Sergeant Bergren and Corporal Hayman could never take from her.

She stepped into the bottom of the jumpsuit and started to work her arms into the top's sleeves, but a hand gripped her shoulder. She stopped dressing, standing motionless, and despite her hard-won detachment, her heart beat harder, for it was Bergren's hand.

"Getting close to arrival day, cell bait," he told her, and his gloating voice was right behind her ear, his breath hot on her bare skin. "Not long before that stiff neck of yours is gonna get a little *longer*." She said nothing, and not a muscle twitched, but he laughed, and his fingers squeezed her shoulder in a mocking parody of a caress. "I'm thinking maybe you'd like a little *comforting* before they haul your worthless ass to the gallows," he said, and his grip tightened, forcing her to turn to face him.

His eyes roamed over her, and she felt the sickness behind them. There was no trace of comparison between the lust *he* felt and what she and Paul had shared. Indeed, Bergren's diseased hunger was worse even than what she had sensed from Pavel Young. Young had hated her. He'd wanted to punish her because her rejection of his advances had humiliated him in front of those he considered his peers. It had been a stupid, shallow hate—the hate of a person to whom other human beings were never people, but simply *things* which existed for his convenience—but at least it had been personal.

Bergren's hate wasn't. It didn't *matter* to him who or what she was, except in as much as her passive resistance had frustrated his efforts to make her fear him. She might have been anyone—anyone at all—for the only thing that truly mattered to him was the infliction of pain. Physical, mental, spiritual . . . that didn't matter to him either, for his need to hurt and punish sprang not from any specific offense anyone had ever committed against him. It sprang from *all* of them, from every real or imagined slight or indignity he had ever "suffered." There was nothing to him *but* hate, and an empty core which hungered to devour and destroy anyone who refused to share his hate.

Her artificial left eye was dead, its pupil fixed and its focus unchanging, but despite all she could do, her right eye flickered with cold contempt for the human-shaped corruption before her, and his mouth tightened in a snarl.

"Yeah, cell bait," he told her, his voice softer and still uglier. "I think you *need* some comfort. So why don't you just open those legs of yours?"

He licked his lips, and his eyes flicked to the female guard. Not that there was any chance she might intervene, for she was as diseased as any of Timmons' male personnel, and *her* anticipation was even more sickening than Bergren's.

"C'mere, cell bait," he whispered, and the hand on her shoulder pulled her closer while his free hand reached for her breasts.

But it never touched them. As he reached forward, Honor's left hand shot up like a striking viper, and he hissed in sudden pain as her fingers locked on his wrist like a vise. He tried to jerk free, but her hand might have been a steel clamp. Her passivity had lulled him into forgetting her heavy-grav origins, just as it had convinced him she would *always* be passive, and sudden fear—darker, uglier, and far stronger for its total unexpectedness—flickered in his eyes as she tightened her grip still further and the right side of her mouth curved in a parody of a smile.

"Get your hand off me."

The five words came out with a soft, dangerous clarity which surprised even Honor after so many endless days of silence. There was steel behind them, and a hunger which echoed Bergren's own, and for just an instant, they froze his blood. But he recovered quickly, and stepped forward, trying to drive her back against the bulkhead.

It didn't work. She scarcely even swayed, and then he grunted hoarsely, as she twisted her hand and the sudden explosion of pain in his wrist drove him to his knees.

"Let him up, bitch!" The other guard stepped forward, reaching for the truncheon on her belt, and Honor turned her head to look into the other woman's eyes.

"Touch me with that club, and I'll break your spine," she said flatly, and the SS woman froze before her total assurance. Then she shook herself.

"I don't think so, cell bait!" she sneered. "You aren't going anywhere even if you do, and you won't like what the *rest* of 'em will do if you even try. Besides, you've got friends topside, remember?"

She stepped forward with renewed confidence . . . and Bergren screamed as his wrist snapped in Honor's grip. She kicked him away from her and turned to face his companion, and the female guard flinched away from the cold, hungry fire in her eye.

"You're right," Honor told her softly. "I *do* have friends 'topside,' and you can make me play your sick little games by threatening them. But not this one. Not even for them. And in case you've forgotten, Ransom wants me 'undamaged,' remember? So play your other games, Peep, but tell the rest of the garbage there are limits." Bergren started to heave to his knees, clutching his wrist, but Honor's right foot shot out, and its bare sole crashed into his mouth. He slammed into the corner, groaning and half-conscious, and the other guard shuddered—afraid, and hating Honor all the more for her fear.

"You can come back with your friends and do whatever you want," she said in that same soft voice. "I know that. But you'd better bring *all* of them, Peep, and after it's over, there's no way—no way in this universe—you'll deliver me to Ransom alive."

The live half of her lips smiled a thin, terrifying smile, and the guard stepped back involuntarily, clutching her truncheon, trying to understand how the balance of power in this cell could shift so totally in such a tiny instant when *she* held all the cards. But then she looked into the single brown eye of the gaunt, half-naked woman facing her, and a wolf looked back at her—a wounded pack leader, starved and weakened, who had been goaded and harried by the hounds on its back trail but would be harried no more. A wolf who would die where it stood rather than be driven further. A wolf, she realized shakenly, who was actually willing—perhaps even *eager*—to die if only it could lock its fangs on the throats of the mongrels howling at its heels.

She looked into that hungry, dangerous eye, and she knew then. Knew exactly how the balance had shifted.

She removed her hand very carefully from her truncheon, and, never taking her eyes from Honor's face, bent down, hoisted a moaning, semiconscious Bergren to his feet, and dragged him from the cell without another word. And as she locked the door behind her, a deeply hidden part of her wondered uneasily if she was locking the wolf *into* its cage . . . or herself safely outside it.

• Chapter Twenty-Six

"So what's on the schedule today?"

Horace Harkness, late of the Manticoran Navy, leaned back in the comfortable recliner, hands folded behind his head, and wiggled his bootless toes at his "escorts" as he asked the question. Citizen Corporal Heinrich Johnson and Citizen Private Hugh Candleman had been assigned as his permanent keepers when he decided to change sides. Their purpose had been plain enough—to discourage any thoughts of inappropriate activities on his part—and Harkness knew the two State Security goons had been chosen because they were big, strong, tough, and well trained in the art of dismantling their fellow man with their bare hands. It was, perhaps, unfortunate that those qualities pretty much exhausted the list of their employable skills, but no one could have everything.

"Not much—I think," Johnson replied. The corporal wasn't as broad as Harkness, but he was several centimeters taller, and he looked impressive in his black-and-red uniform as he fished in his tunic pocket for his memo pad. He found it and keyed the display, then squinted down at it. "Got another HD interview scheduled for thirteen-thirty," he announced after a moment. "Then Citizen Commander Jewel wants to talk to you about the Manties' com systems some more. That's scheduled for, uh, seventeen hundred. 'Side from that, you've got nothing but free time." He shoved the pad back into his pocket and chuckled. "Looks like they must really like you, Harkness."

"What's not to like?" Harkness replied with a lazy grin, and both StateSec men laughed. A prize like Horace

Harkness didn't drop into Public Information's lap every day, and the fact that he was a missile tech familiar with the FTL transmitters mounted in the Manties' recon drones made him even more valuable as a source of technical data R&D would make good use of. But the larger implications of propaganda broadcasts and technological information were beyond Johnson and Candleman's mental horizons. They had their own reasons to be happy Harkness had decided to defect, and those reasons had nothing at all to do with his value to the PRH in general.

"So, you have any luck with Farley's Crossing yet?" Candleman asked now, and Harkness' grin turned from lazy to evil.

"Oh ye of little faith," he murmured. "I told you I could, ah, *enhance* the odds, didn't I? Here."

He drew a data chip from his shirt pocket and scaled it across the compartment to Candleman, who caught it eagerly. The private peered down at the featureless chip as if he thought he should be able to read its data with his unassisted eye, and for all Harkness knew, Candleman *did* think so.

"How's it work?" Johnson asked from where he lounged against the opposite bulkhead, and Harkness shrugged.

"It's a more complicated than the others 'cause there's so many more variables," he said, "and the multiplayer versions complicate things even further. So instead of setting it up so you guys can *predict* the outcome, I set it up so you can *force* the outcome while you're playing."

"Huh?" Candleman put in, and Harkness hid a desire to sigh in exasperation behind another friendly smile.

Technically, both his watchdogs were high school graduates, and Johnson actually had two years of college on his résumé. Unfortunately—or fortunately, depending upon one's perspective—they'd both been Dolists, and their schooling had been provided courtesy of the PRH's educational system. It had been theoretically possible to acquire a worthwhile education from that source, but doing so had required an individual to use the resources available to educate *himself*, because after so many decades of debasing the concept of achievement in the name of "democratization" and "student validation," no one in the teaching establishment had had a clue as to how to truly educate someone *else*.

The problem was that genuinely self-motivated people are rare. Without someone else to explain it to them, most young people don't understand why learning is important in the first place. There are always exceptions to that broad generalization, but the majority of human beings learn from experience, not precept, and until someone experiences the consequences of being *un*educated, he seldom feels a driving need to correct the situation. Creating a desire to learn in someone who hasn't already been caught in the gears requires an entire support structure, a society in which one's elders make it clear that one is *expected* to acquire knowledge and training in its use. And that sort of society was precisely what the prewar Dolists had lacked, for the Basic Living Stipend had been handed over like clockwork however unproductive they might have been. Besides, what had there been for a Dolist to use an education *on?*

Perhaps even worse, the prewar Legislaturalists had gone to some lengths to make the answer to that last question "nothing," for knowledge was a dangerous thing. They hadn't *wanted* the Dolists educated or involved in making the system work. They might have been an almost intolerable, parasitic drag on a moribund economy, but as long as the BLS had sufficed to support their accustomed lifestyles, they'd felt no particular urge to demand the right to participate in the making of political decisions. That, after all, had been the original bargain between their ancestors and those of the Legislaturalists. In return for being "taken care of," the citizens of the PRH had surrendered all decision-making to the people who ran the machine, and until the machine collapsed, no one had felt any need to fix the host of things wrong with it.

On the grand scale, the mutual suicide pact between the Legislaturalists and their education establishment was academic as far as Harkness was concerned, but on a *personal* level, its consequences had become very important indeed, for Johnson and Candleman were typical products of the system from which they came. That meant they suffered from an appalling ignorance few Manticorans would have believed was possible. People who could barely handle basic math or, like Candleman, suffered from what anything but the Peep Office of Education would have called functional illiteracy, were of strictly limited utility to a modern war machine, because maintaining or servicing any equipment more complex than a pulse rifle required at least *some* familiarity with the basic principles of electronics, cybernetics, gravity theory, and any of scores of other disciplines. Anyone could be trained to *operate* modern hardware—simply surviving in a technological society required at least a surface competence—but for people like Johnson and Candleman, that competence was like the math ability conferred by learning to make change in a shopping mall. They had no more comprehension of what went on behind the input keys and the displays than someone from preindustrial Terra would have had.

That was the main reason the majority of maintenance duties in the People's Navy were assigned either to officers or to senior noncoms. If the prewar PN had wanted competent technicians, it had been forced to train them itself, and it simply hadn't had most of its conscripts long enough to overcome the disabilities with which they arrived. Its only real choice had been to train them first as operators and only secondly as true technicians, and that took time. Years of it, in most cases, which meant it was only really practical to train the people who formed its long-term, professional core.

The People's Marines had faced the same problems, though on a somewhat lesser scale. Battle armor and support weapons weren't something one wanted in the hands of technical ignoramuses, and the days when the dregs of an uneducated society could be turned into first-line soldiers without massive remedial training had gone out with the bolt-action rifle, but the Marines had always been a long-service outfit, with a lower percentage of conscripts. Coupled with their (relatively) simpler equipment, they'd been able to impose a more uniform level of training which came far closer to matching the tactical competence of their Manticoran counterparts, although maintenance remained a chronic problem even for them.

But the heavy losses the People's Navy and Marines had suffered in the opening stages of the war—not to mention the officer purges which had followed the Harris Assassinations and the casualties suffered in things like the Leveller Uprising—had cut dangerously deep into the military's trained manpower. The Committee of Public Safety had acted to recall veterans who had completed their terms of service, which had *almost* covered the initial shortfalls, but the only real solution had to be the education and training of the required replacements to a modern standard . . . preferably *before* they got to boot camp. There were enough realists in the PRH to recognize that, and whatever her other shortcomings, Cordelia Ransom had managed to sell it to the Mob, as well. In a sort of insanely twisted logic, the need to fight a war started to preserve a parasitic life style had led to a situation in which the parasites in question were actually willing, even eager, to abandon their parasite status, repair their schools, and learn how to provide the support their military required. It was a pity the thought of making the same repairs hadn't occurred to anyone when it might actually have *averted* the war in the first place.

In the meantime, however, people with real educations remained in critically short supply, and they were needed not just for the military, but also to operate the Republic's civilian and industrial infrastructure. Balancing personnel allocations between the combat arms and the people who made the weapons with which the combat arms fought remained an enormous problem for the PRH. The situation was improving—and far more quickly than the more complacent Allied leaders would have believed possible—

but for the foreseeable future, manpower supplies would remain tight.

But there was at least one area in which people with minimal educations could be readily employed by the State, and that brought Harkness back to Johnson and Candleman. There was nothing fundamentally wrong with the mind either of them had been issued; it was simply that no one had ever bothered to acquaint those minds with their own potentials. They were ignorant, not stupid, and State Security didn't need hyper physicists. For that matter, even with ships like *Tepes* in its inventory, StateSec didn't need an enormous number of missile and gravitics techs, and those could be poached from the Navy with a suitable use of the security forces' absolute priority.

What StateSec *did* need, however, were shock troops and enforcers who could be relied upon to take orders and break the heads of any enemies of the People at whom they might be aimed. Seventy-five or eighty percent of its personnel fell into that category, and it didn't take a lot of education to squeeze a pulser trigger or club a dissenter. By the standards of their peers, Johnson and Candleman were of above average ability . . . and neither of them would have been allowed to serve aboard any ship to which Harkness had ever been assigned anyway. There was a point, after all, where ignorance *became* stupidity, for one could hardly expect people, however inherently bright, to allow for or protect themselves against dangers no one had ever bothered to tell them existed.

And just at the moment, Harkness' watchdogs were demonstrating that very fact.

"Look," he said after a moment, still smiling at Candleman, "Farley's Crossing isn't like the other games I've, um, *modified* for you guys. This one's actually a simplified version of a real Navy training simulator, and that means its parameters are a *lot* more complex than the other packages, right?"

He paused, eyebrows raised, and Candleman glanced at Johnson. The corporal nodded, which seemed to reassure him, and he turned attentively back to Harkness.

The Manticoran felt a brief twinge of guilt as the StateSec thug looked at him with trusting eyes terrifyingly devoid of any understanding of what he was talking about. Harkness had spent enough time in the service to feel confident that anyone StateSec might have assigned to him would have been receptive to the concept of rigging the ship's electronic games library. The combination of boredom, greed, and a very human (if ignoble) desire to put one over on one's fellows had produced the same ambition in virtually every Manticoran ship in which Harkness had ever served, and those factors operated even more strongly aboard *Tepes*. Still, he knew he'd been lucky to draw these two, for Johnson was an operator and black marketeer from way back. He was actually quite competent within the limits of what he knew, but he was also as greedy as they came, and neither he nor Candleman had the background to realize the consequences of giving Harkness access to the games library.

Not that Harkness had leapt right out to make the offer. The possibility of doing anything which might jeopardize his arrangement with Committeewoman Ransom was unthinkable, and so he'd done exactly what was asked of him. He'd recorded dozens of propaganda broadcasts in which he cheerfully perjured his immortal soul with accounts of all the "war crimes" he'd either observed or helped commit. Other recordings, when they were broadcast, would appeal earnestly to his ex-countrymen to follow his example and defect to their true class allies rather than continuing to serve their plutocratic exploiters. And while he'd been careful to warn Citizen Commander Jewel that he was only a technician with a severely limited understanding of the theory behind the grav pulse generators he'd learned to service, he'd also spent hours discussing the system with her and giving her pointers towards how it worked. By now, he calculated, he'd committed at least thirty different forms of treason—certainly enough to make it impossible (or, at least, fatally *inadvisable*) for him ever to return home.

As he'd proved his bona fides to their superiors and received a steadily greater freedom of movement, Johnson and Candleman had come to regard their guard duty as more and more of a formality. The awe inspiring heights his own black market and smuggling activities had attained during his pre-Basilisk career hadn't hurt, either. Once Johnson's guard came down and the two of them began swapping tales of past exploits, the corporal had quickly realized he was in the presence of either a true maestro whose attainments dwarfed anything he himself had ever even dared to contemplate, or the greatest liar in the known universe.

As the tales accumulated, he'd been forced to accept that Harkness truly was a man of enormous talent . . . and a kindred soul. He'd sought advice—cautiously, at first—on certain of his own operations, and Harkness' suggestions had increased his profit margin by over twenty percent within the first week. From there, it had been a natural enough step to introduce him to the gambling empire the corporal helped run on the side. The real head of illicit operations aboard *Tepes* was Staff Sergeant Boyce, but Johnson was one of his senior assistants, and the fact that gambling aboard ship was totally against regulations made Boyce's empire even more lucrative, since no one was likely to go to an officer and complain over any losses he might suffer. But the sergeant was always on the lookout for ways to maximize his profits, and he'd been delighted when Johnson was able to up his take by something like forty percent. He'd also decided not to ask the corporal how he'd managed it—on the theory, apparently, that what he didn't know he couldn't be guilty of—and turned the entire gaming operation over to Johnson.

Which, in many ways, meant he'd actually turned it over to Horace Harkness, for the games in *Tepes'* libraries were far easier to manipulate than any which would have been found aboard a Manticoran ship.

Harkness had been astounded when he realized just how obsolescent they were. Several were actually variants of games he'd first encountered fifty T-years before, at the very beginning of his naval career. He'd always assumed—correctly, as it turned out—that the Peeps' military hardware (and the software that ran it) had to be at least comparable to the RMN's. It was clearly inferior, but if it hadn't been at least within shouting range, the war would have been over years ago. That assumption was the reason it hadn't occurred to him that something which formed the basis for shipboard gambling could be so extremely simpleminded . . . or have such primitive security features. It was a given that any game which could be rigged *would* be rigged, sooner or later, and those aboard Manticoran ships were regularly inspected by electronics teams from Engineering to be sure they hadn't been. Perhaps more to the point, the people who designed those games (and their security features) knew some very clever, *extremely* well-trained people would bend all their formidable talents on *breaking* those security features.

But there weren't all that many well-trained people in the People's Navy . . . and there were even fewer in StateSec. Which meant the games library contained an entire raft of programs with security arrangements which were laughably simple for anyone who'd cut his eyeteeth on *Manticoran* software. Harkness had started out slowly, altering the odds slightly in the house's favor on half a dozen card and dice games. He hadn't needed to do any more than that to prove his point, and Johnson's avarice had taken over nicely from there.

From Harkness' viewpoint, there'd been a large element of risk in the project. Not in fixing the software—that part had been child's play—but because in order to fix it in the first place, he'd had to have access to the library in which it was stored, and if Johnson's superiors had discovered even an *ex*-Manticoran had any such thing, the consequences would have been dire. But Johnson had every reason to conceal what was going on . . . and no idea *why* his superiors would have been upset.

As far as Johnson or Candleman were concerned, the games library was merely that: the *games* library. It was simply a place somewhere in the mass of computers they didn't really understand where the games were stored, and they knew *they* had no access to anything else in the system. But Horace Harkness was an artist. His ability to work the RMN personnel system to ensure that he always wound up assigned wherever Scotty Tremaine was assigned had baffled many an observer, but that was because none of them realized he'd actually managed to hack into BuPers' records. He might have reformed considerably since his first tour on Basilisk Station with Tremaine and Lady Harrington, and he'd certainly abandoned the various contraband operations he'd maintained on the side, but a man liked to keep his hand in. . . . And the security fences which had been erected to block a crew of techno-illiterates from access they shouldn't have were laughable barriers for anyone who'd broken the security on the classified records of the Royal Manticoran Navy's Bureau of Personnel.

Which meant that, for the last two weeks, Harkness had prowled the bowels of PNS *Tepes'* information and control systems almost at will. Aside from tinkering with the gaming software, he'd been careful to make no changes lest he leave footprints which could be tracked back to him, but he'd amassed an enormous amount of knowledge about the ship, its course, its destination, its crew, and its operating procedures. The fact that Johnson and Candleman regarded his hacking activities as nothing short of black magic had helped enormously, for they'd granted him the sort of working privacy which had been the prerogative of wizards throughout history. That meant he hadn't had to figure out a way to carry out his explorations while they looked over his shoulder every second. In fact, they normally left him undisturbed on one side of the compartment, working away on the minicomp they'd been thoughtful enough to provide, while they played old-fashioned poker on the other side. Just to be safe, he'd created his own version of what was still called a "boss program" to instantly shift the display to something innocuous if one of them had decided to get curious, but he'd scarcely ever needed it.

In fact, his biggest problem now was that he'd completed his preparations. Only a fraction of the hours he'd spent on the minicomp had actually been devoted to modifying game software, but Johnson and Candleman assumed his time had all been directed towards the ends they knew about, and if he suddenly cut back on those hours but continued to keep up with their requests for software modification, even they might begin to wonder why it was suddenly taking so much less time. That was why he'd suggested altering Farley's Crossing, which was an extremely simplistic recreation of the last major fleet engagement ever fought by the navy of the Solarian League. Simplistic or no, a game designed to let up to ten players on a side control over six hundred ships was more complicated than the other games by several orders of magnitude, and he'd been confident that the time required to put in the fix would eat up his free time quite nicely.

But now that it was finished, he still had to explain it to his partners in crime, and he drew a deep breath.

"You see," he began, "there are an enormous number of variables in this program, and the fact that, in a really big game, every ship in it is being individually controlled by someone—by another human player, not simply the computer—only makes that worse. That means I've gotta be careful how I come at it, 'cause any brute force approach is likely to be pretty damned noticeable, okay?"

Candleman said nothing, but Johnson nodded.

"I can see that," the corporal agreed. "You figure that if, say, the order of arrival in the Tango Variant suddenly started favoring the Sollies every time it was played, or if one player's ships started disobeying his orders, somebody'd get wise."

"Exactly!" Harkness congratulated him. "So what I did, I set it up so that when you plug one of the user IDs I've flagged into the player queue, you get a little edge. You'll have to be careful using it, but basically, if you double-tap the firing key in an iffy situation, the computer will add a fifty-percent bonus to your probability of scoring a hit."

"Oh boy! *That* part I understand!" Candleman put in happily.

"Figured you would," Harkness told him with a grin. "Like I say, you've gotta be careful not to overuse it, but it should give you a good advantage in a close situation. I've also worked in an adjustment to the damage allocation subroutine. If one of 'our' ships takes a hit, the damage allocator will reduce the damage applied to it. That part still needs a little work to fine tune it, and I've got a few more ideas, but basically, what you guys are gonna have to do is play this one out on a game-for-game basis. 'Course, with this kind of edge, you oughta be able to sharp some poor sucker pretty damned well."

"I'd think so, yeah," Johnson agreed with a smile. "Thanks." He took the chip from Candleman and bounced it in his palm for a moment. "You're all right, Harkness," he said after a second. "And you're worth every centicredit of your cut, too."

"Glad you think so," Harkness said with an answering smile. "I like to think I earn my way wherever I am, Corp, and I always look after my friends."

• Chapter Twenty-Seven

"Message from *Tepes*, Citizen Admiral."

Lester Tourville raised a hand at Citizen Lieutenant Fraiser's announcement, interrupting his conversation with Citizen Captain Bogdanovich and Everard Honeker, and turned towards the com officer.

"What does it say, Harrison?" His voice carried no emotion whatsoever, yet its very neutrality seemed to shout his tension, for *Count Tilly* was six hundred and ninety hours out of Barnett, with the white, G3 furnace of Cerberus-B twenty-four light-minutes ahead of her.

"*Tepes* will continue to a parking orbit around Hades, but we're to place ourselves in orbit around Cerberus-B-3, Citizen Admiral," Fraiser replied respectfully, then paused and cleared his throat. "There's a personal attachment from Citizen Committeewoman Ransom," he added. "She says that you, Citizen Commissioner Honeker, Citizen Captain Bogdanovich, and Citizen Commander Foraker should report to her on Hades by pinnace at oh-nine-hundred local tomorrow."

"Well isn't that just ducky," Bogdanovich grunted with an obvious disgust every member of Tourville's staff understood only too well. Their original orders had been to accompany *Tepes* clear to Hades, and the abrupt change at this late date struck all of them as being almost as incompetent as it was insulting. "They don't want a Navy ship any closer to their precious prison than they have to let her," Bogdanovich went on. "Probably think we'd open fire on it or some goddamned thing!"

The chief of staff's vicious voice carried an outright hatred he would never have allowed to show a month before. It cut like a lash, but Honeker didn't even bat an eyelid. He'd had plenty of time during the voyage here to realize he was just as doomed as Tourville and his officers. He supposed he should blame Tourville for that, but he couldn't. He'd gone into it with open eyes, and he was still convinced the Navy officer had been right. Cordelia Ransom's determination to have Honor Harrington judicially murdered was going to be a disaster for everyone, not just for the people who'd tried to prevent it. The Solarian League would be almost as infuriated as the Manties and their allies, which could have devastating consequences for the movement of technology from the League to the PRH, and altogether too many members of the Republic's own military would be just as sickened and shamed by it as Tourville had predicted. And quite aside from all the pragmatic considerations that made executing her an act of lunacy, trying to keep Harrington alive had been the right thing to do morally, as well.

No, much as he regretted—and feared—the consequences, Honeker couldn't fault Tourville for making the effort or enlisting his own tacit support. And that had produced an odd effect on Everard Honeker. He'd come aboard *Count Tilly*, and before that aboard Tourville's old flagship, *Rash al-Din*, to spy on him for StateSec and the Committee of Public Safety, and though he'd learned to like the aggressive, hard-fighting rear admiral, he'd never forgotten he was Tourville's keeper. That there must always be that sense of separation, of standing apart and watching warily for signs of unreliability.

But the separation had vanished now. Perhaps it was only because Honeker knew they were both doomed, yet it was a vast relief nonetheless. And partly, he knew, it was because he no longer had to lie—to others or to himself—to justify actions he'd always known deep inside *couldn't* be justified. By betraying and condemning him for trying to do his duty despite its own idiocy, the system had finally freed him from his bondage to it, and he

realized—now—that "unreliables" like Lester Tourville
and his staff were far better champions of the cause he'd
once thought the Committee served than people like
Cordelia Ransom could ever be.

Unaware of the thoughts behind his people's commissioner's silence, Tourville simply nodded to Bogdanovich,
for the citizen captain was obviously correct. The entire
Cerberus System was a monumental tribute to the institutional paranoia of the PRH's security services, old and new
alike. Its coordinates weren't even in *Count Tilly*'s astro-
gation database, for the very existence of the system, much
less its location, had been classified by the Office of Internal
Security when the old regime first authorized Camp
Charon's construction. Even today—or perhaps *especially*
today—that information was a fanatically guarded secret
known only to StateSec, and the fact that no one else had
the slightest idea of where to find it was but the first layer
of a defense in depth.

In all his years of naval service, Tourville had seldom
seen orbital defenses as massive as those which surrounded Hades—otherwise known as Cerberus–B-2—and
its three largish moons. The data on it available to *Count
Tilly* was severely limited, but Citizen Captain Vladovich
had given her a fragmentary download when it was
assumed she would accompany *Tepes* all the way in. He'd
had to, for the planet-moon system was literally
smothered with firepower which would have made short
work of any ship which made a single wrong move. Yet
even a cursory glance at Vladovich's information had been
enough to show that StateSec's chronic distrust had
produced a bizarre defensive arrangement whose like
neither Tourville nor any member of his staff had ever
imagined.

There wasn't a single manned fortress in the entire star
system. Shoals of mines—old-fashioned "contact" nukes
designed to kill small craft as well as the laser buoys
designed to shoot LACs and starships, and both seemingly
thick enough to walk across—surrounded the planet and

its moons, seeded with more sophisticated and modern energy platforms for good measure, and he suspected there were ground-based missiles on the planet, at least, if not on the moons. Taken all together, Hades must have had the raw combat power of a full squadron of super-dreadnoughts . . . but *all* of those weapons were remote-controlled from Camp Charon. There wasn't even an orbital cargo station. *Everything* within a good light-minute of the planet was covered by massive amounts of firepower, but no permanent manned orbital presence of any sort had been tolerated, and Tourville wondered why that was.

To be sure, minefields and energy platforms were cheaper than manned systems would have been, and because they *weren't* manned, there was no need to come up with personnel to crew them. Of course, "cheap" was a purely relative term where defenses on this scale were concerned, but even purely relative savings mounted up. He could understand that, just as he understood that StateSec's decision—like that of InSec, before it—to conceal this place's location from its own military had meant they couldn't call in Navy personnel to man its defenses. But surely they could have come up with sufficient personnel of their own to man at least a *cargo* station! That would have tremendously simplified the transshipment of freight (and prisoners) from orbit to surface, so why not do it? Were they so paranoid they didn't trust *anyone*, even their own, in orbit above them?

He didn't know the answer to that, and he doubted he ever would. Nor did he understand why they'd bothered with orbital defenses at all. If they weren't going to let the Navy know where the system was and put a picket force into it, then all the mines and remote energy platforms in the galaxy were ultimately useless, for a planet suffered from one enormous tactical disadvantage: it couldn't dodge. An attacker always knew *exactly* where it was, and that meant a single battlecruiser—probably even a *heavy* cruiser—could take out every weapon orbiting Hades with old-fashioned nuclear warheads launched on purely ballistic courses from beyond the defenses' own range. A few dozen fifty or sixty-megaton detonations would blow gaping holes in the massive, interlocking shells of mines, and not even modern hardening could have prevented the EMP from at least temporarily crippling the electronics of any spaceborne platform that survived outright destruction. He supposed ground-based missiles on the planet or its moons (if, in fact, there *were* some) would survive, but any competent defensive planner knew purely orbital systems— even proper fortresses with bubble sidewalls—were ultimately useless against mobile attackers.

The only explanation he could come up with was that whoever had ordered the immense (and wasted) expenditure to put this abortion together hadn't bothered to *consult* a competent defensive planner. Well, that actually made a sort of sense, didn't it? If you distrusted your own military personnel so much that you refused even to tell them a prison existed, far less where it was, lest they decide to attack it for some unimaginable reason, then you were hardly likely to ask those same people for advice on how to fortify it against *themselves*, now were you?

But whatever the rationale behind the emplacements, Yuri was right; the paranoiacs who'd put them up would never allow a warship manned by anyone except their own people any closer to Hades than they had to. And parking *Count Tilly* clear out around Cerberus–B-3 would put her a full seventeen light-minutes from the prison planet—and condemn Tourville, Honeker, Bogdanovich, and Foraker to an almost three-hour pinnace flight to reach it. Well, at least *Tilly* would be well outside the range of the defensive shell, too. In his present mood, Lester Tourville had to consider that a major plus.

"Very well," he said to Fraiser at last. "I assume Citizen Captain Hewitt already has that information?" Fraiser nodded, and Tourville shrugged. "In that case, inform Citizen Committeewoman Ransom her message has been received."

No one on Flag Bridge missed the fact that he hadn't told Fraiser to *acknowledge* Ransom's message, thus confirming her orders would actually be obeyed. Nor did any of them, including Honeker, fail to grasp that by Navy standards, a simple, curt notice of receipt was, in fact, a none-too-veiled insult to the message's originator. It was possible Ransom might not realize that, but, frankly, Tourville no longer really *cared* what Cordelia Ransom did or did not realize.

Count Tilly's vector diverged gradually from *Tepes'*, and Tourville watched the small, bright dot of Cerberus–B-3 grow slowly on the main view screen.

Horace Harkness twitched as the chrono under his pillow beeped. He'd taken it off his wrist and shoved it under the pillow to keep its sound from waking anyone else, and he swallowed a silent curse as it beeped again. He hadn't been to sleep all night, though no one would have thought it to look at him—or he hoped they wouldn't have, anyway—and he'd set the alarm as the only way he could think of to keep himself from checking the time at compulsive five-minute intervals. He'd been confident the pillow would swallow its sound completely, yet now that the thing had gone off, its muted voice seemed to echo in the darkened compartment like thunder.

But that was all in his mind, he told himself firmly—not that his pulse rate seemed impressed by his firmness. It was only because the beep told him it was time to put his plans into operation. Well, that and the fact that he realized just what a piss-poor chance he had of actually carrying all this off. Unfortunately, they were the only plans he'd been able to come up with, which didn't offer him a lot of options.

The chrono beeped yet again, and his hand darted under the pillow to silence it. Then he drew a deep breath, licked his lips, and sat up in his bunk. He swung his legs over the side and stood very slowly, bare feet silent on the decksole. Heinrich Johnson's deep, slow breathing and

Hugh Candleman's nasal snores didn't even falter, and his jaw clenched. This was the part he'd hated most when he planned it, but he had no choice, and he drifted across the deck like a ghost. The faint glow of the night-light Candleman insisted on leaving on lent a dim illumination to the compartment, which let him watch where he was going as he moved noiselessly towards Johnson's bunk. He reached its head and paused, drawing another of those deep silent breaths, and then he struck.

His left hand snapped out, grasping Johnson's chin and yanking it upward, pushing the back of the StateSec man's head harder into his pillow and arching his neck. The corporal's eyes opened, unfocused and confused, but he hadn't even realized he was awake, much less what was happening, when Harkness' right hand came down like an axe. Johnson started to suck in air, but any shout he might have given died in an agonized wheeze as his larynx shattered. He thrashed and jerked, hands pawing at his throat while he fought for breath that wouldn't come, but Harkness had already turned away. Heinrich Johnson was already a dead man; he simply hadn't realized it yet, and Harkness still had Candleman to worry about.

The second StateSec guard made a snorting sound and stirred sleepily. For all their violence, Johnson's death throes weren't very loud, and Candleman never had a chance to realize what the harsh, choking sounds which *had* penetrated his sleep might portend. He was still moving muzzily towards the boundary of wakefulness when two callused hands locked on his head and twisted explosively. For just an instant, the sickening crunch of vertebrae seemed to completely bury the sounds of Johnson's fading, desperate efforts to breathe, and then those sounds, too, died, and Horace Harkness stood back in the darkness, closed his eyes, and shuddered with sick loathing.

It wasn't the first time he'd killed, but it *was* the first time he'd killed someone he actually knew or done it with his bare hands rather than missiles or an energy mount, and it was different this way. He felt unclean, for neither Johnson nor Candleman had even guessed what was coming. But that had been the point. He couldn't have *allowed* them to guess, and so he'd had to become their partner—their good friend and buddy the venal ex-Manty—so that he could murder them in their sleep.

His fists clenched at his sides, and he stood motionless but for the tiny shudders he couldn't quite still. But then his nostrils flared, and he opened his eyes once more. He'd already been through this when he planned the entire thing, and he'd been right then. He'd had no choice, and he knew it, and however pleasant Johnson and Candleman might have been drinking beer while they planned their next scam, they'd also been StateSec thugs. God only knew how many people they'd helped others of their kind to torture or kill. That thought might be an attempt to salve his conscience, but that didn't make it untrue, either, and he turned away from the dead men to their lockers.

Both of them were locked, but Horace Harkness had opened quite a few locks which had belonged to someone else over the course of a checkered career, and he had the advantage of having watched their owners open these dozens of times. He input the combinations quickly, and his mouth twitched in a hungry smile as the lockers' internal lights gleamed on his dead watchdogs' weapons.

He strapped Johnson's gun belt around his own waist before he drew and checked the pulser. Magazine and capacitor both showed full, and he went quickly through the belt pouches to confirm the presence of extra magazines and power packs. Then he shoved one of the corporal's uniform tunics and a pair of trousers into a laundry bag and turned to Candleman's locker. He made the same check on the private's side arm and hung the second gun belt diagonally from right shoulder to left hip like a bandoleer, then closed the lockers, scooped up the minicomp he'd used to rig the game software, and plugged it into the access slot on the compartment bulkhead.

He used Johnson's password to log on. Had computers cared about such things, *Tepes'* computer might have been amazed by the quantum leap in the programming skills of Citizen Corporal Heinrich Johnson, SN SS-1002-56722-0531-HV. But computers *didn't* care, and Harkness flipped quickly through the pathways he'd established while Johnson and Candleman assumed he was simply rigging the outcomes of games for them.

He hadn't dared make any major changes on the main system lest one of the officers or NCOs who were computer literate stumble across his work, but that hadn't prevented him from making all those changes well in advance on the minicomp. Of course, seeing to it his little packages were activated at the proper time and in the proper order was going to be a bit of a problem, but he hoped he'd taken that sufficiently into account. And there was one bit of programming he *had* been forced to change ahead of time. Now he checked it and grunted in satisfaction; it had activated eighteen minutes and twenty-one seconds earlier, exactly as instructed, and he grinned. There were still a thousand things that could go wrong, but that had been the part that worried him most. Now he had to do the *next* most dangerous bit, and he flicked a function key.

As far as anyone else aboard PNS *Tepes* was concerned, nothing at all happened, but Harkness and his minicomp knew better. Throughout the battlecruiser's electronic guts, half a dozen programs changed abruptly, overwritten by the versions of themselves which Harkness had downloaded to his minicomp and altered—in most cases subtly; in others not so subtly—days or even weeks before.

Despite the size of some of the programs and program groups involved, the substitutions flicked into place with a speed which would have been inconceivable to anyone who'd lived in the days of chips and printed circuits, and the breath Harkness hadn't realized he was holding whooshed out as confirmation of his commands' execution blinked on his display. Then he logged off, pulled the minicomp out of its slot, shoved it into his pocket, slung the laundry bag with Johnson's uniform over his shoulder, and walked quickly to the end of the compartment. The ventilation grille would be a tight fit, but that was the least of his worries at the moment.

Warner Caslet squared his shoulders and straightened his spine as the lift stopped and the doors slid open. The last four weeks had been even worse than he'd expected, less because of any active unpleasantness than because of his complete impotence. He'd known exactly what was going to happen to Honor Harrington and her people, and there'd been no more he could do about *that* than there'd been anything he could do about whatever Cordelia Ransom intended to do with *him*. He was a bit surprised, when he thought about it, that she'd been content to leave her "military liaison" with the prisoners alone for so long, though that might have been because he'd underestimated her intelligence. Perhaps she'd simply realized that the longer she kept the Sword of Damocles suspended above his head, the worse it would hurt when she finally let it fall and proved any hope he'd allowed himself to feel was only an illusion.

But whatever else might be about to happen, *Tepes* was about to cross the perimeter of the satellites protecting the planet Hades. In fact, she was little more than half an hour out of parking orbit, though he wasn't really supposed to know that. He didn't quite understand the point in trying to conceal it from him, unless it was simply part of StateSec's mania for keeping *everything* to itself, but it hadn't proved particularly difficult to discover anyway. And because he knew what was about to happen, he'd decided to pay another visit to Alistair McKeon and Andreas Venizelos.

He shouldn't do it, of course. He'd been brought along specifically to take official responsibility for the prisoners' condition, but deliberately seeking additional contact with them only chipped away at whatever tiny chance of survival he might still have. He knew that, but he couldn't help himself.

Despite his official status, he'd been unable to gain access to Lady Harrington—who, after all, wasn't a military prisoner . . . officially—and his single attempt to ferret out a report on her condition had met with a rebuff so savage that he hadn't dared to pursue it. But he *had* been able to get in to see the people who were still considered military POWs virtually at will. Perhaps that was because he hadn't asked permission; he'd simply taken advantage of his rank and "liaison" duties to bulldoze his way past the StateSec lieutenant responsible for them. He hadn't really expected to get away with it, but apparently the lieutenant hadn't reported his visits to higher authority—unless, of course, said higher authority had decided to give him enough rope for a suitable noose and use the security cameras to record the proof of his apostasy. After all, what legitimate reason could an officer of the PRH have for hobnobbing with captured enemies of the People any more than his official responsibilities absolutely demanded? No doubt the HD chips would prove useful at his trial . . . assuming anyone bothered to give him one.

Now he stepped through the lift doors and nodded curtly to the four guards at the security console halfway down the passage. The StateSec troopers looked up in alarm, straightening their spines and setting down illicit coffee cups, then relaxed as they saw it was only Caslet. Even disregarding whatever the rumor mill suggested might or might not happen to him down the road, he was merely a naval officer, and the duty watch sergeant waved for the others to stay put as he strolled down the passage to greet the visitor.

"What can I do for you, Citizen Commander?" he asked without bothering to salute.

"I'd like to speak with the senior prisoners, Citizen Sergeant Innis," Caslet replied, and the guard shrugged.

"No skin off my nose," he grunted, and waved an arm to bring one of the other three over as he turned to lead the way to the locked hatch. The woman behind the desk answered his gesture, unracked a flechette gun, and crossed to stand five feet back, covering the hatch, and only then did the sergeant input the door lock's combination.

"Look alive, Manties!" he shouted through the opening hatch. "You got a visitor."

The compartment lighting came up as the hatch opened, and Caslet felt a twinge of guilt as sleepy men sat up in their bunks. It was the middle of the night by *Tepes*' clocks, but if he'd waited till morning, they would have been gone before he could see them.

He nodded to the sergeant once more and stepped into the compartment so that Innis could close it behind him. Yawns turned into stillness as sudden, tense speculation replaced sleepiness in the POWs' eyes, but Caslet only stood there, hands folded behind him, and waited for them to finish waking up.

The first time he'd come to visit these men, their welcome had been frigid. He hadn't blamed them for that. Indeed, he'd expected it to be even worse, but that was because he hadn't known "Colonel" LaFollet was in the same compartment. Lady Harrington's armsman had recognized him and introduced him to the others, and the way LaFollet had done it had told them *this* Peep was different. By now, Caslet had actually formed a tenuous friendship with McKeon. Venizelos remained more suspicious, but like McKeon—and, especially, LaFollet and Montoya—he'd been too grateful for Caslet's efforts to obtain additional medical supplies for Nimitz to maintain any active hostility.

Thoughts of the treecat carried Caslet across the compartment towards LaFollet's bunk, and his heart twisted with familiar distress as Nimitz struggled up in the nest of blankets at its foot to greet him. Treecats' bones knitted more rapidly than human bones, but no one in *Tepes*' crew had been interested in providing the tools Montoya would have required to repair Nimitz's injuries properly. The 'cat had regained much of his strength, but his shattered midshoulder and arm were twisted and crippled, "healed" in the merely approximate positions Montoya had been able to manage. The injury had robbed him of his normal, flowing grace, and the pain in his eyes and half-flattened ears as he made himself move was grievous to behold, but the 'cat refused to let self-pity rule him. Now he pushed himself into an almost fully upright position, listing slightly to the right as his crippled side dragged at his balance, and bleeked a welcome to Caslet.

The fact that Nimitz liked and trusted him had been the real final element in the human prisoners' acceptance of him, Caslet knew, and he ran one hand gently over the 'cat's head, then turned to face McKeon.

"I'm sorry to wake you, Captain," he said quietly, "but I thought you should know. We'll be entering Hades orbit within forty minutes." McKeon stiffened, and Caslet felt the same ripple of tension spread out across the compartment. "Shipboard time isn't quite synchronized with local," he went on, "but it'll be light at Camp Charon in about another two hours, and they'll be taking you down then. I . . . thought you'd like to know."

Harkness made a final turn, then stopped, resting flat on his belly, and pulled the minicomp out. The display's moving window was centered on a single portion of the ventilation and maintenance schematic he'd copied from the Engineering subsystem, and he tapped a key, zooming in on the window. The scale shifted, showing him his present surroundings in considerably more detail, and he grunted in satisfaction.

Dirtsiders tended to think of starships as solid chunks of alloy wrapped around passages and compartments, but any professional spacer knew better. Like the human body itself, ships were riddled by arteries and capillaries which carried power, light, air, water, and all the other vital ingredients of an artificial world throughout their volumes. And unlike the human body, they were also provided with inspection hatches and crawlways to provide access to components which might require repair or adjustment.

Needless to say, the presence of such subsidiary access ways was a pain in the posterior for naval architects, who had to provide blast doors to seal *them*, as well as the passages and lifts the dirtsiders knew about, in the event of sudden loss of pressure, but there was no way to do without them. And if a man knew his way around them, and had enough time, he could get virtually anywhere he wanted to without *using* those passages and lifts.

Which was precisely what Harkness had done. Now he switched the minicomp off, shoved it back into his pocket, and slithered down the last few meters of his current ventilation duct. It wasn't quite a perfect way to his destination, but he figured it came as close to one as he had any right to ask for. The grille at its end was set into the long wall of the passage, but it was clear down at the far end from the lifts. No one was likely to be looking this direction—after all, the only thing there was to see was the bulkhead the passage dead-ended into—but its positioning also meant he wouldn't be able to look things over before he acted, and he didn't much like jumping blind this way. On the other hand, he didn't have a lot of choice, and he'd spent enough time viewing the output from the security cameras covering the passage to know what he *ought* to find waiting for him.

He breathed a silent prayer that he was right, worked his way around to get his feet against the grille, drew both pulsers, and kicked hard.

"Why d'you think he spends so much time with them Manties, Sarge?" Citizen Corporal Porter asked.

"Damned if I know." Citizen Sergeant Calvin Innis shrugged and reached for his coffee cup once more. Citizen Private Donatelli saw him reaching and pushed it closer to him, and he nodded his thanks to her before he looked back at Porter. "All *I* know is he's s'posed to be their 'liaison officer,' and as long as nobody tells me he can't see 'em,

I don't give a rat's ass what he's up to. 'Course, if he *hasn't* got authorization to be down here, he's gonna be a mighty sick puppy when Citizen Captain Vladovich finds out about it, don't y'think?"

"Oh, I think you could probably say that," Citizen Private Mazyrak, the fourth member of the detail, agreed with a smile. "Wanna start a pool on how long it's gonna be before he checks into one of the rooms down the hall himself?"

He and Innis exchanged nasty grins, and then the sergeant chuckled and raised his mug. He'd needed the laugh, but he needed the caffeine more, and he grumbled to himself as he sipped. He'd only been on duty a bit less than an hour, and he hated the midwatch. He never seemed to get any real *sleep* when they made him work nights, which was silly, since only chronos gave any meaning to the terms "day" and "night" aboard a starship. But there it was. He always had that sense of fatigue, that stretched-skin feeling around his eyes, which made the coffee especially welcome, and—

A loud clatter chopped off his thought, and he jumped in surprise. Scalding hot coffee sloshed over his tunic, and he snarled a short, savage oath as it soaked through to his skin. His free hand dabbed uselessly at his chest, and he turned his head towards the source of the sound, prepared to flay the skin off whoever had made it.

It wasn't until he'd actually begun to turn that his brain started to catch up with his reactions, and one eyebrow rose in surprise, for the sound had come from his left, and the lifts were to his *right*. But the lifts were the only way into the area, and all three of his subordinates were right here in front of him, Citizen Private Donatelli seated behind the security console while Citizen Corporal Porter and Citizen Private Mazyrak leaned casual elbows on its counter. So if they were all with *him*, and if the lifts were to his *right*, then what the hell—?

He never completed the thought, for even before he saw the ventilator grille still bouncing on the deck, he also saw a human body come feet-first after it. He had too little time to recognize the Manty petty officer who'd defected to the Republic—indeed, he barely had time to realize where the man must have come from—for the apparition had a long-barreled military-issue pulser in either hand, and the very last thing Citizen Sergeant Calvin Innis ever felt was astonishment as a hurricane of three-millimeter darts tore him and his detail apart.

• Chapter Twenty-Eight

"I appreciate the gesture, Citizen Commander, but if we're not supposed to know the schedule, you shouldn't be here." The four missing and two broken teeth his demand to see Lady Harrington had cost him made Alistair McKeon's enunciation a little unclear, but his sincerity came through, and Warner Caslet gave a small, fatalistic shrug.

"I can't get into a lot more trouble, Captain," he said. "You didn't cause that, and neither did Lady Harrington, really. It's just a fact. And since it is, I might as well spend some time doing what I think is right."

McKeon said nothing for a long moment, simply gazed into Caslet's hazel eyes. Then his own eyes softened, and he nodded. In fact, as both he and Caslet knew, there'd been precious little the citizen commander *could* do, but that made what he had accomplished no less invaluable. The small favors he'd been able to procure, like the limited medical supplies Montoya had used to care for Nimitz—and, for that matter, do something about the constant pain of McKeon's damaged teeth—had been welcome enough in their own right, but knowing they came from someone who'd risked providing them because his own sense of honor required it of him, had done more for the prisoners' morale than Warner Caslet might ever suspect. And knowing the price he would probably pay for his decency had only made his efforts on their behalf even more precious.

"Thank you," the Manticoran said softly, and held out his hand. "Dame Honor told me you were something special, Citizen Commander. I see she was right."

"It's not so much that I'm 'special' as that StateSec is a

cesspool," Caslet said bitterly, but he shook McKeon's hand anyway.

"Maybe so. But I can only call them as I see them, and—"

The Manticoran broke off in midsentence, staring past Caslet as the hatch behind the Peep officer opened without warning. Caslet stiffened but refused to turn. There was only one reason for the hatch to open before he ordered Innis to let him out, and he waited for the heavy, contemptuous hand on his shoulder and the voice placing him under arrest for association with the People's enemies. But what he heard instead was only a strange, ringing silence, a suspension of sound and movement, as if no one present could quite believe whatever was happening. And then the stillness shattered.

"*Harkness?*"

The sheer, stunned incredulity in Venizelos' voice sent Caslet spinning around despite his earlier resolve, and his jaw dropped as he, too, recognized the man in the open hatch. The man carrying four heavy flechette guns under his left arm like an awkward bundle while four holstered pulsers and their gun belts dangled from his right hand.

"Yes, Sir," Horace Harkness said to Venizelos, and then nodded to McKeon. "Sorry it took so long, Captain."

"My God, Harkness." McKeon sounded even more stunned than Venizelos had. "What the *hell* d'you think you're *doing?*"

"Staging a breakout, Sir," Harkness said matter-of-factly, as if it were the most natural thing in the world.

"Where *to?*" McKeon demanded. Which, Caslet reflected numbly, was an eminently reasonable question, given that they were a hundred and thirty light-years from the nearest Alliance-held real estate

"Sir, I've got it figured out—I think—but we don't have time to stand around talking about it," Harkness replied, still matter-of-fact but with urgency. "We've gotta pull this off in a real tight time window if we're going to make it work, and—" He broke off, staring at Caslet as if the Peep's presence had just registered, and his mouth tightened. "Oh, *shit*, Commander! How long have *you* been here?"

"I—" Caslet began, then stopped. He didn't have any more idea of what was happening than the Allied officers about him had, but he knew his own status had just changed. He'd gone from being one of their captors, albeit an honorable and respected one, to the lone enemy officer in a compartment full of desperate men. But was that really true? *Was* he their enemy anymore? And, for that matter, could they possibly be any more desperate than *he*'d become over the past month?

"I've only been here a few minutes, Senior Chief," he said after a moment. "Not more than five or ten."

"Well, thank God!" Harkness breathed, and looked back at McKeon. "Captain, will you *please* just trust me and get your butts in gear, Sir? We've gotta haul ass if we don't want to end up with a real bad case of dead!"

McKeon stared at him for another second, then shook himself and nodded sharply.

"You're certifiably crazy, and you're probably going to get us all killed, Senior Chief," he said, taking one of the gun belts, "but at least we know what we're up against this time." His broken-toothed smile was grim, and his eyes were cold.

"If it's all the same to you, Sir, I'd just as soon get out of this alive," Harkness replied. "And I may be crazy, but I think we've got a shot."

"All right, Senior Chief." McKeon waved the others forward, and wolfish smiles blossomed as they relieved Harkness of his load of weapons. Most of them were spattered with bloodstains, despite Harkness' efforts to wipe them clean, and McKeon glanced into the passage and pursed his lips as he saw the lake of blood surrounding the guard detail's mangled bodies.

"Is there a reason we don't already have SS goons coming out our ears, Harkness?" he asked almost mildly.

"Well, yes, Sir. As a matter of fact there is." Harkness handed the last flechette gun to Andrew LaFollet and fished the minicomp out and displayed it. "I sort of hacked into their computers. That's why I was worried by the Commander here." He nodded to Caslet. "I've set up a loop in the imagery from the surveillance cameras in this section."

"A loop?" Venizelos repeated.

"Yes, Sir. I commanded the cameras to go to record mode five minutes into the current watch and stay there for twenty minutes. They started playing that back as a live feed for the folks watching the monitors up-ship about sixteen minutes ago. Unless they send somebody down to look, they're gonna go right on seeing what they *always* see, and according to the Security files, nobody's scheduled to come calling until they send in the goons to collect you and the other officers for transport dirtside. That's what gives us our window—assuming everything goes right. But if I'd caught the Commander's arrival and they saw him come in twice without leaving in the middle, well—"

He shrugged, and Venizelos nodded. But he also turned and gave Caslet a long, thoughtful look, then quirked an eyebrow at McKeon.

"He goes with us, Andy," the captain said firmly. Caslet blinked, and McKeon smiled grimly at him. "I'm afraid we don't have much choice, Citizen Commander. Much as we all like you, and grateful as we are for all you've done, you *are* a Peep officer. It'd be your duty to stop us from— Well, from doing whatever the hell Harkness has in mind. And leaving you locked up behind us wouldn't do you any favors, either, now would it?"

"No, I don't imagine so," Caslet agreed. His grin was crooked, but there was also genuine humor in it, and he wondered if McKeon was as surprised to see it as *he* was to feel it. "They'd be bound to figure I'd had something to do with it, wouldn't they?"

"You've got that right," McKeon agreed, and turned back to Harkness. "Can you open the other compartments?"

"No sweat, Sir. I lifted their combinations from the security desk over there."

He jerked his head at the console, and McKeon suppressed a slight shiver. Not only was the deck coated in blood, but unspeakable bits and pieces of what had been the guard detail were splattered across the console and bulkhead beyond it. To get to the computer, Harkness must have had to stand right in the middle—

The captain looked back out into the passage at the bloody footprints stretching from the console to within less than two meters of the compartment hatch. He stared at them for a moment, then drew a deep breath and returned his attention to Harkness.

"In that case, pass the combinations to Commander Venizelos and let him get them open while *you* tell me just what the hell it is we're doing, Senior Chief," he invited.

"—so that's about it," Harkness said, looking around at the men and women who'd been released from their prisons. Aside from five of the noncoms, he was junior to every one of them, but he had their undivided attention. Especially that of Scotty Tremaine, who couldn't seem to take his glowing eyes off him. "I've got the security alarms shut down throughout most of the ship, and I've got the route to the boat bay mapped, but I couldn't set timers on any of my surprises because I couldn't tell how long it'd take us to get ready. That means we'll have to send the activation code once we're in position, and that means someone's gonna have to get my 'puter here into an access slot at the right time. And I couldn't get into the systems that control the brig area, either. That's the highest security area of the ship, and their computers are stand-alones. There's no direct interface between there and the main system, and just getting there physically's going to be a bitch, Captain. We can do it, but if the brig detail gets time to hit an alarm button, it's gonna go off, 'cause I can't get to it to stop it."

"Understood." McKeon rubbed his chin, looking around at the twenty-six frightened, grimly determined faces clustered around him and Harkness. As a professional naval officer, he thought the senior chief's plan had to be the most insane thing he'd ever heard of, but the really crazy thing about it was that it might just work.

"All right, we're going to have to split up," he said after a moment. "Chief, give Commander Venizelos the memo board."

Harkness nodded and handed over the memo board he'd taken from the security console. He'd downloaded the plans of *Tepes'* air ducts and service ways to it, and he tapped a recall key as Venizelos took it from him.

"We're right here, Sir," he said as the display flashed. "I've highlighted what looks like the best route to the brig, but I'm not sure how accurate the plans are. These fuckers are real paranoids, and I've hit a few places where I'm pretty sure they deliberately incorporated disinformation into their own computers. And even if this—" he twitched the board "—is all a hundred percent, you're gonna have to move fast to make it before the shit hits the fan."

"Understood, Senior Chief." Venizelos gazed down at the display for a minute, then looked back at McKeon. "Who else?" he asked simply.

"I'm going to need Scotty, Sarah, and Gerry in the boat bay," McKeon thought aloud. "And Carson, of course." Ensign Clinkscales blushed as all eyes turned to him. He felt conspicuous and odd in the StateSec uniform, but he was the only person for whom Johnson's clothing was anything like a proper fit, and that was going to be important in the boat bay. McKeon stood a moment, rubbing an eyebrow, then sighed.

"I'm coming at this the wrong way. There's no point sending anyone after the Commodore without a gun, and we don't have enough of them to go around, anyway." He thought a second longer, then nodded. "All right, Andy. You, LaFollet, Candless, Whitman—" Alistair McKeon knew better than to try excluding any of Honor's armsmen "—and McGinley. That's six. We'll give you three of the flechette guns and three pulsers. That'll leave one flechette and three pulsers for the break-in to the boat bay."

"Will that give you enough firepower?" Venizelos asked anxiously.

"We shouldn't need much for the actual break-in, Commander," Harkness reassured him. "And if we get in in the first place, we'll have plenty of guns to hold it."

"All right, then," McKeon said, with a sharp, decisive nod, and smiled grimly. "As Dame Honor would say, people, 'Let's be about it.'"

Thirty-one minutes later, McKeon and Harkness stood panting for breath in a lift shaft with Carson Clinkscales. Scotty Tremaine stood with them, the grim lines which had etched themselves into his face over the past month still evident but no longer harsh and old, and the rest of their party was spread down the shaft behind them in a long line, bodies pressed into the inspection tunnels that grooved its walls. At least a dozen lift cars had passed them during their cautious journey, but none of those cars' passengers had suspected what was moving along the shaft beyond the thin walls of their conveyances. Now McKeon rested a hand on the ensign's shoulder and looked him in the eye.

"Are you up for this, Carson?" he asked quietly, and Clinkscales nodded. It was a choppy, abrupt nod, but there was a strange maturity to it. Carson Clinkscales was still young, but only physically. The last month had burned the youthfulness out of him, and a corner of McKeon's brain wondered if it would ever return. He hoped so . . . but at the moment, what mattered was that the hard-eyed young man in front of him was no longer the awkward and uncertain kid he'd been aboard *Jason Alvarez* and *Prince Adrian*.

"Yes, Sir," the ensign replied, unaware of the thoughts running through his senior's mind.

"All right, then," McKeon said, and pulled out a hand com. Half an hour ago, it had belonged to Citizen Sergeant Innis, and using it constituted a risk, though not an enormous one. All personal communications aboard *Tepes* were recorded as yet one more of StateSec's precautionary measures, and it was remotely possible one of the recording techs would actually be listening in and overhear what McKeon was about to say. But that was a chance they had to take, and he punched in the combination of the com which had once belonged to Citizen Corporal Porter.

"Yes?" Andreas Venizelos answered almost instantly, and McKeon glanced at Harkness and Clinkscales.

"The present is here," he told Venizelos. "Is your part of the party ready?"

"We need another ten minutes," Venizelos replied, and McKeon frowned. It would be better to wait until the chief of staff's group was actually in position, but every passing minute added to the chance that McKeon's own group would be discovered . . . or that someone would discover one of the bodies Harkness had left in his wake. And even if he moved right this instant, it would probably take *close* to ten minutes to put his own part of the operation into action. The problem, of course, was that as soon as either group moved, the fact that escaped prisoners were running around the ship would become quickly evident to *Tepes'* crew.

He thought for ten silent seconds, then sighed. There wasn't really much choice.

"We'll make delivery on schedule, then," he said.

"Understood," Venizelos responded, and McKeon killed the circuit and nodded to Harkness, who handed Clinkscales the minicomp. The senior chief hated the very thought of letting it out of his hands, but he had no choice. Even if every single member of their party had been armed, the odds against successfully storming a single boat bay, even with total surprise, would have been astronomical, and they needed control of *all* of *Tepes'* bays for this to work. And, unfortunately, there was only one way to pull that off.

"Now look here, Mr. Clinkscales," he said in exactly the same calm voice he'd used to generations of junior officers. "All you've got to do is walk into the bay, slide the 'puter into the slot, and hit this function key here. That'll transmit Johnson's access code, log you onto the system, and then execute the programs, got it?"

"Got it, Senior Chief," Clinkscales replied, and Harkness blinked at the sober steadiness of the response. This kid sounded like he meant *business*, and that was good.

"Then go get 'em, Sir!" he said, and thumped the youngster on the shoulder.

Carson Clinkscales gathered himself and bent to step through the service hatch Senior Chief Harkness and Captain McKeon had opened for him. It was more of a fast, awkward crawl than a "step," really—something that had to be done quickly, lest someone happening along the passage see him and wonder what he thought he was doing—and he stumbled on the hatch coaming. He flung out an arm to catch his balance, half-hopping and half-falling across the narrow passage, and for one dreadful instant the memory of every awkward, humiliating disaster of his adolescence seemed like a garrote about his throat. In that instant, he knew, without a shadow of a doubt, that he was going to screw *this* one up, as well, and when he did, all the people counting on him would die.

But then his outstretched hand smacked into the bulkhead opposite the service hatch and he caught himself. Panic hammered in the back of his brain, but there was no time for that, and he ground it under a ruthless mental boot heel. He couldn't do anything about the rapidity of his pulse, yet he straightened his spine and squared his shoulders as he pushed away from the bulkhead which had arrested his fall. He tugged at his tunic sleeves—Johnson's arms had been shorter than his—and looked casually in both directions, and his pulse slowed just a fraction as he realized there was no on in sight.

Well, there shouldn't *be anyone down here,* he told himself. This passage was normally used only to service the docking and umbilical arms of Boat Bay Four. If small craft operations had been underway, there would have been an excellent chance of running into someone, but there were no launch orders on the schedule Harkness had pulled out of the main computers. Even if there had been, they

wouldn't have used Bay Four . . . unless Cordelia Ransom
had decided for some reason that she had to make an all-
up assault landing on StateSec's own prison planet.

Clinkscales actually felt himself grin at the thought, then
drew a deep breath and moved off with a calm expression
and a steady tread which he found distantly surprising . . .
and which anyone else who had ever known him would
have found amazing.

Andreas Venizelos looked at the bulkhead in front of him,
then down at the memo board's display, and muttered a
venomous curse. Andrew LaFollet's head snapped around
at the sound, and the focused purpose in the armsman's
gray eyes hit Venizelos like a fist. That purpose came
dangerously close to desperation—if it stopped short of that
at all—and Venizelos reached out to grip the other man's
shoulder hard.

"We're doing the best we can, Andrew," he said quietly.
"Don't you go taking any stupid chances on me. I need
you, and so does Lady Harrington."

LaFollet nodded curtly, but his eyes held Venizelos',
demanding an explanation for the commander's curse, and
the Manticoran sighed.

"There's a discrepancy in the schematic," he explained.
He took his left hand from LaFollet's shoulder to point at
the alloy which turned the ventilation duct in which they
stood into a "T" intersection. "According to the plans, that
ought to be a four-way intersection, and the one in front
of us ought to lead right to the brig. As it is—"

He shrugged, and LaFollet's grip tightened on his heavy
flechette gun. "So which way do we go instead?" he asked
harshly, and Venizelos pointed to the right.

"That way. But it looks like they did an even more
thorough job of sealing the brig off from the rest of the
hull than Harkness thought. This—" he nodded once more
at the bulkhead that shouldn't be there "—must've been
an add-on. I'm guessing that when they decided to hand
Tepes over to StateSec, they decided to cut off all the cross

connected ventilation shafts as an additional security measure. They could probably get away with that, because this section backs right up against one of their environmental plants. All they'd really need is supply and return ducting to that; anything on this side of the brig would be part of the distribution system for the rest of the ship. But if they were paranoid enough to seal *ventilation* ducts, you can bet they did the same with the service ways."

"Which means?" LaFollet demanded.

The armsman hated being dependent on someone else to plan his Steadholder's rescue, and it showed. But despite all the time he'd spent aboard starships with Lady Harrington, this wasn't his area of expertise. It was Andreas Venizelos', and Venizelos recognized fury born of devotion when he heard it. He kept his own voice calmer and more level than he'd really believed he could and squeezed LaFollet's shoulder again.

"Which means we're not going to be able to sneak in on them the way Harkness did on *our* guards," he said, and punched buttons on the memo board. The display shifted scale, losing detail but showing a much wider area, and he pointed into it. "We're going to have to cross this passage here to the lift, then take the shaft down a deck to the brig. If they're on their toes, they *may* have cameras in the shaft, in which case they'll be waiting for us. We know they've got cameras in the *cars*, but Harkness didn't turn up any sign that the shafts themselves are wired. If they aren't, we should still have the advantage of surprise, but we'll be going in blind whatever we do."

"Um." LaFollet grunted, chewing unhappily on the implications of a blind assault against an unknown number of enemies. Venizelos hadn't had to tell him the change in route was going to put them behind schedule, either. Using the lift shaft should help a little in that regard—it would certainly be faster than moving the same distance through these cramped tunnels—but he didn't like coming into the brig from the most predictable direction. The advantage of surprise should make up for a lot, assuming they actually *had* that advantage when the moment came, but it was still going to be iffy.

"All right, Commander," he said after a moment. "We'll do it that way, but give your flechette gun to Bob." Venizelos' eyebrows rose in question, and LaFollet bared his teeth in a grimace no one would ever mistake for a smile. "He'll trade you his pulser, but when we hit the brig, you and Commander McGinley will bring up the rear." Venizelos started to open his mouth, but LaFollet cut him off with a brusque gesture. "You and she are naval officers. You'll be more useful if it comes to picking alternate ways out of here than me, Jamie, or Bob, so if we have to lose someone—"

Venizelos didn't like it a bit, but LaFollet's logic was unanswerable. So instead of protesting, he slid the flechette gun's sling off his shoulder to hand it to Robert Whitman.

Carson Clinkscales walked briskly up the narrow passage, and the hatch at its end opened at his approach. He strode through it, trying to look completely at ease . . . and hoping no one would wonder what a ground force trooper had been doing wandering around down amid the controls for the docking arms.

There were twenty or thirty people in the bay gallery. It looked as if some of them were carrying out routine maintenance on the pinnace at the head of the bay, and two or three men in flight suits stood in idle conversation near the docking tube that led to one of the enormous armored assault shuttles which filled the rest of the bay. Clinkscales glanced around casually, trying to get his bearings quickly. Harkness had briefed him as well as he could, but actually picking up the access slot without ever having been here before was harder than he'd expected.

There it was! He turned a bit to his left and walked onward, reaching into his tunic for the minicomp which Harkness had turned into such a lethal weapon. He pulled it out with a calm he was far from feeling, and the display blinked as the coupling mated with the slot and the connection brought the minicomp on-line.

"Hey, you!" The shout came from his left. He turned his head, and his heart seemed to stop, for a StateSec sergeant stood twenty meters away, glowering in his direction. "Just what the hell d'you think *you're* doing?" the sergeant demanded.

He sounded more irritated than alarmed, but the ensign felt a moment of total and absolute panic. But then, as suddenly as the panic had come, he felt something entirely different. It was if the universe's entire time scale had just shifted, and a cold, crystalline sense of purpose replaced his choking terror. He was still afraid, but now he was *only* afraid, and the fear was a distant thing, small and unimportant beside his absolute certainty of what he must do.

His finger depressed the function key Senior Chief Harkness had told him to press. The minicomp's display flashed as the stored commands poured through the interface, but Clinkscales wasn't even looking. His attention was on the sergeant, his expression one of casual interest, and he strolled to meet the older man. Their mutual angles of approach turned his right side away from the sergeant, and his right hand fell naturally to his hip. It settled on the butt of his holstered pulser, and he smiled, cocking his head as if to ask the sergeant what he could do for him while the singing, frozen tension in his brain wondered how the hell long it was going to take Harkness' programs to activate, and what would happen when they did, and, Sweet Tester, that sergeant was getting *close* now, and—

PNS *Tepes* shuddered violently as the first explosion reverberated through her iron bones.

Boat bays aren't normally considered especially dangerous places. True, they offer ample ways for someone to do himself in, but so do a great many areas aboard any starship, and the things that pose dangers to the *ship*— like the connections for things like hydrogen and emergency rocket propellant to fuel the ship's small craft, or the stores of ammunition and external ordnance kept in nearby magazines—are safeguarded in many ways. Proper training in operation and maintenance is the first defense, and so is physical separation, keeping one danger source as far from any other as the boat bay's servicing requirements permit. And in addition to all human safeguards, computers monitor the danger points continuously.

Unfortunately for *Tepes*, however, her computer net had been compromised. None of her crew knew it . . . and none of the computers cared. They existed only to carry out their human masters' orders, and the lines of code Horace Harkness had altered made just as much sense to them as the *right* instructions would have made.

The programs already buried and waiting in the main system began to activate as the execution commands flashed into the net from the minicomp plugged into Boat Bay Four's number five access slot, and all over *Tepes* officers and ratings stared at their consoles—first in confusion, and then in alarm.

CIC went first, and the senior tracking officer swore as her holo display went suddenly blank. It was hardly a life-threatening disaster when the ship was safely in orbit around Hades, but it was irritating as hell, and there was no logical reason for it.

Except that there was one. The display had died for the simple reason that there was no longer any input to drive its imagers. For just an instant, the tracking officer felt relieved by the realization that the display's sudden shutdown hadn't been *her* people's fault, but then her forehead furrowed in fresh—and deeper—consternation. What in heaven's name could cause *every* sensor system to go down at once?

The program which had shut down *Tepes'* sensors finished the first part of its task and turned to the second. In the flicker of an eye, far too rapidly for any human operator to realize what was happening, it used CIC's computers as a launching pad to invade the Tactical Department's central processing system, established control . . . and ordered the system to reformat itself.

The tac officer of the watch gaped in disbelief as his panels started going down. It began with Tracking, but from there the failures leapt like wildfire, and display after display blinked and went dead. Radar One, Gravitics One and Two, Lidar Three, Missile Defense, Main Fire Control . . . the nerve center of the ship's ability to fight—or defend herself—died even as he watched. Nor was the damage something which could be quickly fixed. The computers would have to be completely reprogrammed to put them back on-line—a nightmare task in a Navy with so few fully qualified technicians—and it all went so quickly the tac officer barely had time to realize it was happening before it was done.

Other programs capered and danced, exploding through the net like a plundering army. Internal alarms and central communication systems became so much useless junk as the software which ran them was reduced to meaningless gibberish. The ship's helm and drive rooms locked down. "The Morgue," in which every suit of battle armor was stored, suddenly sealed itself . . . and the subprocessers which monitored the ready suits of armor to be sure they were always prepared for instant use sent power surges down the monitoring leads to lobotomize their onboard computers and render them totally useless until teams of technicians spent the hours required to reprogram their software.

And while all that was going on, the computers responsible for monitoring the fueling needs of the ship's small craft received their own orders. Valves opened, and in Boat Bay One a technician who'd happened to be working on a minor glitch in Umbilical Two gaped in horror at what was happening. He leapt for the manual controls, trying to override, but there wasn't time . . . nor would it have mattered. For even if he'd been able to keep the emergency propellant from venting and mixing in Umbilical Two, it wouldn't have stopped precisely the same thing from happening in Umbilical Four.

The binary-based fuel was hypergolic, and even as the

service tech screamed and turned to run, he knew it was pointless. The components mixing behind him were too . . . voracious for that, and *Tepes* bucked like a wounded horse as Boat Bay One blew apart. Twenty-six members of her crew and every small craft in the bay were ripped apart in the explosion, and alarms wailed as the blast blew back into the hull as well. Bulkheads shattered, and another forty-one men and women died as atmosphere belched out of the hideous wound in an almost perfect ring of fire.

Blast doors slammed, more alarms screamed, and officers and noncoms tried to shout orders over the com systems. But the com systems no longer functioned, and then the ship heaved again as Boat Bay *Two* blew up, exactly as Boat Bay One had done.

The sergeant walking towards Clinkscales staggered as the first explosion shuddered through the ship's hull. He threw his arms out for balance, lurching through a dance to stay on his feet which would have looked ludicrous under other circumstances. But there was nothing humorous about *these* circumstances, and as Clinkscales threw out his own left arm, bracing himself against the bulkhead, he saw the sergeant's eyes dart past him to the minicomp still plugged into the access slot. There was no logical reason for it, but it didn't matter. The sergeant didn't know how it had been done, or why, but in that instant of intuitive insight, he knew *who* had caused it. It was as if his mind were somehow linked to the ensign's, for even as the sergeant guessed Clinkscales had somehow caused whatever was happening, Clinkscales knew he had.

There was no sign of the clumsy youngster who'd boarded GNS *Jason Alvarez* with Lady Harrington in the tall young man whose left hand thrust him suddenly away from the bulkhead. His push propelled him towards the sergeant, who was still fighting for balance while he opened his mouth to shout an alarm. But he never got it out, for even as he started to yell, Carson Clinkscales' left fist caught the front of his tunic and jerked him close. The two men went down, with Clinkscales on the bottom, and the sergeant felt something hard dig into his chest. He looked down into Clinkscales' eyes, confusion giving way to hate, but he still hadn't figured out what was pressing into his chest when Clinkscales squeezed the trigger and a burst of pulser fire ripped his heart apart.

The body convulsed atop Clinkscales, drenching him in a scalding rush of blood. He thrust it aside and rolled up on one knee just as the ship lurched to the explosion of Boat Bay Three and Horace Harkness' amplified voice blared through the galley of Boat Bay Four.

"Propellant leak!" it announced. "Multiple propellant leaks! Evacuate the bay immediately. Repeat, *evacuate the bay immediately!*"

It was neither a computer-generated voice nor a stored message, and as panic swept the bay, no one noticed that they didn't have the least idea just whose voice it was. It came from the intercom speakers, and it spoke with absolute authority. That was all they needed to know, and they stampeded for the lifts as red and amber danger lights began to flash. *Tepes* lurched yet again as Boat Bay Five blew up, and the fresh concussion lent desperation to their flight. They piled into the lifts, too frantic to escape even to notice the blood-soaked corporal kneeling beside a dead sergeant, and as Carson Clinkscales watched them go, he knew that for the first time in his life, he'd gotten everything exactly right.

• Chapter Twenty-Nine

Citizen Lieutenant Hanson Timmons was in a foul mood.

He stood ramrod straight in his dress uniform, gloved hands folded behind him, swagger stick clasped in his right armpit, and glowered at the lift doors. A double watch section stood with him, weapons slung, each man and woman as immaculately groomed and polished as he himself while they waited for the camera crews to come collect the single prisoner in their charge. His people had taken special pains with their appearance, and not just because of the impending cameras. Their detail commander's growing frustration had been apparent for weeks, and no one wanted to give him the slightest excuse to vent it on them. Timmons knew that, and knowing they recognized his wrath only made it worse, for in recognizing it, they'd obviously guessed what caused it.

Timmons had been posted to the command of *Tepes'* brig detachment only a few weeks before Cordelia Ransom sailed for Barnett, and considering his relatively junior rank, the assignment had been quite a plum for him. It had also been an indication of the favor in which his superiors held him . . . and of their faith in his abilities. In the course of his career with StateSec, he'd specialized in the management of politically sensitive prisoners, and he'd always delivered them in exactly the desired condition. Usually, that had meant breaking them to heel, reducing them to cringing compliance with whatever StateSec might demand of them, and Timmons was confident he could break *anyone*. After all, a man was usually good at his work when it was a job he loved.

That was, in fact, the reason he'd been assigned to Ransom's personal transport, for the Secretary of Public Information had anticipated an occasional need for the services of such a specialist. But the citizen lieutenant was a frustrated man this time, for Honor Harrington had eluded his best efforts. Of course, he'd been handicapped by Committeewoman Ransom's demand that she be delivered to the executioner in shape to appreciate—and react to—all that happened to her. After all, the cameras would be recording her big moment for later broadcast. But knowing she would be going before those cameras had ruled out the application of much direct physical coercion— it wouldn't do to mark her badly enough to evoke sympathy from the viewers—and Ransom's insistence that she react properly to her execution had ruled out the use of drugs.

Viewed objectively, Timmons couldn't really fault the restrictions. It wasn't as if they were trying to get information out of Harrington, and there was no real need to break her if they were only going to hang her. But that didn't change the fact that he'd *wanted* to crush her. He had his professional pride, after all. Besides, he enjoyed his work, and he'd been confident of his ability to break her as he'd broken everyone else . . . which only made the blow to his pride even more severe when he failed.

It should have been so simple! Even without the cruder forms of physical abuse or drugs, humiliation should have done the trick. He'd recognized the steel at her core, but that had only added to his anticipatory pleasure, for he hated the proud ones. The ones who looked down from the mountains of achievement to sneer at the lesser mortals at their feet. There was a special joy in hurling them down from the heights, and one thing he'd learned dealing with Legislaturalist prisoners was that humiliation's effectiveness as a means of breaking resistance was directly proportional to the power a prisoner had wielded before his fall. Someone accustomed to seeing his orders swiftly implemented, of having control of himself and his surroundings, was far more vulnerable to impotence than someone who had never been in a position of command. When it was borne in upon him that nothing he did could have *any* effect on what happened, that his authority had become total helplessness, the shock and shame struck with crippling power. Timmons had seen it again and again, in civilian and military prisoners alike, and because he had, he'd never doubted that Harrington would follow the same pattern.

But she hadn't, and he couldn't understand it. Other prisoners had tried to escape him by withdrawing into their own private worlds, but none had succeeded. There were too many ways to jerk them back, and they always worked. Except that they *hadn't* worked this time. There was a strange, elastic power to Harrington's resistance, as if by refusing to resist the blows he rained upon her she somehow deprived them of their power, and in a way he couldn't quite define, that made her *refusal* to resist the most potent defiance he'd ever encountered. Most of his mind insisted that if he'd only had more time he could still have smashed that nondefiance, but deep inside, he knew better.

He'd calculated everything so carefully, metered the humiliation so precisely. He'd opted for the death of a thousand cuts, stripping away her defenses with her dignity and her self-confidence with her ability to control her fate, and for a time, he'd thought he was succeeding. But he hadn't been, and he'd slowly realized he wouldn't. What she'd done to Bergren three days earlier only confirmed what had already become obvious to him. This time, he wasn't going to succeed. He'd had her for a T-month, and if he hadn't broken her in that long, then he never would without turning to sterner measures.

And those measures were denied him. What he *wanted* to do was storm into her cell with a neural whip and see how she liked direct stimulation of her pain centers for an hour or two. Or there were other, older-fashioned techniques—cruder, but perhaps even more effective because they were crude—which he'd learned from the ex-InSec personnel who'd trained him. But Ransom's orders not to damage her prevented him from doing any such thing. In fact, he was more than a little afraid of how the Committeewoman was going to react anyway when she set eyes on her prize once more.

Regulations had demanded the deactivation of Harrington's implants, but he hadn't counted on what that would do to her face. Nor had he expected the tech who deactivated them to actually burn them out, leaving no way to reverse the process. He didn't expect Ransom to be pleased to have her prisoner looking like a pre-space stroke victim, nor did he expect her to be happy at how gaunt and starved looking Harrington had become. But that wasn't his fault, damn it! He'd fed her regularly! In fact, he'd—

The ship lurched. It was more of a tremor, actually, but even that was enough to make him stiffen. The battlecruiser massed the next best thing to a million tons. Only something frighteningly violent could send a shock through something that huge, and Timmons turned towards the security console . . . just as a *second* shockwave lashed through the ship.

The second one was more pronounced than the first, and Timmons moved faster. Citizen Private Hayman jumped out of his way as he stepped behind the console, but the lieutenant hardly noticed. He stabbed the com key just as the ship trembled for a *third* time, but nothing happened.

Timmons frowned and punched another key, but *still* nothing happened. He felt ripples of panic beginning to spread through his subordinates as yet another concussion echoed through the ship, and his own panic rose with theirs as he entered still a third com code and got no response at all.

People aboard starships rely absolutely upon their technology, and nothing is more terrifying than to have that technology fail—especially for no apparent reason. Timmons was no exception to that rule, and he snarled at the communicator's dead display, then reached a decision and thrust a hand into his tunic pocket for his personal com.

As the commander of the brig security detail, he'd been issued a personal communicator, to be used only in the direst of emergencies. Outwardly indistinguishable from any other, it had one important difference: it didn't go through the main com net. Instead, it was a secure link to Citizen Colonel Livermore, CO of *Tepes'* ground force and security detachments, via a stand-alone system which had absolute priority.

"*Yes?*"

The single word, without any identification, was hardly correct com procedure, and Timmons recognized the confusion and fear within it. Yet simply hearing it was still a vast relief.

"Timmons, Brig Detail," he said crisply, drawing the comfort of proper protocol about himself. "Our communications are out down here. What's happening?"

"How the hell do *I* know?" the unidentified voice snarled back. "The whole frigging ship is coming apart, and—"

Hanson Timmons never learned what else the voice might have said, for at that moment, the lift doors slid open. His head snapped up, and he wheeled towards them in confusion, for the tone to signal an approaching lift car hadn't sounded. His confusion deepened as he looked into the darkness of the shaft and realized the tone hadn't sounded because there *was* no car . . . and then the first flechette gun coughed.

The brig passageway opening off the lift formed a dog-leg to the right on its way to the cells. LaFollet didn't know if that was a deliberate security feature, but it certainly had the effect of one.

He and Candless had been ready when the rest of the rescue party opened the lift doors manually . . . which was more than could be said for the half-dozen people standing there in their black-and-red dress uniforms. Each had a flechette gun slung over his or her shoulder, and a pulser rode at each right hip, but most of them had been looking *away* from the lifts, at the officer behind the security console at the bend in the corridor. Their heads started to turn as the doors slid apart, and one of them actually shouted something and clawed frantically at his slung weapon, but he was too late. Andrew LaFollet and James Candless had debts to pay—one to their Steadholder, and a very different one to her enemies—and their eyes were merciless as they squeezed their triggers.

Flechette guns were designed for shipboard combat. The modern descendants of pre-space shotguns, their grav drivers punched out masses of knife-edged flechettes. With much lower velocities than pulser darts, they were less prone to dangerous ricochets or punching holes in important pieces of equipment, but they were lethal against any unarmored target. Their projectiles dispersed into deadly patterns, controllable by the "choke" setting on their pistol grips. They could be set to cover a cone over a full meter wide at a range of five meters from the muzzle, or as little as fifteen centimeters across at a range of fifty meters, and flesh and bone meant very little to the razor-cruel flechettes.

LaFollet and Candless had set their weapons to maximum dispersion and full automatic. The cycle time on a flechette gun was much slower than that of a pulser, but that hardly mattered given their wide area of effect. The guns coughed rhythmically, belching death and destruction, and the waiting SS guards exploded in a bloody mist.

"We're under attack! *We're under attack!*" Timmons screamed into his com even as he flung himself down behind the security console. Flechettes slammed into it like deadly sleet, and he scuttled down the passage on his elbows and belly. A single flechette, licking through the gap between the console and bulkhead, caught him just as he rounded the bend, and he screamed as it chewed into his thigh. Slower than a pulser dart or not, it was still traveling at three hundred meters per second, and it sliced the back of his leg like a high-velocity axe. The lieutenant dropped his com involuntarily to clutch at the bloody wound with both hands, and the communicator slithered away across the deck. He heard the shouted questions from the other end even through his own sobs of anguish, but he had no time to worry about answering them. Most of his people were down already, but the two he'd posted as formal guards outside Harrington's cell had been shielded by the bend in the corridor. That pair had been intended as window-dressing for the formal transfer of the prisoner, but stationing them here had had the effect of giving him a reserve, and he bared his teeth in a pain-stretched snarl.

"Get ready!" he gasped at them, and took his right hand from his gashed leg. His fingers were slimy with his own blood, but he drew his pulser and covered the bend as he shoved himself along the deck on the seat of his trousers and his wounded thigh left a bright red blood trail behind him.

"Go!" LaFollet snapped, and Robert Whitman vaulted from the lift shaft into the brig passage. "At least one got around the turn!" LaFollet warned him.

The other armsman nodded, but he never slowed in his dash for the security console. He went down on one knee, weapon ready, and stiffened as he heard a voice.

"Timmons! *Timmons!* What the *fuck* is going *on* down there?"

He realized instantly what he was hearing—and that whoever was on the other end of that com link would be sending help as quickly as he could. Time had just become an even more deadly foe, and he looked back over his shoulder at LaFollet and Candless, just starting to climb out of the shaft.

"Open com link!" he shouted, and then, before anyone could stop him, rolled out of his cover with the flechette gun on full automatic.

Timmons heard the shout and grinned viciously. The bastards knew someone would be coming up their backsides any minute now. All he and his remaining men had to do was hold out, and he suddenly realized how he could do just that. These idiots had to be here to rescue Harrington, so all he had to do was open her cell and drag her out into the middle of the firefight, and—

His thoughts broke off as someone rolled out into the very middle of the passage. His sudden appearance took Timmons totally by surprise, and he gaped at the apparition in shock, unable to believe anyone would *deliberately* throw himself into what he *knew* had to be a deathtrap. But that was because he'd never encountered a Grayson armsman whose Steadholder was in danger. Robert Whitman had only one purpose in life, and his very first shot tore Citizen Lieutenant Timmons to bloody rags.

The two men further up the passage poured fire back, but the bare bulkheads and deck offered no cover . . . for anyone. Deadly clouds of flechettes shrieked past one another, intermingling and then separating, all of them set for maximum dispersion, and there was no place to hide.

"Citizen Admiral?" Lester Tourville looked up quickly, for there was something very odd about Shannon Foraker's tone.

"What?" he asked, and the ops officer frowned.

"I think you'd better look at this, Sir," she said. "*Tepes'* active sensors just went down."

"What?" Tourville said again, in a very different tone, and Foraker nodded.

"Every one of them, Sir." Foraker had gotten even more careless—or deliberate—about her "elitist" vocabulary over the last month, but this time Tourville was certain she'd used "Sir" without even thinking about it. "They shouldn't have done that," she went on. "They're through the main minefields and into orbit, but nobody in her right mind would shut down her radar."

Tourville nodded and walked quickly across the deck towards her station, for she was right. *Tepes* might be in her designated parking orbit, but with so many mines floating around the possibility of one having strayed into her orbital path could never be completely ruled out.

"Anything from her at all, Harrison?" he demanded.

"Negative, Citizen Admiral," the com officer replied. "I don't— Just a second, Citizen Admiral." Citizen Lieutenant Fraiser listened to his earbug intently, then turned to Tourville. "Citizen Captain Hewitt reports that he was receiving a message from Citizen Captain Vladovich, Citizen Admiral. Apparently the transmission was interrupted in the middle of a sentence."

Tourville and Bogdanovich looked at one another, then turned as one to Everard Honeker. The People's commissioner looked back at them, as confused as either of the naval officers but not as immediately concerned. Unlike them, he didn't fully understand just how massive an interruption *Tepes'* systems had just apparently suffered.

Tourville saw Honeker's incomprehension and started to speak, then stopped himself and looked back down at Foraker. The tac officer was bent over her display with focused intensity, and he glanced at it himself rather than disturb her.

The relative orbital positions of Hades and Cerberus–B-3 were such that *Count Tilly* had passed within less than two light-minutes of the former on her vector for the latter. Hades now lay almost exactly three and a half light-minutes off her starboard bow, moving away from her at a little over 26,000 KPS as she continued to decelerate towards Cerberus–B-3, and he glanced back up at Citizen Commander Lowe.

"Assume we go to maximum military power. How soon could we reach *Tepes?*"

Lowe punched numbers into her panel quickly, then looked back up.

"We'll need a little over eighty-three minutes to decelerate to rest relative to Hades, Citizen Admiral. If we go for a least-time flight from that point, we can reach the planet in another hundred and seventeen minutes—call it three hours and twenty minutes total—but our relative velocity would be over thirty-six thousand KPS. If we go for a zero-velocity intercept, it'll add almost another hour to the flight profile."

Tourville grunted and turned back to Foraker's panel. He drew a cigar from his pocket and unwrapped it slowly, never taking his eyes from the data on the display. He had the cigar half-way to his mouth when Foraker sucked in an audible breath and his own hand froze.

"Citiz—"

"I see it, Shannon," he said quietly, and his hand moved the cigar the rest of the way to his mouth. "How bad is it?" he asked almost absently.

"I can't say, Citizen Admiral. But look here and here." She tapped a secondary display at her elbow, and Tourville nodded slowly as he scanned the readouts.

"Stay on it," he told her, then beckoned for Honeker and Bogdanovich to join him.

"I don't know what's happening, but *something* sure as hell just went wrong aboard *Tepes*," he told them in a flat, lowered voice.

"What do you mean, 'wrong'?" Honeker asked tautly.

"Citizen Commissioner, warships don't just suddenly go off the air unless something very unusual happens to them. And Citizen Commander Foraker just picked up debris and atmosphere loss. I'd say she's suffered at least one major hull breach."

"*A hull breach?*" Honeker stared at him in disbelief, and Tourville nodded grimly.

"I don't know what caused it, and the air loss is low enough—for now, at least—to indicate that they managed to seal off the damaged areas. But whatever's going on over there is serious, Citizen Commissioner. Very serious."

"I see." Honeker rubbed sweaty palms together and made himself take a deep breath. "What do you propose to do about it, Citizen Admiral?" he asked quietly.

"What we're seeing now happened at least four minutes ago," Tourville told him, still in that flat tone. "By now, she could already have blown up, and we wouldn't know it. But if she's in serious trouble, she's going to need help."

"And you propose taking *Tilly* to render it," Honeker said.

"Yes, Sir. The only problem is that we don't know what she may have already told Camp Charon . . . or how they may react if we suddenly head for the planet when they told us to stay the hell away from it."

"Understood." Honeker stood another moment, still rubbing his hands together, then looked at Fraiser. "Contact Camp Charon, Citizen Lieutenant. Inform them that we are going to the assistance of *Tepes* on my authority at our best acceleration and request that they confirm the minefields have been safed for our passage."

Honor Harrington rose and faced the door of her cell as it opened, and the right side of her face was almost as expressionless as the dead left side.

It wasn't easy to keep it that way. Timmons had taken great pleasure in informing her that the next time her cell was opened would be for her trip to the hangman. That would have been enough to make maintaining her composure difficult even without the flashes of emotion she'd begun receiving from Nimitz. They were too far apart, their link stretched too thin, for her to tell exactly what the 'cat was feeling, but there was a sense of . . . movement, and sharper flashes of pain, as if the movement hurt him. At first she'd been certain he was being transported to the planet to die with her as Ransom had promised, yet she'd become steadily less positive, for a flush of excitement and a strange, fierce determination seemed to have wrapped itself about all of his other emotions. She had no idea what might have caused it. For that matter, it might all be nothing more than a delusion on her part, inspired by her own fear and half-starved weakness. But whatever else was happening, she would meet Timmons and his ghouls without flinching.

The door lock clacked, and she braced herself as it swung open. And then—

"My Lady! *Lady Harrington!*"

Honor staggered, her good eye flaring wide, as Andrew LaFollet shouted her name. Her personal armsman stood in the open doorway, face haggard and his normally immaculate uniform ragged, and he cradled a flechette gun in his arms.

Not possible, her brain told her calmly. *This is* not *possible. It has to be a hallucination.*

But it wasn't, and she stumbled forward as he freed one hand from the gun and held it out to her. Her working eye misted, making it hard to see, but his hand was warm and firm as it closed on her too-thin fingers. He squeezed hard, and Honor dragged in a deep, shuddery breath and put her arms around him, hugging him fiercely.

"We're here to get you out, My Lady," he said into her shoulder, and she nodded and made herself release him. She stood back, blinking to clear her vision, and saw his face change as he took in her own appearance. The brightly colored jumpsuit seemed two sizes too big for her wasted body, and his gray eyes went harder than steel as he took in the dead side of her face. He opened his mouth, but she shook her head.

"No time, Andrew," she told him huskily. "No time. Later."

He gazed at her for a fraction of a second longer, and then shook himself like a dog shedding water from its coat.

"Yes, My Lady," he said, and nodded to someone else. Whoever it was was to her left, and Honor turned quickly, then inhaled in fresh surprise as Andreas Venizelos stepped to her side and fastened a gun belt around her waist. He looked up from his work to meet her eyes with a tense, strained smile, and she touched his shoulder for a moment, then drew the pulser and checked it quickly.

"This way, My Lady," LaFollet said urgently, and she turned to follow him . . . then stopped. Four bodies lay on the deck, all oozing blood from multiple flechette hits. She recognized two guards whose names she'd never bothered to learn, and Timmons . . . and Robert Whitman.

"*Bob*," she whispered. She started to go to her knees beside him, but LaFollet gripped her upper arm and shook his head fiercely.

"There's no time, My Lady!" If Honor had known him even a little less well, she would have hated him in that moment, for the words came out brusque and harsh, devoid of any emotion. But she did know him, and she recognized the matching anguish behind that mask of nonfeeling as he tugged on her arm again. "We've got to get moving, My Lady. They got the alarm out before Bob killed them."

Honor nodded and tried to clear her mind as Candless appeared on her other side and he and LaFollet half-lifted her down into the lift shaft. Marcia McGinley was waiting to help, and Honor clung to her for a moment while her armsmen jumped down beside her. She tried to speak, but her ops officer only gave her a short, fierce hug, picked up a flechette gun of her own, and vanished into the shaft's dimness on Candless' heels while Venizelos joined Honor and LaFollet.

"At least we've got plenty of guns," the commander told Honor grimly, handing her a flechette gun to go with her pulser. "I stocked up on spare magazines, too."

"Come on, My Lady," LaFollet said urgently, and he and Venizelos urged her into motion.

"They're trying the lift again!" Alistair McKeon heard someone shout, and a grenade launcher coughed in rapid fire.

Three grenades sizzled past him and dropped neatly through the doors the first assault attempt had left jammed half open, and there was a moment of silence. Then the screams began a half heartbeat before the grenades exploded in rapid succession. Their effect in the enclosed lift shaft must have been indescribable, but Jasper Mayhew sent two more after them.

McKeon grunted in satisfaction, but he also looked at Solomon Marchant.

"We need somebody in position to actually see who's coming down that shaft," he said urgently. "The one thing we don't want is to accidentally kill our own people if they come that way with Lady Harrington!"

"I'll take care of it," the Grayson assured him, and waved for Clinkscales to join him as he loped over to the jammed lift. The lift at the other end of the bay gallery appeared undamaged so far, but Russ Sanko and Senior Chief Halburton were camped right outside its doors with a plasma rifle dug in behind a barricade of shattered machinery and equipment pallets.

Another of Harkness' programs had locked all the lifts to Boat Bay Four—a fact the Peeps obviously had already discovered. So far, they were restricting themselves to the forward lift only, and since they couldn't use the lift car itself, they'd come down the shaft and tried to blow the doors into the gallery. They'd partially succeeded, and the explosion when they blew the doors had killed Chief Reilly, but the rest of McKeon's people had massacred the entire assault team before it could clear the shaft. The undamaged rear lift remained a threat, but McKeon had decided against blowing it himself. Honor might need it, and Sanko and Halburton made a pretty effective security measure. Anyone who tried to use it to attack the boat bay might get as far as opening the doors; he certainly wouldn't get any further.

McKeon turned where he stood, watching the rest of his people scurry about their tasks, and even as he barked orders, a corner of his mind continued to marvel at Horace Harkness. The senior chief's "defection" had fooled even McKeon, and the captain fully intended to sit on him, if that was what it took, to get the entire story out of him. But that would have to wait. Just now, all that mattered was that Harkness' crazy plan actually seemed to be succeeding.

The fact that *Tepes* was a State Security ship worked in their favor at the moment. Each of the assault shuttles in the boat bay was configured to drop one of StateSec's outsized infantry companies, approximately seventy-five percent bigger than a Royal Manticoran Marine company, at minimum notice. That meant their onboard guns and external ordnance racks were left permanently armed . . . and that the weapons in their small arms racks were kept charged, with ammunition ready to hand. His people had many times more firepower than they could possibly use, all courtesy of StateSec, and they were employing everything they had the manpower to fire with savage satisfaction.

But not all of them could be spared to shoot bad guys. Harkness had moved his precious minicomp from the access slot Clinkscales had used to the cockpit of one of the shuttles and put it into straight terminal mode to wage war against the Peep computer techs who had belatedly realized what was going on. The senior chief had two enormous advantages: he was a better programmer than any of them, and, unlike them, *he* knew exactly what he'd done in the first place. But he had two matching disadvantages, for there were more of the Peeps and, unlike him, they had physical access to all the ship's systems. After twenty minutes of trying to take control back from him, they'd begun shutting computers down—or ripping them out—and going to manual control.

Fortunately for the escaped prisoners, Harkness had planned his original sabotage carefully. Wherever possible, he'd used the computers to inflict major damage on systems rather than simply locking them down, and *Tepes* was going to require months of repairs before she could possibly return to service. Her crew, unfortunately, seemed to have grasped that, and they appeared to be perfectly willing to inflict massive additional damage on their own ship if that was the only way to get at their enemies.

"Ready to launch, Sir!"

McKeon turned at Geraldine Metcalf's shout. She stood just outside the docking tube to the bay's number two assault shuttle, and he waved acknowledgment. His tac officer swam down the tube while Anson Lethridge unlocked the docking arms. Then the shuttle's thrusters flared as Metcalf sent it drifting out of the bay, and McKeon took a moment to breathe a silent prayer that Harkness really had gotten the Peeps' weapons shut down.

✧　　　✧　　　✧

Geraldine Metcalf took the shuttle up the side of the battlecruiser on reaction thrusters alone. The big assault boat felt logy and clumsy, and a part of her screamed to kick up the wedge and get more acceleration, but that was out of the question. She had a very specific job to do, and any betraying emissions would keep her from doing it.

She settled into position above the ship, passive sensors searching down past its hammerhead bow. If anything came up from Camp Charon, it was almost certain to come in from ahead, and she glanced sideways at Sarah DuChene as her copilot ran her fingers down the weapons panel and green standby lights began to burn an ominous scarlet.

"Message from Camp Charon, Citizen Admiral," Harrison Fraiser announced, and Tourville gestured for him to continue. "Your intention to render aid to *Tepes*, if required, is approved, but Brigadier Tresca says he has no confirmation that it *is* required. He's sending up some shuttles to check, and he'll advise us of their findings. In the meantime, we are not to cross the outer mine perimeter without express permission."

"Wonderful," Bogdanovich growled. "The bastards *still* don't want us anywhere in their sky, do they?"

"Now, now, Yuri," Tourville said mildly, watching Honeker's eyes for any flash of condemnation. He didn't see one, and he filed that away for future consideration . . .

"Down!"

Andrew LaFollet tackled Honor as gunfire suddenly broke out ahead of them. The fall drove the breath from her, and she coughed, fighting for air as the whine of pulsers and the heavier coughing of flechette guns filled the shaft. There were shouts and screams, and LaFollet released her and went crawling up the shaft. She started to follow, but a hand closed on her ankle and she jerked her head around.

"You stay here," Andreas Venizelos told her flatly. She opened her mouth, and he shook his head. "You're a commodore. More to the point, you're that man's Stead-holder, and he didn't come all this way to get you just to have you killed now."

Pulser darts shrieked as they ricocheted from some projection in a shower of sparks, and LaFollet ducked involuntarily. But he never stopped moving, and he quickly caught up with Candless and McGinley. They were bellied down behind a flange supporting one of the shaft's pressers, with an excellent field of fire. Unfortunately, the Peeps further up the shaft had an equally excellent field of fire, which meant the escapees' best covert route to Boat Bay Four was blocked.

More pulser darts screamed down the shaft, and Candless moved to the side to hose the enemy with flechettes in response. He had the dispersion pattern set for medium coverage, and he tracked his fire across the entire width of the shaft. A horrible, gurgling shriek answered, and he drew back into cover just as more darts whined past.

"How many?" LaFollet asked.

"I don't know," Candless replied, eyes sweeping the dimness ahead. "It was pure luck we saw them in time to take cover. I'd guess there're at least fifteen or twenty. No heavy weapons—yet—or they'd already have taken us out, but that's going to change."

"If they can coordinate well enough," McGinley put in. She sounded much tenser than Candless, but then, this wasn't exactly her kind of fight. "If Harkness' sabotage worked, their communications're probably at least as screwed up as ours are."

LaFollet nodded absently. Their own stolen communicators were getting only gibberish, which probably meant Harkness' efforts to cripple the Peeps' central communications net had worked. But the presence of those people up ahead was proof it hadn't worked completely . . . and that somebody on the other side had figured out at least part of what was going on. If they hadn't guessed what was happening, they wouldn't have known to block the lift shaft between the brig and Boat Bay Four, and if they hadn't had at least some communications ability, they couldn't have gotten these people here to do the blocking. But how *much* com capability did they have? If it was any more than fragmentary, he'd never get the Steadholder to safety, because there were simply too many people aboard this ship. If their officers could tell them where to go to intercept the escapees . . .

"I'll take it," Candless said calmly. He hadn't even glanced at LaFollet, and he never looked away from the shaft now, but his conversational tone proved he'd been thinking exactly what LaFollet had. "Head back about sixty meters and try that service tunnel on deck nineteen," he went on. "Commander McGinley can show you."

"Now wait a minute!" McGinley began. "We can't just—"

"Yes, we can," LaFollet said softly. "Here." He thrust the memo board at her, then jabbed a thumb back down the shaft. "Go," he said, and his flat voice held an implacable note of command. McGinley stared at him for a moment, then inhaled sharply, turned, and slithered into the dimness, and LaFollet looked at Candless.

"Are you sure, Jamie?" he asked quietly.

"I'm sure." Candless' reply was almost serene, and he turned his head to smile at LaFollet. "We've had some good times, Major. Now go get the Steadholder out of this."

"I will," LaFollet told him. It wasn't just a promise; it was an oath, and Candless nodded in satisfaction.

"You'd better be going then, Andrew," he said much more gently. "And later, when you've got her out of here, tell her—" He paused, unable to find the words he wanted, and LaFollet nodded.

"I will," he said again, and put one arm around his fellow armsman, hugging him tight. Then he turned and followed McGinley back down the shaft.

It took him only a few minutes to reach Honor and Venizelos. They stood where McGinley had already passed them, gazing up the shaft as a flechette gun coughed again in rapid fire, and he stepped brusquely past them.

"This way, My Lady," he said, gesturing for them to follow him, but Honor didn't move.

"Where's Jamie?" she asked, and he stopped. He stood for a moment, staring after McGinley, then sighed.

"He's not coming, My Lady," he said as gently as he could.

"*No!* I can't—"

"Yes, you can!" He rounded on her fiercely, and she flinched before the mingled pride and anguish in his face. "We're *armsmen*, My Lady, and you're our Steadholder, and you can do whatever the hell it *takes!*"

She stared at him for a breathless moment, unable to speak, and then her shoulders sagged and her personal armsman took her by the hand, almost as if she were a child.

"Come on, My Lady," he said softly, and she followed him down the shaft while Jamie Candless' flechette gun coughed behind them.

• Chapter Thirty

Scotty Tremaine crawled out of the pinnace's electronics bay and scrubbed sweat out of his eyes. He'd never even imagined doing what he'd just done, and the ease with which he'd accomplished it was more than a little chilling. There were many better small craft flight engineers than he—Horace Harkness, for one—but it hadn't taken a genius to carry out the modifications, and that was scary. Of course, there hadn't been any security features to stop him, since no one in his right mind would have considered that someone might do such an insane thing *on purpose.*

But it was done, now, and he hoped to hell that Harkness was as right about this as he'd been about everything else. His track record had been perfect so far—or as far as they *knew*, at any rate—but it seemed unfair to dump so much responsibility on one man.

But we didn't *"dump" it on him, did we? He volunteered himself for it from the get-go. All we* did *was sit around and think he'd really deserted.*

Tremaine felt a fresh, dull burn of shame at the thought, even though there was no logical reason he should. Harkness had played his role well enough to fool the Peeps, and no doubt the reactions of the rest of the POWs had contributed to his success. Yet despite all that, Tremaine couldn't quite forgive himself for having believed even for a moment that Harkness could truly turn traitor.

He made himself shake that thought off and closed the bay hatch. He stood up in the pinnace's passenger compartment and nodded to Chief Barstow.

"This bird's ready," he said. "Now let's go see about *ours.*"

"Base, I have *Tepes* on visual."

Geraldine Metcalf cupped her palm over her earbug as if that could help her hear better. Not that she really needed to; the voice from the lead cargo shuttle was clear and crisp, and she watched the three crimson dots creep closer on her targeting display and wished the assault shuttle's controls felt a bit more familiar. For that matter, she would have traded three fingers from her left hand for the ability to bring her active sensors on-line. The assault shuttle was well concealed, more than half hidden in the visual and radar shadow of *Tepes'* flared bow, and its passive systems *seemed* to have a good lock on the cargo shuttles, but that sense of being in someone else's bird—of not *quite* having everything under perfect control—continued to jab at her like a sharp stick.

She'd logged thousands of hours in small craft, and if she wasn't as hot a natural pilot as Scotty Tremaine, she *was* immensely experienced. That was one reason she'd drawn this assignment, and intellectually she felt confident of her ability to carry it out. But that didn't keep her from wishing she'd had a month or two to familiarize herself with this big brute of a boat. She felt heavy and clumsy, which was purely an illusion but felt no less real because of it. And the truth was that she and DuChene would have been hopelessly outclassed in any sort of maneuvering dogfight. Their lack of experience with their craft would have shown quickly under those circumstances . . . but, then, the entire point of this operation was to keep it from ever turning into a dogfight, now wasn't it? Besides, those trash haulers over there weren't even armed.

"Any sign of external damage, One?" another voice asked over her earbug.

"Negative at this time, Base. I have some debris scatter, but no sign of hull ruptures. I'm assuming they must have blown a boat bay—maybe more than one—but I don't see any indication of anything worse than that. They're certainly not leaking any more air, and I don't have any life pod beacons. It's gotta be some sort of internal electronics failure."

"Yeah?" Charon Base sounded dubious. "I never heard of an electronics failure taking out a ship's whole com net *and* causing her boat bays to blow up, have you?"

"No, but what the hell *else* can it be? If they were in any kind of serious trouble, we'd have life pods and small craft evacuating all over the place up here!"

Metcalf smothered a chuckle at the Peep's exasperated tones. She couldn't fault the logic on either side, but that was only because neither of them had ever heard of an "electronics failure" named Horace Harkness.

"Can't argue with that, One," Charon Base admitted after a moment. "What's your ETA for rendezvous?"

"I make it just under fifteen minutes, Base. Maybe a little longer. I want to do a low pass and get a look at her bays before we try to dock at one of the external points."

"Your call, One. Let us know if you see anything interesting."

"Will do, Base. One, clear."

The voices died, and Metcalf watched the shuttles drift slowly closer. A soft, musical tone sounded, and she turned to look at DuChene.

"Acquired and locked," her weaponeer said, and looked up to meet her eyes. It no longer really matter how good the shuttle's passives were, because the seekers in the missiles themselves had the Peeps now. They were locked on and ready to track, and the smile Geraldine Metcalf shared with Sarah DuChene could have frozen a star.

"Still nothing from *Tepes*?" Citizen Rear Admiral Tourville demanded.

"No, Citizen Admiral," Fraiser replied so patiently that Tourville blushed. He let one hand rest lightly on the com officer shoulder for a moment by way of apology, then crossed back over to Shannon Foraker's station to glare down at the tac panel.

Count Tilly had reduced her velocity relative to Hades

to 10,750 KPS, but she would need another thirty-five minutes to reduce it to zero, and by then she would be over seven light-minutes from the planet. To achieve even that much Citizen Captain Hewitt was running his ship flat out, with zero margin for error on her compensator. Tourville supposed many people would question the wisdom of doing that when there was a planetary base available to investigate, but no professional spacer could ignore a ship he suspected was in trouble. And as the minutes ticked away, each of them left him more and more confident that something *was* wrong—probably seriously. Too many systems must have failed simultaneously to produce this total silence, and he smothered another curse at the dilatoriness of Camp Charon's efforts. Damn it to hell, that was one of *their* ships up there! What the *hell* did those StateSec idiots think they were *doing?*

But there was no answer . . . and *he* was still an hour and twenty minutes away.

"I don't like it," Honor said flatly, crouching to look at the memo board with the others. "It's too exposed."

"I'm not denying that it's exposed, Ma'am," Venizelos replied in an equally flat voice, "but we're running out of time."

"What about detouring through these service ways?" Honor demanded, tapping one edge of the display.

"I don't think it'll work, Ma'am," McGinley replied before Venizelos could. "At least someone knows some of us are crawling around in the lift shafts and ducting. If they've managed to pass the word, the bad guys would expect us to go that way from our last point of contact with them. Besides, Andy's right; we're running out of time. We're going to have to make a dash for it, and this offers us the shortest total exposure."

Honor frowned, kneading the dead side of her face with her fingertips and wishing she could feel it. She was closer to Nimitz now, and the 'cat's emotions crackled in their link. The dark shadows of his physical pain were stronger, but so was his excitement. She could get no clear picture of what was happening, but certainly *Nimitz* seemed to feel things were going according to plan, and she clung to that hope.

But whatever was happening in the boat bay, Venizelos and McGinley were right; they still had to get there somehow, and their options were narrowing. It was just that the route Venizelos had picked ran straight for the nearest lift connecting to Boat Bay Four, and if the Peeps *did* know there were stragglers trying to link up with the rest of the escapees . . .

"Andrew?" she asked, looking at her armsman, and LaFollet shrugged.

"I think they're right, My Lady. Certainly it's a risk, but not as big a one as going the long way 'round. If we take too long, Captain McKeon will either have to leave us behind . . . or, worse, wait for us until the Peeps get *all* of us."

"All right," she sighed, and the right side of her mouth managed a wry smile. "Who am I to argue with the lunatics who planned this whole thing?"

"Here they come . . ." DuChene murmured, and Metcalf nodded. The Peep cargo shuttles were getting so close they'd have to spot the assault shuttle shortly, hiding spot or not. Besides, they were beginning to split up, and she couldn't have that.

She watched for another five seconds, then punched the button.

The range was less than sixty kilometers to the furthest shuttle as her impeller drive missiles kicked free of the racks and brought up their wedges. They couldn't match the eighty or ninety thousand gravities of acceleration all-up shipboard weapons could crank, but they *could* accelerate at forty thousand gravities. The longest missile flight lasted barely .576 seconds, and that was much too short a time for anyone to get a transmission off or even realize what was happening.

✧   ✧   ✧

"What the—?"

Shannon Foraker jerked upright in her chair, staring at her display, then turned to call for her admiral. But Tourville had seen her jump, and he was already halfway across Flag Deck to her.

"What?" he demanded.

"Those three shuttles from Charon just blew the hell up, Sir," she said quietly.

"What do you mean?" Bogdanovich demanded from behind Tourville.

"I mean they're *gone*, Sir. Their drive strengths peaked, and then they blew."

"What the *hell* is going on over there?" Bogdanovich fumed.

"Well, Sir, if I had to make a guess, I'd say each of those shuttles just ate itself an impeller head missile," Foraker told him. "And they must've been fairly small birds, or I'd have seen their impeller signatures from here, and I didn't."

The chief of staff stared at her, as if unable or unwilling to believe what she'd just said, then wheeled to Tourville.

If he'd expected the citizen rear admiral to reject the ops officer's diagnosis, he was disappointed. Instead, Tourville simply nodded and walked slowly back to his command chair. He parked himself in it, and spoke very calmly.

"Shannon, I want you to launch an RD. It can get there a hell of a lot quicker than we can, and I want a closer look at what's going on. Got it?"

"Aye, Citizen Admiral," Foraker replied, and Tourville looked up as Bogdanovich and Honeker arrived on either side of his chair.

"It would seem," he said in a quiet voice accompanied by a tight smile, "that Committeewoman Ransom is being hoist by her own petard."

"Meaning what?" Honeker asked flatly.

"Meaning that the only thing *I* can think of to explain what's going on over there is that her prisoners are up to something."

"But that's even crazier than any other explanation!" Bogdanovich protested—less, Tourville suspected, because he truly disagreed than because he felt *someone* had to do it. "There are only thirty of them, and Vladovich has over two thousand people!"

"Sometimes quantity means less than quality," Tourville observed. "And whatever they're doing, they seem to have completely paralyzed that ship. I wonder how they got to her computers . . . ?"

He frowned, in thought, then shrugged. At the moment, how they'd done it was less important than the fact that they had, and he sighed unhappily as he realized what he had to do. He suspected he would spend a lot of time avoiding mirrors for the next several weeks—or months—but his duty left him no choice.

"Harrison, com Warden Tresca." He looked up and met Honeker's eyes. "Tell him I think the prisoners aboard *Tepes* are trying to take the ship . . . or destroy it."

"Here they come again!"

McKeon wasn't certain who'd shouted the warning this time, but it came not a moment too soon. The Peeps had finally gotten reorganized, and they came storming down the crippled lift shaft behind a curtain of grenades. Pulsers snarled and ripped and flechette guns coughed from the shaft, and McKeon swore bitterly as Enrico Walker took a pulser dart that blew his head apart. The surgeon lieutenant's body went down with the bonelessness of the dead, and he saw Jasper Mayhew thrown backward as a burst of flechettes slammed into his chest. But like all of them, Mayhew had found time to climb into unpowered body armor from one of the assault shuttles, and he dragged himself back up to his knees and his launcher hurled grenades down the Peeps' throats. Another of McKeon's petty officers went down—dead, he was grimly certain— as a Peep grenade bounced out of the open lift doors and exploded directly behind her, but then Sanko and Halburton got their plasma rifle turned around, and a packet of white hot energy went roaring up the shaft. Anyone who got in its way never had time to realize he was dead, but those on the fringe of its area of effect were less fortunate. Shrieks of agony and secondary explosions as ammunition cooked off rolled from the lift shaft like the voices of the damned, and then Sanko fired a second round and the screams cut off instantly.

No more shots were fired from the shaft, and McKeon heaved a sigh of relief. But he knew the respite would be brief. There were limits on the weapons the Peeps would willingly use against them as long as they held the boat bay—the explosions in the other bays had been a pointed reminder that there were things in here which didn't take kindly to combustion—but there were a lot more of them than there were of *his* people. And there were fewer of his than there had been, he thought, looking at Walker's body.

He pushed up and walked over to Harkness. The senior chief's face was drawn and soaked with sweat, but his hands were no longer busy on the keyboard, and he looked up at McKeon's approach.

"Looks like they finally kicked my butt out, Sir," he said, and bared his teeth in a wolfish grin. "But by the time they did, just about everything but life support got slagged right down to glass. Even if we don't make it, they're gonna be a long time trying to put *this* bucket of bolts back on-line."

"So they've got complete control of whatever's left?" McKeon asked.

"Just about, Sir. I don't think they can break my lock on that lift—" he pointed to the intact lift doors through which no attack had yet come "—and there's no software *left* down here in the bay itself. But give 'em another forty, fifty minutes, and they're gonna start getting some sensors and weapons back under manual control. And when they do—"

He broke off with a shrug, and McKeon nodded grimly.

✧   ✧   ✧

"Now remember, Ma'am," Venizelos said, his voice low and urgent as they crouched just inside a ventilation grate, "if Harkness pulled it off, that lift'll be waiting when we get there."

Honor nodded. Their journey through the bowels of the ship had been too rushed for Venizelos to give her many details on Harkness' achievements, but he'd managed to hit the high points, and she was astounded by how thoroughly the senior chief had worked this all out. The fact that StateSec had seen fit to maintain outdated files where the brig area was concerned had thrown a monkey wrench into a part of his plans, but that was hardly his fault. And if the *rest* of them hadn't been working—so far, at least— the Peeps would already have reasserted control of their computers . . . in which case it would all be over by now.

But if it wasn't going to be over, anyway, they had to get to the boat bay—quickly. Andy and Marcia were right about that, and she leaned back against the wall of the duct, panting for breath and hoping none of the others realized how exhausted she was. The weight and muscle tone she'd lost during her confinement dragged at her like an anchor, and she forced her eyes open and gave her people—her *friends*—one of her half-smiles.

"At least I shouldn't have any trouble remembering the code," she said, and Venizelos surprised her with a genuine chuckle, for Harkness had used *her* birthday. She had no idea how he'd happened to remember it, but the senior chief was turning out to be full of surprises.

"All right," Venizelos said, and looked at LaFollet. "Andrew?"

"We go down the passage in single file," the armsman said. "I take point, then Lady Harrington, Commander McGinley, and you. Here, My Lady." He handed the memo board to Honor to take his flechette gun in a two-handed grip.

"You're sure of the route?" she asked.

"Positive." LaFollet took one hand from the gun long enough to tap his temple. "And I want you to have the map if something—"

He shrugged, and she nodded, heart aching for the risks these people—and Jamie Candless and Bob Whitman— had taken for her. She wanted to say something, to thank them, but there was no time and she didn't have the words, anyway. And so she only smiled at her armsman and put an arm around each of her staff officers, hugging them briefly.

"All right," she said then, gathering her own weapon back up. "Let's be about it."

"Warden Tresca thanks you for your warning, Citizen Admiral," Harrison Fraiser reported. "However, he thinks you may be overly alarmed, and he's confident *Tepes'* crew will soon regain control of their vessel. In the meantime, he's ready to deal with any small craft which may attempt to launch."

"Oh, that's just wonderful!" This time the mutter came from Shannon Foraker, not Bogdanovich. Tourville glanced at Honeker, and then, to their mutual astonishment, both of them grinned matching helpless what-the-hell-do-we-do-now? grins at one another.

"How so, Shannon?" Honeker asked after a moment, and Tourville wondered if Shannon even noticed that the People's commissioner had used her first name.

"Well, I was just thinking, Sir," the ops officer replied. "He says he can deal with any small craft that try to launch, right?" The People's commissioner nodded, and Foraker shrugged. "I'd be more reassured by that if they didn't already *have* at least one small craft—and an armed one, at that—in space." Honeker quirked an eyebrow, and Foraker sighed. "Sir," she said gently, "where *else* could the missiles that killed Charon's shuttle flight have come from?"

"Go!"

LaFollet kicked the grate loose and charged out after it, and his flechette gun coughed twice before Honor was out on his heels. Only one of his victims had the chance to scream, and then the armsman was running down the passage with Honor on his heels.

It was hard for her to keep up with him, despite her longer legs. Her heart pounded and her working eye blurred with strain as she fought to match his pace, but it took everything she had, and she cursed her long imprisonment and poor diet. She heard McGinley on *her* heels, and Venizelos after her, and then her blood ran cold as someone shouted behind all of them. Pulsers whined and flechette guns coughed, and despite herself, she turned her head to see Venizelos peel off as he rounded a bend. Her feet tried to stop, fighting to go back to him, but McGinley charged into her from behind.

"*Go!*" the ops officer screamed, and Honor knew she was right, and her legs obeyed her staffer, but oh how her mind cried out against it, and then Venizelos was down on one knee, and the last thing she ever saw of him he was firing steadily, calmly, like a man picking off targets in a gallery, covering her retreat while she ran and left him to die.

More fire echoed, from ahead this time, and she half-stumbled over a body. For a terrifying instant she thought it was LaFollet, but then she saw the StateSec uniform and knew her armsman had killed whoever it was on the run. As he was killing more people.

LaFollet had saved her life once before, from assassins—he and Jamie Candless and Eddy Howard—but Honor had been too stunned by events to truly realize what was happening then. Today was different, perhaps because Jamie and Eddy were dead and her heart of hearts knew LaFollet was damned to die for her as well. She didn't know. She only knew that this time she blinked her eye clear of the filmy blur of strain, and for the first time she saw what a lethal force he truly was.

He ran quickly, smoothly, head turning in metronome arcs to sweep the passage ahead of him. He carried the heavy flechette gun at his hip, the sling over his shoulder to steady it, and his finger stroked the trigger in elegant, precise bursts as astonished Peeps popped up before him, attracted by the clangor of battle exploding in their very midst. He was a wizard of death, dispatching his sorcery in the lethal patterns of his flechettes, for he was fighting for his Steadholder's life and anyone who crossed his path was doomed.

And then he rounded the last bend and shouted in triumph as he reached the lift doors at last.

He spun back the way he'd come, waving Honor past him to enter the command code, and he and Marcia McGinley crouched on either side of the passage down which they'd come, pouring fire back up it. Heavier weapons were snarling back, now, and as Honor hammered the lift button, she heard the distinctive, ear-splitting devastation of a tribarrel slicing bulkheads like a bandsaw.

The doors opened and she leapt through them, stabbing at the panel. Lights flickered on the display, then burned steadily, confirming that Harkness' control of the lift still held, and she turned back towards her friends.

"Come on!" she shouted. *"Come on!"*

McGinley heard her and wheeled, teeth bared in a huge smile of triumph as she ran for the lift . . . and then she seemed to trip in midair, and her torso exploded as the tribarrel sawed through the bulkhead, and Honor screamed in useless denial.

"Go, My Lady!" LaFollet shouted, slamming his final magazine into the flechette gun. *"Go now!"*

He went down on one knee, firing desperately—firing like Jamie had, like Robert and Venizelos and Marcia—and Honor couldn't leave him. She couldn't!

"Come on, Andrew!" she screamed, but he ignored her, and then a grenade skittered around the bend and he hurled away his weapon and flung himself on it. Somehow he reached it before it exploded, and his frantic heave sent it back the way it had come, but not quite soon enough, for the blast picked him up and bounced him off the

bulkhead like a rag doll. He slammed to the deck, motionless, and Honor's heart died within her.

She had to go. She *knew* she had to go. That this was what her armsmen—her friends—had died for. That only her escape would give their deaths meaning, and that it was her duty—her *responsibility*—to go.

And she couldn't. It was too much, more than she had in her to give, and she dropped her own weapon and hurled herself from the lift. The grenade explosion seemed to have stunned the attackers—any who were still alive—and not a shot was fired as she flung herself down beside Andrew. She was weak and wasted, running on adrenaline and desperation alone, and it didn't matter. She snatched him up as if he were a child and flung him over her shoulders even as she turned back towards the lift.

And that was when the Peeps seemed to snap back awake. Pulser darts whined and shrieked, ricocheting from the bulkheads. More grenades exploded. The tribarrel opened fire once more, flaying the bulkheads, and the entire universe was a seething, screaming tide of metal and hate ripping about her ears.

She staggered as a flechette chewed into the outside of her right thigh, but she kept her feet and hurled herself into the lift. She spun on her toes, blood scalding her leg as the wound pumped, and somehow she hit the release button without dropping LaFollet.

The car began to move, and relief rose in her, warring with her grief, but she was going to make it. She and Andrew were going to make—

And that was when the tribarrel tore the lift doors apart.

"The lift! Someone's coming down the lift!"

McKeon whirled at the shout, and his heart leapt. If Harkness' lockout had held, that could only be the people who'd gone after Honor, and if it wasn't—

He beckoned, and Sanko and Halburton turned their plasma rifle back to the undamaged lift while Anson Lethridge dashed across the deck towards it with a grenade launcher.

But then the lift stopped, the doors opened, and Lethridge froze. He stared into it, ugly face blanching, and then he hurled away his launcher and charged into it. McKeon followed on his heels, and the captain gasped in horror at what he saw.

The upper third of the lift car had been torn to bits, not so much shattered as *sliced* by what could only have been a heavy-caliber tribarrel, and bits and pieces of knife-edged alloy—some small as a fingernail paring, others the size of a man's hand—had been spewed out of the lift wall like bullets. He knew they had, for Honor Harrington and Andrew LaFollet lay entangled on the lift floor, and the entire bottom of the car was coated in blood.

Lethridge was already there, lifting LaFollet off his Steadholder and passing the limp armsman to McKeon. The captain took him and passed him out to other, ready hands, but his eyes never left Honor as Lethridge went to his knees in her blood.

It was her arm. Her left arm was shattered just above the elbow, and Lethridge's hands moved with desperate speed as he whipped his own belt around her upper arm, right at the armpit, and yanked the crude tourniquet tight. And then he and McKeon between them picked her horribly limp, blood-soaked body up and ran for the pinnace.

"Bug Out One, this is Bug Two. Say status."

Geraldine Metcalf started to sigh in relief as Captain McKeon's voice sounded in her earbug, but then his tone registered. It was harsh and jagged, with a fury—or a despair—Metcalf had never heard from him, and she turned to look at DuChene.

"Status green," she said into her com after a moment. "I say again, status green."

"Very well," McKeon's voice came back. "Stand by for Falling Leaf."

Two stolen StateSec assault shuttles moved towards one another, hiding in *Tepes'* radar shadow as they used the lobotomized battlecruiser for cover. Some of the ship's systems were coming back on-line under manual control, but not many, and she was still blind, unaware of the two tiny motes gliding rapidly towards her stern on thrusters alone. Nor did any of *Tepes'* crew suspect that Horace Harkness' final—and most deadly—computer programs weren't in the main system at all. They were in the single assault shuttle and pinnace still in Boat Bay Four.

Scotty Tremaine was at Bug Out Two's controls, with McKeon in the copilot's seat, and he watched the digital timer on the instrument panel count down and prayed that Harkness had gotten it right. It felt disloyal to doubt the senior chief, but surely it was too much to expect him to get *everything* right! And if he hadn't—

The third shuttle came screaming out of Boat Bay Four under maximum reaction power. Its carefully programmed flight path brought it whipping up past *Tepes'* armored flank, then steadied down on a course away from Hades with *Tepes* directly between it and the planet. Its impeller wedge came up as soon as it was clear of the ship, and its acceleration leapt instantly to four hundred gravities.

"Impeller signature!" Shannon Foraker barked.

Count Tilly had killed her velocity relative to Hades and started back the way she'd come, but she remained far beyond any range at which she could have intervened in what was happening in Hades orbit. The drone she'd launched was still too far out for good detail resolution, but it was close enough to see the brilliant gravitic beacon of a pinnace streaking for the stars. For that matter, her shipboard sensors easily picked up its impeller wedge, and Foraker clenched her jaw as the small vessel raced for freedom.

"Do they have it from Camp Charon?" Tourville asked urgently.

"They must, Sir," she said grimly, and looked up to meet her admiral's eyes. Then she looked back at her display, already knowing what she would see.

Most of the defenses around Hades were designed to kill starships, not something as small and agile as a shuttle. None of the energy platforms or hunter-killer missiles could target something that tiny—not efficiently—and Camp Charon was in no mood to try. Nor did it need to, for that was why the old-fashioned area-effect mines had been emplaced. And so the ground base waited calmly until the small craft passed almost directly between two hundred-megaton mines, then pressed a button.

"Now!" McKeon said sharply, and Scotty Tremaine gave his thrusters one more nudge that sent Bug Out Two sliding rapidly away from *Tepes*. The shuttle's onboard sensors were temporarily useless, blinded by the enormous power of that explosion . . . but so, hopefully, were those of Camp Charon.

"Should be activating just . . . about . . . *now!*" McKeon said, and looked through the view port at the battlecruiser shrinking against the stars.

The small craft of all impeller-drive navies have at least one thing in common. They may be larger or smaller, armed or unarmed, fast or slow, but every single one of them is fitted with safety features to prevent it from bringing up its drive when any solid object large enough to endanger it—or to be endangered *by* it—lies within the perimeter of its impeller wedge. And above all, it is impossible to accidentally activate an impeller wedge while still within a boat bay.

But those safeguards, while as near to infallible as they can be made, are designed to prevent *accidents*, and what happened in PNS *Tepes'* Boat Bay Four was no accident. The only vessel left in it was the pinnace upon which Scotty Tremaine had labored, and now Horace Harkness' last program brought its systems on-line. But Scotty had made one small alteration: he had physically cut the links between the pinnace's sensors and its autopilot. The flight computers could no longer "see" the boat bay about them. As far as they could tell, they could have been in deepest, darkest interstellar space, and so they felt no concern at all when they were commanded to bring the pinnace's wedge up while it still lay in its docking buffers.

"My God."

Shannon Foraker's hushed whisper seemed to echo and re-echo across *Count Tilly's* flag deck as PNS *Tepes* blew apart.

No, Lester Tourville thought shakenly. *No, she didn't* blow *apart; she simply* came *apart. She . . . disintegrated.*

And that, he realized, was precisely the right word. The battlecruiser's fusion plants blew as their mag bottles failed, spewing white-hot fury amid the wreckage, but it didn't really matter. Nothing could have survived that dreadful, wrenching blow from *inside* her hull. All the fusion plants did was vaporize a few score tons of wreckage and silhouette the rest of it against a star-bright fury, like snowflakes in a ground car's headlights.

He stared in awe at the visual images of the carnage transmitted from their RD to the main view screen, and he knew how it had happened. He'd never actually seen it before, but there was only one thing the Manties could possibly have done to produce that effect, and a corner of his mind wondered distantly how they'd gotten past the fail-safes that were supposed to make it impossible.

Everard Honeker stood before him, even more stunned than any officer on the flag bridge, and Tourville drew a deep breath as he looked at the People's commissioner's back. He glanced around at the rest of his staff and their yeomen—every one of them as hypnotized as Honeker. All except Shannon Foraker, still bent over her display, seemed unable to think beyond the stunning shock of what had happened, but Tourville could, and a strange, vaulting exuberance warred with his horror at so many deaths. He knew he should be as numb as the others, as incapable of thought, but he couldn't help himself, couldn't keep a single thought from tolling through his brain.

Cordelia Ransom was dead. And so was Henri Vladovich

and all the other people aboard that ship who'd known what Ransom had planned for Lester Tourville and his staff. No one else knew, for they'd stopped nowhere between Barnett and here, and Ransom had taken too much pleasure out of keeping them dangling in suspense to tell anyone what she intended. But now she was gone, and all her files and her entire personal staff were gone with her, and if it was wrong to rejoice when so many people had died, he was sorry, but he just couldn't help it.

And then he saw Shannon Foraker's right hand come out of her lap and move slowly, almost stealthily, towards her panel. Something about its movement caught at his attention, and he crossed quietly to stand behind her. She heard him and looked up, and her hand moved away from the "ERASE" key even more slowly—and far more reluctantly—than it had come.

Tourville gazed down over her shoulder at the tactical recording she'd been replaying, and his jaw clenched as he saw what she'd seen: two pieces of wreckage, larger than most of the others, and on a vector which had clearly taken them away from the murdered battlecruiser *before* she exploded. A vector which just happened to look very much like an unpowered reentry course.

He looked at them for another long moment, rubbing his fierce mustache with one finger. Shannon's drone had seen them, but it was highly unlikely Hades' EMP-blinded sensors had picked them up in time, and with the destruction of the "fleeing" pinnace, no one would even think to look for them. He felt a deep flicker of admiration for whoever had thought this one up, but he knew what his duty required of him.

Yes, I know what "duty" requires, he thought, and reached down past Shannon's shoulder to press his own finger firmly on the "ERASE" key. He heard Shannon inhale sharply, saw her head twitch, but she didn't say a word, and he turned away from her panel. He walked across to where Honeker and Bogdanovich stood, both still staring in awe at the visual imagery of the spreading pattern of wreckage relayed by Shannon's drone, and cleared his throat.

"Too bad," he said gravely, and the sound of his voice startled Honeker into turning to look at him. "There can't be any survivors," Tourville told his commissioner, and shook his head regretfully. "Too bad . . . Lady Harrington deserved better than that."

• Epilogue

She woke slowly, and that was very unlike her. Thirty-five years of naval service had trained her to awaken quickly and cleanly, ready to face any emergency, but this time was different. It was *hard* to wake, and she didn't want to do it. There was too much pain and despair waiting for her, too much loss, and her sleeping brain cringed away from facing it.

But then something changed. A warm weight draped itself across her chest, vibrating with the strength of a deep, buzzing purr, gentle with love, that seemed to pluck at the very core of her.

"N-Nimitz?"

She scarcely recognized the wondering voice. It was cracked and hoarse, its enunciation slurred, yet it was hers, and her eyes fluttered open as a strong, wiry true-hand touched the right side of her face with infinite tenderness.

Her eyes widened, and she sucked in a shuddering breath as Nimitz leaned closer to touch his nose to hers. She stared at him with her one working eye, raising her right hand to caress his ears as if the simple act of touching him was the most precious gift in the universe. Her hand trembled, with weakness as much as emotion, and the 'cat folded down on her chest to rest his cheek against hers while the depth of his love rumbled into her bones with his purr.

"Oh, *Nimitz!*" she whispered into his soft fur, and all the remembered anguish, all the fear and despair she would have died before admitting to an enemy was in that whisper, for this was the other half of her own being, the beloved she had known she would never see again. Tears spilled over her gaunt cheeks, and she reached up to hug him close . . . and froze.

Her right arm moved naturally to clasp him tight, but her left—

Her head snapped over, her working eye wide, and her nostrils flared as shock punched her in the belly, for she had no left arm.

She stared at the bandaged stump, and disbelief was a strange sort of anesthesia. There was no pain, and her mind insisted she could feel the fingers on the hand she no longer had, that they still obeyed her, clenching into a fist when she willed them to. But those sensations were lies, and she lay frozen in that moment of stunned awareness while Nimitz pressed still harder against her and his purr burned still deeper and stronger.

"I'm sorry, Ma'am." Her head turned the other way, and she looked up into Fritz Montoya's face. The surgeon's eyes were shadowed, and she felt his mingled regret and sense of guilt as he sat beside her. "There was nothing else I could do," he told her. "There was too much damage, too much—" He stopped and inhaled, then looked her squarely in the eyes. "I didn't have the tools to save it, Ma'am, and if I hadn't amputated, we'd have lost you."

She stared at him, trapped between too many emotions for rational thought. Joy at her reunion with Nimitz, astonishment that she was alive at all, the shock of her mutilation, and behind all that the waking memories of friends who *had* died—who would never wake, as she, to find they had somehow survived after all—crushed down upon her, and she couldn't speak. She could only stare up into Montoya's careworn face while her right arm held Nimitz tight and her soul clung even more tightly to his.

She didn't know how long it lasted, but finally the right corner of her mouth trembled in a fragile, almost-smile, and she freed her hand from Nimitz to hold it out to Montoya.

"Fritz," she said softly, wonderingly. He took her hand

and squeezed it fiercely, and her too-thin fingers returned his clasp.

"I'm sorry," he repeated, and she shook her head on the pillow.

"Why?" she asked gently. "For saving my life—again?"

"He did that, My Lady," another voice said, and Honor gasped. She tried to sit up, but her right hand still held Montoya's, and she hissed in sudden pain as she tried to rise on the left hand she no longer had and the bandaged stump pressed into the firm softness on which she lay.

Montoya started to stand, his face distressed, but someone else's arms reached out to support her. Nimitz spilled from her chest, lying beside her, and she pulled her right hand from Montoya's. Her arm went out, and the pain still rippling through her meant nothing at all as she hugged Andrew LaFollet with all the fierce strength in her wasted frame.

Her armsman returned her embrace, and she felt the terrible power of his own emotions echo and reecho deep within *her*. She tasted his own relief at having survived, his grief for those who had not—and his fierce pride in them. But over and above everything else, she felt his devotion—his love—for *her* and his joy that *she* was alive, and she clung to him as she had to Nimitz.

Such moments were too intense to last, and at last she drew a deep, quivering breath and relaxed her embrace. LaFollet eased his, as well, and started to step back. But she shook her head quickly and reached across her body to pat the side of the bed. The expression on the live side of her face was almost pleading, and he hesitated for a moment, then shrugged and sat beside her. She gazed at him, then at Montoya, and a different sort of disbelief filled her as she looked beyond the doctor and recognized the bulkhead and low overhead of a pinnace or shuttle. It wasn't a design she was familiar with, and someone had rigged curtains to screen in the folded down row of seats which had been turned into her bed, but whatever it was, it definitely was *not* the brig of PNS *Tepes*, and she turned wonderingly back to LaFollet.

"How?" she asked simply, and he smiled.

"We're still figuring that out ourselves, My Lady," he said wryly, "but we know *who* pulled it off."

He looked at Montoya, one eyebrow raised, and the doctor reached for Honor's wrist. He felt her pulse for several seconds, then looked into her natural eye and nodded.

"I think she's up for it," he said. "But you tell the captain that when I kick you all out, you *stay* kicked out."

"Yes, Sir," LaFollet said with a grin, and stood once more. He patted Honor's shoulder, then turned and pushed through the curtains, and Honor began wiggling determinedly up the bed. Montoya started to speak sharply to her, but then he sighed, shook his head, and helped her into a sitting position and propped her with pillows.

She smiled her thanks, but her attention was back on Nimitz as the 'cat moved to lie across her lap. She'd felt the flash of his pain, and her good eye darkened as she absorbed the lurching limp which had replaced his usual smooth gracefulness. She eased him down, settling him as comfortably as possible, and her fingers trembled as she stroked his twisted midshoulder and midlimb. She looked back up at Montoya, and the doctor returned her gaze levelly.

"I did my best with what I had, Skipper," he said, "but the bastards wouldn't give me much. The good news is that aside from the bone and joint damage, he seems to be fine—and if we can get him back home, any good Sphinx veterinary surgeon can repair the bone damage. The bad news is that he'll be in constant low-grade pain, and he won't be climbing any trees until we do get him to a surgeon."

"You're wrong, Fritz," she said, resting her hand lightly on the 'cat's head. "The *real* good news is that he's alive, and I owe you and Shannon Foraker for that, don't I?"

"Foraker more than me," Montoya half disagreed. He

opened his mouth to say something more, then shut it again as someone pulled the curtains back.

Honor turned her head, and her right eyebrow rose in fresh surprise as she recognized the hazel-eyed man in Peep uniform standing beside Alistair McKeon. Warner Caslet grinned crookedly at her and shrugged.

"I didn't expect to meet under conditions like these, Milady," he told her wryly. "Given the alternative—for both of us—however, I'm delighted to have the opportunity."

"Warner," she said wonderingly, then looked at McKeon. The broad-shouldered captain looked almost as worn as she felt, and there were gaps in his teeth when he smiled, but his eyes were bright as he took the hand she held out to him.

"Long way from Basilisk Station, isn't it?" he said, and Honor surprised herself with a chuckle.

"I suppose it is," she agreed, and looked past him at Horace Harkness. The senior chief looked almost bashful, as if he wanted to shuffle his feet while he stared down at his toes, and she looked back at McKeon and raised her eyebrow once more.

"I've got a feeling Sergeant-Major Babcock is going to be proud of her husband when we get him home," the captain said with a grin. "He's the one who got us all out."

"So I understand." Honor turned her gaze on Harkness once more, and this time the senior chief *did* look down at his toes.

"Yes, Ma'am. He sort of, um, convinced the Peeps he'd gone over to them, got access to one of their mini-computers—I'll let him give you the details later—and hacked into their main system. He set up the entire breakout . . . and just as an encore, he managed to arrange things so the Peeps think we're all dead."

"I don't—" Honor began, then stopped. There was too much going on here, and she wasn't in shape to assimilate all of it. That would have to come later, and she suspected it was going to take quite a while for them to tell her everything, but for now . . .

"I want to hear all about it when I'm in shape to

understand it all," she told her subordinates. "But for now, what I really need is a status report."

"Yes, Ma'am," McKeon said, and rubbed his eyebrow for a moment, as if marshaling his thoughts. "Basically, Ma'am, we're on the surface of the planet Hades. Thanks to the fact that Harkness here is probably the most devious hacker outside a maximum security prison—excuse me; outside any *other* maximum security prison—we managed to get off *Tepes* once she was in planetary orbit. More than that, he blew the whole ship the hell up, and the Peeps think we went with her."

"He—?" Honor blinked, then looked at Harkness. "You blew the ship *up*, Senior Chief?" she asked very carefully.

"Uh, yes, Ma'am," Harkness mumbled, turning an alarming shade of red. "Actually, ah, I sort of, well . . ."

"He demonstrated what happens when a pinnace brings its wedge up *inside* a boat bay, Skipper," McKeon told her, and Honor blinked again, with a sort of appalled respect.

"I see," she said, and then the right side of her mouth twitched. "Remind me to never, ever get you angry at *me*, Horace."

Harkness went an even darker crimson as she used his first name for the first time in the eleven years they'd known one another. He started to mumble something, then stopped, looked at her, and shrugged helplessly.

"He also pulled a lot of information on Hades out of *Tepes'* database," McKeon went on, as much to save Harkness from more embarrassment as to bring Honor up to date. "I've been looking it over since we planeted, and I can see why the Peeps figure this is a pretty secure prison."

"Oh?" Honor returned her gaze to him with renewed attentiveness.

"Yes, Ma'am. It's simple enough: there's not a single thing on the entire planet which a human can metabolize." Honor's eye narrowed, and he nodded. "You've got it, Skipper. They don't need to lock anyone *up*; all they have to do is lock the prisoners *out* of the food depot. We don't have figures on the prisoner population, but if the rumors are true, they've been dumping military and political prisoners here for something like seventy years, and most of the people they've dumped had prolong. There have to be thousands of 'inmates' down here, but the Peeps have them spread out across the surface of an entire planet in relatively small packets, and they can't stray far from wherever they were dumped in the first place because that's where the Peeps deliver their rations."

"I see." Honor's fingers stroked Nimitz's ears, and she frowned. "How big is the garrison?"

"Again, we don't have precise figures, but I'd estimate there're around a thousand or fifteen hundred of them. Their main facility is on an island in the middle of Hades' biggest ocean, it's covered by satellite reconnaissance, and according to *Tepes'* database, they've got light and medium antiair defenses around the base. The only contact between there and the rest of the planet is by air, and once they've been shipped down to the surface, no prisoners are allowed on the island." McKeon shrugged. "Since they control the only food source, and the only means to get to that food source, *and* the orbital defenses around the planet, security's never been a real big concern for them."

"I see," Honor repeated, then flicked her hand at the bulkheads around them. "But now?" she suggested.

"Now that might just change," McKeon agreed with an unpleasant smile. "Thanks to Harkness here, we've got a pair of heavy assault shuttles with almost full loads of external ordnance, full small arms racks, and a fair amount of unpowered armor."

Honor felt both eyebrows rise and gave Harkness another respectful look.

"We're also pretty sure the Peeps don't know we're here," McKeon went on. "From what Harkness pulled out of *Tepes'* database, they've got a good satellite surveillance net, but it concentrates on covering their main facility, and we touched down on the far side of the planet. We made dead-stick approaches without using impeller drive, too, and we didn't cut in the countergrav until we were under a hundred meters. There's no way anyone saw us make reentry or land, and this place is covered in triple-canopy jungle, so camouflaging the shuttles once we had them down wasn't exactly hard. Besides, we've been down for over three local days now. If they had any suspicion we'd made it out when *Tepes* blew, we'd be neck deep in recon flights. Under the circumstances, StateSec would probably even have called in *Count Tilly's* small craft to look for us, and we've seen zip air traffic."

"All right," Honor said after a moment. "It sounds to me like you're right about that part of it, but where do we go from here?"

"That's up to you, Ma'am, and frankly, I'm just as happy it is," McKeon said candidly. "We're down and concealed for the moment, and we've got some hardware to work with and enough emergency rations to carry us for up to five months if we're careful. But there are only eighteen of us—twenty, if we count Warner and Nimitz—" he nodded to the Peep officer with a wryly apologetic grin "—and the bad guys have a hell of a lot more firepower than we do. Not to mention an established base, at least a dozen armed pinnaces of their own, and those damned satellites to watch their backs. Any way you look at it, Ma'am, we're pretty damned outnumbered!"

"Outnumbered, Alistair?" Honor leaned back, her thin fingers buried in Nimitz's warm, soft fur. She looked more like a gaunt, half-starved wolf than ever, with her shaved hair, half-dead face, and amputated arm, but the feral gleam of a pack leader glittered in her remaining eye. She swept that eye over the men around her, and the right side of her upper lip curled back to bare her teeth.

"You people got us out of *Tepes* and down to this planet," she told them. "There were two or three thousand people on that ship, with guns and the combinations to our cells, but you still got us out, and we've got a lot more to work with now than you had then, now don't we?"

She held McKeon's eyes until he nodded, then swept

her gaze over the others once more, and she could not have defined or described the wild, fierce flow of her emotions if her soul had depended upon it. But it didn't matter. She didn't *need* to define or describe anything, for she felt the same determination, the same defiance, echoing back at her from her officers. She didn't realize how much those emotions focused on *her*, had no true concept of the way they viewed her as their living victory totem, and that didn't matter either. What mattered was the moment, the sense of naked swords raised in the dawn and the roar of massed voices ready to defy the gods themselves behind her. And as she heard the inner echo of that defiance, she knew it didn't matter at all that she had less than twenty people and only two sublight shuttles on a planet a light-century and a half from the nearest friendly territory, for it was inconceivable that the Peeps could keep *her* people here. Not after all they'd already done.

"If anyone's outnumbered here," Lady Dame Honor Harrington told her friends softly, "it's the Peeps."